GOLDEN FILLY

LAURAINE SNELLING

GOLDEN FILLY

 COLLECTION 1

BETHANYHOUSE
PUBLISHERS

Published by Bethany House Publishers
11400 Hampshire Avenue South
Bloomington, Minnesota 55438

Bethany House Publishers is a division of
Baker Publishing Group, Grand Rapids, Michigan.

Printed in the United States of America

ISBN-13: 978-0-7642-0737-2

ABOUT THE AUTHOR

LAURAINE SNELLING is an award-winning author of over sixty books, fiction and nonfiction, for adults and young adults. Her books have sold over two million copies. Besides writing books and articles, she teaches at writers' conferences across the country. She and her husband, Wayne, have two grown sons, a basset named Chewy, and a cockatiel watch bird named Bidley. They make their home in California.

EDITOR'S NOTE

Originally published in the early 1990s, these books reflect the cultural and social aspects of that time. In order to maintain the integrity of the story, we opted not to impose today's styles, technologies, laws, or other advancements upon the characters and events within. We believe the themes of love of God, love of family, and love of horses are timeless and can be enjoyed no matter the setting.

THE RACE

BOOK ONE

To my daughter, Marie,
who won her race and now wears her crown.

Chapter
01

The rising sun peeked through feathery mist.

Two Thoroughbreds rounded the far turn on the three-quarter mile track at Runnin' On Farm. Side by side, both riders stood high in their stirrups to hold the surging animals under control.

"Now, Tricia!" Hal Evanston, the rider on the gray, shouted above the thunder of pounding hooves.

His daughter, Tricia, nodded, loosened the reins, and crouched back in the saddle, her face almost buried in two-year-old Spitfire's black mane. "Okay, boy," she whispered to the colt's twitching ears. "Let's see what you can do."

The colt leaped forward. He snorted, then settled into ever-lengthening strides. The white fence blurred as Spitfire gained speed. Beside him, old gray Dan'l valiantly attempted to keep pace. Another furlong and the black was stretched out, running free. The gray dropped back, blowing hard.

Tricia urged the colt on, using her hands and feet. She thought about the whip in her hand but decided against it.

"Come on, baby," she crooned. "Let it out. Let's go all the way." The horse gave a little more. His heavy breathing drowned out the thunder of his hooves. As they passed the entrance gate, Tricia remembered her father's instructions. She eased back on the reins.

"That's enough for now, fella." She chuckled as Spitfire shook his head. She pulled the reins tighter, rising in the stirrups to gain more control. Gobs of lather splashed past her as he shook his head again. Tricia ducked her face into his sweaty mane for protection.

"Come on, Spitfire," she coaxed him. "You gotta slow down. We're in cool-down time now. You'll get to race again. I promise."

The feisty colt slowed to a canter, tossing his head and playfully fighting the snaffle bit. The desire to race on around the track screamed from every taut muscle. His blue-black coat was lather-flecked and dripping wet, but he'd finally tasted real racing. Centuries of selective breeding had led to this event. He was a Thoroughbred in every line and hair of his seventeen-hand, long-legged body.

Tricia settled back in her short-stirruped racing saddle as the horse slowed to a trot, then a walk. *Man, oh man,* she thought, *Dan'l's never been this fast. Maybe, no, not maybe. For sure this horse is going to do it for us.* She pushed her goggles up on her head and dreamed ahead. *Only one month to go before the season opens. Twenty-eight days until my birthday. Then I'll be sixteen and old enough to ride at the Portland Meadows Racetrack. To win! I know we can do it. Spitfire and me.*

She stroked the animal's arched neck. "We'll do it, won't we, fella?"

Spitfire danced faster when he felt the reins loosen. His ears pricked forward as he recognized the gray walking ahead of them. The black blew. He tossed his head. He tried to take the bit in his teeth, but Trish foiled his attempt when she tightened the reins.

"Thought you'd try something, didn't you?" She gentled him with her voice. As they came up on Dan'l, Spitfire jogged sideways. His front legs crossed one another, like a dancer in a *pas de deux.*

"Well? What'd you think? Wasn't he fantastic? Oh, Dad, I've never ridden so fast in my whole life. He'll do it for us, won't he?"

"Wait a minute." Hal laughed as he held up a gloved hand. "Give me a chance to answer. Which question is most important?"

Trish chuckled. "He was *so* good!"

4

"Better than just good." Hal nodded. "Makes me more sure than ever that Spitfire's the one we've been waiting for. I think he has the speed to win."

Trish grinned at her father, but her grin turned to a frown as she watched him bend over Dan'l's gray neck. He coughed until he gasped.

"You okay?" She reined the side-stepping black down.

Hal nodded. "Just too much dust." He wheezed as he spat the choking phlegm at the ground. "I'm fine now."

"You sure?"

"Of course I'm sure," he snapped. "Don't start cross-examining me, babe."

Trying to hide her hurt feelings, Tricia jerked the reins. Spitfire reared in surprise, then crowhopped in place. "Sorry, fella," she muttered as she straightened him out into a slow trot again.

"Sorry I barked at you." Hal trotted the gray even with Tricia and her sweating mount.

"That's okay." Tricia shrugged. "But Dad—"

"No buts. Let's talk about something else." Hal tapped her gloved hands with his whip. "How did Spitfire feel when you pulled him up? Did he have more to give?"

"I think so." Trish settled back in her saddle. "But he was tiring."

"That's just conditioning. Did he want to keep running?"

"Did he ever! With another horse pushing him, I think he'd really have gone."

"Well, poor old Dan'l just wasn't in shape to give that youngster a real run for his money." Hal patted his mount's sweaty neck. Dan'l twitched his ears, then tossed his head. As he side-stepped, pulling against the reins, Hal laughed. "I know, old man. You love to run too."

Trish wanted to reach over and hug the old horse. He was her favorite the horse who had helped her learn to be a jockey. She'd been exercising him for the last five years, getting ready for her first race at Portland Meadows Racetrack.

"We're getting close, huh?" She smiled at her father.

Hal nodded, his understanding immediate. So often they read each other's minds, not needing to finish their comments.

"We've got a lot to do." Hal loosened his reins to bring Dan'l into a canter. "Not the least of which, you'll be late for school if we don't hustle."

At that moment she noticed her mother, Marge, and nineteen-year-old brother, David, leaning on the fence by the gate. Caesar, their purebred sable collie, sat obediently at their feet, never taking his eyes off the moving animals.

"David!" Trish trotted up to the gate. "Did you see us? What's the time?"

"Fantastic!" David grinned and held up the stopwatch. "It looks like he did four furlongs in forty-eight and two, and that's with no one pushing him."

Tricia leaned forward as David waved the shiny gold watch on its chain.

At the sight of the unfamiliar glinting object, Spitfire half-reared and whirled to get away. Caught off-balance, Tricia grabbed instinctively around the animal's neck and dug in with her knees. Like a slow-motion picture, she catapulted from the horse's back and thumped onto the loose dirt of the track. Even as she hit the ground, Trish clutched one rein in her hand to keep Spitfire from backing away.

"Oof!" She grunted at the force of the impact. "Oh, no you don't!" She rolled to her feet to control the plunging horse. "Come on, Spitfire. It's only me. You're okay."

Hal swung Dan'l around to block the colt from taking off.

"Tricia . . ." David began.

"I'm fine." She kept her eyes on her horse. "I've been dumped before. Besides, my pride's hurt worse than my rear—I think."

"Well, if your pride's as dirty as your rear, you're in real trouble."

"Thank you, big brother." Tricia held the now-quiet horse's bridle with one hand and dusted herself off with the other. "Hey, Mom. What'd you think?" She looked to the fence where Marge had been standing with David, then at David. "Where'd she go?"

Hal and David shrugged in unison.

Tricia shook her head. "Not a good time to take a flying lesson, huh?"

Hal shrugged again and stared toward the house, disappointment clear in the droop of his mouth and shoulders. "Come on, Tee. These guys are hungry and so am I."

"But, Dad, I didn't get hurt. And Spitfire didn't mean to dump me. It was that stupid watch that scared him."

"I know," Hal answered as he walked his mount beside Tricia. "But you know your mother's worried that you could really get hurt on the racetrack."

"Sure. And a meteor could fall out of the sky and pound me into the dirt."

Hal chuckled.

"Or the school bus could sprout wings and kidnap me . . ."

"Now, Tee."

"Or I might get ptomaine poisoning from my cereal." Trish delivered the last with all the dramatic flair of a seasoned actress.

Hal laughed again. "Well, falls have happened to better jocks than you, you know." He nudged Dan'l into a trot. "But don't worry, I'll call the emergency wagon for you after I wash these horses down and feed them. Think you can hang on till then?"

"I'll try." Trish touched the back of her leather glove to her forehead. The wink her father gave her was all the applause she needed. "David?" she asked as he fell into step beside her. "How am I ever gonna convince Mom that I'm a careful rider?"

"Sure you are." David reached behind her to pat Spitfire's neck. "You just proved it."

"D-a-v-i-d!" She dug into his ribs with her elbow. "That fall was no big deal."

"To our mother it was. You know what a worrier she is. She's always worried about Dad at the track, and now you add to it. Besides, in her mind, girls shouldn't be racing horses, especially not *her* girl."

"Yeah, I should take dancing lessons and wear a frilly tutu. Maybe I should smear makeup on an inch thick too, and chase every guy in sight."

"Knock it off, little sister." David draped an arm around her shoulders. "No one said growing up was easy." He glanced at his watch. "You better move it or you'll be late for school, and you know what happens—"

"Okay. Okay. Don't remind me. I've already been late once and school's been going less than a week." She trotted toward the stables, Spitfire dancing behind her. "David," she called after him as he turned to the house. "You can muck out the stalls. It'll be good for you. Someone once told me it builds muscles."

"Got enough already." David flexed an arm, then whistled for Caesar. Together, they loped up the rise.

Tricia led Spitfire into his stall and cross-tied him. As she reached to loosen the saddle girth, she heard her father start to cough in the adjoining box stall. She pulled the racing saddle from Spitfire's withers, paused, then called, "Dad?" As the coughing continued, she slung the saddle over the lower half of the stall door. In frustration, she jerked her goggles and helmet off her head, only to run trembling fingers through her thick ebony hair. *If I could just go to him*, she thought. *But what if he yells at me again?*

The rattle of her father's struggling breath filled the stalls. Spitfire tossed his head, eyes rolling white at the strange sound.

Tricia crammed her gloves into her pocket and, green eyes flashing, stepped into the sunshine. She swung Dan'l's stall door open. Her father leaned against the wall. His body sagged as he choked for breath.

"Dad . . ." Trish shook his arm. When he turned, she saw bright red bubbles frothing from the corner of her father's mouth.

"Don't worry, Tee." The words rasped in his throat. "I'll be all right."

No you won't, Tricia thought. *Blood means more than allergies or a smoker's cough, like you've always claimed.*

Chapter
02

Dan'l snorted. He shoved his nose into Tricia's back. When that didn't get her attention, he blew in her hair. Feeling a burning in her eyes, she absently rubbed his soft nose.

"Oh, Dan'l," she whispered. "What are we gonna do?"

Hal coughed again. After he spat the choking mucus out of his throat, he pulled a handkerchief from his back pocket and wiped his mouth. When he saw the blood stain, he stared at his daughter.

"Honest, Trish. There's never been blood before." He shook his head. "Guess I better see a doctor right away, spare time or no spare time."

"Guess so."

Hal wrapped both arms around Trish. As he hugged her close, he absently rubbed the early morning stubble on his chin against her forehead.

Tricia felt a little more secure. Her father had always made everything all right. When she was little, he fixed the broken rope on her swing. He kissed her and put her back up on the pony when she fell off. All her life she'd tagged after him and David as they farmed and slowly built a business training Thoroughbreds for the racetrack.

Most of those years Hal had trained horses for other breeders. It was only since Trish had turned ten that he'd had horses of his own to race. They still had horses in the stalls that belonged to other owners, but Tricia liked to work their own animals best. Since Dan'l was getting too old to race, they had Spitfire and his half-sister Firefly for this season and some real promising young stock for next year.

With her head against her father's chest, Tricia could hear the air rattling through his lungs. He wheezed, then gently pushed her aside so he could cough again.

"Short and sweet this time," he tried to joke as he took a deep breath. "See, Ma, no cough."

Tricia wanted to join in their old joke from her bikeriding days. "See, Ma, no hands" had been her password. Now all she could see was her father's pale face with sweat beading on his upper lip. While the horrid red bubbles had been wiped away, a dried-brown smear marked where they'd been.

"Oh no." Hal checked his watch. "It's seven o'clock. I'll get the tack off these boys and you feed them. Then you've gotta get to school."

"I'll be late anyway, so why don't I stay home today? I can catch up on some stuff around here while you and Mom go to the doctor."

"David can do the chores. You're going to school."

"But, Dad—"

"Tricia." Hal gripped her forearms with calloused hands. "I'm going to be fine. Your staying home won't change anything but your grades." Tricia stared into his eyes, seeking an answer to the fear that gnawed like a beaver at the back of her mind.

"Really." He turned her and lovingly swatted her on the seat. "Now get going. These horses are hungry."

Sunlight turned the straw to gold as she shuffled toward the open door. Dan'l snorted. Spitfire whickered. Soft nickers passed down the row of white stalls as the horses begged for their feed. Tricia turned and looked at her father one more time. His tuneless whistle accompanied his hands as he uncinched the saddle. Suddenly, the morning was the same as any other, the telltale dab on his cheek the only sign of trouble.

Sucking in a deep breath, then letting it all out, Tricia stepped into the sunshine. "Be right back, fella," she promised Spitfire as she picked up the buckets and headed for the feed room.

After loading half a bale of alfalfa and the filled grain buckets into the wheelbarrow, Tricia hurried from stall to stall. She measured each animal's allotted grain into their feedboxes and threw a wedge of hay in each manger. After checking to see that all the animals but Spitfire and Dan'l had water, she stepped into the tack room as Hal finished hanging up the saddles and bridles.

"Ready?" she asked.

"Yep, but I don't think we'll race this time."

Tricia nodded. "That's okay. I've beaten you the last three mornings."

"I gave you a head start."

"Sure. Sure."

"You don't believe me?"

"Nope." Trish shook her head.

"What do you think I am?" Her father bent at the waist and with his right hand on his hip limped for several steps. "A rickety old man?"

"Yup," Tricia responded, trying not to laugh. "Just a worn-out, falling-apart, ancient old man." The two paced each other up the rise toward the house.

"See if I give you the fastest horse tomorrow morning," he growled, laughter showing in his hazel eyes. "Lady, from now on, you work old Dan'l."

"Nope. The old horse suits the old man."

Arm in arm, they mounted the three concrete steps to the deck off the back of the house. Vertical cedar siding on the walls set off the blossom-covered fuchsias hanging from the beams. Below the baskets, tubs of ruby begonias raced for first place in the blooming contest.

Tricia paused to look for the hummingbirds that dined every day on the drooping pink, purple, and white blossoms.

"Hustle, Tee," Marge called. "You're late again."

"Dad." Tricia clutched her father's arm. "You'll go to the doctor today?"

"Umm-m-m. See . . . there's a hummingbird. On the other side of the pink basket."

"Don't play games with me." Tension tightened Tricia's jaw. "If you don't tell Mom, I will."

"Now, Trish."

"I will."

"Okay. Okay." He raised his hands in surrender.

"What are you two so serious about?" Marge met them at the sliding glass door. "In case you haven't noticed, my girl, you're late."

Trish glanced at her mother, then stared into her father's eyes. Silence. *Why doesn't he tell her?* Tricia thought. *I'm not going to back down, not this time. I know there's something really wrong.* Unbidden, a prayer surfaced in her mind. *Make him well, God. He's the best father a girl could ever have.*

Hal took a breath, like he was preparing for a deep dive. He patted Trish on the shoulder, then put his arm around Marge and walked into the family room with her.

Trish slid onto the stool by the door.

"It's about this cough I've had." He drew out a chair. "Sit down, honey."

"That bad?" Marge laughed up at him as she sat.

"Ummm-mm, I think so. Ah-h." He rubbed her shoulders. "This morning I coughed up a bit of blood. The pain was so bad I nearly fainted."

"But, Hal, you've always said—"

"I know what I've been saying. But there has been pain. Not much but . . ." He walked to the window and stood looking out. "I think it's getting worse."

"Why haven't you—?"

"I don't know." He ran work-worn fingers through his hair. "I was so sure it would go away. I quit smoking. Thought that would do it."

"But it hasn't."

"No."

Trish felt each word beat against her. His flat "no" rattled in the room.

After a long moment, Marge asked, "What exactly happened down at the barn?"

Hal told her the entire story and ended with, "And there was just enough blood on my handkerchief to scare the living daylights out of me."

"And me," Trish whispered from her perch by the door.

Marge slumped in her chair, one arm over the back.

In the corner, the fish tank bubbled on, as though nothing unusual had happened. As if Trish's world hadn't just had a major hole punched in it. She could hear David singing in the shower. Off key. As usual.

"Guess I'll go wash," she said.

"Yes," her mother acknowledged, not taking her eyes off her husband's back. "I'll call the doctor as soon as the office is open. We'll go right in."

"Don't I need an appointment?"

"I'm sure they'll want to see you right away—" Her mother's voice was cut off by Trish's rap on the bathroom door.

"You about done in there?" she raised her voice to be heard above the warbler.

"In a minute," David interrupted his favorite song to answer.

That means more like five, Trish thought as she leaned her head against the door. "Time for me to eat first?"

"Yeah. Probably."

"Well, take your time. I'm late already." The sarcasm in her voice finally penetrated to the songbird in the shower.

"Hey, what's with you?" David shut off the faucets. "You always eat first. Why should this morning be any different?"

"David." Trish heard the shower door slam. She knew she should head for the kitchen but couldn't force herself to listen to her parents again. Instead she tapped the door again. "David, Dad coughed up blood this morning."

"He what!" Her brother jerked the door open.

"There was blood on his handkerchief and the side of his mouth after a coughing attack. His face was all gray—and sweaty."

With one towel tucked in around his waist, David leaned against the door jamb. Without taking his eyes from Trish's, he reached for another towel and began drying his curly hair. "Does he know what's wrong?"

"No. They're talking about going to the doctor."

"He never goes to a doctor. He must be worried."

"Yeah. Just says he'll wait for the Great Physician to do His job."

"He's always been right. So far."

"Yeah. So far. But . . ."

David draped the towel around his neck. "Hurry up, kid. I'll drive you to school as soon as you're ready. And, Tee . . ." he added as she closed the door behind her, "we better start praying."

"I have been."

A quick shower later, Tricia grabbed beige pants and a matching striped T-shirt from her closet and threw them on the bed. A moment's rummage in the bottom of the closet proved that her shoes were missing— as usual. Still kneeling, she glared around her room. It was in its normal state of disaster. Piles of clothing were strewn on the floor and hid the chair. Finding the mirror would take an act of Congress. So what if she never combed her hair again?

"Trish?" Her mother's voice broke through her concentration.

"Yeah. Yeah, I'm coming." She glared around the room one more time. "Have you seen my rope sandals?"

"They're in the living room, right where you left them," her mother answered. "You know, if you'd pick things up . . ."

"I know. I know," Trish muttered to herself as she slammed the bathroom door shut. "Don't start in on me right now. I don't have time."

Ten minutes later, dressed and with mascara applied to her long dark lashes, Trish brushed her hair back and tossed the brush on the counter. *No time to try anything different today.* But then, when did she have time? The racing schedule would make her life even more hectic. Good thing she had second-year Spanish first thing in the morning. It was an easy class. Her junior year. Well, big deal. Racing was more important.

Trish stopped long enough to slather peanut butter on a piece of whole wheat toast and pour a glass of milk to finish in the car.

"Here's a banana too," Marge said as David honked the horn.

Pushing the sliding door closed with her elbow, Tricia heard her father coughing again. It sounded as though he couldn't get his breath, then he gagged. Trish turned to see him collapse into a chair.

David's honking urged her to hurry.

Torn in both directions, Trish slammed the glass door open again. "Dad?"

"Come on, Trish," David hollered. "You'll be late for second period at this rate."

"Get going, Tee." Her father waved. Sweat beaded on his forehead. "I'll be all right."

Trish turned and ran down the steps. The little red bubbles around his mouth filled her mind.

Chapter

03

The morning dragged like a limping turtle.

All Trish could hear in her mind was her father's choking cough. His white face was all she could see when she closed her eyes.

"Hey, Trish, you all right?" Rhonda Seabolt asked on the way to lunch. Trish and Rhonda had been best friends since kindergarten.

"Yeah, I'm fine." Trish tried to smile.

"You sure don't look it."

"Thanks a lot."

"No. I mean . . . well—"

"Rhonda?"

"What?"

"What would you do if you saw your dad coughing up blood?"

Rhonda stared at Trish's sober face. Hurrying students jostled them as they stopped in the middle of the hall. "I don't know. Are you sure? About the blood, I mean."

Trish nodded. "We were out in the stable after this morning's workout. It happened again just as David and I left for school—"

"Hey, you two," a familiar baritone voice interrupted them. "You're blocking the hall."

Trish glanced up at Brad Williams, their tall, lanky cohort in innumerable escapades. He wrapped an arm around each of the girls and herded them over to the wall. "Now, if your conversation is so all-fired serious, at least you won't get run over."

"Thanks, friend." Trish tried to smile but the corners of her mouth felt stiff. She felt herself gathering to run. What she needed right now was to huddle in the big chair in the living room at home and wait for her parents to return. Maybe, just maybe, the problem wasn't too serious. Maybe some kind of medicine would make her dad well again. Maybe Jesus would make him well right away. She groaned to herself. She hadn't even thought to pray again. Some Christian she was.

"Trish?"

"Ummm-mm."

"What can I do to help?" Rhonda shifted her books so she had a free hand to grab Trish's.

"What's going on here?" Brad looked from one stricken face to the other. "Trish, you look like you lost your first race." He lifted her chin with a calloused finger.

Trish glanced from Rhonda to Brad, then stared at her typing book. The more she talked about it, the worse it seemed.

Taking the hint, Rhonda said, "It's her dad. He was coughing blood this morning."

Brad stared at the wall above Trish's head. He shook his head, took a shuddering breath, and looked deep into her eyes, searching out the pain that lurked behind her self-control. "When did this start?" he whispered.

"Well," Trish tried to think back, "he's been coughing for a long time. Just kept referring to it as 'his smoker's hack.' You know how he is."

Brad nodded.

"Then this morning in the barn . . ." Trish stared at the hurrying mob of students with unseeing eyes. "They're at the doctor's now."

"Would you like me to take you home?"

"I don't know." She pushed her hair off her forehead. "I wanted to go home a minute ago, but here I have something to keep my mind sort of busy."

"Do you need help at the stables?"

"I don't think so. David's there."

"Well, if you need anything . . ."

"Sure, thanks." *What I need, you can't give,* she thought. *No one can.*

"Starving won't help." Brad took both girls' arms. "Let's go eat before the food's all gone."

Trish attempted a smile. She knew Brad was trying to make things easier for her. He'd been that kind of friend for years. Her mother often laughed about having four kids instead of two. David was the oldest, Brad next, and finally the Siamese twins, Rhonda and Trish. All four had dreamed of being jockeys when they grew up, but the boys had grown so big they made jockeys look like midgets. Rhonda had switched her concentration to showing gaited horses, so that left Trish to carry the farm silks to glory. Together they had voted on stable colors, crimson and gold. Hal teased them about being in a rut since those were their school colors, but they had stuck by their decision. Trish would wear crimson and gold all the way to the winner's circle.

Trish and Rhonda made their way to the salad bar. Like a robot, Trish greeted the serving attendant and filled her plate. Her shoulders slumped when she saw other students sitting at their table in the back of the room. There'd be no time for real talking, no privacy.

She felt like hiding. The walk across the room suddenly seemed too far, too difficult. Why, just this morning everything had been fine, and now her favorite person in all the world was . . . She refused to finish the thought.

She juggled her purse and tray to free one hand. With it, she brushed back her wayward bangs. *We're winners,* she thought. *Dad always says "Quitters never win and winners never quit."* She marched across the room.

"You want to sit somewhere else?" Rhonda asked from behind her.

"No. That's okay." Trish set her tray down. "Besides, everything else is full."

A chorus of "hi's" greeted the two as they pulled out their chairs. The familiar din of the lunchroom made talking below a shout difficult, so Trish concentrated on her salad.

"Still watching your weight?" Doug Ramstead, quarterback on the varsity football squad, pulled his chair close so he could shout in her ear.

Trish nodded. "Good thing I love salads."

"How long till you race?" He leaned nearer and lowered his voice. A lazy lock of blond hair fell over his forehead.

"The season starts October first, but we won't be in the first races. Dad has us scheduled for the Meadow's Maiden. That's a race for untried colts."

"Bet you can't wait."

"We're not ready yet. Spitfire still has more conditioning."

"Ugh. Don't even use that word." Doug shoved back his tray and leaned on his elbows.

"Workout was rough, huh?"

"Worse. Thought I was gonna heave my guts out." He rubbed his biceps. "And my arms . . . I've been haying most of the summer, then weight training since the beginning of August. Coach Sey, the new man, makes old Smith look like a kindergarten teacher."

"How's the team look?" Trish chewed on her straw.

"Pretty good. This just might be our year." He turned partway so he could look at her. "What about you? Doing any lifting? I haven't seen you in the weight room."

"Yeah. I've been using David's old set at home. I just can't fit in the time to work out here."

"Could you fit in the party after the game on Friday?" He spoke right in her ear.

Trish felt a tiny shiver as his breath tickled her earlobe. She drew back at the unfamiliar sensation. "Can I tell you later? I'm not sure what my dad has planned."

"Sure." His voice stayed close. "But, Trish, I'd really like to take you."

"Thanks." Trish spun her straw in her milk carton. "I'd like to go with you."

Doug pushed his chair back and stood, at the same time dropping a hand to her shoulder. "See ya."

Trish watched as the broad-shouldered quarterback made his way across the room with his tray. *You'd think he'd be a snob with all the attention he gets*, she thought. But he wasn't. His smile was as real as the hay bales he'd hoisted. And he even said hi to the giggly freshman girls, most of whom pushed Trish's patience to the limit. Going out with Doug Ramstead would be fun. But. There was always that *but* during racing season. Morning workouts came too early for her to stay out late. But just this once . . .

Rhonda poked her in the ribs. "Did he really ask you out?"

"Listening in, huh?" Trish turned her attention back to the table.

"Not really." Rhonda shrugged, then leaned closer as Trish toyed with another bite of lettuce. "You going?"

"I don't know." Trish glanced up to find Brad staring at her from across the table. "It's still a week away."

"David and I thought the four of *us* would go together—like always," Brad said. "It'll be his last night home."

"Of course!" Trish thumped her fist on the table. "How could I forget?"

"All that hunk had to do was say hi, Rhonda laughed, "and your—"

"And my brain went into orbit," Trish finished for her. "I know what you're thinking."

"Well," Brad rocked his chair back on two legs, "that's the way it looked to us, huh, Rhonda? You two were sitting pretty close—"

"Brad Williams, I—"

"Now, don't get your Irish temper up, Tee. It's not good for your digestion." Brad ducked as Trish faked a pitch with her milk carton.

"Sometimes you two go too far." Trish picked up her tray and joined the line to leave it at the dish window.

"Do you want a ride home after school?" Brad asked as they headed back to their lockers. "Or do you have something going?"

"No. I mean, yes, I want a ride home. The bus takes too long. I've got to lunge some colts this afternoon and Dad's gonna shoe . . ." Trish abruptly stopped as she remembered the scene in the stall that morning. With her notebook clutched to her chest, she rubbed her arms as if to warm herself.

"You okay?" Rhonda touched her arm.

Trish turned from staring into the trophy case without seeing.

"Ummm-mm." She nodded. "See you later." She turned the corner to her locker. *Only three classes to go. Maybe, just maybe,* she thought. *No, not maybe.* She could hear her dad telling her to be positive. She had his words memorized: *When you want something really bad, picture it in your mind as already happening.* He'd drilled it into her since she was tiny. *Picture it in your mind.*

Trish swung her locker door open and leaned into the island of shelter it created. She scrunched her eyes shut. The picture she forced onto the backs of her eyelids was familiar: her father kneeling in front of a gray gelding, taping the forelegs. Whistling off-tune. Breathing easily.

Until the coughing attack.

God! Help! her mind screamed. She grabbed her chemistry book and dashed toward the classroom, unaware of the people she bounced against. *Make him better; make him better.* Her mind pounded the beat for her feet.

Trish gritted her teeth to keep the tears from falling. Better wasn't good enough. *Please, God, I don't want him to be sick. He's always said, "You can do anything." Please!*

She slid into her seat as the bell rang.

"Hand in your assignments," the teacher said. "And turn to page 51."

Trish forced her mind to the job at hand. Her groan joined the universal lament of students unprepared.

I forgot it was due today! her thoughts took over again. *I haven't even started it. Great. I'd planned to do it during second period and lunch hour. He'll never let me turn it in late, either.* She looked at page 51. Without the first assignment finished, this one could have been written in a foreign language. In fact, some of the symbols were.

Trish shook her head. And David thought chemistry was fun. She sank lower in her seat and tried to pay attention.

The next class was no easier. By the final bell she'd responded with a blank stare to the teacher's question, mumbled "I don't know" because she couldn't think, and been accused of daydreaming.

The drive home wasn't much better. Even Rhonda didn't indulge in her usual chatter as Brad drove up the curving driveway at Runnin' On Farm. The pickup was gone. David's car was missing too.

Maybe Mom's shopping. Tricia's mind clutched at any idea.

Caesar barked a welcome. Except for him, the place was deserted.

"Do you want us to stay?" Rhonda asked.

"No." Trish shook her head. "I've got too much to do."

"I'll be back over as soon as I change," Brad said, ignoring her comment. "I know you'll need some help if your dad's been gone all day. And besides, he may not feel much like working in the barn after being at the doctor's."

"I've got a dentist appointment," Rhonda said, "but I can come after that."

Trish nodded, grateful for caring friends. "I'll call you if I need you."

"No. I'll be right back. I haven't gotten to exercise horses since David's been home for the summer. He took my job away, remember?"

Trish waved as the blue Mustang pulled away, then leaned over to hug the regal collie. "Mom? Dad?" she called as she opened the front door.

The stillness of the empty house wailed "No one home."

Chapter
04

Trish dropped her books on the entry table and headed into the kitchen for food and messages. David's note, stuck on the fridge door with a strawberry magnet, read, "Trish, Mom called from the hospital. They admitted Dad and she needed someone with her."

Slowly Trish removed the note and read it again. It was pretty plain. "They admitted Dad," she said aloud. *Then,* her mind reasoned, *the doctors think it's serious too. 'Course, that way he can get better faster. But the hospital . . . only Grandma went there—and she died.* Absently, she chose an apple from the bowl on the table, opened the fridge door, took out the milk, and poured herself a glass. She felt like a mechanical doll, doing routine things without thinking.

You said You could take care of everything, God. How about this? Can you really heal my dad, like he says you can? Please, if you could just make it be something simple . . . They've got medicine for everything now. Just let him get the right medicine and come home. I need him!

Eating her snack with little enjoyment, Trish made her way to her bedroom to change clothes. The mess was still as she'd left it. No good fairies came during the day to repair the damage.

Trish dropped the apple core in the wastebasket. On a huge poster on her wall, three Thoroughbreds raced for the finish line, reminding her of the animals and stalls that needed to be taken care of.

"Good thing Brad is coming," she muttered. "There's lots to be done." She glanced around at the piles of clothes, dirty and clean all jumbled together. The unmade bed invited her to take a nap, but instead she tossed her pants and shirt on one of the mounds and scrambled to find a clean pair of jeans. A car horn sounded as she pulled a cut-off sweat shirt over her head.

"Coming," she shouted out the open window, then dashed down the hall to find her boots. At least they were by the door where they belonged. The horn sounded again.

"Brad, you idiot, I'm coming," she muttered to herself. Once out the door, she trotted to where Brad lounged against the fender of his metallic-blue Mustang. "How'd you get here so fast?"

"Fast?" He held up his watch for her to see. "It's been forty-five minutes. What have you been doing? Daydreaming?"

"Uh—huh—I mean, no." Trish shook her head. "David went into Vancouver to be with Mom. They admitted Dad to the hospital."

"I'm sorry, Tee." Brad touched her shoulder. "You want me to drive you in there?"

"No! Not now." She stared off at the stables. "I mean, uh, someone has to do the chores around here. We can't all be running in to the hospital." Trish cleared her throat as she leaned down to stroke the insistent Caesar. "Besides, Dad needs me here. There's so much left to do before the season starts." She took a deep breath, silently promising herself to think about that later.

"Well, then let's get at it." Brad bowed. "Brad Williams, horse feeder, trainer, mucker-outer, at your service."

"The pay's not so good."

"Madam, I am c-h-e-a-p labor. What I do, I do for love." Way off key, Brad crooned one of the latest hit melodies.

"Yeah, love of Mom's cookies." Trish grinned at his antics.

"Speaking of which . . ."

"No way. You get paid after you work, not before."

"You heartless slave driver." Brad tried one more pleading look. "Oh well." He bent over to talk to Caesar. "See how she picks on me?" The dog licked Brad's nose, and he brushed it off with the back of his hand. "Well, let's get at it."

"He's crazy, isn't he, Caesar?" Trish shook her head. The three of them, two long-time friends and the dog, jogged down the slope to the stables. The three white buildings looked peaceful in the late afternoon sunshine.

A chorus of whinnies greeted Trish's whistle. All down the line, horses' heads turned to greet her from the stable doors. Spitfire, in the near stall, tossed his head and wickered again. Dan'l, not to be out done, banged the door with his front hoof.

"Some greeting." Brad laughed.

"You guys just want out, don't you?" Trish rubbed Spitfire's soft black nose. He pushed against her shoulder, then nibbled at her hair. "Careful, goofy, you bit me yesterday." Trish rubbed his ears and stroked down the muscled neck. In the next stall, Dan'l reached as far toward her as his stall door permitted. His nostrils quivered in a soundless nicker.

"You old sweetheart." Trish rubbed his nose and on up to his favorite spot, just under his forelock. Dan'l draped his head over her shoulder, content to be scratched.

"What do you need me to do first?" Brad joined her in stroking the old gray.

"Let's get them on the hot walker, then you can muck out the stalls. I've gotta work with the younger colts and check on the mares. Those other two haven't been worked yet either." She waved toward the two horses they were training for a new breeder.

"Fine with me." Brad grabbed the handles of the deep red wheel-barrow and followed her to Spitfire's stall.

Trish released the bolt and led the high-stepping black toward the hot walker, a circular exerciser that the horses moved themselves. She snapped the dangling lead rope to his halter and as she left slapped him lightly on the rump. The black reared slightly in sheer exuberance, then danced obediently around the worn track.

The girl smiled at his antics. "You're really something," she chuckled, pride in her eyes. Dan'l whinnied sharply and struck the door again. "I'm coming. I'm coming. Hang in there a minute."

After Dan'l and a bay filly joined Spitfire on the creaking hot walker, Trish approached the last stall on the west arm of the stable. "Hey, knock it off," she scolded the bay colt. "You're gonna beat the door to death." The colt glared at her, wild-eyed. Slowly Trish unlatched the stall door. "Easy now. Sorry you're the last."

The colt snorted. Trish slipped inside the door, then waited by the wall for him to calm down. "Easy, boy, easy now," she crooned, her voice gentle like a song. "You're just wasting time. If you'd behave you'd be outside already."

With a toss of his head, the colt stepped forward for the lead rope to be snapped to his halter. Trish rubbed his ears, then swung the door open and led him out.

Just as they cleared the door, a small piece of white paper tumbled by on the breeze. With a high squeal, the colt reared and struck out with one foreleg. The force jerked Trish off her feet.

"Oh, no you don't," she muttered as her boots hit the ground again. Her arms felt like they had grown two inches. This time, as he reared again, she let the rope travel through her fingers. When he started down again, she seized his halter and smacked him on the nose.

Surprised, the colt shook his head and kept his feet planted on the ground.

"You finished smarting off now?" Impatience laced her voice. "That paper was nothing and you know it."

The colt looked around as if surprised at his own actions.

"Bit of a rodeo, huh?" Brad asked as she snapped the bay's lead rope to the hot walker.

"I guess." Trish rubbed her shoulder. "He's a spooky one."

"You sure you want to work him today?"

"Have to." Trish chewed her lip. "We told Mr. Anderson we'd have his horse ready for the first race."

"But, Trish—"

"He'll calm down as soon as he gets to move around some. He always does." She turned toward the pastures. "Come on, Caesar, race you to the mares."

A frown creased Brad's forehead as he hefted the handles of the manure- and straw-heaped wheelbarrow. "Speaking of spooky," he muttered. "Girl, sometimes you worry me. There's nothing wrong with a little wholesome fear."

Having put the incident from her mind, Trish loped across the emerald turf. Two colts raced to the end of their pasture. The three mares in the adjoining paddock ignored the young frolicking in favor of lazy dreaming under the maple tree.

After a quick inspection, Trish patted the sorrel mare's shoulder and started back toward the barns. One of the mares coughed.

At the second cough, Trish wheeled back and checked each animal, ears, eyes, and nose. The sorrel with three white socks coughed again, stretching her nose toward the ground.

"Now what?" Trish stroked the animal's satiny neck. She listened carefully as the mare breathed in and out. "No wheeze, old girl. You just trying to get some extra attention?" Trish chewed her lip as she watched and listened to the animal another minute.

"Remind me to watch her, Caesar old buddy." She patted the dog trotting beside her. "That's what Dad would do." She paused at the gate to the yearling pasture. Two of the colts raced back along the fence line. They plowed to a stop before her, then extended their muzzles to sniff her proffered hand.

Trish laughed at their antics, but her attention zeroed in on the gray filly dozing against the back corner.

"What is this?" she questioned herself. "Sleepy time. Cough time. It's supposed to be training time. And I don't have time for anything else." Briefly she checked the filly for wheezing. She sounded fine. No mucus in her nostrils. But her eyes were droopy.

"Lethargic is the word." Trish closed her eyes to better recall symptoms she'd read in the medical dictionary. Only influenza came to mind. "I'll keep a close eye on you two," she promised with an extra pat. "We can't afford any sick animals."

Like well-trained puppies, the two colts dogged her footsteps back to the gate. When Trish snapped a lead shank on the colt named Samba and led him out of the gate, the other tried to follow. Caesar drove him back with a sharp bark.

"Thanks, old buddy." She swung the gate closed. "I can always count on you." Samba shook his head, then tried dancing in a circle. Playfully he struck out with a snowy forefoot.

"Nope. I've had enough of that kind of behavior today." Trish snapped on the rope. "You settle down right now." The chestnut colt rolled his eyes in mock panic, then ambled along beside her to the stable.

After Trish cross-tied him in an empty stall, she headed for the tack room to get an old soft bridle with a snaffle bit.

"Need some help?" Brad wiped the sweat off his forehead. He parked the wheelbarrow in the breezeway. "That's one job done."

"Thanks, Brad." Trish rubbed the worn bit. "You can be his distraction."

"Great. First I'm a barrow-pushing slave and now I'm a distraction. When do we get to the fun stuff?"

"Like?"

"Oh, like racing two horses around the track. Eating cookies. Drinking Coke. You know, the important things in life."

"Yeah, I know. Your resident tapeworm is acting up again."

"Yup. I've gotta feed Fred at regular intervals." Brad patted his flat stomach. "Poor Fred."

"You nut. Forget Fred. We've gotta put the bit in Samba's mouth now."

The colt didn't bat an eyelash as Trish showed him the bridle with the silvery bit. He sniffed the leather, then looked over at Brad. Trish held the bit carefully to keep it from jangling as she rubbed the chilly metal against the colt's nose. He blinked and tried to shove his muzzle against her chest. Before he knew what happened, Trish had inserted a finger in the space behind his teeth, pried open his mouth, and slipped the bit in place. At the same time, Brad slid the headstall over the animal's ears.

The colt snorted. He rolled his eyes, then shook his head. The bit and bridle stayed in place. With a sigh, Samba lowered his head again and nuzzled Trish for the treats she always carried in her pockets.

"Boy." Trish let out the breath she'd been holding. "That was easy." She palmed a sugar cube. "Here, you earned that, fella."

"Good job, partner." She shook Brad's hand as they left the stall. "We did it. We'll come back later and take that off. Give him time to play with the bit for a while."

"Now for the cookies?" Brad gazed soulfully toward the house.

"Nope. Now for the racetrack. You take Anderson's filly and I'll take the rowdy Gatesby."

"Maybe you should skip him today," Brad suggested. "You've already had one round with the beast."

"Nah-h. He just needs the exercise. Besides, we were supposed to work him into the starting gate today."

"So?"

"We'll need extra hands to do that. Let's just take him up to the gate." Trish studied the colt, now pacing placidly around the ring. "That will give him a chance to look it over."

"Okay, boss lady. Let's go."

Within minutes they had the two animals saddled and ready. The bay colt stood calmly until Brad boosted Trish into the flat racing saddle. Before she could finish gathering the reins, the bay exploded. He reared, then pounded both front feet into the shavings. As Brad grabbed for the bridle, the colt lunged away from him.

Trish clamped her legs and tangled her fists in the colt's mane. "Whoa!" she commanded as she tried to tighten both reins, remain in the saddle, and get control of the plunging animal.

"You crazy idiot!" Brad muttered as he leaped again. "Calm down!" This time he clamped his fist around one of the reins where it clipped to the bit. He jerked savagely. With a last snort, the bay stood still, his eyes rolling white.

"Would you lead him to the track?" Trish whispered as she fought to stop the trembling in her hands.

"You're as crazy as he is," Brad growled. "Put him away for now."

"No." Trish was adamant. "He's got to learn he can't act like this. He can't develop bad habits."

"Trish!"

"No, I'm okay. Lead us out there, then come with the filly. We'll trot a couple of laps, gallop a few more, and then take them to the gates. Maybe he'll get the idea when he sees how easily the filly handles the gates."

Brad glared up at her. "Come on, then, stubborn." He pulled on the bridle.

"You talking to me or the horse?"

"Take your pick," Brad said without turning as he left them on the dirt track, then added, "Trish, be careful."

Willingly, as though he'd never caused a ruckus in his life, the colt struck out in a smart walk.

After both horses had cantered the track several times, Trish pulled the colt back to a walk, waiting for Brad to catch up. "Let's go round once together at a good clip, then breeze 'em once. Okay?"

"Fine with me," Brad replied, his grumpiness gone with the feel of obedient horseflesh beneath him. "Do you want me to push her?"

"Yeah. Let's give this colt a run for his money." She slapped her mount lightly on the shoulder.

At the marker, Trish gave the bay his head. "Come on, fella. You wanted to run so bad, so here goes." With a lunge he lengthened his stride, then settled into the rhythm. His pace quickened steadily as he heard the filly coming up on the inside. Trish tightened the reins, allowing the filly to pull even at the shoulders, then the nose.

The bay tugged at the bit, begging for a looser rein. "Okay, boy. Let's see what you can do." Trish let him have his head.

Slowly the bay inched ahead of the filly. First by a nose, then a neck. As the filly dropped behind them, Trish tightened the reins, slowing the animal's driving pace. Within a few strides, both animals were back to a slow gallop.

"Pretty good, wouldn't you say?" Trish shouted, riding high in the saddle.

"Mighty fine."

They slowed both animals to a walk. "Let's go work the gates while this guy is too pooped to fight." As they reached the entrance into the center field of the oval track, Trish heard a car horn. "We'll do this another time." She trotted back toward the gate, Brad beside her. David came up to meet them.

"How's Dad?" Trish slid to the ground.

"They're still at the hospital." David's voice caught in his throat. "Trish, it's bad."

"How bad?" She couldn't speak above a whisper as she rubbed the bay's nose.

Chapter
05

It can't be bad, Trish thought as she stared at David with unseeing eyes. *I've been praying—praying for this mess to be healed right away. Or at least for there to be some medicine to take care of it. Dad says God can take care of anything. Now Dad's the one that's sick. None of this makes any sense.* She shook her head. Her fingers automatically smoothed the horse's silky hide as she leaned against the colt's shoulder.

"Trish?" David spoke softly at first.

"Um-m-m."

"Listen to me." This time he shook her arm.

"I'm listening." Trish glared at him. "You're not saying anything."

"You were a zillion miles away."

"Well, I'm here now, so tell me what you've found out."

"Here, Trish," Brad interrupted. "Let me take your horse with mine and get them cooled out."

"No. I'll come." She led the colt toward the stables. "Come on, David. We can walk and talk at the same time."

"Dad has cancer."

"Cancer!"

"In his lungs. That's why he's been coughing all this time."

"But people *die* from cancer!" Trish grabbed her brother's arm. "David, you're crazy. That can't be. I prayed—"

"Trish," David interrupted her frantic words. "Let me finish."

"No, David! Dad's not going to die. We've got too much to do here. The horses to train; the season's about to open. This is our year to win. No! He can't have cancer. No! No way!"

As Trish's voice raised to a shout, the colt's ears flattened. The whites of his eyes flashed.

"Trish!"

"No!" Unaware of anything but the pain crushing her heart, Trish jerked the reins.

Slashing black forelegs parted the air as the angry colt blasted his resentment at her thoughtless treatment. He reared, pounded the ground with furious hooves, and reared again.

When he came down the second time, David leaped to seize the bridle. Trish tightened her hold on the one rein; the other flapped in the fracas. Together they brought the quivering colt to a standstill. As one they calmed him, their words running soothingly together.

"I'm sorry, fella," Trish mumbled as she stroked the flaring nostrils. "I forgot all about you. I know you can't understand, but things are really bad for us right now. Easy, I won't ignore you again."

Gatsby stamped one foreleg and blew—hard.

"You're okay now." David stroked the steaming neck on the off side.

"Boy, that was close." Brad dismounted to walk with them.

Keeping a wary eye on the horse, Trish asked, "David, are you sure the doctors said it was cancer?"

"Yeah." David bent his head. "I'm sure." Silently they each contemplated the horror until David blew his nose. "They're doing a biopsy tomorrow, but the X-rays show a growth in both lungs. I saw them." He stopped the horse to face Trish. His red-rimmed eyes pleaded for her understanding to be quick. "They're huge. They said it's a miracle he's kept on so long."

"But when Aunty Bee had cancer, they just operated and took it all out."

"I know. I . . . well, you go talk to them tonight. Dad is expecting you. We'll go in as soon as the chores are done."

Trish shook her head. "I can't," she whispered.

"What did you say?"

Trish and the colt walked faster.

"Trish!"

"No, David. I just don't have time. I have a pile of homework, entry forms have to be filled out, I have to . . ." As they reached the barn, Trish snapped the two-way ties on to the colt's bridle. She filled a bucket with warm water and reached for the sponge and scraper. She wiped a hand across her eyes to clear the blurring. "I can't," she whispered. "I just can't."

David shook his head. "Don't be stupid, Tee. Of course you can." He picked up a scraper and the two guys copied her actions as they worked with the filly. Steam rose in a fluffy cloud when they rinsed the sweat off both horses. Off to the side, Caesar watched patiently, his dark brown eyes tracking Tricia as she swiftly groomed the colt.

On the hot walker, Spitfire nickered for attention.

Trish didn't see or hear any of it. *Think about it later,* one side of her brain cautioned.

Now, God! Heal my dad now! the other side screamed back. Her hands slowed as the war in her mind raged on. *I should have made him go to a doctor when his cough first started. . . . Why didn't Mom do something? . . . Why . . . oh, God . . . WHY?*

"Trish?" David touched her shoulder.

"What!"

"Brad and I'll feed. You go get the horses off the walker."

"Okay."

By the time the feeding was finished and the two Anderson horses were clipped to the hot walker, Trish had calmed the battle in her head. Instead of screaming, she felt numb, like a jaw full of novocaine.

"Does Dad have a phone in his room?" she asked as the three of them walked up to the house.

"Sure, but you can talk to him when we—"

Trish ignored him. "I've got to ask him about a mare that's coughing, and the gray filly is droopy."

"Trish, we'll—"

"No, David. You don't understand." She turned as they reached the steps. Pain clouded her green eyes. "I can't go there . . . to that—that place. At least not tonight." She shook her head. "Not now."

"But . . . but Mom said . . ." David stuttered in his disbelief. "Trish, Dad needs you."

"I'll talk to him on the phone." The sound of the opening door punctuated her sentence. "Brad, you coming in for cookies and a Coke?"

Brad glanced at his watch. "No, think I'll pass for tonight. You gonna need help in the morning?"

"What do you think, David?" Trish stroked Caesar's golden muzzle. The dog whined, low in his throat, always sensitive to her moods. Then he glued his haunches to her leg.

"We'll try to handle it tomorrow. If we can't get all the chores done, we'll call you. Okay?"

"Okay. But you know I'm available for whatever you need. Besides, I haven't gotten to do much riding for a long time. I'm sure Rhonda will pitch in too."

"Somehow . . ." Trish pledged, "somehow we'll get those horses ready. This is our year to win."

"Catch you later." Brad trotted off to his parked car, then turned. "Hey, David. When do you leave for school?"

Trish and David stared at each other.

"Oh my gosh," he muttered. "I'd forgotten all about that."

"Next weekend," Trish whispered. "You're supposed to leave next Sunday."

"What'd you say?" Brad leaned across the shiny roof of his car.

"It *was* next weekend," David called back. "But now? Who knows?"

Groaning, Trish threw herself down on the padded lounge chair. Caesar laid his head on her knee, brown eyes pleading for her to cheer up.

"What are we gonna do, old man?" she whispered, scratching his ears. "We just can't make it all alone. There's so much to be done around here." Her jaw tightened. "Well, we can if we have to. That's what Dad always says. God gives you the time and energy to do what you have to do. Right, David?"

Trish looked up from the dog to see her brother's stocky form propped against the house, his gaze staring across the pastures.

"Yeah, I guess so," he replied absently. David blew his nose again, dug in his pocket, pulled out a nail clipper, and began clipping his nails.

Trish knew nail-clipping was David's way of buying time. Often she teased him about having the best manicure in Clark county. Today was not the time to mention that. Trish leaned over and rested her cheek on Caesar's warm head. His tongue flicked the tip of her nose. Before she got a full face cleaning, Trish turned away. Caesar thumped his feathery tail and dug his muzzle under her chin.

"Good old dog." She gently pulled his ears. "Always gotta get the last lick in."

Caesar put both front paws on her knees. As he stood looking her right in the eye, Trish laughed. "Get down, you big horse. What do you think you are, a lap dog?" The collie dropped to the deck, his nose and forepaws down, haunches and waving tail in the air.

"Can't play now." With one leap she reached the door. "Gotta get the phone." Caesar stopped patiently at the door. "It's for you," she called back to David.

Trish ignored her brother on the phone as she opened a large can of chicken noodle soup, poured it into two bowls, added water, and popped them into the microwave.

"What was that all about?" she asked as she punched the timer.

"Getting rides back to Pullman."

"Sounded like a girl to me. I thought your rider's name was Danny."

"Yeah, short for Danielle. She's nice—blond hair, an education major. I've gone out with her a couple times. Anything else, nosy?"

"Yup. How come you haven't invited her out here to meet us?" Trish leaned against the kitchen counter.

David shook his head. "She's just a friend, for pete's sake."

"Oh sure, just a friend," Trish mimicked his tone. The timer rang. "Ah, saved by the bell. Get the bread out while you're standing there. And the peanut butter." After setting the steaming bowls on the table, Trish returned to the fridge for milk and the raspberry jam. "Want anything else?"

"No, this is enough." David hooked the chair out with one foot.

Trish blew on her soup as she spread peanut butter and jam on her whole wheat bread. "So, what did you tell her?"

"Who?"

"The awesome blond, Danielle." She licked a drip of jam off her finger.

"Knock it off! I said I'd get back to her, but she better look around for another ride, just in case." David slurped a spoonful of soup.

"Just in case what?" Trish stopped chewing and stared directly at David.

"In case I don't go back."

"But, David . . ."

"I mean for right now. You need me here. Mom needs someone with her. And how can I leave Dad? I can make it up later, no big deal."

"But what about your scholarship?"

"They'll have to hold it for later, I guess. Trish, none of that is important now." David shrugged. "It'll all work out, somehow."

"Mom's gonna be mad. Your college comes first with her."

"Not now it won't. All she needs to think about is Dad." David took a deep breath. "Besides, what else can we do?"

Trish went back to eating her soup. "I'm just glad it's not me telling her."

"Not to change the subject or anything, but hustle. We've gotta get to the hospital."

Trish choked on the mouthful of soup. "But I told you, I'm not going."

"Trish!"

"No! I'll call Dad as soon as I finish the horses." She shoved her chair back from the table. Stuffing the last of her sandwich in her mouth, she ran out the door, ignoring David's demands. Caesar bounded across the lawn after her.

Dusk was deepening into dark by the time Trish had returned all the horses to their stalls, wiped down and put away the tack, and headed out to check on the coughing mare. She seemed well enough, so her next stop was the young stock pasture.

"Come on, Caesar," she called as he sniffed around a Scotch broom bush. "Leave the rabbits alone and let's find the filly."

As she climbed the board fence into the yearling pasture, the two colts raced up and skidded to a stop. Both tossed their heads and nosed her for a treat.

"No treats." Trish pushed them away. "You haven't done anything to earn one." Both horses turned and followed her across the field, her flashlight playing out in front, searching for the missing animal.

Tricia crisscrossed the pasture from one end to the other. She checked the fences in case boards were down. The filly lay in the farthest corner. If it hadn't been for Caesar, Trish might have overlooked the animal. Her shivering body blended into the shadows of the slight hollow.

Trish dropped to one knee beside the animal's head. "Oh no," she whispered.

The gray head bobbed with a wrenching cough. Another shiver spasm rippled down the heaving sides. Trish searched her pockets. Not even a lead rope. Nothing.

Chapter
06

With a groan, Trish leaped to her feet. Her mind raced as fast as her pumping legs. *First, get the filly up and walk her to the barn. No. First get a lead rope. Do we have an empty stall away from the other animals? Yeah, I'll fork some straw in after I get her there. Then take her temperature and call the vet. Oh, if only Dad were here. I don't want to make these decisions. What if the filly dies? Oh, God, no—no! I won't think of dying. Please, God, you said you'd help . . . all the time. Why are you so far away when I need you?*

When she reached the stable, Trish flipped on the light. Nickers and rustlings in the stalls told her she had surprised the sleeping animals. The thud of hooves on a wall warned her that Spitfire didn't take kindly to the interruption.

"Easy, fella," she called as she grabbed a lead rope off the nail and dashed back to the pasture. Caesar raced beside her.

"Dear God," she pleaded between harsh breaths. "Help me get her up and into the stall."

The filly still lay shivering in the hollow. When Trish petted the gray neck, her hand came away wet.

"Dew or sweat?" she muttered. "I'm not sure. My feet are soaked enough to make me think it could be dew. Let's hope so."

All the while her soft murmurings seemed to calm the shivering horse. With the lead rope snapped in place, Trish stood and leaned against it. The gray shook her head but made no effort to regain her feet.

"God, please." Trish wiped a hand across her forehead and wrapped the lead rope around her fist. "Come on, girl." The command rang across the hollow. "Get up!" Once more she leaned against the rope, her heels digging into the wet turf.

Caesar barked. The command sharpened when he nipped the filly on the rump.

The horse scrambled to her feet.

Trish scrambled to keep from landing on her seat.

"Wow!" She shook her head. "God, when you answer a prayer, you don't fool around."

"Thanks, Caesar." At his name the dog left his self-assigned position at the animal's hocks and nuzzled his slim nose into Trish's hand. "Good boy," she whispered. "Good job. Now let's get her up to the barn."

Slowly the three made their way to the lighted stables. Every time the filly stalled, a sharp bark from Caesar reminded her of the nip on the haunches. Trish led the droopy animal into the stall farthest away from the stabled horses, one kept for sick animals but rarely used. She clipped the lead rope into one of the barn rings, then snapped the cross-tie in place.

"I know you want to lay down," she stroked the sick animal. "But that will have to come later."

When she unlatched the door to the tack room, Spitfire nickered for attention. "Later, fella," she said as she reached inside the medicine cabinet for the thermometer and petroleum jelly.

The filly was too miserable to even flinch as Trish lifted the horse's tail and inserted the rectal thermometer. Her gray head drooped as far as the lead ropes permitted. The two minutes back-pedaled into what seemed like an hour while Trish's mind flipped pages in the medical dictionary searching for possible diseases.

"Whew! A hundred and four," she read after wiping the glass tube on her pant leg. "No wonder you're shivering, old girl. You've got a fever.

Let's see what else." Swiftly she checked the animal for other symptoms. *Droopy eyes, sweaty, can't hear any strange breathing,* mentally she checked them off.

"Be right back," she patted the steamy neck. "Come on, Caesar. Let's call the vet."

The phone was ringing as Trish slid open the back door. "Runnin' On Farm," she could barely get the words past her gasps for air after the run to the house. "Trish speaking."

"Hi, babe. What's happening?"

"Oh, Dad!" Trish swallowed past the boulder that had suddenly lodged in her throat at the sound of the familiar voice. "How did you know how much I needed you?"

"Hey, we've always said great minds run in the same circles." Her father's voice rasped from a throat raw from coughing. "Now, what's our great minds' problem?"

"It's the gray filly. When I went back out to last-check the stock, she was down. Caesar and I—no, *God*, Caesar, and I got her up and into the barn. Her temp was one-oh-four."

"Slow down. Slow down. Why don't you call the vet, then call me back. Then you can tell me what you mean by God, Caesar, and you. Sounds like a good story." He paused, his voice deepening, reassuring his daughter. "Take it easy, Trish. Everything's going to be all right."

"Thanks, Dad." Trish forced her hand on the receiver to relax. "I'll get right back to you."

Amazing, Trish thought when the phone at the vet's was answered on the first ring.

"Bradshaw here."

"I'm so glad you're home. This is Trish from Runnin' On Farm. I've got a yearling filly with a temp of one-oh-four. She was down, sweaty and shivery. She didn't want to get up."

"First, get her up into the barn."

"I've already done that."

"Good, good. I'll be there in about fifteen minutes."

"Thanks, Doc."

"Oh . . . and Trish?"

"Yeah?"

"Sorry to hear about your dad."

Boy, news sure travels fast, Trish thought as she said thanks and hung up the phone. Then she turned the yellow pages for hospitals. *Ah, St. Joseph's.* She wrote the number on a pad by the phone.

"Hal Evanston's room, please," she responded to the operator.

"That's room 731. I'll ring it for you."

"Thanks." Trish scribbled the number down by the other as she switched the receiver to her other ear. "Dad?" Trish leaped in before he could give a hoarse hello.

"Yes, Trish. What did you find out?"

"He's coming right over."

"Good."

"You don't sound so good." Trish cradled the phone on her shoulder while she pushed up to sit on the kitchen counter. "Been coughing again?"

Her father chuckled, carefully. "Can't get away with much around you, can I? Forget that for now. What's going on around there, and what's this about God and Caesar helping you?"

As Trish finished describing the incident of the nip on the rump, Hal laughed until a coughing spell took his breath away.

"Sorry, Tee. But that was a good one. 'Please God'—and Caesar bites her on the rump." He chuckled more carefully this time. "Guess I don't have to worry about you at all. You, God, and Caesar. What a combination!"

Trish giggled in return. "You be good now. No matter what, we need you around here. Next time Caesar might tune out his heavenly hearing."

"No chance. His ears are perfect. You just keep on praying, that'll do it."

"Thanks, Dad." She gripped the phone like it was the lifeline connecting her to safety. "I gotta get back to the barn. Talk to you later."

"I'll call you. The switchboard won't let calls through after nine. They think we patients need our beauty sleep." He snorted. "As if beauty sleep would do me any good at this stage in my life."

"Hey, is Mom still there?"

"No, she and David left just before you called. They were stopping for hamburgers and then groceries. What do you need?"

"Nothing. Talk to you later." Trish breathed a sigh of relief when she hung up the phone. She wasn't sure what she'd been expecting, but he sounded good, she thought. *Except for that awful coughing.*

The headlights from the traveling veterinary clinic flashed in her eyes as she opened the gate. By the time the vet had parked the pickup and stepped out, Trish had run the distance to the barns.

"This way, Dr. Bradshaw. I've cross-tied her in the isolation box."

The grizzle-haired man quickly unlocked the rear boxes. "Let me get my gear. Sounds to me like you've got everything under control." As he talked, he chose syringes, bottles, and gloves and laid them in a stainless steel bucket. "You've got hot water?" He pulled on his galoshes.

Trish wished she could find the button to shift the deliberate man from low to high gear.

All the horses nickered, their curious faces hanging over the stall doors. Spitfire tossed his head and kicked the wall.

"Later, fella." Trish didn't even take time for one ear rub.

"They all look alert," the vet said. "Good sign."

"So far it's just the filly." Trish paused. "Oh, and maybe one of the brood mares. I'd like you to check her before you leave."

"Sure enough." They opened the stall door. The gray filly didn't even raise her head. She leaned against the ropes, seeming to depend on them for stability.

Trish held the animal's head up while Dr. Bradshaw checked eyes, ears, nose, and throat. A hush fell over the stall as he placed his stethoscope against the filly's heaving ribs.

Make it something simple, God, Trish prayed in the silence of her mind. *So he can give her a shot and make her all better.*

I prayed that for Dad too, she thought, *and look what happened. He's in the hospital. And cancer sure isn't simple.* She rubbed her forehead against the filly's soft cheek. *And there're no shots to cure cancer.*

"This time a shot or two will do," she whispered into the droopy ear. "I know it will."

"Well," the vet said as he removed the stethoscope and patted the gray rump. "Looks like a virus to me. I'll load her up with antibiotics to prevent any secondary infection, but the only cure is good care. And time. You've got to keep her eating and drinking. Especially drinking. So far, the ones I've seen respond pretty quickly when I catch them as early as this. The real problem comes if they go into pneumonia."

Trish felt the weight fall off her shoulders. "I'll watch her."

"Make sure you don't contaminate the other horses. This stuff is highly contagious. Don't even go into their stalls with boots you've worn in this stall. Here, wash your hands before we go check that mare. Can you give injections?" he asked as he scrubbed his hands in the disinfectant water.

"Yes. Dad made me practice. Said every horsewoman had better be able to doctor her own stock."

"Good. Good." Dr. Bradshaw patted her shoulder, his hand accustomed to conveying comfort. "I'll leave this bottle. You've got disposable syringes?"

"Sure, in the tack room."

"Give her fifteen cc's both morning and night. Warm water to drink, and mix her grain with warm water and a little molasses. If she goes down on you, call me right away."

"Got it. Fifteen cc's."

The vet kept talking while he filled his syringe, swabbed the filly's shoulder, and rammed the needle home. Trish gripped the halter extra hard, but the sick animal didn't even flinch.

When Trish unsnapped the tie ropes, the filly's head sank even lower. "I'll get some straw in here right away," Trish promised her with a last pat. "You hang in there."

Outside the stall, the vet removed his boots and stuck them in the bucket. "You keep a pair down here," he reminded her. "Do just like I'm doing."

"Okay. Will spraying the ones I have on with disinfectant take care of this evening?"

"I think so. But galoshes are better." He pulled a flashlight from his coverall pocket. "Let's go look at that mare."

When they reached the brood mares, everything seemed perfectly normal. All of them grazed peacefully, the sound of their munching drowned out by the singing frogs. Trish held each mare's head while the doctor listened to the horse's lungs with his stethoscope.

All was quiet. *Dumb horses,* Trish thought, *of course you won't cough while I have someone here to help you.*

"Can't hear a thing." Bradshaw took back the flashlight he'd given Trish to hold. "But watch them carefully. As I said, that stuff's pretty contagious. Call me if you see or hear anything unusual."

By the time the vet had reloaded his gear and reminded Trish of all his instructions, two sets of headlights turned into the farm gate.

"Looks like you have company." He shut his door.

"Mom and David are just getting home from town," Trish said through the open wondow." Thanks for coming so quickly. I really appreciate it."

"Any time, Trish. See you." The doctor honked his horn and waved as the incoming cars braked in the gravel.

"What's Bradshaw doing here?" David slammed his car door.

"The gray filly has a virus. He says it's really contagious so we have to be extra careful."

"Oh great," David groaned, "that's all we need."

"I'll be up in a minute. Just gotta fork some straw in her stall and get her a bucket of warm water."

"Want me to do it?"

"Naw, my boots are already contaminated. Won't take me long."

"Trish." Dave stopped her. "Better be prepared. Mom's pretty upset."

"About Dad?"

"That . . . and other things."

By other things, he means me, Trish thought as she loped back to the barn. *So what's new?*

Chapter 07

Fifteen minutes later, Trish slid open the glass door and sank into the nearest chair. At the staccato tap of her mother's heels, Trish looked up.

Her "Hi, Mom" trailed into a whisper when she noticed the white line around her mother's tight mouth. With a clenched jaw and hands to match, her mother stopped two feet in front of her.

"I thought you cared about your father, but it's just like I've always said. Those horses come first in your life."

The attack left Trish in a momentary state of shock. "But, Mom." She shook her head, as if to clear her ears. "Someone had to do the chores. You know Dad always says—"

"You listen to me for a change." Marge's words were clipped, each syllable sliced as if with a sharp knife. "Your father is more important to me than anything on this earth. The horses, the racing—I don't care about those. When he asked for you tonight, where were you?"

"But—" Trish was frantic to get a word in.

"I've had it!" Her mother turned toward the living room. She shook her head. "I've just had it with you, Tricia."

"But, Mom!" Trish bit off the plea.

"Horses. All the time! Sometimes I hate those animals."

"That's not fair." Trish leaped to their defense.

"You were needed somewhere else—where were you?"

"Mom! David went with you. Somebody had to take care of things around here." Trish tore her fingers through her hair. "The filly went down and—"

"Mother . . . Trish!" David vainly tried to interrupt.

"Do you think Dad wants everything to fall apart around here?" Trish's voice rose. "He's sick enough, and all you're worried about is whether or not I went to the hospital. Well, you can worry all you want to, because I *couldn't* go tonight." She brushed away the tears cascading down her cheeks. "And I probably won't go tomorrow either."

"That's nothing new. When have you ever done what I wanted?" her mother countered.

"Well, Mom, if I did what you wanted, we wouldn't have a jockey to race this year." The rage welled up within her like a mushroom cloud. "You never want me to do the things I like best. I'd rather be with horses than with people any day!"

"Tricia!" her mother reprimanded.

"You started this, Mother. Dad and I love racing."

"That's fine for a man. But in case you haven't figured it out yet, you're fast becoming a woman. Racing Thoroughbreds is a man's job."

"No! No, it's not! You know there are women jockeys. And they do okay. You just worry all the time. You don't want your daughter to be different." The feelings of rebellion within scared her, but she couldn't stop the flood of words. "Remember, you've said, 'Always tell the truth.' Well the truth is, when it comes to racing, I *don't care* if you don't agree with me!"

"Watch your mouth, young lady!"

"I have a right to say what I think!"

"Trish, go to your room." Her mother took a step closer. "I'll not allow you to talk to me like that."

"You can't stand the truth, can you? When you don't like what I have to say you send me to my room. Maybe I should sleep in the stable!"

"Tricia Evanston!"

"I don't care. Anyplace is better than here." Trish glared through her tears at her mother, then stomped down the hall. The slam of her door echoed through the house.

With a grunt she pulled off her boots and heaved them one after the other against the closet door. The tears blinded her eyes and caught in her throat. If only kicking and screaming would help.

I hate her! her mind screamed. She threw herself across the bed and sobbed. *And I know she hates me. After all I did tonight to help, and she just rips into me. Those horses are our business—Dad's and mine.* The tears raised blotches on her face and soaked circles on her bed. *I'd be better off at the track. Maybe she'd be happier if I weren't here. But where would I go?* She tossed her head from side to side, as if to drum out the furious thoughts. *I hate her. I hate her.*

Her mind went numb. The word *hate* echoed in the dark corridors of her brain. *Hate. I hate crying. I hate fighting. Oh, God, why are things so messed up? I need my dad! You say you love us, but Dad's so sick, Mom's yelling at me. . . . None of this feels like love.*

She gulped down another sob. With one hand she fumbled for a tissue on the nightstand. Tears and nose-blowing soaked that one and the next.

"Trish." David knocked softly on her door.

"What."

"Can I come in?"

"Oh, why not?" She sat up on the edge of the bed, blew her nose again, and mopped her eyes.

"Don't ask me to apologize." She hunched her shoulders, her face hidden in her hands. "Not this time. She started it." Trish could feel the tears clogging her throat again.

David sat beside her on the bed. "Yeah, I know." He rested his elbows on his knees. "But, Tee, things have been awfully rough on her today."

"Sure. And my day's been wonderful? Why'd she have to take it out on me?"

"She really felt we all needed to be together as a family, to give Dad all of our support." He handed her another tissue.

"Somebody had to be here, to keep things going."

"That's true. But if you'd gone in for just a little while—"

"I *can't* go in there." Trish buried her whisper in her fingers.

"What do you mean, you *can't* go in there?" David leaned forward, his hands clasped between his knees.

"I can't. That's what I mean." She fell back on the bed, the back of her hand hiding her eyes.

David stared at her, confusion wrinkling his brow. "Well, if you don't make any more sense than that, how can you expect Mom or anyone else to understand?"

"I don't know." Trish's voice sounded like it came from the closet, far away. "All I know is that I just can't go in there." The silence stretched. "And I hate fighting." She sniffed. "I always feel so guilty afterward, like everything in the whole world is all my fault."

"Then go say you're sorry."

"I hate that most of all." She hiccupped. "Besides, this time it was *not* my fault."

"Tee."

"Well . . ." She could feel the thoughts whipping around her brain like a gerbil on a wheel. A knock at the door brought the wheel to an abrupt stop.

"Trish." Her mother's voice came softly through the door.

"Yeah."

"Can I come in?"

"I guess."

David squeezed her hand.

"Trish—" Marge joined her children on the edge of the bed, three sets of jean-clad knees pressed together. "Please forgive me for unloading on you like that. It was totally inexcusable." She shook her head. "I know you had a terrible day too."

Wordlessly Trish nodded, tears brimming in her green eyes again. When she could look at her mother, she saw tears that matched her own. "I'm sorry too," she whispered. "I hate fighting."

Marge wrapped both arms around her daughter and held her close. "Oh, Trish. I love you so."

Trish felt the steady thumping of her mother's heart. She nestled closer, feeling safe within those protecting arms. Her mother's sweet perfume was somehow an added comfort. "I always say stuff I don't want to when I'm mad." Trish raised her face.

Marge wiped the tears from her daughter's cheek. "I know. We all do." She drew in a deep breath. "How about if I forgive you and you forgive me and we go on from here?"

Trish nodded. "Thanks, Mom."

Both reached for the tissues at the same time.

"Now," her mother went on, "how about the animals? You said you were having a problem."

"Oh dear!" Trish leaped to her feet. "Dad never called back about the filly. I should call him."

David looked at his watch. "You can try, but it's nearly eleven." David gave his sister a push out of the room. "So go call him."

Just as she reached the phone it rang. Trish jumped liked she'd touched a live wire instead of a phone. "Runnin' On Farm." She tried to sound business-like instead of breathless. "Dad! The phone rang just as I touched it. Spooky."

"As I've said, great minds . . ."

"Yeah, same circles. How are you?"

"Could be better, but the real question is how's the filly?"

"Well, Dr. Bradshaw shot her full of antibiotics and said to keep her isolated. I'm to give her fifteen cc's more morning and night for the next couple of days."

"How does she look?"

"Droopy—but the doc said the ones he's treated early like this respond pretty fast."

"What about the rest of the stock?"

"He checked the brood mares and the two colts. All clear, but I have to keep a close eye on everything." Trish cupped the phone on her shoulder as she leaned her elbows on the counter.

"How's your mother?"

"Well," Trish paused to chew her lip. "We're okay . . . now."

"Been fighting again?"

Trish forced her voice to remain calm. "Don't worry about us, Dad. Just take care of yourself." She drummed her fingers on the counter. "Hey, you know what? I have to wear galoshes when I treat the filly. Think what I'll look like in your giant-sized boots. I could put both feet in one and still have room."

"Tee, you nut."

"I'll look nutty, all right. Just call me hoppity."

"Okay, Peter Cottontail, back to the filly." Trish could feel his warm smile over the wire. "Where do you have her?"

"In the isolation stall, where else?" Surprise at his question raised her eyebrows.

"Sorry." Her father sounded sheepish. "I should have known you'd do exactly the right thing."

"You taught me, Dad." Trish hugged the phone closer to her ear, as if the action would bring him closer to her. "That's why I have to wear the galoshes, to keep from contaminating the others. I'll check on her now, before I go to bed."

"Tee, I'm proud of you. But let David check her during the night. He can do the chores in the morning too. You've got to get to school on time for a change."

"Dad . . ."

"You heard me. You can work Spitfire on the starting gates in the afternoon. And David can . . . let me talk to David. You get to bed."

"But what about Spitfire's morning workout?"

"Okay. Gallop him four miles like you've been doing. But leave the rest for David."

"Yes, sir." Trish swallowed a lump in her throat. "And please get better, Dad."

"Keep praying, babe. All of us have to keep praying."

"I'll get David." She laid the phone down on the counter and rubbed her hand across her face.

After David picked up the receiver, Trish slid the door open and stepped outside. Caesar whined for attention, then shoved his cold nose into her hand. She scratched behind his ears, all the while concentrating on her prayer. *God, make my Dad better. Bring him home to us, to me. He's a good person and he loves you. Please make him all right again.*

All the way to the barn *Please, God!* ran over and over in her brain. Soft nickers snapped her back to the present when she reached the stable. Quietly she opened the tack room door and felt on the shelf for the flashlight. The light helped her find the galoshes and slide her wet sneakers

50

into the huge boots. They came nearly to her knees. To keep them from falling off, she shuffled her feet down the row to the filly's stall.

The filly lay asleep in the straw, breathing heavily but no longer shivering. Trish flashed the light into the half-empty bucket.

"Good girl," she whispered as she stooped and ran her hand down the animal's neck. The filly just flicked her ears. "I'll get you another bucket. Drink lots."

By the time Trish's head hit the pillow, the numbers on her digital clock had flipped over 12:00. She set her alarm for 5:30 and snuggled down under the covers.

Oh no! she sighed deeply, feeling it through her whole weary body. *My chemistry—and that essay is due by three.* Like a swallow swooping through the spring sunshine, the thought of getting up and studying flitted through her mind and flew away again.

Tomorrow. I'll catch up tomorrow.

Chapter
08

Dawn hadn't cracked the darkness yet.

Trish squashed her pillow over her ears at the buzzer. She hit the snooze button and jumped when the alarm rang again. Five minutes extra sleep was not long enough; she needed five hours more, at least.

By the time she'd pulled on her jeans and sweat shirt and fumbled for her boots, David tapped on her door.

"You about ready?" His tone didn't sound any livelier than she felt.

"Yeah." She ran her fingers through her hair. The hairdresser called it finger-combing. Trish called it sheer desperation. "Gotta spray these boots first," she said as she came out of her bedroom.

She grabbed the disinfectant spray from under the kitchen sink and her down vest off the hook, and met David on the deck. "Why don't you feed and I'll start working Spitfire." She looked up from dowsing her boots. "That way maybe I'll have time to do something else."

"Remember, Dad said school on time today."

Trish wrinkled her nose. "I know. If I could just take a leave of absence or something." She wiped her nose with the back of her hand. "Phew, that stuff *smells* bad enough to kill germs." She pulled her boots on, and with Caesar trotting beside them, they jogged down to the barns.

The eastern skyline glowed a faint lemon yellow, but overhead the stars still shone valiantly, fighting off their moment of demise.

"Going to be a nice day." Trish filled her lungs with the crisp air. "Sure wish I could stay home."

"Knock it off." David lightly backhanded her arm. "I'll help you mount up. If we hustle, you can work Firefly too. I'll have her saddled so if you're on your way to the house at seven, you should be okay. Mom said she'd drop you off at school on her way to the hospital."

"She's going that early?" Trish bridled Spitfire, ignoring the nickerings on down the line. "Stop that." She slapped the horse smartly when he reached around and nipped her shoulder. "Have to keep an eye on you every minute," she muttered. "Good thing you just got my vest."

David boosted her into the saddle and waited while she gathered up her reins. "Now, you know what Dad said."

"David." She tapped him on the head with her whip. "You make a lousy mother hen. Besides, one mother is enough." Trish loosed the reins enough for Spitfire to crow-hop once before he jigged sideways to the entry to the track. She turned him clockwise and kept a tight hold on his mouth. Her father had taught her well. *No matter how much of a hurry you're in, never—but never—cheat on the warm-up time.* Strained muscles were too easily come by and too costly to cure.

After several laps at the restricted pace, Spitfire was warmed up, both from the easy gait and from fighting for his freedom every step of the way. Trish knew she'd been having a workout. Who needed free weights when she had Spitfire?

The long, slow gallop that built endurance wasn't any more to his liking. Finally, she pulled him down to a walk. "Listen, horse. Just settle down." She rubbed his neck, high on the crest and under his sweaty mane. "You know the routine as well as I do, so behave yourself. There'll be no racing today." Spitfire snorted as if in answer. "I don't care what you think. Those are Dad's orders. Now let's try this again. Slow gallop, you hear me?" The horse's ears twitched back and forth, both listening to her and checking out everything in the area.

Trish walked a final circuit, took him back to the barn, and repeated the process with Firefly. Temperament-wise, she was the exact opposite of her half-brother. Trish could relax more around her; the dark bay filly was always eager to please her rider instead of fighting her way around the track.

Trish slid off the sweaty filly at the end of the workout, threw the reins at David, and dashed up to the house. "Don't forget the shot for the sick filly." She back-pedaled as she shouted instructions to David. "Fifteen cc's and watch her." It was 7:10.

No matter how she hurried, she couldn't make up that ten minutes. The frown on her mother's face as they backed the car out of the garage at 7:55 clouded the ten-minute drive to Prairie High.

"I'm not writing an excuse." Marge checked both ways before they pulled out onto the road.

"Fine," Trish mumbled around her mouthful of peanut butter toast. *Don't bother,* she thought. *If I have to stay after to make up these tardy times, I'll just have to stay after. They're lucky I'm making it to school at all.*

"You know your main responsibility is school and your schoolwork, Tricia," her mother reminded her.

Trish cringed. Her schoolwork. She'd really have to make better use of study hall than she had. Maybe David would have time tonight to help her with her chemistry. All the rest she could manage. She'd write that essay during history and—

"How far behind are you?" Marge's jaw had that iron look.

Trish started to say, "I'm fine," but a look at her mother's face made her mumble, "Not too bad."

"What's not too bad?"

"I'll catch up today," Trish stated flatly. "Don't worry about my school-work."

"Trish . . ." Marge laid her hand on her daughter's knee.

"Don't worry." Trish jumped from the car as soon as it stopped at the curb. She leaned back in to say, "Tell Dad hi for me," and loped away, her books caught under one arm.

The stop at the office made Trish more uncomfortable.

"Where's your excuse slip?" The receptionist glanced up at the clock. "You're seven minutes late."

"I know." Trish chewed her lip, the desire to tell just a tiny fib uppermost in her mind. She shrugged. "I took too long at the barn and Mom refused to write me an excuse. I'd promised her I wouldn't be late again."

"You know this goes on your record?" The woman signed the small pink slip and handed it over the counter.

"I know. Thanks." Trish felt like tearing up the piece of paper but knew she wouldn't get into class without it. She slammed her fist against her locker when it wouldn't open on the first attempt. *Boy*, she thought as she dashed across the quad, *this day is really gonna be a great one*.

Trish used every spare minute, and by lunch time she had even made up one chemistry assignment. Her essay was ready to recopy. She debated skipping, lunch but her stomach reminded her that breakfast had been less than filling.

"How's your dad?" Rhonda asked as they joined the lunch line.

"He sounded pretty good on the phone last night." Trish glanced around the noisy room. "Have you seen Doug?"

"You going to the after-game party with him?"

"No. I won't be going at all."

"Won't be going where?" Brad joined their slow shuffle to the counter.

"To the party," Rhonda answered for her friend. "Tee, how can we help? I know you've got tons to do."

"Well, you could tell Doug I've got mono or something. He'll ask me why I can't go and I hate telling people about my dad." Trish hunched her shoulders. She hadn't let herself think about her father and the hospital this morning. Yesterday had been overwhelming; today she had regained some of her control. Fear that her mother might carry out the no-racing threat made her concentrate on her homework. The last thing she needed was an I-told-you-so from her mother. She *would* manage—somehow.

Rhonda snapped her fingers in front of Trish's eyes. "Hey, Trish, come back. What do you want for lunch?"

"Uh-h, tuna salad, milk, and an apple." She spotted Doug waving at her from a table in the back. She made a face at Rhonda, paid for her lunch, and carried her tray to the seat Doug had saved for her.

"Hi." Her smile felt like it was stuck on with Elmer's Glue.

"Hi, yourself." He pushed his books out of the way to make room for her.

"Doug, I'd love to go to the party with you, but I can't," she blurted. "I need every minute to train for the Meadows, and staying out late— well, you know how it is."

"Sounds like your coach is as tough as mine."

"Tougher. We have a lot of money tied up in these races."

"Yeah, I know." Doug nodded. "Maybe some other time?"

"Sure. After the season. It ends in April." Trish drained her milk. "I gotta rewrite this paper. Thanks for asking me." She stuffed the apple in her purse and rose to take her tray back.

Doug put his hand on her arm. "I'll do that." He looked up at her, his smile wide as the skies. "See you in the winner's circle. We'll all be there to watch your race."

Trish swallowed another lump that clogged her throat. *He is so cool.* "Thanks."

Trish found a bench outside in the sun and began the rewrite. She corrected a couple of sentences, trying to keep her handwriting legible but still writing as fast as possible. Generally she liked writing. She'd even thought about getting on the school paper staff, but as usual there was no time.

The bell rang, but she only had one more side to copy.

"There'll be a quiz tomorrow," the chemistry teacher announced just as the bell rang. "So be prepared. Remember, quizzes total twenty-five percent of your final grade." The groans from thirty students would have done justice to an announcement of thirty days' hard labor, Trish's included. That was all she needed.

Brad was waiting for her as she came out of her last class. "You want a ride?"

Trish nodded. "Thanks. Let me get my stuff out of my locker."

"How'd it go?" Rhonda asked as Trish opened the car door two minutes later.

"How'd what go?"

"With Doug." Rhonda's look suggested Trish had lost her marbles.

"He understood. Just told him I couldn't break training." Trish slammed the door as she settled herself in the front seat.

"Good thinking." Rhonda leaned forward and patted Trish on the shoulder. "Hey, you need any help this afternoon?"

"Probably. Who knows how much David got done."

"We'll be right over then, won't we, Brad?"

"Yup. Maybe today I'll get promoted to exercise boy on a permanent basis." Brad grinned at Trish. "Rhonda can muck out the stalls."

"Thanks, buddy," came from the backseat. "I'm not the one who needs bigger biceps."

Warm from the laughter of her friends, Trish didn't mind the empty house quite as much. Besides, David's car in the driveway assured her someone was home. The phone rang just as she was heading out the door to the stables, peanut butter and jelly sandwich in hand.

A stranger's voice answered her business-like response. "May I speak to Hal Evanston, please."

"I'm sorry, he's not here right now," Trish answered. "Can I help you?"

"This is John Carter. I have two Thoroughbreds and a quarterhorse I want trained and conditioned for the track. I know I'm late getting started, but I just purchased the one. A couple of people at The Meadows recommended Hal. Could you have him get back to me?"

"Sure will," Trish answered. "What's your number, Mr. Carter?"

Dollar signs played tag in her head as Trish ran down to the barn. She found David and Caesar out with the mares. "David," she called as she reached the gate, "guess what?"

"Get me another lead shank, will you?" He was leading the brood mare who'd been coughing the afternoon before.

"She's worse?"

"I think so. We'll take 'em all up and check temps. That's the only way to be sure."

Where are we gonna put more sick horses? Trish's mind raced as fast as her feet. *Guess we better clean out the old barn. They'd be isolated over there all right.*

Brad and Rhonda met them at the barn. Trish had one mare and David the two others. One of them coughed again.

"Looks like you need help for sure." Brad took the lead ropes. "Where do you want them tied?"

"Bradshaw said we have to keep them isolated, so how about the old barn?" Trish looked at David for confirmation. At his nod, she continued. "Rhonda, grab the wheelbarrow and throw in a couple of forks. We'll have to clean those old stalls out. Brad, tie those two to the outside rings and I'll get some straw after I take this one down." She rubbed the coughing mare's nose. "Pregnant as you are, you don't need to be sick too."

"When's she due?" Brad asked as they led the animals out.

"Around the twentieth, I think." Trish rubbed the mare's neck as they walked. "I keep telling Dad that if she foals on my birthday, the foal should be mine."

"Sounds good to me," Brad agreed.

They tied the animals up. While David checked temperatures, Trish helped Rhonda with the cleaning gear.

"We better call Bradshaw," David said when he came into the dim barn. "One temp with those three, and I think another of the yearlings is coming down with it. He wasn't kidding when he said it was contagious."

How do we keep the racing stock safe? Trish thought as she dog-trotted back up to the house to call the vet. *We've got to be able to move Spitfire and the others to the track next week.*

Chapter
09

The phone was ringing as Trish came through the door.

"Runnin' On Farm," she panted. "Trish speaking." She paused and smiled at the response. "Hi, Mom. No, David's down at the barn. We've got a couple more sick ones. I just came up to call the vet. How's Dad?"

"He's in the recovery room," her mother answered. "They did the bronchoscopy about an hour ago. How about you and David meeting me here at the hospital for dinner and then you can visit with your dad for a while?"

"I don't know." Trish felt caught in a trap. "I told you the mare is sick, and so is another yearling. Even with Rhonda and Brad helping, it'll take several hours to prep stalls."

"Where are you putting them?"

"Down in the old barn." At the silence in her ear, Trish swallowed. "We're doing everything we can and . . ."

"Yes, I know." Marge bit off each word. "The horses always come first. But not if your presence here could help make your father feel better."

"Tell Dad I'll call him later . . . when we know more." The line went dead without a good-bye. Why couldn't David have been the one to talk with her? *He always manages to make things better,* Trish thought. *I just make it worse.*

She called the vet and left a message for Dr. Bradshaw to come as soon as possible. Her chemistry book stared up at her accusingly from where she'd dropped it on the counter. She gave it a push. *Somewhere I'll find the time to study.* Her feet dragged on the way back to the stable. She hadn't told David about the Carter phone call. Fat chance they had of taking on any more horses now.

"I left a message on his machine." Trish found David bringing up the other two yearlings. "And Mom wants you to call her. She asked us to come in for dinner. I told her what's going on."

"And . . ."

"She wasn't very happy. Don't blame her. I'm not either."

David tied the two colts to the outside rings. "Why don't you go work Anderson's two. The three of us will get this place in shape. Dad said to put Brad on the payroll again so we can count on the extra help."

"How's the filly?"

"About the same. At least she's drinking."

"I'll call when I need a leg up. Those four been out on the hot walker today?" She nodded toward the horses they'd been training.

"Yup. Be careful with that hellion."

"What'd he do now?" Trish knew immediately that Dave meant the Anderson colt, Gatesby.

"He sure spooks easy."

"I know."

"Be careful."

"Yes, mother hen." Trish laughed as she evaded her brother's swat.

Always one to get the worst out of the way first, Trish cross-tied Gatesby in his stall, brushed him down, then bridled and saddled him. He stood, docile for a change, with only his ears responding to her soft monologue. Trish knew he behaved better for her than anyone, but he sure was a handful. And today they should be training him at the starting gate. Time was running out on getting him ready for the first part of the season.

Brad gave her a leg up when she called for help. The colt just stood there until Trish was settled and she clucked him off. He set out for the track in a flat-footed walk, looking around him with only mild interest.

Trish waved her thanks and concentrated on the warm-up. The entire session, even to walking him around the gates, only drew some snorting and eye-rolling on the colt's part. She patted his neck and smoothed his mane down as they stood a few feet from the starting gates. *That metal monster would be enough to scare anyone,* she thought. *Wait till he's boxed in with gates closed in behind and in front of him.* She rubbed the horse's neck again and turned him toward the stable.

"We'll work you with Dan'l tomorrow," she said as he twitched his ears. "All of us will be at the gate at once. That should make things easier."

The sun had set by the time she finished working Anderson's three-year-old. He'd already raced one season and was being reconditioned after an injury during the summer program in Spokane. He was a willing animal, without the contrariness of Gatesby. Trish breezed him twice around the track for the pure joy of running.

She scraped him down and rinsed the sweat off with warm water. Brad had taken care of Gatesby, so with both animals snapped to the hot walker to cool off, Trish spent a moment with old Dan'l.

"Tomorrow you get to train the kids." She rubbed his head, right behind his ears, a favorite place. "Hope they watch you and learn fast." Dan'l rubbed his nose against her chest and blew softly in her face.

For a moment Trish could pretend everything was all right. Her father was working in one of the other stalls; the exerciser sang its creaky song, and all the animals were healthy. Her mom was up baking cookies and soon dinner would be on the table.

"Where do you have the sick ones now, Trish?" Dr. Bradshaw's question broke her reverie.

She swallowed as she turned away from Dan'l and her dream. "Down at the old barn. I'll show you."

The mercury yardlight had come on before they had all the sick animals in separate clean stalls and the racing stock exercised. Training had been minimal, compared to what Trish knew needed to be done.

"How's your dad?" Rhonda asked as they trudged up the rise to the cars.

"Not coming home right away," Trish sighed.

"Are you going in to the hospital tonight?"

"No, it's too late." Trish kicked a small rock ahead of her, the action slowing her steps so David and Brad pulled ahead.

"That why your mom's mad?" Rhonda stopped beside her friend.

"Yup. She can't understand why I haven't gone to visit my dad."

"Well, why haven't you?"

"I don't know." Trish searched for words to explain her feelings. "I just can't go in there. It's like . . . well . . . if I go there . . ."

Rhonda waited out the silence.

Trish shook her head. "Rhonda, I'm so scared. I'm just so scared." She kicked another rock, viciously this time. "What if he dies?" Tears spilled over. She dashed a hand across her eyes and shook her head again. "I just can't go to the hospital. Dad *has* to come home."

By the time Trish opened her chemistry book that night, she was so tired she could hardly read the print. She took her book into the living room. "David, can you help me with this stuff?"

David was sound asleep on the sofa; his half-eaten sandwich on a plate on the floor. Trish. Threw the afghan over him and went back to her desk.

An hour later Marge found her daughter, head on her chemistry book, fast asleep. "Trish." She shook her gently. "You better get to bed."

Trish felt like she was crawling up out of a deep hole. "Hi, Mom." She blinked and turned in her chair. "How's Dad?"

"We have some good news. After his radiation treatment tomorrow, I may be able to bring him home. They started with chemotherapy today, so it depends on how he's feeling."

Trish spoke out of her fog. "He's better then?"

"Well, we just have to pray the treatments help. We'll know more in a couple of weeks. Tonight he was pretty sleepy from the anesthetic and the medication."

And you didn't even call him, Trish's conscience scolded. *What kind of daughter am I?* she thought. *Maybe Mom was right about wondering how much*

I love Dad. She swallowed against the lump that seemed to be making itself at home right behind her tonsils.

"You better get to bed." Marge rubbed Trish's tight shoulders.

"I have a quiz tomorrow. Gotta study some more." Trish stared at the sparsely filled paper glaring up at her. Three problems done out of ten. Big deal. And she had one more assignment after that. And review for a quiz. None of the stuff made any sense anyway.

"Let David take care of things in the morning. You sleep in," her mother suggested.

"Maybe." Trish picked up her pencil. *Why not have David do my chemistry and I'll work the horses?* she thought. Made a lot more sense. *Oh sure, and he could take the quiz too,* her nagging inner voice jumped back into the act. Trish looked longingly at her bed. Just one more hour. Surely she could study one more hour.

She flunked her chemistry quiz. The score stood one out of ten. Trish stared at the paper in her hand. She'd never flunked anything before. What if her mother asked how the quiz went? She stuffed the paper into her folder and tried to pay attention to the lecture. All those symbols, how would she ever get them all memorized?

Trish had a hard time paying attention all day. Good thing it was Friday. She'd be able to catch up over the weekend. When the last bell rang, she bolted for Brad's car. Give her the horses and track any day.

"Where's Rhonda?" she asked as she slid into the front seat.

"Her mom picked her up so they could leave early for the show this weekend." Brad backed out of his parking place.

"Sure wish I could be there for her. Those are nearly professional jumping classes she's entered. She's up against the big time."

"Be nice if we could all be there." Brad patted her knee. "But don't worry, Rhonda understands."

"I know." Trish sighed. *I just wish I understood,* she thought. *Everything is so messed up. Maybe . . .* her thoughts brightened. *Just maybe Dad will be there when I get home.*

He wasn't. No one was. A scrawled note from David said he'd gone to the hospital to see Dad. He'd be back around four.

"Well, that's great," Trish muttered as she changed her clothes. "You could at least have told me what needs to be done." She gathered up a load of dirty jeans and stuffed them into the washing machine. "No one ever tells me anything around here." She poured a glass of milk, stared longingly at the empty cookie jar, and grabbed an apple. Slamming the sliding glass door took skill, but she managed.

Clouds covered the sun, the gray light matching her mood. Even the horses seemed subdued as she and Caesar approached the barn. Spitfire only nickered. She missed the sound of his hoof slamming the wall.

What if they're all coming down with the virus? She stalked from stall to stall, checking each of the horses in training. They all seemed fine, just dozing. Relief, like water from a hose, washed over her.

She hugged Dan'l, comfort stealing into her bones as he nibbled at her hair. "You guys are all just lazy." She rubbed his ears and smoothed the coarse gray mane. "Wish I had time to ride you today. But you can play teacher with Brad or David to our trainees. How about showing them all you know?"

By the time she had Dan'l and Spitfire groomed and saddled, David and Brad drove up one after the other. Trish left the two animals cross-tied and began on Anderson's three-year-old. Gatesby would have to wait for her. She patted his nose as she went by, only to get a wall-eyed snort in response.

"On second thought." She grabbed a lead rope and snapped it to his halter. "I'll let you work off some of that orneriness on the hot walker."

"Good idea." Brad watched with her a moment as the colt struck out at imaginary shadows with his forefeet, shaking his head at the confining rope.

"How's Dad?" Trish asked as David loped up. "Is he coming home today?"

David shook his head. "Maybe tomorrow. He was sleeping when I left."

"I'll call him as soon as we get back to the house."

David stared at her. "I told Mom I'd bring you in for a visit tonight."

"Well, you should have checked with me before you made any promises." Trish chewed her bottom lip. "I have too much to do."

"I don't understand you." David shook his head. His jawline matched his mother's now. "Well, let's get these guys going. I mucked out and brushed them all down this morning."

"How are the sickies?" Tricia asked as David boosted her into the saddle on Spitfire.

David left the stirrups long on Dan'l's saddle. "Here, Brad, boost me up and then you take Dan'l," he said, settling himself on his horse before answering Tricia's question. "I think they're better. At least no worse, and the filly is eating again." Together they trotted toward the track. "Dad said to give these guys a good workout first, before we try the gate. We may put blinders on Gatesby and maybe even Spitfire."

Trish felt her low mood blowing away with the breeze in her face. Nothing gave her the high that working the Thoroughbreds did. And if working them was this good, what would an actual race be like? Anticipation shivered down her spine.

"I can't believe it." Trish patted Spitfire's steaming black neck. "Good boy, you're fantastic." She felt like hugging the horse who had just walked flat-footed through the open starting gate. It was like playing Follow the Leader. Whatever Dan'l did, so did the others. They walked the horses through a couple more times before Brad dismounted and tied Dan'l to the track rail.

David gave him instructions as Trish brought Spitfire back to stop in the open gates. The colt rolled his eyes and tossed his head but remained standing as her comforting voice rippled past his ears.

When horse and rider entered the stall again, Brad had closed the front gate. Spitfire walked into the open-air stall and snorted at David's mount beside him.

"Okay," David said. "Let's put these two away and bring out the others. Brad, how about if you wash 'em down while Trish and I work Firefly and Gatesby? Then we'll use Dan'l again to teach them their lessons."

Trish felt an unfamiliar gnawing in her stomach at the thought of working Gatesby. He wasn't just unpredictable; sometimes he seemed deliberately mean. She shrugged it off as Brad boosted her into the saddle.

"Now, you be careful with him." Brad kept a secure hand on the bridle. He walked them to the track. For a change, Gatesby seemed more interested in a workout than causing mischief.

Trish let the animal pick up his pace as he settled into the routine. Trot around once, then the long, conditioning slow gallop. "If you just do this well at the gate, we'll call it a great day," Trish spoke into the twitching ears. After breezing him once around, she reined him into the center field beside Dan'l.

Gatesby didn't mind the gate. He rolled his eyes and tossed his head at the close enclosure but followed Dan'l on through. Firefly came right after him.

"Thank you, God," Trish murmured, grateful the tension she felt in her stomach hadn't made it through the reins to her mount. When Brad took hold of the bridle, she rubbed the bay's neck under his sweaty mane. "Good boy. You were super." She shook her head, beaming at Brad. "I can't believe it. Did you see that?"

"I know. That's the way I dreamed of it going, but I can't believe it either."

"Let's put 'em away while we're ahead." David walked his filly toward the track. "Tomorrow I'll move the starting gates out on the track. Since it's Saturday, we can take more time. If it goes like today, we'll be in great shape."

"I can't wait to tell Dad." Trish kicked her boots out of the stirrups and slid off the steaming horse. *He should have been here,* she thought as she unbuckled her saddle. *Heavenly Father, when are you going to bring him back to me?*

Trish felt like someone had socked her in the stomach after her call to the hospital. Her father could hardly talk. Once he'd had to throw up while she waited. There were no jokes, and very little interest expressed in the horses.

"I'm sorry, Tee," his voice rasped just above a whisper. "You're doing a good job. I'll see you later."

"Right. Get well quick," Trish spoke into the dial tone after the receiver had bumped into its cradle.

What are they doing to him? She grabbed two TV dinners from the freezer and tossed them into the oven. *And they think I'm going in there—when he can't even talk on the phone?* She leaned over the sink, her stiff elbows supporting the crushing weight. *Dear God, what's happening to us? Where are you?*

Chapter
10

I said I'm not going back to school. Not right now."

"Oh, David." Marge poured herself a cup of coffee.

Tricia stared at her brother. Why'd he want to ruin a Saturday morning by bringing up something like that? He knew Mom would lay into him, especially when she was still upset about last night. Trish could tell by the way her mother had avoided her.

Marge brought her coffee mug to the table and sat down. She rubbed her fingers across her forehead, as if to erase the lines gathering there.

"I was afraid you'd decide that." She shook her head. "But I hate for you to have to postpone your education."

"I know. But, Mom, it isn't forever. Maybe Dad'll be back on his feet in time for me to go back after Christmas. I'll be missing only one semester."

"Maybe." Marge ran her forefinger around the edge of her coffee mug.

"Besides, what else can we do? Those horses support us."

Trish felt like crying for David. She knew how much he had been looking forward to school again. His dream of veterinary medicine just got put on hold—for who knew how long—and he was talking about it so calmly. Mom was too. Amazing.

"I know." Marge sipped her coffee. "I've thought maybe I'd have to look for a job."

Trish unconsciously dropped her spoon into her empty cereal bowl. The only other sound in the room was the bubbling fish tank.

"Well." Marge pushed her chair back. "I'd better get going. Maybe they'll let me bring Dad home today. Thanks, David." She squeezed his shoulder. "Trish, do you think there's any chance you can clean your room today?"

Trish felt the sarcasm bite. "I'll try."

"And maybe get some extra sleep—in your bed instead of on your desk?" Marge patted Trish's shoulder. "We don't need another sick one around here, and let's face it, you've been burning the candle at both ends and then some."

Grateful to be let off so easily, Trish just nodded.

"Brad will be over about ten," David said after their mother left the house. "Why don't you see what you can do about your bedroom between now and then? I'll get at the stalls and haul the gate onto the track."

"Okay." Trish drained her glass of milk. "David?"

"Yeah?"

"Things sure are a mess, aren't they." It was a statement, not a question.

Trish glared at the disaster in her room. "Horses are more important any day," she muttered as she sorted the dirty clothes into one gigantic heap. She glared at a poster on her wall that said "I'd rather be riding." After switching her wet jeans from the washer to the dryer, she dumped her shirts in the washer and went back to strip her bed. "Might as well do it right," she continued muttering to herself.

Within an hour, she had accomplished miracles. There was a floor there after all. By the time she vacuumed the carpet and hung up her newly washed clothes, she heard Brad's car in the driveway. "Well, at least Mom won't be able to holler at me for a messy room." Trish pulled on her boots and jogged down the slope, relieved to hear horses nickering instead of a vacuum cleaner roaring.

The three of them worked the horses in the same order as the day before. Since morning workouts had been done before breakfast, Trish put Spitfire into a slow gallop just twice around the track. He only snorted at the iron contraption taking up part of the dirt track and kept on at his easy gait.

They followed the same routine at the gates too. Everyone paraded through after Dan'l. The old horse acted bored, his quietness calming the others.

Trish kept up her one-way conversations, all the words and cadence praising Spitfire for a fine performance.

"We'll close the rear gate," David said. "He's doing so well that we'll go ahead and release the front gate at the same time. You be ready, Trish. Let him get the feel of starting."

At David's signal the gate screeched closed. Both horses were penned on all sides. Trish felt Spitfire tremble. He laid back his ears but calmed as she talked to him, her hands steady on the reins.

"Okay, Brad." David spoke in a level voice. "Be ready, Trish."

As the gate clanged open, Trish loosed the reins and shouted, "Go, Spitfire!"

Spitfire didn't need a second invitation. He bolted from the gate like a pro, running straight out within four strides. Trish stood in her stirrups to bring him back to a canter after they passed the second furlong post.

"Wow!" She turned him back toward the gate. "You are some fella."

"That was great." David cantered with her on the three-year-old. "Let's try it again, now that he knows what's going to happen."

They ran through the starting three more times, and with each release, Spitfire smoothed out his strides. He entered the gates willingly, only his dancing front feet relaying his anticipation. Trish made him stop flat-footed before the gate released so that he'd get used to waiting in case another horse was cantankerous.

"Just wait till Dad sees you," she murmured into the flickering ears. "He'll be so proud of you."

They switched horses at the stable, unsnapping Gatesby from the exerciser. As if testing her mood, he nipped at Trish's shoulder. She jerked on the lead rope. The colt rolled his eyes but walked flat-footed beside her. Trish was careful to keep her feet well ahead of his. Gatesby made a practice of stepping on human toes.

Trish could hear her father's voice in her head: *You've got to watch him at all times. Gatesby's just not as careful with his feet as he should be.* Trish thought the bay was more intentional than careless. Somehow they had to break him of the nipping. If he was as persistent in winning as he was in being a pain, Gatesby could be a Derby winner.

When he trotted by the starting gate, Gatesby laid his ears back and spooked to the side. Trish was prepared, her knees clamped and hands firm on the reins as she pulled him back to a walk.

"Now, behave yourself," she scolded as she circled the horse around the metal monster. When he quit snorting she continued around the track, passing the gates several times until the colt ignored them.

Gatesby followed Dan'l through with only a few tosses of his head, but when the time came to stand with the front gate closed, he reared at the screech. Trish smacked him hard with the side of her fist, right between his ears. "No!" she commanded at the same instant. Gatesby dropped back to all fours and shook his head.

"Try it again." She had him reined down so tightly his chin nearly touched his chest. When the gate screeched closed, the horse quivered from ears to tail, but he stood. Trish backed him out and walked him around in a tight circle. "Let's get some grease on that thing," she called to Brad. "It's the noise that's spooking him."

She turned and trotted her mount around the track until the guys were finished. This time Gatesby only danced in place. Trish settled herself more firmly in the saddle. "Okay, Brad, let's do it." As the gate swung open, Trish loosed the reins and shouted, "Go!"

Gatesby paused only a fraction of a second before he leaped at the command. He stumbled on the off forefoot as he cleared the chute but regained his footing in a stride and was running free.

Trish's grin, as she cantered him back to try again, revealed her pleasure. "One more time, then try Dan'l next to him."

Gatesby broke clean the second time and only snorted when Dan'l walked into the stall next to him.

"Are you sure you don't want to quit while we're ahead?" David asked as he settled himself for the lunge.

"Race you two furlongs." Trish grinned over her shoulder. "He's plenty warm enough." She stroked the horse's sweaty neck with one gloved hand.

David hesitated. "You're on." He whispered to Dan'l's twitching ears, "Go for it, old man. When that gate opens, go for it."

Eyes straight ahead, Trish saw the gate swing and felt Gatesby lunge at the same instant. He nicked the gate. Stumbled. Tried to regain his footing. But before Trish could blink, the momentum from his lunge slammed them into the ground.

Trish could feel herself flying through the air, her reflexes commanding her to relax.

She tried.

"Tricia! Trish!"

She could hear the voice, but so faintly she wasn't sure where it was coming from.

"Call 911." She heard no more.

"Oh shoot," Trish mumbled as she pulled herself toward the circle of light somewhere above the black dungeon she floated in. The landscape paled like dawn breaking faint on the horizon. "We did it that time, didn't we?"

"Trish? Are you okay?"

"Yeah, Brad, I'll live." Trish opened her eyes. The light blurred on her goggles. She pushed them up, relieved to see the darkness was caused by dirt on the lenses. She spat some grit out of her mouth.

"How's Gatesby?" She cleared her throat.

"Limping, but all right."

"Well, now I know what it feels like to be knocked out." Trish wiggled her fingers and flexed her feet. Everything worked. It hurt to breathe deep; in fact, she felt like she'd just been slammed into concrete, not a soft dirt track.

"Where's David?"

"Calling 911."

"Oh no. Why's he doing that?"

"Trish, you were out cold. What did you expect him to do?"

Trish raised her head.

"I don't think you should move. You know they say accident victims shouldn't be moved."

"Brad, for crying out loud, I'm no victim. I just fell off a horse." She leaned on one elbow. *Ow, that hurt. Not a good idea.* "Here, help me up."

"No, just lie there."

"I have a lump of dirt poking me in the back, the ground is cold, and all my limbs move. Slowly, but they work." She unbuckled her helmet. "Just help me sit up."

Brad slid one arm under her shoulders and cushioned her back as she leaned against him. She pulled her helmet off.

"Good thing I ride with that, huh?" She tossed it aside.

She blinked at the flashes of light in her peripheral vision. Nope, shaking her head was not a good idea either. She could feel strength returning as she drew in deeper breaths.

"Mostly, I think I had my breath knocked out."

"Trish, it was more than that. You were *out*."

"Well, go tell David . . ."

"Here he comes. You tell him."

"How is she?" David slid to a stop beside them. "They'll be here in a couple of minutes."

"David," Trish groaned. "Call them back. I'm only bruised, not broken. I don't want—" The wail of a siren broke her sentence. "Oh no. What's Mom going to say now?"

Chapter

11

 B ut, Mom, I haven't broken anything."

"What do you call anything? Possible concussion, badly shaken up. Who knows what internal damage. You can hardly move." She spun to nail David with her glare. "What's the matter with you, David? Why didn't you call me?"

"I did."

"After the medics left."

"But, Mom, what could you have done? All I could think of was getting medical help when Trish didn't come to." David twisted his class ring on his finger. "You were too far away to do anything. And after they checked her over, they carried her up to the house."

Marge rammed her hands in her pockets and went to stare out the window. "And the paramedics said they didn't think X-rays were necessary?"

"That's right."

Trish needed comfort, not this. She could feel the tears damming up behind her eyes again. As she fought them down, the pressure seemed to fill her whole head. She shut her eyes against the pain. A tear squeezed out under a closed lid and trickled down her cheek.

Her mother turned in time to see it. "Oh, Trish, I'm sorry." She dropped down on the side of the bed and wiped her daughter's face with a tissue. "But you scared me half to death." She gathered Tricia into her arms. "I've always been so terrified something like this would happen. Or worse."

Trish clamped both aching arms around her mother's waist and let the tears come. She cried until the pounding drum in her head forced her to lie down again.

Marge handed Trish a handful of tissues and wiped her own eyes with another. "Are you sure nothing is broken?"

"I'm sure, Mom. But I hurt all over. David says I landed flat out."

"David, go call your father. I'm sure he's worried sick by now." She turned back to Trish. "Would you rather sleep for a while or would you like a hot bath first? That would help the aching."

Trish tried to think, but her brain felt fuzzy and she couldn't keep her eyes open. "Later," she mumbled. She wanted to ask how the colt was but her mouth refused to cooperate.

She slept soundly for five hours, her mother checking her daughter's eyes several times for possible signs of a concussion. Those times were only a vague memory. It was thirst that woke her. Trish chewed the grit between her teeth for a moment, opened her eyes very carefully, and sighed with relief. The thumping behind her eyes was only a vague impression now.

"Ouch! Ow-w-w!" Every muscle screamed in protest when she tried to sit up.

"Need some help?" her mother asked at the door to her room.

Trish nodded, very carefully.

"I'll get some epsom salts in a hot bath started."

"I'm so thirsty."

"Here, let me help you sit up, then I'll get you a drink. We'll do this in stages." After easing Trish into a sitting position, her feet on the floor, Marge said, "Now, wait till I come back before you attempt anything else."

Trish nodded. No danger of that. At least the room had stopped tilting. She flexed her fingers and toes.

The bathroom might as well have been on the moon, it seemed so far away.

An hour later, after a long hot soak in the tub, the track dirt washed out of her hair, Trish hobbled back to bed under her own steam. She was out the instant her head hit the pillow.

The bed and bathroom were Tricia's domain until she woke late Sunday afternoon. She stretched, gently checking out each limb. Her arms were still sore, her back and legs ached, but her head was clear. Her stomach—starved. She drank the water left on her nightstand, and slowly rolled over, pushing herself up and easing her feet to the floor. Every back and hip muscle screamed in protest as she stood up. She hesitated, then tottered toward the kitchen, in favor of her hunger pangs.

The note on the counter told her David was at the stables and her mother at the hospital. A plate of food was fixed for her in the fridge.

By the time Trish had eaten and taken a hot shower, she felt fairly close to being human again. Getting up and down from a chair was painful, but not agony. She eased herself down in one and dialed the hospital.

"Dad?" She hesitated at the rough voice that answered the phone.

"Tee, how are you?" Rough voice or not, no one but her father said her name just that way.

"I'll live. I think we ought to sue the truck that ran over me, though."

"Thank God you fell so clean. Nothing broken."

"Yeah, I'm lucky."

"Not luck, Trish. You have good guardian angels."

"Yeah, well, it's a shame I didn't land on one of them. It would have been softer than the ground."

"How's Gatesby?"

"I don't know. I just woke up and David's down at the stable."

"Your mom left a few minutes ago. I'm so thankful you're all right."

"How are you doing?" Trish scrunched around on the chair, trying to find a comfortable spot. "You sound awful, but stronger."

"I am. If I do all right through the next three treatments, they're saying I can come home Wednesday."

"Good." Trish nodded. "I miss you." Where were the words to tell him how much she missed him, how much she needed him? The phone was such a poor substitute for the real thing.

"Maybe you'll feel up to coming in tomorrow. I want to make sure none of you are keeping anything from me, like a cast on your arm or leg."

"Dad, we wouldn't do that." Trish grinned at the thought. "The only thing good about a cast would be that you could sign it for me."

"I miss you, Tee." Her father cleared his throat. "Will you come?"

Trish felt the weight of the universe on her shoulders. Her chin sank to her chest. *Go see him,* her little voice nagged. *What's the matter anyway? Scared? What's hard about going to a hospital?*

"Dad, I can't." The words tore at her heart. "I . . . ah . . . I . . ." She fell silent.

"It's okay, Trish, I understand." His voice came softly over the wire. "I'll see you Wednesday, and remember, I love you."

She sniffed and swallowed the tears, almost choking on the boulder at the back of her throat. "Bye." She put the receiver down and her head on her arms. *Why can't I go see him in the hospital? I'm glad he understands, because I sure don't.*

The phone rang again just as she ordered her muscles to stand her up. "Runnin' On Farm."

"Trish, are you all right?" Rhonda's tone carried a note of panic.

"Well, I will be. Right now even this chair needs a pillow. I landed flat out on my back. At least I've learned firsthand how to fall right. How'd you find out?"

"Brad was just here."

"Hey, how'd the show go?" Trish searched for a more comfortable position.

"Well, I placed in the top ten in the open jumping class."

"How far up?"

"Number ten." Rhonda laughed. "But at least I placed. And one of the other breeders talked to me about riding for him sometime."

"They should. You're one of the best." Trish chewed on her lip. "Sure wish I coulda been there."

"I know. But there'll be other events. How's your dad?"

"Maybe coming home Wednesday. He sounds awful." Trish squirmed again. "Hey, my rear's killing me. I'll see you tomorrow. Okay?"

"Bye." The receivers clicked simultaneously.

Trish limped only as far as the kitchen door when the phone rang again. She hesitated only a moment before picking it up. "Runnin' On Farm."

"Hi, Trish," a deep voice said in her ear. "This is Pastor Ron. Just wanted to say we missed you this evening and make sure you're all right."

"I've been better." Trish glanced at the chair and eased her elbows onto the counter instead. "Uh-oh. I just found another bruise."

"Bad, huh?"

"Well, at least nothing's broken. And most of my bruises won't show. I'll probably walk funny for a day or two."

"Trish, we're all praying for your father. The kids met tonight up by the altar for a special prayer session for your dad and for you too."

Trish tried to swallow around her resident lump. "Thanks."

"I'm here when you need me. Remember that."

"Okay."

"I'll see you soon. Tell everyone hello for me. And all of us."

"I will. Thanks." Trish wiped away a renegade tear as she put the phone down.

Trish was back at the barns on Monday morning, and although she was moving slowly, she was moving. "Well, Gatesby, old man," she said as she stopped at his stall, "hear you're in about the same shape I'm in. How about a nice walk this afternoon?" She stroked his neck, keeping a firm hand on his nose. She didn't feel like having another bruise on her shoulder.

"He's not limping anymore." David joined her. "I've been bathing his shoulder in liniment. We should have used it on you."

"Should have." She retrieved her goggles and helmet from the tack room. With her jacket sleeve, she rubbed the dust from the helmet. *Good thing I was wearing this thing,* she thought as she secured the chin strap. She snapped her goggles onto her helmet as she approached Spitfire. *I'm sure glad Dad taught us to use every safety precaution. And how to fall. What if I'd tensed up?*

"Your seat feel up to sitting up there?" David asked as she gingerly settled herself into the saddle.

"Not really, but then the thought of a desk at school isn't too hot an idea either." She leaned forward to rub her horse's neck. "And do you think I can get out of either?"

David shook his head. "Just be careful, okay? Work him long and slow and I'll take care of the others." He led her toward the track. "And you *have* to be on time today. I'll signal you at quarter to seven."

"Yes, *mother.*" Trish turned Spitfire clockwise on the track and grimaced when he switched from a walk to a trot. Maybe that liniment wasn't such a bad idea.

By Wednesday Trish felt like she was behind by three days again. She used every spare minute at school, and if it hadn't been for chemistry, she would have been all right. However, when Brad turned into the drive, her low spirits leaped into high. The family car was parked in front of the house.

Trish just waved in answer to Brad's "See you in a while" and dashed for the door.

"Dad." She barely recognized the man lying in the recliner. Fear clutched her throat and strangled her stomach. She dropped her books on the sofa and tiptoed over to the sleeping figure.

What have they done to you? She almost said it aloud. He looked old and broken, like a toy someone had discarded and then hid under a bright quilt. When she touched his hand, she flinched at the deep purple and black bruises on his raised veins.

His eyes flickered open and a barely familiar smile lifted his sagging cheeks. "Tee." She didn't recognize the voice either. It rasped gray, like his face.

Tricia knelt on the floor beside the arm of the chair and laid her cheek on her father's hand. "I'm glad you're home, Dad." She felt his other hand tenderly smooth her hair back from her face. *God!* her soul raged at the heavens. *What have you done to him? I thought you were making him better.*

"I'm just worn out from the treatment today and the trip home. Tomorrow I'll be better, you'll see," he managed.

Trish nodded. "I better get down and work those beasts." She forced herself to drop a kiss on his head. "See you later."

Trish squared her shoulders and kept her stride steady as she left the room. The same iron control enabled her to change clothes and get out the door. The look she gave her mother could have slashed steel.

"David!" She ignored Caesar trotting by her side. She ignored the nickered greetings from the horses. "David!" Her shout sent Spitfire drumming a heel against the wall. Trish ignored that too. She jogged the length of the stables to find David down in the yearling pasture. She paused a moment while he latched the gate in front of the two curious colts. Her shout, "David!" cut off his whistle mid-tune.

"What's wrong?" He strode up the lane, breaking into a trot at the expression on her face.

"David Lee Evanston."

He stopped short.

"What'd I do?"

"You never told me."

David reached out and touched her arm. "You've seen Dad."

Trish nodded, her jaw set like a pit bull about to attack. "Why didn't you and Mom tell me how bad he is?"

"We tried. But you wouldn't go see for yourself, remember? We tried to ease you into it. Why do you think Mom's been with him all the time? Trish, for heaven's sake, he has cancer and the doctors think he's going to die."

"My dad's *not* going to die." Trish spun around. The tears she held back threatened to drown her. She fought the bitter bile rising from her stomach and burning her throat. In fact, burning was what she felt all over. Her brain, her heart, down to her toes. Like a forest fire out of control.

"Tee." David tried to stop her.

"Don't call me that." Trish spun away and sprinted down the

driveway, her pumping hands pummeling the horror of it all. *Dad calls me Tee, and you say he's dying.* The thoughts were like flames licking up trees. *He can't be dying. No! God, you don't love us. you don't even care. You're a liar. I hate you!*

Chapter
12

You're in no condition to ride," David said.

Trish finished saddling Dan'l with the western saddle. She had run for an hour but the fire still flickered. "I'm just taking him down through the woods." She leaned her forehead against the stirrup leathers. "David, just let me be. I promise I won't be stupid with him."

"Okay." He checked the girth. "I . . . Mom . . . we . . ."

"Later, David." She swung up into the saddle. "I'll talk to you later."

Raged out, cried out, worn out, Trish felt empty, spent, exhausted. She put Dan'l away with barely a pat and forced her boots to carry her to the house.

"Where's Dad?" The quiet house seemed to require a whisper.

"He's in bed." Marge looked at her daughter over the top of her magazine. "I'll heat your dinner while you wash up."

"No thanks." Trish looked around as if in a strange country, searching for a familiar landmark. "I'm not hungry."

"Glass of milk?"

"No. I've got some studying to do. See you in the morning." She closed the door softly after a peek at her father. No, he wasn't better.

When she came up from working Spitfire in the morning, her father was at his place at the breakfast table. While the plaid shirt he wore looked like it would fit his bigger brother, the smile he gave Trish was more like the father she knew.

"You look like you lost your best friend." The rasp was there but his voice was stronger.

"You're up."

"You're right. Very observant for such an early hour."

Trish wasn't sure whether to run and hug him or run outside and dance for joy. She opted for the hug.

"We're going to be all right," he whispered in her ear, his weak arms using what strength they had to comfort her.

Trish blinked back more tears. She didn't know she had any left. "I gotta hurry."

"So what's new?" He swatted her on the behind as she pulled away.

"How's the studying going?" Marge asked that evening after dinner.

"Better." Trish looked up from her chemistry book.

Her mother frowned almost imperceptibly at the piles of clothes in her daughter's room, then sat down on Trish's bed. "Getting better grades in chemistry?"

"Most of the time. It just doesn't make a lot of sense to me."

"It's one of David's favorite classes."

"I guess that's good, since he wants to be a vet." Trish leaned back in her chair. She stretched her arms over her head and yawned.

"How's your back?" Marge cradled her coffee cup in her hands. "You aren't limping anymore."

"No, the biggest bruise on my hip is more green than purple now. I'm sure glad—"

"That you weren't hurt worse?"

Trish nodded, dreading the turn the conversation was taking. "Don't worry so much, Mom," she pleaded. "It doesn't do any of us any good."

"That's easy for you to say." Her mother sighed deeply. "But no matter how hard I try not to worry, it just doesn't work for me. I close my eyes and I see you flying through the air or landing under some horse's hooves. Trish, accidents *do* happen. You can't deny it." She rose and patted her daughter's shoulder. "And you're the only daughter I've got. I'd just as soon keep you around for a good long time."

"Oh, Mom." Trish turned and wrapped her arms around her mother's waist. She couldn't think of anything else to say.

On Saturday Hal rode in the car down to the stables so he could watch Trish work Gatesby and check on the horses that had recovered from the virus. Neither horse nor girl seemed to remember the falling accident as they broke clean from the gates and breezed the oval track twice, Firefly neck and neck with the bay colt.

Trish waved at her father from the last circle of the track as she and David cooled the horses down.

"I think what we'll have to do is keep them here an extra week," Hal said as the four leaned against the fender of the car in a post workout rehash. Brad, their faithful gateman, had arrived at ten. "We just can't handle the trips back and forth to The Meadows in the morning."

"But will that give them time to get used to the track?"

"It's not the best plan, but in this case, we'll have to take what we can get." Hal started to cough and quickly popped a throat lozenge into his mouth. He wrapped both arms around his chest as if to hold himself together.

"I'd better get back up to the house." The rasp was worse as he fought the urge to cough. He climbed in the passenger side of the pickup. "Trish, want to drive me up? Let those two strong backs finish the stalls."

Trish hesitated an instant, resentment flaring briefly that he had to leave right when things seemed almost normal. "Sure." She swung into the driver's seat and turned the key.

"Have you made any plans for your birthday?" her father asked as they headed back up to the house.

"No. Not really. I wasn't sure . . . well, you know . . . who'd be around."

"I know it's been rough on you, Tee. I'd give anything if this weren't so." He sighed. "But it is. Rotten as it seems, we're caught in the reality."

Talk about something else, Trish reasoned in her mind. *Quick, think of something.*

"Uh-h-h, how do you think Gatesby looked?" She stammered in her panic to change the subject.

"Good. You've done a good job with him."

"I still watch him real careful. He nips any chance he gets and spooks at anything. . . ." Her voice trailed off as her father opened the passenger door.

"Decide about where you want to go for your birthday dinner. We'll take Brad and Rhonda if you like."

Trish nodded. "Okay." *What I'd like is for you to be healthy again!* she wanted to shout at his stooped back. *That's all I want for my birthday, for Christmas, the Fourth of July. That's all. God, do you hear me? That's all I want.*

"By the way," her father turned back before closing the door. "A Frank Carter called. Said he'd spoken with you about training some horses for him?"

"Yeah, I said you'd call him back, but with all that's gone on, I forgot to tell you." Trish leaned her elbows on the steering wheel, dreading her father's answer. "What did you tell him?"

"I told him the truth. That I've been mighty sick and if he can find someone else, he should. Otherwise, call back in a month."

Trish nodded, a tiny smile tickling her cheeks. She nodded again. "Thanks." At least he hadn't said "No way." Her lighter mood fluttered away like a moth on a breeze when she watched her father pause on each step, as if the effort to climb three steps was beyond him. He even leaned on the rail while digging in his pocket for a piece of candy.

Trish forced the truck into gear and drove back down to the stables.

Sunday morning the whole family went to church together for the first time in what seemed like months. Trish didn't want to go.

"You're going to make us late," her mother finally snapped. "We'll wait for you in the car."

Trish threw her hairbrush down on the bathroom counter. "I'm coming!" One more honk made her grab her purse and stalk to the car. She paused to see her father sitting on the passenger side. Another change. Too many changes.

She got through the service without really hearing one word. She was amazed at her powers of concentration. In her mind, she'd been at the track with Spitfire the entire time. *So there, God.* So much for worship.

Guilt made her feel like Pastor Ron, their youth pastor, could read her mind as he greeted her after the service.

"See you tonight?" he asked, looking from her to David. "We're playing volleyball at six."

"I wish . . ." Trish looked at David and he was shaking his head too. "I have to spend every spare minute studying so I've time to work the horses."

"We miss you." Ron squeezed her hand. "Take care." He patted David's shoulder. "Both of you."

"That mare is going to foal any time," David said at the breakfast table on Wednesday morning. "I'll bring her up to the maternity stall as soon as I take Trish to school." He glanced at his watch. "You're early, kid. What'd you do, turn over a new leaf for your sixteenth birthday?"

"Yup." Trish didn't admit that the reason was because this was the time of day her father looked the best. After his radiation treatments in the morning, he looked bad again, and he was usually asleep when she came home from school. He said his throat was so sore, he had difficulty eating.

"Did you invite Brad and Rhonda for dinner tonight?" her mother asked.

Trish nodded, her mouth full of toast.

"Where do you want to go? I'll make reservations."

"I thought we could go to The Fish House. Their clam chowder is good." Trish had thought about the Mexican restaurant, but it was noisy and the food too spicy for her dad. He wouldn't be able to eat pizza or Chinese food either. "How does that sound?"

"Sounds to me like we better hustle." David jingled his car keys. "You want to drive?"

As Trish eased the car out onto the road, she thought about her dad helping her drive lately and the fact that she hadn't had time to practice more. *I should be taking my driver's test next week!*

Her friends sang "Happy Birthday" to her in the lunchroom. If looks could kill, Rhonda would have been diced meat. She ignored Trish's red face as Doug Ramstead and a couple of other football players came over to claim a kiss.

"I'll get you," Trish hissed, her cheeks hot. Sweet sixteen—how dumb can you get. But inside she felt warm, glad that her friends cared. They'd even brought her a cupcake with a candle and several small presents wrapped and tied with crimson ribbons.

"You guys are awesome." She ignored the tears brimming in her eyes. "Thanks."

"How long till you race?" Doug asked.

"Seventeen days." Trish swallowed at the thought. "We run two weeks from Saturday."

"We'll be there." Everyone nodded.

"Just think, 'Trish to win,' " one of the football players said. Someone else took up the chant. "Trish to win. Trish to win. Trish to win." The words swelled around the room. Hands clapped. Feet stamped. Whistlers gave it all they had. The walls reverberated with the din.

Brad and Doug hoisted Trish up on the table so she could be seen by all.

Cheeks flaming, Trish waited for the cheers to die. "Thanks, guys." Her voice rang true in spite of that familiar boulder. She grinned at another whistler. "You are totally awesome. Thanks." She climbed down amid more cheers and whistles. She saw the teachers lined up against the wall. They hadn't even tried to quiet the room down.

"Even the teachers were clapping." She shook her head in amazement as she and Rhonda joined the line at the tray window.

"I know." Rhonda dumped her milk carton in the trash. "We all want you to win. No one from Prairie has ever won a horserace before."

The rest of the day raced by. "See you at seven," Trish tossed over her shoulder as she got out of the car.

"What are you wearing?" Rhonda leaned forward on the seat.

"Denim skirt, I guess. And that rust Shaker sweater."

"Okay. I'll wear a skirt too."

"And I'll wear . . ."

"Shut up, Brad," the two girls chorused and slapped their palms together in a high five.

Trish whistled for Caesar as she ran up the walk. What a birthday.

That night at the restaurant, Trish looked around at her family, light from the flickering hurricane lamps reflecting off their faces. She could even imagine her father the same as before in the dim light. Until he coughed.

The six of them had been a family for all the years the kids were growing up. Brad and David, she and Rhonda—the four musketeers.

Trish smelled the carnations in front of her. Both spicy and sweet— just like she felt at the moment.

When the waitress brought a birthday cake with sixteen candles, she wasn't surprised. Everyone sang "Happy Birthday" again and she blew hard, her wish the same as her prayers. *Make my dad well.*

"Oh my!" Her eyes widened as she opened the first of several boxes stacked in front of her. "Racing silks." She lifted the crimson and gold long-sleeved shirt from the tissue paper and held it up. Light glinted off the shiny fabric. She held the shirt to her face, feeling the coolness. "Thanks," she breathed as she laid it back in the box on top of the white pants. She grinned at her father and mother. "They're beautiful."

"Even the right color," Rhonda said. "Open mine and Brad's next."

"A new helmet! Thanks, guys." She smiled and put the hard hat back in its box.

"What do you think mine is?" David pointed at the long, slim package left in front of her.

"You sure didn't try to disguise it." Trish lifted a new whip out of the box. "Thanks, David."

She looked around the table. "Now I'm all set. Think how great this stuff will look in the winner's circle! Thank you, everybody."

"Tee, I have something more for you," her father said when they got home. He went into his bedroom and brought out a flat package. Trish looked at him with a question in her eyes. "Go ahead. Open it."

It was a beautiful book with a Thoroughbred's head on the cover. Inside the pages were blank. Trish had a puzzled expression.

"In all his visits with me at the hospital, Pastor Mort encouraged me to start a journal. Writing things down has helped me in the last few weeks, and I thought it might do the same for you."

She flipped through the pages. The flyleaf read, "To my daughter, Trish, with all my love. Dad."

"I wanted to say so much more—"

"The mare's down and in hard labor." David poked his head in the door. "Should be any time now."

Father and daughter stared at each other a few seconds. Matching smiles creased their faces. Trish grabbed both their down vests and they headed out the door together.

"You want to change first?" Hal shrugged into his vest.

"Naw. Let's get down there. Give me the keys and I'll drive." She paused. "Or would you rather walk?"

"I'd much rather walk." Her father dug in his pocket. "But we'd better drive. Here are the keys."

Hal leaned his head back on the seat even on the short stretch to the stables.

A glance at his face in the light from the dash made Trish aware how exhausted he was. Deep lines from nose to chin creased his face. Without a smile to hold the facial muscles up, his skin sagged. While he didn't wheeze, his breathing was shallow and quick. Any exertion made him stop to catch his breath again.

That ever-present snake of fear slithered back to her mind and hissed, *He's dying and there's nothing you can do about it.*

"Dad . . ."

"Um-m-m"

"Do you think you better go back to the house?" She tossed the keys in her palm. "This could be a long wait."

He opened his eyes and reached for the door handle. "Don't worry. Let's go see that mare."

Don't worry. Such an easy thing to say, Trish thought as their footsteps sounded loud in the quiet barn. *And such a difficult thing to do.*

Together they leaned over the stall door. David sat in the deep straw, stroking the mare's head.

"Good thing she recovered so quickly from that virus. She had time to get her strength back," Hal murmered.

"Will that affect the foal?" Trish asked.

"No, it was far enough along to be safe."

As they watched, her body shuddered with the force of a contraction. Two tiny hooves emerged, then withdrew.

"I brought you a stool." David nodded toward the corner. "Trish, come take my place so I can pull if I need to."

"She's progressing well," Hal said softly as another contraction forced the hooves out again. The three of them took their places, ready for an emergency, but relaxed, caught now in a rhythm as old as life.

The mare groaned at the next spasm and a nose joined the hooves. Three more contractions and the foal slid out onto the straw, securely wrapped in its protective sack.

David took a cloth from his back pocket and cleaned the foal's nostrils of mucus. The foal snorted and shook its head.

"It's a filly." He picked up some straw and began scrubbing the foal clean.

"Good girl," Trish praised the mare, who lay still through the contraction bringing forth the afterbirth. Then the horse surged to her feet, gave a mighty shake, and began nuzzling her offspring. Trish got up slowly and carefully walked around the two to sink in the straw again at her father's knee.

"What'll we name her?" Trish asked.

David left off his scrubbing as the mare took over, cleaning the foal with her tongue. Instead, he tied off the umbilical cord and clipped it with scissors that had been waiting in the pail of disinfectant.

"You name her. She's yours," Hal said.

"Mine?"

"Well, she was born on your birthday. I'd say that old mare gave you a pretty special present."

"Oh, Dad . . ." Trish couldn't get any more words past her resident throat lump.

"I know what to call her." David draped his arms around his knees as he joined them in the corner. "Miss Tee. You know, capital M-i-s-s capital T-e-e."

"Perfect. Trish, meet your namesake." Hal hugged Trish and kept his hand on her shoulder.

Trish watched each movement the foal made. The three of them laughed as Miss Tee propped each toothpick leg and tried to stand. Within an hour she was on her feet, wobbling to her mother's udder and enjoying her first meal. Her tiny brush of a tail flicked back and forth.

The three left the box stall. While David went to get a bucket of warm water for the mare, Trish and Hal leaned on the door to watch the nursing foal.

"With her bloodlines, you should have a real winner there." Hal rested his chin on his hands. "I can see your entry in the programs. Owner, jockey, Tricia Evanston."

"Our entry. We'll have so many by then, Runnin' On Farm'll be famous from Seattle to San Diego. Breeders from all over will be bringing their stock to be trained by Hal Evanston."

Hal remained silent.

Trish trailed off. They had built this dream together, talked it into reality. Spitfire was their great hope this year but next . . .

"Funny how . . ." Hal's voice was a low murmur, like he was talking to himself, "how God brings new life in as old life fades away."

"God didn't do it," Trish snapped. "The mare did." *And quit talking about life fading away,* she wanted to shout at him.

"I'll drive you up." Her flat tone cut each word clean.

Chapter
13

Trish didn't talk to her father for two days.

The morning after her birthday he wasn't at the table.

"Your dad had a bad night," Trish's mother explained. "He's finally sleeping."

When Trish pleaded homework in the evening, she wasn't lying. She'd gotten a D on that day's chemistry quiz. And midterms were coming up.

She spent every spare minute with the foal. Miss Tee accepted Trish as part of her family and already loved being rubbed behind her ears.

That afternoon Trish brought a soft brush into the box stall. With Miss Tee nearly in her back pocket, she began grooming the mare.

"She's a beauty," Rhonda whispered as she leaned against the stall half-door.

The foal scampered to the far side of her mother at the sound of a new voice. "Isn't she." Trish continued brushing with long, sure strokes. The mare flicked her ears, shifted to relax the other hind leg, and went back to drowsing contentedly.

"Do you think she'd let me help you?"

THE RACE ♘ Chapter 13

"We can try. There's another brush in the tack room. I'd like to take her out today."

The mare turned to face the newcomer as Rhonda opened the stall door and slipped inside. Rhonda stood perfectly still but carried on a singsong conversation while the horse sniffed her proffered hand, the brush, up her arm, and finally blew in her face.

"You smell other horses," Rhonda said. "And me—I'm no different, just haven't ridden you for a long time." When the mare relaxed again, Rhonda rubbed behind the horse's ears and stroked the brush down her neck.

The little filly peeked out from behind her mother's haunches. She twitched her pricked ears to free them from the veil of her mother's long, black tail draped over her face.

Trish chuckled. "What a sweetie."

The two girls chatted quietly, the mare dozed, and the filly became a little bolder toward the strange person who had entered her world.

"You look better now," Rhonda said as they dropped their brushes in a bucket.

"How'd I look before?" Trish asked.

"Bad. What's happened?"

"Well," Trish chewed on the inside of her lower lip, "it seems every time things start to get better, my dad talks about dying or . . ." The tears that seemed to stay right behind her eyelids gathered again. "Or he . . . umm—he's too sick to come to the barn." Straw rustled as the mare moved to the water bucket. The slurp and gurgle of her drinking seemed loud in the otherwise silent barn.

"Rhonda, sometimes I don't even want to talk to him. I don't want to see him . . . see how sick he really is. I *hate* all this." Trish rubbed her fist across her eyes. "And I shouldn't be angry at *him*. Not my dad." She leaned into the mare's neck and let the tears flow.

Rhonda patted Trish's shoulder, her own tears running down her cheeks. "It's not fair," she whispered. "You and your dad, you've always been so special to each other. But, Trish, you can't give up. You know we've all been praying. God can work miracles. You can't give up."

"I haven't." Trish sniffed the tears away. "At least not all the time. I pray and keep saying God knows what He's doing and I feel better. Then something happens that knocks me right down again. I feel like a yo-yo. Up and down. Up and down." She felt a tiny soft nose brush her hand. Miss Tee stretched her neck to sniff again.

Trish and Rhonda stood still and let the foal come to them. One tentative step at a time, all the while poised to dart back behind the safety of her mother's tail, the filly approached the two girls.

Trish sneezed.

The foal wheeled on spindly legs and disappeared behind the mare.

"She's just perfect." Rhonda wiped the moisture from her face.

"Yup. At least something's perfect in my life right now." Trish grasped the mare's halter. "Come on, old girl. Let's give you some exercise." She snapped a lead shank on the halter, slid the bolt on the stall door, and led the mare out of the stall. The filly glued herself to her mother's shoulder, trying to see everything but keeping herself hidden.

Rhonda opened the small paddock gate so Trish could lead the mare and foal through. The mare braced all four legs and shook herself as soon as the lead shank was unsnapped. The filly darted around the far side of her mother, tiny ears pricked and eyes wide.

Trish and Rhonda leaned against the fence, smiling at the colt's antics.

"Well, I better get going with the others. You want to work Firefly?" Trish asked.

"Sure." Rhonda glanced at her watch. "I've got time. I have to work out in the arena tonight. Dad doesn't like me taking the high jumps without anyone there. Besides, it takes too long to set the poles again by myself."

"Don't knock 'em down and you won't have to get off so often," Tricia teased.

"Thanks for the advice." Rhonda punched her friend on the shoulder. "At least they haven't had to call the paramedics for me."

"Don't be jealous." Trish stroked first Spitfire and then Dan'l after all the chores were done that evening and she'd led the mare and foal back into their stall. "I haven't been ignoring you. Miss Tee's just a baby

94

and babies need lots of attention." She dug in her pocket for a piece of carrot for each of them.

Morning workouts with Spitfire were spent in long conditioning gallops with a final breeze around the track. He fought to go all out, but Trish kept him to the schedule her father had set. Unless he sweated up because he was hyper, the black colt was in superb condition, rarely lathering by the end of the run.

On Friday night, Trish's father knocked on her door. "Trish, I think it's time we had a talk."

Bent over her chemistry book, she answered, "Sorry, Dad, but I've got to finish this assignment."

Opening her door slowly, her father spoke softly, "I know you've been angry with me."

"Dad, it's not you." Trish turned to face him. "It's this whole . . ." She searched for a good word.

"Mess?"

She nodded. "But please, I can't talk tonight."

"Okay," he agreed. "But I've missed you these last couple of days."

Trish chewed her lip. "I'm sorry." The words didn't come easily.

"Well . . . how about we move the Anderson horses to the track tomorrow? Gatsby's race is only a week away. I ordered the supplies in today."

"Hope he loads okay." Trish perked up now that the discussion was on the horses.

"We'll hood him if we have to. Get to bed early tonight." He pressed her shoulder with a comforting hand.

Trish leaned her cheek on the back of his hand. "I'll try."

That night Trish managed to stay awake for more than a short sentence-prayer. She thought about the good things that were happening: Miss Tee, the workouts, her dad at home, and all the friends who helped out and cheered them on. "Thank you, heavenly Father," she said and named each one. "Thanks, too, for loving me. I'm sorry I've been so angry. Please forgive me? I don't know how to deal with all this. And sometimes I'm so scared. Please make my dad all right again. Amen." She punched her pillow into the right shape, then added, "I almost forgot. Please, God, help Spitfire and me to win the race."

The morning fog rolled back as Trish trotted Gatesby out on the track for his early workout. He snorted and slashed at fog tendrils with his front feet.

"Feeling your oats, aren't'cha." She laughed as he leaped sideways at something only he sensed. After a couple of laps, he settled down for the long gallop, repeatedly tugging at the bit whenever he thought Trish might not be paying full attention.

Spitfire gave her the same kind of ride. "What's with you guys today?" She smoothed his mane as they trotted the cooling circle. "David feed you dynamite or something?" Spitfire jigged sideways for a furlong before he settled back to an easy trot. Flecks of lather flew back from where he kept working the bit.

By the time she'd finished Firefly and the three-year-old, Trish felt like she'd done fifty push-ups a hundred chin-ups. She rubbed her arms as she shucked her jacket at the kitchen door.

"Hard workout?" her father asked as she slid into her seat at the table.

"Yeah. They're all really feisty today." She rubbed a particularly tender spot on one shoulder. "And that clown Gatesby snuck by my guard. He wasn't just nipping either."

"He got me when I was cleaning his hooves." David joined them. "And it wasn't my shoulder."

The laughter felt like a little piece of heaven to Trish, and the French toast her mother set in front of her tasted as good.

The comforting scene ended too soon with her father's "Well, let's load 'em up. That way you can work them both real easy on an empty track this afternoon."

"They're all taped and ready." David shoved back his chair. "You coming with, Dad?"

"Yes. If I get too tired, I can sleep in the truck."

The loading went amazingly well. When Gatesby saw his stable-mate walk right up the ramp and into the double-wide horse trailer, he followed with only a rolling of his eyes. The shallow pan of grain Brad held out might have contributed to the success.

"You want me to stay here and muck out stalls?" Brad asked as they slammed the tailgate shut.

"Of course not. That's why we have a king cab, to take all of us." Hal waved toward the pickup. "You deserve a break with the rest of us."

"Trish, run in and tell your mother we're leaving," her father said as they stopped at the house.

Why me? Trish thought as she stepped from the vehicle. *This'll give her another chance to worry at me.* She slid the glass door open and leaned inside. "We're leaving, Mom. See you later."

Her mother wiped her hands on a towel and joined her at the door. "Trish, please watch out for your father." The two of them descended the stairs together. "He gets so tired and I—"

"I know." It felt strange to be on the comforting side for once. "I'll try." Trish climbed back into the truck relieved.

"You all be careful," Marge cautioned when she shut the truck door.

"We will," the three chorused as David shifted into low gear and eased the rig down the drive.

A thrill of excitement, pleasure, and suspense rippled up Trish's spine as they entered the bustling stable area of Portland Meadows Racetrack. When they stopped in front of their five designated stalls, she felt like she'd come home. *My second home, that is,* she hastily amended the thought.

Gatesby backed out of the trailer with his ears flat against his head and hooves thundering on the ramp. Trish handed one lead shank to David and kept up her low murmur, soothing the high-strung animal. Between the two of them, they worked him into his stall. They left him cross-tied in the box, but he let them know his displeasure by a tattoo of hooves on the back wall.

"We'll let him settle while we go do the paper work." Hal joined Trish after they moved the three-year-old in next door. "John Anderson will be here about two o'clock to watch you work out."

"You mean he's finally back in the country?" She kept her voice light in spite of the knot that tightened her stomach. Riding in front of an owner for the first time was as bad as giving a speech in front of a room full of classmates.

"Right. I know he's gone a lot. But an absentee owner makes it easier for the trainer. You haven't had him trying to tell you how to train his horses."

"True." Trish drew in a deep breath. The mixture of horse, shavings, straw with an overlay of hay, and grain dust smelled better than any perfume to her. She stuck her hands in her back pockets. They were here, and her race was only two weeks away. Right about now she and Spitfire would be riding to the post. She studied a circle she'd drawn in the shavings with her booted toe.

"Scared?" Her father's gentle question penetrated her reverie.

"No. Yes." She grinned up at the smile she saw on his face. "Can I be both at once?"

Hal nodded understandingly. "Let's go up to the office and then grab some lunch. Come on, you two."

David and Brad finished moving the tack into the spare stall where their feed and hay had been delivered. Lawn chairs joined buckets along the wall and their two wardrobe-style tack boxes took up another. They hung the Runnin' On Farm sign on the door and joined Hal and Trish.

Back at the barn after a satisfying lunch and with their passes in their pockets, Trish felt pure relief at the sight of a note taped on their door that read Anderson wouldn't make it today.

"That's fine with me too." Hal smiled at Trish. "I'm going to rest in the truck for a while. Why don't you start with the three-year-old and come get me when you're ready to work Gatesby." He glanced over at the bay. "Looks like he's calmed down some."

Much to Trish's surprise, the gallops for both animals went smoothly. Gatesby checked out every strange sight, smell, and sound, but once he'd been around the track a couple of times, he acted like an old hand. Trish breathed a sigh of relief as she kicked free of her stirrups and slid to the ground.

Several trainer friends of Hal's had gathered around the box. While the boys groomed the horses, Trish eased over to stand by her father's shoulder. *You're so tired you can hardly spit,* she thought of her dad. *How are you going to get strong enough to get through a race day even as a spectator?* She glanced down the aisle to where David and Brad worked like two arms of the same man. *Guess it's going to be the three of us.* Her jaw tightened. *But we can do it—can't we?*

Chapter

14

All Trish wanted to do was crawl back into bed.

She'd fed and watered all the home stock while David took care of the two at The Meadows. When she cross-tied the mare in the alley to clean out her stall, Miss Tee explored her new domain, her tiny hooves dancing through straw wisps and thudding back to hide behind her mother.

Trish threw new straw in the stall, refilled the water bucket, and led the mare back in. Miss Tee started her spooking-at-the-straw game all over again.

"You're so silly." Trish dumped a measure of grain into the feedbox. While the mare munched, Miss Tee lipped a bit of hay. Trish tugged a couple of strands of straw out of the filly's brush of sorrel mane. "You look like someone gave you a Mohawk." She smoothed the bitty forelock. "Hard to believe you'll ever be big enough to race." Miss Tee whiskered Trish's hand, her nose softer than velvet to the touch. "I'd better go." Trish latched the stall door as she heard the pickup return. "Or they'll be down to get me."

Her mother glanced pointedly at the clock when Trish slid open the glass door. "You've less than an hour," she said as she placed a plate of pancakes in front of her daughter.

"How's Dad?"

"Ready and resting. We don't want to be late to church."

Trish flinched at the implied criticism. She wasn't late *all* the time.

Trish's concentration failed her during the sermon. She was right in the middle of a workout with Spitfire when Pastor Mort's voice broke in on her daydream.

"God loves each of us so much He sent His only Son to die a miserable, degrading death—death on a cross. Even Jesus felt abandoned when He cried, 'My God, my God, why have you forsaken me?' "

Trish tried to put herself back up on Spitfire's back. She couldn't. *Does everyone have to talk about dying?* she thought. But the pastor's next words grabbed her back.

"That's how much He cares for you. For each one of us. Look for His promises when you're trapped in the hard spots of life, when everything seems hopeless. Your Bible contains all the promises God has made to His people for all time."

Some care, Trish's thoughts kept pace. *Some promises.*

But you don't know His promises, her inner voice began a debate. *I know some of them,* Trish countered. *Not enough,* the voice insisted.

"Memorize the verses," Pastor Mort continued. "So the Holy Spirit can bring them to your mind when you need them. It is a certain thing that there will be times in life when you need His help, when you need His Word."

Trish got so caught up in the argument in her head, she missed the rest of the sermon. Still, a feeling of warm comfort seemed to settle around her shoulders and snuggle into her mind. How would she find the promises? She didn't have time to read *all* the Bible right now.

"Wake me in half an hour." Trish tried to stifle the yawn that threatened after lunch. "I need to study before chores."

"And your room?" her mother asked. "If you'd hang up your clothes when you take them off . . ."

"I know." Trish headed down the hall. "I just don't have a lot of extra time." She surveyed the disaster, promised herself to catch up later, and fell on the bed—asleep before she could even roll over.

She awoke two hours later. Silence surrounded her as if she were the only one in the house. She checked David's room. He was sprawled across the bed like a puppet without strings. She peeked into her parents' room. Both of them lay sound asleep too.

Relief flooded through Trish, making her aware she'd been holding her breath. She breathed deeply, returned to her room, and opened her chemistry book. *Might as well use the bit of afternoon remaining.*

She sat down at her desk before she saw it. A green three-by-five card was set against her lamp. In her father's block printing were the words *"Cast all your cares on Him, for He cares for you" (1 Peter 5:7).* She push-pinned the card to the wall so she could see it whenever she looked up.

Trish's alarm rang at 4:30 Monday morning. She stumbled out to the pickup with her eyes half closed and didn't really wake up until David parked the truck at The Meadows. She rode both horses, left them on the hot walker, and was back home at exactly seven.

Her first class after lunch was pure agony. Her umpteenth yawn felt like it would crack her jaw. She got a drink between classes, but the chemistry symbols ran together during study hall.

Her head cleared by the time she had Spitfire out on the track, but the evening at her books was an absolute failure. Her mother tapped her on the shoulder. "Trish, you'd sleep better in bed."

Thursday afternoon she fell sound asleep in history class. Rhonda poked her in the back. Trish jerked awake to find the teacher staring at her.

When it happened again on Friday, the teacher said, "Tricia, would you stay after class a minute, please?"

"Oh no," Trish groaned.

"Tricia, this isn't like you." The teacher leaned against her desk. "I know you're getting ready for the race, but your first responsibility is here, in class."

Trish nodded, her cheeks feeling like she was standing in front of a bonfire. The teacher sounded just like her mother.

"I'll try harder, I really will," she managed.

"I hope so. Otherwise I believe I'll have to talk with your parents." The teacher signed a tardy slip as the bell rang. "Think about it."

"Yes." Trish picked up the paper and left the room. *Oh sure,* she thought. *Talk to my mom. That's all I need. As if I don't have enough on my mind without this. Who needs history anyhow?*

Rhonda waited for her outside their last class. "How bad?"

"She threatened to call my parents if I don't shape up."

"What are you gonna do? You do look beat." Rhonda held the door open for her friend.

"I don't know, but if she tells my mother, that'll be the . . ." Trish slung her denim jacket over one shoulder. "Let's get out of here." Together they jogged out to Brad's car. "At least it's Friday."

"Don't ask," Trish said to Brad's questioning look.

Trish opened the back door of the house to the aroma of fresh chocolate chip cookies. Her mother pulled a cookie sheet from the oven just as she entered the kitchen.

"Wow, these are great!" Trish relished every morsel. "Thanks, Mom."

"How was school?"

"Okay." Trish poured herself a glass of milk. "Where's Dad?"

"Down at the stable." She turned to put more scoops of dough onto the sheet. "So, what went on today?"

Trish dug a piece of dough out of the bowl with her finger and stuck it in her mouth.

"You might wash your hands first."

"Um-m-m, that tastes good. Seems forever since I've come home to your baking and cooking."

"I know." Marge sighed. "This hasn't been easy for any of us. And Trish, I *am* grateful for all you've done. Even when I don't seem so."

"Thanks, Mom." Trish felt her smile begin way inside and work its way out.

You should have told her about your teacher, the voice admonished.

Well, I got out of that one pretty good, she thought as she went to change her clothes and head for the barn.

"I've hired Genie Stokes to ride Gatesby tomorrow," Hal announced at dinner that night. "I decided to stay with a woman since you're the one who trained him, Tee."

"She'll be good for him." Trish laid her fork down. "She taught me a lot last year when we exercised horses together."

"I know. And she has the same light touch you do." Her father leaned his chin on his steepled hands. "She's going to do morning workouts for us too."

"But—" It was hard for Trish to hide her disappointment.

"You're too tired, Tee," he said, glancing toward his wife. "Your mother and I have decided no more morning workouts at the track during school days."

"But what about when we move Spitfire there? We can't have someone else work him."

"I figured we'd move him after school on Wednesday. We'll make an exception for those next two days. Your mother will take you over to ride him and bring you right back. On the condition that you get to bed early both nights."

Trish was afraid to say any more, grateful for the reprieve the two days before the race. No one else had ever ridden Spitfire.

"What about when we have an entry during the week?" she asked.

"Genie will ride then." Marge's voice was firm, to match her expression.

That's not fair! Trish wanted to scream. *They'd let me out of school. My grades are always good enough.*

Oh really, the inner voice intruded. *Flunking chemistry is good enough to get breaks at school?*

Trish looked from her mother to her father. He took his wife's hand in his. "Sorry, Tee. We really believe this is what's best."

Maybe for you. Trish bit her lip to keep the words inside. *But not for me.* "May I be excused, please?" At her parents' nod, she pushed back her chair, rose, and left the room, her booted heels beating a staccato pout.

Saturday morning Trish worked the two horses at home before she and Brad went to pick up Rhonda and head for The Meadows. David had gone in at the usual six o'clock, and Marge and Hal would be coming closer to post time. Breakfast had been pretty quiet as Trish ate quickly, keeping her eyes on her food to avoid her parents' gaze.

"I'll see you about an hour before post time," her father said. "Then we'll watch the race from the box with the Andersons."

Trish nodded.

"I've already talked with Genie. She knows what I want her to do."

"Fine." Trish left the room without a backward glance, even when she heard her father's deep sigh. *He should be at the track with us all of the time. He's never watched from the box before. And how is he going to do all that walking?* Her thoughts chased around her mind, like chipmunks on a log.

Trish rode old Dan'l on the parade to the post that afternoon. Gatesby seemed to respond well to his new rider—he'd only tried to bite her once. While he jigged sideways, his legs crossing in perfect time, his perked ears showed more interest than orneriness.

"Good luck." Trish waved to the rider as she released the lead. All the instructions had already been given. Trish felt a stir of pride as Gatesby walked easily into the starting gate.

He broke clean at the clang of the gates, his jockey keeping him free of the pack as they rounded the first turn. In this race for maiden colts, he was easy to spot, running slightly to the front. By the fourth furlong, it was obviously a race between Gatesby and a sorrel.

"And they're neck and neck," the announcer intoned. "Numbers five and seven. And they're in the backstretch, ladies and gentlemen."

"Go, Gatesby!" Trish shrieked from her position high on Dan'l's back. Rhonda's shouts joined Trish's from her spot by Dan'l's shoulder. David handed her his binoculars. "Five to win. Come on Gatesby." They chanted in chorus. At the last length, the sorrel surged ahead to win by a nose.

"Oh no," Trish moaned along with a good part of the crowd.

"For pete's sake, Tee, he placed, didn't he?" David smacked her on the knee. "That's fantastic! See what a good job you did with him?"

"If you'd been on him, he'd have won," Rhonda said when Trish dismounted and they led Dan'l back to his stall. "Genie may be a good rider, but you know Gatesby."

Trish and David were washing the steaming horse down by the time their father and the Andersons arrived at the stables.

"You've done a fine job with him." John Anderson shook Trish's hand.

"Thank you." Trish grinned up at him. "But it was all of us. We're a team, Dad, David, and I. Oh, and Brad and Rhonda too." She tapped Brad's shoulder as he wielded the scraper. "Besides, Gatesby's a good horse."

"Good and mean." Anderson kept a safe distance from Gatesby's head. "He tried taking a hunk out of me when he was just a little thing."

They all laughed, since each of them had been nipped at one time or another.

"How about you up on him the next time he's out?" Anderson tapped his program on Trish's shoulder. "You trained him, you ride him. Even though the silks will be blue and white instead of crimson and gold. Think that'd be a problem for you?"

"No, sir." Trish shook her head. "No problem at all."

"I'll pay you the standard percentage, of course."

Trish fought to wipe the grin from her face. "That'll be great. Thank you."

"Good for you," her father whispered in her ear as he left with the visitors. "See you at home."

Trish caught the look on her mother's face. Both worry and sadness creased her forehead. *Be happy for me, Mom, will you please?* Trish wished she could have said the words out loud.

Trish ignored the uneasiness she felt around her mother and embraced the thrill of future mounts to herself as she finished helping with the cleanup. She was on her way to being a professional. Her first mount on a paying basis. The only cloud on her horizon was the gray of her father's face. He looked totally exhausted.

Hal couldn't make it to the dinner table that night, so the family carried dinner to him. He was propped up on pillows, and the pallor of his face matched the pillowcases, but his smile brightened the room. David parked his TV tray in front of the rocking chair in the corner and Marge pulled up the ottoman.

Hal patted the bed beside him. "Here, Tee. You sit here."

Trish propped pillows against the headboard and wriggled herself into a comfortable position, her tray balanced on her knees. The play-by-play rehash of the day, even though in a different setting than the usual, was the perfect end to an almost-perfect day.

That is, until the others left the room and her father said, "Trish, we have to talk."

Chapter
15

In a puff the glow left the room.

Trish stalled for time. "Let me go to the bathroom first." She slipped off the bed. "I'll be right back."

She stalled longer, washing her hands, brushing her teeth, and combing her hair. When she finally returned to the bedroom, her father was slumped against the pillows—sound asleep.

"Good night, Dad," Trish whispered as she shut off the light.

The next afternoon when they returned from church, Hal remained in the front passenger seat. "Come on, Tee. Show me how your driving's improved. Don't rush lunch," he said to Marge as she got out of the car.

"When do you plan to take your test?" he asked Trish as she pulled the car out onto the main road.

"I don't know. When do I have the time?" Trish settled back and relaxed. She loved to drive.

"Probably not this week." Hal rubbed his hand across his face. "Why don't you make an appointment for next Thursday?"

"I have to take the written first, before they'll even schedule my driving test."

"Okay, then plan for the written that day. Are you studied up for it?"

"I think I have the book memorized." Trish flashed a grin at her dad. "Rhonda and I quiz each other."

"Good. Let's stop and get a milk shake at the Dairy Queen and go on out to Lewisville Park."

Trish nodded. She loved the drive to Battle Ground. On a day like today, decapitated Mount St. Helens stood sentinel against the clear blue sky. Vine maple ran rampant up the banks along the road, already flashing vermillion and burgundy.

"Two chocolate, then?" she asked as she stopped the car.

"Yeah. Make it malts."

They pulled into a secluded parking area, easy to find since few picnickers were out this late in the year. For a few minutes the only break in the silence was the slurp of milk shake through their straws.

"How much has your mother told you about my condition?" her father finally asked.

"Not a lot." Trish stirred her shake with the straw.

"Well, the good news is the radiation is shrinking the tumors."

"How much?"

"I couldn't see the difference, but the doctor assured me he saw progress. I keep picturing my lungs healthy, and claiming God's love and healing."

"But David . . . the doctor said . . . but what if you die? How would *that* show God's love?" Trish stammered over the words.

"I don't know."

"What do you mean you don't know? Aren't you mad? Don't you want to live?"

"Of course. And yes, I have been angry. Angry that this could happen to me. Furious that I kept on smoking even when I knew it was wrong and bad for my health." His sigh came from the pain deep within. "I blamed myself, blamed God, blamed the doctors for not making me well right away."

"But you've always said God can do anything."

"He can."

"And that He loves us."

"He does."

"But what if you die?" Trish gripped the steering wheel like she'd tear it off the column. "How does that show God's love?"

Her father rubbed her shoulder with the hand he'd draped over the back of the seat. "There are no easy answers, Tee. If I die, I get to go home to heaven. I'm with Him then. If I live, I get to stay home with you. Then He's with me. Either way, I'm—we're in His care."

"But I need you here." The cry tore from her heart.

"I know." His voice softened. "I know. And that's my choice too." He gathered her close.

Trish could hear the wheezing as she leaned her head on his chest. *God,* she smothered the thought deep inside her. *If you let my dad die, I swear I'll hate you forever.*

"But, you see, it's not God's fault." Her father had been reading her mind again.

"Then whose fault is it?"

"Sickness isn't anyone's fault. It just exists as long as we're on this earth."

"But . . ." Trish couldn't put her thoughts into words. "I hate cancer."

"So do I."

Trish stared at the container in her hands. "I told God that I hate Him," she whispered.

"I'm sure He understands. He knows our feelings better than we do."

"But—"

"He forgives you, Tee. And He'll never let you go. No matter how much hate and anger you have, He'll take care of it—and you."

"Thanks, Dad." The silence echoed in Trish's thoughts. She looked through the windshield, her gaze focused somewhere beyond the drooping cedar trees. "You always said God answers prayer."

"He does."

"I've been praying for you to get better."

"So have I. And a lot of other people. You heard Pastor Mort in church this morning."

Trish didn't answer. She'd been careful not to hear much of the service.

"Tee, whichever way it goes, remember that I love you. You'll never know how thankful I've been for the times we've spent together. No man could be prouder of his daughter than I am of you."

Trish let the tears flow. Great sobs shook her entire body as she clung to the father she adored. Tears fell from his eyes too, but he managed to keep from coughing.

When the emotional storm passed, they dried their eyes and attempted to smile. Trish sat up straight and dropped her head on her hands against the steering wheel.

"I still have a hard time seeing that God loves us through all this." Trish turned the key to start the engine.

Her father stayed her hand. "Tee, I've lived my whole life knowing that I am His and He is mine. Why would that change now? I need Him more than ever."

"And I need you."

"I know." He let her turn the key. "But remember that death isn't the end of life."

Trish drove home carefully, her mind a whirlwind of her father's comments.

On Monday Trish got to sleep in, and woke to find another card on her desk. This one said *"Do not be afraid—I am with you! I am your God— let nothing terrify you! I will make you strong and help you; I will protect you and save you" (Isaiah 41:10).* She tacked it up above the other one. *How,* she wondered. *How will He do all that?*

David spent Monday and Tuesday evenings coaching her on her chemistry, and his explanations made sense.

"You really like this stuff, don't you?" Trish stared at David as if he were some strange creature from outer space.

"Sure." David scrunched the pillows up behind him against the headboard. "Math and chemistry are orderly—the equations remain the same, if you do them right."

"Yeah, right."

"And yet there are all kinds of realms to explore, like medicine, for instance."

"Well, since I have no desire to work in medicine or math . . ."

"Besides that, it's good discipline for your mind. You work out to develop your muscles, right?"

"Of course."

"Well, consider this information as a workout for your mind."

"Whether I like it or not, right?" Trish flipped the pages of her chemistry book back and forth. "Do you think Dad's getting weaker?"

David didn't answer her.

Trish raised her head in time to see and hear her brother draw a ragged breath that seemed to catch on something in his throat.

"Well?" Trish hated the silence filling the room. She knew if David disagreed, he'd have said so immediately.

"Tee." David swung his feet to the floor, but slumped rather than standing up. "That's part of the disease. Dad said the treatments were about as bad as the cancer. They both make him weak."

"I feel like crying all the time. I hate it." Trish slammed her book shut. "I just hate it!"

"I know."

"You too?"

David nodded.

"But you don't . . . I mean, well . . ." Trish met her brother's gaze. The pain she saw mirrored her own. But being of a different nature, he suffered in silence.

On Wednesday, Trish earned a B on the quiz. Things were indeed looking up—in that department of her life, at least.

Snatches of the conversation with her father intruded on her thoughts at odd moments. Like when she was in the shower, or working Spitfire. Or now, when she was supposed to be studying in study hall. *God, he has such faith in you. And he's so sick.*

Last night her father had slept through the workout he'd planned to clock, and right on through the evening. Today he'd gone for a transfusion. And they were supposed to transport Spitfire and Firefly to the track when Trish got home.

"It's amazing what new blood and extra rest can do." Her father closed his Bible and brought his recliner upright as Trish came through the door.

"You look lots better."

"Feel lots better." He dug in his pocket for one of the perpetual throat lozenges. He didn't wait anymore for the cough to come, but sucked on hard candy or cough drops almost continuously.

"I'll hurry and change."

"Good. David's waiting for us to help load."

Spitfire had to show off a bit as Trish and David led him toward the trailer. He tossed his head and reared with both front feet only inches from the ground.

Trish jerked his lead rope. "Get down here, silly." She gripped the shank right under his halter. "Who're you trying to impress?"

The colt shook his head, his mane flying in every direction. He laid his ears back at the drumming of his hooves on the gate but walked in like an old hand.

Firefly didn't like the idea a bit. As soon as her front feet thudded on the ramp, she backed off with a whinny of protest. Trish led her up to the ramp again and waited for the filly to sniff the ramp. David shook a pan of grain right in front of her nose.

Acting as if she'd never hesitated, Firefly thumped her way into the trailer. Trish breathed a sigh of relief.

"You sure never know what to expect, do you?" Hal shook his head. "You two did a good job with her, with both of them."

"We had a good trainer." Trish shot home the bolt on the tailgate.

After they unloaded the two horses at The Meadows, Trish saddled Spitfire and took him out on the empty track. The colt paid attention to her voice and hands, but his twitching ears recorded all the new sights and sounds. He shied at a blowing program and snorted at the snapping flags on the infield. Trish kept him at a slow jog.

"This way there'll be no surprises for you, old buddy." She stroked his neck with one gloved hand. "You just check it all out now, 'cause Saturday we're going to be going so fast you won't have time to look."

That night Trish woke to the sound of her father's coughing. She got up and tiptoed down the hall. Her parents were both dressed.

"I'm taking your dad in to Emergency. We can't get the coughing to stop," her mother said as she helped her dad into his jacket. "I'll call you as soon as we know anything."

"You want me to drive?" David stumbled from his room.

"No. You stay with Trish." Marge tucked her purse under her arm.

"Don't worry, you two," Hal rasped between breaths. "I'll be at the track even if it's in a wheelchair."

Trish had a hard time going back to sleep. *God, he looks so awful. Please don't let him die now. Please. Please.*

When her alarm went off, she could smell bacon frying. Trish peeked into her parents' room on her way to the kitchen. Her father was asleep in the bed, a portable metal tank on the chair beside him, and a tube with prongs to his nose.

"What happened?" Trish asked when she entered the kitchen.

"They gave him some medication and oxygen, and tried to keep him there. But, as you see, your father is pretty stubborn." Her mother slipped the platter of bacon into the oven to keep it warm. "So hurry up now. I've made a good breakfast this morning."

Trish felt like the four musketeers were together again as she and Rhonda prepped Spitfire, and David and Brad worked on Firefly for the afternoon workout. They saddled Spitfire first.

"Loosen him up with a couple jogs around, slow gallop twice, and let him out for four." Hal gave Trish specific instructions. "We'll clock him."

"Forty flat," her father said before Trish could ask. "Do you think he was all out?"

"No." Trish smoothed her mount's sweaty mane. "He does better on the longer distances and with someone else pushing him."

Genie Stokes had joined the group at the rail. "He sure looks good, Trish. Did you know I'll be riding against you Saturday? That'll be a great race."

Trish could feel her insides tighten up. Any mention of Saturday brought the same reaction.

"Hey, don't worry." Genie patted Trish's knee as she guided Spitfire back to the stalls. "You'll do just fine."

"Thanks." Trish dropped to the ground and let David take the colt to his stall and begin cooling him down. "How's Gatesby doing?"

Genie rubbed her shoulder. "You sure you want to know?"

"Up to his old tricks?" Trish laughed. "You gotta watch that Gatesby."

"Can you two come for dinner?" Hal nodded at Brad and Rhonda when they were all ready to leave. "We'll get some take-out pizza."

Trish and Rhonda grinned at each other. Brad nodded.

"Good. Stop and get whatever you want." Her father stuffed some bills in Trish's hand. "Get some soft drinks too."

Feels like old times, Trish thought, after most of the three giant pizzas had disappeared. A fire snapped and crackled in the fireplace. Her father rested in his recliner, her mother's rocker creaked familiarly. All four young people lounged against floor pillows, and David fed the empty paper plates and pizza boxes into the fire. It felt so good, Trish was able to ignore the gray lines on her father's face.

"I want to thank all of you for all the extra work you've done around here," Hal said. "We couldn't have made it without you. Brad, Rhonda, you've been like my own kids ever since you were young."

"Yes, I had four chicks to worry about, not just two." Marge joined the laughter. "You've been busy kids."

"Still are," Hal added. "I'm really proud of all of you. And now, I'm going to call it a night." He brought his recliner upright. "See you at the track tomorrow."

"Thanks for the pizza," Rhonda said, finishing her drink. "Come on, Brad. Trish needs her sleep."

"Yeah, so she'll look beautiful in the winner's circle tomorrow." Brad tossed his paper cup in a wastebasket.

Trish hugged the warm glow of the evening around her as she snuggled under her bed covers. *Just like old times. Thank you, heavenly Father. Thank you.* Repeating the words lulled her to sleep. She felt like she'd just dozed off when she felt someone shaking her.

"Trish. Wake up." David shook her again.

"What?" She sat up, blinking at the light from the hallway.

"Dad's bad again. He and Mom are about to head back to the hospital."

Trish leaped from her bed and padded down the hall. She could hear her father fighting to breathe as she reached their room. He sat hunched over on the edge of the bed, the oxygen in place. Trish noticed a blue tinge to his lips. She took his hand, wrapping it in both of hers to warm it.

"I'll—see—you—in—the—morning." He panted between gulps of air. "Or—at—the—track." He draped his arm across her shoulders as David helped him to his feet. Between the two of them, they helped him to the car and swung his legs in. Trish dashed back into the house for a quilt.

"Here," she said, wrapping the blanket around him and hugging him once more.

David draped his arm around her as they waved at the receding taillights. "Pray for all you're worth," he said.

Chapter
16

Her parents' bedroom was empty when Trish checked in the morning.

She'd fallen asleep just as dawn pierced the darkness of night. Now everything looked gray, overcast, fog hugging the hollows. Trish felt gray inside, even though her resident butterflies were already up and about.

"Has Mom called?" she asked as she joined David in the kitchen.

"No." He checked his watch. "Can you be ready in half an hour?"

Trish mixed a glass of instant breakfast and forced it down. The thought of chewing even a piece of toast made her gag. After her shower, she packed her silks—the crimson and gold high-necked shirt, the white stretch pants. She snapped the silky cover in place on her helmet and tucked it in. She'd carry her boots and whip.

By the time they arrived at the back gate she'd chewed two fingernails down to the quick. The guard waved them through.

Trish could see that Brad had been hard at work when they opened the door to their tack room. All the stalls had been mucked out, and all four of the animals were out on the hot walker.

"Thanks." Trish patted her friend on the back as he forked the last of the clean straw back into one of the stalls. "How'd you get done so fast?"

"Slave labor." Rhonda squeezed past the wheelbarrow and stuck her pitchfork in the heap of straw and manure. "How're you doing, Trish?"

"I don't know." Trish shook her head. "One minute I think I'm going to throw up and the next that I'll faint. I've never had the shakes so bad."

"Better get 'em over with now." Brad leaned on the handle of the pitchfork. "Once you start working with the man," he nodded at the black colt playing with the ring on the walker, "you'll be fine. He's in great form today."

"I keep telling myself this is our day for winning. Dad and I . . ." her voice choked.

"He'll be here, Trish," Brad promised. "He said he would, and you know what an iron will he has."

"Something like yours," Rhonda finished as she gave Trish a hug.

Brad wrapped his arms around both girls. "You and your dad, you're two of a kind, Trish."

Trish leaned into the comfort and warmth of her friends' embrace. As she breathed deeply, she inhaled all the aromas of the track, and Brad's woodsy aftershave. She made herself take even breaths, and with each exhalation, the tension drained away, bit by bit.

"Thanks again." She hugged first Brad, then Rhonda, and drew herself up to her full height. "Well, Spitfire, let's get at it."

When they'd finished grooming Spitfire, the rising sun sparked blue highlights in his black coat. He tossed his head and nickered at the horses passing back and forth in the aisle. When David picked up Spitfire's front hoof to clean it, the colt gave him a nudge that sent him to his knees.

"He's just having fun." Trish giggled at the look of disgust on her brother's face. "He thinks it's time to play."

"Well, you can do your playing out there on the track." David planted his feet more firmly as he raised the next hoof. "Trish, hang on to him."

When they were finished, they draped the sheet over the perfectly groomed horse and cross-tied him in his stall.

"You want to get some lunch?" David asked.

Trish stared at him as if he'd lost his marbles.

"Just thought I'd ask." He sat down in one of the chairs in the tack room. "Brad, you want to saddle Dan'l for the post ride?"

"Sure thing."

"And lead them in the parade to the post." David glanced at Trish. "That okay with you?"

"Fine." Trish swallowed. The butterflies were back.

"Here." Rhonda handed Trish a neon-pink plastic water bottle. "It's lemonade. I'm always thirsty just before an event and cola makes me more hyper."

"Thanks," Trish said before taking a deep swallow through the attached straw. "You're right. This was just what I needed."

"How are the butterflies?" Rhonda rolled her eyes to make Trish laugh.

"Fluttering."

"Noon," David announced after glancing at his watch. "You better get over to the dressing room. "I'll call the hospital before I bring Spitfire over to the saddling paddock. We'll see you there."

"Okay." Trish gathered up her carryall, whip, and boots. "You'll bring the saddle and pad?"

"And your number. Three was a good draw."

"Dad's favorite number." Trish chewed her lip. The walk across the infield to the stands and the dressing rooms seemed like a mile. Or more.

"You want me to help carry your stuff?" Rhonda asked.

"You ready, Trish?" Genie Stokes stopped at their door.

"Sure am." Trish breathed a sigh that sounded strangely like a swimmer who'd just snagged a lifebuoy. "Thanks anyway, Rhonda. See you guys over there."

"I remember what my first race was like," Genie said as they walked past the stables. "I was absolutely sure I was gonna throw up. And then I was afraid I wouldn't. Did you eat something this morning?"

"Yes." Trish found herself answering in monosyllables.

"Good. I'd grab a bite with you after the race, but I'm riding three different horses today. Pretty good, if I do say so."

Laughter and the pungent odor of liniment hit them as they opened the door to the women's dressing room. Trish hung her things on a hook and joined Genie in an open area where several women were stretching out. She felt her stomach relax as she touched her head on her knee for hamstring stretches. The familiar routine warmed her body, and the jokes flying around brought first a smile, then a giggle.

Genie introduced her to the others and helped her begin to form a routine of her own.

When Trish left the room to go pick up her saddle, she took one last glance in the full-length mirror. No one would know she was a novice from her appearance. She brushed a hand through her dark hair and snapped the helmet in place.

Brad whistled under his breath as he handed her the saddle.

"Let's walk before I weigh in." Trish checked her watch. "I have extra time. How's Spitfire?" she asked. "And Dad?"

"Spitfire's ready to race and no report on your father. David couldn't get hold of your mom."

"That must mean they're on their way here." Trish nodded.

"You look totally awesome." Brad stepped back to look her up and down. "Wait till the team sees you."

"They're here?"

"Right on the other side of the paddock. Can't you hear them?"

"Trish to win. Trish to win." The chanting grew louder as they walked down the tunnel.

Trish waved as they paused in the entrance to the paddock. The saddling stalls formed a circle like spokes of a wheel. On the other side, spectators could come to watch behind-the-scenes action. Students from Prairie High lined the rails.

"You better go quiet them down," she told Brad. "I have to go weigh now." She waved to her cheering audience one more time. "See you in a bit."

"Good luck." Genie shook Trish's hand after they'd both been weighed in and lead weights inserted in the slots of their saddle pads.

"Same to you." Trish carried her saddle over for David to settle it just behind Spitfire's withers. As he tightened the girth, she stroked Spitfire's muzzle one more time. "This is it, fella." She smoothed his forelock. "So give it all you got."

"You can do it." Rhonda accompanied her assurance with a hug. "You're winners, both of you."

"Thanks." Trish felt like her smile might slide off and get buried in the dirt.

David boosted her atop her mount and held the stirrup while she settled her feet in place. "Now, you remember all Dad's instructions?" He patted her knee.

Trish nodded and took another deep breath before she picked up the reins. She patted Spitfire's neck again as David untied the lead rope and handed it over to Brad. After snapping her goggles in place, she nodded again.

Dan'l stepped smartly into the number three place in line when the bugle called the parade to the post. As they cleared the dim tunnel and came out into the sunlight, Trish blinked and checked the box reserved for Runnin' On Farm. It was still empty. Her father wasn't standing along the fences leading to the track either.

Trish had no more time to search. Spitfire danced sideways in his personal ballet. "Easy, boy." Her continual murmur seemed to entertain him as his ears flicked back and forth at her words. His black hide gleamed, already damp from the excitement.

As they pulled even with Dan'l, Brad grinned at her. "You're gonna do it, buddy." He snugged the lead rope down to keep Spitfire from drawing ahead. "You two look better than anything out here." He unsnapped the lead shank as they turned and slow-galloped back toward the gates. His thumbs-up signal to Trish meant "to win."

God, take care of my dad was Trish's only thought as she snuck one last glance at the empty box. Spitfire strutted into the gate and only blew when the metal clanged shut behind him. Trish felt him settle for the break. She concentrated on the space between his cocked ears, willing both herself and the horse to victory.

The shot and the opening clang of the gates sent the field surging from the gates. Spitfire broke at just the right moment, with a mighty thrust that gave them the rail in three strides. Horses one and two disappeared in the melee.

Trish leaned over the colt's withers, her face buried in his blowing mane. As they rounded the first turn she sensed a horse on their right, coming up strong. "Let's go, fella." She loosed the reins a bit and was rewarded with another lengthening of the colt's stride.

She could hear her father's voice: *Save him for the final stretch, if you can. But he likes to be out in front, so do what feels right.*

They rounded the far turn with Spitfire running easily, his ears up and twitching between Trish's running cadence and his observing everything around him. He tugged at the bit but didn't fight when Trish kept her hands firm. Still she felt him settle a bit deeper as his stride lengthened.

Coming down the final stretch, Trish became aware of a horse pulling up on the outside. He was flattened out, the jockey using the whip to bring out the last reserves.

"Go, boy!" Trish shouted to her mount. "Come on."

As they flew across the finish line, Trish wasn't sure who'd won. They'd pounded the last yards nose and nose. She stood in her stirrups to bring Spitfire down to a canter and circled back toward the stands.

"I'm sorry, fella." She tightened the reins as he tugged on the bit. "I should have let you go when you wanted. Your hearing is better than mine. If we lost, it's my fault, not yours."

"We have a photo finish, ladies and gentlemen," Trish heard the announcer. "That's numbers three and five. A photo finish—we'll have the results for you in just a couple of minutes, so hang on to your tickets."

Trish wiped lather from her cheek and let Spitfire trot around in a circle. The other horses, except for number five, had left the track.

"Trish! Trish! Trish!" The chant gained momentum as the cheering crowd quieted. The block of crimson-and-gold-clad teenagers roared from their seats. "Trish! Trish!"

Trish smoothed Spitfire's mane and allowed herself a glance at the stands. The box was still empty. She started to check the fences, but the announcer's voice cut into her concentration.

"And the winner of the first race today for maiden colts is *number three*. Spitfire—bred and owned by Hal Evanston and ridden by Tricia Evanston."

Trish's response to her victory was different than she thought it would be. As she walked Spitfire into the winner's circle, all she could think of was her father. Her eyes scanned the box one last time. It was empty.

And then she saw him. Straight ahead, between Spitfire's twitching ears, her father shuffled forward, braced by David on one side and her mother on the other. Trish's smile was brighter than the flashing of cameras as she slid to the ground.

While the steward settled the horseshoe of red roses over Spitfire's withers, Trish clutched the reins right under her mount's chin with one hand and reached for her father's hand with the other.

"Good job, babe." He squeezed her hand. "I knew you could do it." Spitfire snorted and rolled his eyes as the flashbulbs flared. He nosed Hal's shoulder, then lipped the hair that fell beneath Trish's helmet. When he tossed his head, a gob of lather landed on Marge's cheek.

"You goof." Trish rubbed the colt's soft nose. "You're a celebrity now, so act cool." She caught her mother's eye as she wiped the lather off her face.

"Good race, Trish," Marge said as she wiped her hand on her husband's sleeve. "Thanks a lot, Spitfire. I needed that."

Trish, David, and Hal looked first at Marge, then at each other. While they tried to appear professional for the final shots, laughter linked them as securely as the arms that locked them each to the other.

The Evanstons had won their race.

EAGLE'S WINGS

BOOK TWO

To my son Kevin,
who I just realized
is my pattern for David.

Would that every girl
could have a
big brother
like him.

Tricia Evanston searched the crowd for her mother, a tall woman pushing a wheelchair. Her father had slumped in that chair the moment he sat down again. But he'd been on his feet for the pictures in the winner's circle. Trish and their two-year-old Thoroughbred colt, Spitfire, had won their first race. But now her father was gone. Panic welled up.

"Come on, Rhonda." Trish grabbed her life-long friend's arm. "Maybe they're back at the stables."

"Tricia Evanston?" A well-dressed man blocked their way.

"Yes?" She found herself looking up and up.

"I'm Jason Rodgers, owner of Rodgers Stables." He extended his hand. "I've known your father for a long time. It's a real pleasure to meet his daughter."

Trish shook hands with him, wondering where the meeting was going.

"I heard about Hal's illness. It was a relief to see him here today. But let me get right to the point, since I know you have a lot to do. I have an entry in the ninth race tomorrow that I'd like you to ride. Would you be interested?"

Trish nodded before her mouth had time to answer. A mount for Rodgers Stables. The enormity of it walloped the pit of her stomach. "I'd love to but . . . but—" she clamped her lips on the brief stammer. After a deep breath, she started again. "That'll be fine." She hoped she sounded grown-up—and professional.

But what about Mom and Dad? The thought hit after he'd left. He had already told her when he'd meet her the next day. *I should have asked them first, but then, they never said I couldn't ride for someone else. And I am riding Gatesby for John Anderson. And that crazy horse tries all kinds of shenanigans. But then, I've been training him.*

The thoughts dipped and darted around in her head like bats just out of their cave for the evening.

She looked at Rhonda. The startled look on her face was a mirror of Trish's. Their "All right!" burst at the same moment.

Both girls turned and loped down the dirt path cutting across the nine-hole golf course in the infield. They met the horses being walked to the saddling paddock for the next race.

"Have you seen Dad?" Trish asked when they reached the stables.

"Your mom took him back to the hospital right after the race," Brad Williams said. Tricia's mother always referred to Trish, her friends Brad and Rhonda, and her brother, David, as the four musketeers. "He looked pretty bad."

"Where's David?"

"He and Spitfire are still at the testing barn." Brad glanced at his watch. "Should be back any minute."

Trish pulled off her helmet and fluffed her springy dark bangs with the other hand. "I didn't even get a chance to talk with him."

"Yeah, all that crowd from Prairie kind of took over." Rhonda winked at Trish. "Now you know how the football heroes feel when they get hoisted up on shoulders."

Trish could feel the red heat creeping up her neck again. Doug Ramstead, their high school's star quarterback, had lofted her on his shoulders. All the kids at the track had cheered. It *had* been pretty exciting. Until she saw her father was gone.

At that moment nineteen-year-old David trotted up with Spitfire on the lead line. "You told her?" he asked Brad, then turned to Trish. "Mom said we should come to the hospital as soon as we're done here."

Trish felt like the earth gave out beneath her. "But . . . but you know I can't go in there. I just . . . I . . ." Her gaze darted from Rhonda to David and around the stalls, as if searching for a place to hide. "I can't . . . not to the hospital . . . not now. I'll . . . I'll stay here . . . and . . ." She could feel the tears biting behind her eyelids.

The look David gave her spelled disgust in capital letters. Brad and Rhonda busied themselves on the other side of the cross-tied horse.

Trish leaned her forehead against Spitfire's neck. *Why'd they have to mess up this day? Everything has been perfect so far. Well, not really.* She remembered the empty box in the grandstands. Her father hadn't arrived at the track before the race began. He'd been rushed to the hospital the night before, hardly able to breathe.

It wasn't his first time at the hospital. But she hadn't been able to make herself go to the hospital when he'd been there for several weeks after the cancer was first diagnosed. No matter how hard she'd tried. Or how angry her mother got.

The warm, comforting smell of horse intruded on her thoughts. She stepped back so David could finish rinsing and scraping the water off the animal's blue-black hide. When David unclipped the cross-ties to take Spitfire to the hot walker, Trish took the lead rope. "Let me have him. I'll walk him out."

"You want me to come with you?" Rhonda asked.

Trish shook her head. She swallowed hard and led the weary colt out the stall door.

The noises of the stable receded as they ambled past the last stalls. Trish heard the roar of the stands as another field left the starting gates. She and her dad should be hanging over the fence, studying each horse and rider as they surged around the oval track. He should be pointing out strategies for her as he trained her in the art of becoming a jockey. No one knew racing like her father.

She swiped at a tear that meandered down her cheek. Nothing had been the same since the diagnosis. Her father had lung cancer. And he had talked about the possibility of dying. *And I let him down by not visiting him in the hospital,* Trish scolded herself.

"God, why am I such a chicken?" She aimed her question at the heavens. "Why can't I go see my dad in the hospital?" She kicked a clod of dirt ahead of them.

Spitfire snorted at the interruption. His flicking ears heard all the sounds around them, but he was too tired to react. Trish rubbed his nose in a reflex action, her mind on her troubles rather than the horse.

Her mother's accusation, *"You love those horses more than anything,"* joined the battle raging in her mind.

People go to the hospital to die.

Hogwash! People go there to get well.

My dad's not well.

He's better than he was.

Not really. They had to hold him up for the pictures.

Yes, but he made it to the track.

God is supposed to heal him.

Give Him time, you idiot. You want everything right now.

And her mother's voice, *"You love the horses best."*

"No! I don't!" The words burst out of Trish, along with sobs that wrenched her in two.

She leaned into Spitfire's neck and let the tears pour. It wasn't as if she could stop them. All the fear, the anger, the worry, the nagging little doubts that plagued her. All merged with the tears and soaked Spitfire's now dry hide.

The voices died.

Trish hiccupped. She wiped her eyes on her sleeve.

Spitfire bobbed his head, a spear of grass dangling from his teeth. He reached around and nuzzled her shoulder.

When she ignored him, he pushed a bit harder, then blew on her neck.

Trish sniffed again, followed by a deep, shuddery breath.

Spitfire rubbed his muzzle in her hair and licked the remaining salty tear away.

Trish reached up to rub the colt's favorite spot, right behind his ears. He draped his head over her shoulder in contentment.

A new voice seemed to speak in her ear. *If your father could make it to the track for you, weak as he is, we can handle a visit to the hospital for him. No matter what.*

It was as if someone reached over and lifted the killing weights from her shoulders.

Trish nodded. "Come on, Spitfire. I know you're hungry. And Dad is waiting."

She clucked to the colt and the two of them jogged back to the stables.

"If anybody's got any money, we could pick up pizza on the way. I've heard hospital food is terrible." Trish unsnapped the lead line and ducked under Spitfire's neck. Fetlock-deep straw, full water bucket, grain measured, and hay in the manger; all mute evidence that the others had been busy. "Well?" She bit back the slight wobble in her chin as she faced her brother and two best friends. "Let's go."

David threw home the bolt on the stall door. "I have ten dollars, that'll buy one."

"I'm broke but hungry." Trish wrapped her arm around Rhonda's waist.

"Five from me." Rhonda hugged her back.

"I've got eleven dollars." Brad checked his pockets. "And seventy-six cents. Let's get outta here."

The four piled into the pickup when they reached the parking lot. Brad draped his arm along the back of the seat and whispered in Trish's ear. "I'm proud of you, Tee."

Trish felt a warm spot uncurl and blossom into little stars right down in her middle. She swallowed a couple of leftover tears and rolled her lips together.

Rhonda's hand on her knee telegraphed the same message. They knew she'd fought a private war—and won.

"Hal Evanston's room, please," David said when they stopped at the information desk at the hospital. The aroma of pepperoni and Canadian bacon wafted from the flat cardboard containers Trish and Rhonda carried. Brad had charge of the soft drinks.

The woman at the desk tried to hide a grin as she gave them instructions to room 731.

Shadows hugged the corners of the room where Hal slept in a white-blanketed hospital bed. Marge napped in a chair-bed by his side. Monitors bleeped their rhythm of life, assisted by the slow drip of the IV tube attached to the back of Hal's hand.

Trish wanted to turn and run. Escape down the halls, out the door, and back to the barns where life smelled of horse and hay and grain. Where janglings and whinnies and slamming buckets chattered of evening chores and life in the horse lane. That's where her dad should be.

Not here. All was silent and gray. The shadows seemed to have slithered over the rails and painted themselves on his hair and face. His chest barely raised the covers as he breathed in through the oxygen prongs at his nose and out through a dry throat that rasped with the effort.

Trish now knew what an animal felt like in a trap. Why they gnawed off a paw to escape. Only her iron will kept her in the room. *He's going to die. He's going to die.* The words marched through her mind.

"It's not as bad as it looks." Marge rose from her chair to stand by her daughter. "He's just exhausted from going to the track." She put her arm around Trish and hugged her. "You'll never know how glad I am you're here. We have good news. An infection caused this setback and he's responding to the antibiotics."

Trish nodded. She leaned closer to her mother, as if afraid to touch the hand of the stranger sleeping in the bed.

"Maybe we should just go on home and let him sleep," David whispered.

"No." Marge shook her head. "He made me promise to wake him when you got here." She took the drinks from Brad. "You two find some more chairs. We'll have our own celebration right here. Go ahead and wake him, Tee."

"Dad," Trish whispered. When there was no response, she darted a look at her mother.

Marge nodded.

"Dad." This time Trish sounded more like herself. The word wasn't lodged behind the boulder in her throat.

The man in the bed blinked as if his eyelids weighed two pounds each. He frowned in an obvious effort to corral a mind that wandered in exhausted sleep. When he recognized his daughter, a smile crinkled clear to his eyes and sent the shadows skulking back to their corners.

"Congratulations, Tee. You won the race." While faint and scratchy, her father's voice unleashed Trish from a prison of fear. She threw herself into his arms.

"It's okay, babe," Hal whispered into her ear as one hand stroked her wavy midnight hair. "I'm going to be all right." His murmur flowed like Trish's when she calmed a frightened horse, soothing and somehow magical. She had learned the music from years of watching and listening to the father she adored.

As her tears subsided, Hal patted her back again. "Hey now, let's get me raised up so we can all talk." He sniffed. "And besides, I smell something good."

Trish wiped her face with a corner of the sheet. She gulped back the remaining tears and sat up on the edge of the bed. "We brought pizza." She heaved a deep breath. "Will they let you . . . I mean . . ."

"No problem." Hal settled himself against the angle of the raised bed. "I'm not in prison, you know."

Trish's grin wobbled but spread. "Coulda fooled me. What'll we use for a table?"

"Improvise." Hal shifted his legs to one side. "We even have a white tablecloth. Hi, Rhonda. Glad you could come." The boys returned with two chairs each and set them around the foot of the bed where Marge had opened the pizza boxes.

Trish scooped out a piece of Canadian bacon with pineapple and handed it on a napkin to her father. Hal bowed his head. "Thank you, Father, for food, for family, for your continued and most needed presence. Amen."

At the unanimous "Amen," they attacked the pizzas. After fingering a stretch of cheese back onto her piece, Trish bit into the gooey concoction as if she hadn't eaten for a week. She licked her lips and took a long drink from her icy Coke.

"How does it feel to win your first race?" Hal asked.

Trish thought a long moment. "Good, great, awesome . . . there just aren't enough words." She shrugged her shoulders. "Spitfire was fantastic. But I almost blew it. I held him back too long."

"Well, you were only doing what I told you. You'll develop a sixth sense about what's best and what your horse can do."

"I hope so." Trish licked her fingers as she finished off her pizza.

"Two men I heard talking were really impressed with Spitfire." David reached for another slice of pizza. "They thought he had a lot more to give."

"And did he?" Hal directed his question to Trish.

She nodded around another mouthful of food. Trish continued to eat as the conversation swirled around her. She could feel the tiredness start at her toes and work its way up her body. She snagged her wandering attention back to the group when she heard her name called.

"I entered Firefly in the seventh race for maiden fillies," Hal said.

Trish nodded.

"Tomorrow."

She jerked upright. "Great. She's ready." *And what about your race tomorrow?* her inner voice prodded. Trish took a deep swallow from her Coke. "That means I'll have two mounts tomorrow. Mr. Rodgers asked if I'd ride for him in the ninth." She grinned, pleased with the honor. "Good, huh?"

Beeping monitors punctuated the silence.

"But you've never ridden that horse before." Marge rose from her chair. "You don't know anything about it."

"But, Mom, that's what all jockeys do."

"No, not my daughter. I only agreed to your riding our horses."

"You should have talked with us before you accepted the mount." Hal leaned against his pillows, lines deepening around his mouth.

"I know, but there wasn't any time." Trish shoved her fingers through her hair. "And besides, you weren't there to ask." She paused and chewed her lip. "I thought you'd be proud of me."

"Oh, Tee, I am." Hal reached for her hand. "It's just that . . . well, things aren't normal and . . ."

"You call Mr. Rodgers and tell him no, thank you." Marge interrupted.

"Dad!" Trish leaped from her chair.

"We'll talk about it." Hal coughed on a deep breath.

"We better get home and get the chores done." David folded the cover on the empty pizza box. "Come on, Brad, let's put these chairs back."

Trish glanced at her mother. Marge stood looking out the window, her back to the room. Her hand rubbed her elbow as if to warm it. *Or to keep from slamming something or someone,* Trish thought. She knew how much her mother hated the thought of Trish racing. This was just the latest in a long line of discussions.

Then her inner nagger leaped into the battle. *You just went ahead and accepted, before thinking it through.*

Trish had to admit this was true. She'd been so excited at being asked that she hadn't really considered what her mother would say. Until now.

Trish leaned over the bed to kiss her father good-night. Before he hugged her he slipped a three-by-five card into her hand. "Hang on to this," he whispered.

Trish hugged him. "See you tomorrow."

As the others said their good-byes, Trish looked over at her mom.

"We'll talk more when I get home." Marge clipped her words.

Trish wasn't sure if that was a threat or a promise. She left the room, pausing briefly to read the words on the card before she strode down the hall. *"Always giving thanks to God the Father for everything, in the name of our Lord Jesus Christ"* (Ephesians 5:20).

Right, she thought, as she stuffed the card in her pocket. *Thank you, God, that my mother is ready to kill me . . . again?*

Chapter 02

I'm in for it again, Trish thought.

Dusk softened the outlines of trees and fences as the pickup turned into the drive of Runnin' On Farm. Falling dew raised ground mist that puddled in the pasture hollows and lapped up the ridges. Caesar barked a welcome, frisking beside the truck as David braked to a stop.

Trish pulled her frame upright and slid from the cab. "I'll change and be right down." She turned toward the house. "Come on, Rhonda." Trish bent over to give Caesar his expected strokes, scratching behind his pointed Collie ears and fluffing his white ruff. A flash nose lick thanked her.

"You think you'll get it bad?" Rhonda asked as they sprinted up the three back steps.

"I could tell Mom's really mad, but Dad knows how important riding is to me. To the farm. We need the money now that Dad's so sick." She pulled off both high boots at the bootjack by the sliding glass door. "I just hate having her mad at me. You know how much I hate fighting . . . of any kind."

"Yeah." Rhonda nodded soberly. "Me too."

The usual disaster area greeted them as they entered Tee's bedroom. She ignored the unmade bed and dug a pair of jeans out of the pile of clothes tossed on the chair. A minute's rummaging located a sweat shirt at the bottom of another pile.

Rhonda stared at the mess. "Maybe you should just stay up here and clean your room." She shook her head. "That would make her happier than anything."

"Later." Trish inspected the spots on her white racing pants. "Gotta remember to throw these in the washing machine. I'll need them tomorrow."

Thoughts of her mother and the coming argument flitted away on the evening breeze as Trish trotted down to the stables. A deep breath told her someone was burning leaves. Caesar leaped in front of them and whined for attention. Both girls stopped to stroke the dog's sable coat.

The stables seemed empty with the racing string at the track. "Miss Tee and her mother need some exercise." Trish measured grain into a bucket for the mare and handed Rhonda a hunk of hay. As they left the feed room, she stuck a currycomb in her back pocket and dropped a soft brush on top of the grain.

A nicker greeted them when they entered the shadowed barn. Trish flicked on the light switch and the bay mare blinked at the glare. She nickered again at the sight of the grain and hay.

"Hungry, are you?" Trish held out a handful of grain. "You need to get out first, then eat." The mare lipped the grain, then nudged Trish's chest, begging for more. Trish took the lead rope down from its hook and clipped it to the mare's halter. "Hi, Miss Tee, whatcha hiding for?"

Rhonda giggled at the month-old filly who peeked out from behind her bay mother, whose long black tail hairs whisked over Miss Tee's face. "You should know me by now." Rhonda's soft voice set the foal's ears flicking.

Trish offered the lead shank to Rhonda and opened the stall. She smoothed the mare's shoulder as she slipped inside. "Come on, baby. You don't need to play hide-and-seek with me."

The foal stretched her nose as far as she could, then took two steps. When Trish touched the soft muzzle, Miss Tee leaped back. She shook her head and stamped one tiny forefoot.

"Okay for you." Trish turned her back. "Hand me that brush, will you?" When Rhonda handed her the brush, Trish stroked it down the mare's neck. She winked at Rhonda and whistled a little tune, all the while ignoring the foal.

Step by step Miss Tee left her hideout and approached her owner. Finally she rubbed her forehead on Trish's arm.

"Silly baby," Trish crooned as she gently rubbed the filly's ears. "Just have to play out your games, don't you?"

"What a clown." Rhonda laughed as she swung the stall open. "Does she always act like that?"

"No, only when I haven't paid enough attention to her. The last couple of days have been kind of crazy."

"You're telling me." Rhonda rolled her eyes.

"Why don't you walk them and I'll muck out this stall."

"What a deal." Rhonda took the lead rope. She clucked to the mare and the three trotted out of the barn. Miss Tee stopped at the door and looked back at Trish as if asking why she wasn't coming too.

"Go on, run a bit. You don't have all night." Trish shooed the filly out and reached for the pitchfork.

It was eight o'clock by the time the four of them finished all the chores and Brad drove his blue Mustang out the drive.

"I'm beat." Trish shrugged her shoulders up to her ears to pull out the kinks.

"Me too." David scratched Caesar's head. "I'm going to bed."

I wish, Trish thought. "You could do my chemistry problems."

"In your dreams, girl." David threw her a big-brother's-pained-with-his-sister look. "That's not how you learn the stuff."

"Thanks. I don't seem to be learning it too well anyway."

"Tell you what, I'll help you tomorrow night. If you have any questions, hold 'em."

Trish nodded. She took another deep breath on the way to her room and rotated both shoulders again. Her feet felt like they each weighed a ton. As did her eyelids. She groaned at the state of her room. With one hand she scooped up her racing silks, both top and pants, then grabbed some other good pants and shirts to add to the wash load. She didn't dare ask her mother to wash clothes, or even come into the room. It was bad enough arguing about racing, not to mention their ongoing fight over Trish's housekeeping habits. Or lack of them, as the room attested.

After starting the machine, Trish bit her bottom lip. This once wouldn't hurt. And besides, studying was more important than a clean room. Wasn't it?

She opened her closet door and tossed in the pile of clothes off the chair. The two stacks on the floor were quickly shoved under the bed. Maybe a Diet Coke would help her stay awake. Back down the hall. And an apple.

"I thought you had to study," David growled from the couch where he was stretched out watching TV.

"I am. I mean, I do." Trish stuck her head in the open refrigerator. "Did you drink all the Diet Coke?" Not waiting for an answer, she located the last one, behind the milk. She polished the apple on the front of her sweat shirt and bit into the shiny red skin. "Thought you were going to bed," she commented around chewing the apple.

"Don't talk with your mouth full."

"Yes, Mother." Trish ducked the pillow he threw at her and headed back to her room. At least it *looked* better. She set her Coke down on the desk and pulled out the chair. Papers slid to the floor. With a groan she picked up the pieces of her term paper. *That* was ready for a rewrite. The card from her father caught her eye as she plunked down on the chair. The hard, uncomfortable, stiff chair. She looked longingly at the bed.

Hard to do, she thought, as she tacked the card up above the desk. "Give thanks in everything." Sure. Even chemistry?

With a yawn she opened the book.

You've been stalling, her little voice scolded.

"I'm just tired," she caught herself answering aloud. "So shut up."

The first problem made sense. Now, that was some kind of break-through. Trish sipped her Coke, mentally rehearsing the list of chemical symbols. The next problem took a little longer. The fourth problem . . .

"Trish, wake up." Marge shook her for the second time.

"Huh-h-h." Trish blinked her eyes open. She stretched her neck where it crinked from lying on her crossed arms, on top of her chemistry book. "Hi, Mom."

"Get to bed." Marge patted her daughter's shoulder. "You aren't getting anywhere this way."

"What time is it?"

"Ten."

Trish blinked again. Everything seemed furry around the edges. "I need to finish this assignment."

"Bed." Marge closed the book.

Trish wanted nothing more than to shut off the alarm what seemed like only minutes after she'd pulled the covers up.

"You'd better hustle." David knocked on her door.

Trish slept on the way to the track. Even the chill of a drizzly morning failed to wake her. She had reached the truck with her eyes half-closed and promptly fallen back asleep.

"Well, Sleeping Beauty, you better wake up now or Gatesby'll do it for you." David pushed her toward the door.

The thought brought her alert—immediately. You didn't sleep or even blink around Gatesby. The least you'd get would be a nip on whatever part of your anatomy the crazy horse took a shine to. The worst . . . well, so far the worst had taken a week to heal. At least neither one of them had broken anything in that fall on the home track.

Spitfire slammed a hoof against his stall door. His whicker was not a plea but a demand.

"I'll saddle Firefly while you get him ready," David nodded at Spitfire. "Then you can ride Gatesby and I'll take Final Command. We should be done in an hour that way. Dad said to keep it slow and easy this morning. Just loosen them up. They deserve a day of rest too."

Some day of rest, Trish thought as she brushed and saddled the restless black. *We're rushing like crazy and I have two races this afternoon.* She felt her butterflies stretching their wings . . . right in her middle.

"You were fantastic, fella." She rubbed Spitfire's ears before leading him out of the stall. "Ready, David."

The workout ran smoothly except for one brief shy at a blowing paper. While the drizzle had stopped, gray clouds and a bone-penetrating wind made Trish think of hot chocolate and warm blankets. At least she'd remembered her gloves. Spitfire showed only slight traces of sweat when she returned to the stables. Trish pulled the saddle off and clipped him to the hot walker.

Gatesby appeared in a good mood. The bright sorrel nickered when he saw her and even kept his ears forward when she stepped into the stall. Trish clipped the cross-ties to his halter and turned around for the saddle she'd left on the stall door.

"Ow-w-w! You ornery idiot! And here I thought you were happy to see me." She rubbed her left shoulder. It stung even through the wind-breaker, down vest, and sweat shirt.

Gatesby flung his head as far up as the shanks allowed and rolled his eyes.

"He's laughing at you." David handed her the bridle.

"Yeah, I'm sure he thought it was a love bite," Trish grumbled as she finished tacking him up.

"Naw, he just loves to bite." David had his cupped hands ready as she led the dancing horse out of the stall. "Now, you be careful with him."

"David." Trish put both hands on her hips. "You're beginning to sound just like Mom. Worry, worry, worry. You know I watch this guy like a . . ."

"Right. And how's your shoulder?"

Gatesby perked his ears toward the track as Trish loosened the reins. While he never succeeded in a flat-footed walk, at least he skipped any crow-hopping or sudden lunges. Trish reined him down tight any time another horse galloped by. Gatesby wanted to race, not slow-gallop.

Trish made the mistake of wiping her drippy nose on her sleeve and had to manhandle the bit out of his teeth before he made more than ten strides. "Sneaky, aren't you? Well sorry, boy, but the boss said an easy lope. You're working up a lather just fighting me. Now settle down."

Gatesby snorted and tossed his head but quit fighting. When they returned to the stables, he blew in her face, as if in gratitude for a good ride. Quickly they clipped Gatesby and Final Command on the hot walker, forked the manure piles out to the wheelbarrow, and filled water buckets. Trish measured grain and tossed hay wedges in the mangers as David returned the animals to their stalls.

"See you guys later." Trish blew Spitfire a kiss as she climbed back in the truck. She glanced at her watch. "You better gun it, Davey boy. We used up our breakfast time and showers are out."

The creases on Marge's forehead warned them to hurry when they reached home. One glance at her watch took the place of a thousand words.

"I know. We're hurrying." Trish shucked her jacket and boots. *One thing I know,* she thought as she changed clothes with the speed of a frantic shopper, *I never have time to worry.*

The car seemed empty without her father. And she hadn't even called him last night. But then she hadn't done a lot of things last night. She finished the peanut butter toast her mother had handed her on the way out the door and wiped her mouth with the napkin. *I'd think that with all the stuff going on, we could miss church one Sunday. Surely*—She shut the rebellious thoughts down. Today her attitude had better be perfect. She got out of the discussion last night, but knowing her mother, the war wasn't over yet. If *only* she wasn't such a worrier. And liked racing better. Like Hal and Trish did. Then life would be so simple.

Trish greeted her friends as they entered the church. One of these days she'd like to go back to youth group too. There just wasn't enough time for everything. She grinned at Rhonda when Marge led them into the pew just behind the Seabolt family.

"Can you come to the track?" Trish whispered as they sat down.

Rhonda shook her head. "My grandmother's coming for dinner."

Marge's frown canceled their conversation.

Trish's eyes drooped during the Scripture reading. She perked up when the folk group sang a new song. The chorus played in her mind long after the song was finished. "And He will raise you up on eagle's wings. . . ."

Trish felt herself jerk. She'd gone to sleep. Her mother's warning "Trish" came just as David drilled her with his elbow. Trish blinked and squinted. She'd slept right through the sermon.

One more thing to add to her mother's list.

Chapter
03

Trish breathed a sigh of relief.

"We'll see you at the track." Marge paused just before going out the door. "Trish, be careful. You know I . . ." She shook her head, her forehead furrowing again. "David, just make sure she's safe."

"Don't worry, Mom. You take care of Dad." David gently pushed her out the door. "We'll be fine."

Marge nodded, obviously not convinced. She dropped a quick kiss on both David's and Trish's cheeks and left.

Trish's deep breath seemed to give her butterflies a boost instead of calming them. *Saved again,* she thought. *Maybe if we keep postponing, she'll forget to holler at me.* No, if there was one thing her mother did well, it was worry about Trish's racing.

She chewed on her lip. "Oh no! My silks. They're not dry."

"Well, you better get a move on," David shouted from his room, where he'd gone to change clothes.

"Yes, Mother." Trish stuck out her tongue. He sounded too much like Mom for comfort. The list of all she needed to take ran through her mind as she hurried to the laundry room. Her silks, shirts, and pants all hung on hangers on the bar above the dryer, ready to take. "Thanks, Mom," Trish breathed as she grabbed the hangers. A twinge of guilt at the mess on the floor attacked her when she hung the clothes in her closet. *Soon,* she promised herself. *Soon I'll get all this cleaned up again.*

Her mother's advice, more like nagging in Trish's opinion, ran through her mind. *Just hang your things up or put them in the hamper when you take them off and your room will stay neat.*

"You ready?" David knocked on his sister's door. "I'm going down to the barn to check on things, so you have five minutes. Oh, and remember to call Dad."

Trish packed the last of her gear in her sports bag and slipped the garment cover over her silks. Her glance fell on the cards tacked to her wall. The verses, written in her father's square printing, reminded her to pray. "Please, make my dad well." She picked up her bag. "And take care of us today. Thanks for everything." She turned off her light. "Oh, and help me win. Amen."

She didn't recognize the voice that answered the phone in her father's hospital room. Though weak and scratchy, it had to be Hal. No one else shared his room. "Dad?"

"Good morning, Tee." He cleared his throat.

"You sound awful."

"I know. I just haven't talked much yet." He coughed once, gingerly, as if his chest hurt.

"Mom's on her way there. David and I are leaving in a couple of minutes."

"Good. We've drawn the post for Firefly, so you need to get her out in front and let her go. How was the track?"

"Dry. It didn't rain, just mist, and it looks like it may clear off."

"That's great. And, Tee, take some time and go over to see Rodgers' mount. Get to know him a little. Jason'll tell you how he wants the race run so you can concentrate on the horse. You've a gift there, so use it."

"Thanks, Dad." Trish heard the truck horn honking. "Gotta go. See you at the track."

Trish focused on relaxing during the drive to Portland Meadows. She took deep breaths and held them before exhaling. The butterflies delighted in the extra oxygen. She scrunched her shoulders up to her ears. Her fluttering friends did aerial flips.

Trish shook her head. Might as well watch the sailboats on the Columbia River for all the good her efforts did.

"Uptight?" David asked as they crossed the I-5 bridge between Vancouver and Portland.

"Yep. This is the first time I'm racing a horse I haven't ridden before."

"I know. And only your third race."

"Thanks for reminding me."

"You want a hamburger before we get there?" David pointed at the Golden Arches off to the right.

Trish gave him her best my-but-you're-dumb-big-brother look.

"Okay. Okay. I'll just get one for me." David pulled off the freeway.

"I'll take a Diet Coke," Trish added to his order.

Sipping the drink seemed to help. *Maybe butterflies like Diet Coke,* Trish thought.

David flashed their passes as they entered the stable area to the east of the track. "Trish," he said, slowing for a blanketed horse being led across the drive, "you *will* be careful."

"About what?"

"When you're racing, dopey."

"Now you sound like Mom. You want to be a worrier too?"

"Well, just don't take any unnecessary chances."

Trish snorted. "What do you think I am, dumb?"

"No, you just want to win . . . a lot."

Brad had three of their horses working the hot walker while he cleaned their stalls. Only Gatesby and Spitfire pleaded for release when Trish hung her gear in the tack room. Old Dan'l whickered a greeting from his place on the exerciser.

"Boy, you've been hard at it," Trish greeted her friend. "How come you left those two inside?"

"Right. And thanks to you too." Brad leaned on his pitchfork. "I didn't want to break his record. Why, Gatesby hasn't had a bite out of anyone for nearly twenty-four hours."

Trish chuckled as she entered Spitfire's stall. The black colt nuzzled her shoulder and dropped his head against her chest to have his ears rubbed. Trish obliged, enjoying the ritual as much as her horse. She'd cared for him since he was foaled, trained him, and finally they'd raced. She was the only rider he'd ever had. With her he behaved, most of the time. He wasn't named Spitfire for nothing.

Trish stroked his coarse black forelock and smiled at his sleepy-eyed contentment. "What a baby you are," she murmured as she snapped a lead shank to his halter. "How about some time outside?"

The horse perked up. His ears pricked forward and he snorted in her ear as she led him outside. She clipped him to the hot walker and laughed as he half-reared and shook his head. David finished laying the straw bedding as she led Dan'l back into his stall.

"Come on, I'll help you with Gatesby, then you get over to meet Rodgers' horse while we groom these guys."

Trish gave Dan'l a last pat. Guilt over her neglect of her old friend nibbled at her mind. There just wasn't enough time for all she *had* to do, let alone the things she *wanted* to do.

"Now, you behave!" She snapped the rope on Gatesby's halter. David copied her motions so they had him cross-tied between them. Gatesby walked out of the stall and over to the hot walker without even a snort. He joined the other horses in their circular path, plodding like an old plowhorse.

"Is he sick?" Trish flashed back to the infection that had raged through their stables a month ago.

"Nah-h-h." David shook his head. "Just disappointed cause we were ready for him."

"Okay. Well, I'll be back in a while."

The Rodgers Stables sign creaked a greeting in a puff of breeze. All the stalls and walkways showed the detail to attention of a first-rate stable. *Why would he ask you to ride?* her inner voice whispered in her ear.

Any jockey's anxious to ride for him. Trish shrugged. As her dad always said, never look a gift horse in the mouth. Or in this case, a gift ride.

"Your mount's down here," the trainer said after asking Trish about her father. "We've always thought this old boy had more to give, but somehow he's never come in higher than fourth. He's a good horse, gentle as can be, and from a good line. His registered name is Prancer's Dandy but we call him Dandy."

Just needs a fire under him, Trish thought as she dug in her pocket for the chunk of carrot she always kept there. The dark bay lipped it off her palm and munched the treat. Trish stood still in front of him, waiting for the horse to finish his inspection of her. When he'd sniffed her hand, up her arm, and then her hair, he tossed his head as if giving a nod of approval. Trish grasped his blue web halter with one hand and rubbed up behind his ear with the other.

"So we're gonna race today, Dandy boy." She knew it wasn't what she said but the tone of her voice that set the dark ears twitching. She kept up her singsong rhythm as she stroked the wide white blaze between his eyes and down over his muzzle. "You're a sweetheart. You know that, don't you?" Dandy nodded, leaning into her magic fingers.

"I see you've made a friend." Jason Rodgers joined them.

"Good morning, Mr. Rodgers." At his greeting Trish felt one or two of her butterfly troupe somersault. "He sure is a friendly horse."

"True, but we need some fire from him. I may enter Dandy in a claiming race if he doesn't do something soon. Make sure you have a whip with you today. I want you to do all you can to make him want to run his best."

Trish took a deep breath. "Yes, sir. Well, Dandy," she scratched him under the throat one more time, "see you in the saddling paddock."

Trish missed having Rhonda along as she headed for the dressing room under the grandstand. She, David, and Brad had spent the last hours grooming their horses. Firefly fairly gleamed from all the brushing. While she wasn't the blue-black of Spitfire, her four white socks sparkled against the dark color of her legs. A small diamond between her eyes left white hairs whenever the filly rubbed against Trish's shoulder. Today Firefly was ready to run. It was as if she knew her turn was coming, the way the filly looked to the grandstands every time the roar of the crowd announced another start.

The women's locker room was a total disaster as Trish entered the door. Towels, bags, boots, and tired women draped everywhere. Liniment and lather from earlier races vied for supreme billing on the moisture-heavy air.

"Hi, Trish." Genie Stokes, the jockey who exercised for Runnin' On

Farm in the mornings, waved from a bench in the corner. "There's room for you over here." She pushed a bag and jacket out of the way.

"Thanks." Trish hung her silks on the hook above the green bench. "Congratulations on that win today. You riding again?"

"Yeah. Against you in both the seventh and the ninth."

"Oh."

"Don't worry. You'll do fine. Firefly is posted as a favorite." Genie stretched her arms over her head and twisted from side to side. "How's your dad?"

Trish felt the heavy weight settle back on her shoulders. She'd been hoping her father would make it to the stables before she left to dress. But he hadn't. And their box in the grandstand was still empty too. "He says he's feeling better again. They plan on being here today."

"Your dad's a good man. You're lucky he's trained you, you know."

"Yeah. Thanks." Trish slipped to the floor to begin her warm-up routine. Hamstring stretches, curl-ups, push-ups, her body followed the patterns, and the rhythms bottled up the fears trying to crowd her mind.

Once she was dressed and weighed in, and lead weights had been inserted in the saddle pad slots, she flexed her arms. The silky fabric felt cold against her heated skin. "Thank you, Father," she prayed as she ambled down the tunnel to the saddling paddock, "for the chance to race again. Help me do my best. And please make my dad better." Her soft voice disappeared in the noise from the stands. Horse racing was not a quiet sport.

David and Firefly occupied the first stall since they'd drawn the post position. He buckled the saddle girth and cupped his hands to boost Trish up. "You can do it." He patted her white-clad knee. "Brad's waiting for you."

Trish took a deep breath and let it out slowly. She gathered her reins and leaned forward to rub Firefly's shiny neck. "Okay, girl. This is it. Let's use those eagle's wings." The melody of the song trickled through her mind like a calming stream on a summer's day.

Firefly liked the crowd. She pranced beside Dan'l like a queen bowing to her subjects. Ears nearly touching, chin tucked to her chest, she danced down the track. At the turn, when Brad loosened the lead shank,

24

Firefly broke into a canter, her body collected, every muscle and sinew primed for the breaking strides.

She entered the gate, again behaving like the lady she was. Firefly even remained flat-footed when the horse next to her reared and nearly unseated the jockey.

The hush fell, that moment when all the world seems to wait on tiptoe for the shot.

Trish crouched forward. The gun, the gate, and Firefly's burst for freedom seemed to explode at the same moment. Her "GO!" disappeared in the thunder of the race.

Firefly took the post like a veteran. Each stride lengthened, hurtling her forward. Trish concentrated on her horse, at the same time staying aware of the horses on her right.

Firefly tugged at the bit. Her ears swept back and forth listening to Trish's encouraging song. The horse flattened out, reaching for the finish as each furlong post flashed by. As they crossed the wire, Firefly was still begging for more slack. No other horse even came close. They won by a furlong.

The stands went wild. Trish heard the roar now that she could relax. "Wow! Oh, baby, you're awesome." She patted the steaming neck, then settled back in the saddle so she could snap her goggles up on her helmet. "You not only won, you ran away from the pack." Firefly jogged sideways on her approach to the winner's circle, her neck curved, head high, as befits a reigning monarch.

She posed for the pictures, as if nodding to the flash. Trish and David grinned at each other. But their father's place in the picture as owner was empty.

"Mom called," David said as they led Firefly away. "Dad's okay but they decided since yesterday wore him out so bad, they'd skip today. They're waiting for you to call when you're done. He said good luck on your next race too."

Trish hugged Firefly one more time before David led the filly off to the testing barn. "If only Dad could have seen this," she whispered to her steaming mount. "He'd be so proud of you. And here we thought Spitfire was our big winner."

Trish felt strange in blue and green silks. Even her butterflies didn't like the new colors. She felt like a royal battle waged in her middle. The whip in her hand didn't help either. But Mr. Rodgers had insisted that she carry—and use it.

The saddling paddock—round with stalls radiating out like spokes on a wheel—felt different without David and Brad there to cheer her on. She gathered her reins after the boost into the saddle. Dandy pricked his ears at her voice. She leaned forward to stroke his neck and smooth his black mane to one side.

"Ready?" At Trish's nod, the trainer untied the slipknotted rope and backed Dandy out of his stall. They joined the parade to the post, in the middle of the pack, position number three.

"Lord, we really need those eagle's wings this time," Trish included the prayer in her monologue. "Sure hope you have more than one pair. Firefly flew on hers." They broke into a canter at the turn. Dandy seemed alert and raring to go. *But he doesn't have the class of our horses,* Trish thought as she guided him into the gate. *Guess I'm already spoiled.*

Her whip hit his haunches as the gate swung open. Dandy bolted forward, his ears laid back. "Sorry, fella, but that's the way it goes." Trish leaned forward, her goggles brushing his mane. "Come on now!" Dandy settled into an ever-lengthening stride. As they rounded the first turn, Trish encouraged him again, this time taking him to the rail, just behind the front runner. When a horse came up on their right, Dandy lengthened his stride again. And kept his position.

The far turn found the field bunched behind them. When Dandy slowed a bit, Trish tapped him with the whip again, her voice commanding in his ears, "Come on, Dandy, give it all you've got." He laid his ears back again and drove down on the front runner.

They finished second, by half a body length.

"Wow-ee!" Trish felt like throwing her whip in the air and screaming for joy. They hadn't won, but Dandy'd been tagged as last in the field. What a long shot.

"Incredible." Jason Rodgers shook her hand. "He's never run like that.

How about riding for me Wednesday? If you can get Dandy to run like that, I'd like you on my other horses too." He handed her an envelope.

"Thank you, and I'd love to." Trish shook his offered hand. "What race?"

"How about the third and the seventh?"

Trish stopped in her tracks. The third? School wouldn't be out yet. "Sorry." She shook her head. "I could do the seventh but I'm not out of school till after three."

"That's fine. I'll see you then."

But what's your mother going to say when she hears this? her inner-nagger gloated.

Chapter 04

You're awfully quiet." David steered the truck into the hospital parking lot.

Trish's sigh originated somewhere down about her toes. She'd agreed to ride for Rodgers before she had asked her parents. And her mom was upset over today's ride. What would she say about riding Wednesday? *But I won't be missing any school. At least I thought of that.* She tried to make things all right in her mind before she needed to explain to anyone else, but it wasn't easy. In fact, she knew she was in the wrong. Again.

"It's nothing, really," she answered David with a shrug. "Just tired, I guess."

The hospital corridors seemed to close in on her as she and David left the elevator. While she tried to walk quietly, her booted heels tapped out echoes to match those marching in her mind. *You better get a smile on,* she ordered herself. *You're a winner, remember?*

"Hi, Dad, Mom." Trish leaned over the bed to give her dad a hug. "You look better than yesterday."

"Sorry we didn't make it to the track." Hal pressed the button to raise his head, then shifted to a comfortable position against the pillows.

"The doctor gave him a choice of going home a day earlier or going to the track today," Marge explained.

"And I *need* to get out of here." Hal patted the bed beside him. "Congratulations, Tee. Sounds like you and Firefly ran some race."

"She was having fun out there." Trish gave a little bounce. "You should have seen her. That horse loves the crowd—you'd think all the applause was for her. And now that she knows how much attention she gets for winning . . . well, just try to keep her back."

"And we'd counted so hard on Spitfire. Now we have two winners. That's wonderful!" Hal took a sip of water to soothe his throat. "How'd you do with Rodgers' horse?"

"A second. Mr. Rodgers could hardly believe it. And he gave me this, besides what I'll get as part of the purse." She handed her father the envelope. "Every little bit will help with the entry fees."

"No, Trish. That's your money. You earned it, you bank it."

"But, Dad."

"No, I mean it. We've never expected you kids to help with the bills and we won't start now."

But this is different, Trish thought. *You've never been sick before and you've always had so many horses to train, you've turned some away. Now we only have Anderson's two.* She glanced over at her mother but, seeing the frown on her face, wisely left it at that.

After some casual banter about other things, Marge finally asked, "Have you kids eaten yet?"

"No, but we'll fix something at home." David rose from his chair. "We've got the chores to do."

"Where's Brad?"

"He had to do something with his mom and dad tonight, so we're it."

"How much homework do you have?" Marge turned to Trish.

"Not much." Trish rolled her lips together. She wasn't lying, exactly. It all depended on how you defined much.

"Well, David, you do the chores so Trish can study."

"Why doesn't *he* do my chemistry and I'll feed the mares." Trish knew she'd made a mistake the minute the careless words were out of her mouth. "Just a joke." She backtracked as fast as she could. "Come on, Mom. Just a joke."

"When will you learn?" David asked as they walked back down the hall after their good-byes.

Trish just shook her head. And *he* didn't know the half of it.

Trish fixed tuna fish sandwiches when they got home. She took hers into her bedroom and, after changing clothes, sat down at her desk. The glow from the desk lamp pooled on her chemistry book and the paper with only two problems done. She'd better hit it hard.

Two hours later she rose and stretched. Chemistry caught up. Spanish reviewed. Only one composition to go—and that only two pages. But her eyes felt like someone had thrown a handful of sand in them.

She thought longingly of a hot bath as she stumbled to the kitchen for something to drink. David was sprawled on the sofa, dead to the world, while the TV flickered in the corner.

"Hey, why don't you sleep in bed." Trish prodded his shoulder.

"Um-m-m." David didn't even open his eyes. "Just waiting for Mom."

Car lights flashed in the window as Trish poured herself a glass of milk. She felt like sprinting down the hall and hiding in her room.

Marge hung her coat in the closet. "Hi, kids. Any messages?"

"Forgot to check." Trish looked at the answering machine. "It's flashing. I gotta finish a paper." She left her mother to deal with the machine and headed back to her books.

Another hour, and she slipped her recopied paper into her notebook. What a way to end a winning day; all her homework caught up. Except reviewing history—but the test wasn't until Tuesday, she reasoned. No more studying tonight. Her bed was calling.

" 'Night, Mom." Trish took her plate and glass back to the kitchen. Marge was still on the phone.

Trish slung her jeans and sweat shirt over the chair. She planned on putting them on again in the morning, so why hang them up? She'd just turned out the light when Marge tapped at the door.

"Trish?"

"Yeah, I'm awake." *Here it comes,* Trish thought. *And what do I do about Wednesday?*

Marge turned the lamp back on. She started to sit down in the desk chair but frowned at the clothes draped across the back. Instead she sat at the foot of Trish's bed.

"Your father and I've been talking. . . ."

I'll just bet, Trish thought as she folded her arms behind her head.

"You *know* how much I hate your racing at the track."

"Yeah."

"But I agreed to go along with what your father said. You could race *our* horses."

"But, Mom . . ."

"No, let me finish." Marge paused, as if searching for the right words. "Trish, I don't want you racing for other stables. You don't know those horses and you haven't had a lot of experience yet."

"But that's how I'd get more experience." Trish couldn't keep her mouth closed.

"You're only sixteen. You don't need more experience racing; you need time for school. Your studies have to come first."

"But, Mom." Trish sat up and hugged her knees. "Racing is all I want to do, and I'm doing okay in school too."

"Okay isn't good enough. You are too bright to waste your brain riding horses. You can pull straight A's when you work at it."

All Trish heard was "waste." "What do you mean *waste*? You think Dad wastes his time training horses? That's our business, Mom, and his dream. We've always talked about when I could jockey for our horses. And now all *you* want is for me to go to school. Other kids go out for sports—mine is just a different one." Trish could hear her voice getting louder. She knew she should calm down, but she couldn't. "And besides, I made good money today."

"Trish, let me finish."

"Why bother? All you do is try to take away the thing I love most." Trish turned her head, struggling to keep the tears back.

"Listen to me, I was trying to explain . . ." her mother went on. "I didn't want you racing at all, but I went along with *our* horses. Your father said you can race for other farms, but you have to talk it over with him. That's not my idea, but he *is* your father." The deep furrows creased her

31

forehead. She spit the words out as if she were holding something back. "No matter how hard I try to talk sensibly with you, you get upset."

"I didn't start this." Trish thumped back on her pillow. "Racing is *not* a waste!"

"That's enough!"

"No! If I got a job at the Burger Palace, you'd think that was okay. But I made more money in one race . . . than . . . than . . ." Trish couldn't think far enough. "And you call it a waste. We *need* the money. You know that."

"That's enough. If you can't talk to me without yelling . . ."

Look who's talking, Trish corralled her thoughts. *Just leave me alone.* She glared at her mother through tear-filled eyes.

Marge stood to leave. "Genie Stokes will be working all the horses at the track in the morning. David will do the chores both here and at The Meadows. And you will go to school . . . *on time for a change.*" The click of the closing door sounded like a gunshot in the stillness.

Great. Trish rolled on her side and pulled the covers up. *I'm the only one who's ever ridden Spitfire. Let 'em find out the hard way.* I am *going to ride.*

But what about Wednesday? her little voice asked.

She shrugged off the thought and drifted to sleep. When she awoke in the morning, Trish realized her dreams hadn't been pleasant ones. She felt like she'd been in a battle all night. What *would* she do about Wednesday? How would she get to the track? She'd given her word to Mr. Rodgers. She wouldn't be missing any school. *But* she didn't have her parents' permission. What would they do when they found out? They really needed the money; she knew the bills were stacking up. But her mother didn't want her racing at all. Let alone for another stable—and on a *weekday.*

The arguments chasing each other around her brain made her want to go back to bed and pull the covers over her head.

SHE HATED FIGHTING!

So, she needed to apologize to her mother and ask for forgiveness. That was just as bad. The thoughts were a flock of scavenger crows tearing her peace of mind to pieces.

"I'll drop you off at school on my way to the track." David joined the family at the breakfast table. For a change Trish wasn't grabbing peanut butter toast on the run.

"I'll be ready in five minutes." She set her cereal bowl in the sink, then went back to the table, where Marge sat drinking a cup of coffee. "Mom, I'm sorry I yelled at you last night. I . . ."

"Me too." Marge drew her daughter into the circle of her arm and hugged her. "Have a good day. And, Trish, I *am* proud of you."

"Thanks, Mom. Give Dad a hug for me. When do you think he'll be home?"

"Probably Wednesday afternoon."

"Oh." Trish nodded. The hand of fear grabbing her throat kept her from saying anything else. "Gotta run. See ya."

What was she going to do? Halfway to school she turned to David. "I need a favor, big brother."

"What now? More chemistry?"

"No. I need a ride to the track on Wednesday right after school."

"What for?"

"To ride for Rodgers. He asked me on Sunday after he was so pleased with the race. He wanted me to ride twice but one was during school. This one's about four."

"Have you asked Mom and Dad?"

"No. But we need the money."

David shook his head. "Trish, I won't lie for you."

"It's not exactly a lie . . . just not telling them everything."

David shot her one of his big-brother looks. "You better call Rodgers and tell him you can't."

"Thanks for nothing." Trish opened the door when the pickup stopped at the curb. "You're all heart."

Now what do I do? she thought as she crossed the wide sidewalk to the school entrance.

Shock stopped her dead in her tracks as she stepped through the doorway. A computer banner, the block letters filled in with crimson and gold, said "Way to go, Trish. On to the Derby." The banner stretched from post to post. Another sign hid half the trophy case.

All the way to her locker, students congratulated her. Even the principal said congratulations when he passed her in the hall. Another sign, this one announcing "#1 Jockey," taped her locker closed.

Rhonda leaned against her own locker. "So, what do you think?"

Trish just shook her head. "You guys are awesome." She carefully removed the taped sign so she could get into her locker, and folded it to save. "You must have spent all night on this stuff."

"I had lots of help. In fact, it was Doug's idea."

Trish blinked. "Come on."

Rhonda nodded. "Yup." She leaned real close. "I think he likes you."

The funny glow in Trish's middle stayed through the day. So many kids stopped by their table at lunchtime that Brad threatened to eat somewhere else—in peace. And when Trish aced a chemistry quiz, she felt like she'd used her eagle's wings to top a mountain.

When the final bell rang, she took the sign from the shelf in her locker, grabbed the books she needed, and headed for Brad's Mustang.

The Runnin' On Farm pickup was parked at the curb, motor idling. David pushed open the door. "Hustle, Trish. There's trouble at the track."

Chapter 05

Whatt happened?" Trish tossed her books in the cab.

"Spitfire threw Genie. He's gone crazy. Won't even let me near him."

"Is he hurt?" Trish slammed the door behind her.

"No! Just nuts!"

"Where is he?"

"We got him back in his stall. But he still has the bridle and saddle on. I dropped Genie off at the hospital to have her shoulder X-rayed. She's hurting pretty bad."

"Have you talked to Dad yet?"

"Yeah." David cruised through a yellow light. "He said to get you, and get that crazy horse home tonight if we can. Who knows when Genie can ride again."

Trish shook her head. "You better slow down. A ticket isn't going to help us any."

David let up on the gas but shot her a dirty look.

"Hey, it's not my fault. If they'd just let me work the horses like we're all used to, things would be fine."

"Yeah, and if Dad wasn't sick, I'd be in Pullman and not worrying about all this . . . this stuff. I'm not a trainer. How're we gonna load him?"

"Spitfire'll behave for me." Trish chewed on the inside of her cheek.

"You better hope so. You didn't see him go crazy like I did."

"Let's bring Gatesby home too," Trish continued as if she hadn't heard him. "Dad'll know of someone else to work the other two. They're easy to manage."

Trish leaped from the truck as soon as it stopped at the racing stables.

"Be careful, Trish," David hollered after her as she sprinted to Spitfire's stall. Both halves of the door were closed. A rapid tatoo of hooves on the wall and a high-pitched scream left no doubt that Spitfire hadn't forgotten the incident.

"Hey, fella, easy now. You know better than to act like this." Trish slid back the bolt on the top half of the door. A hoof slammed against the wall again. "Come on, Spitfire. This is me. I'm gonna open the door and let some light in." Trish followed her words with actions. Spitfire whinnied, but the sound was more greeting than anger.

As the light hit him, he tossed his head, ears laid flat. The bit jangled. His nostrils flared so wide they glowed red in the dimness. The whites of his eyes glimmered against his black hide.

"You've really made a mess of things, haven't you?" Trish leaned on the stall door. She kept her tone low and her body relaxed, as if nothing were wrong.

Spitfire exhaled, the whuffle sound blowing through his lips. He shook his head, his forelock brushing from side to side. After an all-over shake that set the stirrups clapping against his sides, his ears pricked forward. The colt stretched to sniff Trish's proffered hand and blew again, as if letting out all the tension. Finally he stepped forward to drape his head over Trish's shoulder.

"Good boy." Trish rubbed behind his ears and down the arched neck. Dried lather and sweat crusted his fine black coat. A raw spot on his lower lip from fighting the bit hadn't had time to scab over. Spitfire trembled when Trish opened the lower door and stepped inside the stall.

"Let's get this bridle off." She worked as she talked and slipped the web halter back over his nose. As soon as the colt was cross-tied, she checked his legs for swelling.

"Want some help?" David asked from the door.

Spitfire laid back his ears and stamped one forefoot.

"No, let me get him cleaned up and calmed down. Then we'll see. How're the others?" Trish removed the saddle and slung it over the stall door.

"Gatesby missed me today but bit Genie a good one, so he's about normal. Genie worked all three of them before she and Spitfire got into it."

As David and Trish talked, she could feel Spitfire relaxing. She brushed while she spoke, finishing one side and moving around to the other.

"She sure has that touch," Trish heard someone say to David outside the stall. "I wouldn'ta' gone in there with that black for nothin'."

"He really put on a show," another voice chimed in. "How's Stokes?"

"I don't know." The voices faded away.

Trish finished grooming Spitfire and went to the tack room for tape to wrap his legs. She hung up the saddle and bridle and dug a handful of grain out of the bin.

On the way back, she stopped at Dan'l's stall. The gray nickered and rubbed his forehead against her shoulder. As he lipped the grain from her hand, Trish rubbed his ears and the poll of his head. "You old sweety, you'd never do anything like that, would you?" Dan'l's eyes closed in bliss. "You don't get nearly enough attention here." Trish dropped a kiss on his nose and went back to working with Spitfire.

The black rested his weight on three legs so a rear one could be bent and relaxed completely. His head drooped as far as the cross-ties allowed. Eyes closed, he slept, worn out from all the excitement.

What a change, Trish thought as she leaned on the door. *You just don't like another rider, do you? I didn't realize how much you are my horse.*

"But you know," she continued her thoughts aloud as she swung open the door, "you've got to let another jockey ride you, just in case something happens to me sometime." Spitfire shook his head. Trish chuckled as she squatted to firmly wrap the white tape from fetlock to just below the knee.

"The trailer's here." David kept his voice soft, but Spitfire flicked his ears.

"Okay. We're ready. Come on in and take one of the ties so we both have hold of him."

As David entered the stall the colt raised his head. David held out a palm of grain. Spitfire munched happily, as if the day's events had never happened. He whuffled, then licked David's hand for the salt.

"You coulda behaved like this earlier, you know." He rubbed the droopy black face and ears. David unclipped the ropes and handed one to Trish. Spitfire thumped his way into the trailer without even a glance at the other activities in the area.

"Let's get Gatesby. We'll walk him double-tied too." Trish knotted the lead ropes with a bow that could be pulled loose with just a jerk on the end of the rope. She patted Spitfire on the rump as she pushed him over so she could get out. *Thank you,* God," she breathed as she strode down the ramp.

Gatesby nickered a greeting. His black ears touched at the tips they were pricked so far forward. When Trish reached for his halter, he rolled his eyes and tipped his head sideways, ready to nip.

"Knock it off!" Trish clipped the lead ropes to the halter ring while David held the opposite side of the halter. "You just have to get your licks in, don't you?" Gatesby dropped his head, asking for an ear rub. Trish obliged, all the while keeping a wary eye for any shenanigans.

Gatesby stepped smartly out of the stall when David swung open the lower door. Ears flicking to catch all sounds, including Trish's comforting voice, he ambled between them, until his front feet thudded on the trailer gate.

The ropes burned through their hands as the bay lunged backward.

"Oh, for pete's sake!" Trish clutched the remaining rope in her hand. "You've done this before." As one, she and David jerked their lead lines. Gatesby shook his head. Trish smacked him on the nose as his front feet started to leave the ground. "Now behave yourself!" The bay shook all over and pricked his ears again. When he blew in her face, Trish shook her head and led him forward. This time he thumped his way into the trailer with laid-back ears.

"Ow-w!" Trish yelped. She slapped the bay's shoulder. "Get off my foot!" The sneaky look on Gatesby's face told Trish he'd stepped deliberately. She shoved against his shoulder to force him to move over and limped out of the trailer. "One of these days you're gonna be dog food," she muttered as she pulled off her boot and massaged her toes.

David slammed the tailgate in place. "Let's feed so we can get outta here."

"Easy for you to say, you can walk." Trish flexed her foot.

Both horses seemed glad to get home when Trish and David led them to their stalls. The workout passed without a hitch, but by the time all the animals were fed, dusk had deepened into darkness. Trish spent a few precious minutes playing with Miss Tee before she limped up the rise to the dark house.

The message light flashed on the phone when she walked into the house. Bob Diego had two mounts for her on Wednesday. Trish called him back. "I'd love to," she said.

That night in bed the argument took over her mind again. One side demanded, *You've got to tell your parents about the mounts on Wednesday.* The other side blasted back, *You can't. They'll never let you ride.* "But we've got to have the money!" Trish turned her pillow over and smashed it with her fist. There was no insurance. She'd heard her mom and dad discussing the medical bills. The hospital had eaten up their savings just like the cancer ate up her father's body. And they had no income. Her dad wasn't training enough horses. That only left the purses they won and her percentage as a jockey.

But you have *to tell them,* her nagging voice intruded. *You can't lie, you know you can't. And besides, how are you going to get to the track?*

Trish flipped onto her back and locked her hands behind her head. When she tried praying, the words seemed to bounce off the ceiling and fade like falling stars on a clear night.

Well, God. She took a deep breath. *You promised to take care of us, but as far as I can see, you're not doing too good a job.* She paused, an idea tiptoeing into her mind. *Maybe my being offered mounts is God's way of taking care of us.* She grinned with satisfaction as she turned on her side. *Of course!* She ignored the muttering of her nagger as sleep hit her like a sledgehammer.

David had broken all speed records to get her to class before the bell. She hadn't even had time to stop at her locker, just run from the car to class in spite of her sore foot.

Spitfire hadn't been feeling too well that morning either. There was some swelling in his front leg and tenderness in a rear hock where he'd probably banged himself in all the ruckus.

"Serves you right," Trish had scolded him. All she needed was a lame horse right now.

The lunch bell rang before she saw Brad. She leaned her forehead against her locker. The cool metal eased the pressure she felt building behind her eyes.

"Now what?" Brad stopped beside her.

"More problems."

"Is it your dad?"

"No . . . yes . . . well, sort of."

"That tells me a lot."

"Come on, you guys." Rhonda joined them. "The food'll be all gone." The look on Trish's face stopped her. "Now what?"

"I've been asked to ride in two races tomorrow afternoon."

"Wow! That's great." Rhonda looked from Trish to Brad, who shrugged his shoulders.

"But you know what Mom's said about riding."

"Yeah, that's right." Rhonda paused. "So what are you gonna do?"

"Ask Brad to take me to the track."

"Naturally." Brad shook his head. "What did David say?"

"Plenty. But the bottom line was no way." Trish raised her head, her jaw clenched tight. "I *have* to get there. I gave my word. . . ." Her voice dropped to a whisper. "And we need the money."

Brad rubbed his forehead with one tanned hand. "I'll take you," he said finally. "But I think you should talk this over with your dad first."

"I can't. What if he says no?" Trish started down the hall. "Are you guys coming or what?" She walked backward so she could watch her friends catch up to her. "Thanks."

"So. When *are* you going to tell your dad?" Rhonda asked as they entered the lunchroom.

"Not till I have to, I guess."

Chapter
06

Study halls are usually intended for studying.

What a joke! Trish felt like smashing her books to the floor. *I can't study today.* She stared out the window. The Oregon liquid sunshine misted the trees at the corners of the quad. The dismal outside matched her dismal inside. *I'll just have to tell them I have something after school tomorrow.*

But that's a lie! Her nagger wriggled out from under his rock.

Trish pushed her fingers through her bangs. *I can't help that.*

You'll be sorry.

So, what's new? I already am. But I have to ride. We need the money.

What if you lose?

Trish's pencil lead snapped against her paper. *That* hadn't entered her mind before. She slid from behind her desk and headed for the pencil sharpener. She glanced at the clock. *Five minutes till the bell. What a relief.*

At Runnin' On Farm, wind blew the drizzle into sheets that drifted across the track during the afternoon workout. While her windbreaker provided some protection, it failed to prevent icy water from dripping down the back of her neck. Her nose ran faster than the horses.

She pulled the saddle off Gatesby and slung it over the door. "Good job, fella." The pat on his neck spoke more warmly than the words. Gatesby shook; drops from his mane spattered her face. "Way to go."

"I'll finish here." David set down his bucket with scraper and water. "You go on up and get warm."

Trish nodded. "You need me anymore?"

"Nah. I'm almost done. Mom wants us to come to the hospital for dinner."

"Okay. But we can't stay long. I've got a ton of homework."

"You're awfully quiet, Tee." Hal leaned forward in his wheelchair. The four of them sat around a small table in the hospital cafeteria. They'd already discussed the horses both at the track and home.

Trish took a deep breath. "I . . . ah . . ."

Tell him! her nagger commanded, the voice so loud in her ears she was afraid her father had heard it.

"Ah . . . when are you coming home?"

"Not till Friday, it looks like. I think the doctor likes having me here." Hal smiled. "Think I'll start charging him for the racing tips."

Trish grinned at him. "Yeah, I think you better. Make your fees as much as his." She pushed herself to her feet. "Come on, David, let's hit the road. My books are waiting."

"I'll be home soon," Marge said.

"Bye, Dad." Trish hugged her father. Instead of the usual horses and hay, he smelled like hospital. That old familiar boulder blocked her throat. And he was so thin. His navy blue robe hung on his bony shoulders. "Get better."

"I love you, Tee," he whispered in her ear.

Don't say that! she almost screamed the thought as she left the room. *God, when are you going to make him better?*

Trish felt the load lift from her shoulders as she walked down the hall. Friday—he wouldn't be home until Friday. Now she wouldn't need to lie.

43

The next day flew by. Trish felt like someone had cranked up her treadmill to sprinting speed. She'd packed boots and helmet in her duffel bag and told David it was some stuff for Rhonda. She'd lied after all, but at least not to her parents.

"You're sure you want to do this?" Brad asked when she slid into the front seat of his Mustang.

"Too late to back out now. Those owners are counting on me. Where's Rhonda?"

"She took the bus home."

"At least it quit raining." Trish broke the long silence on the drive to Portland. Butterflies took turns doing aerial flips in her midsection.

"But the track may still be muddy. Trish . . ." Brad turned to face his friend as she opened the car door. He'd stopped right in front of the gate closest to the dressing rooms.

"It's okay, Brad. I'll be careful." She paused and stuck her head back in the door. "Meet me here right after the seventh race, okay? I've gotta gallop Spitfire and Gatesby as soon as I can get home."

"Are you Tricia Evanston?" a young man in a black windbreaker asked just as she reached the locker room.

"Yes."

"Here're your silks. Bob'll meet you in the paddock as soon as you're dressed." He handed her the shiny black-and-white shirt and helmet cover.

"Okay. Thanks." Trish took the hanger and pushed open the door. The now-familiar, liniment-scented steam tickled her nose. Even though this was only the fourth race of the day, the room had already adopted the cluttered look. It reminded Trish of her own room. Except for the smell.

"How's Genie?" she asked one of the other jockeys.

"Should be back by the weekend. Good thing she only dislocated that shoulder rather than pullin' the muscles or breakin' it." The jockey twisted her long blond hair and pinned it on top of her head. "You're Tricia Evanston, right?"

Trish nodded.

"And it was your horse that threw her?"

"Yeah. Spitfire doesn't seem to like anyone else on his back. I didn't know he was such a one-person horse. Sure sorry Genie got hurt."

"Happens to the best of us." The woman settled her helmet in place. "You take care now."

The brief conversation left Trish feeling both bad about Spitfire and happy Genie was okay. She would take care . . . but she needed the win.

This time she hadn't met the horse before the race. While she knew her father's advice was sound, she also understood that pre-meets weren't always possible.

Her mount had drawn the number five position. Right in the middle of the pack. Bob Diego stood to the side of the trainer as Trish entered the stall.

"Good afternoon." His voice had the precise inflection of one to whom English was a second language. "Permit me to give you a leg up."

Trish smiled at him. "I'd like to meet your horse first, if that's okay?"

Diego nodded, a smile tugging at the corners of his mouth. "Be my guest. This old man here is called Hospitality, otherwise known as Hoppy. He's five years old, won some, lost more, and back after an injury in California. He likes to come from behind, but is never pleased with a muddy track."

Trish stood quietly in front of the leggy blood-red bay and let him explore first her hands, then her arms and up to her helmet. His breath in her face signified approval, and she extended a hand to rub along his head and up to his ears. He had the chiseled bones and large eyes of a mature horse, not the teenage look of her own string. She brushed his forelock aside and rubbed between his ears.

"You've made a friend for life," Diego said. "He doesn't usually take to newcomers quite so easily."

Trish listened hard to the trainer's reply, trying to pick out words she knew from the rapid Spanish. *Muy bueno* she knew meant very good.

Trish mounted and settled herself in the saddle. So he didn't like mud. Well, he'd get a lot of that today if they came from behind.

Hoppy tugged against the bit as they filed on the post parade. Trish rose in her stirrups, testing his mouth, feeling him bunch under her. His ears twitched in perfect time to her singsong.

As they entered the gates, she stroked Hoppy's arched neck. His ears pricked forward. He blew, tensed for the shot, and exploded from the gate. Within four strides he broke ahead of the pack and leaped for the first curve.

Trish crouched over his shoulders, giving him all the encouragement she could while keeping a firm hand on the reins. She didn't want him to tire before the stretch, but he was running with his head up. He tested the bit, lengthening his stride when she relaxed even a little.

As the marker poles flashed past, Trish listened for her competition. At the three-quarters point the pair running a length behind made their move. With hooves thundering up on both sides of her, she loosed the reins. Her mount's surge of power carried him another length ahead. He seemed to be laughing as they crossed the finish line two lengths ahead of the mud-covered second-place contender.

"So you don't like mud in your face, eh, Hoppy?" Trish laughed as she pulled him down to a canter. "And you like to come from behind. Sure fooled me." She turned him back toward the winner's circle. "And your owner."

"Sorry, Mr. Diego," she said as she slid to the ground. "Keeping him back when he'd broken so clean just didn't seem the right thing to do. And he was having too much fun in front."

Bob Diego smiled and nodded, but Trish could feel his black eyes assessing her.

He'll probably never ask me again, since I didn't follow his directions. She snapped her goggles up to her helmet. *But I just knew what the horse wanted. And needed. And we won.*

After the trainer led Hospitality away to the testing barn, Trish fell in step with Bob Diego as he spoke. "You have the insight, that special gift, do you not?" He rubbed his chin between forefinger and thumb.

"Wha . . . what do you mean?"

"It's rare. That ability to get the best out of a horse. Some say they can read the horse's mind or else the horse can read theirs. Whichever. It is not important how, but that you can."

Trish took a deep breath. "I don't know, Mr. Diego. About the gift, I mean. I always thought it was only because I was around our animals so much; they know me and I know them. But your horse today . . . well, I'm just glad I didn't make a mistake."

Robert Diego nodded. "Now, about this next race."

Trish could feel the explosive energy of the colt she mounted next. He fought her all the way to the post and back to the starting gate. "Now, if you think you can get away with all this, you're crazy," she instructed his twitching ears. "I ride Gatesby, and you don't have a chance on winning the sneakiness trophy next to him. Settle down. Your time is coming."

When they entered the gate, the colt snorted and reared. Trish backed him out and walked him in a tight circle, all the while using her voice and hands to calm the fractious beast. "You're wasting your energy," she commanded. "Now just behave and let's get on the other side so you can run."

She felt him relax. They stopped for just a moment, time for both of them to expel a deep breath. This time he settled for the break, his weight on his haunches as it should be.

This was the first time Trish and her mount were caught in the middle of the pack. As they rounded the first turn, she pulled him back and out of the box of surging horseflesh and swinging bats. The colt shook his head at the restriction but settled again at the sound of her voice.

She could hear Bob Diego's voice in her ear. "I like my horses to come from the rear. Save them for the stretch, then use the whip if you have to."

First one, then another horse dropped back as they rounded the far turn. The pace had been stiff, but when Trish let up on the reins, the colt extended his stride. He was running easily, ears flicking both to hear his rider and to look forward.

With the final two horses neck and neck in front of them, Trish let the colt have his head, her hands on the reins to support, not control him. They swept across the wire, winning by half a length.

"You did it!" She felt like hugging the prancing horse. *And no whip.* The thought brought a grin of satisfaction. The other two jockeys had laid on the whips for all they were worth, but her mount won.

They posed for the pictures and Trish gave the colt one last pat.

"Congratulations." Diego shook her hand. "That one, he gave you a hard time at first, no?"

"We had a bit of a discussion about who was boss. Guess I convinced him we should work together." Trish stepped off the scale and handed the saddle to the trainer. She wiped a chunk of track off her cheek. "But coming from behind on a muddy track . . . well."

The owner laughed. "I have one tomorrow in the fourth. Can you ride for me again?"

"Sure."

"He's a problem sometimes. Seems to do better with a woman on him. This will be his third race, but he's never won. If he doesn't at least show, I'll enter him in a claiming race next."

"I'll do my best."

"Here." His smile gleamed beneath a well-trimmed mustache as the man handed Trish an envelope. "Tell your father he's done a good job, both as a trainer . . . and as a father."

"Th—thanks," Trish stammered her surprise. *If he only knew.*

Jason Rodgers joined her in the winner's circle after Trish rode his horse to win also. It had been an excellent day, if only she could tell her dad about it.

Even though Trish changed clothes as fast as she could and Brad drove more than the speed limit, it was dark when they turned at the Runnin' On Farm sign.

"You want me to ride Gatesby?" Brad asked as they trotted down to the stables. The dark house and vacant drive had given Trish a brief relief. No one else was home yet.

"No, I better. Just help me saddle up. David must be at the hospital yet, so if you'd feed it would sure help."

Trish had just dismounted from her final circuit when David stomped up. "How come you're so late? You should have been done hours ago. What's been going on?"

Anger and guilt clipped each word as Trish turned on her brother. "Who made you my boss?"

Chapter

07

Where were you?"

"Where do you think?" Trish faced him—hands on her hips, her jaw tight and eyes flashing.

"You rode after all."

"You bet I did. We *need* the money, haven't you figured that out yet?"

"How . . . who . . . ?"

"Who cares? I rode and I won. Someone in this family has to be making some money. You know how much everything costs. And I didn't miss school."

"No, but you lied to Mom and Dad." David grabbed her arm.

"No, I didn't. They didn't ask and I didn't say anything. But I could have had another mount if I had skipped. Dad says to use my gift and I am." Trish whirled away. "I'm doing the best I can, David, so leave me alone."

"All right! I will! Just don't come crying to me when they find out."

"Yes, *Mother*."

"You're not funny."

"Oh, r-e-a-l-l-y. You're so bossy. Think you always know what's best."

"Stupid kid."

"Takes one to know one." Trish couldn't believe they were hollering at each other like this. She and David never fought. But right now she felt she could strangle him with her bare hands. Calling her stupid. All the feelings of guilt and resentment rushed up from her toes and erupted.

"Leave me alone, David Lee Evanston!" she yelled. "If you know what's good for you."

"And what'll you do about it, if I don't?" Red flamed up into David's face. His fists bunched at his sides, ready to punch. Instead of at her, he slammed one fist against the barn wall.

Trish froze. Tears welled behind her eyes, clogged her throat, and spilled down her cheeks.

David grunted with the pain. He doubled over, cushioning his injured hand with the other.

"David, I . . . I'm sorry." Trish put her hand on his shoulder.

David stepped back. "Haven't you done enough?" Clamping his hand against his chest, he headed for the house.

Brad held Trish while she cried. As the deluge dried to drips, she pulled away and wiped her eyes on her sleeve. "I just don't know what else to do," she finally muttered. "We need the money. Dad'll understand."

"When are you going to tell him?"

"When he gets home, so we can talk by ourselves." She drew another shuddering breath. "Well, I better get at the horses." She looked around, as if coming into new territory from a far land.

"I put them all away."

"Thanks."

"We need to feed. I don't think David will be back down."

"I know. Hope he's icing that hand." Trish chewed her lip. "Do you think he broke anything?"

"You're lucky he didn't break you."

Trish nodded. Her deep breath snagged on a clump of tears still stuck in her throat. "I'll do grain and you get the hay." She felt like a ton of alfalfa sat on her shoulders. If she didn't start moving, her knees would buckle under the load, and once she went down, how would she ever get up?

David's door was shut when she finally got up to the dark house. She warmed two bowls of leftover spaghetti in the microwave, buttered some French bread, and poured two glasses of milk. After arranging all the food on a tray, Trish carried it down the hall and tapped on David's door.

"Yeah."

"I've brought dinner." She bent one knee to balance the tray and struggled with the doorknob. Almost upsetting the milk, she kicked the door open with her foot. "Whew, that was close."

Only the clock dial glowed in the darkened room. Light from the hall showed David huddled on the bed, facing the opposite wall.

Trish set the tray down on the desk and switched on the lamp. "David, I'm sorry for hollering at you like that."

"Yeah." He flinched when he tried to push himself against the head-board. "Me too."

Trish could tell he'd been crying. Was he feeling as wretched as she was? Did he ever get mad at God and the cancer like she did? If so, he never said anything about it. Was he mad that he didn't get to go back for his second year in college? If only she dared ask him all these questions.

"Here's your dinner," she said instead, handing him the bowl and bread. "I'll get some ice for your hand."

As she wrapped the ice bag in a towel to hold it in place, she asked, "Do you think anything's broken?"

David shook his head. "No."

"What's Mom gonna say?"

"I'll just tell her it was an accident." He spilled some spaghetti on his shirt.

Any other time Trish would have giggled at the look of disgust on his face. Her neatnick brother didn't spill. But then he hadn't had to eat left-handed before.

"David," Trish paused, trying to choose the best words. "About the racing . . ." She met his gaze, not willing to back down. "I . . . I wouldn't

51

have done it if we didn't need the money so bad. It's just like other kids who have jobs after school."

"Yeah, but other kids have their parents' permission."

"I know. And other kids don't make near the money I do."

"That has nothing to do . . ."

"With it? Yeah it does. For us it does." She picked up the empty dishes. "I'm not gonna race forever—without permission, I mean. I'll talk to Dad as soon as he gets home."

"Are you going to ride again?"

She nodded. "Tomorrow."

"You racing again?" Rhonda asked at the lunch table.

"Um-mmm," Trish mumbled around a bite of tuna salad. "You want to come with me? You could help exercise in the evening too. Gatesby needs a rider, and it's so late when I get home."

"Okay. I've a show this weekend, so I won't be jumping tonight." She picked up her tray to leave. "You told your mom and dad yet?"

Trish shook her head. "Dad's coming home Friday. I'll tell him then."

"Hard, huh?"

"Yeah. I've always told him everything. Last night David and I really got into it. I've felt like screaming at anything . . . and everybody. Or crying. But if I start, how'll I ever stop? The only time I ever feel good anymore is when I'm on a horse."

Trish really felt good after the first race. Another win. The horse exploded under her in the backstretch and they won by two furlongs. Mr. Diego slipped her an envelope with fifty dollars in it. That was on top of her share of the purse.

Her second mount was for Rodgers Stables, so she changed silks quickly. She was ready when the trainer brought a gray gelding into the saddling paddock.

"Hey, you look like Dan'l." She waited for the horse to finish inspecting her. "He's one of my best buddies." She kept up a flow of conversation while she stroked the horse's neck and head.

"Dundee's been racing for three years," Rodgers said when he joined them. "He had a bad spill last season and strained his shoulder, so this is his first time out again."

Trish listened carefully to the instructions, but her hands never ceased their stroking and rubbing, communicating her care for the horse. Her favorite fragrance filled her nose—horse, along with dust and saddle leather.

The noise of the crowd faded into the background, replaced by jangling bits, stomping hooves, and the sharp whinny of a high-strung contender.

The gray blew in her face, his breath warm and damp. Trish mounted, feeling like she and the horse were already one. The gray settled deep on his haunches as the gate clanged shut. Trish stroked his neck one more time, the thrill of the moment tingling through both of them.

Dundee broke clean, but within four strides was trapped in the middle of the field. The only alternative was to pull back, away from the surging haunches in front and around them. Just as Trish tightened the reins, Dundee stumbled, clipped by another horse.

Trish instinctively held his head up, using all her strength and determination to keep the animal on his feet. He faltered. Stumbled again.

"Come on, Dundee," Trish pleaded. "You can do it." By the time he regained his footing, the field had left them a furlong behind.

Dundee straightened out again, ears laid back. Each stride and heave of his mighty haunches hurled them closer to the trailing pack. One by one, he passed the spread-out field. By the stretch he inched up on the third-place rider. Trish rode high over his shoulders, giving him every advantage.

"Come on, Dundee, you can do it." She felt him reach further. He settled deeper, intent as they pulled into second place. They caught the front runner by the last furlong pole. Nose to tail, nose to haunches, nose to neck.

The other jockey went to the whip.

They flew across the finish line stride on stride.

"And that's number four to win and three to place." The announcer's voice could barely be heard over the heaving of her mount.

"Sorry, boy, you gave it all you had. If the race had been even three

53

yards longer, you'da made it." Trish pulled him down to a slow gallop, then an easy canter as she swung back to the exit gate. Dundee pricked his ears and tossed his head.

"Some race, Trish." Jason Rodgers met her at the weighing platform. "I thought for sure he was going to go down, but you kept him on his feet."

"Sorry we didn't win." Trish stepped on the scale. "But that horse is all heart. He gave it everything he had, we just ran out of track."

"I know." Rodgers slipped her an envelope. "You earned it," he said at her surprised look. "And I have a mount for you Saturday, and one on Sunday."

"I'll have to check what races we're in."

"I already did. Thanks, Trish." He started to leave. "Oh, and say hi to your dad for me. Tell him thanks for raising such a promising jockey."

"Thank you, Mr. Rodgers." Trish waved as the tall man strode off.

"Are you Tricia Evanston?" A voice by her side brought her back. "Yes."

"Come on, Trish." Rhonda handed Trish her bag. "Brad's got the car waiting outside the gate."

"Okay. Okay." She turned to the slender woman who'd asked her name. "I've gotta hurry."

"I'll walk you out. How many races have you won now?" The woman fell into step beside Rhonda and Trish.

"Uh . . ." Trish counted in her head. "Six, I think."

"And how long have you been racing?"

"A couple of weeks."

"Why do you think you're doing so well?"

"I just seem to understand the horses, I guess," Trish said. "You a jockey?"

"No, I'm a . . ."

"Come on, Trish," Brad hollered. "It's gonna be dark soon."

"Sorry, I gotta run." Trish dashed across the gravel to Brad's car.

"Who was that?" Brad asked as he drove out of the parking lot.

"Beats me." Trish and Rhonda both shrugged.

When Trish settled deeper into the seat, the words of Jason Rodgers came into her mind. *His compliment sure felt good.* She pulled the envelope from her pocket and opened it. "A hundred dollars!" She swiveled in the seat to stare at Rhonda.

"Wow!" Rhonda grinned at the sight of the five twenty-dollar bills. "Hey, there's a note too."

Trish read it aloud. "I know things are tight right now for all of you. Hope this helps a little. Thanks. Jason Rodgers." Trish felt the sting of tears behind her eyes. What a wonderful thing for him to do. If only she could show the note to her father right now.

At least she wouldn't be visiting him tonight. It was hard enough to keep the information from him when they spoke on the phone. *I never knew lying could take so much time and energy,* she thought. *What a mess I've gotten into.*

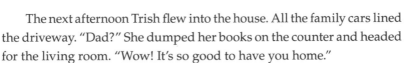

The next afternoon Trish flew into the house. All the family cars lined the driveway. "Dad?" She dumped her books on the counter and headed for the living room. "Wow! It's so good to have you home."

Her father raised his recliner with a thump. There was no smile on his face. His arms remained at his sides.

Trish dropped to her knees beside the chair. "Dad?" her voice squeaked.

Hal handed her the sports section of the local newspaper. The headline read "Local Girl Rides to Win."

Chapter
08

So much for a happy homecoming.

Trish skimmed the first paragraph, and knew. The photo of her and Bob Diego in the winner's circle was a dead giveaway, one she couldn't argue with. She kept her eyes on the paper, but rather than read the rest of the copy, her brain scrambled for an out.

"Well?" Her father prodded.

"I was going to tell you as soon as you got home." Trish dropped the paper on the hearth and straightened her shoulders. She could feel the tears gathering at the back of her throat. She swallowed—hard. No crying this time.

"All I'll say now, Tricia . . ."

She swallowed again. It had been a long time since her father used her full name, and in such a stern voice.

" . . . is that I'm—we're"—he took her mother's hand—"disappointed, deeply disappointed, in what you've done. I know you have to load those horses, so we'll discuss this when you get home. Understood?"

Trish nodded. One glance at her mother's flashing eyes and rigid jaw warned her that the discussion would *not* be comfortable. Trish looked at her father again. He'd leaned back in the recliner, eyes closed, as if he didn't want to look at her.

Trish ran from the room before the tears spilled over. *She would not let them see her cry.*

David had an I-warned-you look about him when she got down to the stables. He'd already backed the trailer in place for loading.

Trish leaned against Spitfire, both arms around his neck. The colt bobbed his head and rubbed his chin against her back. With her cheek against his mane, she breathed in the comforting odor of warm horseflesh. The quiet stalls, except for Gatesby rustling straw in the adjoining box, offered her the peace of mind she needed to handle the hours ahead. Trish took a deep breath. *Well, Dad. I did the best I could. I guess—no, I know I should have gone to you first, but I didn't. All I can say is, I'm sorry.* With the decision made, she clipped the lead to Spitfire's halter and led him out and into the trailer.

"Want help with Gatesby?" David asked.

Trish nodded.

Ears flat, Gatesby threw up his head when she reached for his halter. "Oh, knock it off," she ordered as she reached again, this time clamping firm fingers around the blue webbing. "We don't need any trouble from you today."

David snapped a lead rope on the opposite side as she paused before leading the colt out the opened stall door. Gatesby jumped around, rolling his eyes and spooking at anything that moved, including shadows. But at the echo of front feet on the trailer gate, he lunged backward. The bay planted his feet like trees. No matter what they tried—grain, a carrot, kind words—the horse wouldn't budge.

When David got behind Gatesby to push, the horse lashed out with one rear hoof, barely missing David's knee.

David muttered some words Trish knew he hadn't learned at home.

Gatesby glared at Trish. He even pulled away when she stroked his neck and rubbed the spot behind his ear.

"I'm hooding him." David stalked off to the tack room.

"You dummy." Trish felt the urge to smack the stubborn horse with her whip. "You could use a whip right now, and we don't even keep one down here at the barn."

57

Gatesby shivered when David slipped the hood in place. He dropped his head and sighed, a deep sigh that melted all resistance, then followed his two leaders into the trailer.

Trish wisely kept her mouth shut. The look on David's face matched the one she'd seen earlier on her father's.

By the time they'd unloaded the horses and fed all the stock, darkness blanketed the landscape. A drizzle blew in on the evening wind. David decided to cut the workout, so Trish gave Dan'l an extra bit of rubbing attention before they unhitched the trailer and headed for home.

"I'm starved." Trish stuffed her cold hands in her pockets. "Let's stop at Mac's for a burger."

David obligingly took the roads to I-5 and stopped at the drive-through window. With Coke and hamburger in hand, David completed the circular on-ramp back to the freeway. Traffic ground to a halt, and flashing signs overhead announced the raising of the bridge to allow a ship to pass up or down the Columbia River.

"Sorry." Trish hid behind her Coke. The glare David cast her way was enough to melt the ice in her drink.

Maybe Dad'll be asleep by the time we get home. Trish allowed that and other dreamy thoughts to occupy her mind. They were better than those of her nagger. She'd heard enough from him the last few days to last a lifetime.

Just tell the truth, and I'll let . . . It was her nagger again, getting in his nickel's worth. Trish tried to concentrate on Saturday's race.

"Sure hope Gatesby settles down by tomorrow." She slurped the last bit of soft drink.

"Hmm-mm." David settled further down in the seat. He finished his food and thrummed his fingers on the steering wheel.

Trish jabbed her straw to the swish of the windshield wipers. All she could think about was the confrontation ahead.

David grabbed the container out of her hand. "For pete's sake . . ."

"Sor-ry."

Traffic began moving again.

"David?"

"Yeah."

"What do you think they're gonna do?"

"Mom and Dad? I don't know. They're both hurt and mad."

"And disappointed."

"Yeah."

Trish chewed on her lip. "What do you think I should do?"

"Just get it over with. You want to be treated like an adult, here's your chance to act like one."

Trish settled lower in the seat.

When she arrived home, Caesar greeted her, then followed David to the barn, where he'd finish the evening chores. The fire crackling in the fireplace was warm and inviting when Trish opened the sliding glass door. The fish tank bubbled comfortingly in the corner. She pulled off her boots at the jack and shrugged out of her jacket. She could see her father lying in the recliner, his eyes closed. Her mother's rocking chair sang its familiar creaky tune.

Trish took a deep breath.

"There's dinner in the oven." Marge didn't look up from her knitting.

"Thanks. I'm not hungry." Trish crossed the room to sit on the field-stone hearth. "Is Dad . . ."

"I'm awake, Tee. Just start at the beginning."

"Well, last Sunday Mr. Rodgers asked me to ride for him on Wednesday. I told him yes before I even thought because I was so happy to be asked. Then I . . ." Trish told everything she could think of, including her load of guilt. "And I'm sorry for lying—not telling you all the truth. But, Dad, I know how bad we need the money." She studied her hands hanging between her knees. Neither of her parents had said a word the entire time.

When she sneaked a look at her mother, Trish could see the still-tight jaw. Her knitting needles seemed to jab into the yarn.

"Well . . . why don't you holler at me—anything. Say something!" She dropped to her knees beside her father's chair. "Please, Dad, I'm so sorry." The tears came, silently dripping onto her hands that clenched the recliner arm.

Her father lifted a hand and stroked her bent head. "Trish, this hasn't been easy for any of us. But we've trusted you kids to be honest with us. You broke that trust."

"But I . . . I . . ." Trish tried to talk around the tears.

"I know. You did the best you could. And you did a good job, but the bottom line is you did something you knew was wrong. Honey, it's not your job to take care of this family. We've always trusted God to provide and He has. He will. Trish, you should have come to us first."

"But I was . . ." Trish paused to swallow. She dropped her head further. "I was afraid you'd say no."

"And I would have. Trish, when will you learn that we only want what's best for you?" Marge dropped her knitting in her lap. "You're exhausted. Your grades are suffering. You've been snappy. And accidents happen when people are too tired."

"Mom, I've been trying my best."

"I know."

David came in and sank down on the sofa.

"What if I promise never to do anything like this again? If I swear to always come to you first? Dad? Mom? I can't handle the guilt."

Hal nodded as he brought his recliner upright. "I know, Trish. That's why God gave us Jesus. To rid us of the guilt and teach us forgiveness."

Marge made a little sound in her throat.

"I know how hard you all have been working. And I'll never be able to tell you how grateful I am—we are." Hal included Marge, smiling at her. "I wish I could say things will get better soon." He shook his head. "But I can't." He stopped to swallow and lick his lips. With one weary hand he rubbed the creases in his forehead.

Trish felt the tears stinging again. One trickled down her cheek to match the one on her father's.

The fire snapped in the fireplace. David sniffed and got up for a tissue.

Hal blinked, then sighed.

It seemed to Trish that the weight of despair crushed her father further into his chair. She took hold of his hand and raised it to her cheek, wishing and praying that her strength would help him. *Could* help him.

"We'll just have to continue to take one step at a time. You're right,

Trish. Money is a big problem. We have no health insurance and the hospital bills have already wiped out most of our savings."

Trish leaped up and dashed to the closet for her jacket. "Here." She dropped the envelopes into her father's lap. "And I'm not sure how much my check will be for the races. Over a couple thousand dollars, I think. It'll help, Dad."

Hal smiled as he read the note. "My good friends." He smoothed the bills and handed Marge the note. "Trish, this should be your money, but thanks."

Marge smiled over the note, then raised her head to smile at Trish. "I hate to take your money too." She shook her head. "But . . . well . . . thank you, Tee."

Trish felt a warm glow spreading through her midsection.

"I have thought of getting a job myself," Marge said after rereading the note. "But I'm not really trained for anything. However, Trish, you simply *cannot* miss school to race." Her mother's tone allowed no argument. "I know you can make the best money—if you win—but school *has* to come first. The minute your grades fall, weekday racing goes."

Trish drew a deep breath. *They weren't going to make her quit riding for other farms!*

Marge continued. "We've given you a lot of freedom in the past, but now we'll want a complete report every Sunday evening. We'll sit down for a family meeting and talk about the past week and what's coming up. There will be no more half-truths; we *must* know what's going on around here."

Hal nodded. "Your mother's right. We have to be able to trust each other. And we can't afford to have anyone else sick around here. I know how important it is for me not to worry too. We all have to believe that God knows what He's doing. He's always taken care of us in the past, and now is no exception. He *will* provide, but we have to work together." He looked intently at each member of the family.

Trish felt her eyes fill again. She swallowed past the lump in her throat and nodded.

Hal let his hands fall at his sides and resettled himself in the chair. "Now, Trish, how many mounts do you have for tomorrow?"

Chapter
09

Trish crawled into bed that night with her father's "I forgive you, Tee" ringing in her ears. She could also see her mother's face, the grim line about her mouth. Family meetings every week. No more fibbing about how school was going. Total honesty—or pay the consequences. She knew there would be no more stretching the boundaries. Besides, she'd learned that cheating of any kind hurt too badly. Not only herself—but her whole family.

"Thank you, heavenly Father, for bringing Dad home again. And for helping to clean up the mess I made. God, please make my Dad well again. And help me to win tomorrow. Amen." She thumped her pillow and turned over. Morning would be here before she had half enough sleep. A brief snatch of song drifted through her mind, *"Raise you up on eagle's wings."* She smiled her way to dreamland.

Hal sat with a cup of coffee cradled in his hands at the breakfast table the next morning. His smile made Trish think the sun had broken through the heavy overcast. Her mother humming in the kitchen, bacon sizzling in the pan, David singing off-key in the shower; all seemed normal—like life was supposed to be at Runnin' On Farm.

She hugged her dad, squeezed her mom around the waist, and slid into her chair. Her grin felt like it might crack her face. "Waffles!" The grin got wider. "Thanks, Mom." Crispy golden waffles were joined by two strips of bacon and an egg, easy-over, just the way she liked it. Trish buttered her waffles and poured the syrup.

"You could say grace first." Her father smiled.

Trish grinned back at him and silently bowed her head. All she could say was *Thank you, thank you, thank you.*

"See you at the track." Her father hugged her before she picked up her bag and boots. David honked the horn. "In the winner's circle."

"Be careful," her mother added with a hug. Worry lines still creased her forehead.

"Sure, Mom. And thanks for the good breakfast." When Trish glanced back, Marge had leaned into the protective circle of Hal's arm. Trish suppressed the wish that her father could come along, and hung her silks behind the seat. "Let's go," she said, slamming the pickup door.

🐎

Trish could see the outline of the sun through the clouds as she trudged the path to the dressing room. Horses for the first race of the day were being led to the saddling paddock. Her mom and dad hadn't shown up at the track yet, but she, David, and Brad had Spitfire and Gatesby in prime form. After the ruckus he'd caused the evening before, Gatesby had clowned around, tossing David's hat, dribbling water on Trish's back when she tried to pick his hooves. Trish smiled at the memory.

"You look happy." Genie Stokes caught up with her.

"I am. Dad says he'll be here today." Trish grinned at the other jockey. "How's your shoulder?"

"Stiffens up some." Genie swung her arm in an arc. "But the pain is gone. That Spitfire sure didn't like having someone else on his back."

"Sorry."

"Hey, it's not your fault. By the way, you heard what they're saying about you?"

"No. Who?"

"Oh, here and there. They say either you're luckier'n anyone or you just talk those horses into winning. Not too often someone comes along with that special touch, but I think you got it."

"I . . . I just do what seems best." Trish shifted her bag to her other hand. "Are the other jockeys . . . ?"

"Well, there's some griping. You know how people can be—but most everyone is glad for you. They know about your dad and all."

Trish slowed as they reached the slanted concrete tunnel to the dressing rooms. "Thanks, Genie. You've helped me a lot."

"Just repaying the favor. You know your dad has helped plenty of people around this track. Both with advice and money when times are tough. Me included. He's a good man."

Trish felt a glow of pride. She'd always known her dad was the best. Genie's words just proved it. "Thanks."

At the whiff of dressing room, her butterflies woke up and began their warm-up routine just like the one she was about to perform. Trish had forgotten to appreciate their long nap. They'd even slept through a waffle breakfast. What a day!

Spitfire nickered when he saw Trish waiting in the saddling stall. He seemed to dance on the tips of his hooves as he followed David. Head up, ears pricked, he caught the attention of the railbirds, those watching the saddling process. At their oohs and aahs, he lifted his nose higher, like a movie star with fans.

"You silly." Trish laughed as David tied the slipknot in the stall. "You think everyone came just to see you."

Spitfire nodded. He shoved his nose against her chest and snuffled her pockets. Trish held out both fists. When he licked the right one, she gave him the hidden carrot.

"I dare you to do that with Gatesby." David fastened the saddle girth.

"Sure. And lose my hand. How could I ride then?" Trish smoothed Spitfire's forelock. When he begged for another carrot, she laughed and pushed his persistent nose away. "After you win." She looked him straight in the eye. "Now give it all you've got, Spitfire. We need the money."

David boosted her into the saddle. "Watch that far turn. It seemed wet." He patted her knee. "You can do it."

"Did you see Mom and Dad?"

"They're up in the box." David backed Spitfire out and handed the lead shank to Brad mounted on Dan'l. He patted Spitfire on the rump. "Go get 'em."

As the bugle blew parade, Spitfire danced to the side of the gray. He flung his head up at the flags snapping in the breeze. When the crowd roared, he turned his head, accepting their accolades.

"Should have named you Prince or King." Trish laughed in sheer joy. "Or maybe Ham."

Brad laughed with her as he released the lead. "Ham he is. See you in the circle."

At the post position, Spitfire settled for the break. Within three lengths after the shot, he was running easily at the head of the field. No other horse even came near him. Trish felt like they were out for a private gallop. She heard the announcer call Genie Stokes as rider of the second-place finisher.

"Congratulations," Trish called as they cantered their horses back to the circle.

Genie stopped her mount. "Did he even go all out?" She pointed her whip at Spitfire.

"I don't think so. But he sure had fun." Trish smoothed Spitfire's mane. "He wasn't too happy about quitting."

"You might be thinking first Saturday in May." Genie grinned. "He's some horse, even if he doesn't like any other riders."

Trish felt a tingle go up her spine and then race down again. *The first Saturday in May. Kentucky Derby Day.* While she and her dad had dreamed about it, someone else mentioning it made the dream more of a reality.

She slipped from her horse's back and removed the saddle. Standing between her father and David with Spitfire's head over her shoulder felt right. This was where they all belonged—in the winner's circle.

"Congratulations, Tee." Her father kissed her cheek. Spitfire nudged Hal away, as if he were jealous. Laughter from the crowd, another popping flash, and then Trish got on the scale. She could get to like this.

Trish changed silks, weighed in again, and joined David and Gatesby for the next race. "What'd you feed these guys today?" she asked after the colt tried to pick the silk covering off her helmet. When she scolded him, the horse gave her his *Who—me?* look.

"They're sure full of spunk today. Leading him over here was tougher than an hour on the weights. And that was with Brad on the other lead. All you'll have to do is point him in the right direction and hang on today."

"Thank you for making my job sound so simple." Trish thumped her brother on the head with her whip. "Is Anderson here?"

"Up in the box. He came by the stable, but says you know Gatesby better than he does. So just do your best. Dad says since you're on the outside, stay there. And he'll see you in the circle again. He said to tell you this could get to be a habit. A nice habit."

"Yep." Trish gathered her reins as David led them out. Gatesby didn't think he should wait until the end of the line. All those horses in front of him and . . .

"Knock it off, you big goof." Trish pulled him back to a walk. When he crowhopped, Brad jerked on the rope. Trish snugged the reins down until Gatesby's chin met his chest. Even then, he pranced sideways instead of walking.

"How're your arms?" David released the lead.

Trish laughed. "See ya."

"In the circle."

Gatesby walked into the gate flat-footed and settled for the break, all business now that the time was at hand. When the gates clanged open, he erupted, running flat out within four strides. Trish kept him on the outside, letting the field spread itself. Gatesby pulled on the bit, running smoothly, his concentration focused on the horses ahead of him.

As they passed the halfway pole, Trish gave him more rein. He passed the third-place runner, caught the second, and reached for the first as they entered the final stretch.

"Now, go for it!" Trish commanded. "Come on, Gatesby!"

"And the winner by a nose, number seven, Gatesby, owned by John Anderson and ridden by Tricia Evanston." The announcer confirmed what Trish already knew. She had won again. And Gatesby had lived up to her expectations. "Good boy! You were great."

"Knock it off, you dummy," Trish hissed at the horse when John

Anderson flinched. Gatesby acted as though the bruise on Anderson's shoulder had nothing to do with him. So what if he was in the winner's circle. A shoulder right next to his nose was too good a target to pass up.

Anderson rubbed the bruise as David led Gatesby away to the testing barn. "He never gives up, does he?" John turned to Hal. "Thought you could break him of that."

Hal and Trish looked at each other and shook their heads. "We tried. At least he doesn't bite hard anymore. Just nips." Trish stepped off the scale. "He thinks he's being funny."

"Some joker. Thanks, Trish. You did a good job."

As Anderson disappeared into the crowd, Trish joined her mom and dad at the rail. Hal sank back into his wheelchair. "That's enough for one day." He looked up at his wife. "Ready to go home?"

"Sure was good to have you here." Trish walked beside him. "Even if Spitfire doesn't like that kissing stuff."

Hal chuckled. "He's your horse all right. See you at home."

Trish felt a letdown after the next race. She brought Bob Diego's horse in second. While the owner was pleased, Trish missed the winner's circle. But she knew she'd ridden a good race. The horse had done his best too. The winner had just been better.

"Hey, two out of three's not bad." Brad joined her in the lawn chairs in the tack room. He handed her a can of soda. "Drink this and let's get out of here."

It was hard to hit the books after such an exciting day. But when Trish thought of her bed, she remembered the discussion from the night before. Her grades *had* to stay at a B or better. The cards on the wall caught her eye. "Give thanks." "He cares for you." She picked up her pencil. *Chlorine, Cl; Chromium, Cr. . . .*

The next morning in church Trish chose to pay attention. The praise hymns suited her mood. Praising God wasn't so hard when her father was next to her in the pew. During the offering they all sang a new song, "He will raise you up on eagle's wings, bear you on the breath of God." She listened hard for the words. The tune seemed planted forever in her mind. She decided to look up the verse later.

Firefly won that afternoon. *Maybe this is God's way of helping us out right now. Giving us the money we need.* Her thoughts leapfrogged ahead of her feet as she walked back to the dressing room to change for the next race. *Just now we need horses that are able to win, and we have them. And I can ride, so we don't need to pay jockey fees.* She shook her head. *Amazing.*

"If you can get her in the money at all, I'll be pleased," Jason Rodgers said as he boosted Trish into the saddle for the seventh race. "There's a tough field out there."

"Well, old girl," Trish said as she stroked her mount's neck on the way back to the scale. "I know you did your best, so it's a good thing your boss will be happy with a show. Third place isn't my favorite, but . . . guess it's better than no money at all."

"Good job." Rodgers shook Trish's hand. "I have two on Wednesday's program. Both late in the day. Can you ride them?"

"I think so, but I'll let you know later this evening."

"That's fine. Sure was good to see Hal here yesterday. Tell him hello for me. He got away before I could get to him."

Trish felt that familiar pride straighten her tired shoulders. She had to remember to tell her dad what Genie had said. It was a shame he couldn't have been there to see Firefly win, but yesterday had worn him out.

Marge had dinner ready to put on the table when Trish and David walked in the door. Trish couldn't believe her eyes when she sat down. Roast beef, mashed potatoes, gravy—her mother must have spent all afternoon cooking.

"Smells wonderful!" Hal laid his napkin in his lap. After grace he raised his head and looked at Trish. "Now, tell me how the day went."

Trish talked between bites. "Mom, this is so-o-o good." She and David related all the happenings of the afternoon, and Trish finished with Genie's comments. "She said you've helped lots of people when they needed it."

"I just do what I can." Hal leaned back in his chair. "You know we've always shared what we have. And God's been good to us."

Trish looked at her father. His plaid shirt hung loosely on his once-broad shoulders. The circles under his eyes had deepened to dark hollows. Even his thin hair seemed to have grayed, matching the lines in his face. And purple and black bruises covered the back of one hand from the IVs. After all he'd been through the last couple of months, her dad could say, "God's been good to us." *Maybe he means for the past—not for now.*

"I mean it, Tee." He seemed to read her mind. "God is good to us right now—today and every day. I'm here, aren't I?"

Trish nodded. Saying thanks for winning was easy. But her father said thanks no matter what.

"Now. How many mounts have you been offered this week?"

Trish told him about the offers. "But I said I'd let them know tonight." She looked at her mother. "And while I have more studying, my chemistry is caught up. I'm okay for this week."

"So far." Marge sipped her coffee. "See if you can get to bed early tonight."

"What about the rumors you mentioned, David?" Hal pushed his chair back. "Let's go in the other room where the chairs are more comfortable."

"Diego wondered if you were considering Spitfire for the first Saturday in May. He said to call him if there was any way he could help."

Trish snuggled against the pillow she'd stuffed between her back and the stones of the hearth. "Genie asked the same thing. We've said this is our year."

"I know." Hal sighed. "I just . . . well, we have to take one step at a time. The Futurity is the next milestone. That's a mile and an eighth, close to the Derby. Spitfire needs plenty of conditioning to run that far."

Trish sizzled with excitement. "You mean we're gonna try for it?"

"God only knows, Tee. God only knows."

Chapter

10

S o. What all happened?" Rhonda blocked her way in the school hall.

"Well, I won."

"All right!"

"Three times."

"Three times? On who?"

"Spitfire, Gatesby, and Firefly. Got a second and a third on the other two." Trish twirled the dial on her locker. "And I have two rides for Wednesday."

"Did you tell your dad . . . about the . . ."

"Extra racing? Yes."

"And you're still alive—and still riding? Trish, for crying out loud, quit stalling and start talking."

"And start walking." Brad wrapped an arm about each of them and herded them toward the lunchroom. "I'm starved."

It took the entire lunch period to fill her friends in on all the details. Brad added a few of his own. "And so," Trish finished, "we start seriously training Spitfire for the Futurity and then we'll see about . . ."

"The first Saturday in May?" Rhonda couldn't stand still and remain cool. Brad finally put both hands on her shoulders to calm her down.

The bell rang. Rhonda hugged Trish and dashed off.

Trish had to order her mind to quit dreaming of the Derby. Her classes came first. She needed every bit of concentration she could scare up.

When she got home, Trish found her father in the recliner reading his Bible. He put it down when she entered the living room. "Come sit here a minute." He patted the hearth in front of the snapping fire.

"Wait a sec." Trish raised her book bag. In the bedroom she dropped her load beside the cluttered desk. Her room seemed to grow piles of clothes when she wasn't looking. She shut her eyes on the mess and went back to her dad by way of the kitchen for milk and an apple.

"How was your day, Trish?"

"Good." She offered him a bite of her apple. "Finals are this week, so the teachers kind of let up today."

"I've been thinking about the logistics around here. You need to get your driver's license so people don't have to keep hauling you around."

"All right!" Trish's grin nearly cracked her jaw.

"Do you have time to take the test soon?"

"Well, my chemistry final on Thursday is my last hard one. I only have history on Friday, so Thursday afternoon would work. We have Anderson's horse running on Friday and I have one other mount."

"Fine. Your mother will pick you up at school on Thursday afternoon, then." Hal returned her grin. "Just make sure you pass the first time."

"Da-a-d." She drained her glass of milk. "Gotta go work those beasts. You been down to see Miss Tee yet? She's really growing."

Hal shook his head. "I'll be down to watch tomorrow afternoon."

Trish spent the week studying. Every spare minute she reviewed Spanish vocabulary, chemistry symbols, and Shakespeare for English. Her two mounts on Wednesday finished in the money but not the winner's circle. While she was disappointed, Bob Diego congratulated her for good rides. He offered her two more on Saturday and one on Sunday.

"Sorry you can't ride during the day," he said. "I'd like you up on Friday afternoon."

"Me too."

Another trainer asked Trish to ride on Saturday.

I'm going to have to keep a calendar, Trish thought on the way home. *In fact, I need to be better organized. Somehow, I've got to keep my room clean. That'd make Mom happier than anything . . . other than quitting my racing, that is.*

Trish was up till three Thursday morning. Even though David coached her in the evening, she felt she hadn't done enough. All the equations and symbols ran together—mixed with racing times, and how many feet one must dim the car lights for an oncoming vehicle.

Trish slept right through her alarm. When she finally heard the insistent buzzer, the clock read 7:10.

"Trish, you're going to be late."

"I'm up."

"That's what you said fifteen minutes ago." Marge wiped her hands on a dish towel as she leaned against the door frame.

"I did?" Trish shook her head and tried to blink her eyes open. "I don't remember."

"How can you stand . . ." Marge cut off her words, but Trish knew what she wanted to say. One glance at her mother's face after seeing her totalled room said it all.

Not today. Not this week. Trish stumbled down the hall to the shower. *Maybe I'll have time to clean it up Saturday.*

The hot shower helped wake her up, but her eyes still felt gritty, as if she had to force her eyelids to stay open.

"Control to Trish, come in, Trish," David teased her in the car.

"Umm-mmm," Trish yawned for the umpteenth time. "I should go out and run the track." She picked up her book bag. "I just can't wake up."

"I noticed."

She felt good about her Spanish test. The essay went well too. But she felt totally defeated by the chemistry test. *Why can't I get this stuff?* Tears of frustration pricked the backs of her eyelids. *I've never studied so hard for anything in my life.* She slumped into her seat in history class. The hour was slated for review, with the teacher answering questions and approving topics for term papers next quarter. Trish opened her book. Panic swept over her. She hadn't even thought of a topic yet.

Half an hour later the teacher shook her awake.

"I'll have to call your parents right after school," she warned. "You're just too tired, Trish. Something has to give."

Trish just shook her head and muttered as she left the room. She felt like slamming her fist into her locker door when it wouldn't open. A perfect end to a perfect day? Right!

Trish waved at Rhonda and Brad, then tossed her book bag in the back seat of the family car.

"Feel like driving?" Marge opened the door and stepped out.

"I guess so."

"Pretty bad day, huh?"

Trish just nodded as she slid into the driver's seat. The nagger added to her weariness. *You better tell her. You know you promised.* Trish felt like twisting his scrawny neck, if he had such a thing. *I planned on it,* she answered. *Give me a break, will ya?* She bit her lip. That wasn't quite true. She *had* thought about postponing telling her mother.

As they turned onto 79th Street, heading west to Hazel Dell, Trish glanced over at her mother. Marge sat half-turned in the seat, studying her daughter.

"I did fine in Spanish and English, maybe flunked chemistry, and fell asleep in history." Trish got it all out in a rush. "Mrs. Smith will call you to set up a conference. She's probably trying to get you now."

"Oh, Trish." Marge patted her daughter's arm. "I'm sorry."

Yeah, I'll bet. The words popped into Trish's mind. Then she scolded herself. It wasn't as if her mother didn't care.

"I tried *so* hard." She ground her teeth together. "And it didn't do any good."

"When will you know your grades?"

"Tomorrow."

Marge nodded. "Are you sure you feel up to your driving test today?"

"Yeah." Trish took a deep breath. "Mom, I *have* to ride tomorrow. I gave my word."

"I know. But remember the agreement, nothing below a B. You can ride tomorrow because the grades aren't posted yet, but don't accept anything beyond that—until you know."

Trish groaned.

"And falling asleep in class . . ." Marge straightened in her seat, took a deep breath, and shook her head. "Your father and I will talk with Mrs. Smith." She looked at Trish slumped behind the wheel. "How about something to eat before you go in there?"

"Afterwards, okay? I just want to get this over with."

Trish didn't need to tell her mother she'd passed the written driver's test. Her grin said it all when she emerged from the room. "My behind-the-wheel appointment is next Tuesday." She slid into the driver's seat. "I can't believe I got one so soon. They had a cancellation." She reread her score sheet. "I missed the questions on numbers again—four of them. They all had to do with number of feet and speeds. I *hate* numbers." She stuffed the sheet into her purse. "Let's go eat."

"Mrs. Smith called," Marge said when Trish came back to the house after working the horses that night. "Our conference is for Monday right after school"

"Me too?"

Marge nodded. "Dinner's ready."

Trish started to get ready for bed early that night, resenting the hour she'd spent on history. She felt that if she didn't do well on that final, it would be another strike against her in Mrs. Smith's eyes. She glared at her notes.

Reaching to turn out the light, she stared at the open book on her desk. With a groan she threw back the covers, stomped to the desk, and grabbed the book. Propping her pillow against the headboard, she began reviewing—again. She *would* get an A on this one.

Or close to it. When she'd finished the test, only two true-and-false questions were in doubt, and the written part looked good. At the end of the day Trish slammed her locker, and she and Rhonda dashed to the parking lot. Even a mud bath from a sloppy track would be better than the last couple of days. But then, anything to do with horses was better than finals.

"What'd you get in chemistry?" Rhonda leaned on the back of the front seat.

"C minus. One point away from a D." Trish slumped in the seat. "At least they won't ground me today. But I'll have to tell Diego I can't ride Wednesday."

"Maybe your mom and dad will change their minds."

"No." Trish shook her head. "No chance. And they're meeting with Mrs. Smith on Monday. I'll probably have to quit racing on weekdays all together."

"It's just not fair."

"Tell me about it."

"Your dad coming to watch?" Brad asked.

"I don't think so. David's already there to get Final Command ready. My first mount is for Diego."

Trish rode to win the fourth race. While the pouring rain washed half the mud off her black and white silks, her grin still sparkled. Wet or dry, she loved the winner's circle.

Final Command fidgeted in the gate. "That's not like you, fella," Trish crooned as she stroked his neck. "I know you don't like the rain, so let's just get this over with."

The horse on their right refused to enter the starting stall. It took two assistants to finally get him in. Trish hunched her shoulders to keep the rain from running down her neck. She crouched forward, making herself small, hugging all her body heat close. Mentally she called the stubborn horse every name she could think of.

"If only we were on the outside, boy." She spoke to her mount's twitching ears. "But we're right in the middle."

And in the middle was where they were six lengths out of the gate. Right in the middle with horses slipping all around them. She felt a bump on one side and pulled back on the reins to get them out of the melee before something happened.

At that moment, she heard the crack of a bat. Her mount leaped forward. They slammed into the horse on their left.

Someone had struck her horse!

Chapter

11

Pure strength of will kept her horse on its feet. Trish ignored the stumbling animals around them and kept her mount's head up. He slipped in the mud but regained his footing. As the way cleared ahead of them, Trish talked him into running the race. Far ahead the two leaders rounded the turn. One other horse left the pack and ran with her.

Trish brought the animal over to the rail, and as she encouraged him with heart, hands, and voice, they ate up the furlongs. While there was no way to catch the lead runners, she made sure that they took third place. As they raced around the track, her mind returned to the thwap of a bat on *her* mount's haunches.

"I'm sorry that someone hit you, fella. I know you're not used to the whip. You don't need it. But who hit you? And why?"

That was her question to her father that evening. "Why, Dad? Why would someone hit my horse? And who? Who would do such a mean thing? It's illegal, too, isn't it?"

"Did you report it?"

"No. I don't know how. And it was such a mess out there, I . . . I just wanted to get home." She leaned even closer to the roaring fire. She wasn't sure she would ever feel warm again. On the outside anyway. Inside she was hotter than the snapping logs.

"It's just so unfair!" Sparks from the fire reflected in her eyes.

"Trish, life isn't fair. Racing isn't fair. There will always be those who do underhanded things. Those who take advantage of others. Even to the point of cruelty. That's part of racing. Part of any business."

"And that's why I'd rather you weren't racing." Marge stepped into the room, handing her daughter a steaming cup of hot chocolate.

"But, M-o-m."

"One of the horses went down, and it could easily have been you." She raised her hand to stop Trish's answer.

"I know you're a good rider. And I thank God you weren't injured, that no one was seriously hurt. But accidents happen. And maliciousness. You felt it firsthand." She turned back to the kitchen. "Dinner'll be ready in about fifteen minutes. Set the table, please, Trish, as soon as you finish your chocolate."

Trish cupped the hot mug in her hands.

"She's right, you know," her dad said.

"I know, but . . ."

"Tomorrow we'll file a complaint, so you know how."

"That's not all." Trish swirled the remaining cocoa in her mug. "I got a C minus on my chemistry test."

"I'm sorry, Tee."

Not half as sorry as I am, Trish thought as she got up to set the table. *I'm the one who has to tell those men I can't ride. And that's gonna shoot down my paycheck for next week.*

Trish enjoyed picking up her check each week from the head office at the track. Giving the money to her father made her feel like all the hours she put in made a difference for their family. No matter how much her father grumbled about her not keeping the money, she knew the bills were being paid. And that made his life easier.

"I want to make Dad's life easier, so he can get well, Father," she prayed that night. "Thank you for the money, and for keeping me safe."

She snuggled down in the covers. "And please help me find out who whipped us today. Amen."

When Trish came up from working the horses in the morning, her mother had scrambled eggs with bacon ready to put on the table. She pulled a pan of bran muffins from the oven as Trish slid into her place.

"Those guys were sure rarin' to go this morning." Trish rubbed her arms. "I feel like I did a hundred push-ups."

"How would you know?" David asked. "You've never done that many at one time." He put his plateful of food down on the table. "Thanks, Mom. This smells great."

Trish stuck her tongue out at him. "Well, you work four horses and see how your arms feel."

Hal buttered a muffin. "What time do you have to be at the track?"

"One or so. I ride in the third and fifth."

"Good. David, I want you to bring all the horses home today. I know that's not the best, but it will be easier for you to have them all here. Plus we won't have to pay the extra help at the track."

David nodded.

"And, Tee, how about showing off that little filly of yours right after breakfast?"

"Um-m-m." Trish scrunched up her face. "I've got something I have to do first."

Surprise raised her father's eyebrows. "Okay. Let me know when you're ready."

Trish attacked her room with a vengeance. Some clothes ended up on hangers for the first time in days while others landed in the washing machine. The jumbled bed took on a completely new look when the bedspread was smoothed into place. And her desk—there really was a flat surface under all those papers.

An hour later she folded her underwear and stacked it in the proper drawer. A quick swipe with the dustcloth and even the chest of drawers shone. "God, help me keep this up," she prayed as she looked around the orderly room. "Even I can't stand the mess anymore, let alone Mom." She gathered a pile of shirts off the chair and headed for the laundry room. "I'm ready." She turned the dial to start the last wash load.

Miss Tee still spooked when someone else tried to approach her, but she came right up to Trish. The bright morning sun made her blink as Trish led the mare out of the barn and turned her loose in the paddock. When the mare snorted and rolled in the wet grass, the filly danced over to Trish and, hiding on the opposite side from Hal, rubbed her forehead against Trish's arm. When she peeked around to keep that strange man in sight, Trish chuckled. Hal coughed. Miss Tee darted away, her hooves skimming the grass. She skidded to a stop behind the standing mare, then peeked out, her nose and ears visible through her mother's tail.

"She's a beauty, all right." Hal leaned against the fence, resting his elbows on the board rail. "But she should be with her bloodlines. Full sister to Spitfire. Only shame is her birthday. She'll be barely three months old January first."

"Yeah, but legally she'll be a year. It's crazy that all Thoroughbreds are considered a year old on January first, no matter when they were dropped." The filly tiptoed back to Trish. She reached around, tentatively sniffed Hal's arm, and shook her head.

Hal laughed. "Come on, Tee. We've got work to do."

Just for a moment, if she didn't look at her father, Trish could pretend things were just as they used to be. But then he coughed again. He turned toward the house, his once-broad shoulders hunched against the chill of the morning, and his face slashed with new lines and gray like the fog.

But at least he's down here with you and not in the hospital, her nagger reminded. *Don't you ever take a nap?* Trish snapped back, but then smiled at herself. She knew she needed to remember to be thankful.

That afternoon she won both races. Both owners seemed as pleased as she was. The best part was that her father had watched from the special bleachers built by the barns for owners and trainers to observe morning workouts.

Trish could feel her Irish temper flare when he told her what he'd heard. The jockey whose horse went down the day before had filed a complaint against Trish for knocking him down.

"You can't prove someone struck you," Hal said when Trish fumed. "I told them what happened, but . . ."

"No good." Trish drew circles in the shavings with her booted toe. She chewed on her bottom lip. "At least my side is written down too, right?"

Hal nodded.

Trish was silent as they loaded Firefly and Dan'l. She checked Final Command's legs before leading him into the trailer. At least he hadn't been hurt in the accident.

But it wasn't an accident. She climbed into the truck cab beside her dad. *We were slashed on purpose.*

The organ was playing her song when they entered the church sanctuary the next morning. Trish hummed along. Eagle's wings. She sure needed them. She glanced at her father. So did he.

After church she took her Bible and checked the concordance. Isaiah 40:31. She looked up the verse and wrote it down—twice—on two cards. *"But those who wait on the Lord shall renew their strength; they shall mount up with wings like eagles, they shall run and not be weary, they shall walk and not faint."*

Her father was sound asleep in his recliner. Trish slipped the card into the Bible lying on the end table by his chair. Picking up the quilt, she covered him gently. *Wish you could come along, Dad. I need you there. And get better. I need you here.* She felt the plea so powerfully, she was afraid she'd spoken out loud. Then Trish changed clothes and left for the track. She had three mounts ahead.

A stiff breeze had the flags on the infield snapping. That same western breeze trailed mare's tails across the washed-out blue sky. While bringing in more wet weather, it had also helped dry the track.

Trish took time with her first mount. She hadn't ridden the mare before, but Rodgers had assured her the horse had every chance of being in the money. Still, she was a long shot on the boards.

"Well, old girl, let's go for the top. You'll look good in those pictures." Trish gathered her reins and settled her goggles in place. She needed a win as bad as the horse. Thoughts of the whip from the day before flitted into her mind as the gates closed, but she shut them out and concentrated on her mount.

That concentration paid off—handsomely. The purse was a large one. But Jason Rodgers still handed her an envelope. "I can't believe it," he said after the pictures were taken. "You brought her in two lengths ahead of the favorite."

"She just wanted to run," Trish laughed with him. "And I let her. Thanks for . . . for . . ." She touched her pocket.

Rodgers nodded. "Tell your dad hello for me."

By the end of the sixth race, Trish was jubilant. Two wins, a second, and no whip. Surely yesterday had been a freak.

Her good humor lasted until the family meeting that evening. Even though her mind knew she would be grounded for her chemistry grade, her heart kept hoping her parents would change their minds. They didn't.

If I hear "It's for your own good" one more time, I . . . I . . . To not race was *not* for her own good, she was sure, and it *would* hurt the entire family. They needed her share of the purses.

Calling Jason Rodgers and Bob Diego were two of the hardest things she'd ever had to do. "I'm sorry, I can't ride for you during the week," she said. To answer their *why*s she was tempted to blame her parents, but honesty won over. "I let my grades go down, but I can still ride Saturdays and Sundays." She felt like slamming the receiver down but instead grabbed her jacket and slammed out the door.

Caesar shoved his cold nose into her hand, but after no response, he trotted beside her down to the dark stables.

"It's just not fair," she sobbed into Dan'l's mane. "I'm trying my best and it just isn't good enough. It's not fair."

An hour later, all cried out, she slipped back into the house and crawled into bed. "God, you said you would help me. Where are you?"

"It happened, didn't it?" Rhonda didn't need more than one look at Trish's face to know. "Until when?"

"My grade comes back up. And today we have the conference with Mrs. Smith." Trish leaned against her locker. "You'd think all my good grades would count for something, but no. One crummy . . . I hate chemistry!"

Trish felt like she was invisible as Mrs. Smith and her parents discussed her grades, her exhaustion, her future grades, and what she planned to do with her life. Nobody asked her.

She swallowed a smart remark. When she shifted in her chair for the third time, her father turned his head and winked at her. A warm glow, like a hug, circled her heart.

She caught herself just before a yawn. That's all she needed. To fall asleep during the conference.

"So, we'll set up a conference with our counselor, Mrs. Olson, the principal, and Trish's other teachers, if that's all right?" Mrs. Smith asked.

Trish jerked completely alert. *Now what?*

At her parents' nod, she continued. "Would tomorrow be possible?"

"No." Hal shook his head. "I have another treatment tomorrow. I won't be in any shape for a meeting. How about Thursday?"

Trish cleared her throat. "Will you need me there?"

The three nodded.

"I'll call you then," Mrs. Smith finished. "Thank you for coming."

The next afternoon Marge picked Trish up after school.

"How's Dad?" Trish asked as she slid behind the wheel.

"Sleeping. The doctor gave him a new medication for the nausea, so he shouldn't be so sick this time. He's gained a couple of pounds—that was good news."

Trish tried to concentrate on her driving. Surely the driver's test wasn't much different than a horse race. Her butterflies didn't need to try anything new. The old antics stirred her up enough.

"You can do it." Marge smiled through the open window after she'd slid out of the car.

The uniformed instructor who took her place looked as if a smile might shatter his face. *Maybe the frozen look is in for testing instructors.* Trish swallowed . . . hard. Her left hand refused to leave the wheel when the man told her to test the turn signals. At his second gruff order, her hand finally obeyed.

Trish relaxed as the driving got under way. She followed each instruction, but every time the man wrote something down, her butterflies did flips.

"You did just fine," he said when she parked the car back at the station. He handed her the sheet. A big red 90 stood out at the top. "Now go inside to line B to have your picture taken, and pay your fee." He almost smiled. But not quite.

Trish didn't know if her feet were touching the ground or not. When she got back in the car, her grin told her success.

"Congratulations, Trish. I'm proud of you." Marge reached across the seat to hug her daughter. "How about a banana split to celebrate?"

"You're on!" She bounced on the seat and thumped the steering wheel. *I should run around the block. I am s-o-o excited.* Instead, she carefully checked both ways before pulling out on the street.

As soon as they arrived home, Trish called Rhonda. "You are talking to a *licensed* driver," she said with a haughty note. Rhonda's squeal matched the one stuck about mid-throat for Trish. "Gotta run," she cut the conversation short. "Have to work the beasts."

Her dad wasn't in his recliner, but lay curled on his side in bed, asleep. The pan on the floor reminded Trish of how sick he could be. She tiptoed out without sharing her good news. This was life—since the cancer. Her dad wasn't there to share her news, good or bad.

Chapter
12

The weight bearing Trish down seemed even heavier on Wednesday. She hadn't been able to concentrate the night before, so instead of acing her chemistry quiz, she flunked it. Even though the sun played hide-and-seek with the scurrying clouds, she saw only gray. And rain.

Dumping her book bag on the chair at her desk, she looked around her bedroom. It seemed strange to see uncluttered carpet, undraped chairs, and a *made* bed. At least *one* thing in her life was going right. Not training horses in the morning gave her the extra few minutes to put things away. *Yeah, sure,* she responded to her nagger. *Be thankful for small favors.*

Downstairs, her father asked from his seemingly permanent place in the recliner, "You got a minute, Tee?"

"Yeah," Trish answered on her way to the kitchen. "Umm-mmm, smells good." She sniffed the glorious aroma. "Wow, homemade rolls!"

Marge had just lifted the pan from a plate of caramel-cinnamon rolls. Trish scooped a golden glob of the gooey concoction from the waxed paper. "Whoa! That's hot!"

Marge turned from the sink. "Pour some milk, and I'll fix a plate of these for you and your dad. This should tempt his appetite."

"Does mine. Where's David?"

"Down at the barn, where else? He's trying to get some training in for the yearlings. We think we have a buyer for one or two of them."

Trish caught her glass before it cracked on the counter. *Selling the yearlings! Those are our investment for next year.* She swallowed the words before they could burst forth. Setting the glasses of milk and plate of rolls on a tray, she carried them into the living room.

"I know, Tee." Hal had heard and knew she was upset. "But I don't know what else to do."

"You could let me race more!"

Hal closed his eyes. He shook his head. "I know, but . . ."

"Don't say it."

A tiny smile lifted the lines around his mouth. "All right, I won't, but even if you're racing four days a week, you can't always count on a win. We can't depend completely on what you make."

"There's the money from Anderson."

"I know. That helps with the feed bill." He took a bite of the cinnamon roll. "Ah, now this is good. Your mother sure knows how to bake."

Trish huddled on the hearth. Today, even the glowing fire didn't warm the chill of foreboding that seeped into her mind like fog tendrils in the pasture hollows when the sun goes down.

"Trish, you can't carry the weight for all of us." He pulled her card out of his Bible. "Eagle's wings," he mused. "I've loved this verse for so many years. And when the pain's been at its worst, this promise lifts me up. God does what He promises, Tee. He gives us new strength for each day, but He won't take care of tomorrow until it comes. And we can't either."

Trish nodded. "I guess so."

"I don't just guess, I *know*." Hal patted her hand. "Now, eat your roll before it's cold." He wiped his mouth. "And thanks for the card. Finding this promise has meant the world to me."

Trish sighed. She wrapped her arms around her legs and rested her chin on her knees. "It just seems crazy to keep me from racing when we need the money so badly."

"We need *you* more."

The phone rang. After a few minutes, Marge leaned around the door to the kitchen. "That was Mrs. Olson. Our meeting is being postponed until next Thursday."

Trish wasn't sure if she was happy or sad about the change. "After all, I don't even know what the meeting is really about," she confided to Caesar as he loped beside her to the stables. A sharp bark assured her that he was listening. "I sure don't need anyone yakking about my grades again, or making a big deal of my falling asleep in class."

"Hey, can you sleep over tomorrow night?" Trish asked Rhonda on the way to the cafeteria the next morning. "We're trailering Firefly and Gatesby to the track right after school, then I need to gallop Spitfire and you could ride Final Command. I already asked my mom."

"Don't know why not. I'll ask and call you tonight."

"Maybe we could rent a movie."

"What about me?" Brad thumped his hand on his chest. "All I do is work all the time. I *never* get invited to the parties."

Trish and Rhonda rolled their eyes at each other. "You can bring the soft drinks."

The horses loaded without a hitch. After David and Brad rolled out of the driveway, Trish and Rhonda galloped the two at home, fed all the stock, and still had time to play with Miss Tee.

Only twinges of I-wish-I-were-at-the-track nipped at Trish's mind. If she were forced to admit it, the break felt good.

And the party felt better. For a party it was, as Hal teased Rhonda about her latest boyfriend, and *everyone* hassled Trish about *the* Doug Ramstead. Marge served hamburgers and French fries, with ice cream sundaes for dessert. By the time they brought in the popcorn, Trish felt as if she might pop.

Halfway through the movie, Rhonda had an attack of the giggles. Her face turned red and tears streamed down her face.

"It must be a v-v-virus," Trish tried to talk around her own laughter.

"Knock it off, you two." David threw a pillow at Rhonda.

"We can't hear the movie!" Brad raised his hands in protest.

Trish was rolling on the floor. Rhonda thumped her feet. Neither of them could breathe.

"Don't look at me!" Trish plumped the pillow on Rhonda's head. "Or I'll never stop." Their laughter erupted again.

Trish took a deep breath. When she looked up at her dad, he winked at her. She lay on her back, staring up at the pine-board ceiling. Her stomach hurt from all the laughter. What a good feeling!

Later in her bedroom, Trish leaned over the side of her bed. Rhonda lay snug in a sleeping bag spread on foam cushions, her head propped on her hand. "We haven't gone crazy like *that* in a long time."

Trish shook her head. "Too long."

They talked for a while longer, until Rhonda didn't answer. Trish was too sleepy to prod her.

The next afternoon, Trish rode two races before Gatesby—winning one and placing fourth in the other. Just the thought of having her dad in the stands sent an extra thrill down her spine as she and Gatesby paraded to the post. The rain had stopped, but the track was still wet. A brisk wind bit through her silks and snapped the infield flags.

Gatesby wanted to run. He'd already worked up a lather before Brad turned them loose at the gates. Trish laughed at the bay's antics as the gate squeaked shut behind them. Gatesby spooked at the sound, then settled for the break. In a split second Trish noted who rode on either side of her. Genie grinned back on the left.

Gatesby pulled ahead by the quarter pole and stayed there. After the finish line Trish had to fight him back to a trot. He shook his head at her command and sent gobs of lather to decorate her silks. She scraped a glob off her cheek as she slid to the ground in the winner's circle and wiped her hand on the colt's nose. "Looks better on you," she said, and held his bridle tightly under his chin. John Anderson gripped the other side the same way. Neither of them wanted a new bruise.

When the announcer called Firefly's race, Trish gladly slipped into her crimson and gold. She didn't get to wear their own silks half as much as she'd like. She smoothed the sleeve and snapped the colors on her helmet. Another win would sure feel great. She raised her shoulders up to her ears and relaxed them to get the kinks out.

By the time they paraded to the post, the drizzle had returned. Trish hunched her shoulders again, this time against the dampness. When they entered the starting gate, the drizzle deepened to a downpour. Firefly shook her head and laid back her ears.

"I don't like it any more than you do." Trish rubbed the filly's neck. "So let's just get this over with." Firefly paused an instant after the gates clanged open, then leaped forward. Within six strides they were boxed in. Just the spot Trish hated and feared. A horse behind them kept her from pulling back.

She could hear her father's advice in her ears. *Just ride it out and watch for a hole.* Firefly skidded a bit in the turn. The harsh thwap of the whip and the squeal of pain sounded at the same instant.

Firefly leaped ahead, thudded into the horse on their right and clipped the hind feet of the mount in front of them. Trish fought to keep the filly's head up as horses grunted and stumbled around them. Jockeys swore, horses squealed. Seeing daylight in front, Trish drove for the opening and by sheer willpower kept her mount moving and upright.

Feeling Firefly loosen up and lengthen her stride, Trish checked the track ahead. One horse rounded the far turn. "Let's go for it, girl," she shouted. She ached to look back and see if anyone was injured. That had been too close. Who had struck Firefly? And why?

They pounded into the stretch, gaining on the leader. Rain drove in Trish's face. The horse ahead appeared and disappeared in the sheets of silvery, icy rain. Suddenly the first-place runner stumbled, almost went down, then limped along the rail in obvious pain.

Trish pulled Firefly up on the far side of the wire. They'd won—but at what cost to the other entries?

Hal wrapped a jacket around his daughter as she slid off her horse. The pictures were taken with an umbrella over the owners and cameraman.

"What happened?" her father asked as she stepped off the scale. David led Firefly away to the testing barn.

"Someone hit us! Dad, what's going on? What about the rest of the pack? And what happened to the lead horse?"

"I haven't heard. All I could think about was you."

"I'm okay. But someone caused all that. It was no accident."

Wouldn't you know, Mother would be here to see this one, Trish thought as she stepped into the hot shower back in the dressing room. She wasn't sure if the shakes were caused by the cold or left over from the race. Anger, fierce and unrelenting, burned her from the inside as the water pounded her skin. Someone had whipped her horse, and maybe caused the injuries of other horses and riders. What sort of person would do such a thing? Poor Firefly. She'd never been struck with a whip in her entire life—until today. Trish ground her teeth. The filly's squeal of pain echoed in her ears.

Trish and her father filed their complaint before they left the track. Trish was still so angry, she could hardly give the correct information.

"They acted like it was *my* fault!" Trish railed on her father as they left the office.

"Easy, Trish. They'll look in to it. The rain made it difficult for anyone from the stands to see what was happening. At least no one was hurt. Let's be thankful for that."

"Except that horse broke a leg."

"Yes, but that had nothing to do with your situation. Sometimes bones just crack. It's one of the hazards of racing Thoroughbreds." Hal snapped open the umbrella as they reached the exit. "Let's get back and check on Firefly."

The filly nickered at the sight of Trish. "I'm going to find out who did this," Trish muttered as she rubbed down the horse's neck and behind her ears. "I promise."

Chapter 13

A complaint against *me*? Again?"

"I know. But your horse bumped the others. No one saw anyone strike Firefly. The rain made everyone extra cautious and visibility was nil."

"But, Dad, that's not fair!" Trish could feel herself losing control. She wanted to scream and pound someone—the someone who caused this. Twice now. Someone had struck her horses twice. "What are they saying?"

"That you're young and inexperienced." He dropped his voice. "And you'll do anything to win."

Trish stepped back as if struck. "But . . . but that's not true!"

"I know. I think someone is starting rumors too. Those who know us won't believe it, but others? Well, you know how it goes."

Trish stared at her father, her eyes wide with shock. She licked her dry lips and tightened her jaw. "What are they going to do about it?"

"Continue investigating."

Trish replayed the race in her mind—moment by moment. Nothing. All she could remember was disgust at being boxed in, and trying to keep Firefly on her feet. The reel played as she worked the horses around the home track; when she took a shower; and in a nightmare that left her shaking.

On Tuesday morning Trish found a new card. *"I can do all things through Christ who strengthens me" (Philippians 4:13). I suppose that means not wanting to beat up whoever is doing this.*

Her nagger seemed to congratulate her, *You're right!*

And I can study in spite of everything? she asked.

Right on.

Even chemistry?

You got it.

Trish smoothed the covers on her bed and read the card again. She pinned it above the others. There was quite a list of promises. Now, to hang on to all of them.

A trailer truck drove out of the yard when Brad dropped her off after school Wednesday afternoon.

"Who was that?" she asked.

Hal studied his hands. "He bought Samba and the gray filly."

"You mean they're gone? Already?"

Hal nodded. "He met my price, Tee. Those two yearlings just bought us some breathing room."

Tears prickled at the back of Trish's eyes. She swallowed. "But I didn't even get to say good-bye."

"I know." Hal put his arm around her shoulders. "I know."

That evening Trish had to turn down another mount when a trainer called her. His "Thanks anyway," when she told him she'd be glad to ride for him on the weekend didn't help.

And now I'm supposed to study chemistry. Trish slammed the book shut. Standing up suddenly sent her chair crashing to the floor. She stomped to the window and jammed her hands in her back pockets.

Fog drifted past the mercury yard light, creating a shimmering, circular glow. Rocks glistened in the driveway. Moisture beads on the car roof sparkled in the soft light. Trish sighed and returned to her desk. *Where are my eagle's wings tonight?*

The new card caught her eye. She gritted her teeth and opened the book again. "Please, God. It says *all things.*"

The next afternoon Trish got a B on the chemistry quiz. *Well, that means a D average for this quarter.* She felt like putting her head down and bawling. *When will I ever get to race again?*

Trish met her parents by the trophy case near the main doors. "Mrs. Olson asked me to take you to the conference room. She said the others would be there in a few minutes."

Trish pulled out a chair by her father. "I don't know what good this is gonna do," she muttered under her breath.

"Trust us." Her father patted her knee.

Trish nodded and smiled as all her teachers, the principal, and Mrs. Olson, her counselor, took their places. After general greetings and exchanges, a hush fell on the room. Trish squirmed in her seat. *I'd rather be home working the horses. At least that might do someone some good.*

Her father cleared his throat. "I think you all are somewhat aware of our situation. I have cancer, and . . ."

Trish forced herself to straighten up in her chair. The expression she wore masked the thoughts that whizzed through her brain. *Why does he have to tell everybody what's happening in our family? This is our business.*

But maybe they can help, her nagger offered.

Sure. She pulled herself back to the meeting.

"And so, I'm hoping you may have some suggestions of ways we can make life—and school—easier for our daughter."

The group nodded and spoke among themselves.

"Let me offer some ideas." Mrs. Olson smiled at Trish and her parents. She outlined several things they could do, including tutoring, summer school, and planning ahead for the times when Trish would be absent because of family matters.

"What do you suggest?" Marge asked the counselor.

"I suggest we take Trish out of chemistry," Mrs. Olson continued.

"She can drop up to four credits without damaging her GPA. She's a good student." The other teachers nodded. "And I think we should do all we can to help her succeed. None of you"—she smiled at Marge and Hal—"need any extra pressure right now. Trish can make up chemistry this summer at Clark College or choose to take another science. This will give her another study hall until next semester. That should cut her homework even more."

Trish couldn't believe her ears. *Drop chemistry! Wow!* She looked at each person around the table. They were all nodding and smiling. Trish peeked at her parents. Her mother wasn't smiling but looked relieved.

Relief didn't begin to describe Trish's feelings. She felt like a helium balloon, let go. Yes, bumping on the ceiling might be a close description. This was almost as good as the winner's circle.

That evening Trish took time to play with Miss Tee when she brought the mare and foal back into the barn. They spent their days out in the paddock now.

"I don't have to do chemistry tonight," she sang to the filly while brushing the mare. "All my homework is done." She hugged the inquisitive filly and kissed Miss Tee's soft nose. Trish got a lick on the cheek in return. Soft, tiny lips nibbled her hair. She cupped both hands on the filly's cheeks and rubbed noses. "Oh, you sweetie. I love you so much."

"It's good to see you so happy." Trish looked up, surprised to see her mother. Miss Tee retreated behind the mare's haunches. Then braver, she inched her way over to Trish and peeked around her mistress.

"Isn't she beautiful?" Trish laid her arm around the foal's neck.

"Yes, she is. Dinner's ready."

"Okay." Trish rubbed her baby's ears one more time and slipped out of the stall. When she leaned back across the half door, the filly nickered, a soft little sound that barely moved her nostrils. "Keep that up and I'll never leave." Trish stroked her one more time. "Remember, you're a winner." She turned off the lights, and together she and her mother left the barn.

"I'm really proud of you, you know," Marge said.

"Why, Mom?"

"Oh, lots of things. Your efforts in chemistry, all the hard work you do with the horses . . . keeping your room so neat and clean now."

"Thanks. I like my room better now too. I've been praying to be better organized. Mom, I feel free tonight. Like a two-ton weight has been lifted off me. No more chemistry!"

"It was that bad, huh?"

"Yeah."

Matching strides, an arm around each other, they topped the rise to the warmly lit house.

"Tonight, when Spitfire breezed that half mile, he didn't even look winded at the end." Hal leaned against the counter as Trish loaded the dishwasher.

"He wasn't. He's ready for the mile and a sixteenth, easily. Probably could do the mile and a quarter." Trish placed the last dish in the rack and shut the door.

"Well, Saturday will tell. How many mounts do you have this weekend?"

"Only four, so far. And Spitfire." Trish wiped off the counter. "Have you heard any more about the race last Sunday?"

"No, thought I'd check into it tomorrow." The two of them walked into the living room. "You worried?"

"A little." Trish crossed her legs and sank to the floor beside the recliner. "Aren't you?"

"Well if *you're* not worried, you should be," Marge joined the conversation. "Otherwise, I've got it covered."

Trish smiled. It was good to hear her mother joke about being worried. There hadn't been much joking in the family lately—not for the last few months.

"Just think—the Futurity's only a week and two days away. When he wins that one . . ." *First Saturday in May. Clear across the country to the Kentucky Derby!*

"Take one race at a time, Tee." Her father stroked her hair. "One day at a time."

Just before she fell asleep that night, Trish heard her father's voice, *"One race at a time."* Did that mean he wasn't planning on the Derby anymore?

She'd already said her prayers, but she quickly added another. *Please, God, the Derby.*

Even though it rained all day Friday, Trish still felt like the helium balloon. Lighter than air, she drifted through her classes—especially the extra study hall. She used it to begin research for her history term paper.

Even though Gatesby did his best to spoil her good mood, Trish laughed at his bad humor . . . and stayed away from his teeth. A good hard workout took the starch out of him and made Trish feel even better.

Only when she galloped Firefly did the nagging worry creep back in. What if Spitfire was slashed tomorrow? So far, neither she nor her horse had been hurt, but what if their luck was running out?

She remembered what her father had said so many times. *For us, luck doesn't count. Only God counts. And His care.* "Well, I sure hope He's got lots of guardian angels around us tomorrow. If I could just get my hands on whoever . . ."

Trish awoke suddenly from another nightmare. She breathed deeply and wiggled her fingers and toes. She and Spitfire had fallen, with her catapulting over his head. She woke up just before hitting the ground. Dawn cracked the black sky in the east before she fell asleep again.

When her alarm buzzed, Trish dragged herself out of bed. Instead of the usual butterflies, lead weights clanged together in her middle. They wouldn't have to insert weights in her saddle pad. She already had them.

Trish galloped the horses at the farm, but even the breeze couldn't blow away her worry.

"Let it go," her father said when she came back up to the house. "You can't let Spitfire know you're scared. Or the other horse that you'll ride first. No jockey in his right mind would be so foolish to attack again. Not with all the questions the racing commissioners have been asking. Just go out there and ride your best race ever."

Trish felt better after the pep talk. Her father was good at that. *And he's right. Nobody would be stupid enough to try something again.* She stuffed the nagging little doubt down—out of sight and mind. The purse was a good one today. And Runnin' On Farm needed a good purse.

Trish rode high in her stirrups, controlling the dancing Spitfire while scanning the other jockeys. She'd been in the winner's circle once already. Twice would be better than nice. Spitfire snorted and fought the bit.

Trish switched back to the monologue the colt was used to and put the other entrants out of her mind . . . again. "Okay, fella, this is our chance. A long one today, and are you ever ready." Spitfire twitched his ears in cadence with her voice. He shied when a plastic bag flitted past and bonded to the fence. "Now behave yourself. Dad's got the glasses right on us."

On the canter back to the gates he shied again, this time at something only he could see. "Easy now, you're wasting your energy." Trish guided him into the number-five gate. "Now, we're going for the outside, you hear me?" As the horses settled for the gun, Trish crouched high on her mount's withers, ready for the thrust.

At the shot, Spitfire leaped through the opening. Instead of minding Trish's hands on the reins, he pulled toward the rail, aiming for an open space just to the left. Trish pulled him back, bringing his chin nearly to his chest, her arms straining with the effort. They were boxed in again. Horses in front and on both sides.

Both Trish and Spitfire saw the opening at the same moment. As Trish loosened the reins, the dreaded sound of a whip stung her ears. Spitfire screamed and leaped into the slight opening, knocking hard against the horse on the left.

Like dominos, two horses thrashed to the ground, one rider flying under their feet. Spitfire leaped over the balled-up jockey and landed hard on his right foreleg. At his grunt of pain, Trish knew her horse was in trouble. But Spitfire refused her commands to slow. He leveled out, running free, chasing the three horses running in front.

While it seemed to Trish they'd been held back forever, they were only a furlong behind the leaders. Spitfire lengthened his stride, his belly low to the ground. Trish rode high over his withers, no longer fighting but assisting him all she could.

They drove past the third-place runner, then the second. At the mile post they caught the straining leader. Even with the saddle, neck and neck, each stride brought the black colt closer to victory.

The whip did the other horse no good. Spitfire ran him right into the ground to win by half a length. When Trish pulled him down to a trot, he began to limp. His heaving sides told her the effort he'd put forth to take the race. By the time they got to the winner's circle, Spitfire could harldy touch his right front hoof to the ground. Trish slid off him and ran her hand down his leg. The swelling popped up as she stroked.

"Dad, they did it again!"

Chapter 14

Did you see anything? Could you tell who did it?"

Hal shook his head. "I must have moved the glasses off you just that second. The next thing I knew both horses were going down. It happened so quickly."

Trish smiled for the photographer, then turned her attention back to Spitfire. "Easy, fella." She smoothed his forelock and rubbed behind his ear. Spitfire leaned his head against her, all the while keeping his weight off the injured leg.

Hal stood after his inspection of the injury. "I'm pretty sure it's not broken, but we'll get an X-ray to be on the safe side. Let's get him back to the barn. Trish, you have another mount, right?"

"Yeah, I'll come down to the stalls as soon as I'm done." She shook her head as Spitfire limped slowly away. *There goes the Futurity.*

Scenes flashed in her mind as she trotted over to the dressing room. *If only I'd pulled back harder. I should* not *have let us get caught in that box. A good* jockey *keeps her mount out of trouble. What's the matter with me?* She jerked open the door. The familiar aroma of liniment-steam, shampoo, and perfume greeted her. Today *she* smelled of mud and horse.

Trish quickly changed to the black-and-white silks, snapped the helmet piece in place, and picked up her whip. The thought of using it on some well-deserving jockey brought a grim smile to her face. *If only they could find out who hates my performance so much they'd whip my horse.*

"You okay?" one of the women asked.

"Yeah. How's the jockey that fell?"

"Broken arm. He must've gotten kicked by one of the other horses."

Trish gritted her teeth. "I'm sorry to hear that." *Now a jockey's been injured too. Does a jockey or a horse have to get killed before this stops?* She was sure she felt a coolness from the other jockeys. *Do they think I'm at fault?* The new thought brought a lump to her throat. She left for the scales.

"Now, you be careful, hear?" Bob Diego gave her a leg up. "Something funny is going on out there."

Trish nodded. "You don't think I . . . um-mm . . . that is . . ."

"No. Once—maybe an accident. Three times?" He shook his head. "Just bring this old lady up from behind. She doesn't mind mud in her face and she likes to chase the leaders, wear 'em down." He patted his mare's shoulder.

Trish did exactly as she was told. She held the mare back so she was slow coming out of the gate. Reins tight, Trish let the field pull ahead. When the runners strung out along the fence, she let the mare have her head on the outside. Every stride brought them closer to the trailing horse, past him, and working on the next. Trish grinned. *This old lady sure knows her stuff.* Trish felt like she was only along for the ride.

When they passed the second-place runner, the rider went for his whip. Trish closed out her instinctive flinch and shouted her own encouragement. The mare stretched out even more and caught the furiously lunging lead. The number-one animal dropped back, spent before the finish line. The mare crossed a length ahead.

"Thanks." She slid to the ground in the winner's circle and handed the reins to Diego's trainer.

"Thank you." Bob Diego smiled for the flash and turned to Trish. "You did a good job. She was due for a win."

Trish trotted across the infield to the stables. She met horses on their way to the next race. "Please, God" kept time with her feet, but this time it was for her horse.

Hal and David already had the leg wrapped in medicated mud bandage strips. Spitfire rested the tip of a hoof on the ground, taking all his weight on the remaining three good legs. He nickered when he saw Trish.

"No, it's not broken," Hal said before she could ask. "Let's get him home so we can work with him." Hal leaned against the wall. "David, you get the truck, and Trish, you lead him out."

Hal rested his head on the back of the seat as David drove out the back gate. By the time they reached Highway 205, the weary man snored softly.

Now, alone with her thoughts, Trish's anger came rolling back, threatening to drown her. She clenched her fists and jaw. *How could anyone deliberately hurt someone else—man or horse?* When her mind played with what might have been, she shuddered. "I didn't file a complaint!" She kept her voice low so her father wouldn't wake up.

"Dad did," David whispered.

"Good."

As soon as they arrived home, Hal went straight to bed and slept through the evening. Trish and David took turns applying ice packs to Spitfire's leg.

"What'd Dad say about his chances for the Futurity?" Trish asked as they turned off the lights for the night.

"Said not to give up hope, but chances are slim."

"It's just so unfair, so . . . so . . ."

"Bet the jock with the broken arm is ticked too."

"And Mom?"

"What do you think?"

Trish chewed on her bottom lip. She could imagine what her mother was thinking.

Marge gave her daughter a quick hug, I-told-you-so written in her expression.

The next morning Trish wanted to stay with Spitfire, but wisely dressed for church, and was ready on time.

God, you're supposed to be taking care of us. That's what Dad always says. When she simmered down a bit, her nagger whispered almost imperceptibly, *You weren't hurt, were you? It could have been a lot worse.*

Trish couldn't think of a good answer. And with so much on her mind, she didn't hear much of the service.

With the extra study hall, Trish didn't have to bring books home, but it also gave her extra time to brood. *Who, and why? And why hasn't the racing commissioner reported it yet? What is going on?*

Rhonda, Brad, and Trish worried over the situation like dogs with a bone. They dug up every memory and fact they could, discussed every jockey, and then repeated the process again. Nothing. They just didn't have all the pieces to the puzzle.

Trish spent every evening with the horses—packing Spitfire's leg and galloping the others. Every time she saw the colt flinch or limp, she wanted to grind the culprit who caused the injury into the dirt.

"Trish, you've got to let this thing go," Hal told her one evening. "It's not your place to solve this. And *you* aren't the one to mete out justice or punishment." He smiled at her troubled expression.

"How can you be so calm? Don't you want to . . . to . . ."

"Get even?"

Trish nodded.

Hal shook his head. "Then I'd be just as guilty as they are. No, Tee, it's not worth it. Just let it go. And do your best."

By Wednesday the swelling was gone, and on Thursday Spitfire's leg was cool to the touch. When they clipped him to the hot walker, he still favored the leg but he was walking straight. Within half an hour, the leg heated up again. It was back to the barn for packs.

Friday morning Trish found a new card on her desk. *"Vengeance is Mine, I will repay"* (Hebrews 10:30). Her father had added a line of his own. *"He's better at it than we are."*

Trish smiled grimly. *Then why doesn't He get on it?*

Friday the leg stayed cool after an hour on the walker.

"I think we're okay." Hal carefully felt every muscle and tendon. "But not working at all this week, I don't know, Tee." He shook his head. "I just don't know."

"You think we should scratch him?"

"He seems sound, but racing could injure it again." He patted Spitfire's neck. "Well, old boy, I guess we'll make the decision in the morning."

Trish had been praying all week, but her prayers that night included a note of panic. She'd been so sure God would heal her horse in time.

Saturday morning Spitfire trotted around the hot walker, snorting and playing with the ring and lead shank. Hal rubbed his chin once. "Let's do it." He turned and headed up to the house for breakfast. Trish danced beside him, much like Spitfire, in her exuberance. At one point she jogged backward, arms raised in a victory clench.

"So you're going to do it." Marge shook her head, a frown creasing her forehead.

Trish knew her mother had been hoping they would give up the idea. But if they won the Portland Futurity . . . the next step would be the Santa Anita in California. And after that, the first Saturday in May.

Trish won on both mounts that afternoon. And while she watched carefully, no one bothered her. No whips, no screams of pain. No falling horses or jockeys. On the ride home, she voiced something that had been lurking at the back of her mind. "The attacks come only when I'm riding *our* horses."

"Naw," David disagreed. "The first time you were up on Anderson's gelding."

"I know. But he's from our stables. Maybe the dummy didn't know any differently."

"You may have something there," Hal agreed that evening when they were doing their post-race hash-over.

Trish went to bed with a solid weight in her middle. Tomorrow she would be back up on Spitfire—their own horse. She tried to swallow with a parched throat. *What if . . .* She shut her eyes tight against the "what if's" and tried to picture Jesus hugging the children. *I bet He loved horses too!*

It was Sunday morning. "Clearing by noon," David's clock radio announced as Trish padded down the hall to the shower. *That's one good thing,* she mused. It had been dry for three days. At least the track wouldn't be muddy. She let the hot water beat on her tight shoulders. Even her butterflies felt dormant. No aerial flips today, just heavy weights.

Halfway through the church service, the pastor announced that Hal Evanston would like to share a few words. Trish scrunched her legs against the pew so he could get by. At the same moment, she shot him a questioning look. What was going on?

Her father scanned the members of the congregation and smiled at his family. "I want to publicly thank all of you for your continuing support and prayers. I'm here today because our loving Father listens and cares for His children. The doctors were sure I would go fast, but they shot all their weapons at the cancer anyway. You, we all, prayed. That's an unbeatable combination—and Friday, the X-rays showed the proof. The tumors are receding."

The congregation broke out in spontaneous applause.

Hal waited. "We always know God is at work in us and for us even when we can't see what He is doing. This time He's allowed us to see the results. Again, thank you for your faithfulness to me and my family, and thank you, Father, for the gift of life." He bowed his head. "Amen."

Marge gripped Trish's hand. "He wanted to surprise you," she whispered.

Trish let the tears roll down her cheeks. They caught in the corners of her smile.

There wasn't a dry eye to be seen after the service. By the time everyone had hugged her father and mother, Trish felt full, to the point of spilling over.

Rhonda danced in place. She grabbed Trish's hands, then dropped them to hug her. "I am *so* happy."

"Me too." The words didn't begin to say what Trish was feeling. No words could.

The glow stayed with her all the way to the track.

Spitfire was in good spirits. When David lifted the colt's front hoof, Spitfire nudged him and sent him sprawling in the straw.

"Knock it off!" David picked up the hoof again.

Brad rubbed down the colt's opposite shoulder with a soft cloth. Spitfire reached around, nipped off Brad's crimson and gold baseball hat, and tossed it in the corner.

Trish caught the giggles. She doubled over laughing at the looks on the guys' faces. Then Spitfire gave her a shove that toppled her on her rear in the straw.

This time David and Brad joined in the laughter. Spitfire pricked his ears and blew, reaching down to shower Trish with his warm, misty breath.

When Trish was back on her feet, the horse nudged against her chest, then rubbed one eye against her shoulder. She rubbed all his favorite places, all the while telling him how wonderful he was. He nodded in contentment.

"That horse is almost human." Rhonda leaned on the stall door. "Sorry I'm late, but it looks like you managed without me."

"You missed the clown act." Trish let herself out of the stall. "Come on, I've got another race before the Futurity. See you guys at the paddock." She picked up her bag in the tack room.

By the time she'd changed after the first race, Trish's butterflies were frisking full force. Until she saw her father in the saddling paddock.

"Just let God handle the race," he said as he boosted her up.

"Reading my mind again?"

"No, your face." He patted her knee. "And I know how you think and feel. Just go out there and do your best. That's all you can do. Let God take care of the rest."

Trish leaned forward to give Spitfire a big hug. She smoothed his mane to one side and gathered up her reins.

She tried to keep the black to a flat walk to conserve his energy, but Spitfire would have none of it. He jigged sideways, pulling against the lead rope in Brad's hands and against the reins.

"He sure is ready," Brad said from his perch on Dan'l's back.

"I hope so," Trish answered. "But he's never raced this far before." *And he's been penned up all week.*

A slow canter brought them to the gates. Trish took a deep breath and released it along with her plea, "Please, God." The two words said it all.

Spitfire broke clean at the shot and drove straight down the middle of the track. He ran easily, as if nothing had happened. His twitching ears kept track of Trish's song, sung from high on his withers, and the horses around him. The field spread out going into the first stretch, and when Spitfire eased over to the rail, Trish let him. By the three-quarters mark, Spitfire was running stride for stride with another horse. A sorrel and a gray ran two lengths in front, also side by side.

At the mile post, their running mate fell back and Spitfire gained on the two ahead, now running head to tail. Stride by stride the colt eased past the second place and gained on the front runner. The leading jockey went to his whip.

Trish could feel Spitfire waver. His breath came in thundering gasps. "Come on, fella," she shouted. "This is it. We're almost there. Come on."

Spitfire reached out one more time and hurtled over the finish line.

"And the winner by a nose is—number three, Spitfire. Owner, Hal Evanston, and ridden by Tricia Evanston."

"You did it. You did it!" Trish pulled Spitfire down to a canter. Lather covered his shoulders and flew back when he shook his head. He slowed to a walk, still gasping for air. His sides heaved. Trish patted his neck, comforting him. As his breathing slowed, his head came up again. By the time they entered the winner's circle, he pricked his ears and rubbed his itchy forehead against Hal's arm.

Trish slid to the ground. Her knees wobbled so bad she hardly had the energy to unbuckle her saddle girth. David grinned at her. Hal hugged her and they all posed for the pictures. Trish plucked a rose from the wreath and handed it to her mother.

"Save this one for me, will you?"

Marge nodded, relief evident in the smile that fought the tears for first place.

Santa Anita, here we come, Trish thought as she stepped off the scales. *And after that . . .*

That evening David turned to the sports section of the local paper. The headline read, "Jockey on Probation." He read the article aloud. "Investigation has revealed that Emanuel Ortega, nineteen-year-old jockey at Portland Meadows, is the alleged attacker on Tricia Evanston and her mount on three occasions during the last several weeks." David rattled the paper. "All right!"

The article continued with a quote. " 'People like her keep the rest of us from riding,' Ortega said. 'She's from a rich family and since she's the daughter of a owner, she gets the breaks we don't.' "

"Rich!" Tricia burst out. She stared at her father. "Rich!"

Hal shook his head. His laugh started down deep in his chest. David joined in, then Marge.

"But we are, you know." Hal tousled Trish's hair as she sat at his feet. "We're rich beyond measure."

ACKNOWLEDGMENTS

My thanks to Adele Olson, Prairie High counselor and friend to students and their parents. Also to Tex Irwin, trainer at Portland Meadows, who so willingly shared his expertise. And thanks to Ruby MacDonald: reader, critiquer, and blessed friend.

GO FOR THE GLORY

BOOK THREE

To my son Brian,
  my friend.

Chapter
01

Icy rain trickled down her neck. Tricia Evanston, sixteen-year-old wonder jockey at Oregon's Portland Meadows Racetrack, crouched higher over her mount's withers. "Come on, girl," she sang to the filly's twitching ears. "Let's do this one. You know we like winning."

The dark bay filly settled deeper on her haunches. Firefly's ears pricked forward, nearly touching at the tips. She not only liked winning, she acted as if all the spectators came just to watch her. Besides loving to run, she was a natural performer.

The horse next to them refused to enter the starting gate. The memory of slashing whips flitted through Trish's mind. But the jockey who'd caused those accidents had been barred from the track.

Trish sniffed. In the cold, her nose ran nearly as fast as the horses. "Come on, get him in," she muttered.

The rear gates slammed shut. Trish and Firefly both tensed for the shot. The front gates clanged open. The filly burst from the stall, her haunches thrusting them ahead of the horse on their left. Three powerful strides and they had the rail.

Trish kept a firm hold on the reins. Pouring rain meant a slippery track, no matter how much sand the crew worked into the dirt. The marker poles flashed past. By the six-furlong post, Firefly was running easily in the lead. She never seemed to care if the track was muddy or dry. She ran for the pure joy of it. Trish loosened the reins and let the filly have her head. She won by a furlong and was still picking up speed at the wire.

Trish laughed as she pulled her mount down and turned back to the grandstand. "You're fantastic!" She stroked the filly's wet neck, then rose in the stirrups for the slow gallop back to where her brother, David, and father, Hal, waited in the winner's circle. "Shame there wasn't a bigger crowd for you to dance for," she teased her horse. "Too many people stay home when it rains."

Trish glanced up at the glass-fronted grandstand. The sheeting rain made everything look dreary. But with a win like she'd had, it was as if the sun shone brightly.

Trish slid to the ground and unhooked her saddle, almost in the same motion. Firefly posed for the camera. David thumped Trish on the arm and her father gave her a quick hug.

"We should take Firefly with us to Santa Anita," Trish said, grinning at her father. "She needs a bigger crowd."

Hal nodded as he stroked the filly's nose. "She sure struts her stuff. And she's not even tired. What'd you do, just take her out for a Saturday stroll?"

Trish laughed again as she stepped on the scale. "She was still picking up speed at the wire. I couldn't believe it. David, you better give her a treat; she earned it."

"Yes, ma'am." David touched the rim of his hat in a mock bow. "You mind if we get out of the rain now?"

Trish returned his arm thump. "At least you've got a dry stall to work in." She looked skyward. "I've three more mounts—in this."

"Nobody said life was easy, or dry." David tugged on the filly's reins. "Come on, horse." He stopped after they'd taken only a couple of steps. "You be careful, Tee. All those horses aren't mudders like this one here."

"Yes, *Mother.*"

David shook his head and trotted off to the testing barn with Firefly.

"He's right, you know." Hal fell into step beside his daughter.

4

"Da-ad."

"I'm not being over-protective, Tee. I've seen some pretty nasty spills on days like today. Just keep your guard up." He stopped at the entrance to the dressing rooms. "And, Tee, that's not a bad idea."

Trish replayed his last comment in her mind as she entered the steamy room. She knew he'd been referring to her suggestion about Santa Anita. She and her father had that kind of mutual understanding. Sometimes it seemed they could almost read each other's mind.

Trish pulled her crimson and gold winter silks over her head. Her long-sleeved insulated underwear top was wet around the neck, but the waterproofed silks kept her body dry. She toweled the edges of her dark hair and, grabbing a brush out of her sports bag, gave it a good brushing. The longer length felt good.

Trish stared longingly at the steamy shower room where someone was singing as she soaped. A quick glance at her watch settled it. No hot shower. She put on the black-and-white diamond-patterned silks and headed out for her next ride. On her way out the door she applied a thick coating of lip balm and grabbed a handful of tissues to stuff up her sleeve. She would need them for her runny nose.

Rain blew over the track in sheets as they entered the gates for the sixth race of the day, Trish's third. The race was for maidens under four, making it this colt's first race. And he didn't like the rain.

"Don't worry, fella, the rest of us don't like this any better than you do, so let's just get the job done." A horse two stalls over reared and backed out of the gate.

"Not now, you crazy thing." Trish kept her mutterings in the singsong cadence that always soothed her mount. She tightened her shoulders up to her ears. *Man, it's cold*, she thought.

As the gates swung open, her mount slipped before regaining his footing. Trish kept his head up and let him gather himself together before urging him on. They were already two lengths behind the field.

Once he was running smoothly, she brought him up along the out-side. They went into the far turn in fourth place with Trish encouraging him to reach for the leaders.

The horse on the rail slipped and bumped the one next to him. That horse went down, the rider flying over his mount's head.

Trish's horse skidded. He shied to the right. Trish caught herself, arms wrapped around his neck and nearly on his head.

The colt slipped again but veered around the jockey in the mud. Trish scrambled back in the saddle and yelled in his ears. "Now get on with it, we've still got a race to run."

The horse bobbled again but straightened out and crossed the wire with a show. "Third place is sure better than a fall," Trish consoled both him and herself as they cantered around to the winner's circle.

Her hands were still shaking when she stripped off her saddle and stepped on the scale.

"Bad 'un out there," the steward said. "You handled him real well."

"Anyone hurt?" Trish shivered and ducked her chin in her collar.

"Not so's you'd notice. One good thing about the mud, it cushions a fall."

"Yeah, well thanks." *But that was awful close,* she thought. *Good thing Mom wasn't here to see that one.*

By the end of the day Trish was nearly frozen, and exhausted, but higher than the flagpoles standing at attention in the infield. Three wins on four mounts. And in weather like this. She ignored the shaking and hugged the happiness to herself as she trotted out to the car where her father waited for her. David and his best friend, Brad Williams, who worked for their Runnin' On Farm, would load the horses in the trailer and meet them at home.

Hal snapped his seat upright when Trish turned her key in the lock. By using every moment to rest, he was able to keep up the restricted schedule the cancer treatments imposed on him. "Congratulations! You set yourself a record."

"I can hardly believe it." Trish tossed her sports bag in the backseat, then slid into the driver's seat. "And Firefly won a good purse too. That should help the old checkbook."

"It will. You hungry?"

Trish shot him a tolerant look. When wasn't she hungry after a day of racing? "Are you?"

Hal nodded. "But you know Mom will have dinner ready."

Trish took a deep breath. She mentally finished his thought. *And she'll be worrying about us too.* "So we'll go to the drive-in window. I won't tell if you don't." The entire family had an unwritten pact. Anytime they could get food into Hal, they did. The chemotherapy killed his appetite along with the disease.

The rain had stopped by the time they crossed the I-5 bridge between Portland and Vancouver. Car lights reflected off the wet girders and shiny asphalt. Trish sipped her Diet Coke. The warmth of the car and the pleasure of her father's company mixed with the day's wins to create a perfect moment in time. She shot a thank-you heavenward.

"I think we'll do it," Hal said, slurping his chocolate shake dry.

"Take Firefly?"

"Um-m hm-m. We'll check out the stakes book when we get home. The Santa Anita Oaks for fillies on Saturday would be a great race for her. Taking two won't be much more expensive than one."

"Does Bob Diego have room in his van for more than one?"

"Should have. I think he's taking just one horse."

Trish felt like hugging her father. Taking their colt Spitfire to the Santa Anita Derby in Southern California was exciting enough, but riding three mounts at that track? *Wowee! What if all our horses win?* She corrected the if. *What'll we do when they all win?* Not only would the money be fantastic, but not very many women raced at that prestigious track. And few of those ever won.

She resolutely pushed aside thoughts of what her mother would have to say. Marge had been even more against her daughter riding since the incidents with the jockey striking their horses during several recent races.

Hal patted her knee, knowing her thoughts. "It'll be okay, Tee. I'll handle your mother."

Trish flashed him a grateful smile.

Surprisingly, Marge didn't have a lot to say, other than "Congratulations" accompanied by a quick hug. She just shook her head when Hal mentioned taking Firefly along to Santa Anita. But her tight jawline revealed more of her true feelings.

Trish overheard her mother talking to her father when she passed their room on her way to the bathroom later that night.

"It doesn't matter what I think," Marge said. "You and Trish will do what you want to do anyway. You *know* how I feel. It's bad enough for her to race here, but California and then Kentucky scares me to death."

Trish shut her bedroom door. She didn't want to hear any more. Her mother's fears always managed to take some of the joy from her racing.

The next morning the Evanstons sat in their usual pew at church, right behind the Seabolts. Rhonda winked over her shoulder at Trish. The two had been best friends since kindergarten.

When the pastor spoke about not being afraid, Trish wanted to nudge her mother. *How much easier life would be if Mother weren't such a worrier!*

Pastor Ron repeated the verse. "Be not afraid, for I am with you."

Trish's mind flitted back to the times her horses had been struck. By the third incident, she'd known what fear was. And anger. But it hadn't slowed her down any, in spite of Marge's anxiety.

Trish shook her head. Why couldn't her mother quit worrying?

She shuddered again when her father's name was said during the prayers for healing. Why did *everyone* have to know their business? Now people would ask about the chemotherapy and her father would tell them how things were going. It made her want to melt into a little puddle and seep into the ground. It was *so* embarrassing.

"I'll be over after lunch," Rhonda promised as they left the church. "Then you can tell me all about yesterday. Three wins. Awesome!"

"And you can quiz me for our history test. I *hate* memorizing dates."

"Both of you can muck out stalls in your spare time." David grinned as he interrupted them. "Keep you from getting bored."

"Right!" Rhonda and Trish laughed when they said the word at the same time.

That afternoon the weak sun split the clouds just above the western horizon as the girls headed down to the barns to visit Miss Tee, Trish's two-month-old filly.

She nickered at the sound of Trish's voice. While she still dashed behind her mother when strangers approached, she came forward when Trish called. Rhonda stood still and let the filly come to her. She extended the grain in the palm of her hand. The filly nibbled the oats, her soft nose whiskering Rhonda's palm. With a final lick not a trace remained.

Trish hugged her baby and scratched behind Miss Tee's tiny, pointed ears. The foal rubbed her head on Trish's chest.

"You are so-o-o lucky," Rhonda said. "She's about the prettiest thing around. And what a sweetie."

"I know. She's special all right. And she should be fast. Look at Spitfire. Miss Tee's his full sister." Trish turned and stroked the mare. "You've done a good job, old girl." The mare shifted to rest the other back foot and leaned her head against Trish for more scratching.

After one last pat, Trish snapped a lead rope on the mare's halter and handed the shank to Rhonda. "Here, you lead her and I'll bring Miss Tee. She's not too happy yet when I lead her by herself. This way we'll fool her. Let's take the trail to the woods."

"Take your time, the work's all done anyway," David called as they trotted down the two-track dirt road.

"Thanks, we will." Rhonda grinned at Trish. "Has he always been so bossy?"

"He's gotten worse." Trish tugged on the lead rope. "Come on, Miss Tee. You need a run."

Half an hour later the girls came back up the rise with the horses. Trish was still puffing when she unsnapped the leads and put the mare and her foal back in their stall. She took a deep breath. "I'll get the feed if you'll fill the water bucket."

Rhonda's deep breath matched Trish's. "Boy, we need to do some running again. I can see weight training isn't enough."

"Yeah, and I haven't even had time for that lately."

"How come you had the afternoon off?"

"They scratched my two rides yesterday. One had shins and the other spiked a temperature. Maybe it's this yucky weather."

The weather became the topic of conversation at dinner that evening when Hal talked about their nomination for the Santa Anita Derby. At his mention of sunny California, Trish closed her eyes for a moment and tried to remember what warm sun felt like on bare skin.

"Maybe I can get a tan while we're down there."

Her mother's frown made Trish bite her lip.

"I'm sending in our nomination for the Kentucky Derby also," Hal said. "That six hundred dollars includes the rest of the Triple Crown too."

The Kentucky Derby! Trish ignored the thought of Belmont and the Preakness. It was like her dreams could only reach so far.

"Even if we don't get to go, better six hundred now than forty-five hundred later."

"They sure up the fees when the race gets closer," Trish said, leaning on her elbows. "Doesn't seem fair."

"Since when did fair count?" Marge muttered as she rose from the table. She clattered the dishes into the sink and poured herself a cup of coffee. "Racing here is bad enough, but clear across the country? There are so many things that can go wrong. Driving over the mountains. Transporting a horse in an airplane. All the time Trish will miss from school. And how are we going to keep up with everything else around here? David isn't a superman, you know."

"*Mom.*" David shook his head. "We'll do just fine. They'll be going to California over spring break, and we just won't race any of our horses then. By the time they leave for Kentucky, the racing season here in Portland will be over."

Marge sat down again and slumped in her chair. "As far as I can tell, the season is never over around here. For the first time in my life, I swear I'll leave home if I don't hear something besides horse racing."

Hal took her hand. "You don't mean that."

"No, probably not." She shook her head. "But then I never dreamed my daughter would be racing Thoroughbreds around the track either. And scaring me to death. Like an idiot, I thought we'd be doing a few girl things together." She shook her head again. "Crazy, huh?"

Trish bit her lip. Would she and her mother *ever* see eye to eye?

Chapter 02

Gatesby was unhappy.

Trish stared the cantankerous bay right in the eye. "Now, you listen to me." Her tone brooked no argument.

Gatesby snorted. He tossed his head and reached for her shoulder with bared teeth.

Trish smacked him on the nose with one hand and caught his halter with the other before he had time to jerk his head back. "I mean it. I have no time for your mule-headed mean mood. Now, you behave!"

Gatesby blew in her face as if to apologize. He dropped his head so she could reach his favorite scratching place. Trish obliged.

"You dunderhead. I don't know why we put up with you." She gave him another pat, clipped both lead lines to his halter, and began a quick grooming so she could saddle him for the morning work.

Brad, part-time stable hand and full-time friend, kept his six-foot frame out of range of Gatesby's teeth. "Need any help?"

"Yeah, a few minutes ago. Where've you been?" Trish's smile took the sting out of her words.

"Sor-ry." Brad touched his fingers to the bill of his Seattle Sonics cap. "What can I do to help you, ma'am?"

Trish tossed him the brush. "You could finish while I go get the saddle."

Brad handed the brush back to her. "I'll get the saddle."

"Can't understand why nobody trusts you," she spoke to the colt as she slipped the bit into his mouth and the headstall over his ears. "Hard to believe you're the same ornery goof that greeted me."

"Now, you be careful with him," Brad cautioned as he boosted Trish into the saddle.

"Brad, even *you're* beginning to sound like my mother. Is worrying a contagious disease?"

Brad sidestepped a sneaky nip by Gatesby. The look Brad flashed Trish spoke volumes.

Trish walked the colt out to the track at Portland Meadows. Dawn whispered its presence through a crack in the eastern cloud cover. The morning breeze, fresh from the rain during the night, carried the aroma of horse and hay and—Trish sniffed again. *Mm-m-m-m. Bacon already frying over at the cafeteria. If only I could spend all my mornings here at the track instead of rushing off to school.* She shrugged. *Well, at least Saturday is better than never.*

Gatesby pricked his ears and tugged at the bit.

"Sorry, fella, but the boss said walk today and jog the last lap. You get to run this afternoon."

And run he did. Gatesby hated dirt kicked in his face, so when Trish gave him some rein he surged around the outside as though the other horses were out for a Sunday trot. He won by a length and a half with his ears pricked forward and head up.

He didn't try to nip anyone until his owner, John Anderson, failed to pay attention to him in the winner's circle. When he turned his back on the colt he paid with a bruise.

"I swear he's laughing," Trish said after she scolded the colt. "Look at his eyes."

"I think I'd be better off watching his teeth," Anderson said, rubbing his shoulder. "You'd think I'd have learned by now. That was a good ride, Trish. You've really brought him along. Thanks, Hal." The two men shook hands and David trotted Gatesby back to the testing barn.

"See you later," Trish said as she headed for the dressing room. She had three more mounts on the day's program.

When she met her father for the ride home, she'd brought in a second win and a place, but her final mount faded at the six-furlong mark on the mile race.

"He just wasn't in condition." Trish tossed her sports bag in the back as she spoke. "What's wrong with trainers that don't keep their horses up to their peak?"

"Well, that one just wasn't ready after an injury. You know it takes time."

"Do I ever know. But then he shouldn't have entered the horse."

"True. But sometimes owners put the pressure on, Trish. You know there are countless reasons why a horse is entered—or scratched. Besides, what are you grumbling about?"

Trish flashed her father a guilty grin. "I hate not being in the money."

Hal chuckled. "I know how you feel."

"What do you think about Firefly? David's been keeping the ice packs on both her front legs, so she shouldn't have shin problems. We've made sure she's in peak condition."

"You never know." Hal shook his head. "Just happens sometimes, especially with two-year-olds. They're still growing, and racing too. We'll bring her home and give her plenty of rest."

And then she won't be ready for Santa Anita, Trish finished in her mind.

"Santa Anita is more than four months away." Her father read her thoughts again. "You know how things change for horses; you just do the best you can and pray for the rest. God cares about our business, Tee. You know that."

Trish nodded. Her father had such faith. Maybe strong faith came when you got old.

The next morning in church they sang Trish's favorite song. All the way home the words repeated in her mind. *"And He will raise you up on eagle's wings. . . ."* We'll have to name a colt that sometime.

All afternoon Hal looked like he was guarding a secret.

13

"All right, Dad, what's going on?" Trish nailed him as they walked back up from the barns.

"Whatever do you mean?"

"Da-ad!"

"Can't a person just be happy?"

"Sure. But you look like the night before Christmas."

"Well, Christmas *is* coming."

"That's not it and you know it."

"I'll never tell." Hal distracted her by pointing to a V-formation of mallard ducks flying overhead. Their quacking echoed and drifted on the evening breeze.

The two stopped to watch as the birds angled west to the swamp beyond the horse pastures. Needle-topped fir trees stitched the sunset in place and a maple cradled a bird's nest in its naked arms. Caesar, their sable collie, shoved his nose into Trish's hand and whined softly.

Trish absently stroked his head, watching as the sun slipped its bindings and slept beyond the horizon. She inhaled the moment, then leaned her head against her father's shoulder.

"It's times like this I wish I were an artist." Hal hugged her with both arms and rested his chin on the top of her head. "God sure makes a wondrous world, doesn't He?"

Trish nodded, afraid words might break the spell. The molten gold of the sun flowed into pinks and fuchsia, washing the gray clouds with flaming color.

"Dinner's ready," Marge called from the house.

Trish and Hal turned, and with matching steps, arms locked, they stepped over a puddle and kicked the mud off their boots before mounting the three concrete steps to the back deck.

Hal couldn't hide the twinkle in his eye through dinner. David and Trish exchanged puzzled glances. *What is going on?*

Marge hummed a little tune as she cut the apple pie she'd baked for dessert. "Anyone for a la mode?" She paused at the refrigerator door.

Trish groaned at the thought of the scale at the track. But then, she *was* down a pound or two—she shrugged as she glanced at her father. He nodded vigorously. Trish cast her yes vote along with the others. It had been a while since they'd had apple pie and ice cream.

14

"Well, Trish, do you have your report for the week?" Hal asked, savoring the pie.

She nodded. Each time her father asked for a report it brought back memories of when she'd ridden without permission. While the family meetings weren't always easy, even she had to admit that some of the strain had disappeared with everyone talking things out.

It's good to feel trusted, isn't it? her little voice whispered. Trish could only agree.

"I'm caught up on all my homework," Trish began. "And I've started one of the two papers due before Christmas break. I need to do some more research for the one on constitutional amendments before I begin writing."

"And your grades?" Marge took another sip of coffee.

"Nothing less than a B since I dropped chemistry."

"Good." Hal smiled at her. "How many rides do you have this week?"

Trish ticked them off on her fingers for a total of thirteen. "And if we could get Anderson's gelding Final Command to want to win as much as he likes running *with* the winners, it'll be a great week."

Hal nodded. "Let me think on that. Marge?"

"I mailed the entries for both Santa Anita and the Kentucky Derby."

Trish knew how hard it was for her mother to do that. Marge had been against the idea of racing on distant tracks from the beginning. But she went along with the family decision. She'd also taken over all of the bookwork and accounting since Hal had become sick.

Marge spoke again. "All the bills are paid and we have some money in the savings account again."

"Thanks to the two of you." Hal beamed at David and Trish. "Because of all your hard work, we have something special for each of you. David, you will now be on a regular employee basis. We'll pay you each week, just like we pay Brad and the other employees."

"Are you sure we can afford that, Dad?" David's eyes sparkled with hope.

"Yes, son. I'm just sorry it's taken so long. Maybe your missing college this year won't be a total waste—at least not financially."

"Thanks, Dad, Mom."

"And, Trish, all the money you earn riding will be yours to keep."

"Dad!"

"That's right. You've been a tremendous help. And if we need money again—we know where to find you."

Everyone chuckled.

"Thanks!" Trish leaped from her chair to hug both her parents.

"That's not all." Marge picked up two envelopes. "These are for you too. Call it a bonus or reimbursement—whatever." She handed one to each of them.

Trish opened hers first. "Five hundred dollars!" Her mouth dropped open in shock. She stared at David. His look matched hers as he gaped at the check in his envelope.

Hal smiled. "You both earned it. I just wish it could have been more."

Marge cleared her throat. "You'll never know how much we appreciate you both and all that you've done." She reached across the table to squeeze their hands. "Thank you."

"Just in time for Christmas shopping!" David stuffed his check back in the envelope. "And my car needs new front tires. I'll stop by and check on prices tomorrow."

"Maybe you could drop Rhonda and me off at the mall at the same time." Trish pushed her chair back. She paused for David's nod before heading to the phone.

"We're on," she announced on her return. She hugged first her father, then her mother. "Thanks a lot. I wasn't sure what I was going to do about Christmas presents this year."

What to buy for each one whirled in her mind through dishes and homework. After shutting off the light in her room, she stared at the reflection of the yard light on her ceiling. "Heavenly Father," she prayed, "help me find the perfect present for my dad this year. Something with *meaning*. And help me find it tomorrow. I don't have many chances to shop. And thank you for making him better. Amen."

A sweater? Huh-uh. Shirt and tie? Na-aa. New jacket? He sure needs one. Maybe. Trish fell asleep before the list got any longer.

The next day she turned more ideas over in her mind during her spare moments. It *had* to be the perfect gift.

"You're not going to spend *all* that money, are you?" Rhonda pushed her new glasses up on her nose.

"I don't know." Trish stuffed her books in her locker. "Let's get some lunch, I'm starved." For a change they were ahead of the crowd pouring into the lunchroom. They picked up their loaded trays and crossed the room to their favorite table.

Brad folded his lanky frame onto the stool next to Trish. "You two broke the speed record getting in here today. What's up?"

"Christmas."

"Not for over two weeks, last time I looked at a calendar."

Rhonda rolled her eyes and shook her head. "Shopping—you know, as in buying presents? I suppose you've got yours all done!"

"Right. And wrapped."

"Already?" Trish's voice squeaked in surprise. She coughed and took a swallow of milk to ease her throat.

"Hey, don't go into shock over it." Brad thumped her on the back. "Some of us have learned to be organized." He ducked the balled-up napkins they threw at him. "Can I help it if some of us are more perfect than others?" He leaned way back to avoid the milk Trish threatened to pour on his head. "Now, ladies." He held up both hands as if to fend them off. "Don't mess with me, you may get hurt, you know."

"Ri-ght!" Trish picked up her tray. "Come on, Rhonda, we wouldn't want to get hurt, would we?"

A few minutes later they were combing their hair at the mirror in the rest room. No matter how much Trish brushed hers, the ebony strands bounced up around her face. She clipped the longest strands back and shoved her brush back into her purse. "Hurry out after class. David is meeting us right out front."

Rhonda picked up her purse. "We haven't gone shopping like this since before school started. We never have time for anything anymore."

Hours later, when Trish still hadn't found just the right gift for her father, she groaned as she shuffled the packages she'd already bought. "Let's get something to eat. I've about had it."

"Burgers or pizza?"

"Neither. Let's get a sandwich at Nordstroms. That's in about the middle of the mall."

Exhausted, they tucked their packages under the table and sank down in the chairs. "How come I get more tired shopping for a couple of hours than riding all day?" Trish rubbed an aching foot. "And I still don't have anything for my dad."

"Are you going to buy that turquoise ski jacket for yourself?" Rhonda asked just before the waitress brought their order.

"Depends on how much money I have left. That's over a hundred dollars—on sale." She took a long drink of her Diet Coke.

"It looked good on you."

"I know, and my other one's falling apart. Maybe I better put a new jacket on my Christmas list." She took a bite of her BLT. "What do I get my dad?"

They tossed ideas back and forth as they munched on chips. Nothing seemed just right; nothing was even close to right. Trish glanced at her watch. "We've got half an hour. Let's go."

She found it at the top of the escalator. Artists and craftspeople had set up booths throughout the mall, creating a holiday feeling. Trish almost walked on by. Sculptures weren't on her list of possibles.

But the eagle appeared to fly free. Each feather in the carved wood seemed alive, with the wind riffling through it. Trish stroked the eagle's head and across an extended wing. The grain of the wood lent color and depth. The song whispered through her mind, *"Raise you up on eagle's wings . . ."*

She was afraid to look for the price.

Rhonda picked the carving up and checked the sticker on the bottom. "Oooh-h." She flinched.

"How bad?"

"Two hundred dollars."

Trish closed her eyes. This was the perfect gift. She thought about the jacket she'd tried on. She couldn't afford both.

With a deep breath she pulled out her wallet. "Do you have a box for the eagle?" she asked the woman behind the counter.

Trish tucked her prize down in the middle of the Meier and Frank shopping bag. How could she keep such a secret till Christmas? Her dad had always guessed what she'd gotten him before. But not this year. This was the perfect gift. It would be a fantastic surprise.

But all surprises aren't so wonderful, as Trish learned after breezing Spitfire around the track on Wednesday.

"His right knee is hot," David informed her at the dinner table. "Did he stumble or anything when you were running him?"

Chapter 03

Spitfire's leg didn't get better.

Two days later, Trish trotted down to the barn as soon as she'd changed clothes. Each of the horses nickered at the sound of her voice. Dan'l tossed his head, begging for attention. Trish gave him a piece of carrot and stood rubbing his ears for a minute.

"You old sweetie, you." She stroked his nose and smoothed his coarse gray forelock. "I haven't ridden you for so long, I can't remember the last time." Dan'l rubbed the side of his head on her shoulder.

Next door, Spitfire banged a hoof against the door.

"Stop it, you'll re-injure that leg!" she ordered the pure black colt as she offered him his piece of carrot. The heavy canvas ice pack was still Velcroed in place around his right foreleg. The pack reached from his ankle to well above the hot knee. Water leaked down over his hoof and into the straw.

Trish inhaled the familiar aroma of horse and straw with overtones of liniment. Spitfire draped his head over her shoulder, his eyes drooping as she rubbed his cheek and behind his ears. Firefly nickered for her turn, and beyond her Gatesby snorted and thumped the wall.

Caesar parked himself at Trish's knee, hoping for some attention too.

"You gonna just stand there moonin' around or what?" Brad's teasing voice broke into Trish's thoughts. "Where's David?"

"I don't know. His car was gone and Mom and Dad are off somewhere too." She gave Caesar a shove to get him off her foot. "I'll take Gatesby and you work Final Command, then I'll do Firefly and you can give Dan'l a gallop. He's been getting lazy lately."

"Yes, ma'am." He grinned at her. "Anything else, ma'am? You want me to—"

"Knock it off, is what I want." Trish shook her head as she entered the tack room. "Can't you ever be serious?"

"Maybe, why?"

"Oh, I don't know." She glanced back at him at just the wrong moment. Gatesby slipped in a quick nip and jerked his head up, ears back, ready for his scolding. "Ouch! Now see what you did?" This time she'd grabbed the horse's halter before yelling again at Brad.

Both Brad and Gatesby wore the same "Who me?" look.

Trish rubbed her upper arm one more time before Brad gave her a leg up.

"You watch him now." Brad unsnapped the lead shank as Trish straightened the reins.

"Thanks a lot—now. If I'da been paying attention to him earlier, I wouldn't have this bruise."

"Yeah, you'd think you'd have learned by now." Brad sidestepped as Trish nudged the colt forward. "Hey, you trying to make him step on me by any chance?"

"Make him? Whatever gave you that idea?" Trish's laugh floated back on the breeze. "Hurry up and we can gallop together."

Spitfire looked clearly dejected when all the other horses were out and he still stood in the stall. Trish gave him some extra affection as she measured out his grain. "Sorry, fella, but you gotta get better. Maybe tomorrow David'll take you out for a walk."

After dinner that evening they finished decorating the noble fir that David and Marge had bought. When they placed the angel on the treetop, it nearly touched the slanted pineboard ceiling. A fire crackled in the fireplace; fat, red winterberry-scented candles flickered on the broad mantel, and Christmas carols drifted from the stereo.

"Needs something more on the left side," Hal pointed from his recliner. Marge attached a shimmery red bell and a revolving star to the branches he suggested and stepped back to inspect her handiwork. All the ornaments they'd collected through the years twinkled in their own special places.

Trish hung the last of the crocheted and starched snowflakes, then sank down, her legs crossed, in the middle of the floor. She propped her elbows on her knees and her chin on her fists, the better to gaze at the tree. Each year the ritual was the same, and she loved every minute of it. She glanced over at the manger scene displayed on a low table to the side of the front window. When the tree lights went on, the star of Bethlehem above the stable would light up too.

Marge settled onto the arm of Hal's recliner. "Okay, David, turn them on."

For an instant Trish held her breath, then let it out as the twelve-foot tree shimmered into glory. "Oh-h-h, isn't it beautiful?" She felt the old, familiar tightening in her throat. All the colors, the special ornaments, the lights both twinkling on the tree and reflected in the window, all of the pieces came together to make each tree they'd had the most beautiful ever. She swallowed around the lump as she looked at her father. And most important, the family was all together.

Hal cleared his throat. "That's got to be the most perfect tree we've ever had."

"That's Mom's line," David said.

"Then I'll say it too," Marge replied softly. "Truly, this is our most beautiful tree ever." She laid her cheek on the top of Hal's head.

That night in bed Trish thought about their gathering around the tree. *We were all a bit weepy,* she thought. *But that's okay. Tomorrow night I'll put my presents under the tree.* She chuckled to herself. *And I'm not going to put name tags on them so no one can guess which is theirs.* She thought of the beautiful eagle wrapped in silver paper and a royal blue ribbon. *Dad'll never guess this time!*

With Christmas break only a week away, Trish burned the midnight oil to finish her two papers.

"Trish, it's after two o'clock," Marge said one night.

"I know, but I'm nearly done."

Marge frowned as she shook her head. "You know if you weren't riding so much, you'd have time for your studies. How many times have we reminded you that school *has* to come first?"

Trish gritted her teeth. "In case you haven't noticed, Mom, I didn't ride after school this week. I spent my extra time at the library."

"Well, you just can't leave things to the last minute like this."

"Right." Trish leaned back in her chair. She clamped her lips on the rest of the things she'd like to say. "Good night, Mom. These go in tomorrow, on time."

"I'll just have to make it up over vacation," she told Rhonda one evening on the phone. "Just think, I'll be able to ride the entire weekday programs, not just a couple of races after school. That way I can get my bank account back up."

"And since Christmas is on Monday, we can go shopping on Tuesday because you don't have racing that day. Maybe that jacket'll still be there."

Trish stretched as she hung up the phone. This was going to be a fantastic vacation! And tomorrow morning she'd be able to ride Spitfire around the track, even if it was only at a walk. His leg hadn't been warm for two days now.

"Can you help me with some more baking tomorrow?" Marge asked as Trish poured herself a glass of milk.

"Yep. I'll get the morning workouts done early, and I don't have to be at the track until two." Trish wished she hadn't mentioned the track when she saw a frown wrinkle her mother's forehead. "I'll have plenty of time. You haven't made sugar cookies yet, and I'll do the Rice Krispies bars too."

"And fudge." David took the milk carton out of her hands. "We need lots of fudge." He poured his glass full and chose a brownie off the plate Marge had left on the counter.

"You can help us decorate the cookie trees and stars and stuff. You missed out last year," Trish told him.

"Just make extra fudge. With lots of nuts in it."

Marge and Trish laughed together at the silly grin on David's face. "Seems to me we sent several care packages of fudge to you at college last year." Marge indicated the milk carton on the counter and pointed to the refrigerator.

"Yeah. And I had to fight off half the dorm to get any." David ducked his head as he reached for the carton to put it away. "I thought maybe Trish wanted more."

"Ri-ght!" Trish rinsed her glass in the sink and set it in the dishwasher. "See you in the morning, brother dear."

She paused a moment in front of the tree. *That is the most gorgeous tree we've ever had.* She heard her father cough as she passed his closed bedroom door. He'd gone to bed right after dinner. *God, please make him completely well,* she thought as she fell asleep.

Trish helped with the baking Saturday morning. The house smelled so good she hated to leave. At the track she'd already had one win before she joined her father and John Anderson in the saddling paddock. The gelding Final Command pricked his ears and blew in her face before rubbing his forehead on her silks.

Trish snapped rubber bands over her cuffs to keep the wind from blowing up her sleeves. While the sky was clear, the temperature was dropping and the wind felt like it was blowing right off a field of snow.

"Trish." John Anderson tapped her knee. "I want you to do something today that I know you're going to disagree with."

Trish stopped gathering her reins and stared first at John, then at her father. Her dad nodded.

"What is it?"

"I want you to use the whip on him. We all know that this old boy just likes to run with the bunch, so when you get him up with the front runners like you did last time, I want you to go to the whip. Make him *want* to win."

"But. . . but you know he—I . . ." Trish swallowed the rest of her argument. At her father's nod, she patted the horse's neck and unclenched her jaw. "If you say I have to."

As soon as they trotted onto the track, the wind knifed through Trish's winter silks and the long johns she wore. Her nose was already dripping as they passed the grandstand on the parade to post, and only the horse's warm neck kept her hands from freezing.

"Well, old boy," she said as he walked placidly into the starting gate. "Don't blame me, but they said we gotta light a fire under you. I promise you this, you run like we both know you can and I won't have to use the whip."

By the time the last stubborn horse finally entered the gate for the third time, Trish couldn't keep from shivering. But as soon as the gates clanged open and the field surged forward, she forgot the cold.

The gelding ran easily, about midway in the pack as the horses spread out by the halfway point. At Trish's urging, he gained on the fourth place, then the third.

"Come on now," she shouted at the four-furlong marker. "Go for it!" The gelding lengthened his stride to catch the second-place horse, hanging on the tail of the leader.

Trish hesitated for only an instant. She brought the whip down on his shoulder at the same time that she shouted, "Go!"

The gelding bolted forward. Trish whapped him again. With his ears flat against his head, the horse pounded across the finish line, nose and nose with the gray who'd been leading.

"A photo finish!" Trish galloped him a bit farther around the track before pulling him down and around. "Well, I guess we gave it our best shot. Maybe I should have given you the whip sooner."

The gelding shook his head. Trish kept an eye on the board as she walked him in circles. The icy wind sneaked past her concentration and made her shiver. *Man, it's cold.*

"And the winner is number five—" Trish ignored the rest of the announcement and trotted the gelding over to the winner's circle. She gave him one more pat as she slipped off.

"I hate to say I told you so, but—"

"He told you so," Hal finished, laughing. "Good job, Tee. We always knew this old bugger had a win in him."

"Congratulations and thanks." Anderson shook Trish's hand. "Just think, we don't even have to worry about bruises with this guy."

Trish hugged her saddle to block the wind when she stepped on the scale. And she still had another ride to go.

After a place in the eighth race, Trish jogged back to the stables to ride home with David and Brad. They had the gelding all loaded, but dusk was falling by the time they drove away from the track. David turned the heater on full blast when he felt Trish shiver beside him.

"Sure glad I'm not riding tomorrow if it stays this cold." Trish rubbed her hands in the warmth pouring from the vents. "Maybe we'll have snow for Christmas."

"That's all we need."

Trish got her wish. Thick snowflakes drifted down while the Evanstons enjoyed Christmas Eve dinner. By the time they left for church, the ground was white.

"At least it's warmer," Trish said as she slid into the backseat of the car. "And there's no wind."

"True." Hal pointed at the huge flakes sparkling past the yard light. "Had to warm up to snow."

It was a candlelight service. Votive candles flickered in the iron sconces spaced along the walls. Tall white tapers banked the platform. Only the Christ candle remained to be lit on the cedar-bough Advent wreath suspended by chains behind the altar. White and gold chrismons and miniature white tree lights adorned the tall fir beside the pulpit.

Trish held her unlit candle while she glanced through the bulletin. All her favorite carols were being included in the service. She slipped her free hand through her father's arm. This was her most favorite service of the year.

A hush fell, as if all the world were waiting on tiptoe for the Christ Child to come. The organ burst into "Angels We Have Heard on High" and the congregation rose and began to sing as with one voice. Trish sang each "Gloria" sure that the angels couldn't sound any better. The church was full to overflowing and so was her heart.

Outside after the service, Rhonda handed Trish a package wrapped in Snoopy paper. "Call me after you open your presents." She leaned close and whispered in Trish's ear. "Has he guessed yet?"

Trish shook her head. "Not even close." She gave Rhonda a narrow, flat box wrapped in silver paper. "Merry Christmas." After hugging

Rhonda, she turned to give Brad his present when a snowball splooshed on her shoulder. She ducked the next one, this time from David, handed the package to Brad's mother, and scooped up the snow from the stair railing. Just as Brad turned, her barely packed snowball caught him on the cheek.

The fight flew fast and furious, quickly involving all the teenagers. Even an adult or two joined in, and those that didn't cheered for the others.

David and Trish were still puffing when they joined their parents in the car after shouting "Merry Christmas" to everyone.

"Well, having a snowball fight is sure a different way to end the Christmas Eve service." Trish laughed as she slumped against the backseat and flicked a remaining clump of snow off David.

By morning the snow had stopped falling, but all the fir trees drooped low with its weight. Trish and David hurried through the chores, making sure each horse got a handful of chopped carrots as a treat. Miss Tee preferred a handful of feed.

"Do you think we'll get more snow?" Trish asked as they slogged their way back up to the house.

"Possibly. Those clouds look mighty heavy." David kicked his boots against the steps. "Won't be much moving around today."

"Good. Let's hurry so we can open presents."

Marge had scrambled eggs with bacon and cheese ready when they walked through the door. Steaming mugs of hot chocolate with marshmallows were set at each of their places. The sliced round loaf of *Julekage*, Norwegian Christmas bread, was placed in the center of the table, flanked on either side with bright red candles.

"Oh, Mom." Trish breathed deeply. "This smells wonderful."

"Wash your hands and we're all set." Marge checked the table once more.

Hal bowed his head as they all joined hands. "Heavenly Father, all I can say is thank you. You have given us everything, but most importantly, you've given us yourself. Thank you for the food and for each other. Amen."

Trish squeezed both her mother's and David's hands. "Remember the year we got up at three-thirty?"

"And I sent you back to bed with threats of no presents." Hal shook his head. "I'm sure glad you've learned to sleep in."

The meal couldn't pass quickly enough for Trish. But she knew the more she tried to hurry them, the slower her parents would be. "I get to be Santa this year." She gulped the last of her cocoa.

Chapter
04

You are the slowest people on earth, Trish thought.

"Patience, Tee." Hal smiled as he settled back in the comforting arms of his recliner.

"Is there any time you *can't* read my mind?"

"I'll never tell. Why don't you use some of that tamped down energy and throw another log on the fire?"

Trish put two logs on the fire while darting disgusted looks toward the kitchen, where Marge and David dawdled with the dishes—or something.

"Maybe you should bring in a couple more chunks of wood before—"

"Da-ad."

Hal laughed. "Just kidding." He held up a hand in a plea for peace. "Come on in here, you two, before Trish has a conniption fit. You'd think something was under the tree for her the way she's carrying on."

That's not the problem this year, Trish thought. *This time I can't wait until you open your present from me.* She sank to the floor in front of the tree and hugged her knees. Sparks snapped their way up the chimney from the blazing fire. Strains from "O Holy Night" drifted from the stereo and mingled with the song about eagle's wings in Trish's mind.

She watched the gold disks of an ornament catch and reflect the light as it revolved in the heat above a glowing red light bulb. The winged angel at the top seemed to smile right at her. Trish smiled back. This was a good morning for smiling.

"Here we are." Marge set a tray with steaming cups of hot chocolate on the coffee table. Roly-poly snowmen danced around each mug topped with whipped cream and a candy cane for stirring.

Trish crawled on hands and knees to the table, then sank back on her haunches. She shook her head. "You outdid yourself, Mom. How pretty."

"I thought we all needed something extra special today." She carried a mug over to Hal. "Here, dear. Merry Christmas." She leaned over and kissed him.

Trish watched them over the rim of her mug. The warm glow in the middle of her stomach had nothing to do with the hot chocolate. She hadn't even sipped it yet.

"Well, let's begin." Marge settled herself in her rocking chair and blinked away the tears that threatened to overflow and run down her cheeks. "Trish, let's start with the oldest first this year."

Trish searched the name tags for one for her father, then passed a shoebox covered with red and green holly paper to him. The tradition of each person opening a present while the others watched had begun. She planned to save the eagle for last.

David let out a yelp when he opened his first present. "Tires!" He waved the coupon in the air. "I haven't had time to buy mine yet."

"Good thing." Trish laughed along with him.

"Thanks, Mom, Dad."

Her laughter stopped when she opened a large flat box from her mother and father. "How did you know? Rhonda told you—oh, it's beautiful." She held up the turquoise ski jacket with hot pink and white slashes on the sleeves. "Thank you, thank you," she repeated, hugging the jacket to her chest.

"Sorry you aren't happier with your present," Hal teased as he licked his candy cane. "This stuff sure is good, Marge."

The unopened gifts under the tree dwindled as the wrapping and ribbons littered the floor. Each one had opened several presents until only those for the neighbors were left—plus one. Trish drew the square silver box from behind the tree and carried it to her father.

"No tag?" He turned the box looking for a card.

"It's from me." Trish sank down on the hearth and leaned her elbows on her knees.

Hal carefully slit the paper.

"You *could* hurry a bit."

Please like it, the little voice inside her whispered.

Her father folded the paper and slit the tape on the heavy cardboard box.

Trish clenched her eyes and hands shut. The rustle of paper forced her to open them again.

Hal carefully lifted the eagle from its packing nest. He turned the burnished wood sculpture each way to look at it from every angle.

"Oh-h-h, Trish." Marge rose from her chair and knelt beside the recliner. "It's magnificent!"

Hal pressed his lips together and blinked rapidly. In spite of his efforts, a tear meandered down his cheek. He drew a forefinger across the lifted wing.

"D-do you—um-mm . . ." Trish studied her father's face as he studied the eagle.

He likes it, you dummy, her little voice chanted. *Can't you tell?*

But Trish needed to hear his approval. "Well?" her voice steadied this time.

Hal handed the eagle to Marge and reached both arms for his daughter. "Thank you, Tee," he said into her hair as he gathered her close to his chest. "Where did you ever find anything so perfect?"

"You—you said that was your favorite verse too." Her voice was muffled against his shirt. "And the song, it keeps playing in my head."

David took the eagle from Marge so he could examine it. "It's really something. Each feather is carved so perfectly. It looks alive."

"Remember when we saw the eagle flying up the gorge?" Marge said, taking the bird from David and handing it back to Hal. "Looking at this, I can almost hear it screeching. Thanks, Trish, for something we can all enjoy."

Trish rested her elbows on the arm of the chair and watched her father study the bird again. A smile flitted from his eyes to mouth and back again. "So wild and free," he murmured as he finally set his gift on the table by his chair. Light from the brass reading lamp made the burnished wood glow even more.

"Merry Christmas, everyone." Hal's smile lingered a bit longer on Trish. "And thank you all." He stroked the soft wool of the heather green sweater David had given him. "And now, are there any refills on that delicious chocolate, Marge?" He hoisted his mug. "All this makes a man thirsty." Eyeing the platter of cookies he said, "And hungry."

"Why don't you pick up in here, Trish, while I get the refills going?" Marge caught Trish's glance at the fireplace. "And don't throw it all in there. We don't need another chimney fire."

"That one was David's fault." Trish pulled herself to her feet and followed her mother into the kitchen. "Do you think he *really* liked it?" she whispered as she pulled two folded grocery bags from the rack under the sink.

"Oh, Trish, how can you doubt it?" Marge shook her head as she reached to hug her daughter. "He—I almost cried too. The eagle was absolutely perfect." Marge leaned back so she could look Trish in the eye. "Did it take *all* your money?" she whispered.

Trish shook her head. "Not *all* of it. It's just a good thing I'll have more coming from the track next week. But once I saw it, I just *had* to buy it. I'd been praying for that special gift and there it was." A grin turned up the corners of her mouth. "And besides, it was twenty-five percent off."

"So you got a bargain, then." Marge smiled as she filled the teakettle at the sink.

"Well, you taught me to be a careful shopper." Trish ducked away from the playful swat aimed at her.

After they'd straightened the living room, and the presents were neatly arranged under the tree, Hal finished his hot chocolate and stretched his arms over his head. "How about the two of you letting the horses out in the pasture to play in the snow. They'll enjoy it as much as you did the snowball fight last night."

"Miss Tee too?"

"Of course. Give her a taste of winter. And, David, keep an eye on that mare. She isn't due until about the tenth but she's a sneaky one. She'll head for the far corners when she's ready to foal. I think I'd better keep this chest out of that cold. I'll help your mother with dinner."

Marge rolled her eyes. "Thanks a whole lot."

David and Trish looked at each other and laughed. Everyone knew that Hal was *not* a cook. "See if you can keep from burning the potatoes this time," Trish called as she headed down the hall to change.

Caesar barked a welcome when they opened the sliding glass door. Puffy snow blanketed the deck and pillowed on the hanging baskets. A blue spot peeked from between the low-flying clouds, but to the west, heavy gray clouds promised more snow.

"We'd better hustle." David nodded at the sky. "I'll feed the outside stock while you let the racing string out." With the collie bounding through the snow beside them, the two followed their early morning tracks to the stables.

"I'll let Miss Tee out first and then the others." Trish gave Caesar a push, then tried to leap ahead of him. When he bounded back at her, she tried to sidestep but slipped and fell on her back in the snow. The collie put both feet on her chest and swiped a couple of licks across her nose.

She grabbed his white ruff and rolled him off her. With her laughing and Caesar's barking, the entire stable erupted with whinnies and hoof slammings.

David quit trying to be heard. He put two fingers in his mouth and blew hard. A piercing whistle split the icy air.

Trish started to giggle. Caesar quickly licked her chin. The giggle turned to a hoot. When she finally quit laughing, she could hardly get her breath. She raised up on her elbows, shaking the snow off her stocking cap. Caesar sat beside her, his tail feathering the snow, and like a perfect gentleman, he extended one paw.

Trish crashed again, overcome by giggles.

Spitfire whinnied, a high, demanding cry for some of the attention she was wasting on the dog.

David stood over her, arms crossed, trying to either keep or regain a straight face. "Do you think you could come help me before dark, at least?"

Trish scooped a handful of snow and tossed it at him. When another caught Caesar full in the face, she crossed both arms above her head to protect herself, both from her brother and the dog.

David reached down and hauled her to her feet. "Come on, snow bunny, we've got work to do."

"Want to make angels?" Trish punched him in the side. "Or are you too grown up for snow angels?"

Old gray Dan'l stretched his neck out as far as the closed stall door would allow. He nickered, a plea for attention impossible to ignore.

"Nope, but explain the wait to your friends there."

Trish dug pieces of carrot out of her pocket and gave each horse both a treat and a pat as she went down the line. "Be right back," she promised before she headed across to the old barn.

Miss Tee plowed to a stop when her hooves hit the snow. She bent to sniff, then tossed her head when the cold touched her muzzle.

"Come on, silly," Trish called as she led the mare out to the paddock. Miss Tee raised each foot high, trying to step over the cold powder. She leaped but still found herself up to her knees when she came down. Then the filly discovered the best way was to follow her mother's trail.

Trish gave her baby an extra pat as the filly finally tiptoed through the gate. The mare immediately buckled her knees and rolled back and forth, grunting in pleasure.

Miss Tee stood stock still. If horses could talk, her look said it all; she was sure her mother had lost her mind.

Trish laughed her way back to the row of stalls where the racing string waited. One by one, she led them out to the board-fenced pasture. And just like the mare, each of them rolled and scratched, then shook all over upon standing up.

They snorted and blew, tossed their heads, and charged across the snowy field, just like a group of kids let loose from school on a snow day. Trish leaned on the fence, enjoying their antics. *If only you could see them, Dad*, she thought. *You need a good laugh too.*

You can be thankful he's alive, her nagging little voice said as if perched on the snow-capped fence post beside her. *You know he . . .*

"Oh, shut up." Trish spun on her heel and headed up to the barns. "Mucking out stalls is better than listening to you." Caesar cocked an ear. "No, I'm not talking to you." She tugged his ruff. "And I'm not going crazy either."

Snowflakes began drifting down again by the time they had all the stalls clean and the animals back in and fed. The twinkling lights of the Christmas tree in the front window beckoned them back to the warmth. The aroma of baked ham met them at the door, along with their mother's voice.

"Dinner in about fifteen minutes. I've made spiced cider to warm you up."

Trish hung her jacket in the closet and laid her gloves and hat on the warm air vent to dry. She glanced in the living room. Her father's chair was empty. "Where's Dad?"

"Sleeping. He'll be up in a few minutes."

"Sure smells good in here." David pulled off his boots at the jack by the door. "Here, Tee, hang up my jacket too."

"Did you ever hear the word please?" She stood with her hands on her hips.

David dumped the denim coat over her head. "Please. And thank you. In advance."

Trish pulled the thing off her head, muttering around the grin she tried to keep hidden. "Muck the stalls, hang up my coat; you don't want a sister, you want a slave."

"Oh, and could you pour me a mug of that cider?"

David sidestepped her punch and laughed his way down the hall to his room.

That night, after spending nearly an hour on the phone with Rhonda, Trish snuggled down in her bed. *No homework, a day that can never be topped, extra rides coming up to pad my bank account, and best of all, no school for nine days!* And tomorrow she and Rhonda were going shopping and to a movie. That is, if the roads cleared.

If only Dad didn't have to go to the hospital tomorrow for another treatment.

Chapter
05

"Mom says I can't drive." Rhonda moaned over the phone the next morning.

"I know. The roads are just too slick. David's taking Mom and Dad to the hospital in the four-wheel drive."

"Another treatment?"

"Yeah. About the time he's feeling pretty good, they knock him down again. Just going outside in the cold air made him start coughing." Trish slid to the floor so she could lean back against the cupboard. "Why don't you walk over and help me and Brad with the chores."

"Thanks a lot. I wanted to go shopping."

"Mm-mm. You coming or not?"

"All right."

Trish didn't mind staying home. She didn't have much money left, and now she didn't need to buy a jacket. "And you don't really *need* anything else," she reminded the face in the mirror as she brushed her hair. A movie and lunch out would have been nice. And who knew when they'd have time for that later.

She finished straightening up her room, tossed the dirty clothes in the washing machine, and shrugged into her jacket. A quick check outside and she switched from leather boots to rubber ones. It had begun to rain.

"You be careful out there," Brad cautioned as he boosted her into the saddle on Spitfire.

"No problem. We're just walking today. Rhonda's coming over, so why don't you saddle Firefly for her. If you'd like, you could work Anderson's Final Command."

"That's okay. I'll get the stalls cleaned out. Then we'll all be done about the same time. Maybe we'll get to that movie yet, the way the snow's melting."

Spitfire shied when a load of snow swooshed off a fir branch and thwunked in the snow. He spooked again when another tree dumped its load. Trish hunched her shoulders to keep the drizzle from trickling down her neck, but she never took her attention from the frisky horse. She stroked his neck with one hand and kept up a running commentary on all she saw. He settled after one round of the track and seemed as relieved as she when they turned back to the stables.

"Better late than never," Trish teased her friend who'd arrived while Trish stripped the saddle off Spitfire in his stall. "You want Gatesby or Firefly?"

Rhonda gave her a have-you-lost-your-marbles look.

Brad chuckled as he boosted the slender redhead into the saddle. "So you don't want a blue-and-green from Gatesby, eh?"

Rhonda stared down at him from Firefly's back. "A blue-and-green?" She started to laugh. "That's a good one, Brad. No, I don't want a Gatesby bruise, or to get dumped either. I don't know how Trish puts up with him."

"With who?" Trish stopped Final Command in front of Firefly's stall.

Gatesby nickered in the stall next to them. To look at the blaze down his long face and the soft eyes, no one would guess him to be ornery, until he laid back his ears and reached for Trish's jacket.

"Him!" Brad backed up the gelding so his back was out of range of Gatesby's nipping teeth. He gave Trish a leg up. "You should have put him on the hot walker to work off some of his meanness."

"I'm starved." Brad closed the door and shot the bolt on the tack room when they were finished. "I'll go home and change, then we can go."

"I gotta call my mom first. She'll probably say okay now that it's warmed up and I'm not driving." Rhonda sniffed. The cold had made her nose run too.

"Well, we better hurry. I have to be home in time to feed, in case David doesn't get back. We could get hamburgers at the drive-in window at Burgerville. That way we can make the matinee." Trish pushed open the sliding glass door. While they waited for Rhonda to call home, she slipped out of her jacket and hung it over the back of a chair to dry. "Want a cookie, Brad?"

"Just one?"

"No, you nut. The whole plate. I don't care how many you eat. Help yourself. Mom musta known you were coming. She left some of each kind."

"Man, oh man!" Brad popped a brownie in his mouth while he picked out several other kinds. "Your mom is the best baker."

"Hey, she didn't do it all. I helped."

Brad pretended to gag.

"Don't worry. She made the brownies. Just don't try the Rice Krispies bars. I did those."

"I can go!" Rhonda gave a little skip as she entered the room. She looked down at her wet jeans. "You got some clothes I can borrow?"

"See you in fifteen minutes." Brad swallowed the last of his cookies and grabbed a couple more. "To keep me from passing out." He laughed as he went out the door.

They slid into their seats just as the opening scenes of the matinee appeared on the theater screen. Brad passed the popcorn tub over to Trish and pulled off his jacket. After propping his knees on the seat-back in front of him, he pushed up his sleeves and reached for some popcorn.

"You think you can settle down now?" Trish whispered.

"Sure, who's got the Coke?" He popped a handful of popcorn in his mouth. "Anybody get napkins?"

"Shush." Rhonda giggled as she handed him the tall drink. "We should never let you out in public."

"Hey, I'm driving, remember?"

A woman in front of them turned to frown at Brad.

Trish was afraid to look at Rhonda for fear they'd never be able to quit laughing. It was a good thing the movie was a comedy. It was a giggly kind of afternoon.

But that night Trish didn't feel like laughing. Her father had been throwing up for five hours straight. In between that he had coughing spells.

By the time Hal finally fell into an exhausted sleep, Trish felt like her own throat was raw. "I thought they'd found some medicine that would keep him from being so sick." She slumped in her dad's recliner with her feet across the arm so she could warm her toes by the fire.

"This time none of that seems to help." Marge leaned her head back in the rocking chair. "I think the cold air made things worse because it started the coughing."

"Just when he was finally feeling better too."

"I know. But at least he is getting better. We've got to be thankful for that."

"Mm-mmm." Trish bobbed her toe to the beat of "The Little Drummer Boy" on the stereo. "It just doesn't seem fair."

"I think that storm is hitting earlier than they predicted," David said, entering the room to rub his hands in front of the fire. "I've just been down to check on the animals. I think it's dropped about twenty degrees out."

"Is it still raining?" Marge asked.

"More like sleet now. I turned the light on in the pump house and blanketed all the racing stock."

"We'd better store up some water in case the electricity goes out. Trish, you could fill the bathtub. I'll fill some jugs in the kitchen. Want some hot chocolate, David, or coffee?"

When Trish tiptoed in to kiss her father good-night, she had to hold back a sob. His gray look was back—in fact, his face looked almost green.

Dark shadows shrouded his eyes and hollowed his cheeks. The curved plastic basin on the nightstand was a grim reminder of hospital days.

"I love you," she whispered as she dropped a kiss on his forehead. Her father's eyelids flickered and he nodded ever so slightly, as if any movement might bring on the vomiting again.

Trish met her mother in the doorway of the bedroom.

"Don't worry, Tee. He'll be better tomorrow."

Trish wished her mother's words carried more conviction. And who was *she* to say not to worry?

Trish chewed her bottom lip as she entered her own bedroom. Her gaze went to the verses printed on the cards she'd pinned on the wall: " . . . *on eagle's wings.*"

She spun out the door and back to the living room. The carved eagle stood on the mantelpiece, its wings spread wide over the pine boughs. Trish carefully lifted it down and went to the door of her parent's bedroom. Marge was holding a straw to Hal's mouth so he could sip a drink. The room was dim with only the light of a small lamp on the nightstand.

Trish tiptoed around the end of the bed and made room for the eagle near the lamp. A smile lifted the corners of her father's mouth as he whispered, "Thanks."

Trish awoke sometime during the night to put another blanket on her bed. She closed the small crack in the window that she always left open. No more snow fell in the circle of the yard light. At least that was good news. She snuggled back into her bed and fell into a deep sleep.

The next day was dark and foreboding. Clouds hovered, shading from gun-metal gray to pussy willow. A biting wind whistled through the bare trees as David and Trish took care of the animals. All racing had been canceled due to the weather.

"Dad looks terrible," Trish blurted, slamming the bucket down in the tack room.

"At least he's not coughing or throwing up," David tried to console her.

"Yeah, thank God for small favors."

"Knock it off, Trish. Mom said—"

Trish spun around and glared at her brother. "I don't care *what* Mom said. She should have left him at the hospital where someone could help him."

"She tried. Dad wouldn't stay."

"Oh." Trish felt like crawling under a tack box.

"If you're through with your temper tantrum, maybe we should go up for dinner, before Mom comes down to see what happened to us."

"Sorry." Trish closed the door behind them. A few minutes ago she would have slammed it. And that would have startled the horses. They didn't like having both halves of their doors closed any more than she did. And right now Trish felt like all kinds of doors were closing on her.

The wind slashed at their jackets and snapped at their faces all the way to the house. Trish caught herself when she slipped on the sidewalk. Sliding could be fun, but not now.

"If that wind would just die down, I'd sprinkle some ashes on the sidewalk and steps," David said. "You almost went down."

"I'm just glad I don't have to go out again tonight." Trish gave Caesar a pat. "Do you think we should bring him in?"

"No. He's got a good, warm doghouse. You'll be fine, won't you, boy?" David rubbed the dog's ears and scratched the white ruff. Both he and Trish stamped the snow off their boots before they stepped inside.

"Dad's still in bed," Marge said before Trish had a chance to ask. "But he did eat some chicken noodle soup."

Trish felt the sadness lift, just a bit.

"Now how about ham sandwiches and chicken noodle soup for you two? It's all ready. You look frozen. Get in front of the fire and I'll bring it to you on trays."

Trish shivered when she took her jacket off, then sat down on the hearth with her back as close to the crackling logs as she dared.

Marge handed her a steaming mug of soup. "Maybe this will help."

Trish felt much better when she was finally warm, had eaten, and checked on her father. Some color had returned to his cheeks and he was breathing more easily.

Pulling her quilt up over her shoulders in her own bed, Trish waited for her body heat to warm the sheets, then said her prayers. It was easier to thank God when her dad looked better.

When daylight came, she stuck her nose out of the covers. The room was cold even with the window closed. She glanced at her clock. It had stopped at two. No electricity! Trish threw back the quilt and sprinted to the window. The tree branches hung low to the ground, buckling under a blanket of ice. Even the cars were entombed.

Trish's world was frozen over.

Chapter
06

Come on, Tee. I need help." David tapped on her door.

"What's wrong?" David was down the hall before Trish could ask any more. "Besides no electricity, that is," she muttered as she pulled on her long johns, then jeans. "Man, it's cold in here!"

"Where's David?" Trish pulled a sweater over her head as she entered the living room.

"He said to find him in the pump house. He's trying to get the generator going." Marge closed the glass doors on the roaring fire, then stood and rubbed her hands together. "At least we can heat part of the house."

"How's Dad?"

"He's okay. I wanted to get it warm out here before he gets up."

Trish pulled on her jacket, a stocking cap, and gloves. She grabbed a flashlight and stepped out the sliding door. The wind caught her as she rounded the corner. She pulled her collar up as far as it would go and headed for the pump house that squatted on the rise halfway to the barns.

"I've never seen so much ice," she said as she bent down at the open door. David was kneeling inside, tinkering with the red gasoline generator. "Here's another flashlight. What can I do to help?"

"This blasted thing won't start. Dad's the one with the magic touch. If I don't get it going pretty soon, the pump will freeze and we'll really be in trouble." David slammed a wrench onto the concrete. "I'm just not a good mechanic." He tucked his bare hands under his armpits.

"Didn't you bring gloves?"

"Sure, but I can't work with them on." His breath blew out in puffs, even inside the tiny building.

Trish knew to keep her mouth shut. David's anger wasn't directed at her. It took a lot to get him angry, but when he did—

"Hold that light so I can see over here."

Trish hunkered down and tried to direct the beam to where David indicated.

"Trish, for pete's sake, can't you hold that thing still?"

Trish swallowed a retort.

"Hand me that screwdriver."

Trish looked through the array of tools in the toolbox and spread out on the floor. "Which one?"

"The Phillips."

She passed him the first one she saw.

"Not that one, the big one with the brown handle."

She passed it to him, but in doing so lowered the beam of light.

"Thanks a lot. Now I can't see anything. Can't you at least keep the light in the right place?"

Trish clamped her teeth together. *You try to do both and see how you do, brother,* she thought.

"Okay, see the pull cord?"

"Yes."

"It pulls hard so give it all you've got."

Trish set down the light, grasped the wooden grips, and jerked hard. She banged her head on the top of the door frame and sat down, *thump,* in the snow, the cord in her hand. "Ow-w-w!" She blinked back the tears that surged in response to the blow on the back of her head.

"What happened? You okay, Trish?" David crawled from behind the generator and stuck his head out the door.

Trish held up the cord with one hand and rubbed the spot on her head with the other. She was glad her mother wasn't there to see their predicament.

"What are we gonna do?"

"I don't know." David crawled the rest of the way out and rose to his feet. He kicked the door closed and turned the knob. "Maybe Dad can come look at this thing. We better get that tank loaded on the truck and go get some water. All the animals need a drink and I know the water troughs must be frozen.

"You go get the pickup and I'll start the tractor."

Trish blinked against the pain in her head and handed David the broken cord. "Here, we better not lose this." She extended a hand for him to pull her to her feet. "Wow, that was a shocker."

"You okay?"

"Yeah, great. I feel like my head is separated from my body, I'm freezing cold, and I love having you holler at me. Anything else? Sure, I feel great."

"Sorry, Tee. The keys are in the truck."

Trish rubbed her head again before stuffing her gloved hands into her pockets. *What a miserable morning. And what a vacation!*

When she tried to open the truck door, it wouldn't budge. She couldn't push the button in. She tried again. Nothing. She slammed her hand against the door. Still nothing. *Is it locked? No, the button is up.*

She went around to try the other door. Both of them were frozen shut.

Then she heard the roar of the tractor coming to life. *Well, at least something's working around here.* She carefully made her way down to the barn, watching the icy patches. She didn't need another bruise.

"The truck doors are frozen," she announced.

David slammed his hand against the steering wheel. "What more can go wrong?" He shut off the tractor and leaped to the ground. "Let's hope Mom has some water heating in the fireplace."

Whinnies and nickers from behind the closed stall doors meant a plea for both light and morning feed.

"Why don't I take care of these guys while you go thaw out the truck door?" Trish nodded toward the stables. At David's okay, Trish

45

went down the line, opening doors on her way to the feed room. Horse heads popped out like jack-in-the-boxes, all of them eyeing Trish like they hadn't been fed in days.

Trish filled the two five-gallon feed buckets and set them in the wheelbarrow along with the remainder of a bale of hay. Each time she swung the lower half of a stall door open, she had to push by an eager horse to get to the manger.

"Where are your manners this morning?" she complained as Spitfire snatched a mouthful of grain from the scoop. "What's gotten into all of you?"

She grabbed Gatesby's halter with one hand, then poured his grain and tossed hay in the rack with the other. "Sorry, guy, I don't feel like any new bruises today. I already got my share." In each stall she checked the water buckets. Those that weren't dry were chunks of ice.

By the time she finished with the outside stock and Miss Tee, she could feel her own stomach rumbling. Caesar didn't seem to mind the cold wind as he danced beside her. "Sorry, no time to play," she said when he crouched in front of her with nose on his front paws and plumy tail waving in the air.

"What's the holdup, David?" she called when she walked back into the house. Closed off from the living room, the kitchen was cold, but it sure beat the wind outside. Trish stamped the snow off her boots and stepped into the living room, where the fire blazed in the hearth. She pulled off her gloves and extended her hands to the warmth. The cast-iron teakettle rested on its metal frame to the side of the burning logs.

"Morning, Tee," Hal said from the comfort of his recliner. "You look about frozen."

"Hungry too, I'm sure," Marge added.

"Yeah, I am. Where's David?" She tossed her jacket at the sofa.

"He's waiting for the water to heat so he can thaw out the truck doors."

David stepped into the room as Marge spooned instant cocoa powder into a mug.

"And I'm going to see if I can't get that blasted generator running," Hal spoke over his mug of coffee.

"Dad, you shouldn't go out. . . ." Trish's comment faded away at the glare from her brother. *Looks like they've already had a discussion about that.* Her thoughts finished her sentence. *You shouldn't go out in that wind and cold.* She wanted to tie her dad to the chair.

"Why don't you wait until I get back with the water tank so I can help you." David shrugged into his jacket. "Trish can water the animals while we fix the generator."

"Heard anything from Brad?" Trish turned so her backside would warm up at the fire.

"Can't. The phone's down too. They've probably got about the same situation we do. Thought I'd swing by there on the way into town in case I can fill the tank there." David brought a half bucket of water from the bathtub and added water to it from the steaming teakettle. "Got a pitcher, Mom?"

Marge spoke as she searched the cupboard for a larger pitcher. "Trish, get some cereal, and there's juice in the fridge. Dad's been toasting bread on the long forks, if you want some. Here you go, David. Anything else?"

"Yeah, warmer weather." He pulled on a hat and gloves and left with the bucket and pitcher.

Trish got her breakfast and huddled on the raised hearth to keep warm while she ate. Her dad offered her some of the bread he'd toasted. "Mm-mm. Thanks, Dad. That's really good. Sure beats toast done in the toaster."

"At least I'm good for something around here."

Trish caught the insinuation that her father felt helpless, even though he smiled when he spoke. She glanced at her mother and father, catching a look that passed between them. While Marge kept her opinions to herself, Trish knew her mother was really worried. And this time she had real reason to be.

"How are things down at the barn?" Hal sounded raspy and short of breath.

"Fine. The horses are frisky, wired. They don't like having their stall doors closed."

"Too bad. How's your head?"

Trish felt for the bump. "Saw stars for a minute. Probably should have put some snow on it but I was already too cold. That wind is awful."

"The radio says more of the same, and colder tonight. They're sanding the main roads, but you could help David put chains on the truck. With those and the four-wheel drive, he ought to be able to get to Orchards and back if he drives slowly." Hal coughed carefully.

The truck roared to life out in the driveway. "Well, that's one problem solved." Trish drank the last of her hot chocolate. "You need anything from the store, Mom?" she asked as she bundled into her gear.

"No, thanks." Marge rubbed her elbows as she stared out the front window. She turned and forced a smile. "Now you be careful."

How often have I heard those words? Trish thought as she slipped her way down the sidewalk. Right now, her father was the one who needed to be careful. He didn't need all this cold and extra worry. And he certainly shouldn't be out working on the generator. *God, you've sure sent this crummy weather at a bad time. Do you have something against us?*

David had pushed the truck seat forward and was pulling the chains out when Trish reached him. He handed her a chain. "Here, just lay this out behind the back wheel and make sure everything is straight. Then we'll back over the chains and hook 'em on."

Trish did as she was told and miraculously it worked. David only got angry once when one of the links refused to close. At least he had plenty of light to work with. Trish was about to tease him, but one look at his face told her to keep her comments to herself.

"Okay," he grunted as he pulled himself up by the rear bumper. "Now let's get that tank loaded."

Within a few minutes they had strapped the tank to the bucket of the power lift on the front of the old red tractor and hoisted it above the pickup bed.

"Now when I get it lowered in place, you release those straps," David instructed. "Make sure you keep your hands and feet out of the way because that tank'll roll."

You sound more like Mom every day. Worry, worry, worry, Trish grumbled to herself as she climbed up over the pickup bed. She leaned over and tugged on the strap catches.

Nothing happened.

"Get over here by the bucket. That'll give you more leverage."

Trish squeezed by the head of the five-hundred-gallon tank and braced herself against the tractor bucket. She reached over, snagged the black webbing, and pulled.

The strap released.

Trish hung in the air for a fleeting moment. Her arms windmilled to try to catch her balance, but the ice on the fender sent her toppling to the ground.

"Ooooff."

"I told you to be careful!" David leaped down from the tractor. "Are you all right?"

Trish took a deep breath. And let it all out. This getting dumped on her butt was beginning to get to her. "I'm fine, David. Just fine."

He reached a hand down to pull her to her feet. "You sure you're not hurt?"

"No, at least the snow is good for cushioning." She brushed the snow and ice off her backside. "How's the water tank?"

David climbed up and released the other strap so the tank could roll into place. "Do you think you can back the tractor up without getting into trouble?"

Trish stuck her tongue out at him as she stepped aboard the tractor, released the gear on the hoist, and backed the bucket away from the truck. She shifted gears, drove the tractor back to the barn, and parked it in the center aisle just down from Miss Tee's stall.

She stopped a moment to rub the filly's forehead. A few white hairs swirled a miniature star between the baby's eyes. Trish kissed the soft muzzle. "No time to play today, but you be good." She patted the mare. "I'll bring you a drink pretty soon."

"Tri-ish!"

"I'm coming." She trotted out of the barn, being careful not to slip on the ice. She didn't need another spill.

The temperature seemed to be dropping by the time they got back with the load of water. David parked the truck at the stables and both of them filled buckets from the spigot on the bottom of the tank and poured water into all the horses' water buckets.

Then they drove out to the aluminum water troughs in the pastures. Since those all had automatic floats, the tanks were full—of solid ice.

David leaned his head on his hands on the steering wheel. He took a deep breath.

"I'll go get the pickax." Trish scooted out the door before he could even ask her.

The ice was only about six inches thick, so chopping through it didn't take as long as she'd feared. The mares and yearling stood in a semicircle watching the action until Trish brought them each a bucket of water while David chopped. The horses drank deeply.

But the Hereford beef stock in the next pasture were too spooked to drink from the buckets. Their plaintive moos begged David to chop faster. When the water was clear, they pushed and shoved to get their turn.

"We'll empty both of these when they're done and then water them again tonight. That way the troughs won't freeze up." David climbed back into the truck. "I'm going to take some of this up to the house and fill the bathtub again. So we'll have water for the house."

Trish slammed the door after joining him. "You know, Davey boy, you're pretty sharp."

He shot her a quizzical look.

"The way you seem to know all the right stuff to do."

"I couldn't get the generator going."

"No, but like dumping the troughs. I never would have thought of that."

"Just common sense." David parked the truck as close to the house as he could. He smiled at her. "Thanks, Tee."

David and Hal were still struggling with the generator when Trish went down to the barn to feed and water the animals again. Darkness was falling when she got back up to the house.

"Did you empty the hauling tank?" David asked.

"No, I didn't think of it." Trish turned and went back outside. She opened the valve and watched as the water drained out on the ground, freezing as it formed a puddle. She wrapped both arms around herself to keep out the biting east wind that whipped down the gorge, bringing the cold from the Rockies. When the trickle stopped, she closed the handle and trudged back to the house.

"No luck, huh?" she asked David after removing all her gear.

"No." David shook his head. "And when we called about renting a generator, they were all gone. Besides that, now we'll have to thaw out the pump too. And who knows how many pipes are frozen."

"How's Dad?"

"Terrible."

Chapter
07

I told him he shouldn't try to fix it."

"I know, David." Marge spoke softly so as not to wake Hal, who slept soundly in the recliner. "I tried to tell him too, but you know how stubborn your father is. He was determined to fix that generator."

"I'll take it in to be repaired tomorrow." David rubbed his hands over his forehead and through his hair.

"Just buy a new one. Your father kept that thing running with baling wire and chewing gum. It's time to lay it to rest."

"Why, Mom, I—"

"We'll deal with your father later. I should have had the nerve to say this earlier today and saved him all this." Marge waved her hand toward her husband.

She'd spread a comforter over the recliner, then a quilt and another comforter. With all that it still took a long time for him to get warm.

Trish listened to their conversation with one ear and kept the other tuned to her father's shallow breathing. Even with the help of the oxygen tank by his chair, she could hear the struggle. And with the oxygen he couldn't be close to the fireplace, so they'd moved the recliner over by the sofa.

He looks shrunken in those quilts, Trish thought. *I thought you were helping us, God! He keeps telling us you're making him well, but he sounds awful.* She chewed her lip to hold back the tears.

Hal coughed then, a deep wrenching cough that shook the chair.

"Here, Dad." Trish unwrapped a throat lozenge and held it to his mouth. "This'll help."

Hal nodded. His eyes fluttered open and a tiny smile lifted one corner of his mouth. "Thanks, Tee." His eyes closed again. "Don't worry. I'll be better in the morning."

"I'll take the sofa and you two get your sleeping bags," Marge said after settling Hal into the chair for the night. "The bedrooms are much too cold, and at least we can keep the fire going in here. Trish, get some quilts and you can use them as pads under the bags."

The glow from the kerosene lamp looked warm but didn't make a difference in the arctic bathroom. By the time Trish had brushed her teeth, she was glad to get back into the living room.

The candles on the mantel, the two lamps, and the glow from the fireplace held them all in a circle of light. Trish looked up at the angel on the tree. She couldn't see its smile tonight; in fact, she could hardly see the angel in the dimness. It didn't surprise her.

She snuggled down into her sleeping bag.

"Our Father, who art in heaven . . ." Marge said softly after blowing out the lamps. Hal's whisper could barely be heard as he joined in the prayer.

Trish felt like plugging her ears. She was glad when they said "Amen."

How would she ever be able to go to sleep, listening to her father fight to breathe?

"Trish. Trish!" David shook her.

"Wha—what's the matter?" Trish pulled the sleeping bag off her head.

"I'm taking Mom and Dad in to the hospital. He's started to run a temperature."

Trish shoved the bag down and sat up. She could hear her father's wheezing like it was in her bones. "What time is it?"

"Two. I've just put more logs on the fire. I should be back in an hour or so."

"Where's Mom?"

"Packing a bag. I've got the truck warming up." He handed her an alarm clock. "I've set this for four. If I'm not back, stoke the fire."

"I'm ready, David." Marge pulled on her coat. She handed him the suitcase. "Why don't you take this out first."

"What can I do?" Trish crawled out of her sleeping bag.

"Pray for us, for a safe trip on all that ice." Marge gave her a quick hug. "And for your dad."

With the recliner levered upright, it still took both Marge and David to get Hal to his feet.

With both of them supporting him, Trish wrapped the long wool scarf around his neck. She gave him a two-arm hug around the waist and, after kissing his cheek, secured the scarf over his mouth and nose. "I love you." She bit back the tears that stung her eyes. "Come home quick."

Trish watched from the door as the three carefully made their way down the steps and navigated the sidewalk. Without the yard light, she could only see them in the lights of the truck. David opened the door, and they boosted Hal in and placed the portable oxygen tank at his feet. Marge tucked a quilt around him and climbed in.

Trish kept watch until the red taillights turned in the direction of town. Caesar whined at her feet. "Come on in." She slapped her leg. "You can keep me company."

The room seemed huge with everyone gone. She blew out one lamp and climbed back into her sleeping bag. The sofa would be more comfortable, but the bag was closer to the fire. Caesar stretched himself beside her, his head on the sleeping bag, assuring Trish she was not alone.

"I don't know, old boy," she whispered. "I just don't know."

All she could think was *Please, please, please take care of my dad.* As she finally drifted off to sleep, their theme song floated through her mind.

Ah, yes, eagle's wings. You promised eagle's wings. And my dad really needs them—right now.

David hadn't returned by the time the alarm went off. Bleary-eyed, Trish poked the remaining coals with the iron log turner and laid a small chunk of wood on the resurging flames. Eyes closed, she drowsed in front of the open doors. When the wood started to snap, she laid on two large chunks and crawled back into her sleeping bag.

The chill had already seeped back into the room, so she shivered as she scrunched down and pulled the edge of the bag over her head. But the chill wasn't just in the room. The *please, please* rampaged through her head.

The wind whistled and groaned around the corners of the house, pleading at the windows for entry. Caesar snuggled closer. It felt like forever before Trish fell asleep again.

"You let the fire go out!" David's voice snatched away her sleepiness.

Trish sat up, but as soon as her nose felt the temperature of the room, she pulled her sleeping bag up with her. Daylight had lightened the room to gray. It was still early.

"How's Dad?"

"They're keeping him there." David knelt in front of the fireplace, poking and prodding the logs in search of live coals. "He was able to breathe better as soon as they gave him a shot. There." A small flame flared around the edges of the crumbling log. He added some kindling from the basket and a couple of small pieces of cedar.

Trish wrinkled her nose as a puff of wind blew smoke out into the room. "Did they say what was wrong?"

"They think bronchitis, maybe pneumonia again. Anyway, he's better off there where he can stay warm and eat right. I take it the lights haven't come back on?"

Trish shrugged. "The heat didn't, so I guess not."

"Well, let's get going. I stopped for water so we can get the chores done. Then I've gotta get the new generator and see how badly we're frozen up." David leaned his forehead on his fist as he sat on the hearth. His shoulders slumped. When Caesar shoved his nose into the other hand, David stroked the dog's head. It was an automatic reaction, but Trish could tell her brother was far away in his mind.

"David?" When there was no answer, Trish disengaged herself from the sleeping bag and reached up to touch his hand. "Is Dad worse than you're telling me?"

"Yes. No. I don't know. He's so sick again. It just doesn't look good." David swallowed and rubbed his eyes. He turned to poke the fire one more time. As the flames danced higher, they glinted on a tear at the corner of his eye. He pushed himself to his feet.

"Come on, Caesar, time for you to go outside. Hustle, Tee." He let the dog out then headed down the hall to the bathroom.

Trish wrapped both arms around her legs and rested her chin on her knees. *Dad's gotta get better. Please, God, he's gotta get well. I need my dad!* She stared into the flames, scenes from the last few days fast-forwarding through her mind. The Christmas Eve service, opening presents Christmas morning, her dad sick from the treatment, the sound of his fight to breathe.

"No! He's going to get well again. Heavenly Father, please." She rubbed her eyes hard with her fists. "This is no different than any other time he's been in the hospital. All I have to do is keep on going."

And keep on praying, her little voice reminded her.

How are we ever gonna do it all? Trish wondered as she pulled on her cold jeans and sweater. She'd slept in her long johns and wool socks to make dressing easier. When would she get to wash her hair again? she wondered. Or take a shower? When would they *finally* have electricity again?

She turned on the portable radio. " . . . still have power outages over much of North Portland and Clark County. Crews are working around the clock to restore power."

"Tell me something I didn't know."

"Some schools are open for emergency housing for those that need assistance." A list of schools followed.

"Well, at least I could go for a shower." Trish tugged on her boots.

"But people are encouraged to stay off the roads. Only drive if it is an absolute necessity."

"My hair is becoming a necessity."

"How about filling the teakettle before you leave?" David strode through the living room and out the door.

"Do you mind if I go to the bathroom first?" Trish grumbled. "And maybe brush my teeth?"

Only the wind answered her, and its whine made her want to crawl back into the sleeping bag.

By the time the animals were fed and watered, Trish was more than ready to return to the house. Her nose felt about frozen off. She carefully checked the mare that was due to foal. They'd moved her into the big box stall when the weather turned bad. The mare attacked her feed and drank deeply when Trish filled the bucket.

"Good girl." Trish stroked down the horse's neck and over her belly. Right in front of the mare's warm flank, Trish felt the foal kick. She held her hand firm but didn't feel it again. "Impatient, aren't you, little one?" She could feel the grin that creased her face. What a thrill to feel that yet-to-be-born life. "But you take your time, you hear? You're not due for another ten days, so hang in there." She patted the mare once more and left the stall.

She gave Miss Tee and her mother extra grain for a treat and hugged the little filly close. Miss Tee sniffed Trish's face and whiskered her cheek. "I'll be back to clean your stall." Trish stroked the satiny nose and tickled the whiskery place on the filly's muzzle. "You be good."

Miss Tee nodded. Her tiny ears pricked forward as she watched Trish latch the stall door. A baby nicker followed Trish out the door. The nicker was much friendlier than the biting wind.

As soon as they had eaten their cereal, David left for Battle Ground to pick up a generator at the co-op. Just as Trish was getting into her coat, the phone rang.

"Hallelujah!" Trish bounded into the kitchen. "Runnin' On Farm."

"Hi, Trish."

"Brad, what's happening? . . . You too, huh? We figured that when you didn't show up yesterday."

"What's going on there?"

Trish caught Brad up on the events of the previous day and night. "So how about I call you when David gets back. That is, if you're sure you can come help."

"I'll be over in a few minutes. Except for no power, everything's okay here."

Trish hung up the phone, a warm, fuzzy feeling in her midsection. It sure was good to have friends who just volunteered when you needed help.

She had four horses clipped to the hot walker by the time Brad got down to the stable. "Shoulda just walked," Brad said as he grabbed a pitchfork. "Almost ended up in the ditch turning into your driveway. I've never seen the roads like this."

"Yeah, David said it was bad, and he has chains and weight in the back of the pickup."

"You aren't going to work any of them, are you?"

"No. Just the hot walker. If it warms up some, I think I'll let them out in the pasture." Trish pitched straw and manure out the stall door as she talked. Steam rose from the pungent pile.

Caesar's barking drew her attention to the house. Two camper pickups were following David up the driveway. "Who do you suppose that is?"

Chapter

08

Curiosity may have killed the cat, but it made Trish stick her fork in the manure pile and trot up to the pump house, where all three vehicles had parked.

As David climbed from the cab of the farm pickup, four people slammed doors on theirs.

"We heard you needed help." A burly man tipped his hat back and extended his hand.

"Mr. Benson, Fred." David shook hands with the four guests. "How did you . . . I mean . . . why are . . . ?"

"Don't be surprised, son," Frank Johnson said. "Pastor called and when he told me your situation, why, I figured you could use some extra hands. And places to heat water so we can thaw those pipes out." He pointed to the campers. "You know your dad's always been the first to help when needed, so we'd kinda like to pay him back."

"You don't mind, do you?" Benson asked.

"Why no, I . . ."

Trish could tell David was embarrassed as all get out. She blinked her eyes a couple of times. Who'd want frozen eyelashes?

"Good to see you, Trish." Frank Johnson smiled at her. "Hear you've been doing real well riding the ponies. We're real proud of you, you know. Just like one of our own kids, since we've known you all your growing-up years."

"Thank you." Trish could feel the blush staining her cheeks even redder than the cold had. "Well, uh, I've gotta get back to the barn. Thanks for coming." She hesitated only to watch two men pull the new red generator off the truck bed and carry it over to the pump house. "Wow! Who'dve thought today'd be like this?"

Well, you asked for help, didn't you? her nagger chuckled gleefully in her ear.

All the stalls were clean and horses groomed when one of the men came down to the barn. "We've got lunch up at the house. You hungry?"

Trish and Brad looked at each other. "Sure," she said.

"My wife figured you'd be about tired of hot dogs by now so she put a hot dish in the oven and salad in the fridge. Those campers come in handy when the power goes out."

Trish heard the chuckle in her ear again.

The women had even sent over paper plates and plastic forks. With the fire roaring in the fireplace and seven people laughing and talking, the house seemed almost like normal. Trish passed around the cake someone had sent for dessert and refilled coffee cups from a thermos. They'd thought of everything.

"Did you pick up the sleeping bags and stuff?" she asked David under cover of someone's joke.

"Yeah, when I came up to take care of the fire."

"Good." Trish breathed a sigh of relief. When she'd left the house the living room looked like a bunch of third graders had had a sleepover.

"Can you believe these guys? They've got the generator running and the pump thawed out. Now we've gotta find where the lines are frozen."

David seemed like a different person than the one Trish had known early that morning. She was glad to see the load lifted off his shoulders for a while.

When all the men went back to work, Trish carried the phone into the living room and closed the kitchen door again to keep the heat in. Holding the receiver to her ear was like wearing an ice pack. She dialed the hospital and asked for Hal Evanston's room.

"Where can they be?" she muttered after the third ring. "Come on, answer." After the sixth ring, the operator broke in.

"There doesn't seem to be any answer."

How'd you ever guess? Trish almost said aloud. Instead of screaming "Where's my dad?" like she wanted to, she bit her lip and said politely, "That's my father's room. Do you have any idea where he might be?" Her stomach clenched like it did just before the starting gate opened.

"Not for sure, but he could be down in X-ray. Can I leave him a message?"

"Please tell him or my mom that Trish called. We have a phone again but no lights yet. I'll call again later. Thank you." Trish clunked the phone back on the cradle. *What is going on there? Is Dad worse? Where's Mom?*

Her thoughts still at the hospital, Trish went out to the back deck to bring in wood for the fireplace. She brought in three loads before brushing the bark and sawdust off her sweater. She was just closing the glass fireplace doors when the phone rang.

"Dad?" She clutched the receiver to her ear.

"No, silly. It's Rhonda. What's the matter?"

"Dad's back in the hospital, and when I called they didn't know where he was." Trish slumped against the wall and slid to the floor.

"Oh, Trish, I didn't know."

"No one did. David took him in in the middle of the night. He looked awful when he left here. You know my dad. He had to work out in the cold to try to get the generator running. We don't have lights yet, and no water."

"We're basically in the same boat—we have water, but that's all. And a phone, as you can tell. Dad's gone on a business trip, so Mom and I are kinda stuck here."

"Do you need anything?"

"No. Just company. This sure wasn't the way I planned to spend my vacation."

"Tell me about it. The only races I'm winning are with Caesar, and I don't tell him where the finish line is."

Rhonda chuckled.

"And if I don't get a shower pretty soon, no one will dare come near me."

"Gross. I know."

"Well, I gotta get back down to the barns and start the afternoon chores. Let me tell you about hauling water to all these animals. I don't think they ever drink this much. They just like to see me slave."

"Is Brad there?"

"Yeah, he came this morning. And there's some guys from church helping David with the pump and stuff."

"Say hi to everyone. Hey, Tee. You decided what to do for New Year's yet?"

Trish groaned. "Nope. Haven't even thought about it. Let's hope we're thawed out by then."

Hanging up, Trish debated whether to call the hospital again. Even while trying to talk herself out of it, her finger dialed the number. This time it was answered on the second ring.

"Mom?"

"Trish, oh, I'm so glad we have a phone again. What about the electricity?"

"Not yet. How's Dad?"

"Sleeping. We just got back from X-ray. And they've been giving him alcohol rubs to cool him off. We don't know a lot yet."

"Oh." Trish paused. "How did Pastor Ron know we needed help?"

"I called him this morning to have us put on the prayer chain again. Why?"

"Some men showed up to help. They even brought hot lunch in their campers. I couldn't believe it when I saw them drive in."

Trish could tell from the sniff she heard over the line that her mother had teared up. All of them seemed to be on the verge of bawling most of the time lately.

Marge blew her nose. "Tell them thank-you from Dad and me. And Trish, call back this evening. I'm so worried about you two."

"You better worry more about Dad. We're okay. Brad is helping me, and David expects to have water pretty soon. Love you." This time Trish set the phone down gently. The hospital seemed so far away.

As she stood up, she heard water running. She dashed into the bathroom. The toilet tank was filling. She checked the faucet. Water!

Then the kitchen. Not yet.

"No water in the kitchen," she hollered out the door. "But the bathroom works."

By the time she and Brad had finished the chores, the men had left. They had running water all the way to the barn, and the house lines were clear. Thawing out the kitchen pipes had been the most difficult, she'd heard.

When Trish and Brad turned over the water tanks in the pastures after the cows and horses had a good drink, Trish said, "Maybe we can go skating tomorrow. Bet the pond is frozen solid by now."

Brad reached down and scratched Caesar's ruff. "I'll bring my skates. You need help with the chores in the morning?"

"Maybe. Ask David."

Trish didn't get a chance to talk to her dad before she crawled into her sleeping bag that night. He was sound asleep when she called. Her mother would stay the night in the hospital next to her husband.

David was snoring long before Trish could shut her mind off enough to even think about sleep. When she turned over and scrunched her pillow behind her head, she felt the bruise she'd gotten at the pump house. And her tailbone still hurt from the fall off the pickup. But worst of all, her dad wasn't better. Some vacation.

The dim light of morning made the living room seem even colder. This time David had let the fire nearly go out. Trish turned her head. On the sofa David looked like a huge blue slug buried in his sleeping bag.

Trish stood up, keeping her bag around her. She sat on the hearth to poke the coals. When she saw a bit of red, she balled up newspaper and added it with a few small pieces of kindling. Finally she leaned forward and blew on it, trying to get a flame started.

"Come on, you," she both begged and ordered. When flames licked the wood, she added larger pieces and finally two small chunks. Trish watched as the fire grew, huddled in her sleeping bag and wishing for something hot for breakfast. Like her mother's fresh cinnamon rolls, or scrambled eggs or—

She waddled back to her mattress of quilts and lay down again. Maybe they could at least go out for lunch.

The phone woke them both sometime later.

David beat her to answer it. "Dad's a bit better," David said across the receiver. "Temperature's down." He listened again. "Mom wants to know if you want to come and shower there and stay for lunch."

Trish rolled her eyes heavenward. "Thank you, God, for small favors."

David smiled. "I think she said yes."

When Trish stepped outside, she could hardly believe her eyes. The sun had finally woken up and turned the ice to diamonds that dazzled everywhere—dangling from tree branches, icicles, and fence posts. The "gems" glittered on bushes and sparkled off the pump house roof.

While the thermometer read only sixteen degrees, the sun would warm things up a bit. And better yet, the wind had died. Trish whistled, a sharp sound that brought an answer from the barn.

Trish skated her way down, deliberately choosing the icy patches to slide across. Arms waving, she almost took a tumble but righted herself. "No sense adding to my bruises," she informed a yipping Caesar. Spitfire progressed from a nicker to a full-blown whinny.

"All right, you guys, knock it off." Trish opened the top halves of stall doors as she made her way to the feed room. "You'd think I hadn't been down here in a week."

"Trish, come here!" David hollered from beyond the barn where he'd taken the truck to deliver water to the field stock.

"Now what?" She dropped the handles of the wheelbarrow and dashed around the corner. At the cow tank, David waved her on.

"Oh wow!" Trish stopped at the fence. A fountain of ice hid the trough, turning a fir tree into a free-form statue. A broken waterpipe had shot water into the freezing air, sculpting the glistening work of art.

"Well, at least I know where this pipe's frozen." David shook his head. "Better drag another trough down here. Why don't you go up and get the camera. Dad'll enjoy seeing this."

After the chores were done, Trish packed clean clothes and shampoo into her sports bag.

"You better bring towels too," David reminded her. "I don't think the hospital is planning on us."

Once they reached Fourth Plain Boulevard, the road was clear.

"I shoulda taken the chains off." David grimaced at the clackety-clack in the wheel wells. "When we get there, you go on up and I'll take them off."

Trish didn't mind being the first to shower, but the old panic tried to strangle her as she inhaled the hospital odor at the front door. She swallowed hard and took the elevator to the third floor.

Hal was asleep when she tiptoed into the room. Marge put down her knitting and rose to give Trish a hug. "You look as bright as that sun out there." She hugged Trish again. "Hal, wake up. The kids are here."

Trish picked up her father's hand. "Dad, can you hear me?"

Hal's eyes fluttered open. He squeezed Trish's hand lightly, a good sign. "Hi, Tee." His voice seemed lost in the beep and whistle of the tubes and machines surrounding him. A slight lift of one side of his mouth could have been a smile.

Trish wheeled on her mother and mouthed the words, "Is he going to die?"

Chapter
09

No, Trish. Actually he's better."

"He doesn't look it." Trish stroked the back of her father's hand with her thumb.

"I know. But he could be a lot worse." Marge rubbed the back of her neck with one hand. "Where's David?"

"He decided to take the chains off." Trish could hardly get the words past the lump in her throat. She wanted to fling herself across her father's chest and plead with him to wake up. To smile at her and tell her everything would be all right. To get up out of that bed and go home.

She tried to hold it back, but one tear escaped and rolled down her cheek. *Come on, Dad. Wake up! See, I'm here to take a shower. You have no idea how bad I need a shower.*

Hal squeezed her hand faintly, but Trish felt it. Clear to her bones she felt the love in that small squeeze.

"Guess I'll hit the shower before David gets up here." She stuck her head back out the bathroom door. "You sure they don't mind? About us using the shower, I mean."

Marge shook her head. "No. They all know how many are still without power and water."

When Trish stepped under the stinging hot spray, she felt the worries of the last few days slither off her shoulders and flow down the drain with the soapy water. She shampooed once and then lathered up again. The water beating down on her head and shoulders felt heavenly. Finally she turned her back to the spray and let it pound on her upper back.

A knock sounded on the door. "You gonna take all day?" David sounded more than just a bit grumpy.

Trish turned to let the water stream over her face again, then shut off the spray. She wrapped one towel around her hair and dried off quickly with another. She looked with distaste at her clean long johns but put them on anyway. It would be time for chores when they got home and getting colder again.

Dressed in a plaid shirt and jeans, with a towel still around her head, she popped out the door. "Your turn, Davey boy." She grinned at him. "And take your time."

"Feel better?" The rasp in her father's voice told of the effort it took for him to speak.

Trish dropped her boots by the chair and whirled to his bedside. "Now I do." Her grin brightened the entire room. "Amazing how good a shower can feel. I'll never take hot water for granted again."

Hal's smile made it to his eyes this time.

"Everything's pretty good at home." By the time she'd told him about the ice sculpture, his eyes had drifted closed again. But his hand still clenched hers.

When she felt his hand relax, Trish dropped into the chair to pull on her boots. She rubbed most of the moisture out of her hair, then brushed and combed it into some semblance of style. After stretching both arms above her head, she dropped them to the floor and finally wrapped them behind her legs and pulled so her forehead rested on her knees.

"Oh, to be able to do that again," Marge said.

Trish stood upright and shook out her shoulders. "I haven't taken the time to stretch lately. I'm really tight."

"Couldn't be because you've had anything else to do, could it?"

"Yeah, we've just been sittin' around." Trish wrapped both arms around her shoulders and pulled, rounding the kinks out of her upper back. "David gonna take forever? I'm starved."

"Look who's talking."

Trish heard the blow dryer in the bathroom. It wouldn't be long now.

A short time later they filed through the hospital cafeteria line. Trish felt like having one of everything. From the looks of David's tray, she was sure he had. "You gonna eat *all* that?" She stared at him in mock surprise.

"Just watch me."

God, let there be lights, she pleaded as they neared the farm drive a while later. But when Trish opened the sliding glass door, it didn't take a genius to know that her prayer hadn't been answered yet. Even the living room was cold because the fire had gone out. *Back to the real world.* She sighed at the mess scattered about: sleeping bags, blankets, clothes, dishes. *Well, at least we have running water. Even if it is cold.*

While David started the fire again, Trish picked things up and put them away. She stacked the bedding by the sofa. "How come this house feels so empty when Mom and Dad aren't here?"

David shrugged. "Beats me."

Another night without lights. The next morning the battery-operated radio promised a warming by the afternoon. And the weather delivered. A chinook wind followed the sun, and soon everything was dripping. The eaves, the trees, the frozen layer on top of the snow dribbled away. By the time the sun fell and took the temperature with it, Trish felt like spring had come.

When they walked into the house, the warmth hit their faces, and Trish could hear the familiar hum of the refrigerator.

"No hot dogs tonight!" Trish shouted, whirling down the hall to her bedroom. "And I get to sleep in my own bed!" She flopped back across it. "Fantastic!"

She could hear David in the kitchen listening to the answering machine.

"Call Rhonda," he told her when she entered the living room. "Maybe she'd like to work horses with you tomorrow."

"And maybe we'll have time to go skating. The ice won't melt that fast." Trish and Rhonda talked for half an hour.

" 'Bout time." David shook his head when she finally hung up the receiver. "Who ya calling now?"

"Brad. To remind him to bring his skates. We're going to have some fun for a change."

It was noon before the temperature rose above freezing, but not for lack of effort by the sun. The world glittered everywhere.

Trish hooked Gatesby to the hot walker while she rode Final Command. As Brad and David worked their way down the stalls, the piles of manure and straw grew, flavoring the air. Trish could hear them teasing each other as she walked the gelding back from the track.

"Who's next?"

"Let's do Gatesby. I want to enjoy the afternoon."

"Sorry I'm late." Rhonda trotted down the rise. "Dad's coming home tonight, so Mom had all kinds of extra stuff for me to do. D'you think he ever notices that all the furniture has *just* been polished? Or that the shower was scrubbed? All he cares about is Mom's home cookin'.'"

"So she's doing some baking?"

"Yep. And I brought you all some." Rhonda pulled a packet of caramel rolls from inside her jacket. "I even kept them warm for you."

Trish pushed her horse's nose away when he tried to take a bite of her roll. "No way. This is for me."

"Tell your mom thanks." David wiped his mouth. "That was great."

"Sure." Rhonda smiled. "Okay, who we doing next?"

"You take Firefly and I'll do Gatesby. Then we can finish with Spitfire and Dan'l." Trish talked while she stripped the saddle off Final Command and slung it over the door. She ran a hand over his chest and down his front leg. "He's not even warm." She patted the sorrel neck. "Are you, fella? If only that next joker were as easy as you."

Gatesby rolled his eyes when she unclipped him from the hot walker. "Just be cool!" Trish ordered with a snap of the lead. She led him back to the stall and cross-tied him for good measure. Even so, she was quick on the sidestep when his ears went back and his bared teeth reached for her shoulder.

When she had him saddled and bridled, she unsnapped the leads and led him out by the reins, her hand clamped right beneath his chin.

"Watch him." She let David take her place at the head. Brad cupped his hands to boost her up. Just as she started to spring up, the horse scrambled to the side. Trish floundered for her footing.

"You—" She couldn't think of a name to call him.

Gatesby perked his ears and looked around at her as if he wondered what could be the matter.

"Now stand still. You know better than that." This time when Brad boosted her, Trish landed in the saddle. She gathered her reins and settled her feet in the stirrups.

"Okay?" Brad looked up at her, concern in his eyes. "Maybe you should ride Dan'l and lead this clown."

"No. We'll be fine. He just needs a good workout. You ready, Rhonda?"

"Thanks, David." After the leg up, Rhonda settled her helmet in place and picked up her reins. "Maybe Brad's right."

For an answer, Trish nudged Gatesby forward. He walked flat-footed toward the track. "See, he's already gotten rid of all his meanness."

Trish kept a close eye on Gatesby's ears as they walked halfway around the track and then slow-jogged two more laps. Both horses snorted at the snow a couple of times.

Once Firefly crowhopped. Rhonda clamped her knees and laughed as she pulled the filly back down. "Thought you'd get away with something, didn't you?"

Gatesby twitched his ears and shook his head.

"How's your dad?" Rhonda kept Firefly even with Trish's mount.

"Mom says he's better but I can't tell. He can hardly talk on the phone." Trish glanced over at Rhonda. "Let's gallop but keep it slow."

Gatesby tugged at the bit but settled into a steady pace at Trish's command. The two horses matched stride for stride.

Trish let him out a bit and glanced over her shoulder at Rhonda.

With a loud whoosh, snow cascaded off a nearby fir tree and thumped to the ground.

Gatesby exploded. He leaped forward; his front feet slid in a patch of snowy mud. As he went down to his knees, Trish felt herself flying through the air.

A loud crack shattered the stillness as the top fence board crashed beneath her weight.

Chapter

10

Trish struggled to her feet.

"Are you all right?" Rhonda leaped off Firefly and, dragging the filly behind her, ran to her fallen friend. "Trish, are you hurt?"

Trish shook her head and blinked her eyes. "Just the breath knocked out of me, I think."

"There's blood on your face. You've been cut."

"I'm okay." Trish felt like she was talking through a tunnel. "How's Gatesby?" She leaned against the fence post she'd just missed in her flight.

Rhonda looked around. "He must have gone back to the barn. You want me to get David?"

"No! I'm okay. I'll—" Trish took one step and the pain blasted from her arm to her brain. "Yeah, you better get David. Tell him to bring the truck." Rhonda was on Firefly and off before Trish knew what was happening.

Trish blinked against the shock. She looked down. Her right arm dangled at her side. She could feel warm liquid oozing down her wrist. When she tried to raise the arm, she bit back the scream that ripped clear up from her toes. A deep breath to clear her mind knifed another pain through her side and chest.

She tried to concentrate on the ground in front of her. The sun that had been so welcome now blinded her, reflecting off the snow and ice.

You're not going to faint! she commanded herself. She shifted her feet. Agony thundered through her body and left her breathless. *Take a deep breath.* The side pain struck again. *Dumb idea!*

Brad leaped out of the truck before it stopped moving. "Trish! Trish! Oh no!"

She tried to smile around her gritted teeth. "It's both my arm and my side. You better get me to the hospital—quick."

"Call 911," David told Brad, trying to remain calm. "Trish, there's blood soaking your sleeve."

Brad jumped back in the truck and gunned it. Mud and slush sprayed up from the back wheels.

"I know. Remember where the upper arm pressure point is?" She swallowed the bitter taste at the back of her throat. "We're going to put our first-aid class to work." She spoke each word slowly, separately, as if hearing herself from a distance.

"Remember? Right above the elbow." She ground her teeth against the pain when David touched her arm. "Careful!"

"I can't, Trish!"

"Yes, you can. Just pinch it hard." She felt her knees begin to sag. She clutched the post with her left arm. "Can you feel the pulse?"

"Yes." David clamped his fingers around her upper arm. He wrapped his other arm around her so she could lean against him. "Would you be better off sitting down?"

Trish shook her head. "Is Rhonda taking care of the horses?"

"Yes."

Trish leaned her head on David's chest. Between his arms and the fence she felt secure.

"Maybe we could just go in ourselves. Do you think we could make it?"

"Tri-ish. How would I get you into the pickup?"

"Just toss me in." The fog seemed to be rolling in—everything looked hazy. "You know, like a bale of hay or a sack of feed."

The truck plowed to a stop in front of them and Brad leaped out. "Here, I grabbed some blankets and a sleeping bag. If she goes into shock, we're in real trouble."

"We're in . . . real . . . trouble . . . now," Trish murmured.

"Lay that sleeping bag out and then help me get her down," David instructed. "I can't let go of her arm."

Trish could hear David talking ever so faintly. The fog rolled in and out. "No-o-o!" She moaned as Brad lifted her as carefully as possible and, with David bracing her arm, laid her on the sleeping bag and covered her with the other blankets.

The siren wailed in the distance.

"Rhonda'll show 'em where we are," she heard Brad say.

"Mom's . . . really . . . gonna be mad." The pain wasn't so bad if she didn't move.

David knelt beside his sister, his fingers locked on the pressure point. "Don't worry about that."

"Mm-mmm."

They cut the siren and the ambulance pulled up beside the threesome. Trish could hear doors slamming and then a woman's smiling face was close to hers.

"Decided to take a tumble, eh?" The voice matched the smile.

"Okay, son." A man's voice carried the same degree of comfort. "You can let go of her arm now."

"My ribs too—I think." Trish barely lifted her head to see what they were doing.

"Just take it easy, Trish. I'm going to cut this sleeve off so we can look at that arm." The pain changed from pulsing to piercing. "Compound fracture of the right radial," he spoke to the woman jotting down the diagnosis. "Bleeding is slowing, we'll splint and bandage."

"Here." The woman slipped a length of tubing around Trish's head and adjusted the prongs in her nose. "A little oxygen is going to make this next part a bit easier for you."

Trish gritted her teeth so hard she thought her jaw would break. She wasn't sure whether it was tears or perspiration running into her ear.

When the arm was stabilized the medic said to her, "Now, you mentioned your ribs. Right side?"

Trish nodded. The lightest touch made her clench up again.

"Okay, let's get you on a board and brace your neck."

"Why? That doesn't hurt." Trish was puzzled.

"You've had what is called an ejection trauma. There could be spinal damage. We've got to take precautions. You don't mind, do you?"

Trish nodded.

With efficiency and precision the two picked up the corners of the sleeping bag and hoisted her onto a wheeled gurney.

"I'll follow you in the truck," David told her.

"Sorry we can't go skating," Trish said when Rhonda leaned over the gurney.

Rhonda bit her lip. "Just take it easy, buddy. We'll go skating another time." She patted Trish's good hand. "See you there."

"Rhonda," Trish called just above a whisper. "How's Gatesby?"

"Ornery as ever, and my shoulder will be fine after a week or two."

Trish smiled at her. "Thanks."

"Ready?" the woman asked.

Trish nodded and they slid the whole contraption into the ambulance.

"Okay," the woman spoke again. "I'm going to start an IV before we get rolling, so you'll feel another prick." She tied a rubber strap around Trish's left arm. "How about a fist now? There, you're an easy one." She taped the needle and tubing in place and started the drip. "Okay, let's roll."

No matter how carefully they drove, every movement vibrated in Trish's arm. The bumps in the road, slowing at intersections, then rolling the stretcher out at the hospital. Trish nearly fainted when they transferred her to an examining table in the emergency room.

She kept her eyes half closed to fade out the bright lights overhead.

"I'm going to get the rest of your clothes off," a nurse spoke as she began removing Trish's jeans before she could respond.

"It's a bad break, isn't it?" Trish forced herself to ask.

"Yeah, honey, you did it up royal this time." The nurse smiled down at her. "But don't you worry, we're gonna fix you up just fine."

Trish smiled back at the friendly dark face.

"Your mom's here." The nurse stepped back as Marge entered the room.

"I always knew I'd find you in the emergency ward someday." Marge kissed Trish on the forehead. She looked at the nurse. "How bad is she?"

A man brusquely entered the room. "Once we take care of that arm, she'll be fine. I'm Dr. Burnaby, and we've called in an orthopedic surgeon. We'll get some X-rays, then as soon as we get the operating room ready, we'll be on our way." He stepped to the head of the gurney and spoke to Trish, "How's that sound to you, young lady?"

Trish tried to smile around her tears.

With Trish flat on her back, the hospital took on a strange appearance for her. All she could really see were the ceiling tiles as they pushed the gurney through the halls.

When they entered another brightly lit room, they transferred her to another hard surface.

A man dressed in baggy green clothes took her hand. "I'm Dr. Johanson, your anesthesiologist. We're going to put you to sleep for a while, Trish. And when you wake up, your mother will be right here, okay?"

Trish nodded. *Do I have a choice?*

"Hi there."

Trish wished the voice would go away and let her sleep.

"Do you know what your name is?"

Trish forced her eyes open. "Tricia . . . Evanston." Her mouth felt like it was full of cotton. It hurt to swallow. "Can I have a drink?"

"Not yet, but here's an ice chip to suck on."

The bit of liquid helped. Trish fell back into the chasm she'd been drifting in.

"Welcome back." Marge smoothed the hair back from Trish's brow.

"Hi, Mom." Trish blinked her eyes open. This time the weights weren't so heavy. And the light didn't blind her.

Marge held a straw to Trish's mouth. "I think a drink will make you feel lots better."

Trish nodded as she sucked on the straw. "How come my throat is so dry?"

"From the anesthetic and the tube they put down your throat during surgery."

"How's my arm?"

"They had to pin and plate the bones back together. You have stitches where the broken bone pierced your arm and where they put the pin in."

Trish thought a moment. "That's why I was bleeding, huh?"

"Yes. You cracked a couple of ribs too, so you probably won't want to laugh much for a while. Oh, and they put two stitches in that cut on your chin."

"How come I'm so cold?"

"Could be that ice pack around the cast on your arm. Here, let me put another pillow under it so you won't feel the cold so much. And I'll get another blanket."

Trish felt her eyes drooping again. "Won't be riding for a while, right?"

"Right." Marge patted her daughter's cheek. "You sleep and I'll go tell your dad how you're doing. I love you, Trish."

Trish smiled. "Me too. Tell Dad I'm okay." She didn't even hear her mother close the door.

The next twenty-four hours passed in a blur of pain, sleep, ice, faces coming and going—and thirst.

"Trish, you have company," she heard her mother's voice as if in the distance.

She blinked till she could see Rhonda, Brad, and David surrounding her bed. "Hi, guys."

Marge placed the straw in Trish's mouth again and she drank deeply.

"Boy, you sure scared us." Rhonda shook her head.

"Me too."

"We brought you something." Brad set a ceramic horse planter on her bedside table. Three helium balloons were tethered to the horse's neck with bright ribbons. Red carnations dominated the variety of plants in the planter.

"That's really cool. Thanks." Trish turned her head to look. "Mom, how do I make this bed go up, so I can see better?"

Marge pushed the button clipped to the sheet beside Trish's head. "Let's dangle this thing over the rail so you can see where it is."

Trish winced as the rising bed shifted her arm and ribs. "Guess I won't be running any races for a few days."

"Yeah, you were kinda hard on the fence too." David tapped her toe.

"How's Gatesby?"

"Sore, but he'll live to bite again."

"He already has." Brad rubbed his arm.

Trish started to laugh at the pained look on his face, but immediately decided a smile would do. "Please don't make me laugh. It hurts."

"Can I bring you anything else?" Rhonda asked when they got ready to leave a few minutes later.

"I'll call you if I think of anything. Thanks for coming." Trish pushed the button to lower her bed again. "Mom, when can I go see Dad?"

"I don't know. We'll ask the doctor when he comes in."

"They oughta put Dad and me in the same room. It would be easier for you." Trish felt her eyelids drooping again.

"Good idea. I'll be sure to ask. If I'm not here when you wake up, you know where I'll be."

Trish and her father went home together on January second.

"At last," Marge sighed as she leaned back in her rocker after everyone was settled. Trish lay back in the recliner. Hal was sound asleep in his bed. "What a way to start the New Year."

"Mm-mmm." Trish scratched her scalp. Her arm itched too, under the cast that extended from her upper arm to the palm of her hand. "Mom, how am I gonna manage at school?"

"It won't be easy. How are you at writing with your left hand?"

"Lousy. You saw how I did at eating." Trish wriggled her toes in her slippers. "And I haven't even tried to put real clothes on yet."

"We'll just have to take one day at a time. The doctor said it would be at least a week at home. Maybe I should go buy you a couple of sets of sweats. They'd be comfortable and you could use the bathroom by yourself."

Trish groaned. "I hadn't even thought about that."

"What color would you like? I'll get extra large tops so you can get them on easily and have plenty of room for the cast and sling."

"And I'll look like a dork."

"Mmm. Whatever that is. Why don't we go to the hairdresser tomorrow and get your hair washed. It would be a lot easier than the kitchen sink."

"Do people really live for six weeks without showers?"

"I'm sure they do."

One week later Trish stared into the dancing flames lapping at the logs in the fireplace. This had to go down as the worst Christmas vacation in history.

Two mornings later Trish stared in the mirror. *Good thing I don't wear a lot of makeup. I can't see myself putting mascara on with my left hand.* Her new forest green sweats made her look like a jock. *Maybe I'll start a new fad—the one-arm look.* The sling held the cast close to her body, and Marge had tucked the right sleeve into the armhole so it wouldn't get in her way.

"Come on, Trish, you're going to be late." David had just come up from the barn. "I'll take you."

"You going to be okay?" Rhonda asked when they met in front of their lockers.

"I've got to be." Trish leaned her forehead against her locker. "Rhonda, I never dreamed anything could be so hard. Having only one good arm is the pits."

At noon Trish called for her mother to come and get her. "I hurt so bad." She bit back the sobs; they only made her ribs hurt worse.

Chapter
11

You're late again."

Trish slammed her hair brush into the sink. It bounced out, knocking a glass bottle of hand lotion into the sink. It sounded like the entire medicine cabinet had come crashing down.

"What on earth? Trish, are you all right?" Marge tried to open the door. It was locked. "Trish?"

Trish propped her weight on her good arm and stared at the sink. "I—I'm fine, Mom." At least the bottle hadn't broken, but it *had* chipped a piece out of the sink enamel. She turned to unlock the door. Tears puddled in her eyes and ran down her cheeks. *Everything is so unfair!*

When Trish opened the door, she was looking straight at her mother. Trish sniffed.

"Can we talk about it?"

"No, I'm late. I'm always late because everything takes twice as long. Getting dressed, combing my hair, brushing my teeth. I couldn't even get the cap back on the toothpaste because I was dressed, and my arm was under my sweat shirt." Trish paused to blow her nose. "I can't even blow my nose right."

Marge followed Trish to her bedroom.

"And when I get to school, I can't open the door if I have books in my arm. I'm sick and tired of asking people to help me!" She dropped to the edge of her bed.

"Anything else?"

"Yes! It's been three weeks since I've ridden and the doctor said it'll be another three."

"Actually, I think you've done pretty well."

Trish glared up at her mother. "Right!"

"Trish, I know it's hard, but let's not fight about it." She handed her a tissue. "Here, I'll go write an excuse."

"Can't I just stay home?" Trish knew her question would be ignored.

You don't really want to stay home, her little voice whispered. *Remember how bored you got the week before you could go back to school?*

Trish stuffed her books into her bag, slung it over her shoulder, and grabbed her jacket with one finger. Marge helped her put it on. Trish slumped in the passenger's seat. *I wish I could at least drive!*

It had been a miserable three weeks. At first all she wanted to do was sleep because of the pain—then the boredom. She felt terrible, she looked terrible, and everything seemed too difficult—too hard to bother doing. At least if she stayed in her room she didn't have to impress anyone.

She tried to put on a good front at school, even managed to laugh sometimes. But it felt as if heavy plaster casts were stacked on her shoulders—like the one on her arm. Her arm still ached at times, especially by the end of the day. All she wanted to do when she got home was go to sleep.

"You comin' down to the stables to watch us work the horses?" Brad asked on the way home.

"No."

"But, Trish, it's about time—"

"I said no."

Rhonda leaned forward on the back of the car seat. "Maybe watching training would cheer you up, make you feel better."

"Thank you, Dr. Shrink." Trish gritted her teeth. "Just don't get on my case, okay?"

The remainder of the drive was silent.

Saturday Firefly was scheduled to run in the fourth race and Final

Command in the seventh. Genie Stokes had worked both of them and would ride in the races.

"Aren't you ready yet?" Hal asked after lunch. This would be his first time back at the track since Christmas. "I'm really looking forward to the races. See, the sun even came out just for us."

"That's nice. But I've got homework to do," Trish managed. "It takes me forever to write a paper, you know."

"Trish, go get ready," her father said sternly.

"No thanks." She left the table and headed for her bedroom.

Hal found her lying on her bed, staring at the wall. "I'm asking you to get ready and go with me."

"Please." Trish covered her eyes with the back of her hand. "I really don't feel up to going."

"All right. But this has gone on long enough, Tee. You and I are going to have to talk tonight."

Hal was worn out when he came home and went straight to bed.

I didn't think he was strong enough to spend all that time at the track, Trish thought indignantly.

At least he tried. Her nagger was becoming a permanent resident in her ear. *You've been—*

"Just be quiet!" Trish ordered. She flexed the fingers of her left hand to ease a cramp before picking up her pen again to finish her paper. It took real effort to form some of the letters. *Well, at least I can use Wite-Out. It's better than throwing a page away and starting over.* She blocked out the words that looked too bad and blew on the white liquid until it was dry. One thing she'd found handy was to fasten her paper to a clipboard. That way it didn't scoot all over when she tried to write.

Trish went to church the next morning under much duress. From the looks on her parents' faces when she asked to stay home, she didn't dare ask again. *But I don't have to listen,* she promised herself. *I don't think God cares anymore, so why should I?*

Everyone was happy to see Hal back. They reminded him of their prayers for him as well as for Trish. Gritting her teeth was getting to be a necessary habit. She got so weary of saying "I'm fine" when people asked "How are you?" that she went to sit in the car. *I should tell them how I really feel.* Her thoughts continued in a negative vein.

You want to know what I think? her nagger chimed in.

"No. Not really." Trish slumped lower in the seat.

I think you're just throwing a pity party—poor Trish.

"Easy for you to say." Trish wished she could put her hands over her ears in an attempt to drown him out.

"Stay in the car," Hal told Trish when they arrived home. "You and I are going for a drive."

"I—uh—I have to use the bathroom," Trish scrambled for a way out.

"Okay. I'll wait for you here." Hal settled himself behind the wheel. "Why don't you bring a couple of your mother's fresh cinnamon rolls? That should hold us till dinner."

"We'll be ready to eat about three," Marge said before shutting the door.

"Now, where would you like to go?" Hal asked when Trish returned to the car. Her mother had had to push her out the door.

"I don't care." Trish struggled with the seat belt.

"How about Lake Merwin?"

Trish shrugged.

"Want a milk shake in Battle Ground?"

"Not really." She chewed her bottom lip. "But if you want one . . ."

Trish looked out the window without really seeing the scenery. What she *wanted* to do was take a nap. Life was so much simpler when she was sound asleep.

She felt the car come to a stop. When she opened her eyes she could see the blue lake glistening in the winter sun. Hundred-foot-tall fir trees sighed in the breeze. She examined her fingernails.

"You haven't been down to see the horses much lately." Hal turned in his seat and picked up a cinnamon roll. "They miss you."

"It's easier not to."

"That's not like you, to choose the easiest way." He waited for an answer. When Trish remained silent, he continued. "Why don't you tell me what's bothering you?"

Trish shrugged.

"You're not eating."

"Guess I'm not hungry."

"Come on, Tee. Let me in so I can help you."

"Isn't it obvious?" Trish angled her body to face him. "I can't ride. I can't write. I'm clumsy. And when I bang into things, I hurt. I'm tired all the time. I—" She drew circles on her pant leg with her fingernail.

"Yes?"

"I feel ugly and stupid and I'm sick and tired of these sweats and . . ." She sniffed the tears back. "And I *hate* blubbering all the time and . . ."

"And?" Hal's voice was soft, gentle, the voice he used around the horses so they wouldn't spook.

"And . . ." Trish swiped her hand across her eyes. Her voice dropped to a whisper. "I'm scared." She raised her gaze to meet her father's. "Dad, I'm so scared."

Hal reached over and closed his hand over hers. "Scared of what?"

"What if my arm doesn't get better before the Santa Anita trip? What if I can't race or even work Spitfire before then? He'll be out of condition and won't have a chance down there."

"Anything else?"

"And you were so sick. I thought for sure you were going to die." Tears brimmed over and ran down her cheeks.

"Trish, I didn't even come close to dying."

"But you were so weak."

"Yeah, infection and lack of oxygen do that to me. I did a stupid thing, working on the generator in that cold. I should have listened to your mother and just bought a new one in the first place. I'm really sorry I put you all through the extra worry just because of my pride. Will you forgive me?"

Trish stared at him. "But it's not your fault."

"Trish, we aren't responsible for the things that happen to us, but we *are* responsible for the way we react to them. Take, for instance, your broken arm. Now, that was an accident, right?"

"Well, I should've been paying closer attention."

"Maybe. But we can *all* play the 'shoulda' game. It just doesn't get us anywhere. Just like I 'shoulda' stayed out of the cold. You can't change what has already happened."

Trish felt like one of the weights had been lifted from her shoulders.

"Now, about your arm healing. Is there any reason why it shouldn't heal?"

"No, I guess not."

"Have you been praying about it?"

She chewed her lip. "Sorta." She swallowed the word.

"Been a little bit mad at God, have you?"

"Well, if He won't help us, can't He at least just leave us alone?" The words spewed out, harsh and biting. "We pray and pray and still things go wrong. You're sick, I'm broken, the ice storm, the . . . the . . ." She huddled back in the corner by the door, appalled at what she'd said.

"Oh, Trish, I know things have been bad. But look at all the good things. Remember that blank book I gave you? One of the good things about a journal is that you can go back and read what you felt in both good times and bad. Jesus never promised us there wouldn't be any trouble, just that He'd carry us through it. I can't even begin to comprehend how bad things could be or might have been without Him."

Trish pointed to her casted arm. "I have enough trouble trying to keep up writing for school right now without adding another writing project."

"True, for now. But think with me of some good things."

Trish frowned. She licked her lips, stretched her neck. "Uh-h-h, the snow and ice are gone."

"What else?"

"You're better. But now it's time for another treatment and you'll be sick all over again."

"Maybe. But not for long. Keep going."

"I'm learning to be ambidextrous." A grin tried to escape the corners of her mouth.

"True. Who knows when that could come in handy?"

"The eagle I gave you for Christmas."

"True. That's a symbol for all time."

Trish drew in a breath that went all the way to her toes. "I've been pretty awful, haven't I?"

"Let's just say I'm glad this side of you doesn't come out very often."

Trish leaned her head back on the seat. "At least Mom hasn't had to worry about my riding."

"I think at this point she'd rather be worrying about your racing than your depression."

"Really?"

"Really. And, Tee, talking things over always makes you feel better. You don't have to carry the whole world by yourself." He started the car. "Let's go home for dinner."

David met them after they'd parked the car in front of the house. "The mare foaled sometime while we were gone. A colt, a real strong one."

"Come on, Trish. Let's go see him." Hal patted her hand. "And greet all your lonesome friends down at the barn."

The colt was nursing when they approached the stall. His tiny brush of a tail flicked back and forth while his mother watched the visitors carefully.

"He has four white socks and a diamond between his eyes that doesn't quite make a blaze. There's another tiny diamond on his muzzle. Wait till you see his face." David leaned on the door next to his father and Trish.

"So what do we name him?" Trish rested her chin on her forearm against the stall door. "Star Bright? Diamond Dan? Uh-m-mm."

"How about Double Diamond?" Hal looked at them.

"I like that. Double Diamond to win. And the winner of this year's Kentucky Derby is Double Diamond, bred and owned by Hal Evanston and ridden by Tricia Evanston." Trish fell into the cadence of a race announcer.

"Sounds good." David nodded. He slid open the bolt on the door and took a bucket of warm water in for the mare. "Easy, girl. You've done well."

Trish visited with each of her head-tossing, nickering, and whuffling friends. Even Gatesby seemed glad to see her. He didn't try once to take a nip. Spitfire draped his head over Trish's good shoulder and closed his eyes in bliss as she scratched his cheek.

Miss Tee hung back until Trish opened the stall door and slipped inside. She extended a handful of grain, and after lipping that, the filly allowed Trish to cuddle her.

"She almost forgot me," Trish moaned as they walked back up to the house. "Guess I better get down here every day."

The countdown till cast-off day began when Trish had two weeks left to go. Every morning she marked another square off on the calendar. And each day she reviewed the cards on her wall. Her father's latest addition was from Proverbs 17:22. *"A cheerful heart is good medicine."*

Trish reminded herself of that one when she felt the weights try to pile up on her shoulders again.

"Tomorrow, tomorrow, I'll love you tomorrow," Trish couldn't stop singing. The cast would come off tomorrow. After the visit to the doctor's office, she would be able to wear *real* clothes again. And take a shower. No more washing her hair in the sink.

The next morning in the doctor's office, the buzzing of the saw sent shivers up and down her spine. *What if he slips and cuts my arm while cutting through the cast?*

"Don't worry, Trish. I haven't cut off any arms yet," the doctor said, reading her mind. He turned off the saw and separated the two pieces of the cast.

"Yuck!" Trish looked from the stark white arm up to her mother and back again. "It looks terrible!"

"Let's get that X-rayed," the doctor said, inspecting the incision. "Then we'll see what happens next."

Trish laid her arm on the X-ray table. She stared at the grungy line around her thumb and across her fingers where she hadn't been able to scrub. She really had a scar too, right along the top of her forearm.

"Okay." The technician pushed open the door. "Got some good ones. You can go back up to the doctor's office and wait for him to read them."

Trish slipped her arm back into the sling with Marge's help. Visions of riding again filled her mind as they waited for the elevator to reach the right floor. And tomorrow she'd wear the new sweater she'd gotten for Christmas. And jeans.

"I'm sorry, Trish." The doctor studied the X-ray. "We're going to have to cast you again. That bone just isn't strong enough yet to take a chance on it."

Chapter 12

"Another two weeks?"

"I'm sorry, Trish." The doctor did look sorry. "But if you broke it again now, it would be a lot more than two weeks. We have to make sure that bone is healed properly."

Trish gritted her teeth and rolled her eyes toward the ceiling to keep the tears from falling. *There goes the next race for Spitfire. That's next week.* Despair clogged her mind.

"You said *at least.* Does that mean it could be longer?" Trish looked the doctor full in the face.

"Let's hope not. I'll put the cast back on today and we'll schedule another appointment in two weeks."

Trish brightened. "Can I ride anyway? If I'm careful?"

The doctor thought a moment, then shook his head. "You'd be taking a pretty big chance. Better wait. The two weeks will go by quickly."

"I'm sorry, Trish," Marge said on the way home. "I know how much you were counting on having the cast off."

Trish let the tears run down her cheeks. She didn't try to fight them back; she didn't mop them up. It was just too much.

One look at her face when she walked through the door and Hal knew the verdict. He put both arms around her and asked over the top of her head, "How long?"

"Minimum of two weeks," Marge answered for her.

"Okay." He drew Trish over to the fireplace and sat beside her on the hearth. "I know this is throwing you right now, Tee, but here's what I suggest. I'll call Genie Stokes tonight and ask her if she can come out here tomorrow afternoon. We'll try her up on Spitfire with you standing there to help control him. Maybe he'll listen to you."

Trish leaned over and pulled a tissue from the box on the end table. She blew her nose, wiped her eyes, and tossed the tissue in the fireplace. With each movement, she sat straighter, shoulders back and head up.

She took a deep breath and paused for a moment, thankful deep breathing didn't hurt anymore. *After all, two weeks isn't forever. I made it this far, I can go the distance.*

"What if we hooded him?" She thought for a long moment about her idea, her chin resting in her hand. She'd braced her elbow on her knee. "Maybe he'll be okay if I lead him around for a while."

"That's my girl." Hal patted her knee.

Trish called Rhonda as soon as school was out. "Bad news, buddy," she said. "I'm recasted."

"Oh no-o-o." Rhonda's moan echoed through the receiver. "How could they?"

"Real easy. He just wrapped that gooey stuff round and round and said, 'See you in two weeks.' "

"Can you ride anyway?"

"No. I tried that idea out on him but no go. Rhonda, I was so mad I felt like punching him or something. He's ruining my life! At this rate, the racing season will be over before I get back up on a horse. We shoulda made you ride Spitfire all along so he would allow someone else on his back."

"What're you gonna do?"

"Well, I'm *not* going to take a nap! I've got horses to groom and a filly to train. And Double Diamond is almost as cute as Miss Tee. Come on over."

"Can't. I have horses to work too, you know."

89

"I know. Just had to give you my *wonderful* news. Yuck!" Trish hung up the phone. *Will raise you up on eagle's wings.* Like a melting snowbank, the song trickled through her mind. She stopped in front of the mantel in the living room and stroked the carved feathers on the eagle's wing.

"Thank you for the healing going on in my arm," she whispered in prayer that night. "And in my Dad." She thought a moment. "And in my mind. Amen!"

Genie Stokes drove in the drive right after Brad dropped Trish off the next afternoon. Genie opened her door and stepped out. "Tough luck, Trish. I sure know how you're feeling."

"Come on in. I don't know where Dad is, but Mom probably has the coffeepot on. How've you been doing?" Trish led the way up the walk.

"Not bad now that the weather's cleared up. We were all really sorry to hear about your accident. You never know what will happen next in this crazy business. Hi, Mrs. Evanston. Mm-mm, it smells wonderful in here."

"Hal and David will be right back. You've got time for a snack if you'd like. There's coffee, hot chocolate . . ."

"Diet Coke, juice." Trish dug caramel off the wax paper and stuck it in her mouth. "And cinnamon rolls."

Down at the barn half an hour later, David saddled Spitfire and held him for Genie to mount. Trish stood right beside the colt's head, scratching his ears and explaining what they were going to do.

Hal boosted Genie into the saddle.

Spitfire snorted. He laid his ears back.

"Easy, fella, you don't mind what we're doing," Trish consoled.

Spitfire threw his head up, ripping the reins from Trish's hand.

"Get back, Trish!" Hal barked the order.

"Spitfire, no!" Trish clamped her good hand over the horse's muzzle. The colt snorted. His eyes rolled white. He jerked his head back, forcing Trish to stumble to the side. She went down on one knee, still trying to calm the horse with her voice.

"Trish, Trish," Hal muttered as he lifted her to her feet.

When Spitfire's front feet left the ground, Genie vaulted lightly to the dirt.

"Let's try the hood." Trish turned to get her father's reaction.

"We'll try it, but I don't think it'll do any good." Hal shook his head. "I just can't take the chance on his injuring someone."

Trish soothed the trembling horse. "Come on, fella, no one's gonna hurt you. You know we wouldn't do that." She led him around in a circle until he rested his head on her shoulder.

He was worse with the hood in place. He lashed out with both front and back feet as soon as Genie settled in the saddle. Nothing Trish said or did made any difference.

"That's it," Hal said. "I'll scratch him. Thanks for trying, Genie."

"Don't worry, Tee," Hal said at dinner that night. "The forced rest won't hurt him any. We'll think about a race in early March, just depends."

Yeah, Trish thought. *Depends on how my arm does. Why didn't I have Rhonda ride him once in a while when we were training him? Then we wouldn't have this problem.*

The countdown to cast-off narrowed to three days, then two and finally it arrived. But this time Trish wasn't so confident. The doctor had said the two weeks was minimum.

"I'm scared," Trish told Rhonda and Brad in the lunchroom. "I can't stand the thought of more time in this thing." She thumped on the cast with her left hand. "What if . . . ?"

"Knock it off." Rhonda took another bite of her tuna sandwich. "This is the day. After three-thirty you will be a free woman."

"That's it! Rhonda has spoken." Brad patted her on the head as he stood to take his tray back. "Your mom picking you up?"

Trish nodded. "Sure hope you two are right."

They were. The X-rays showed the bone had mended.

Trish winced as the doctor cut off the cast. That whirling blade was awfully close to the skin on her arm.

"Now, don't go falling off any more horses." The doctor grinned at her. "And take it easy on that arm for a while. You may still have occasional pain if you over-extend yourself." He handed her a red rubber ball. "Use this to rebuild those muscles. Just clench and release it. Start with about five at a time and work up."

"Thanks." Trish stuck her arm in the sleeve of her sweat shirt and zipped up her jacket with her right hand. She felt like she was floating out the door.

"You want to stop for a celebration sundae?" Marge asked as they got back in the car.

"Nope!" Trish shook her head emphatically. "I'm going home to take an hour-long shower and wash my own hair. Then I'll call Rhonda and tell her the good news."

Marge chuckled. "Hope the hot water lasts that long." They headed for home. "But remember, the doctor said to take it easy at first. I think that means no riding for a couple of days at least."

Trish refused to comment. Her mother's worrying would *not* take the spangle off this day.

The shower was everything she'd dreamed it would be. She stood with her back to the spray, enjoying the feel of hot water pounding on her neck and shoulders. She felt really clean for the first time in two months. When the water cooled, she turned off the tap and wrapped a towel around her head, drying off with another.

She could hardly find the mirror in the steamy bathroom, but she saw enough to compare her right arm to her left. It was definitely thinner. And all that dry, flaky skin? Yuck! She slathered on hand lotion, then studied the scar.

"Well, at least it'll shrink with time. And a suntan." She nodded at the grinning face in the mirror. "And *you* are going to California in five weeks—to get that suntan."

Back in her room she found she needed her left hand to snap the closure on her jeans. But now she had two hands that worked together to button her shirt and tie her shoes. She felt like cheering at the thought of being back in *real* clothes.

She squeezed on the red ball while she waited for Rhonda to answer the phone.

"Hello?"

Trish deepened her voice. "Rhonda Seabolt, you're talking to a free woman. This prisoner has dropped her chains."

"All right!"

When they hung up half an hour later, Marge extended a hand to pull Trish up from her place on the floor, propped against the cabinets. "Well, free woman, how about setting the table? Your dad and David are on their way up."

"What smells so good?" Trish lifted the lid on a steaming kettle. "You made spaghetti! Yum-mm." She stretched both arms above her head. "And this time I won't make such a mess eating it."

The next afternoon Trish headed for the barn as soon as she'd changed clothes. She dug carrots out of her pocket and fed each horse down the line, only spending a minute or two with each, until she reached Spitfire's stall, where he was cross-tied and already saddled.

"Hello, fella, looks like you're ready to go." She smoothed his forelock and scratched his cheek.

"Dan'l and I already galloped him a couple of rounds to take the edge off him. He's gotten real used to being led around the track." David joined her in the stall. "Are you sure you should be doing this?"

Trish just shook her head. Another worrier.

After the first lap at a walk, she loosed the reins enough to let Spitfire jog the next round. Two new unpainted boards in the fence replaced those she'd broken in her accident, making it easy to tell where she'd gone airborne.

"What a bummer," she said as she stroked Spitfire's neck. "If I *never* do something like that again, it'll be too soon." Spitfire's ears flicked back and forth, listening to her voice and checking out everything around them. "I don't know which is better, the shower yesterday or riding today."

Spitfire snorted.

"Yeah, you're right. This is better."

"No, it's too soon!" Marge slammed her hand down on the kitchen counter a week later. "Your arm isn't strong enough for you to race yet. Trish, this time I won't back down."

"But, Mom!"

"No. I don't care what you say. The answer is no!"

"Dad?"

Hal shook his head. "I'm afraid your mother's right."

"But other jockeys get back up with casts and braces and all kinds of things."

"It's different if you have to earn your living riding. You take more chances that way." Hal shrugged.

"But that's not the case here." Marge crossed her arms. "Give it at least another week."

"That's the day I ride for Bob Diego, on the mare he's taking to Santa Anita. I *have* to do that!"

"Okay."

Hal stroked his chin. "Think I'll put Gatesby in the third race that day. That'll give you two mounts and that's plenty for your first day back. Working everybody here will give you enough exercise in the meantime."

Gatesby was up to his usual tricks when they loaded him in the trailer on Friday night. He flipped David's baseball cap off his head and snorted with the first thud of his hooves on the ramp.

"Life is never dull with you around, is it?" Trish kept one hand on the horse's halter as David tied the knot and tugged it tight.

"Get over, horse." David slapped the bay's shoulder. Gatesby had swung his weight so David was pinned against the side of the trailer. He pushed and thumped him again before Gatesby moved over. The horse turned, looked over his shoulder, and nickered at Trish and David as they left the trailer.

"Same to you, you stubborn, ornery hunk of . . ."

"Now, David." Trish swallowed her giggle. "Remember what Dad says. Patience is a virtue."

"Yeah, patience."

Trish slid the bolt home after they raised the tailgate. She'd had a few names for Gatesby herself when her arm was casted.

Real, honest-to-goodness sun brightened the windy March day as Trish bagged her silks and packed her sports bag. Yellow daffodils lined the walk, nodding and bowing her out to the car. Caesar yipped and frisked around her, acting like a puppy on the loose.

"You have everything?" Marge asked as she slid into the passenger's side.

Hal grinned over his shoulder at Trish. "Of course she does. Portland Meadows, here we come. Tricia Evanston is back!"

And being back felt like a huge hunk of heaven. Trish couldn't stop grinning. She laughed when Gatesby tried to nip David in the saddling paddock and beamed at Brad when he took the lead rope. Flags snapped in the breeze and Mount Hood speared the eastern sky. Gatesby pranced for the surging crowd. He arched his neck, ears pricked forward. He was ready to run.

"You'll do great!" Brad gave Trish the thumbs-up sign when he passed the lead over to the handler at the gate.

The field of eight entered the starting gate easily. Trish gathered her reins. A few butterflies flipped around in her midsection, reminding her that they were still resident.

The gates swung open and Gatesby hesitated enough to put them a half a length behind the others. Trish kept him on the outside, giving him time to hit his stride.

"Okay, fella." She loosened the reins and leaned forward. "Let's make up for lost time." Gatesby stretched out. One by one he passed the field now strung out going into the turn. He pulled even with the third-place runner, then the second as they came down the home stretch.

The jockey on the gray in front went to the whip as they thundered down the last furlongs.

Gatesby pulled even with the horse's shoulder, then they were neck and neck.

"Go, Gatesby!" Trish shouted.

One more giant thrust and Gatesby pushed ahead to win by a nose.

"I think you just know how to stick your nose out straighter," Trish said as she let him slow for the turn back to the winner's circle. "You almost blew that one, you know."

Gatesby tossed his head and jigged sideways.

"Good job, Trish." John Anderson shook her hand and patted her shoulder. "I didn't think you were going to pull it off that time."

"I had my doubts too." Trish kept an eye on Gatesby's nose as they posed for the picture. "Watch it, Dad!"

Hal flinched away just in time. "You . . ."

"There aren't enough names to call him," David muttered as he clamped his hand on the reins. "Come on, horse."

Trish felt wonderful to be back in the locker room changing her silks. The familiar steamy liniment smell, someone singing in the shower, friendly greetings and "welcome backs," all combined to make her good mood even better.

She stroked the mare's neck after Bob Diego gave her a leg up in the saddling paddock.

"You know how Marybegood runs," Bob said. "She's really ready and this is a good field for her. I think you should win it."

"We'll do our best." Trish patted the mare's bright sorrel neck again. "Won't we, girl?"

Trish let Marybegood run easily in third place after a clean break from the gates. With a half a mile to go, she moved up into second and encouraged the mare to stretch out after they rounded the turn. Within two lengths they caught and passed the leader.

Suddenly Marybegood stumbled.

Trish caught herself, one foot out of the stirrup and her left arm clamped around the mare's neck.

At the same time, she tried to keep the mare's head up so they wouldn't go down and be trampled by the hind runners.

Marybegood refused to put any weight on her right hind leg. As soon as the last horse passed them, Trish vaulted to the ground.

"Easy, girl, help'll be here soon." She ran her hand down the leg where swelling had already started.

The horse ambulance pulled up beside them.

"I think it's broken," she told them, hardly able to keep the tears from her voice.

Chapter
13

I'm so sorry, Bob," Trish said for the third time.

"Trish, look at me." Bob Diego grasped her chin between his thumb and forefinger. "This break is not your fault. There was nothing you could do; these things just happen."

"Maybe if I'd . . ."

"No." Hal placed a firm hand on her shoulder. "You couldn't have done anything differently. You stayed aboard and kept her from going down."

"Will you have to put her down?" Trish bit her lip.

"I think not. The vet can pin it, and while she won't race again, she'll be an excellent brood mare."

Trish breathed a sigh of relief. "Good. I'll see you after I change, Dad." She turned back. "Where's Mom?"

"In the car." Hal raised his eyebrows.

And not very happy, I'll bet, the thought flitted through her mind.

Hal waited for Trish outside the dressing room. "Bob offered us his horse van for the trip to Santa Anita," he said as soon as Trish met him. "But we'll have a lot of talking to do to make this work."

Trish nodded. "I know."

Conversation never had a chance at life when they got to the car. It didn't take a genius to tell a storm was coming.

Marge whirled on them as soon as they entered the house. "How many times have I said that racing is just plain dangerous? Today it was the horse that got hurt, but you could have been injured again. Hasn't all you've been through taught you anything?" She paced back and forth, her arm slicing the air as she spoke.

Trish glanced at her father and understood his signal. She kept her mouth closed. If only she could have shut down her brain too. Her thoughts whirled like leaves caught in a feisty fall wind.

You're not being fair. I wasn't hurt this time. You can't keep me safe by preventing me from racing. Mom, quit worrying!

Hal stepped in front of Marge to stop her pacing. He put his arm around her and Marge dropped her head on his shoulder.

Trish huddled in the corner of the sofa.

"It's okay." Hal rubbed Marge's back and brushed the hair back from her face. "That was scary for all of us, but Trish did a good job out there. She's an excellent rider, you know that."

Trish went over to the recliner for the box of tissue and handed it to her mother. "Come on, Mom. Maybe it was all those guardian angels that kept me from falling."

"Somebody sure did." Hal led Marge to the sofa and sat her down, then sat beside her.

"I don't want you to go to California," Marge stated flatly after blowing her nose.

"I know." Hal nodded. "But let's talk about that later."

Much later, Trish finished the thought. *And I don't even want to be around for it.*

On the Thursday program, Trish had only one other mount besides Firefly. This would be the filly's last race before Santa Anita. A drizzle blew in veils across the track as the filly danced her way to the starting gate. She broke clean and ran easily, holding the lead until about three quarters of the way around the track.

Trish felt Firefly falter.

Another horse caught them, driving hard on the outside.

Firefly strained forward, throwing herself across the finish line.

"And that's a photo finish, ladies and gentlemen," the announcer's voice boomed over the PA system.

Firefly seemed to be walking gingerly. Trish cut short any extra circling and stripped off her saddle outside the winner's circle.

"Something's wrong." She stooped to run her hands down the filly's front legs. They were already hot.

"All I can say, girl, is you got heart," Trish murmured to Firefly as they posed for the picture.

"I think she won that by a whisker," Hal said. "I'll meet you down at the barn, David."

Trish took a show with her next mount. As soon as she could get away, she trotted across the infield to the back lot.

"It's shins again," Hal answered her question as they met in the filly's stall. "I'm afraid that does it for her this season."

Another Santa Anita scratch, Trish thought. *Are we caught in a string of bad luck, or what?*

She dreaded the Sunday night family meeting that week. And it wasn't because of her grades. The big discussion would be Santa Anita.

In church that morning her prayer was simple. *Make my mom let us go. Help her to stop worrying so much. Please, please, please!*

Trish spent most of the afternoon on her homework so the evening would be free. She set the table without being asked and volunteered to make the salad.

Marge gave her a one-raised-eyebrow look and shook her head.

Trish caught the edge of a smile as her mother turned to stir the gravy. She tried to think of something to say while they worked together in the kitchen, but everything seemed forced or fake. Like, *You know, Mom, how would you like to go to Santa Anita with us?* Or, *How do you feel about your sick husband and young daughter driving that huge van all the way down I-5 to Southern California?* But Trish already knew the answers.

Dinner was quiet. Trish finally pushed her half-eaten roast beef and mashed potatoes to the side.

"You feel okay?" Marge glanced from Trish's face to her plate and back.

"I'm fine."

Sure you are, her nagger chuckled in her ear. *Your stomach is doing flip-flops and your hands are shaking. But you're just fine!*

"Why don't we have dessert later?" Hal shoved his plate toward the center of the table so he could prop his elbows in front of him. "No, leave the plates." He laid a restraining hand on Marge's arm as she started to rise.

He cleared his throat. "Okay, let's begin the discussion. David, I'd like to hear from you first."

"I think we should go for it. Brad and I can handle things here while you and Trish are gone. We don't have any of our horses racing that week so it should be easy." He smiled an apology at his mother.

"Trish?"

"I won't miss much school 'cause that's spring-break week. If we don't go, we don't have much of a chance for the Kentucky Derby, and who knows when we'll have a three-year-old as good as Spitfire again? I think he—we deserve the chance."

"Marge?"

Marge took a deep breath. "I know all your arguments. I know this race is important to Runnin' On Farm as a business. I know how strong you are and how quickly you can get sick." She grasped Hal's hand. "Mostly I know how terrified I am that something terrible will happen. Every scene imaginable has played itself over and over in my head."

Hal covered her hands with his.

She continued. "And I know that the only thing holding you back is your concern for my feelings." She looked around the table, holding the gaze of each for a few intense seconds. "So I say, when do you leave?"

Trish leaped from her chair, slamming it back to the floor in her exuberance. She threw her arms around her mother. "All right, Mom! You won't be sorry, I just know you won't."

Marge hugged her daughter back. "I'm probably already sorry, but let's get on with the planning."

Trish picked her chair up and sank onto it. *We're going! Please, God, with no more hold-ups. We're going to Santa Anita!*

"Thank you, dear. And I had all my arguments so carefully planned out." Hal smiled at her.

"Way to go, Mom." David patted her arm. "You and I can hold down the fort just fine."

"The way I see it," Hal continued after taking a deep breath and letting it all out, "is that we'll leave early Saturday morning and stop in Yreka that night. We'll drive to Adam Finley's farm at Harrisburg on Sunday and stay over there to give Spitfire a rest. Tuesday we'll drive on down to Arcadia. That way we can walk him Wednesday to get him and Trish used to the track, breeze him Thursday, and jog Friday. Then Saturday's the race. We'll start home Sunday morning, be back here by Monday night. What do you think?"

"All right!" Trish bounced on her chair.

"Well, *I* think we better get some motel reservations made and make sure you have all you need." Marge counted the days on her fingers. "We only have five days to get ready. Trish, how many mounts do you have this week?"

"Two Thursday and one Friday. Looks like I'll cancel the one for Saturday."

"Good enough. Anything else?" Hal looked at each one of them. "Then what's for dessert?"

"Thank you, thank you, thank you," was all Trish could say that night in her prayers.

🐎

The week took wings and flew off before anyone could catch it. On Wednesday Hal brought the horse van home and took Trish out for a driving lesson. He taught her about the extra gears with a floor shift and double-clutching to make down-shifting smoother. They drove high in the hills above Hockinson where Hal had her stop and start again in the middle of a steep grade.

"I've always said you were a natural driver." Hal patted Trish's knee as her shifting became smoother and her ear tuned to the sounds of the engine. "I think we better find you a good pillow though so you can relax. Even with the seat all the way forward, you're straining a bit."

"Need longer legs," Trish said as she turned the van back into their driveway. "But I like driving this rig."

"Hopefully you won't have to." Hal pocketed the key when she turned off the ignition. "But we're prepared, just in case."

They loaded the van, all but the horse, on Friday night. Hal had slept in the afternoon and been coughing at dinner, but he assured everyone it was just a tickle in his throat.

"Don't worry," he said. "I've packed extra lozenges and even anti-biotics if I need them. Really, I'm fine."

Trish could see worry lines deepen on her mother's brow, but Marge didn't give voice to her fears this time.

Trish was afraid she'd have a hard time going to sleep that night, but she conked out right after her head hit the pillow. The next sound she heard was her alarm. It felt like she'd just fallen asleep.

"Breakfast's ready," Marge called as Trish gave her hair a last brush through. She tugged her rust sweater in place and winked at the smiling face in the mirror. *On to Santa Anita!*

There was a knock on the front door just as she headed for the table. It was Brad and Rhonda.

"We had to see you off." Rhonda threw her arms around Trish. "Oh, I wish I were going too."

"Pull up your chairs," Hal said from his place at the head of the table. "You're just in time."

Marge flipped more bacon in the pan. "You can start with your juice. Two eggs for you, Brad? Rhonda?"

"We didn't come for breakfast." Rhonda hesitated for just a moment.

"Have you eaten yet?" Hal asked. At the shake of her head, he added, "Then sit down. You know you're always welcome here."

An hour later they were loaded and ready to roll. Spitfire, blanketed and legs wrapped, walked up into the van like a pro. Trish hugged her mom, then David, Rhonda, and Brad. "You guys are something else. Thanks for coming. And, Mom, I'll call you tonight as soon as we stop." Trish's send-off was her mother blowing kisses in spite of her tears, and the other three with their fists raised for victory.

"Eight-thirty, not bad," Hal said as he wheeled the van out onto the county road. "Once we get on the freeway, how about pouring me a cup of coffee?"

The sky was overcast but the rain held off while they drove down the Willamette Valley to Eugene. Trish and her father talked about all kinds of things: her school, gossip at the track, raising and training Thoroughbreds. But by noon, Trish could tell her father didn't feel well. His cough became more frequent and he rubbed his forehead repeatedly.

They stopped in Roseburg for lunch and gas.

"You're looking a bit gray around the edges," Trish said when she sat opposite him in the booth at the restaurant.

"Feeling a bit gray too." Hal rubbed his head again. "All I need is a bug now. Well, I've taken some stuff that should help. What do you want for lunch?"

Trish watched him carefully while she ate her BLT. After he paid the check, she asked, "Do you want me to drive?"

"No, I'll be okay. The break helped."

They opened the rear door of the van to check on Spitfire. He stood drowsing in the deep straw.

"You sure look peaceful," Trish said. "See you later."

By the time they reached Grant's Pass, Hal admitted to needing a break. They stopped at a rest area beside the freeway, and after a visit to the rest rooms and a walk around to loosen up, Trish took over the driving. Hal propped a pillow behind his head and immediately fell asleep.

Trish hummed to herself as she drove along about sixty. She felt herself part of the parade of semis carrying their cargo toward the southland. When she left Ashland, she glanced at her watch. They should make Yreka easily by six o'clock.

She joined the semi-rigs as they shifted down on the snaking four-lane highway up toward the California border and the Siskiyou Pass. Wisps of fog obscured the forest-clad peaks and filled the valleys. As they climbed, the fog closed in on the highway and she had to turn on the lights.

Trish glanced over at her father. *Should I wake him up and let him know what's happening?* She shook her head. *No, he needs to rest so we can keep going.*

A few miles later, just after the check station south of the California border, a fog curtain dropped across the highway. All she could see were the red taillights of the rig in front of her.

Chapter 14

W hat do I do now?" Trish whispered.

Possibilities chased each other through her mind. She could pull over and wake her father up. *No, he needs to sleep. If he hasn't wakened by now, he must be sicker than he said.*

She could give in to the tears of fear and frustration that pricked at her eyelids. *No, if I'm having a hard time seeing now, what would it be like through tears?*

She could pray. *I'm already doing that!*

She could do just what she was doing—follow the taillights in front of her. When it came right down to it, that was the only avenue as far as she could see—she smiled grimly to herself—which wasn't very far.

Father, I sure need your help now. Please take care of us.

As the miles slowly passed, Trish had no idea where they were. She was concentrating so hard on the road that she missed seeing the signs, shrouded as they were in the soupy fog. She blinked repeatedly because squinting to see made her eyelids tired—and ache.

Fear slipped in the window and pinched her shoulders. It snaked down and stirred up the butterflies roosting in her stomach. Fear wrapped around her hands and bonded them to the steering wheel.

Trish swallowed hard. Her throat felt dry. She needed a drink of water, but she didn't dare take her eyes from the road to reach for the water bottle.

God, help me!

Singing helps. For a change her nagger was being helpful.

Trish began with "Eagle's Wings" and followed it with every song she'd learned in Sunday school, Bible camp, and youth group. She sang "Jesus Loves Me" and all the verses to "Michael, Row the Boat Ashore."

As her mind tried to remember the words to all the songs, her hands kept the truck on the road, still following those wonderful taillights.

She sang Bible verses, and when she ran out of ones she knew, she sang her favorites over again.

When fear raised its ugly head, she shoved it down again with the name of Jesus. Just repeating His name kept her chin from quivering.

Trish wanted to check the time but couldn't take her hands from the wheel to turn on the light. *How much farther, God? Shouldn't we have been there long ago?*

But there was no place to turn off, and she didn't dare lose those taillights.

If the truck pulls off, I'll stop and ask him where we are. Having a plan of action helped. She picked up where she'd left off on "Jacob's Ladder."

The trucker flashed his turn signal for a right exit. Trish did the same. She glanced up just in time to see Yreka on a sign and missed the rest. They stopped at a stop sign and she could vaguely see the word Motel outlined in large letters up ahead. When she pulled up in front of it, she read the sign: Traveler's Rest.

"Where are we?" Hal raised himself upright and peered out the window. "Good, Tee. You found the right place. Did you have any trouble?" He stared out the side window. "How long has the fog been this bad?"

"Forever." Trish leaned her forehead on her hands still clutching the top of the steering wheel.

"Why didn't you wake me?"

"I figured if you were sleeping that hard, you must need it. So I followed some trucker's taillights. He turned off here. Do you think God uses truckers as guardian angels?"

"I'm sure He does, Tee. I'm sure He does."

Trish turned on the interior light. "Nine. Why do I feel like it's about one in the morning?"

"Could be four hours of the most miserable driving conditions in the world. You hungry?"

"Starved." She reached for the water bottle. After a long drink, she wiped her mouth on the back of her hand. "Boy, I needed that."

"Why don't you feed Spitfire while I go in and check on our room?" Hal stepped down from the truck. "Do you have any idea where that trucker went?"

"He's parked at the edge of the parking lot."

Trish watched her father cross the asphalt. The fog glistened in the lights of the motel. She could barely see the truck.

Carefully she flexed her fingers. Her arms ached from clenching the muscles for so long. She opened the door and stepped down. Spitfire nickered. She heard him moving about.

"Okay, fella. I'll get you some dinner, then it's my turn." She stuck a flashlight in her rear pocket, measured grain, and separated a couple leaves of hay from the bale. When she opened the people entrance on the side of the van, Spitfire greeted her with both a head in her chest and the soft whufflings that barely moved his nostrils.

"Hey, I only need three hands, now get back, you big goof." She put the hay down and pulled the flashlight from her pocket. By its beam, she set the bucket in the manger and dumped the hay in the sling. A quick flash showed her an empty water bucket.

Spitfire needed attention more than feed. Only when she'd rubbed his face, scratched his ears, and stroked his neck did she finally shove him toward the feed. He reluctantly left her to begin his dinner.

"I'll get you some water." He left the feed bucket and followed her to the door. "No, now get back. You'll get out after you've eaten."

"We're right in front," Hal said, meeting Trish after she'd filled Spitfire's water bucket. "Number 106." His cough sounded as if it were painful.

"Did you tell that trucker that he was a guardian angel?"

"Yeah. He said that was the first time anyone had *ever* called him an angel—of any kind. But he was glad he could help. Says he drives this freeway every other day but even he gets confused in the fog."

"Why don't I run over and get us some hamburgers?" Trish pulled her small bag from behind the seat. "And you get out of this cold, damp air."

"Okay." He handed her some money.

"You want anything special?"

"A chocolate shake?"

"Now, how come I'm not surprised?" Trish gave him her bag. "I'll be right back."

Hal was already asleep on one of the beds when she returned with two sacks of food.

"Dad, come on, you gotta eat." Trish shook him gently.

Hal rubbed his eyes and pulled himself up against the headboard of the bed. "Thanks. I can't get over how sleepy I am. Must be that medication I'm taking. While it helps clear my head, it puts me right out."

After they ate, they went back outside and lowered the ramp. Spitfire clattered down the ramp, eyes rolling and ears pricked forward. He danced in a circle around Trish, snorting at the truck, the fog, the shadows, anything that caught his attention.

"You want me to take a lead too?" Hal asked.

"No, you get inside. We'll be fine. He'll settle down pretty quick." Trish clucked to Spitfire and the two of them trotted off around the parking lot. When Trish started to puff, she pulled him down to a walk.

"I'm not used to the altitude," she told him. "And besides that, I haven't done any running for a long time." Spitfire nodded his agreement. Before long he walked with his head drooping over her shoulder.

"I can't carry you and me too." Trish pushed him away. "So let's get you to bed."

Spitfire snorted and back-pedaled as soon as his front feet struck the metal ramp. "Oh, no you don't." She led him around in a tight circle, and this time he walked right in. Trish gave him a last hug and shut and locked the door. When she tried to slide the ramp back on its rollers, it was too heavy.

"Now what?" She studied the ramp. As soon as the thought hit, she spun and headed for the office. "Could you please help me?" she asked the man at the desk. "I can't get the ramp up and Dad's already asleep."

"Be glad to." He followed her outside and together they slid the ramp home. "You sure were lucky to make it this far in that fog."

"Yeah, thanks to that trucker." Trish pointed across the parking lot. "He turned out to be my guardian angel tonight."

"Oh. Well—ah—good night then."

Trish shrugged and raised her eyebrows. *Maybe he doesn't believe in guardian angels.* But she sure did.

Hal had left her a note. "I called home. Said we hit a little fog. Sleep well."

No problem there.

It was still foggy in the morning, but after feeding Spitfire, cleaning out the manure, and trotting around the parking lot a few times, they got themselves some breakfast and back on the road. Hal drove, nowhere near as slowly as the night before, until they reached Redding and the end of the fog.

Trish took over the wheel there. It wasn't long before the sun beating on the windshield made her roll down the window. After a morning Coke break, she took off her sweater and let the warm sun shine on her bare arm, resting on the door.

Hal slept some more, and when he woke he pointed out the rice fields, the almond and walnut orchards. They stopped for lunch outside of Sacramento, the state capital.

"We aren't too far from Adam's now, only a couple of hours. No need to take Spitfire out." Hal swung down from the truck cab. "But make sure he has water."

The van was plenty warm, so Trish opened all the vents and removed the horse's blanket. Spitfire shook hard, making the whole van shudder. She refilled the water and left him with a last pat. The colt whinnied as if being deserted.

Trish laughed as she joined her father. "Feel that sun? I just know I'm gonna get a tan. Everyone'll be jealous. Ha!"

"Just don't get burned. You're not used to summer sun yet."

"Am I ever? You know what they say about us Washingtonians: We don't tan, we rust."

Trish couldn't believe her eyes when her father drove into his friend's horse farm. "Has this guy got bucks or what?" She stared at the Spanish architecture. The house, the barns all looked like pictures she'd seen of haciendas in old Mexico, with white stucco walls and red tile roofs. Blooming scarlet roses lined all the boundary fences. She could see mares and foals in one section and what looked like yearlings in another. The paddocks seemed to go on to the horizon.

A pair of huge Rottweilers announced the truck's arrival.

"Don't worry about them, my friend." The smile on their host's face was about as wide as the man was tall. He'd obviously been a jockey at one time but now had gained a bit in the girth. "Hal, I can't believe it's really you. How many years has it been?"

"Too many." Hal shook the proffered hand. "Adam, this is my daughter, Trish. Trish, after all the stories you've heard about him, you finally get to meet Adam Finley."

Trish felt her hand taken over by the warm grasp of her father's friend. His blue eyes twinkled, as if the leprechauns of his homeland lived inside.

"Let's be getting that horse of yours settled, and then I'm sure you'll appreciate the cold drinks my wife has ready up at the house. And, Trish, in case you'd be interested, we have a swimming pool out to the back."

Trish looked at her father, her eyes wide, and shook her head. *I could learn to like this*, she thought.

Trish led Spitfire down the ramp and around an open area a few times before leading him into a roomy stall, apart from the other occupied stalls.

"I'm thinking all your hard work has paid off." Adam nodded his head. He scratched Spitfire's cheek and ran his hands over the sleek shoulder and down the colt's legs. "And you say he goes as good as he looks?"

"He does."

"Well now, and I sure am looking forward to seeing that race on Saturday."

"You'll come all the way down there to see us run?" Trish couldn't keep the amazement from her voice.

"Wouldn't miss it." Adam tucked her hand in the crook of his arm and led them toward the sprawling house. "Now, let's go get those drinks I promised you."

The next thirty-six hours passed like a dream. Trish could have listened to Adam and her father swap stories all night, but finally she went to bed.

After walking Spitfire around the three-quarter-mile dirt track a couple of times, then turning him loose in a grassy paddock, she spent the rest of the morning lying by the pool. And playing in the pool. And most of all, lapping up the sunshine. She *did* take heed and slather on the sunscreen. Her dad was right, she couldn't afford a bad burn right now.

When the time came to leave, she felt like she'd known Adam and his wife, Martha, all her life. "Maybe they'd like to adopt me as a grandkid," she said to her father as they drove out the driveway on Tuesday morning. "What a place! And what horses!" She sighed. "I sure would love to ride for him sometime."

"You never know." Hal smiled at her. "I have a feeling that someday you'll have your pick of any mount, at any track."

"You really think so?"

Hal nodded.

Trish re-ran every moment of their visit as they drove on south. What a treat it had been.

Oil derricks at Bakersfield looked like giant grasshoppers nodding above the land. She couldn't get enough of the palm trees, and when they took time for lunch, the riot of flowers around the restaurant stopped her in her tracks.

"Mom would love those," she said. "What are they?"

"Don't ask me." Hal shook his head as he held the door open for her.

He laughed at her awe when they drove the Grapevine on their approach to Los Angeles. Freeways in every direction blew her away.

"Now watch for the signs for Pasadena," Hal told her. "I have to keep my eyes on the traffic."

"I'm sure glad you're driving and not me."

The Pasadena freeway wound up through rough hills, covered with bushes but no trees. A yellow-gray haze hung in the valleys and blurred the mountaintops.

"That's good old L.A. smog," Hal said in answer to her question. "Some days are clear and others are—well, others are downright awful."

They passed exit signs for Pasadena and Trish saw one for the Rosebowl.

"Now watch for Arcadia and the Baldwin Avenue exit. There should be a sign for Santa Anita Park."

"There it is!" Trish exclaimed a few minutes later. As they left the freeway they wound through a beautifully wooded area.

"This used to be all one estate," Hal said. "But now this area is a well-known arboretum and park. See, there are the stables off to our left."

Trish sat with her mouth open as they rounded the street into acres of parking lots. The grandstand soared green and enticing above the palm trees ahead and to the right.

"This place is . . . is . . ." She turned to stare at her father. "It's humongous!"

"Baby, you ain't seen nothin' yet."

Chapter
15

Brian Sweeney's stables?" Hal asked the gate guard.

"Straight ahead, number 26, third barn on your right." The uniform-clad man pointed up a dirt road with low-roofed green barns butting against it. As they drove up the road, Trish could look down lanes leading to the track or deep-sanded walking areas that separated each long barn.

"This is beautiful," Trish whispered, trying to see everything at once.

Since they arrived in the late afternoon, the day's program was nearly over. A couple of horses were being led toward the grandstand. As they stopped the van at barn 26, they heard the roar of the stands. Another race had just begun.

Trish felt like a little country mouse come to the big city. Obviously, horse racing was on a different plane here than up in Portland.

"Brian, how are you?" Her dad shook hands with a dark-haired man who wore a ready smile. She could hear a British accent in the return greeting.

Spitfire nickered as he heard their voices. The van shifted as the colt moved around.

"Brian, my daughter, Trish."

"Good to meet you." Brian shook her hand. "Welcome to Santa Anita. Let's get your horse unloaded so you can move the van. We've a stall all ready for him." The two men pulled out the ramp and opened the back door.

Trish took a lead shank and met Spitfire at the door. He stared out, ears pricked forward. Sun glinted off his blue-black hide. He whinnied, announcing to the world that he had arrived.

Horses answered from stalls around them. Spitfire tossed his head. Trish laughed as she snapped the rope to his halter.

"You're a show-off, you know that?"

Spitfire blew in her face and followed her down the ramp.

"Looks like he traveled well," Brian said. "Why don't you take him to that ring there and walk him for a while, Trish. Loosen him up a bit." He pointed to an oval area between the barns, deeply sanded and with a groove worn by horse hooves.

"You want some help?" Hal asked her.

Trish shook her head. "I need the exercise as bad as he does. Come on, fella. You can check out the sights as we walk."

About half an hour later, Trish led Spitfire down the aisle between the stalls. Each barn was four stalls plus two aisles wide. The aisles had been raked earlier and the cool dimness felt good after the walk. It felt more like a summer day in Portland than early April.

Deep straw bedded the dirt stall. A sling of hay hung on the open upper door, and green webbing took the place of the lower door half. Spitfire inspected everything, drank from the bucket in the corner, and came back to stand by Trish to get his scratching. She obliged, all the while listening to her father and Brian catch up on the years since they'd seen each other.

I never knew he had so many friends in other places, Trish thought as she stroked Spitfire's head and neck.

"Let's feed him now, Tee, and then we can get settled at the motel."

"You needn't worry about a thing in the morning," Brian said. "My men will take care of him until you come to work him out on the track. We have to be done with morning works by nine-fifteen, so you have plenty of time. Take it easy, you've had a long trip."

Trish thought back to the fog. *And you don't know the half of it.*

"We're going to stay here?" Trish looked up at the bell in the Spanish tower of the Embassy Suites Hotel. Her father smiled.

"All right!" She gawked even more when they walked through the inner courtyard on the way to their room. Lush greenery surrounded a waterfall and running creek. Brick walks, benches, and white-clothed tables were scattered throughout the airy, two-story room.

Laughing children played around an outside swimming pool, shaded by stucco and brick courtyard walls. Trish knew where she wanted to spend part of her day.

"I can't believe all this," she told her mother that evening after she and Hal had dinner in the dining room. "Oh, I wish you and David were here too."

In the morning they ate breakfast at the buffet in the courtyard and headed back to the track.

"That parking lot is bigger than our whole farm," Trish pointed out.

"And that's only one of several. Santa Anita has quite an interesting history. You should go on one of the guided tours; you'd learn a lot." This time they parked by other trucks outside the gate.

Spitfire announced his pleasure at Trish's return as soon as he heard her greeting Brian.

"He's already been groomed," Brian said. "We probably should clip him this afternoon. Looks pretty shaggy compared to our horses down here."

Trish tightened the cinch on her saddle. *Yep, they do things differently in California.* Once mounted, she followed the two men past lines of barns and out to the huge track.

"Just walk him," her father said. "We'll be up getting a cup of coffee." He pointed to an open restaurant area to the right.

It was a good thing Spitfire was behaving because Trish had a hard time concentrating on him. Off to her left, across a palm tree–dotted infield, the San Gabriel Mountains seemed to butt right against the track. A turf track and another dirt working track also circled the infield.

The stands to her right seemed to go on forever and clear up to the sky.

Spitfire didn't manage a flat-footed walk. He jigged and pulled at the bit. He snorted and reached out to join those horses slow-galloping or breezing by them. Trish got a better look at the stands from the far side of the track.

"There's gonna be an awful lot of people here on Saturday. We've got a big race to run." The enormity of it all dried her throat right up.

By the time Brian took them on a tour of the facility, Trish was even more thunderstruck.

"This area is designed after the English paddocks," Brian said as he pointed out over a landscaped area that looked more like a park than a racetrack. Two sculptures of horses were carved out of bushes. He called them topiary. "They do a lot of that kind of thing in Europe. And that's Seabiscuit over there under the awning."

Trish saw a bronze, nearly lifesize statue of a horse on a pedestal. White-clothed tables surrounded the statue.

"They entertain special groups there, serve fancy lunches and programs." Brian led them through the saddling stalls and showed Trish the women's dressing area and where to weigh in in the men's dressing room. "We'll bring Spitfire out and lead him through all this a couple of times during the other races. That way nothing will surprise him."

Or me, Trish thought. *This is all so much more complicated than at home.*

She and her father registered that afternoon for their licenses as trainer and jockey in the state of California. They stood in line in the racing secretary's office under the grandstand and paid their fees, including the final $6,000 race fee.

"One thing about California, everything costs more." Hal shook his head as he put his checkbook back in his pocket. "Well, come on. Let's go get that horse of ours clipped."

The foreman was just finishing as they arrived back at the stables. "Good horse here." His smile flashed bright against the tan of his face. He, like most of the grooms and stable boys, was of Mexican or South American descent.

Trish was tempted to try her Spanish but chickened out. She'd been able to pick up some of the conversations, but they all talked so fast. She ran her hand over Spitfire's shoulder. While the hair was short now, it still had the fuzzy feel of heavier winter coating.

"I'm not used to someone else doing all the work like this," she said as she and Hal walked down the aisles to the track. "But it's nice. David would love it here, don't you think?"

Hal smiled at her. "Let's watch a couple of races, then head back to the hotel."

"Fine with me. You still don't feel good, do you?"

"Not great, but better."

At least the race is the same everywhere, Trish thought as they watched a field break from the gates. After the horses swept by, she looked up behind them to the cantilevered roof of the stands, five stories above them. Crowds thronged both the grandstands and the infield, where there were betting windows, food stands, and a children's play area. *Better keep my mind on the horses.*

Trish fell asleep stretched out on a lounger by the pool. When she awoke in the shade, the first thing she thought of was sunburn. She felt her neck and the backs of her knees and let out a sigh of relief.

"Dad woulda killed me," she muttered as she gathered her towel and slipped her sandals back on. "Hope he's ready for dinner, 'cause I'm starved."

Back at the track the next morning, she trotted Spitfire through the gap and onto the track.

"Take two laps at a slow gallop, then let him out at that pole." Hal pointed to one of the furlong markers. "We'll clock him at three-eighths of a mile."

Trish did as her father said. Spitfire seemed to have understood the instructions too, at least the part about running that day. But he wanted speed from the very start.

By the time she'd fought him twice around, Trish could feel her right arm beginning to ache. "Go for it!" she hollered as they passed the designated furlong post.

Spitfire didn't need any further urging. He flattened out in three strides, reaching his sprinting speed in a couple of seconds. Trish crouched high over his withers, her face blurred by his mane. After the third post she pulled him down gradually, then continued around the track, slowing to a canter, then a jog.

"I know, that wasn't long enough." She sat back in her saddle and stroked his neck. "But Saturday is almost here, and then you get to show 'em what you can do."

At the mention of Saturday, Trish's butterflies took a couple of test leaps. She met her father and Brian at the gap.

"We've got the post breakfast in half an hour, so you better hustle." Hal smiled up at her.

"I think he likes running here," Trish said. "Maybe it's the sunshine."

"Whatever it is, he's ready. Stopwatches were clicking around us, so the word will be out right away about 'that Oregon horse.' "

"Da-ad, we're from Washington."

"I know that and you know that, but since he's only raced at Portland Meadows, that's where his times will come from."

"Oh." Trish licked her lips. She had so much to learn.

At the breakfast, she felt about as welcome as a toothache. It was easy to see who the jockeys were, and there wasn't another female among them.

"This is put on specially for the owners, trainers, and jockeys," Brian was saying.

Trish looked around the room again. She stopped and looked back. Sure enough. She pulled on her father's jacket sleeve.

"Dad, that's Shoemaker, isn't it?" She nodded at a gray-haired, jockey-sized man across the room.

"Sure is," Hal answered.

"Would you like to meet him?" Brian smiled at her. "He retired here at the track and has gone into training. Come on."

When Shoemaker shook her hand, Trish's "Pleased to meet you" came out in a stutter.

"Good luck in your race tomorrow," the great man said. "You have a mighty strong field out there."

"It includes one of yours, doesn't it?" Hal asked.

"That's why I can't wish you too much luck." Shoemaker smiled as he spoke. As another person asked him a question, Trish stepped back and watched.

How she would love to hear some of *his* stories, of horses he'd ridden, of races won and lost. He'd been injured more times than anyone cared to count, but he went on to become one of the winningest jockeys in racing history.

Number seven became their post position at the ceremony during breakfast.

Nothing else seemed important after that.

Until they started schooling Spitfire that afternoon. Following Sweeney's instructions, Hal led the colt over to the receiving barn, where a farrier checked the colt's shoes. From there they entered the line of saddling stalls where horses for the next race were being saddled. Spitfire danced some when he was led around where the spectators could look him over.

Trish walked beside the colt, talking to him, explaining what was happening and how he should behave.

"I think you must talk horse," Brian teased her when she led Spitfire back into one of the open stalls. They stood there for a while, giving Spitfire all the time he needed to become comfortable.

The next stage was the walking paddock where the jockeys mounted and again spectators could view the entrants. Spitfire walked around the circular railed area with the other horses. When the bars opened for the mounted animals to proceed to the track, Spitfire watched them leave.

Trish watched the majority of the crowd stream back into the grandstand to prepare for viewing the race. "Something to see, isn't it, fella?" She looked up on the grandstand where stylized tan horses adorned the forest green siding. A flashing light board announced the odds on the horses running.

Around them, sculptured ancient olive trees offered shade to those sitting on the benches. A circular fountain, surrounded by stunning bright flowers, spouted water in a perfect arc.

"You know you're racing where some of the greats have been, don't you?" Trish said. Spitfire rubbed his forehead on her shoulder. "John Henry ran here, and Seabiscuit. Aren't you impressed?" Spitfire shook his head and acted bored.

"I think he's seen enough." Hal leaned over the rail. "Let's leave it until tomorrow."

Friday followed much the same pattern. By now Spitfire acted like he'd always raced at Santa Anita.

That afternoon Trish took some time in the gift shop by the front gate to buy sweat shirts for David, Rhonda, and Brad. She couldn't decide what to get her mother. There were T-shirts and hats, pictures and jewelry. Even jackets, all with signs and slogans about Santa Anita. Finally she chose a T-shirt with a picture of a mare and her foal on it. "Mother Love" was the caption.

Sure wish you were all here, Trish thought as she paid for her purchases. *I need all of you to tease me out of my willies.*

When she called home that night there was no answer.

"That's funny," she said, turning to her father.

"What is?"

"They're still not home. I've tried a couple of times."

"They must have gone to a movie." Hal switched off his light. "How are you feeling?"

"Scared spitless."

"Well, spitting isn't polite anyway."

Trish threw one of her pillows at him. "You know what I mean."

"All you have to do is give it the best you can. If God wants you to win, you will. That's why you don't have to be afraid."

"But all those people. And if we don't win, we won't go to the Kentucky Derby."

"True, but that's part of this business. You win or you don't win, but you go for the glory anyway because you love racing. It gets in your blood."

"But, Dad, I want to win so-o bad."

"So do I, Tee. So do I."

Trish snuggled down under her covers. *Please, heavenly Father, help me do my best tomorrow.* The roar of the crowd filled her ears as she finally drifted off to sleep.

Chapter
16

Trish found a card propped against the lampstand in the morning. *"I can do all things through Christ who strengthens me" (Phillipians. 4:13).* Trish read it through several times.

"Thanks, Dad." She slid into the seat across from him in the dining room. "I needed reminding."

"We all do." Hal sipped his coffee.

"Now if we can just convince my butterflies. . . ."

Spitfire trotted out on the track for his morning workout like he owned the world. Ears pricked, neck arched, he surveyed his kingdom and found it to his liking.

Trish breathed in the cool, crisp air. Bits of cloud still hovered on the mountains, but the sun was quickly drying dew that sparkled on the grass of the turf track. The weather report was for low eighties with a slight breeze.

"No rain down our necks today, fella." Trish rubbed his neck along the high poll. "Nice fast track. Who could ask for anything more?"

I can, Trish thought later, after Spitfire was polished to the nth degree.

Even his hooves shone. *I wish David were here. And Brad on Dan'l to lead us to the starting gate. And Rhonda screaming for us.*

"I even miss Mom telling me to be careful," she said to Hal as they walked out to the truck to get her silks and their racing saddle. "Can you believe that?"

When the crowd roared at the start of the first race, Trish's butterflies flipped and flopped. *Sure is easier when I have several mounts,* she thought. *Then I don't have so much time to stew.*

Worried are you? her nagger's voice accused.

No. Trish tightened her lips. *Scared stiff!*

"What's causing the tight chin?" Hal asked as he handed her a Diet Coke.

"All those other jockeys. Some of them are world-class. They've been racing for years."

"So?"

She cocked her head to the side. "So, Spitfire and me, we're gonna show them that Washington horses are every bit as good as they are." She nodded her head. *If I say it often enough, maybe I'll begin to believe it.*

When Hal and Brian led Spitfire off to the receiving barn, Trish followed and walked around to the women's dressing room. Contrary to the bustling scene in the dressing room at home, she had this one all to herself. There were lockers, a sofa in front of a TV, and even a lighted makeup mirror; but nobody singing in the shower, no one wise-cracking about the last race.

She dressed, locked her things in one of the lockers, and left the quiet room.

Brian knocked on the door to the men's dressing room for her. "Woman coming in!" he hollered to alert the jockeys.

Trish clutched her saddle to her chest and stepped on the scale, carefully keeping her eyes down. *Talk about humiliating!* She could feel the red creeping from her neck all the way to her forehead.

"That's one hundred twenty-two," the steward said after slipping ten pounds of lead into her saddle pad. "Good luck."

Trish fled the room.

The field of ten were all present in the stalls, along with a couple of schoolers. Trish handed her saddle to Brian Sweeney and walked a round with Spitfire. When he nudged her arm, she rubbed his neck.

Back in the stall, Brian squatted down to check a leg wrapping. Spitfire flipped the man's hat off.

"Up to your old tricks, are you?" Hal asked the horse.

Trish fetched the hat. "Sorry, it's kind of a game with him. Guess you can feel part of the family now."

Brian brushed the sand off the tan brim. "Thanks, old man. I needed that."

Spitfire tossed his head. Trish could tell he was laughing.

Hal tightened the over-cinch on the racing saddle just before the number-one horse led the way to the walking paddock. They hung back a bit because the horse in front of them was skittish.

Suddenly a woman screamed as the Thoroughbred's hind feet struck for the stars, throwing clods of dirt over the crowd along the railings.

"Never a dull moment." Brian smiled, shaking his head. The horse in front of them acted like nothing had happened and walked on ahead.

After Spitfire snorted his way around the paddock once, Brian held the colt while Hal gave Trish a leg up. She settled her feet in the stirrups and looked down at her father.

He patted her knee. "You know what to do. I'm proud of you."

Trish swallowed. One of her butterflies flipped a cartwheel while another commanded order.

"Trish! Trish!"

She looked out over the crowds. Who could be calling her name?

Then she zeroed in on a leaping figure, arms waving above a bright-red head. Trish stared in disbelief. "It's Rhonda! And Mom! And David! Dad, they came!" She felt like jumping from her horse and charging out to meet them. "They came! They really came! Hey, you guys!" Trish waved her hand above her head, not jockey protocol or cool, but who cared at this point?

Rhonda pushed through the crowd to lean over the rail, and the others followed. "We were scared to death we wouldn't make it in time."

"Would have been here an hour ago except some idiot had an accident and tied up the freeway." David reached over to pat Trish's knee. "How're you two doing?"

"Great! Mom—I—all of you . . ." Trish blinked away the sting in her eyes. "I can't believe it! You all came!"

Marge had to blink too. "We decided we just *had* to be here. And we wanted to surprise you, Trish."

"That you did!" Hal smiled and turned to Brian. "I'd like you to meet the rest of my family." He introduced Marge and David and then Rhonda.

"You'd better get in line," Brian said after greeting everyone. "It's time."

"Go for the glory, Trish!" Rhonda gave her the thumbs-up sign.

Trish swallowed hard and grinned at them all. "Thanks." Hal led her up the padded walk to the cavern through the grandstand where riders waited to lead them to the post.

Trish heard the bugle blast. A woman rider on a gray peeled away from her spot by the wall and took the lead shank. They broke out of the shade and onto the track.

The sun glinted sparks off Spitfire's shiny hide. The saddle blanket with a number seven flapped in the breeze. The riders led them past the grandstand and on around to the far side of the track.

Trish forgot the crowds. She forgot the famous jockeys. She concentrated on Spitfire—and began to relax.

The blue and white starting gates were moved in position about even with the gap, and she and the other entrants trotted forward.

"If you win this, you'll be the first woman to win the Santa Anita Derby," her rider said. "So go for it!" She handed the lead over to the official in slot seven.

Trish waited for the number six horse to settle down before she entered the gate. After their assistant unsnapped the lead shank, Spitfire looked straight ahead. He settled himself, ready for the shot.

Trish crouched tight over his shoulders.

And they were off!

Spitfire broke clean. He ran easily, head out, ears tracking those around him. By the quarter-mile post, the field had separated and Spitfire was running with the front four.

"Come on, baby," Trish encouraged him with her musical patter. "Let's move on up."

Spitfire lengthened his stride. As they went into the far turn, the four appeared to run neck and neck. Coming out of the turn and entering the stretch, a bay made a bid for the lead.

"Now, Spitfire!" Trish gave him his head.

One horse dropped back. They eased up on the second place. Passed that one and headed for the leader.

Trish used her hands and voice to cheer him on.

The other jockey went to the whip. Spitfire caught him at the mile marker. The two ran stride for stride, thundering down to the wire.

Spitfire eased ahead.

The other horse pulled even.

Spitfire reached again, each stride demanding the lead. They won by a head.

Trish rose in her stirrups to bring him back down. "You did it! We did it!"

She turned and cantered him back to the flower-box-bordered winner's circle. She slid to the ground and fell into her father's arms as David grasped the reins. Trish tried to stop the tears streaming from her eyes, but that was no more possible than controlling the grin that split her face.

"We did it! We did it!"

When they led Spitfire in front of the risers, Marge and Rhonda joined them on the second tier. Hal accepted the trophy and Trish wrapped the floral blanket given to jockeys over her shoulders. Flashbulbs popped, and Brian led Spitfire off to the receiving barn for the mandatory testing.

"How does it feel?" A reporter stuck a mike in front of Trish's face.

"Fantastic! One of these days I'll come back to earth—but not too soon." Trish linked arms with her mother and father.

"Are you planning on the first Saturday in May?"

"Are we ever! Kentucky, get ready!"

"Do you know how much you won?" Rhonda asked her as they walked back under the grandstand. The dim tunnel was the entrance for the race horses.

"Two hundred and seventy-five thousand dollars!" Trish grabbed Rhonda's arm. "I can't even count that far."

"I'm just thankful you're safe," Marge admitted, hugging Trish again.

"I get so scared and so excited at the same time. I think I beat David's arm to death."

David rubbed his bicep. "I think so too. She was jumping and screaming as bad as Rhonda was on my other side. They both used me for a pounding board."

Trish smoothed her hand over the flowers across her shoulders. "Wish this would last. We gotta get lots of pictures. Hey, all of us were in the picture! We won't have any."

"Don't worry," Hal said. "I'll get them from the track. They always give copies of the official pictures to the owner, breeder, trainer, and jockey. That should give us a few."

"Congratulations, Hal, Trish." Adam Finley stepped in front of them. "My girl, you rode like a veteran on that one." He shook her hand, then gave her a hug. "Hal, you've got some rider here."

Trish tucked his words in the back of her mind to ponder later. Praise from a man like Finley was something to cherish.

Brian Sweeney added his congratulations when they got back to the barn. "You handled him well, Trish. You and the colt are a good team, even if he is a bit of a clown."

Trish told David what had happened in the saddling stalls.

"So he got you too?" David shook his head. "Usually I'm the brunt of his clowning, but at least he doesn't bite. Not like another horse I know."

"Gatesby," Rhonda and Trish said at the same time.

"I wish Brad could have come too," Trish said as she looked around their group.

"Somebody had to stay home and do chores," David said.

"And I wanted our whole family together for this." Marge linked her arm with Hal's.

"That's the bad part of farming," Hal added. "Someone has to be there to do the chores."

Later that night they gathered in the dining room at the hotel. Hurricane lamps flickered on white-clothed tables. Heavy wrought-iron chandeliers and wall sconces lit the beamed ceilings.

After a dinner that left everyone groaning from over-indulgence,

Rhonda asked Hal, "Have *you* ever been to the Kentucky Derby, Mr. Evanston?"

"No, almost made it once—as a spectator—but something happened and I didn't go. I've never had a horse this good before."

"It'll be *some* trip then." Rhonda's eyes widened at the thought.

"Sure will. And we'll be flying there." Hal smiled at Trish. "No fog that way."

"Fog? You told me on the phone it was a problem. But is there more you didn't happen to mention, Hal?" Marge wondered.

"Not really, Mom. But there'll be no fog this time. Only eagle's wings." Trish giggled at the look of confusion on Rhonda's face. "You know our song, don't you?"

Rhonda nodded.

"Well, the airline's called *Eagle Transport*, so it looks like we'll be flying on eagle's wings after all!"

Hal nodded. "Haven't we always?"

ACKNOWLEDGMENTS

My thanks to Brian Sweeney, Thoroughbred trainer/owner at Santa Anita, who so willingly shared his time, expertise, and love of racing with me. Thanks also to Director of Communications Jane Goldstein and staff for assisting me in my research at Santa Anita.

Gordon Tallman, Public Relations Director at Portland Meadows, has been an ongoing, invaluable aid with his knowledge and enthusiasm for the sport.

Friends of writers never know what they'll be called on to do. Barbara Rader learned more than she ever dreamed she wanted to know about horse racing in our two days of research at Santa Anita. Thanks for being caring and curious. We had fun.

Thank you to Ruby MacDonald, friend, fellow-writer, and critiquer, and to my husband, Wayne, who is always game for new adventures.

And finally, editor Sharon Madison and the Bethany House staff make me feel like someone special. Thanks, folks.

KENTUCKY DREAMER

BOOK FOUR

To Wayne,
whose love and support
make it possible for me to fly.

Chapter
01

They must have talked half the night.

Tricia Evanston stretched and yawned. It felt as if she had just fallen asleep, but she knew that since the birds were already singing, her Thoroughbred horse Spitfire, winner of yesterday's Santa Anita Derby, would be wanting his breakfast. She tossed a pillow on the body sleeping in the other bed.

"Go 'way." Her best friend since kindergarten, Rhonda Seabolt, knocked the pillow to the floor.

"Well, if you'd rather stay in bed—but I need to eat breakfast and get to the track. If you're coming, you'd better hustle." Trish hit the floor running. "Dad said he'd meet us in the lobby at seven," she called from the bathroom.

Trish stared at her image in the mirror. *Wow! Winning jockey of the Santa Anita Derby!* How come her face didn't look any different? She finger-combed her dark, wavy hair up off her face. *Shouldn't you look, well, more grown up than sixteen when you and the true-black horse you've raised from a colt have just won the Santa Anita Derby? When you've met and defeated world-famous jockeys—and their horses?* She shook her head. Her bangs fell over one eye.

A moment later, with toothpaste fuzzing around her mouth, she checked her face again. Nope, no change. She spit and rinsed.

"You about done in there?" Rhonda, of the carrot-red mop, hammered on the door.

"Do you know who you're yelling at?" Trish opened the door and leaned against the frame. A grin attacked the corners of her mouth and winked in her hazel eyes.

"The winner of the Santa Anita Derby." Rhonda pretended boredom just before she grabbed Trish in a bear hug and danced her around the room. The two girls flopped back on the bed. "You really did it! You and Spitfire showed 'em all." They stared up at the ceiling. "So now what?"

"Now we rush downstairs and meet my dad."

"No, silly." Rhonda punched her on the arm. "Do you go for the Triple Crown, or what?"

Trish let the question sink in. "I wish I knew," she whispered. "I just wish I knew."

Reporters met them at Spitfire's stall. After all the questions and pictures right after the race, Trish was surprised to learn there were more to come. She left them to her father while she measured the grain for Spitfire's morning feed. She'd already realized that the tall, ebony colt hid her from the inquisitive journalists.

"So, how does it feel?" her curly-haired brother David asked as he picked Spitfire's hooves.

"I'll tell you when I figure it out." Trish kept on brushing.

It seemed only moments later that she and her father, Hal, were waving good-bye to Rhonda, David, and her mother. They were driving home to Vancouver, Washington.

Marge kissed her husband and hugged Trish. "You two drive carefully now." Her chronic worrying always stole some of a day's happiness from Trish.

"Don't worry, Mom." Trish halfheartedly returned her hug. She and her mother didn't see eye to eye about a lot of things, like Trish driving the big horse van or racing Thoroughbreds.

Trish rubbed her forehead. A headache thumped behind her eyes. She finished packing for the return home.

"You about ready?" Her father massaged her shoulders.

Trish let her head drop forward. She took a deep breath and relaxed under his ministering fingers. "Yeah, anytime you are."

"We'll fill that ice pack one more time, as soon as we load Spitfire." Hal dug out the tension in her neck with his thumbs. Spitfire leaned over the green-web harness across the stall opening and nuzzled her hair. When she didn't respond, he lipped a curl in her bangs and tugged.

"Ouch!" Trish shoved the black nose away. "You did that on purpose!" Spitfire rolled his eyes in mock fright. He blew in her face, then rubbed his forehead against her chest, begging for the scratching she performed so well.

"We should form a line here." Trish stroked her horse's neck while her father finished smoothing the knots of tension from her own.

"You need anything else then?" Brian Sweeney, long-time friend of Hal's who had invited them to stable in his barn at the track, asked in his slight Canadian accent.

"Just more ice after we load this guy." Hal clipped a lead shank to Spitfire's halter. "Here, Tee, take him up."

Trish led the colt out the open entry of the green stables and to the foot of the loading ramp of their borrowed horse van. Spitfire didn't even hesitate this time when his feet thudded on the padded ramp. He followed her right up.

"Good fella." Trish knotted the half-hitch to hold him in place while her father Velcroed the canvas ice pack to the colt's right foreleg. The knee had been warm ever since the race, but at least it wasn't hot and swollen like times in the past. If it didn't heal in the next few weeks, a hot knee could keep them from the Kentucky Derby the first Saturday in May.

Hal and Trish thanked Brian one more time before climbing into the truck and buckling up. Hal put the rig in gear and eased down the hard-packed dirt road to the gate. The guard waved them through.

"We'll be back," Hal promised as they followed the curving street back to the freeway. Trish turned for a last glimpse of the imposing green

Santa Anita grandstand. Straight ahead it looked as if they were driving smack into the San Gabriel mountains. One more look back and all she saw were the tall spindly palm trees that decorated the infield. Santa Anita certainly had an aura all its own. What would Churchill Downs, home of the Kentucky Derby, be like?

By the time they hit I-5, Trish was deep into her history book. She should have studied more while at the track, but since it was spring break, she only had a couple of days' assignments to do.

The first day they drove as far as Adam Finley's stunning ranch in the foothills above Harrisburg. They had stopped there on their way south, and the Finleys already seemed like old friends to Trish too. She sucked in her breath again at the Spanish splendor of the breeding farm. It seemed strange to see roses blooming already, but the scarlet-covered plants lining the exterior fences didn't know that it was barely spring in Washington State.

The two Rottweiler dogs announced the truck's arrival, and just like before, former-jockey and now renowned trainer Adam Finley directed them to park and showed them to the stable.

"Ah, I see you're havin' a bit o' leg trouble." He pointed at the pack covering Spitfire's knee.

"It's getting to be a chronic thing with him," Hal said as Trish led the colt down the ramp. "It's been worse before."

Trish halted the horse so her father could remove the wrap. "I'll just walk him around a bit to loosen both of us up."

"I'm thinking you better not let him loose in the paddock this time," Adam suggested. "He might jump and strain that knee even more. Soon as you're done, Trish, there're cold drinks and dinner up at the house. Martha's been looking forward to your coming."

Trish walked Spitfire a good half hour before she let him loose in a stall deeply bedded with straw. She Velcroed the newly filled ice pack around his leg and gave him a last pat as he buried his nose in the grain bucket. "Pig out, fella, you earned it." Spitfire blew molasses-smelling grain in her face and went back to his meal. "Thanks." She wiped the mixture of grain and slobber off her nose. "I needed that."

She reached down and petted the two black and tan dogs that met her at the stable entry. They gamboled in front of her, darting back for more ear scratchings and nipping at each other to get her attention. Trish laughed. This was like home, only their collie Caesar had a lot more hair.

Trish took a deep breath as she strode up the brick walk to the stucco ranch house. Curved arches shaded the entry and served as a trellis for flaming bougainvillea. On the trip down, she'd learned that the sweet smell came from the orange trees lining the sides of the house. She also remembered the swimming pool in the backyard. Maybe she could get a dip in before they left in the morning.

"I have a proposition for you," Adam Finley said after they'd finished a barbecued steak dinner. "How'd you like to come down here and ride for me this summer? I know your season up there will be done by the end of April, and after the races back east and school's out, you could bring some of your string down here." He nodded at Hal. "Then she could ride for both of us."

Trish stared from the rosy-cheeked man to her father and back again. "I—ah—it would—ah . . ." She had no idea what to say. This would for sure be a chance to build a reputation in the big leagues. And their horses were every bit as good as those in California. Spitfire had just proved it. She raised stricken eyes to her father. What would her mother say about something like this? She'd just as soon her daughter quit racing altogether. Trish sighed. Her mother would *never* let them do this.

"Thanks for the vote of confidence," Hal said as he leaned his chair back. "Marge and I'll have to give this some thought. You know, with this bout of cancer and all the chemotherapy treatments, I have a hard time being away from home much, and, well, Marge isn't too excited about Trish's racing as it is." He rubbed his chin. "I had thought about coming down for a race or two."

Trish stared at him in astonishment. He'd not mentioned to her about coming back to California so soon.

"The purses are better than Longacres in Seattle, and since they're going to tear that track down, the only other races up in our neck of the woods are Yakima and the county fairs," Hal continued.

"Besides that, man, your colt has put you up in the big leagues. You'd be doing him an injustice not to race him again with horses of equal caliber," Adam reminded him.

"I know," Hal agreed.

7

"On top of that, it would be wonderful to have a young girl around again," Martha added. "We've plenty of room for you in our condo in San Mateo." She patted Trish's hand. "I'd promise your mother to take good care of you."

"Thank you," Trish said. Her smile didn't begin to relay the pleasure she felt at the warm invitation. Just think, living in California for the summer.

Don't think about it, her little nagger said. *You know it's impossible. Remember, you have chemistry to make up too.*

The next morning in the truck, Trish felt cranky and out of sorts. She knew it was the letdown after all the excitement, but that didn't help much. A nap did though.

"Bay Meadows sounds wonderful," Trish broke the long silence the next morning after their overnight in Ashland.

"Don't get your hopes up."

"I know. Mom won't . . ."

"Trish, she can't help her worrying. You know as well as anyone that we're involved in a dangerous business."

"And *she* doesn't think *her* daughter should be racing." Trish felt the resentment dig at her good mood. *I'll never tell my kids to be careful,* she promised herself.

"You finished your homework?"

"Now you sound like Mom." She caught the puzzled look her father sent her. This time it was a good thing he couldn't always read her mind.

"Just thought maybe you'd like to drive."

Little fingers of guilt pinched her. She *should* have noticed he was getting tired rather than sitting there griping. They made good time though, arriving home about three o'clock Tuesday afternoon.

It felt good to be home.

Brad—David's best friend, who worked for Runnin' On Farm—and Rhonda drove in just as Trish led Spitfire into his stall after a walk that loosened them both up.

"Hi, guys." Trish flashed them a grin as she unsnapped the lead shank. "You didn't waste any time getting home from school, did you?"

"Look who's talking." Rhonda threw her arms around her friend. "How was the trip?"

"Rhonda's described the race in *detail*," long, lean Brad said. "And I've read all the newspaper articles, which I kept for you. Now I want to hear *your* version. *And* answer the *big* question."

Perpetual-motion Rhonda couldn't keep still another minute. "When do you leave for the Derby?"

Brad gave her a pained look. "No, that's not it. Are you going for the Triple Crown?"

Trish shrugged. "Dad says take it one step at a time. He'll decide on the other two only if we win the Derby."

"Not *if*. When." Rhonda poked Brad in the side. "We—none of us, nobody says 'if.' We only say 'when.' Trish and Spitfire are going to *win* the Kentucky Derby. No doubt about it."

That night in bed, Trish wished she could feel more secure about the big race. "All I can do is ask you to help us," she prayed. "You know everything that can happen between here and there. Please keep Dad healthy and make his next treatment go easily. And we can't go if Spitfire's leg isn't all right, so please take care of that too." She thought for a time. "Thank you for a safe trip home and for the win. Father, help change my mother's mind about my racing. Help her quit worrying so much. Thanks. Amen."

When she thought back to the evening just passed, she hugged a happy glow to herself. Marge had made a wonderful homecoming dinner and they'd talked about the trip, the race, and the people in California—everything except the proposal from Adam Finley. She knew her father would choose the best time and place for that. However, she'd had to bite her tongue to keep from blabbing to the other three musketeers down at the barn.

Wednesday morning she was back in the groove, nearly late to school. She rushed in the main door and skidded to a stop. "On to the Kentucky Derby" proclaimed a banner strung between two posts. Another one across her locker said she was "#1 Rider." Trish folded that one and struggled with her combination lock. The bell rang before she got her books switched, so she was late to class. English lit stood as a body and applauded.

Trish could feel the heat all the way from her toes to the top of her head. "Thanks," she croaked as she slid into her desk.

That afternoon she received a standing ovation when her name was announced as a jockey at Portland Meadows. She was riding to the post on her first mount and could feel the waves of approval wash over her from the grandstands. She raised her whip in the air and waved, thankful for the brisk wind blowing the heat away from her face.

All the jockeys she'd met offered their congratulations and best wishes for the first Saturday in May. Genie Stokes, who sometimes rode for Runnin' On Farm, summed it up in the dressing room: "We're all rooting for you," she said. "Your dad has worked long and hard for this chance. It couldn't happen to a nicer guy, and his daughter is no slouch."

It didn't hurt to win two races and place in a third either. Trish hurried home to work the horses there. David and Brad had already taken care of them all, even contrary Gatesby.

"And we didn't get any new bruises," Brad bragged as they walked back up the rise to his blue Mustang.

"How's Spitfire's leg?" Trish leaned down to scratch the insistent Caesar as she asked.

"Still warm as soon as he walks on it much," David answered.

"Did you lead him with Dan'l?" He was the horse that had trained her as she exercised him.

"No, just walked him around the area. Dad said to take it real easy, not even let him out in the pasture."

"Well, we gotta go. See you guys." Brad and Rhonda slammed their car doors shut. Trish and David waved good-bye and turned toward the house.

"How's Firefly?" Trish reached her arms above her head and stretched to pull the tiredness out of her muscles.

"No swelling. Hasn't been any for some time."

"Wouldn't it be something to take her to Kentucky with us, to run the Oaks?" Trish leaned against the deck railing. "I wonder if Dad's thought about that at all?"

"He said she was done for this year because of the shin problem."

KENTUCKY DREAMER ♫ Chapter 01

"I know. But she is such a great horse, and the Oaks runs the day before the Derby. It's only for three-year-old fillies. She hasn't really had a chance to prove what she can do."

"Trish, don't get any off-the-wall ideas."

"Well, it's worth thinking about." She shoved open the sliding glass door. "And talking about." She heard retching coming from her father's bedroom. *I forgot!* The thought tore at her. *Dad's sick from his treatment and all I could think about was my day—my wins. What kind of daughter am I?* She tiptoed into the darkened bedroom.

Hal lay with one hand across his forehead. His eyes flickered open when he heard Trish whisper his name. "I'm doing okay," he said. He reached again for the basin on a chair beside his bed. The biting odor of bile from his dry heaves made Trish swallow and wish she hadn't bothered him.

Sure you are, her thoughts jeered at his words. *You're just fine and dandy.*

Hal wiped his mouth and smiled past the green tinge to his face. "Really, Tee. This time isn't anything like the last one. I'll be up and going by tomorrow. Now, tell me about your day. I hear there was a surprise waiting for you at school. And how did you do at the track?"

Trish filled him in, her excitement returning as she told him each detail. She paused at the end and licked her bottom lip. "Have you thought about taking Firefly with us to Kentucky?"

"You never quit, do you?" Hal patted his daughter's hand.

"Well, it wouldn't be a whole lot more expensive to take two horses."

"No, just plane fare, entry fees . . ."

Trish heard him but continued. "It's just a shame she's never raced against horses as good as she is, and since she missed out on Santa Anita . . ."

"Dinner's ready," Marge called from the kitchen.

"Go eat." Hal turned on his side.

When Trish checked on him later, he was sound asleep.

Trish had five mounts for Saturday's program. That was after morning works at Runnin' On Farm. Her father had surprised—and thrilled—her when he told her to gallop Firefly also. He'd been up and around, just like he promised.

11

"Don't get your hopes up," he'd said when Trish grinned down at him from the dark filly's back. "Let's see what happens."

Even though they didn't have a horse running that day, Marge and Hal drove Trish to the track.

"Meet you at the front gate after your last ride," Marge said. "We'll all go out for dinner."

Trish nodded and grinned her agreement, then dog-trotted off to the dressing room.

The sun kept ducking behind clouds coming from the west as though afraid to be seen too long in one place. Trish thought of the constant warmth of California as she snapped the rubber bands around her cuffs to keep the cold wind from blowing up her silks. The track was wet but not muddy.

"Be careful on that far turn," owner Bob Diego said as he gave her a leg up for the second race of the day. "Keep off the rail, it's worse there."

Trish nodded. She leaned forward and stroked the neck of her mount.

"And, Trish, I cannot tell you how pleased I am for you and your father. You rode an excellent race."

"Thank you. I still get excited when I think about it."

Trish again felt the warmth of his words as she moved the horse into the starting gates. All the animals seemed keyed up. She had to back her mount out and come into the gate a second time. But the horse broke cleanly and surged to a secure spot in second. Trish held him there until the last furlong of the short race, moved up on the lead, and with hand and voice encouragement, swept under the wire ahead by a length.

She won the next one for Jason Rodgers also.

"We missed you," the tall, always perfectly dressed Rodgers told her in the winner's circle. "But we're sure proud of you. Not many riders make a mark like you did down south. And thanks for a good win today. Meet you here again in an hour or so?"

Trish grinned at him. "Sounds good to me." And that's exactly what she did. She and another Rodgers horse won the fifth.

"Looked like you had a bad time on that far turn," Rodgers said after the pictures had been taken and the horse led away to the testing barn.

"Yeah, we got caught on the rail and bumped around a little. The maintenance crew needs to work that spot some more."

Trish stood in line for the scale after changing silks again.

"So how does it feel to be back after a win like the Santa Anita?" veteran jockey Phil Snyder asked her.

"Cold." Trish hugged her saddle closer. "I loved the sun down there."

"And winning?" Laugh lines crinkled around his eyes.

"You should know." Trish grinned back at him. She leaned closer to whisper, "I loved every minute of it, even when I was terrified at going against the big-name jockeys. You couldn't exactly call them friendly but"— she shrugged—"I met Shoemaker. And beating the others—well—"

"You can't wait to do it again." They laughed together.

"How's your new baby?" Trish asked as they walked toward the saddling paddock.

"Growing like a weed," Phil said. "I'll have him up on a horse before you know it."

Trish felt the tension in her mount as soon as she approached the saddling stall. She knew this was the first race for the colt because she'd talked to the owner earlier. The horse tossed his head and rolled his eyes when Trish reached to stroke his neck.

"Easy, fella," she crooned to him. "You don't have to act this way. Come on now." The colt stamped his foot but calmed as she kept up her easy monologue. When she mounted, she could feel him arch his back as if to buck. She stroked his neck, murmuring all the while. "You certainly live up to your name, don't you?" She gathered her reins and nodded at the owner. Spice of Life couldn't have been more descriptive.

"Watch him closely," the trainer said as he handed the lead shank over to the woman riding the horse that would parade them to the post. "And you be careful, Trish."

Trish felt the horse settle down about halfway to the post, and when they cantered back toward the starting gates, he quit fighting the bit. His gait smoothed out, so she didn't feel like she was riding a pile driver.

"That's a good fella," she sang to the flicking ears. "Whoops! Not so good! Whoa now!" Her commands seemed to spin off into thin air as the frightened colt backed out of the gates as fast as he should have been breaking forward. The handler led him back in.

Spice of Life snorted and shook his head. Trish settled herself in the saddle. She'd almost been ready to bail off.

"Come on, fella, let's concentrate on running, not tearing things up." The horse seemed to finally hear her and stopped shifting around.

"Good job, Trish," Snyder said from the stall to her right.

"Thanks." Trish concentrated on the space between the horse's ears. Now to get him running straight. The gates swung open and the colt hesitated before he lunged forward. His stride was choppy, so Trish held him firm to give him a chance to catch his balance.

When she finally had him running true, the field was bunched in front of them. As they rounded the first turn, Trish caught the six horses running together. When she tried to swing the colt around the outside, he fought her. He checked, stumbled, gained his feet again.

At that same moment a horse somewhere in front broke down. As he crashed, a second horse fell over him. Bodies flew every which way. Spice of Life smashed into the screaming and kicking mass of downed horses and riders. Trish felt herself flying through the air.

Chapter
02

Relax! flashed from Trish's mind to her body. By now it had to be a conditioned response, or it wouldn't have happened in that split second of catapult time.

She struck the ground at the same time her mount did. The screams of horses and humans echoed in her ears as she plowed through the soft dirt and bumped against a fallen horse's back. Then all went black.

She wasn't sure how long she'd been out. Drawing air into her lungs took major concentration. She wiggled her fingers and toes, doing a body check while she waited for her head to clear. She heard someone moaning. Someone else was either cursing or praying in rapid Spanish. A horse snorted nearby.

The sound of a motor whining around the track must surely be an ambulance. It was.

Trish rolled into a sitting position but quickly dropped her head between her knees. She wasn't sure which was worse, a rolling stomach or a woozy head.

"Just stay where you are," a male voice ordered softly. "We'll get to you as soon as we can."

While it seemed like forever, it was only a minute or so before Trish could open her eyes and focus on the carnage around her. A horse lay just beyond her feet. It must have been what she bumped against. It hadn't moved.

Trish swallowed—hard.

She looked up to see the EMTs loading a covered stretcher into the ambulance. *Covered!* The thought flashed through her own misery. Was someone dead? Two others were working over a jockey who groaned when they moved him.

By the outside rail, a horse stood, head down, not putting any weight on a front leg. Trish could see blood running from the open gash caused by a compound fracture.

She gritted her teeth. They'd probably have to put that horse down.

"Just take it easy," a voice from behind her said. "We have another ambulance on the way."

"I'm fine." Trish turned her head very carefully so her stomach would stay down where it belonged. "I don't need an ambulance."

"Why don't you let us be the judge of that?" The first ambulance pulled away, lights flashing. "Now, any pain here?" The blond-haired young man pressed on her legs.

Trish swallowed again. She spit out some of the track dirt. When she lifted her hands to remove her helmet, the world spun around like an out-of-control carousel.

"Take it easy and let me help you." The blue-uniformed man squatted in front of her, still checking her arms and legs. He finished unbuckling her helmet and handed it to her. "Now, how's the head?"

"Hurts, but not bad. I just feel dizzy when I move." Trish ran her fingers over the dent in the side of her helmet. Someone had kicked her—big time. No wonder she felt funny.

"Let's get you on a back board and brace your neck for the ride in, just in case you've broken something in your neck or spine." The EMT smiled at her as another person brought over the equipment.

"Do I have to?" Trish pleaded. "I've been through this before. I'm okay, really." She kept insisting but didn't have the strength to fight them, especially since every time she moved her head, the world tilted.

The ride to the hospital was mercifully short. The worst part was the lump of dirt digging a hole in her left hip. Once she'd removed that, the rest of the ride was fairly comfortable.

"How bad is she?" Marge asked as the attendants pulled the gurney out of the ambulance. Her voice sounded rigid, as if she had to force her words from between clenched teeth.

"Hi, Mom." Trish raised her head and reached for her mother's hand. "You got here awfully fast."

"It's not hard when you're following an ambulance." Hal took her other hand. He leaned down and kissed his daughter's cheek.

Trish felt a tear slip from her eye and run down into her ear. She sniffed. "I'm okay, except for a dizzy head. Make them let me up, please. I don't want to go through X-rays and everything again."

"Just be patient." Marge clamped on to Trish's hand as if her daughter might be ripped away from her. "It's better to get checked out just—just in case—there's more."

"Mo-o-m!"

"No, she's right, Tee. We'll be right beside you," her father assured her.

The EMTs pushed the gurney through the hospital's automatic doors and into a curtained cubicle. On three they lifted her, board and all, to a hospital gurney.

"By the way," the cheerful blond man said before he left, "you're one whale of a rider. I've been watching you since last fall, and if I had a horse, I'd sure want you riding it. You take care, and good luck at the Derby."

"Thanks." Trish waved back as he left the room. She rolled her head to the side to smile at her mom and dad. One look at her mother's frozen face and Trish knew there was deep trouble. "B-b-but, Mom, this wasn't *my* fault."

"It wasn't anyone's fault, Tee." Her father squeezed her hand. "That's what your mother has always tried to tell you. Accidents—serious accidents—often happen through no one's fault, but people and horses can get hurt. Seriously hurt. Or even die."

Marge rubbed her arms above her elbows as if seeking some kind of warmth. Hal put his arm around her and hugged her into his side.

"Die?" Trish remembered back to the track. "That horse I fell against. It died?"

Hal nodded. The sorrow in his eyes as he kissed his wife's hair penetrated the fuzziness Trish felt when she moved her head.

"That's not all." It was more a statement than a question.

Her father shook his head. "Phil Snyder was killed too. Broke his neck in the fall."

Marge shuddered and hid her face in Hal's shoulder.

Trish bit her lip on the cry that tore from her heart. Tears welled in her eyes and ran through the mud on her face and into her ears. She stared up at the square blocks of ceiling tile. "But—but I was just talking with him before the race—and he has a baby—and—and . . ." She didn't have the courage to look at her mother.

"Well, Trish, so you're back again. We're going to have to quit meeting this way." The doctor stared from her face to Hal's. "Is she worse than they told me?" His question was low, meant for Hal's ears alone. Hal shook his head.

The doctor paused.

Tears slid silently from Trish's eyes. She clenched her fists at her sides on the narrow gurney. *Do not fall apart now! You're tough. Hang in there!* Her orders seemed to be working. She could swallow again.

"I'm sorry, Trish." The doctor picked up her hand and checked her pulse while he spoke. "Phil Snyder was a fine man, besides a good rider. That was a terrible accident." He shifted into a more professional tone. "Now let's see how you're doing. They said concussion. Your vision a bit foggy?" Trish nodded. "And movement makes it worse, right?" he answered when a grimace squinted in her eyes. "Nausea?"

"Some. But it's better now. How about just letting me go home? I'll be—I'm fine. Really, I am." Trish sniffed the offensive tears back.

The doctor moved her arms and legs, all the while asking, "Hurt here? How about here?" He checked her eyes again. "Any pain anywhere else?"

Trish took a deep breath, almost shook her head, and caught herself just in time. "No, not really. Please, no X-rays. Just let me go home."

The doctor studied her for a moment. "Does this feel any different than the last concussion you had? Now be honest with me, Trish. You know what that other concussion felt like, and I can't find anything else."

"About the same. I don't feel like running track right now, but Dad's always said I have a hard head. Guess this just shows he's right."

The doctor rubbed his chin. He extended his hand. "Well, let's get you upright and see how you do. Easy now." He helped her sit up and swing her legs to the side.

Trish gulped and squeezed her eyes shut. She took a deep breath, slowly raised her head, and swallowed again. The room stayed in one place. Her mother and father didn't fade in and out like before.

The doctor nodded. "You'll call if you notice anything different?"

"Yes." She kept her head still. She'd learned that trick pretty quickly.

"We'll have the nurse wheel you out." He shifted his attention to Trish's parents. "Call me if you need me?" He studied Marge's pale, set face. She hadn't said a word throughout the examination.

Trish saw him glance from Marge to Hal, a question on his face. Marge looked like she'd shrunk. Her shoulders, arms, and neck seemed squeezed inward as if she were trying to disappear. When the doctor touched her shoulder, she flinched and tucked her face into Hal's shoulder again.

"We'll be fine," Hal answered the unspoken question. "I'll get them both home and to bed. We've had a pretty big shock today." He turned toward the curtain opening. "We'll get the car."

"I can give her something," the doctor said. "Make it easier."

Hal smoothed a gentle hand over his wife's hair. "I'll let you know." Marge seemed to shuffle as they left.

Trish wanted to scream, but instead she asked the question quietly: "What's wrong with my mother?"

"An accident like this can cause shock to family members too. Besides, you've all been through a lot these last months. Sometimes the body needs a break."

"That's all?"

"That's plenty. You'll call me if you feel worse?"

Trish nodded as she allowed the doctor and nurse to help her into the wheelchair. "Thanks."

"Yeah, changing altitude'll get you. Let me know now." The doctor patted her hand. "About your mom too."

Silence filled the car on the way home. Trish lay down in the backseat, her head resting on her bent arm. The last she heard were the tires howling across the metal treads on the I-5 bridge across the Columbia River.

"Come on, sleepyhead, we're home." Her father patted her shoulder gently.

Trish sat up very carefully. "Where's Mom?"

"I already took her into the house and put her to bed. That seemed the best thing to do." Hal extended his hand to help Trish from the car.

"Why? Dad, what's really wrong with her?"

"Shock, I think. She'll be okay."

As Trish slowly changed altitudes, Hal put his arm around her shoulders so she could lean against him. Together they mounted the steps to the front door, with Trish feeling like stopping at each level. She tightened her jaw and kept on, in spite of the woozies attacking her head.

Never had her bed looked more inviting. Hal folded back the covers, then pulled off Trish's boots. "Now, you call me if you need anything else," he said.

"Where's David?"

"He and Brad are down at the barns. I'm going down to tell them what happened and check on our animals, then I'll be right back. You just get some sleep so you feel better."

"What about the horses I'm riding tomorrow?"

"First of all, you're not riding tomorrow. Give me the owners' names later and I'll call them."

"Who rode my last mount today?" Trish could feel her attention slipping.

"I'm not sure. We left right after the accident."

"Oh." His comment brought the sounds and feelings cascading back.

After he left, Trish slipped out of her silks and under the covers. The bed welcomed her battered body. *I need a shower—bad.* She was asleep before she could dwell on the thought.

Screaming horses. Groaning people. Ambulance sirens. Trish jerked awake. She took a deep breath and let her gaze rove around her room. Light from the mercury yard light cast shadows across the floor. It had been a dream, but the dream mirrored reality. Tears started again. Phil was dead—what about his family? Horses were killed. She'd never heard even the old-timers talk about an accident as bad as this one.

"Oh, God, thank you for taking care of me out there." She stopped the prayer. *Why me? Why did Phil die and not me? Who makes the choices? And why? It all happened so quickly—and so senselessly. None of it makes any sense.* She tried to shut out the thoughts. But when she clenched her eyes closed, the pain in her head came back.

Her little nagging voice snuck by her resolve: *Now you know why your mother worries so much. No matter how well you ride, an accident can happen.*

Trish wished the voice would go back to sleep. She wished *she* could go back to sleep. "And, Jesus, please help my mom. I know she is hurting too. And the Snyder family, help them and all the others hurt in that mess. Thanks again. Amen." She pulled the covers back up to her chin, and slept.

Trish felt the bathroom urge sometime in the dark hours before dawn. As she passed her parents' bedroom, she heard them talking.

"I can't take any more," her mother said between gut-wrenching sobs. "It could have been Trish out there. She *was* out there."

Trish could hear her father's soothing murmur.

"I—just—can't—take—any more!"

Trish slipped into the bathroom and quietly shut the door.

It's all your fault, she heard her nagger accusing her.

It was light out when she staggered up to go to the bathroom again. If she took things easy, it wasn't so bad. She nearly freaked when she looked in the mirror. She hadn't washed her face, and mud from the track still outlined where her goggles had been and smeared across her cheeks and chin. She scrubbed a wet washcloth across the worst of it and went back to bed. The house was strangely silent for the 8:00 a.m. that the clock read.

Maybe she'd dreamed that her parents talked in the night. *I hope so,* she thought. *What if they make me quit racing?*

Hunger pangs woke her at ten. She entered an empty kitchen after a careful walk down the hall. One thing was sure, she felt much better than last night. But where was everybody? Had they left for church without telling her? She poured cold cereal and milk into a bowl and sat down at the table. After the cereal and a piece of toast, she searched for a note by the phone. None.

She looked out the window at the driveway. All the cars were parked in their normal places, so Dad and David must be down at the barn. Shivering, she headed back to her bed. On the way she opened the closed door and glanced into her parents' bedroom. In the darkened room, a mound raised the covers on her mother's side of the bed.

Trish stopped at the door. "Mom?" No answer. What could be happening? Her mother never slept late. She was always the first one up because she loved early mornings. And to miss church? Could something really be wrong with her mother?

Is Mom sick?" Trish confronted her father when he walked in the door.

"Well—" Hal took the time to hang up his coat before replying. "That depends on what you call sick. She doesn't have the flu or a cold."

"So?"

"I think she just needs some time out."

"Because of the accident?"

"That, and all the rest of the stress that's been going on around here." Hal sank into his recliner and patted the hearth beside him. "Sit down, Tee. Maybe you can help me with some ideas."

Trish sat down very carefully, because changing altitudes still caused her stomach to flip. Besides, she sported a couple of bruises from where she'd hit the ground. She stared at her father, waiting for him to quit fidgeting and begin. *Please, please, don't let him ask me to quit racing,* she pleaded to her heavenly Father.

"I think we have to give your mother the kind of care she's always given us."

Trish clenched her eyes shut and gritted her teeth. *He can't ask me to quit. He just can't!* She opened her eyes again. Tears burned behind her eyelids.

"I know you don't feel too well, but if you start the dinner, I'll help you with it."

Dinner! The word smacked into her brain and exploded in red, white, and blue streamers. *Dinner!* She released the streamers in a laugh and a hug. "Sure, Dad. I'd be glad to."

Trish felt like dancing into the kitchen. She was dancing in her mind even though she walked carefully. She stared into the freezer. Yep, she could thaw and fry the chicken. Potatoes—her dad could peel those; there were plenty of vegetables, corn would be good. All the while one part of her mind thought *dinner,* the other rejoiced. She'd still be racing!

But by dinner her mother hadn't come out of her room. She refused a tray; said she wasn't hungry. While Trish and her father had a good time making the dinner, it just wasn't right. Her mom had always been there. If she'd been gone—but that was the problem, she wasn't gone. She was right in the bedroom, and Dad said she wasn't really sick.

David didn't have a lot to say at dinner either. No one did.

"How's Spitfire's leg?" Trish looked at David.

"Uh, better."

"The ultrasound is helping?"

"I guess."

Hal stared at his dinner. "Thanks, Tee." He shoved the half-full plate away. "Sorry, but guess I'm not too hungry after all. Think I'll go sit with your mother for a while."

A knock changed his direction from the hall to the front door. "Why, Pastor Mort. How good to see you. Come on in. We were just finishing dinner. Can we get you a cup of coffee?"

Trish started to leap up, but stopped mid-jump and pushed herself up slowly. "Quick, David, clear the table. I'll put the coffee on and . . ."

The two men entered the dining room.

"How are you, Trish?" Pastor Mort extended his hand. "I heard you were part of that horrible accident yesterday." He squeezed her hand and patted her shoulder. "Had to come myself to make sure you were okay. Hi, David. It's good to see you." He glanced into the kitchen. "Marge around?"

"Have a seat," Hal said. "I'm glad you came by."

Trish picked up her dishes and escaped to the kitchen. "I'll get some coffee going." She listened to the friendly talk with one ear, kept her hands busy filling the coffeepot with water, and still had time to think that she looked worse than a drowned rat. At least she'd taken a hot shower, which got the kinks loosened up and the dirt off her face. But she was wearing the gross sweats she'd worn when her arm was broken. She set out mugs and arranged peanut butter cookies on a plate. As soon as the coffeemaker stopped gurgling, Trish carried the tray of refreshments into the dining room.

"Thanks, Trish." Pastor Mort smiled at her when she handed him a mug of coffee. "Black, just the way I like it."

"You're welcome." Her smile slipped a little as her nagger reminded her she'd forgotten to ask if he took cream and sugar. Her mother didn't forget things like that. *She* should be out here. "Dad, anything else?" She set his mug on the table.

The twinkle in her father's eyes told her he knew *exactly* what she was thinking. "Thanks, Tee."

"Well, I'd better get down to the barn and start chores." David snagged a cookie off the plate as he stood up. "Good to see you, Pastor."

Trish started to clear more dishes from the table, then stopped. Maybe if she got out of there, the two men could talk about how to help her mom. Maybe Pastor Mort could get Marge to come out of her room. "I'll be down in a minute," she told David.

"There's plenty more coffee," she said as she picked up the bowls of leftover food.

"You ready for the big one?" Pastor Mort asked.

"Hope so. If Spitfire's leg gets better, and if—" she glanced at her father. "Or, rather, when." Hal grinned at her. "I have to keep reminding myself that 'if' doesn't count." Trish smiled back at the contagious grin on her pastor's face. She was quoting his own words.

"Good for you, Trish." The balding man nodded as he spoke. "You've got the right attitude, and I know it hasn't come easily."

"Thanks. See you later."

Trish grabbed some carrots from the fridge before she went out the door, and broke them into pieces on her way to the barn. Caesar met her halfway, barking his approval and begging for attention. Trish slapped her chest with both hands and the dog responded by planting his forefeet by her hands. Trish scratched his ears and tugged on the white ruff.

"You ol' sweetie." Her nose got a quick lick. Then her chin. "Hey, knock it off. I washed my face today." Caesar grinned his doggy grin and gave her another quick one before he dropped to the ground.

Trish took a deep breath. Nickers escalated to whinnies when her stable friends heard her voice. She heard David talking to them as he moved from stall to stall with the evening feed. A pheasant rooster called out in the field. Trish searched the fence rows toward the west, trying to locate him. Another deep breath took in the aromas of spring—growing grass, freshly turned dirt, all overlaid with a tinge of stable. She grinned down at the dog sitting at her feet. "Come on, fella, let's go see the kids."

She gave each of the racing string a bit of carrot and a quick scratch as she walked down the line. Spitfire smeared grain on her cheek as he blew in her face. Gray Dan'l begged for more—both carrots and loving. Even Gatesby acted glad to see her, a wuffle warming her fingers as he picked up his carrot.

Trish left them behind and headed for the paddock behind the old barn where the two foals played at grazing along with their dams. When she whistled, Miss Tee, the filly born on Trish's birthday in September, trotted up to the fence. She'd lost her baby coat and was deepening into a dark bay, with one white sock and a narrow blaze down her face. Double Diamond, the January-born colt, hesitated before following the filly up to the fence.

"You two are absolutely the neatest babies anywhere." Trish rubbed Miss Tee's ears and stroked down the brush of a mane. She kept an eye on Double D, waiting for him to tiptoe up. Miss Tee nudged Trish in the chest. "Knock it off, silly. Pretty soon you'll be big enough to knock me over that way." Trish stroked her baby's soft nose and tickled the whiskery upper lip. Miss Tee tossed her head, then nibbled on Trish's fingers. She sniffed Trish's jacket pockets, searching for more treats.

Trish snapped a lead rope on the filly's halter, then opened the gate to do the same for the mare that ambled up for her treat. As she walked the two of them to the barn, Double D and his mother whickered their protest. "I'll be back in a minute," Trish assured them.

A few minutes later, with both pairs shut in their stalls with feed and water, Trish strolled back outside. She could see David down in the pasture checking the outside stock. As she watched, he clipped a lead rope on the pregnant mare and led her up the lane. Trish turned back into the barn to prep the foaling stall.

"You think it's tonight?" she asked as David led the mare into the newly strawed stall.

"Better safe than sorry." David unsnapped the rope and gave the mare a pat on the shoulder as he eased by her. "Her milk's in and she seems kind of restless. I'll check on her a couple of times tonight."

Trish leaned her chin on her arms crossed on the top of the stall door. She studied the mare that pulled hay from the full manger and munched contentedly. "They sure are tricky, aren't they? To think a horse can stop labor at will, or even choose when to drop her foal."

"Yeah, it all helps, especially if you're wild and trying to keep away from predators."

"I know. Adam Finley had video cameras in his foaling stall, and a sound system so he could hear if the mare started panting. You should see that spread, Davey boy. It's unbelievable."

"Well, things like that would make our lives easier too, but with only one or two foaling at a time, it would be mighty expensive."

"I know, but we can dream, can't we?"

David patted her on the shoulder. "Come on, dreamer. Say good-night to your friends and let's get out of here."

"See you two later," Pastor Mort called as they came up the rise. They waved back and watched his car move down the drive.

"You think he talked with Mom?" Trish scuffed her boot toe in the gravel.

"I sure hope so. I've never seen her like this." David tucked both hands in the back pockets of his jeans.

"Scary, huh?"

"Yeah."

"How's Mom?" Trish asked after they'd shut the door.

Her father shrugged and shook his head.

When Trish stepped into the dark bedroom a while later and whispered, "Mom?" there was no answer. She left quietly, wishing she could say or do something that would help.

Trish had barely closed her eyes after her prayers when the nightmares rolled over her again. She felt herself flying through the air. "Oh!" She jerked upright. Blinking her eyes, she tried to clear both her vision and her head. Her mouth felt like horses had been racing through it. Her heart pounded as if she'd been the one racing.

With a sigh, she lay back down and stared up at the leafy patterns reflected on the ceiling. Shadows from the branches swaying in the breeze danced above her. Trish willed her eyes to stay open, knowing that the terrible sounds and pictures would return when she slipped into sleep.

Remember the name of Jesus, her helpful inner voice whispered. *That worked in the fog, didn't it?*

Trish smiled to herself. *That's right, it did.* It was nice to get some inner help for a change. "Jesus, Jesus." When she closed her eyes, she pictured Him sitting on a rock with children around Him. He was laughing.

She slept. In peace.

When her alarm went off, Trish stretched and yawned. She certainly felt better than yesterday. The house was silent when she padded down the hall to the bathroom. Her parents' bedroom door was still closed.

"Hi, Tee," her father said when she peeked around the corner to the dining room table.

"Is Mom . . ."

Hal shrugged. He rubbed his forehead with his fingers as if he had a headache. "I don't know." He took a deep breath. "David's down at the barn with the mare that foaled, so I'll take you to school. It's a filly," he answered the question before she could ask. "And yes, she's fine, and no, you haven't time to go see her before school."

"You could at least let me get a word in edgewise."

"Why? Then you'd try to talk me into letting you see her."

Trish grinned at the accuracy of his statement. She thought about her mother all the time she was showering and dressing. What was going on? Her mother couldn't just check out like this, could she? Maybe she really was sick and not telling them. The thought stopped her toothbrush cold. Mom couldn't be sick too. She just couldn't. Didn't they have

28

enough problems with her father's cancer? Her stomach clenched, like a bad charlie horse.

"You taking Mom to the doctor today?" she asked just before getting out of the car at school.

"We'll see. You make sure you talk with Mrs. Olson now. You know you have to set up a homework schedule for while you're gone."

"I know." Usually the thought of the Derby made her float about eighteen inches off the ground. Today her feet were encased in concrete. "See you." She waved as she slung her book bag over her shoulder.

By afternoon Trish had a headache of her own. The doctor had warned her about trying to read, and boy, was he ever right. Sentences jumbled together, and words—well, it was like looking through a waterfall—all blurry. Besides, so many kids had asked about the accident. She felt like a celebrity in reverse. And every time she thought about Phil and his family, the tears stung the backs of her eyes.

"Bad time, huh?" Mrs. Olson patted Trish's hand when she sat in the chair by the counselor's desk. "I can tell you're not feeling so great, so how can I help you?"

"We'll be shipping Spitfire to Kentucky about the twentieth, and then I'll fly out there on the twenty-second. The Derby is on May sixth." Trish paused.

"And then?"

"Then, I don't know. See, the problem is no one else can ride Spitfire, so we'll decide about the other races depending upon what happens at the Derby."

"So, if you win you could miss more school?"

"I guess." Trish was having trouble concentrating. Her head had gone beyond just hurting and was now in serious pain.

"Trish, you're turning green right before my eyes. What's wrong?"

"I got a bit of a concussion on Saturday and . . ."

"And you should be home in bed." Mrs. Olson shook her head but smiled at the same time. "Why don't you go lie down in the nurse's room." She checked her watch. "The bell will ring in about half an hour. I'll let Brad know where you are."

Trish nodded—carefully. "Thanks."

"And, Trish, I'll let your teachers know about our talk so they're ready to help you with a schedule."

"Bad, huh?" Rhonda said, after she and Brad walked with Trish out to Brad's metallic-blue Mustang.

"Better now than a while ago." Trish slid into the front seat and dropped her head back against the headrest. The pain pills she'd taken seemed to be helping.

She opened her eyes when the car stopped in her yard. A strange car was parked beside the family sedan. "See you guys."

"I'll be back for chores in about half an hour. You aren't riding, are you?" Brad asked.

"I was planning on it, but you and David'll have to do the honors." She shut the door without a slam.

She stopped as soon as she shut the door into the house. The car belonged to Pastor Mort, and he and her parents were in the living room praying. Trish added her own amen, greeted them, and headed for her bedroom. The bed welcomed her with open sheets. *At least Mom was sitting in her chair.* The thought flitted away as her eyelids slammed shut.

Dinner was another silent affair. "Your mother's sleeping," Hal said. Trish squelched her questions when she looked at her father's face.

"Tomorrow's the funeral." Hal looked from Trish to David. "You don't have to go if you don't want to."

"I'll go," David said.

Trish felt her stomach cramp again. "I'll go," she whispered. *But I've never been to a funeral before,* she wanted to cry out.

Chapter 04

I can do all things through Christ who strengthens me." Trish repeated the verse over and over. "All things. I can do all things, even go to a funeral." *But I don't want to go. I don't want Phil to be dead.* She stared at her tear-stained face in the mirror.

Morning had come too soon. David and her father sat in the dining room eating breakfast. Marge still hadn't come out of her room. And Trish—all she wanted to do was hide her head under the pillow. If her mother could, why couldn't she?

She stuffed the thought back down where she hid the questions too hard to think about. Her mother really must be sick. What if something *was* wrong and no one was telling her? Maybe her mother had a terrible disease. Why hadn't she gone to the doctor? Another question to stuff.

"I'm so scared," she finally admitted. Bracing her arms on the counter, she let her head drop forward. So scared. So worried. *Just like my mother.*

Trish blotted her eyes and tugged the brush through her hair. Even that was harder to do now that she'd let her hair grow longer. She gritted her teeth. Obviously this was going to be one of *those* days. She *had* to talk to her mother, that was all there was to it.

When she opened the bathroom door, she could hear the men talking in the dining room. She tiptoed across the hall and knocked on her parents' door. When there was no answer, she opened it anyway and walked into the darkened room. As her eyes adjusted to the dimness, she could see her mother lying on her side facing the window.

"Mom?" She padded around the end of the bed and scrunched down beside the still form. "Mom?" A little louder this time.

Marge opened her eyes.

"Are you sick, Mom? What's wrong? Can I get you something?"

Marge shook her head. "No, just leave me here."

"But—but—you haven't eaten. You—you—we need you." Trish reached out to touch her mother's shoulder.

Marge flinched away. "I can't—I don't want to talk now." She shut her eyes again.

Trish stared at the pale face framed by limp and matted hair. "But, Mom . . ." Her words trailed off. Trish slumped back on her haunches. What were they going to do?

Tears slipped from beneath her mother's closed lashes and ran unheeded onto the pillow. Trish drew a staggery breath. The tears so close to the surface today burned her eyes and made her sniff. She chewed her bottom lip as she pushed herself to her feet. "I'll talk to you later, after the funeral." She wasn't sure if the words were a promise or a plea.

Trish shut the door behind her and headed for the kitchen. On her way past the cold, gray ashes in the fireplace, she glanced at the mantel. The carved wooden eagle she'd given her father for Christmas had become a symbol of strength for all of them. She clutched the eagle to her chest as she tiptoed back into her mother's room and set it on the nightstand where Marge couldn't miss it. Eagle's wings—if anyone needed them now, it was her mother.

"I can do all things," the words kept time with her feet as she mounted the broad concrete steps to the church where the funeral was being held. She clutched her father's arm with one hand and David's with the other. Even rolling her lips together failed to stem the tears that persisted.

Flowers of various colors banked the altar and surrounded the closed casket at the front of the sanctuary. A blanket of red roses like those presented to a winning rider covered the shiny wood. Organ music floated over and under the murmur of voices from people in the packed pews. Trish recognized owners, trainers, jockeys, and stable hands. It seemed everyone connected with The Meadows was present.

The hymns, the sermon, the words spoken by Phil's friends, all passed in a blur as Trish fought her own battle against the sobs that threatened to break through. One verse stayed in her mind: *"I have fought the good fight, I have finished the race, I have kept the faith. Finally, there is laid up for me the crown of righteousness. . . ."*

Hal handed her a handkerchief. "I brought an extra," he whispered in her ear as he wiped his eyes.

Six jockeys, all wearing silks, carried out the casket.

After the pastor spoke the final words at the cemetery, a red-coated steward raised a long brass bugle and blew the parade to the post. Trish felt like saluting. Instead, she wiped her eyes and, like the others, turned back to the cars. The women of the church had prepared a buffet luncheon for everyone.

Trish felt proud of her father as he placed their sympathy card on the table. She knew it contained a check for $2,000, the Runnin' On Farm's contribution to a fund for the grieving family. Jockeys, owners, and trainers from all over the country would send money to the fund, whether they knew the person in trouble or not. Like other jockeys, Trish donated the fee from one mount. That was the way of the track.

But her father had a reputation for helping those in need. He'd said it was his way of paying back some of the blessings God had given them. The warm glow wasn't drowned out by the tears Trish sniffed when she shook Mrs. Snyder's hand.

Back home, she changed her clothes and looked longingly at her bed. Instead of a nap she walked slowly down to the barn. She should go to school for a couple of hours, but it was too big an effort. She stopped to pat each of the stabled horses. Soft nickers and wuffles greeted her, as if they were surprised to see her.

She leaned against Spitfire's shoulder after opening the stall door and slipping inside. She wrapped both arms around his neck and rested her cheek on the coarse black mane. *"And He will raise you up on eagle's wings. . . ."* The song trickled back in her mind. "I wonder," she whispered to no one in particular, "if that's what death is like?" Spitfire's ears twitched and he nuzzled her shoulder, as if to agree with her.

"God, thank you for making my dad better." She let the song continue in her mind. *"And hold you in the palm of His hand."* Trish found herself humming the tune as she scratched Spitfire's ears and left the stall. The parade to post echoed in her mind as she ambled over to the paddock where the two foals grazed with their dams.

"What are we going to do about Mom?" Trish confronted her father that evening after they'd had a motherless dinner again.

"Keep praying."

Tell him you'll quit racing if it would help, her little voice whispered in her ear.

I can't do that! another part of her cried.

Not even if it would make your mother okay again? Trish clamped her lips together. If only covering her ears would quell the argument.

Trish glanced up to catch the look of love and understanding on her father's face.

"Don't worry, Tee. It'll be okay."

Funny thing, Trish thought as she crawled into bed that night. *Dad telling me not to worry. That's what Mom does—worry. People can't get sick from just worrying—can they?*

The next afternoon, mounted on her first ride since the accident, Trish wasn't so sure. Every time she closed her eyes, the scream of horses and humans came back to her. She clenched her teeth to keep them from chattering.

She concentrated on the trainer's instructions. "He's really ready; you should do well today. He hates dirt in his face, so he'll go for the front. Go to the whip if you have to."

Trish nodded. She hated using a whip. As the parade to post echoed over the tinny loudspeaker, her stomach did a couple of flips. A sharp, bitter taste clawed at the back of her throat.

"You okay, Trish?" the rider on the lead pony asked.

"Yeah. Yeah, I'm fine." Trish nearly choked on the lie. She wasn't fine.

She knew she'd better get control of herself or she'd never keep control of her horse.

You're afraid, her nagging voice jeered in her ear. *You're scared!*

The horse jigged and snorted as the handler at the starting gates took the lead shank. When the gate clanged behind them, the horse threw up his head. Trish tightened the reins. Her voice trembled at first, but she forced herself to continue the soothing monologue. It calmed both her and the horse.

The last horse entered the starting gates. Trish focused on the spot between her mount's ears. And they were off.

Her horse paused a moment before his leap out of the gate. Then he bobbled. Trish tightened her reins to keep him on his feet. The field surged ahead of them.

"Come on, lazy bones, you're the one who doesn't like a face full of dirt." Her horse lengthened out, settling into his stride. "Come on, baby, let's make up for lost time here."

They came out of the first turn gaining on the horses bunched ahead of them. Trish saw a gap between two other mounts and aimed hers right down the slot, until they drew even.

She couldn't do it. Echoes rang in her head. Screams. Horses falling.

Trish pulled her mount back and swung out to go around.

They didn't even come in the money.

Trish could hardly look the owner and trainer in the eye. "I'm sorry." She clutched her saddle to her chest and stepped on the scale. She'd buckled.

She wanted to throw up.

Chapter
05

The next race wasn't much better.

"Are you all right, Trish?" owner Bob Diego asked in his precise accent. "You seem unlike your usual self."

"No, I'm fine—really." Trish clenched her hands on the reins and took another deep breath. Maybe she *should* have thrown up.

"It is sometimes difficult for a rider after a bad accident. You would tell me if this were the case?"

Trish felt the sting of tears again. Oh, if only her father were here. She swallowed. "No, no, I'm okay."

Her horse reared in the starting gate. Trish managed to stay on, but visions of getting crushed against the rear gate did nothing for her nerves. They broke bad, ran poorly, and placed sixth out of a field of eight.

Trish hated to say "I'm sorry" again, but what else could she say? The bad race wasn't really the horse's fault, even though he'd been acting erratic the entire time. Usually she could talk a horse out of that kind of behavior and get him running. That's what made her a gifted jockey. She rubbed her arms, sore from fighting with the cantankerous beast all around the track.

She didn't have a ride again until the tenth and final race of the day. *Maybe if I call Dad he can help me get over this.* She shoved the thought away. How could she tell him she was afraid?

Afraid? You're scared stiff. She heard the nagging voice accusing her again. This time he seemed to have brought his entire family to stage a shouting match in her head.

Trish exited through the front glass doors of The Meadows and angled across the asphalt parking lot. The voices kept pace with her marching feet.

Scaredy cat! Scaredy cat!

Now I know what my mother feels like.

If you were a real *Christian you'd let God take care of this.*

Worry and fear are really the same thing.

The Bible says don't be afraid.

Trish clenched her hands over her ears. Her father always said God could take care of things, but if that were so, why was her mother sick in bed? Was *she* scared to death? Were this yucky stomach and shaky hands what her mother felt when she watched her daughter ride?

Trish held her hands out in front of her. She couldn't stop the trembling. She couldn't ride another horse this way. Turning, she stared across the acres of cars to the front of the grandstand. She couldn't let another owner down. She'd have to go back in there and tell Jason Rodgers he needed to find another rider.

"No!" the cry tore from her heart. "God, please help me. I can't get back up and I don't want to chicken out." She looked around. She was alone with her tears. Trish kept on walking, the sobs shaking her shoulders. *Please help me. You promised you would.*

Remember the fog? a soft voice whispered.

Trish nodded. She thought about the guardian-angel trucker who'd turned off the fog-bound freeway at the exit that led to their motel on their trip to Santa Anita.

She leaned against a parked car and closed her eyes, picturing the verses printed on three-by-five cards and pinned to the wall above the desk in her bedroom. *"I will never leave you nor forsake you."*

"If you mean that, Lord, how come I feel so alone? How come I was so scared?"

"I am with you always, even to the end of the age."

Boy, I feel like the end's here right now. She wiped the tears away. *It feels like I'm broken in pieces, scattered all over the place. Maybe Mom would be all right if I'd just quit racing. She's never had problems like this before, but how can I quit?*

An old familiar song floated through her mind, like a wind chime in a gentle breeze. *"Jesus loves me, this I know. . . ."*

Trish raised her head and looked around her. It was so real she thought a stereo must be playing.

"God, I know you are real. And I know you hear me. I don't know what's going to happen but—well—you've been there for me in the past so I guess you'll be there for me now." She looked up as if expecting a cloud to open. It didn't.

She held out her hands. No shaking. She swallowed. Her stomach stayed down.

Trish jogged back to the grandstand, yanked open the door, and strode back to the women jockeys' room.

Enveloped in the steamy hubbub, she mentally chanted the verses as she wrapped both arms around her shoulders and, rounding her back, pulled the tension out. The chant continued as she dropped forward from the waist and hugged her knees.

"You okay, Trish?" Genie Stokes sat down on the bench beside her. Genie, a veteran rider of ten years, rode for Runnin' On Farm when Trish couldn't.

"I am now." Trish unclipped her hair and tousled it with her fingers. As she massaged her scalp, she glanced sideways at the woman beside her. "I—I really was scared." The words came haltingly.

"It hits the best of us. Mine was after I broke my collarbone in a really bad fall." Genie patted Trish's shoulder. "Besides, sometimes a little fear is a healthy thing. Keeps you from making stupid mistakes."

"Yeah, but this is more than a little fear." Trish turned to look at her friend. She paused. "Ah—when you've been scared—um—did you ever—ahh—" Trish cleared her throat. Her voice dropped. "I went around out there. I couldn't drive down between two other horses and the opening was big enough for a truck."

"So?"

"So we didn't even get in the money and we should have. *I* lost the race for that horse, that owner."

"Okay. You made a mistake. You were scared. But you're smart enough to talk about it. I'll bet dollars to doughnuts you'll think about this again, but you'll go on and do what you know is right. Being afraid, especially after a terrible accident like we had here, isn't a crime. It doesn't say you're a bad rider or you failed." Genie held out her hand. "Welcome to the real world of racing."

Trish dug up her sleeve for a tissue and blew her nose. "Thanks, Genie." She glanced up at the round clock on the wall. "I gotta get out there. I'm up again in the tenth."

They won. By a nose, even after being caught in the pack up the back-stretch. Trish slid off the sorrel gelding and nearly threw her arms around Jason Rodgers. She stopped herself in time to just shake his hand.

His smile felt like a hug. "I knew you could do it, Trish. You've passed a big milestone."

When Trish got home, she stopped at the closed bedroom door. She hesitated, shrugged, and then went in. "Mom."

There was no answer from the mound in the bed.

Trish sat down in the chair by the bed. She bit her lip. "Mom, you gotta get up and talk to us again. How can we help you if we don't even know what's wrong?" She waited, hoping for an answer. "I blew it today. Lost two races because I was scared." She leaned forward and touched her mother's shoulder. "Mom? Please wake up and talk to me. Get mad at me or something—anything."

Marge blinked her eyes. She stared back at Trish, then reached out to pat her daughter's hand. Her eyes drifted closed again.

Trish sighed. She shook her head and left the room. What were they going to do?

In bed that night, Trish thought back over the day. Even her mother's not talking to her didn't dampen the thrill she felt. She'd gone to the Source for help and He'd answered. She could race again.

He always answers, her little voice whispered. *You just don't like it when He says no or to wait.*

Trish thought about that. She turned over and snuggled the covers tight around her shoulders. So, how did you know when He said to wait?

What about her mom? Had she been praying about her worrying? Would it help if Trish quit racing? Life sure could be confusing. Her prayers that night were half thank-yous and half what-do-I-do-nows. She fell asleep with a smile on her lips.

Thursday morning on the home track, Trish rode Spitfire for the first time since Santa Anita. His leg had been cool for two days. The blue-black colt crowhopped twice between the stable and the track. He tossed his head and danced sideways, tugging at the bit.

"Oh, no you don't." Trish kept a tight rein. "You're not gonna go and mess up that knee again. We'll take this morning slow and easy. Just listen to the birds sing. See, the sun's even out for you." She took a deep breath and let it out. What a four-star, incredible morning. Green, growing spring smelled like nothing else in the world.

By the second circuit of the three-quarter-mile track, Spitfire walked flat-footed with only an occasional high-step to let off some pent-up energy. Trish settled into the saddle and leaned forward to stroke his neck.

"You leave for the Derby in less than a week—I hope," she told the twitching black ears. "So you gotta get back in shape." Spitfire nodded. Trish laughed, her joy winging away with the robin that flew from the fence after serenading them.

Thursday evening they had a family meeting—without Marge.

"I'll be honest with you kids," Hal said sadly. "I don't know what to do. The one thing I do know is that I can't go off and leave your mother while she's in this condition."

Trish stared at her hands gripped together on the table in front of her. "You mean no Derby." Once the words were out she clenched her teeth. *It just isn't fair.* They'd worked so hard. Here her dad was better, Spitfire's leg was cool again, and now this.

Hal reached over and covered her hands with one of his. "I know how you feel, Tee. Please try not to be angry with your mother. She can't help what's going on either."

She doesn't seem to be trying too hard, Trish wanted to say but bit back the words.

"I'll be here to take care of her—of things—if you think you could go, that is," David said.

Trish looked from David to her father. Both of them looked worn down, tired.

"Thanks, David, but it wouldn't work. I couldn't concentrate on the horse when all I can think about is your mother. And, Trish, if some miracle happens and we do go, I've decided to not even consider taking Firefly. We just can't handle the extra strain right now."

Trish slumped on the edge of her bed a while later. Just yesterday she'd felt as if God were really there, and now He seemed to have slipped off again. She stared at the verses on the wall. Was this a no or a wait? She sighed. She'd settle for a wait until it was too late to go. And a wait meant keep praying. So she did. Even when she woke up in the middle of the night, and the first thing when she got up in the morning, and in disjointed moments after working Spitfire. *Raise you up on eagle's wings,"* floated through her mind while she brushed her teeth.

"Your mom any better?" Rhonda asked when they met at their lockers before lunch.

Trish shook her head. "But something's gotta give." She told Rhonda and Brad about the meeting the night before.

"You really mad?" Rhonda asked.

"I guess. Sometimes. And other times I try not to think about it. But we keep praying." She plunked her tray down on the table. "I just know God's gonna work this out—somehow."

"You going to the track?" Brad asked around a mouthful of sandwich.

"Yeah, I have two mounts. David wants you to come help him get Final Command loaded and over to the track. He runs in the fifth tomorrow."

"Sure. When're you working at your place?"

"We're not. After Saturday everyone is out to pasture except Spitfire. Dad says we'll think about summer racing after the Triple Crown is over. All the horses will be better off with a good rest."

When Trish got home, the pastor's car was in the drive again. He and her father were sitting in the living room talking when she stepped through the door.

"Come here for a minute, Tee." Her father motioned her over.

"Hello, Trish." Pastor Mort smiled at her.

"Hi." She looked back at her father. "What's up?"

"I—we—" Hal nodded at the serious-faced man on the sofa. "We've talked with the doctor and decided on a pretty serious course of action. There were two choices—either put your mother in the hospital or . . ."

"The hospital? Is she worse?"

"No." Hal rubbed his forehead. "Your mother has chosen the second plan. Tomorrow morning, with God and Pastor Mort's help, we'll all go to the track and talk about what happened the day of the accident."

Trish sank down on the hearth. "All of us?" Her voice squeaked on the last word. *The nightmares have finally quit. Will they start up again?*

Hal nodded. "I think it'll help you too."

Trish shrugged. "Okay." She wet her lips. She could hear the fish tank bubbling away in the dining room. She stared at her hands clasped between her knees. "Um-m-m, I've gotta get to the track. I've got two mounts." She rose to her feet as though she were pushing up barbells in the weight room. Her gaze flicked from one man to the other. "You're sure this is the best way?"

They both nodded.

Trish fled to her bedroom.

Chapter
06

Trish battled monsters all night.

"Yeah, I'm coming," she answered David's knock groggily. She could hear her brother go on down the hall. Instead of getting up, she flopped over on her back. Today they were *all* going to the track. Right after breakfast. The thought of food made her stomach turn over. What was going to happen to her mom? To all of them?

Trotting Spitfire around the track blew the cobwebs away from Trish's mind. The morning air was brisk but without the bite of winter. Spitfire tugged at the bit and every few yards danced sideways, tossing his head and snorting.

Trish laughed. "You big goof. You know I'll let you run again when you're ready. Right now, Dad says jog, so jog it is."

Spitfire shied at something only he could see.

"Knock it off." Trish automatically clamped her knees and flowed right with him. "You didn't see anything; you made it up." Spitfire snorted again. He wasn't even warm when they trotted back to the stable.

"You two looked like you were having fun," David said with a grin.

"You should have saddled Dan'l and come too."

"Naw. Need to get all this done so we can leave." He waved at the pile of straw outside Spitfire's and the gray's stalls.

His comment brought Trish back to reality with a thump. "Yeah."

"Look on the good side. This could be the thing that snaps Mom out of this." David stopped stripping the tack off Spitfire and stared at her.

"I know." Trish drew a circle in the dirt with her boot toe. Spitfire blew in her ear and nudged her shoulder. She reached up to scratch his ears and rubbed her cheek against the silky skin of the colt's cheek.

"Well?"

"Well, it's scary."

"For you or Mom?"

Trish sorted through her confused thoughts. "Probably both. I just don't want the nightmares to keep on forever."

"They won't."

"How do you know?"

"I'm your big brother. I'm paid to know these things." David handed her the saddle and bridle. "Don't worry, Tee. It'll be all right."

I wish people would quit telling me not to worry, Trish thought as she hung up the gear. *I'm not a worrier.*

Oh no? She was sure she heard her little nagger chuckle.

Her mother was up and dressed, huddled in the recliner with her eyes closed, when Trish walked back into the house after pulling her boots off at the bootjack on the deck.

"Hi, Mom." Trish started to go to her mother, then thought better of it.

Marge nodded and blinked her eyes open as if weights had held her eyelids closed.

Trish noted the hollows in her mother's pale cheeks, the stringy hair. She changed directions and knelt by the chair. "You want me to help you wash your hair before we go? You know how much better that always makes us feel." *Come on, please. Let me help you like you always helped me.* She bit her tongue to keep the words from escaping.

The seconds seemed to stretch to hours.

Marge nodded. "If you want to."

"I'll get the towels and shampoo." Trish felt like tap dancing on the ceiling.

With her supplies in place, she walked back into the living room and picked up her mother's limp hand. "Come on." She tugged gently. "You'll feel much better." Trish felt like the parent as she led her mother by the hand into the kitchen. She adjusted the water temperature and drew the spray nozzle out.

"Lean over." Trish patted her mother's shoulder.

Marge followed Trish's orders as though she didn't have the energy to resist. "Umm-m-m," she said as Trish massaged her scalp with her strong fingers. "Feels good."

Trish felt like she'd just won the Derby. She rinsed and shampooed again. It seemed so strange to be on the giving end rather than the receiving. But it felt good.

"How about if I blow-dry it for you?" Trish asked as she toweled her mother's hair.

Marge reached up and wrapped the towel around her head. She smiled at her daughter for the first time in what seemed like months. "Okay."

Trish wielded dryer and brush like an expert. Her years of horse grooming were suddenly giving way to a new profession.

Marge closed her eyes. A deep sigh, as if from her toes, seemed to fill the bathroom and drown out the angry-bee hum of the dryer.

"You okay?" Trish stepped back to view her handiwork. She could see strands of gray that she was sure hadn't been there three weeks ago. The dark waves of her mother's hair feathered back on the sides and waved to the right on top. "You look nice." Trish held her hand over her mother's eyes and sprayed. "I think this is the first time I've ever done your hair."

"Probably." Marge sighed. "Thank you, Tee."

The ride to the track was a silent affair. Each of the family seemed lost in their own thoughts. Trish stared out the window. Her mother's eyes were closed again. She hadn't said anything since the bathroom. Her father kept darting glances at Marge, as if afraid she might back out. David chewed on a knuckle.

Trish tried to picture the verses on her wall. They were so fuzzy she couldn't read them. Good thing she knew them by heart by now. She repeated "I can do all things through Christ who strengthens me" under her breath—over and over.

The sun had gone behind the clouds by the time they parked outside the chain-link fence at Portland Meadows Racetrack. Golfers were still playing the nine-hole course on the infield. Morning works were over, so the tractor and drag were grooming the track. Pastor Mort's white car was parked next to a pickup where a golf cart trundled up into the bed.

Trish felt like crawling under the seat and hiding as her father got out of the car and walked around to help Marge out. David followed his father, and between them Marge appeared smaller, as if she'd shrunk in the last week. The three of them walked toward the fence. Trish shoved open her door and stepped out. She felt anchored to the asphalt.

Pastor Mort turned, as if sensing her fear. He came over and took her arm. "Come on, Trish. It will be okay, I promise you."

Trish gritted her teeth. She *would not* cry. Together they followed the others around the outside of the track.

When they reached the spot just beyond the first turn and stopped, Pastor Mort looked at each of them. "I'd like to start with prayer." At their nods, he began, "Heavenly Father, you know how hurting we are. You made us and we are yours. Our minds and our feelings are gifts from you and today we ask . . ."

Trish's mind tried to check out, but she clamped her jaw tight and forced it back to the present.

" . . . that you bring healing to this family, to Hal and Marge, to David, to Trish. You know what they need and we thank you for your healing mercy. Amen."

Trish swallowed hard. "Amen."

"Tee, why don't you come over here by me," her father said as he reached out his arm to her.

Trish nodded. His arm felt good around her, made her think she wouldn't fly apart after all.

After a moment of silence, Pastor Mort continued. "Now, Marge, I'm asking you to go back to that day, that afternoon at the track. Close your eyes and picture the track." He paused. "See the parade to the post." More silence. "See the horses enter the starting gates. Can you see it?"

Trish sensed rather than saw her mother's nod. Trish closed her eyes tighter so she could remember too.

"The horses broke from the gate and pounded in front of the stands. You were down by the rail." Pastor Mort's soft voice stilled.

Trish could feel the clumps of dirt banging into her and her mount as they came up from behind. She'd already pulled down the first pair of goggles and the second pair was darkening with dirt. She felt her mount stumble and herself flying through the air. The cry she heard wasn't from her mind.

Marge buried her face in Hal's shoulder, her sobs tearing at Trish's heart. She turned and began rubbing her mother's back. She could see the tears streaming down David's face through the waterfall of her own.

"And what do you see?" the pastor asked Marge quietly when the tears diminished.

"They've lifted Trish onto the stretcher. They've covered her face! Oh no!" Marge thumped her hand on Hal's shoulder, and the tears resumed in intensity. "They think she's dead! No! Not my Trish. No! No!"

"Mom, Mom, it's okay." Trish forced her words out around her own tears. "I'm right here. I'm all right. I didn't die. I didn't even come close to it."

"I can't handle any more. You could have died. . . ." She looked up into Hal's face. "All I could see out there was Trish on a stretcher . . . and then she was in the hospital—sick—hurt. I've been afraid of that all along."

Trish tried to say something but Pastor Mort put a hand on her shoulder. "Let her cry it out," he whispered.

"Sometimes I get so angry at God—why is He doing this to me? And then I feel terrible. I know worry is a sin. I should—I have to—trust more."

Trish continued to rub and pat her mother's back. She looked up at her father. He buried his cheek in Marge's hair and held her tight to his chest.

God, help us, Trish pleaded.

It seemed her mother would cry forever. At times she was almost incoherent, muttering and sobbing as if her heart would break. Hal continued to hold her. Trish clung to his arm as she rubbed her mother's back, David on the other side, doing the same. Finally she fell silent, shuddering every once in a while.

Then Marge lifted her head from Hal's shoulder and took a deep breath. Hal dug a handkerchief out of his pocket, wiped her eyes and cheeks. She appeared to be past the deep grief she experienced at reliving the incident. "God, forgive me for what I have done to my family," Marge said. She kissed both David and Trish, then Hal.

"He does," replied Pastor Mort. "You know He does. And He'll help you put this behind you."

"I'll take you home." Hal wrapped both arms around his wife and hugged her close. "Unless there's more, Pastor?" The two men exchanged looks.

"No. We'll talk again on Monday, Marge, if you'd like." She nodded. "Good then. God bless you all." He hugged each of them in turn. "Remember, if you need me, all you have to do is call."

"I know." Hal shook the pastor's hand again. "Thank you."

Trish felt like a puppet with all the strings cut. She walked back to the car with her family and slumped in the backseat. *Now what will happen?* She rubbed her eyes with her fingers. After taking a deep breath, she glanced at her watch. The first race of the day was less than an hour away.

David leaned on the open car door and announced, "I've gotta get down to the stalls. Mom, you okay?"

Marge nodded. "I will be. You and Trish go ahead. We'll go on home." She leaned back against the seat, closed her eyes, and reached back to squeeze Trish's hand. "You'll be okay—after all this, I mean?"

Trish lifted her mother's hand to her cheek. "Yes, Mom." She grabbed her sports bag and slid from the car. "I've missed you so." She whirled away before the tears could overwhelm her again.

"See you later." David backpedaled as he talked, then turned and caught up with Trish. He put his arm around her shoulders. "You *really* all right? I mean, you'll be able to get beyond this and ride your mount?"

Trish nodded. "I feel like—like maybe there's hope now."

"Well, if I *never* go through something like that again, it'll be too soon."

"I know." Trish turned and watched as their family car was lost in the incoming vehicles. She shrugged her shoulders up to her ears and relaxed them. "See ya in the fifth." She turned left at the gate into the track, and David loped across the infield to the backside.

Trish was mounted on the favorite in the first race. Bob Diego's sorrel mare nickered when she saw Trish.

"I think you have a friend here." He shifted so Trish had room to stroke the mare's head and murmur sweet promises in the twitching ears.

"I like her too." Trish smiled back. "And today we're due for a win, aren't we?" She scratched the mare's cheek and up behind her ears.

"Two out of three would be a good number, no?" Diego boosted Trish into the saddle.

"Yes." Trish settled into the seat and gathered her reins. "See you in the winner's circle."

The sun had broken through the cloud cover to turn the horse hides into dazzling colors. From the echoing bugle of the parade to post until the gates shut behind them, Trish knew there was no place on earth she'd rather be.

They broke clean at the shot and came off the pack by the end of the first turn. Trish sang to her mount, holding her steady about a half length ahead of the second place. She heard the cries of the jockeys and the grunts of the straining horses. When the other horse drew even with her stirrups, she loosened the reins. The mare settled lower, lengthening her stride. They pounded into the far turn, a two-horse race with the others trailing.

The other jockey went for his whip with a furlong to go. Trish leaned forward even more. "Go for it, you beauty. Come on. Now!" The mare turned it on and drove across the finish line three lengths ahead.

"I knew you could do it. And this was a nice fat purse too. You earned your feed for another year." She cantered on around the track, then dismounted at the winner's circle.

"An excellent ride." Diego shook her hand.

"I hate to say I told you so . . ." Trish grinned up at him.

"You're welcome to say that anytime."

They positioned themselves for the camera and Bob held the trophy aloft. The mare sniffed the silver bowl just as the cameras flashed.

"That oughta be a good one." Trish waved as she headed for the dressing room.

The next race didn't go as well, but with the quality of the horse Trish felt a place was pretty good. So did the owner, a man Trish hadn't ridden for before. She and the trainer exchanged smiles as the owner's wife stepped close enough to get sprayed by dirt when the horse shook.

In her next race John Anderson stood with David in the saddling paddock with his gelding Final Command. "Good to see you, Trish." He shook her hand. "I'm sorry to miss your dad, but I know you two know this old boy better than anyone else. Just remember, I insist you use the whip if he needs it." David boosted Trish up and handed her a whip. He hid his wink in the horse's mane and backed the sorrel gelding out of the stall. They all knew how much Trish hated to use a whip, but this old boy seemed to need encouragement. He liked to run with the pack; winning wasn't on his list of priorities.

"We're gonna turn this into one of your priorities," Trish muttered at the flickering ears. "You and I both know you can run better than you've let anyone else guess."

Trish almost waited too long. Command ran neck and neck with another horse, letting the leader pull away. "Too bad," Trish hollered as she brought the whip down on his shoulder—twice. A spurt of speed brought them up with the leader coming out of the turn. With a furlong to go, Trish whapped him again. Now the race was on. They thundered down the stretch, whisker to whisker.

The other jockey struck his horse again and just the thwap of it sent Command surging ahead—to win by a nose.

"Well, that's the first time I'll have to thank another jockey for making my horse run faster," Trish commented to John Anderson when she slid to the ground.

"What happened?"

"This old boy didn't want to be hit again, so when the other jockey went to the whip, we ran faster." She wiped sand out of her eyes. "Wish he didn't mind being behind. It gets mighty dirty that way." She patted the gelding's muddy face. "Thanks, old boy. We done good."

Trish whistled her way across the infield after changing clothes.

"You sound mighty happy," Brad said as Trish dropped into a chair in their tack room.

"Good day. Fattened up my bank account some and had fun doing it. David still at the testing barn?"

"Yeah, should be here any minute. You hungry?"

"Starved."

"Good, let's hit the cook shack. I'll buy."

"No, I'll buy. We'll celebrate two out of three."

By the time they returned, David had Command all rinsed off and was scraping him down. Brad took over the job while Trish handed David a ham sandwich and a can of soda.

"Thanks. To what do I owe this generosity?" David took a big bite out of one half.

"My wins." Trish sipped her Diet Coke. She poured some in her hand for Final Command to lick. "I just feel so-o-o good." She handed Brad the sheet to throw over the steaming horse. "Here, I'll walk him. Then we can load and go home."

Hal lay dozing in his recliner when Trish and David walked into the house after finishing the chores. With only the gelding, Spitfire, and the foals to care for, chores didn't take long.

Trish's mind flew back to the months when Hal had been too weak to do much more than lie in his recliner. But his smile chased the fears back into hiding, even though she knew he was scheduled for another chemotherapy treatment on Monday.

"Where's Mom?" Trish asked.

"Sleeping."

"Is she . . . ?"

"No, no." Hal shook his head. "She's just resting. This has been a terribly exhausting day. But she put the roast in the oven before her nap, said we'd eat about six-thirty."

Trish felt the sigh reach all the way down to her toes. *What a relief.* She plunked down on the sofa and stretched her hands over her head.

"Well, how did you do?" Hal asked.

"Two wins and a place." She went on to tell her dad the story of Command and the whips. They were laughing together when Marge yawned her way into the room.

51

The entire evening felt like evenings should feel, as far as Trish was concerned. No more mention was made of the morning at the track.

Until Sunday night. Trish knew her mother had a hard time during church, but she also knew if she let down, she'd have been sniffling too. She'd only had a place and a show at the track, but winning all the time didn't carry quite the urgency it did before the accident. Still, with the horses she'd ridden, those paying positions had been nothing to be ashamed of.

"Did you see this?" Hal asked when Trish walked in the door after chores. He handed Trish the sports section from *The Oregonian*, Portland's major newspaper.

A colored picture of her and Spitfire driving for the finish line covered most of the top half of the page. The headline read, "Can This Girl and Her Horse Win the Derby?" Trish grinned at her father over the top of the paper and then read through the article. Most of it seemed pretty accurate.

"They think just because no other woman has won the Derby, we don't have a chance."

"You're going to hear that a lot."

"But most of it depends on Spitfire. He does the running." Trish shook her head and finished the article. "They don't give him too much of a chance, do they?"

"You know Seattle Slew was a shocker because he came from the Pacific Northwest. The racing world doesn't think we have too much going out here."

"Humph." Trish snorted her opinion. She went back to reading the article—again. "At least they mention that Spitfire is a son of Seattle Slew. You'd think that would carry *some* weight. And how about the way he won the Santa Anita Derby? What's the matter with the jerk that wrote this?" She looked for the byline at the top of the article.

"Ken Davis is known as the best sportswriter in the area."

"He's a jerk."

"He's said plenty of good things about you in the past."

"Half a jerk, anyway." Trish grinned at her father.

"You better get used to it, Tee. You're going to hear, read, and see all kinds of stuff in the weeks ahead. Remember what they say, you're in trouble when you begin to believe your own press." Hal reached for her hand to pull him up from his chair. "Let's eat."

The family gathered for their weekly meeting after stuffing themselves with a fine meal of pork chops, potatoes, and gravy. Marge's apple crisp added the final touch.

"Sure beats mine and Dad's cooking." Trish rubbed her stomach as she leaned back in her chair.

"You ain't just a kiddin'," David affirmed.

"Thanks a lot." Trish tossed her napkin at him. "I didn't see you in the kitchen, buddy."

Marge steepled her fingers together under her chin. "Thank you all for what you did for me and for all of us during the last several days. Trish, the eagle meant a lot to me, even if I didn't say so. And all the times each of you tried to get me to talk." A tear ran down one cheek, and she wiped it away. "Please forgive me."

Hal handed her a tissue. And then one to Trish. He and David got by without—just barely.

What about the Derby? Trish wanted to ask, but she bit her tongue and kept silent. Just having her family all together was enough for today.

Chapter
07

I think you should go," Marge said quietly the next morning.

Trish darted a look at her father. He had that deep, considering look on his face. She wanted him to hurry and say "Yes, we're going to the Derby" so she could finish getting ready for school.

"How was Spitfire?" He turned to look at Trish.

"Rarin' to go. You said we might gallop tonight."

"Um-mm. We'll talk more after we see how that goes. Come on, Marge. Let's drop Trish off at school on the way in to the hospital."

Trish's good humor thumped back to earth. What kind of shape would her father be in when she got home? Would he be vomiting and weak again? If only he could wait for a treatment until after the Derby. Better yet, if only he never had to have another treatment. But she knew that was impossible. Since the cancer was receding, they didn't dare play around with the schedule the doctor had set up.

"No decision yet," Trish answered Rhonda's question as they stuffed books into their lockers.

"But at least your mom is better. Man, I was beginning to *worry*." Rhonda slung her purse strap over her shoulder.

"Don't even say that word." Trish slammed her locker door shut. "Let's eat before the food's all gone."

Brad joined them at their table a few minutes later. "You won't believe this." He shook his head as he tucked his long legs under the table.

"What's up?" Rhonda spoke around a mouthful of tuna salad sandwich.

"I won a scholarship. Mrs. Olson just told me about it. My dad is gonna freak out."

The girls threw their arms around his neck and each one kissed him on the cheek.

"That's fantastic." Trish kissed him again. "You deserve every penny."

"For how much?" Rhonda was always practical.

"And where to?"

Shock stole over Brad's face. "I don't know. Guess I just tuned out at the word *scholarship*."

Trish turned when she felt a hand tap her shoulder.

"Hi, Trish, my name is Lisa Jones, and I write for the sports section of the *Falcon Flyer*."

Trish nodded.

"I'd like to interview you for next week's paper, if that would be all right?" The thin girl tucked a strand of long, dark hair behind her ear. "Do you have time?"

"Sure." Trish shrugged. "When?"

"Would right now be okay?"

At Trish's nod, Brad moved over one seat. "Here, we even have a spot for you."

Lisa smiled at him and sank down onto the seat as if afraid he might jerk it out from under her.

Trish answered the questions easily.

When had she started riding? How long had she been racing?

She really got into it when she started describing the thrill of winning and what she liked best about her sport. The words flowed so fast that Lisa asked her to slow down a couple of times. It was a relief though when the bell rang—it kept Lisa from asking about the accident.

Or at least that was what Trish was afraid the young reporter would ask. "Scared to death" wouldn't look too good in the paper, but it would have been an honest answer.

But she'd worked through the fear, hadn't she? Trish sent a thank-you heavenward.

Trish and Rhonda were still laughing and teasing Brad about his memory lapse over the scholarship when Trish got out of the car at Runnin' On Farm.

"Why don't you come ride with me?" Trish stuck her head back in the open window. "I'll be galloping Spitfire."

"Okay. Give me half an hour," Rhonda replied.

"What about me?" Brad assumed his soulful look.

"You know David'll find something for you to do."

"Great. I need the money."

"It's up to you." Trish waved as Brad pulled away. Caesar shoved his cold nose into Trish's hand. She scratched the top of his head, then jogged up the walk to the front door. Late-blooming red tulips filled two large pots on the sides of the concrete step. She hesitated before turning the brass doorknob. Both cars were in the drive, so she knew her parents were back.

Chicken, her nagging voice whispered. *Waiting isn't going to change anything.*

"I know." She stooped down to give Caesar a big hug. His tongue flicked her nose before she could pull back. "Still the fastest tongue in the west, aren't you, old boy?" To prove her point, he caught her chin the next time.

Trish straightened up. "Just what I need, a clean face."

Caesar's feathery tail thumped his answer.

Trish opened the door and stepped into an empty living room, then the kitchen. Nope, no one in there either. She stopped at the door to her parents' room. It stood ajar, and she peeked in. A deep breath didn't help the fluttering in her stomach.

Hal lay on his back in the dimness, one hand across his forehead. A large bowl sat on a chair by the bed.

When he didn't move, Trish turned to leave.

His voice, raspy but stronger than usual, stopped her. "I'll be okay by morning, Tee. Tell me how Spitfire's gallop goes."

"I will. Where's Mom?"

Hal started to answer but instead had to roll to the side and grab the yellow bowl. The sound of his gagging and spitting followed Trish down the hall.

Trish stopped in surprise when she entered her bedroom. Her mother lay soundly sleeping in Trish's bed. Trish tried to set her book bag down quietly, but Marge's eyes blinked open at the faint rustle.

She yawned and stretched her arms above her head. "Hi. Thanks for your bed. I didn't want to bother your dad, and the sun shining in your window was so inviting." She yawned again.

"You feeling okay?" Trish sank down on the edge of the bed and turned to face her mother.

"Just needed a nap. I think all that lying around zapped my strength." She sat up and scooted her back against the pillows. "How was school?"

"I got interviewed for the school paper." Trish leaned over to unlace her tennis shoes. "Oh!" She jerked upright. "Brad got a scholarship. And he forgot to ask for how much."

"Where to?"

"He didn't ask that either. Said he zoned out in shock at the word *scholarship.*"

Marge laughed, then swung her legs over the edge of the bed. "Well, I'd better go bake that boy some cookies. He's coming over?" At Trish's nod, Marge stood and stretched again. "Chocolate chip, I suppose."

Trish heard her mother open the door and check on Hal, then continue into the kitchen.

Trish had no trouble giving thanks to God as one of the cards on her wall admonished.

Spitfire wanted to race when Trish trotted him out on the track a while later. Old Dan'l even crowhopped a couple of times to give Rhonda a bit of a thrill. Neither horse was happy with the slow jog of the first lap.

"Knock it off," Trish ordered when the black colt lunged forward a couple of times. "Whaddya think you are, a charger?"

Spitfire shook his head, spraying gobs of lather from around the bit. One hit Rhonda in the face.

"Thanks a million," she said around her giggles. She wiped the sticky stuff onto Dan'l's shoulder.

"Dad says slow gallop once around and then jog again." Trish eased up on the reins but had to pull Spitfire back down as he argued for a full-fledged race. Trish didn't dare let her mind wander for even an instant. It would be too easy for him to strain that knee again, and then it would be all over.

"Let's walk a loop," Trish said when they finished their jog. "Then we won't have to cool 'em out." She slid to the ground and started leading the colt around the track. Spitfire rubbed his sweaty forehead on her shoulder, nearly sending her flying. "Careful, you goof." She held the reins more tightly under his chin. By the time they finished the circuit, Spitfire had his head over her shoulder, right in his favorite place.

"Hard to believe he's a Derby contender when you see him like that," Rhonda said. "He looks more like a kid's pony right now."

"Yeah, let's just hope he gets a chance to run it."

After the chores were finished, the four teens took their cookies and milk out onto the deck. Marge brought a full plate to pass around again and joined them. Brad became the brunt of their teasing this time.

Trish felt as though she were standing off to the side watching what was going on. This happy scene had played out many times before in the years they'd all been growing up. You just never knew who would get teased the most and at what time. The only one missing was Trish's father. Caesar sat at her feet, eyes pleading for another piece of cookie. She tossed a chunk in the air and the collie caught it with a snap.

They didn't discuss the coming race until Tuesday evening. Trish felt as if she'd been walking on pins all day. They were scheduled to ship Spitfire in only two days.

"I've already given my opinion," Marge said at their family meeting around the dining room table. "I think you should go."

"Are you sure?" Hal clasped her hand between both of his.

"All that we've been through this past week, the talks with Pastor . . ." She paused and raised their clasped hands to her cheek. "I've realized I can't go on like I have been. I know I'm a worrier by nature—my mother was too, remember?"

Hal nodded.

"But I've got to turn it over to God. He says He can handle anything, so somehow He's going to teach me not to get myself sick worrying. He can take better care of you than I can." Tears glimmered in her hazel eyes. "So, I say go." Her voice dropped on the last word. She took a deep breath. "Besides that, I wrote to Mother, telling her they could meet you in Louisville to watch race. That's not too far from Florida, even though Daddy hasn't been feeling well."

Trish felt hope leap in her chest. She stared from her father to her mother. "Do you think they'll come?"

"Who knows." Marge just shook her head.

Hal smoothed the hair back from his wife's cheek. "Well, that certainly puts a new slant on things. What do you say, David?"

"Mom and I'll handle things here. You go. Who knows if we'll ever have a Derby-quality horse again."

"And you, Trish? I know it's a waste of time to ask." His smile caused the dimple to show in his right cheek.

"Well, I don't want Mom to be sick again."

"I won't be."

"And you and David'll come for the race?"

Marge flinched, as if she'd been struck. "I—I don't know." Tension weighted the silence.

Hal cleared his throat. "That's not a decision that has to be made right now. We'll talk about that later."

Trish noticed the relief that caused her mother's shoulders to sag. So it really wasn't over yet. She swallowed the lump in her throat. "Kentucky, look out. We're on our way."

"David, I packed a lot of the tack today." Hal picked up as if there hadn't been a stress point in the conversation. "We'll load the pickup tomorrow, then let Trish work some of Spitfire's kinks out Thursday morning early. After that he should be easy to load. Our flight's scheduled for one-thirty so we should leave here about ten."

Trish tried to listen to the plans, but a new song played like a brass band marching through her head. *We're going. We're going. We're going to Kentucky. We're going. We're going.* The beat continued. She bounced a little bounce on her chair, then gripped the seat with both hands. Maybe she and the chair would just fly up out the roof.

"Thanks, Mom," she whispered as she hugged her mother good-night.

"You get right to sleep now. No Derby daydreaming." Marge hugged her daughter back.

Trish grinned at the words. "What? No homework first?"

A tiny frown lighted between Marge's eyebrows. "You're not behind, are . . . ?" Marge caught herself. She swatted Trish on the behind as Trish tried to dodge away. "Good night, Tricia Marie Evanston."

Trish leaned over and hugged Hal, who was seated in his recliner. "Maybe I should stay home on Thursday and help load him."

"No, you're going to be missing too much school as it is. We'll be just fine. Now get to bed."

Trish didn't think she'd ever be able to fall asleep that night. She read each of her verses, then snuggled down under the covers. She never even got into the "pleases" in her prayer, there were so many "thank-yous."

She'd expected Wednesday to drag by, but thanks to a pop quiz in history and an in-class paper in English, the day flew by. Trish and Spitfire enjoyed a good gallop, and there was even time to work with Miss Tee for a while. The little filly still hesitated at leaving her dam, but once away she pranced along on the lead as if she'd never dug in her tiny hooves and almost landed on her rump due to a bad case of stubbornness.

"Have you started packing, Trish?" Marge asked at the dinner table.

"No, I don't go till Saturday."

"Never hurts to start early. You'll be racing Thursday and Friday, won't you?"

Trish nodded. Her mouth was too full to talk.

"I've got all your things ready." Marge smiled at Hal. "You just need to add your shaving gear in the morning."

"Bless you." Hal squeezed her fingers.

"And I put your tickets, maps, and reservations in your briefcase. The camera too."

"I wish you were coming with, Trish," Hal said. "One of these days we're going to have to take a vacation. Maybe next year we can hire someone to manage here and we can all go to Santa Anita, or wherever."

"Let's think about *wherever.* I'd love to do something *not* associated with horse racing for a change." Marge's tone was wistful, as if she were reluctant to share *her* dream.

"You're right." Hal nodded.

You need to think of others' interests once in a while, Trish's little nagging voice punched her guilt button. *Not everyone wants to talk horses all the time.*

Trish felt a sigh of resignation creep over her unbidden.

"We'll be there for the race," David assured them while reaching for his mother's hand. "Maybe we'll have time for some sightseeing. I'd like to visit Claiborne Farms and see their veterinary setup."

"You giving up on dogs and cats?" Trish looked at him in surprise. David had always talked about a small animal veterinary practice after he graduated from school.

"No, not really. Every vet has those. But maybe I should think of an equine specialty. I've sure gotten plenty of practice around here."

"And you've done an excellent job," Hal said. "You seem to have a sixth sense for what's ailing a horse like Trish does for riding. Maybe you should think about Tucson. Their equine research program is outstanding."

Besides the guilt that continued to nag her, Trish had two more things to think about when she went to bed. At least when David had been at Washington State University, they'd been able to go visit him. Arizona was a long way away.

Her thought switched to the scene at the table. Her grandparents had been invited to see her race. When they'd visited last summer, her grandmother hadn't been excited about Trish riding the Thoroughbreds. In fact, she worried more than her daughter. Was worrying an inherited disease?

And was it really fair to ask so much of her mother? It was true that racing was the main topic of conversation in their home. *Why can't she love horses as much as Dad and I do—or at least like them?*

It isn't the horses, her inner voice reminded her, *it's your riding—in races.*

"Thanks a bunch!" Trish took a deep breath, held it to the count of ten, and let it all out. Her shoulders and rib cage seemed to melt into the mattress.

Light from the mercury yard light showed her half-full suitcase on the chair. In the morning she'd ride Spitfire for the last time before Kentucky. *Please, God, make everything go all right tomorrow* was her last conscious thought.

Spitfire was ready to play when she got down to the barn in the morning. He snatched her riding gloves out of her back pocket when she bent over to pick his front hoof, and tossed them in the corner.

"Whaddya think you're doing?" Trish scolded him.

Spitfire rolled his eyes and gave her a nudge when she bent over to pick up her scattered gloves. She caught herself before she went sprawling in the straw.

"Da-v-i-d." Trish called in the reserves.

"What's wrong?" David leaned over the stall door.

"Just hold on to his head, okay? He thinks he's Gatesby today."

"Or a clown in the circus?"

"Take your pick." Trish looked down at the tool in her hand. "Better yet, here. *You* pick and I'll hold."

They quickly had the colt cleaned and saddled. Trish waved as they trotted off to the track. Spitfire spooked at a gopher mound and shied when a bird flew up. He snorted and pranced, nostrils flaring red-pink as he tugged at the bit.

"You might as well give up," Trish told him. "You're not running today, just jog and loosen up." He danced sideways, reaching, pleading for more slack.

Each time he tugged, Trish pulled him down to a walk again. "See, I warned you." He shook his head. The next time she loosened the reins, he jogged peacefully all the way around the track and back to the barn. Mist had dampened both his hide and Trish's face. She could see steam rising from her horse when she slid to the ground.

"You better hustle or you'll be late for school," David greeted her.

"I think I should stay home until we get him on the plane."

"Dad said school."

Trish groaned but gave Spitfire one last hug before she raced for the house. Caesar beat her by one leap onto the deck.

"I'm hurrying." Trish correctly interpreted the look Marge gave her. She slid into her seat at school just as the final bell rang.

"That was close," Rhonda whispered from across the aisle. "Thought maybe you'd decided to go along."

"Don't I wish." Trish opened her book.

"Put your books away and take out paper." The teacher turned to begin writing on the board. "This quiz will count for twenty-five points."

The class groaned, Trish adding her share.

She'd just started the last question when an announcement came over the intercom. "Will Tricia Evanston please report to the office."

Trish and Rhonda stared at each other.

"Don't panic," Rhonda ordered.

"Yeah." Trish grabbed her books and dashed out the door.

"Your mother will be here to pick you up. There's an emergency at home." The secretary looked sympathetic as she gave Trish the message.

Chapter

08

Trish flew out the door. She jerked open the car door before Marge brought the vehicle to a full stop.

"Trish, don't panic. No one's hurt," Marge said as Trish bounded into the seat.

"Then what . . . ?"

Marge laid her hand on Trish's knee. Her quiet voice calmed her, the same way that Trish's voice quieted a nervous horse. "They're having trouble loading Spitfire, so instead of fighting with him, Dad said to go get you."

Trish slumped in the seat. *They should have let me stay home with him in the first place,* she thought, but was wise enough not to say it aloud. Her stomach returned to its normal place, rather than remaining parked up in her throat. "Man." She shook her head. "That message scared me out of a year's growth."

"Sorry," Marge answered as she looked both ways before pulling out onto 117th Avenue. "I didn't mean for them to scare you, just have you at the door by the time I got there."

"When they call your name over the intercom, you die, no matter what." Trish fluffed her bangs with her fingers. "Everybody in school is gonna wonder what's wrong now."

"In our case, it's what you do right. And that's handle Spitfire."

Please make it that simple, Lord, Trish prayed all the way home.

She leaped from the car before it completely stopped beside the pickup by the stables.

"Where is he?"

"Easy, Tee." Hal came from behind the horse trailer. "We put him back in his stall. He's all right."

Trish took a deep, calming breath before she walked up to Spitfire's stall. He poked his head out the door just as she reached for the latch. A silent nicker tickled his nose. He wuffled in her face, then rubbed his forehead on her chest.

"You crazy animal," Trish crooned as she rubbed his ears and smoothed the coarse black forelock. "What'd you cause such a fuss about?" She adjusted the travel sheet that rode high on his neck.

"Well, let's get this over with." Hal stopped beside her. "You and David both take the leads, even though he looks calm as a kitten right now. I don't know what your magic is, Trish, but it sure works."

"Just love." Trish kissed Spitfire on the nose.

The colt stepped out calmly when Trish swung open the stall door. He draped his head over her shoulder and only hesitated at the edge of the ramp. After a gentle tug on the rope, he followed Trish right into the trailer.

"Don't even say it," David growled as he slip-tied the lead rope.

"You mean, I told you so?" Trish hid her grin as she tied her rope. "I wouldn't dream of it." She patted Spitfire's shoulder and slipped out of the trailer.

Hal and David lifted the gate in place and threw home the bolts.

"I think you'd better go with us to the airport," Hal said. "Just in case. We're late now so let's get a hustle on."

"You be careful now," Marge said as she hugged Hal one more time. "And call me as soon as you get settled."

"I will. And I've plenty of help on call so you needn't worry."

"Easy for you to say," Marge muttered under her breath.

Hal hugged her again. "You're doing great." He climbed up into the cab. "Let's roll."

Trish felt as if she were in one of the old Westerns. Her dad was the wagonmaster with "Let's hit 'em up and roll 'em out," but that wasn't exactly what he said.

"Make something good for lunch," Trish called as she waved to her mother.

David poked her in the ribs with his elbow. "Smart aleck."

"You remember what school food is like. If I'm home, I take advantage of it." Trish settled herself between the broad shoulders of the two men. Good thing they had a large pickup.

The drive over the I-205 bridge to the airport passed with Hal giving them last minute instructions for the horses at home.

"I don't know why I'm telling you all this," he finally said. "You know what to do. And, Trish, you won't have time for anything. Saturday'll be here soon." He turned the truck into a driveway marked Eagle Transport.

A guard stopped them for their names, then waved the truck through after giving Hal instructions for finding their plane. It was the only one on the concrete in front of the hangars. A ramp led up to a wide cargo door on the silver body of the aircraft. An emblem of a flying eagle adorned the vertical section of the tail.

Hal parked the trailer near the ramp and pulled his briefcase from behind the seat. "You two wait here until I get checked in. Don't let me forget my suitcases."

"Is he excited or what?" Trish turned to David with a serious look on her face.

David shook his head. They could hear Spitfire moving around in the trailer. A jet roared up into the sky from the east-west runway just beyond the loading area. They could hear the trailer creak in protest to Spitfire's shifting.

"You better get back there with him." David peeled out the door. "You know he doesn't like strange noises."

Spitfire whinnied when Trish opened the front door and ducked under the bar to stand beside him. At the roar of another jet under full thrust, he threw his head up as far as the ties permitted.

Trish sang her comfort songs to him, stroking the colt all the while. She rubbed his ears and neck, feeling the sweat popping out from his tension. Spitfire rubbed his head against her shoulder and shuddered when another plane took off.

"Keep up the good work, Tee," Hal said as he stuck his head in the door. "We'll get the tack boxes loaded first. How's he doing?"

"Better. Just like schooling at the track. Maybe we should have brought him here a few days ago and let him get used to the noise. Walked him through the process."

"Too late now. We'll be just a few minutes."

She could hear him giving orders to David and someone else. Spitfire flinched when the tack boxes screeched during the unloading. Another jet took off. This time the colt just shifted his feet. Trish checked the thick leg wraps that David or her father had secured on all four legs to keep the horse from injuring himself. The crimson and gold travel sheet covered Spitfire from behind his ears to his tail.

"You look good," she murmured to his drooping ears. He only jerked his head when another jet lifted off. "They sure send plenty of planes out of here."

"Okay, Trish." David stopped at the door before going to the rear to drop the ramp. "We're ready."

"This is it, fella." Trish jerked the loose end on her lead shank and freed the other. David slipped in on the other side as soon as the ramp was down. "Here." Trish handed him one of the ropes. "Okay, Spitfire, back up."

Once out on the concrete, Spitfire raised his head and looked around. David and Trish let him look, watching his ears and eyes for any sign of tension. When he relaxed, they started walking toward the plane ramp. Spitfire looked from side to side, observing the activity around him.

When Trish and David started up the padded ramp, he followed like a docile puppy. Until another jet, a huge one, thundered into the air not a hundred yards away. Spitfire reared. As he went up, Trish let the rope slip through her fingers, then leaped for his halter when he came down. His feet slipped.

Trish flinched at the pain in her leg where the colt's flailing legs had struck her. But she didn't let go and didn't stop talking to him.

When he tried to go up again, she clamped her hand over his nostrils.

"No!" Her order penetrated the black's fears. His front feet stayed on the ground this time. They stood at the edge of the ramp, the horse and Trish both shaking, and David scolding the colt under his breath.

"That was close." Hal kept his voice low and soothing. "Walk him around a bit and let's try it again. He was fine until that plane took off."

Trish didn't have any spit to swallow. Her mouth felt like she'd been sucking on cotton balls. She nodded, and coaxed Spitfire to follow her.

When they approached the ramp again, Spitfire followed them up and into the dimness.

"Good fella," Trish encouraged him. "Just keep it up now until we get the stall up around you." They tied their ropes to one side of a padded wooden stall that was guy-wired in the center floor of the plane. Quickly, the airline crew bolted and wired the remaining three sides around the shivering colt.

Eyes rolling, nostrils flaring, Spitfire tossed his head when Trish started to leave the stall. His tail twitched and all four feet created their own staccato dance step.

Trish stepped back to his head and kept on rubbing, soothing him with her voice and hands.

"How close to packed is your suitcase?" Hal stroked Spitfire's neck under the soaking sheet.

"Why?"

"I don't think you better leave this stall. I've got a tranquilizer along but I hate to use it. You never know how he might react. So-o-o, the way I see it, we better take you along."

Trish rose on tiptoe to kiss her father's cheek. "What's Mom gonna say?"

"Probably plenty, but I don't know what else to do. David, unhitch the trailer so you can make better time. I'll call home and make the arrangements. Trish, you just keep a lid on the kid here. I'll be back to help you as soon as I've made the call."

"Dad, you need to make a list of the things to tell Mom. Like, my silks are hanging in the closet, along with the hang-up clothes I planned to bring. My makeup's in the bathroom, shampoo and stuff. Oh, and my sports bag."

"We can buy things there if you need more." Hal looked up from his list. "David can pick up your books and lessons at school and ship them, plus whatever else you need from home."

"Is this gonna make Mom mad, or sick again?"

"No. It's only two days early. Maybe a shock, that's all. You forget, she's really been praying about her worrying, and besides, she's much better."

"I know." Trish chewed on her bottom lip.

"Anything else?"

Trish looked up to see her father smiling at her. She could feel the love shining from his eyes.

"No. I'm—we're fine."

Hal patted her shoulder and headed toward the door.

"Tell David to bring some carrots," Trish called to his retreating back.

Spitfire shuddered again as another jet began its journey. "What are you gonna do when that's us taking off?" Trish asked. "You won't just hear it, you'll feel it."

Spitfire draped his head over her shoulder. His sigh matched the one Trish felt squeeze past the cotton in her throat.

Two more planes had lifted into the sky before Hal returned. "All set." He handed Trish a soft brush. "See if you can brush him dry. I'll get a dry sheet as soon as we're airborne."

"What did Mom say?"

"That she loves you and she's praying for all of us."

"Did you tell her how Spitfire acted?"

Hal raised one eyebrow. "I'll hold him while you brush."

"We need to get this crate off the ground pretty quick." A man from the airline approached Hal. "How long till your son gets back?"

Just then Trish heard a truck door slam. David bounded up the ramp, clutching Trish's suitcase, plus Hal's garment bag from the back of the truck. Marge followed right behind him with Trish's garment bag and her sports bag.

"Mom!" Spitfire lifted his head when Trish raised her voice. "You came." Trish's grin lit the entire interior of the plane.

"You think I'd let you get away without a hug?" Marge reached over the stall and suited action to words.

Trish clung to her for a moment. "Thanks for getting all my stuff together. Good thing you told me to pack early."

Marge smiled. "You call me tonight if you need anything else. And I'm sure they have stores in Louisville too." She hugged her daughter again. "Just in case."

"Excuse me, folks," the airline representative interrupted. "The captain says he's behind schedule, so we need to get the doors closed."

"Behave yourself."

"You talking to me or the horse?" Trish raised her eyebrows at her brother.

"Both." David punched her shoulder. "See you at the Derby."

Trish hugged her mother again. "Please come," she whispered. "It wouldn't be the same without all of us together."

"I know." Marge's hug bordered on the fierce side. "Take care of your dad."

Trish felt that familiar lump in her throat when she watched her parents say good-bye. It wasn't as if they wouldn't be together again soon. Why did she feel so close to crying? She wiped her cheek against Spitfire's mane.

As they closed the doors, Hal climbed over the stall. "Just in case you need another couple of hands."

Spitfire nosed Hal's pockets. "Smarty." Hal pulled out a carrot and broke it in chunks. Spitfire chewed the first piece as engine number one roared to life. He shifted front feet at the surge of number two. Head up, nostrils flaring, he ignored the carrot Hal offered as engine three thrust awake.

Trish pulled his head back down and rubbed his ears and cheek. Spitfire shuddered along with engine four.

"Easy, fella, easy." Both Trish and her father kept up the easy flow of words, all the while alert for any sudden moves on the colt's part.

The plane taxied forward, engines building as they turned onto a side runway and trundled down to the takeoff point.

Spitfire shifted restlessly. His front feet beat their own tattoo in the deep straw.

The plane turned again. The engines crescendoed and the plane shuddered as it built speed.

Spitfire shook. His muscles twitched and his eyes rolled white. But he stood firm under Trish's loving hands.

With a final roar, the plane lifted off the concrete and thrust itself into the sky. Trish braced against the slant. Spitfire nickered and threw his head up as far as the ropes allowed.

"Easy, come on, it's almost over." Trish breathed a sigh of relief when she felt the plane level out. She yawned to release the pressure in her ears and looked over at her father. His look of I'm-sure-glad-that's-over made her grin.

Spitfire took another piece of carrot.

"You're glad too, aren'tcha fella?" Trish whispered in his ear. She smoothed his forelock, grateful she could unclamp her hand from the halter. She flexed her fingers.

"I'll get some hay and water in here for him." Hal climbed over the wall. "And how about something to drink for you too?"

"I could use that." Trish yawned again. Her left ear popped this time. She frowned. "I think I liked the noise level better when I couldn't hear."

Hal chuckled as he rummaged in their supplies. He handed a dry sheet over the wall after the drinks. "You want some help changing that?"

Trish just shook her head. There was plenty of room to move around in the stall so who was he kidding? She'd been grooming horses since she was ten. She stripped off the damp sheet and brushed the now-weary horse down again. With the dry sheet buckled on, she stepped back to view her handiwork.

When Spitfire finally cocked one rear foot and dozed off, Trish sank down in the corner. She didn't dare leave the stall in case something happened, but sitting sure beat standing. She didn't realize she'd dozed off until she heard the engines change and the plane begin its descent into the Louisville airport.

Spitfire flinched when the wheels touched down, but other than that he remained quiet. Even when the men broke down the stall around him, he just watched, his head draped over Trish's shoulder.

Hal took the other lead rope just in case, but Spitfire walked off the plane like he'd been traveling in such style all his life. He walked right into the horse van waiting for them. Trish unsnapped the ropes so Spitfire could inspect his new quarters. After a quick hug, she shut the door and leaped to the ground.

"How about dropping me off to pick up my rental car and then I'll follow you to the track?" Hal asked the van driver.

"Sure." White teeth flashed as a smile split the man's fudge-colored face. "That's a ma-aghty fine lookin' colt you have there. Been hearin' some about him."

"Fred, this is my daughter, Tricia." Hal laid a hand on her shoulder. "Trish, Mr. Robertson."

Trish extended her hand as she'd been taught. Her fingers disappeared in the width of the man's hand.

"Just call me Fred." He tipped his hat after releasing the handshake. "You the young miss they all in a sweat about? Say you and that black colt maaght make racin' history."

Trish grinned back. "Winning the Derby will be kinda exciting."

She heard little nagger snort. *Kinda exciting?*

The three of them climbed up in the high cab. Trish felt the truck rock as Spitfire continued his inspection. She listened as Fred and her father talked about the area and what had gone on so far at the track. Nomatterwhat, the sorrel favorite they'd beaten at Santa Anita, had arrived the weekend before. Dun Rovin', a Kentucky-bred colt that took the honors at Gulf Stream in Florida, had arrived on Wednesday. Equinox, the current favorite, was shipping in on Saturday.

Trish felt two shivers chase each other up and back down her spine. She was *really* in Kentucky. It wasn't just a dream or a wish any longer. The race was two weeks from Saturday, sixteen days away. Sixteen days of butterflies.

"Trish, you ride with Fred in case you're needed, okay?" Hal hesitated before shutting the truck door. At Trish's nod, he slammed the door and waved.

"This your first trip here?" Fred turned off the engine.

"Uh-huh. My first racing season too. Spitfire's the first colt we've had this good. Dad's been training for a long time, but only in the Northwest."

"And this colt brought you into the big time." Fred leaned back against the door. "Y'all must be maaghty proud."

"You been hauling horses long?"

"Seems like all my life. This way ah get to be part of the business."

"Tell me about some of the horses you've seen."

"Why, I hauled Secretariat himself. Now that horse, he knew he was king." Fred chuckled. "Course ah was a bit younger then. Summer Squall, now he looked ma-aghty good too. You seen Seattle Slew, haven't you?"

"No, but he's Spitfire's sire."

Fred waved back when Hal walked from the car rental building to the burgundy four-door car. Fred turned the key and the engine surged to life. He hummed a little under his breath as he pulled out onto the road. "Now, ah remember when . . ." His stories kept Trish enthralled all the way to the freeway and over the surface streets following the signs to Churchill Downs. Huge trees shaded the houses along Central Avenue. Traffic increased as they neared the track.

"Last race about done," Fred commented. "You watch ahead, we're almost there."

Trish checked her side mirror to make sure her father was still behind them. Horse trucks and trailers filled a lot on their right and concrete-block stables lined the chain-link fence on their left.

Fred shifted down and signaled his turn. They had arrived. The guard at the gate waved them through. Fred eased the truck down the main road running between stables.

Trish could see the track off to her right, the triple cupolas that marked the famed racetrack visible on the roof of the grandstand.

It seemed like they drove forever. Trish tried to see everything at once as Fred pointed out the steward's office, the media building, the first-aid station, and finally barn 41. This barn at the back of the backside housed all the Derby contenders. With a green roof, white trim, and concrete block walls, the stable seemed to stretch out a mile. Everything looked freshly painted, even to the green and white sawhorses that marked parking restrictions.

Fred laughed softly. His contagious chuckle brought a grin to Trish's face too.

"Well—" Trish took a deep breath and let it out. "Thanks for such a great ride." She unbuckled her seat belt. The truck shifted as Spitfire moved around. He nickered.

"Y'all take care now, you hear?" Fred opened his door. "And I'll be a-watchin' you, 'specially in that winner's circle."

"Thanks." Trish stepped down and went around the truck to unload. Two men already had their microphones in front of her father's face, asking him questions. Trish helped Fred let down the ramp.

Spitfire whinnied, a shrill announcement that he had arrived. Horses down the lines answered.

"He's tellin' 'em, 'Look out. Ah'm here.' " Fred chuckled again and shook his head. "That boy not gonna take nothin' from nobody."

"Back up," Trish ordered when she opened the door. Spitfire nuzzled her shoulder and did as he was told. His flaring nostrils showed that he knew this was a strange place and he was ready to check it out. "Just take it easy now," she talked as she snapped the two shanks on his halter, slipping one chain section over his nose in case he got rowdy.

Spitfire posed in the doorway. Head high, ears pricked forward, he surveyed his kingdom. He answered another whinny from a stabled horse, then blew in Trish's face and followed her down the ramp.

"Are you Tricia Evanston?" a voice called.

Chapter
09

Spitfire danced in a circle around Trish, effectively scattering the three people who waited. "Behave yourself now," she ordered sternly. "Sorry, but he's had a long day."

"We're in stall five, halfway down." Hal checked the paper in his hand. "Let's get the sheet off him, then you can walk him and get the kinks out while I get us settled."

"If you've got as many kinks as I do, we're in deep trouble," Trish said as she led Spitfire after her father. The horse rubbed his forehead on her shoulder. He seemed to be walking on tiptoe as he paraded after her, eyes and ears checking out everything around him.

The colt shook all over like a wet dog when Hal pulled off the crimson and gold sheet and folded it to air over the open half wall that fronted the stalls. Hard-packed dirt aisles and shade from the overhanging roof kept the interior cooler than outside.

"Come on, fella." Trish didn't need to tug on his lead rope. As they left the building Spitfire raised his head and whinnied again. "Knock it off. You want to break my eardrums?" Trish watched him for any nervousness but Spitfire seemed calm. He was just letting everyone know he was there. They strolled up and down the wide areas between barns. Some were gravel, some deep sand. Some stables were decorated with hanging flower baskets, others displayed signs. Bandages, blankets, sheets, all the gear of any track hung drying on the lines strung between the posts on the half walls.

The sun was setting behind the barns when Trish and Spitfire found their way back. Hal had set up their room at the end of the barn; deep straw filled the stall, with a hay net hanging in a corner. Spitfire walked to the bucket and took a deep drink. While he buried his nose in the grain pan, Hal stroked down the colt's legs, checking for any heat or swelling.

"We'll leave the wraps on tonight in case he gets restless, but I think he's ready for a good night's sleep." He patted the horse's shoulder. "I know I am."

"You know how to get where we're going?" Trish asked as she hooked the web gate over the stall entrance.

"Sure." Hal grinned at her questioning look. He patted his pocket. "I have a map."

"Can we eat soon? I'm starved." Trish looked around their office for her suitcases. "Where's my stuff?"

"In the car. Fred helped me get everything moved around."

"I didn't get to tell him good-bye. He was such a neat man."

"He said he'd see us again before the race. He thought you were all right too." Hal put an arm around her shoulder. "Let's hit the road."

Birds twittered their night songs in the stately oak trees that shaded the backside track entrance. A horse whinnied off to their left and another answered. Somebody picked a guitar, the simple tune floating on the gentle breeze. It was a track settling down for the night. It could be any track, but it wasn't. They were at *Churchill Downs*. Trish gave a little skip as she rounded their car.

Hal handed her the map when they were inside. "Here, you navigate." He pointed to the circular mark indicating the racetrack, and then pointed out the streets that led to the hotel. "It's right off the freeway, back the way we came in, so we shouldn't have any trouble."

Trish glanced through the brochure. "Jacuzzis in each suite? All right!"

"Just pay attention to where we're going," Hal teased her. "We'll think about hot tubs later." He waved at the guard at the gate and turned right. "You want to eat before we check in, or wait and have dinner at the hotel?"

"Let's eat now."

Trish sighed as she climbed back into the car after dinner. "Funny, I knew about southern accents, but I feel like an idiot saying 'Huh?' or 'Excuse me?' all the time. I gotta listen up."

"It never seems like we have an accent, but we must," Hal said. "That waitress asked us right away where we were from."

"I never think of saying Washington *State*. Kinda forget there's another Washington." Trish glanced from her map to see where her father was turning. "Should be one more exit, and then ours."

Hal parked under the portico of the New Orleans–style building with wrought-iron trim.

"I think I'm gonna like it here." She gave her father the thumbs-up sign.

"I *know* I'm gonna like it here," she repeated as she stared at the huge oval, rose-colored Jacuzzi tub in their bathroom. She almost needed a step stool to get into it.

"Think it'll be okay?" Hal asked after tipping the bellboy. "Good grief, that thing is almost as big as a swimming pool."

"And I'm getting in right away." Trish read the instructions on the wall. She picked up the little bottles nesting in a basket of tri-folded pink washcloths. "There's even bubble bath." She turned on the taps and adjusted the temperature. The bottle of blue gel she dumped in began to foam immediately. "Now I'll hang up my stuff. That thing'll take forever to fill."

A sitting room with a sofa hide-a-bed separated the two bedrooms of their suite. Horse pictures, both racing and fox hunting, decorated the walls. French doors opened onto a grilled balcony overlooking the central courtyard where glass-topped wrought-iron tables awaited the breakfast buffet crowd.

Trish flopped on her back across the queen-size bed in her room. Even with her arms spread-eagle she didn't touch the sides. She raised on her elbows and looked at herself in the mirror above a chest of drawers. She stuck out her tongue at the grinning face in the mirror, and got up to empty her suitcases into the drawers and closet. Her tub was not even half full yet.

"Tell Mom hi for me," she said as she closed the bathroom door. "And tell her I'm soaking in this monstrous tub. Maybe that'll convince her to come."

Trish pinned her hair up on top of her head. The waterline was finally above the jets. The water churned to life with a turn of the dial on the wall. When she was ready to climb in, she rolled one towel to put behind her head, and sank into the hot, bubbling water up to her neck. Her toes just touched the opposite end. She flexed one foot over a jet and played with another with her hand. This was living!

By the time she forced herself to get out and get ready for bed, her father was already fast asleep. Trish thought about turning on the TV, but when a huge yawn stretched her entire jaw, she crawled into bed.

She screamed and screamed again but no sound came. She couldn't get enough air. The horse was dead. A jockey too. Ambulance sirens. More screams. Something was holding her prisoner; she couldn't move. Why was her mother fading away?

"Trish, Trish, it's all right now. You're dreaming." Hal shook her gently. "Wake up, Tee."

Trish jerked upright. She sucked in a huge gulp of air. She shook her head and blinked her eyes. "Where's Mom?"

"At home. Trish, everything is okay. You had a bad nightmare."

"I sure did." Trish slumped against the pillows. "I thought those terrible dreams were all over. Dad, I was so scared. I thought I was dying—and Mom wouldn't talk to me—and . . ." She buried her face in her hands.

"And?"

"And I shouldn't be so scared. My Bible verse says, 'Fear not,' so if He's with me why am I so scared? And I keep thinking that if I didn't race, Mom wouldn't worry so much."

"And so you feel guilty too." Hal smoothed her hair back from her forehead.

Trish nodded. She sniffed and reached for a tissue on the night-stand. "Yeah, it's like I have this little voice in my head that keeps yelling that everything's all my fault." She rubbed her temples with her fingers. "Sometimes I even get a headache from it all."

"Tee, I think you have a serious problem."

"I know."

"No, look at me." He tipped her chin up with a loving finger. "Your problem is—you're human, just like the rest of us."

"Da-a-d."

"No, I mean it. The fears and the guilt are all part of our humanity. And teenagers seem to attract guilt like a magnet. So do those who don't really understand God's grace."

"I know He takes care of my fears." Trish told her father about the time at the track. "I went on and rode that day. And it's been better ever since."

"That's wonderful."

"I know. But then the nightmare makes it all worse again."

"So you claim your verses again, confess your fears, your guilt, and go on. That's what it takes to build faith. Just like you stretch your muscles; they get sore but they also get stronger. Faith is really like a muscle. Use it or lose it."

"You make it sound so simple." Trish twisted her fingers in her lap.

"Remember the rest of the 'Be not afraid' verse?"

Trish nodded. "For I am with you."

"He never gives an order without a promise." Silence wrapped comfort around them. "Be right back." Hal returned in a few moments with the carved eagle and set it on her nightstand. "Just a reminder. For when *you* need those eagle's wings."

Trish threw her arms around his neck. "I love you."

Hal hugged her back. "And I love you. Good night, and good dreams this time." Trish nestled back down in the bed, and Hal pulled the covers up over her shoulder. Then he switched off the lamp.

The next thing she knew, her father was knocking at her door. "Time to get up. I'll be waiting for you downstairs by the buffet."

Trish stretched both arms above her head and then all the way to her toes. The nightmare seemed dim and faraway, like most dreams do upon waking. She glanced at the eagle, spiraling where the air currents led. Her feet hit the floor running. What a great day to be alive.

Downstairs, she grabbed an apple, toast, and a strip of bacon. "I'm ready."

Spitfire was ready too when they got to the track—ready to eat. Trish measured his grain and refilled the water bucket. "There you go, enjoy." She patted his shoulder as she went by.

Shoulder to shoulder, she and Hal leaned on the track fence and watched the morning works already in progress. *I don't know anybody here,* Trish thought as she watched one rider argue with her horse. *At Santa Anita we weren't there long enough, but here . . ."* She shrugged. Maybe she'd get some sun and studying done this way. "Did you remind David to pick up my books? And assignments?"

"He did that yesterday afternoon. They'll be here Monday."

"Good—I think."

Hal nodded. "You'll have to work hard next week. Derby week'll keep us plenty busy."

Trish watched another horse breeze by. "Sure hope Mom comes. Do you think she will?"

"I keep praying. And I know she is too." He checked his watch. "Spitfire oughta be done by now. Let's get him out on the track."

Spitfire rubbed the grain stuck to his whiskers on Trish's cheek and blew some more in her hair.

"Thanks." She wiped off what she could. "Do you want to pick or brush?" She offered her father the choice. It seemed so strange to be working with him instead of David. The thought made her think of home again. Here she was, already missing her brother and mother. *Great!*

"I'll pick." Hal handed her the brush. He lifted a front hoof and bent to the task.

Trish hummed to herself as she brushed her way around the horse. Even in the dimness of the stall, Spitfire's coat shone with health and good care.

Her father leaned against the wall after he'd finished his job.

"You okay?" Trish paused in her brushing.

"Yeah. Just not used to bending over so much. You and David have spoiled me." Trish heard a slight wheeze when he talked.

"Here." She tossed him the brush. "I'll take off the bandages while you get the saddle."

"No, leave 'em on." He unhooked the web gate and left.

"He worries me sometimes," Trish confessed to Spitfire's twitching ears.

There you go again, worrying, her little nagger whispered. *See how easy it is?* Trish shook her head and rolled her eyes toward her eyebrows.

Spitfire stood quietly while she adjusted the saddle. He even dipped his head down for her to slip the headstall over his ears. Trish smoothed his forelock in place and took a deep breath. "Well, let's go, fella. Your public awaits." She led him out the stall and turned right. The horse on the end, stall one, stuck his head over the gate and nickered. "Who's that?" Trish asked.

"Nancy's Request. He's owned by that singer down in Hollywood. Haven't heard much about him 'cause he might not run."

"Problems?" She waited for her father to give her a knee up.

"Some. Keeps coming up sore behind and they're not sure why." He boosted Trish aboard. "Now you take him slow and easy. Walk one to let him see everything, and then jog." He patted her knee.

"Tell *him* that." Trish stroked Spitfire's neck. She clucked him forward and Hal walked with them up to the entrance to the track. Then he continued on to the wooden bleachers set up for trainers and media people to watch the horses.

Trish let Spitfire stand watching the action. Other horses came and went. An exercise rider hit the dirt just past the gate and her horse galloped on around the track. She stood up and dusted herself off, disgust written all over her face. It took the red-jacketed assistants several tries to catch the runaway. The horse proved adept at dodging.

When Trish nudged Spitfire forward, he walked flat-footed out onto the track. They kept near the outside rail so as not to get in the way of those working faster. Trish felt like both she and Spitfire had swivels in their necks as they tried to see everything at once. The stands stretched from just past the first turn to the other. A turf track lay inside the dirt oval and its grass was as green as that on the infield. All the official tote boards sported a fresh coat of dark green paint, and the two-story hexagonal building that centered the horseshoe-shaped winner's circle glistened white. Stairs inside led to the celebrity viewing area up above. Churchill Downs, lettered in gold, graced the base of the building. A bright red horseshoe of flowers set off the green turf around it. Just beyond that, gold knobs topped the two tall round posts with "CD" and "Finish" lettered in gold.

"Impressive, huh, old boy?" Trish turned her head to see the rest of the floral plantings in neat rows of yellow, red, and orange. "You look that horseshoe over good, 'cause we want to be standing there when this is all over."

A horse galloped on by them, drawing her attention to the fountain that jetted a column of water ten feet in the air. "Awesome. Totally awesome."

After jogging their two laps, Trish rode back to their barn. She'd expected to meet her dad at the gate, but when she didn't see him they kept on walking. She found him leaning against the wall, struggling to breathe. The half-cleaned stall told her what he'd been doing.

"What's the matter with you?" she scolded. "You know better than to work in that dust." She planted both hands on her hips, still clasping the reins in one. "Just leave that and—"

"Yes, boss." Hal touched a finger to his cap. His sarcasm cut off her tirade.

"Sorry." Trish handed him the reins. "Why don't you walk him out and I'll . . ." She stopped again. Her father didn't need to do that much walking right now either. *David, I need you.* "No. You put away the tack and I'll walk him. Then you can hold him while I clean. Okay?" She unbuckled the saddle and bridle while she talked, deliberately not looking her father in the eye. She knew how much he hated to admit any weakness.

She heard him coughing when she brought Spitfire back into the barn.

Chapter 10

"Dad? If you can hold him, I'll finish the stall."

Hal nodded. "The water is helping." He took another drink and, leaning against the block half wall, held out his hand for the reins. Spitfire nosed the cup. When he started to nibble the rolled paper edge, Hal shook his head. "Not for you, old man. Yours is in the bucket."

Trish left the two of them discussing the water cup, and attacked the dirty straw. By the time she'd loaded and trundled out a couple of wheelbarrow loads, sweat was running down her neck.

When she started to load a straw bale on the barrow, a voice stopped her. "Why don't you let me do that?"

She turned to look into the bluest eyes she'd ever seen, except in the movies. He had curly red hair—not carrot, but deep auburn, and he was grinning at her. She couldn't resist grinning back.

"They call me Red but my name's Eric." He hefted the bale and dumped it in her barrow. "Another?"

"Yeah, thanks. I'm Tricia Evanston, Trish." Before she could pick up the handles, he had the wheelbarrow in motion. "You don't have to do this. I *can* manage."

"I know."

"Stall five." She kept pace with him.

"I know. You ride Spitfire and you're from Washington, as in, state of. This is your first time to Kentucky, and most people think the world will end if a girl should win the Derby."

"How . . ."

"I can read. They do teach us southern boys how to read before they let us up on horseback. But me, I was riding before I started reading." He lifted the bales out one at a time and dumped them in the stall.

Trish snapped her mouth closed. She looked at her father in time to catch a slow wink.

"Gotta go. See y'all later, maybe down at the track kitchen. Only one more mount this morning." He walked off whistling.

Hal took one look at Trish's face and started to laugh. Even a cough in the middle didn't make him quit chuckling.

"What's so funny?" Trish cut the baling wires with a pair of pliers, pulled out the wire, and wrapped them together to throw away. Then she took a pitchfork and broke up the bale. Tossing the straw in the air to separate it sent clouds of dust billowing up. "Don't know what made him think he could do this stuff," she muttered as she worked. "There must be someone here we can hire to help."

"Kinda takes your breath away, doesn't he?"

"Who?" Trish pulled her leather gloves off and stuck them in her back pocket. She wiped her forehead with her sleeve. "Where'd you find that water?"

Hal pointed to a hose outside. "That jockey who helped you."

"Jockey? He was probably just an exercise boy." Trish downed a cup of water.

"Don't you know who he is?"

"Red, or Eric. That's all he said. I didn't *ask* him for help, you know." Spitfire rubbed his forehead against her shoulder, then lipped the cup. "Get away, your drink's in your stall." She pushed his nose away.

"Do you care who he is?"

"Not particularly. Right now I'd rather eat." She squatted down and started unwrapping the thick bandages Spitfire still wore. As she finished each one, she handed it to Hal, who hung it over the wire strung between the posts. When she finished that, she checked the stall. "Dust's down. He can go in." She led the colt into his stall and let him loose. "Be good now." One last pat on his rump, and she slipped out of the stall while he drank.

Trish picked up the bucket with brushes, scraper, and sponge to store in one of the wardrobe-size tack boxes. She added her pliers, gloves, and helmet, then glanced around to make sure nothing was left lying around. Her father had taught her well; loose gear meant lost gear.

In the car Hal leaned back against the headrest with his eyes closed. His breathing was shallow with an occasional wheeze. He handed Trish the keys. "You better drive, at least on the grounds here."

Trish adjusted the seat for her shorter legs and turned on the ignition. "Am I legal in this car?"

"Not really. Should have had you sign on the contract just in case." Hal opened his eyes. "I'll be okay after some hot coffee and food."

Trish found a place to park right in front of the brick building shaded by massive oak trees. Track Kitchen read the sign above the white double-wide doors. White shutters at the windows and white bricks outlining the flower beds and trees made it look more like a nice home than a cafeteria.

Trish headed for the restroom before getting in line for her food. One look in the mirror at her dirt-streaked face and she groaned. Great way to meet a new guy.

Thought you weren't interested, her little nagger chuckled teasingly.

"I'm not—I mean, I—" Trish stuffed the wet paper towel in the trash. She pulled a comb from her back pocket, combed her hair, and refastened the clasp holding it back. Her bangs lay flat, mashed by her helmet. She dampened her fingers and fluffed her bangs.

Of course! You always go to all this trouble for breakfast. Hee, hee, the voice persisted.

Trish stuffed the comb back in her pocket, wishing she could stuff the voice in the trash can along with the paper.

A man with the look of a reporter had joined her father for a cup of coffee. Hal introduced him as a writer for the *Blood Horse Journal.*

"How about if I get your breakfast too?" Trish held out her hand for money. "Your usual?" At Hal's nod, she joined the line and waited to order. Trish studied the menu printed above the counter, in case there was something new she'd like to try.

"Told you I'd see you here," a voice said behind her.

She whirled around. Eric reached past her, picked up two trays, and handed her one. "They make good hot cakes here. You need to pick up forks and stuff right there."

"I can handle it, thank you." Trish shook her head. Who did he think he was, telling her what to do? But his grin was easier to catch than a cold.

"My sister says I'm bossy."

"She's right." Trish tried to stop them but the words just leaped out.

"Y'all gonna order or what?" The man behind the cafeteria-style counter settled back to wait.

Trish felt a blush creep up her neck. "Two orders. One egg over easy, bacon, and hot cakes."

"Short stack or tall?"

"Huh?"

"You want two hot cakes or four?" His dark eyes laughed at her.

"Two. And put two eggs on the second order. Same way, over easy." She reached for a carton of milk and shoved her tray along the line. Why'd she feel like these two guys were ganging up on her? By the time she paid for the orders, the two plates of food appeared on top of the stainless steel counter. She loaded her tray and headed back to the table where her father was deep in conversation. He took the plate she passed him, nodded his thanks without breaking eye contact with the reporter.

"Don't mind Sam." Eric set his tray down beside Trish's. "He likes to give pretty girls a bad time. Once you get to know him, you'll like him." He pulled out the chair and sat down. "Actually, he likes to give everybody a bad time."

Trish looked at him, astonished. When she opened her mouth, no words came out. She watched as he attacked the scrambled eggs and dry toast. Who'd he think he was—her big brother? She already had one of those, thanks.

Trish spread butter and syrup on her hot cakes and seasoned her egg. She bowed her head for grace, and when she looked up again she could feel Eric staring at her.

"That takes a lot of nerve," he said softly.

"What?"

"Grace in public. That's just one more reason why I think I like you." He winked at her over the edge of his milk carton, then drank it half down.

Trish felt her mouth open—then close. Butterflies fluttered in her middle. As she ate her meal, she tried to both listen to her father's conversation and answer Eric's comments. Finally she gave up on her dad and enjoyed listening to Eric tell her about the people in the room. Famous trainers, world-class jockeys, renowned media, all were there and all were talking horses. She wished she could be a little mouse at each table, but then her mother had tried to teach her not to eavesdrop.

When she pushed her plate away, Eric stacked it on top of his, loaded the trays, and returned them to the proper place.

"Tomorrow it's your turn," he announced as he sat down again, a cup of coffee in hand. "You want some?"

"No, thanks. And what makes you think we're—I mean, I'm—"

"Having breakfast together?" He took a sip of coffee. He shrugged. "We just are. You coming to the races this afternoon?"

"I—uh—I don't know." She turned to her father. He'd just finished his interview with the writer and heard the question.

He extended his hand. "Hi, Red, I've heard a lot about you." He answered the question on Trish's face before she could ask it. "This is Red Holloran, leading apprentice jockey in the country."

Trish felt even more like someone who forgot to come in out of the rain.

"And about the races, I think not today. We've got to get licensed, and then I'd better rest awhile. Trish, you could stay if you'd like."

Trish shook her head. She could see the tiredness around her father's eyes. That coughing fit in the barn hadn't helped any, and yesterday had been a rough day.

"Then how about dinner?" Eric looked right at Trish. "I could meet you back at the barn after the program is done for the day."

Was he asking her for a date? Trish looked to her father, not sure if she even wanted to ask permission.

"Maybe another time." Hal pushed his chair back. "After you get to know each other a bit more."

Trish breathed a sigh of—relief—disappointment? She wasn't sure which.

Chapter

11

Hal slept all afternoon.

Trish slathered on sunscreen and lay out by the pool. *It would have been fun to watch Red race*, she thought. *And dinner? He probably meant hamburgers. But maybe not. Maybe it would have been a real date.* After a couple of hours of turning and toasting, she pushed herself to her feet. The spots she saw before her eyes reminded her of the last concussion, but they left as soon as she moved around some.

After changing clothes, she ambled out the door to the shopping center that surrounded the hotel. She spent an hour in the card shop, chuckling to herself as she chose cards to send home. But it wasn't as much fun without someone to show them to.

A T-shirt caught her eye in the next store, but she didn't have enough money along. There'd been no time to go to the bank before she left home. She'd have to ask her dad for some money.

By the time she bought a Diet Coke from the hotel pop machine and reentered the room, it was time to leave for the track for evening chores. She shook Hal awake.

"Dad? It's time to go feed Spitfire." She noticed the lines that had deepened around his mouth. "Dad?"

Hal groaned and blinked his eyes. "I didn't plan on sleeping the day away."

"Guess you needed it. I can go by myself if you want."

"No. You're not a legal driver for the rental car yet," he reminded her as he swung his feet to the floor. "We'll stop by the airport on the way back and get your name on that contract. Just in case you need to run an errand or something." He reached for her soda can and glugged a couple of swallows. "Now, that tastes good."

He seemed more himself on the drive back to the track. Spitfire welcomed them with nickers and head tosses. "You walk him around a bit," Hal said as he sat down in a lawn chair. "I've got some paper work to do."

By the time Trish and Spitfire returned, a couple of men had pulled up chairs and were visiting with Hal. Trish could hear them talking horses as she passed.

"Trish," her father called to her. "There's someone here I'd like you to meet."

Trish turned and walked back to the tack room.

"Patrick O'Hern, this is my daughter, Trish." Hal put his hand on her arm. "I can remember reading about this man years ago, Trish. He retired from a good career as a jockey and went on to become a renowned trainer."

Trish shook hands with a rounded man no taller than she. His blue eyes twinkled above Santa Claus cheeks as he removed a battered fedora hat to greet her.

"So you be the lass they're all hummin' about." His brogue surprised Trish. "I'm pleased to meet you."

"Do you have a horse here?" Trish asked. From the abrupt silence she knew she'd said the wrong thing.

"Nay, lass, that was years ago."

Trish flashed a questioning look at her father. At the slight shake of his head, she nodded at the old trainer. "It was nice meeting you. I've gotta go feed a hungry horse." As she left, she could hear the conversation pick up again. *Now what was that all about?* she wondered. Putting her curiosity aside, she went about the evening chores.

"Now you sleep well," she told Spitfire after forking out some dirty straw. She filled his water bucket and measured the grain, then leaned against his shoulder, stroking his neck while he ate. "It's strange not to be so busy that I don't know if I'm coming or going. Wish Rhonda were here, or Brad or David."

Trish really wished for help in the morning when she had to feed, ride, clean the stall, cool out the horse, and tape his legs again. The early morning breeze touched her face with cool, velvet fingers, but by mid-morning the air felt heavy. Sweat ran down her back and neck.

"I'm sorry I can't help you more," Hal apologized. "I didn't plan for things to happen like this."

"I know. Don't worry about it. I needed some good old manual labor anyway." She rubbed her shoulder. "Now let's eat. I'm starved."

Trish had just finished saying grace when she felt a person take the seat next to her. She brushed a strand of hair back as she glanced sideways.

"Hi, sorry I wasn't there to help you this morning." Red grinned his irresistible grin.

Trish felt a tingle down to her toes. "Hi, yourself. I managed quite well, thank you." She laid her napkin in her lap. "How did you do yesterday?"

"One win, a show, one fourth, and we won't discuss the other." He took a bite of his scrambled eggs. "Is your dad feeling better?"

"How'd you know . . ."

"I read, remember. Besides, one look at him yesterday and I could tell he was having a hard time breathing."

"Yes, I . . ." Trish turned in her chair so she could really look at the jockey next to her. *I'd like to tell you what I'm worried about. No, I refuse to use the W word. It's about what's happening with my dad. I need a friend here.* "He needs a lot of rest and has to stay out of the dust."

"That's tough, the dust, I mean. Well, the resting too."

"He didn't think it would be this hard, or we probably wouldn't have come." Trish kept her voice low so her father, who was talking with someone else, wouldn't hear her.

"Glad you told me. Does he need you with him all the time?"

"No. Not really, why?"

"I can help you some in the mornings, and maybe we can, I mean, I can show you some of the country when I'm not riding. Have you seen everything here at the track yet?"

"No. I—we—uhhh . . .'"

"How about I show you and your dad around after we finish eating?"

"That'll be fine," Hal said when Trish asked. "We need to stop by the race office first and get our licenses. Are you riding today?"

"Not till late, so I won't have to be up in the jockey room so early." Red finished his milk in a long swallow. He raised an eyebrow at the question on Trish's face. "We have to report in two hours before our first race and return to the jockey room between races until we're finished for the day. Derby Day you'll have to check in about nine-thirty."

"But why?"

"Track rules. Don't worry, I'll introduce you to Frances Brown. She runs the women's room. You'll like her."

Trish felt a sinking in her stomach. She wouldn't be able to help get Spitfire ready. Good thing David would be here by then.

The Evanstons filled out the paper work and paid their fees. Trish flinched at the cost of final entry. They were now officially listed as Derby contenders.

Eric proved to be a knowledgeable guide as they walked slowly around the track and through the tunnel under the grandstand. They saw the empty saddling stalls and walking paddock, fenced but open to viewers, as well as the owner's and trainer's lounge with a large screen for watching the races. They took the escalator to the jockey rooms.

"Wait here," Red told Trish at the entrance doors. "I'll call Frances."

A few moments later, an attractive woman with white hair smoothed back and tied at her neck introduced herself. "I'm Frances Brown, kind of the room mother here. Mr. Evanston . . ."

"Hal."

Her smile felt warm and welcoming. "Hal, you go through those doors and Red will give you the tour. We'll meet you back at the coffee shop. Trish, the scales are through those double doors too. You need to let them know when you're going in so everyone's decent."

Trish couldn't believe her eyes as Frances showed her around. The men's jockey room at Portland wasn't as nice as this. Lockers, showers, a room with beds in case someone was tired, a whirlpool for injuries, sauna; and then they walked through a short hall to the recreation room with a snack bar for men and women. Some guys were already shooting pool and a TV flickered in one corner. The track monitor was showing videos of past Derby races.

Hal and Trish looked at each other and shook their heads. Things sure were different in Kentucky.

"Y'all come on up and visit and I'll introduce you to the other women jockeys around here," Frances invited. "We get into some pretty good story swappin' up here."

"I'd like that," Trish replied.

"You shown them the museum yet?"

"Nope, that's next," Red answered. "We'll meet you back outside, Trish."

"Thanks, Frances," Trish said as they turned the corner back into the women's room. "I'll probably see you next week."

"Any questions, you just ask," Frances said. "I'm here, seems like all the time."

The museum was located just outside the main gate. Trish realized immediately it would take hours to go through it. She glanced in the gift store just enough to know she'd like to spend more time there.

"Wait till you see the show in here on Thursday morning when they draw post positions." Red waved to a two-story oval room with other wings branching off. "This is the best museum on Thoroughbred racing anywhere. Y'all oughta take the tour if you can. There's a library here and you can watch all the previous races that were filmed on video."

Trish stood in the center of the room and slowly turned around. Pictures, statues, displays, lists of all the Derby winners, all about the sport and industry she loved. She felt as if she were in the midst of greatness.

"Wow!" She closed her eyes to picture Spitfire's name on the list of

Derby champions. When she opened them again, she saw Eric watching her. His grin surely matched her own. She could feel her cheeks stretching.

"That horseshoe out there is used only for the Derby," Red told them as they left the dimness of the tunnel under the grandstand. He showed them another place to their left, also banked with flowers but not nearly so grand. "The rest of the time this is for the winners. That seating area right up above it is for owners and their wives."

"Hey, Red," another jockey called. "If you're up on the first, you better get up there."

"See y'all later." Red smiled from Trish to her father. "Your badges will get you in anywhere." He walked backward as he talked. "Enjoy the races."

"Nice guy," Hal said as they followed the fence line to the backside.
"Yeah."

Even if he is bossy, her little voice chuckled.

Sunday morning two bales of straw were stacked by stall five when they arrived. Eric had the stall half mucked out when Trish returned from walking Spitfire.

"Gotta run." He grabbed up his helmet as he left.

That afternoon Hal felt much better, so he and Trish drove to Lexington to see the bluegrass country.

"People around here sure must love to mow." Trish had mild whiplash from trying to see both sides of the manicured highway at once. "See, even the pastures look like front lawns."

"Better'n our yard," Hal agreed with her.

"And the fences. I thought they'd all be white, but some are black. And look at those barns."

"Even the barns are fancier than our house." Hal pointed out a particularly impressive structure on the top of a rise.

Trish rolled her window down. "It even smells good. I never believed what they said about the grass being blue, but it is." She pointed to a field that hadn't been mowed. The breeze rippled waves of deep blue-green across the stand of grass.

Hal pulled off the main highway so they could drive slower. He stopped at one field where a group of mares and foals grazed peacefully.

"Aren't they something?" One youngster kicked up his heels and soon three raced across the rolling pasture. "Already in training for the races."

"So many at once." Trish rested her chin on her hands on the window. "I've never seen so many foals at one time."

"And look at the field of babies, all those yearlings." Hal pulled the car forward to the next pasture.

"Seems funny to call them babies."

"I know." Hal checked his watch. "We better head back. We'll try to come back tomorrow or Tuesday and visit the Horse Park."

"Maybe Mom and David'll want to see that too."

"If they get here in time."

By the time they'd finished chores, Red hadn't made an appearance. Trish refused to admit she felt disappointed. After all, he hadn't said *when* he'd see her again. She decided to call Rhonda when they got back to the hotel, and tell her about the Jacuzzi. She slumped in her seat. Much as she loved being with her father, she did miss the rest of the four musketeers.

"You better cut it off." Hal tapped his watch later that evening. "Half an hour on long distance is enough."

"Okay," Trish sighed. "Dad says I gotta go. No, I'm not taking a picture of Eric. Rhonda, knock it off. He's just being nice to a stranger. Tell Brad all that's been going on. Bye."

She slumped against her pillows. There was a three-hour time difference. Right now Washington seemed terribly faraway. She moped into the bathroom and started the water running in the tub. A hot soak would feel mighty good, and while it was filling she could talk to David and her mother. Her father had dialed home as soon as she'd hung up.

Sadness pulled Trish down into a puddle of lament after the call home.

Marge still wouldn't say for sure she was coming.

Chapter 12

Monday's paper carried a story about Trish and Spitfire.

"Can't these guys get anything straight?" Trish folded the paper and handed it back to her dad. They were sitting in their tack room about ready to go for breakfast.

"What don't you like?"

"I don't know, just a feeling, I guess. Like they think I don't ride anything but Spitfire. That anything else I ride is just accidental. You know I've been doing all right at The Meadows."

"You and I both know you're an exceptional rider, but the rest of the racing world won't think so until you ride other horses at other tracks. That's just the facts." Hal shrugged his shoulders. "Let's go eat."

Eric didn't join them at the track kitchen like he usually had.

Trish caught herself looking around for him. The two bales of straw had been by their stall, so she knew he was at the track.

Oh, so you're missing him, are you? her little nagger snickered. *Thought you said he was bossy.*

Trish wiped her mouth with her napkin. Eric was just a friend, that's all. *And I need a friend here. Everyone else is so far away.* She picked up her father's tray and returned it with hers to the washing window.

"You want to go to the Horse Park today?" Hal asked as they drove out the gate.

Trish looked out her window. Heavy dark clouds covered the western sky. A brisk wind tossed trash in the air and whipped the branches of the huge shade trees around.

"I don't know. The weather doesn't look too good."

By the time they looped up onto the freeway, lightning forked against the black clouds. A few seconds later, thunder crashed louder than the sound of the car engine.

"Dad, let's go back to the track. You know Spitfire doesn't like loud noises."

"And he's never been through a midwest thunderstorm."

"Neither have I."

Jumbo raindrops pelted their car by the time they returned to the track. Lightning had just split the sky when Trish bailed out of the car by barn 41. She heard Spitfire scream as the thunder rolled over them, rattling the metal roof like a giant kettledrum.

Trish unhooked the web gate and slipped into the stall just as Spitfire reared, slashing the air with his hooves. She felt the wind of it on her cheek.

"Easy now, come on, Spitfire. We're here." She grabbed for his halter, all the while murmuring his name and comforting words.

Eyes rolling white, nostrils flared red, Spitfire trembled under her calming hands. The rain pounding on the roof above them drowned out her voice to any but the horse's ears. But that's who the singsong was for.

"Here, Trish." Hal handed her a lead shank. "Run the chain through his mouth in case you need some control."

Trish did as she was told, and finished just as lightning turned the stable area blue-white. Spitfire threw up his head, but Trish clamped one hand over his nose and clutched the strap tight against his jaw with the other. She hunched her shoulders, waiting for the coming boom.

The crack sounded right overhead. Spitfire's front feet left the ground, but Trish stayed right with him. "Easy, boy, come on now. Nothing's gonna hurt you." He quivered as she stroked his ears and neck. Sweat darkened his hide.

"The storm's heading east, so maybe this won't last much longer." Hal stood on the opposite side of the colt, copying Trish's calming actions.

"Hope so. You sure this building's safe?"

"Lightning goes for the high points. The two spires on top of the grandstand would attract it away from here."

Trish sniffed. "What's that funny smell?"

"Ozone. From the lightning. That last one was right above us."

"Thanks."

Spitfire snorted like he was relieved too. When the thunder rolled again, it was far enough away that he only flinched. The rain changed instruments from kettledrum to keyboard, singing off the eaves and thrumming on the gravel.

Trish took a deep breath. She wasn't sure if her hand shook of itself or because it strangled the colt's halter. She unclamped her fist and flexed her fingers.

Spitfire draped his head over her shoulder, shaken by an occasional quiver, just as a person shuddering after a crying spell.

Hal handed Trish a brush, and started on the other side with another one. "Let's get him dried off."

"You okay here?" one of the track assistants asked.

"Now we are." Hal left off brushing and stood at the door.

"Yours wasn't the only horse shook up."

"Yeah, we don't get thunder and lightning much at all at home, and never like that."

"You need anything, you let us know." The man moved off.

Now that Spitfire was calmed down, Trish realized she was soaked. She hadn't been able to run between the drops during that downpour. She looked up from her brushing in time to see her dad shiver from the breeze that whipped down the aisle. He'd gotten wet too.

"How about we go back to the hotel and get into some dry clothes?" She finished the brushing and gave Spitfire a last pat. "Come on, Dad." Shivers attacked her too as soon as she left the warmth of the stall. "Turn the heater on." She flicked the knobs herself as soon as she got into the car.

The heat pouring out the vents didn't make Hal quit shivering. Trish bit her lip as she heard his teeth chatter on a bad shake. "You want me to drive?" she asked.

"No. I'll hit the shower as soon as we get to the hotel, and you can make some coffee. Hot liquid inside and out oughta do it."

Trish turned the shower on as soon as she entered their suite so the bathroom could steam up. She filled the automatic coffeepot, and when it quit gurgling brought a cup to her father, who was still in the shower.

"Your coffee's here on the counter."

"Thanks, Tee."

Trish noticed the message light winking on the phone. When she dialed the desk, they told her there was a package downstairs for her. By the time she got back up, the shower was quiet.

"Dad?"

"In bed. How about bringing me another cup of coffee?"

Trish poured a cup and carried it in to him. "My stuff came." She plopped the package down on his bed. "Think I'll study for a while since the sun's hiding. You gonna sleep?"

"Ummm. Can't believe how cold I got. I forget that my internal thermometer doesn't work the way it used to, thanks to the chemotherapy."

"Want something to eat or anything?"

"No, thanks." He handed her the cup. "Oh, maybe you better hand me those antibiotic pills in the amber bottle. Between the dust and the rain, I better be safe than sorry."

Trish wrote a paper for English, read two chapters in her history book, and took a nap. Her father was still sleeping when she got up, so she left him a note and drove back to the track to feed Spitfire.

"Where's your daddy?" asked the man at the gate. "He all right?"

"I hope so," Trish answered.

Spitfire was glad to see her, but it sure was lonely without her father.

The sound of his coughing greeted her when she opened the hotel room door. *Oh, God, what do I do now?* Trish thought of calling her mother, but what good would that do? She knew her father would just tell her to be patient; he'd feel better in the morning.

But he didn't.

Trish had set her alarm for six, and when she went to check on him, her father admitted to a temperature.

"Should we call a doctor?" Trish crossed her arms, hugging her elbows.

"No. Just give the antibiotics time to work. But I better stay in bed today. Trish, I can't tell you how terrible this makes me feel." The old, ugly rasp was back in his voice.

"No problem. I'll get someone to help me at the track. We can order room service for you."

"I don't feel much like eating. Maybe some orange juice and toast when you come back." He rubbed a hand across his eyes. "Are you sure you can handle things out there?"

"Da-ad. It's not like I haven't done all those chores before." She set two glasses of water on his nightstand. "Drink. I'll be back as soon as I can."

Trish hated to ask for help. Thoughts of how to take care of the horse and clean out the stall all at the same time nagged at her. She waved at the guard when she drove in and parked the car. Spitfire greeted her with his usual nicker. She poured his feed in the bucket and leaned against the colt's shoulder while he ate, trying to figure out what to do.

"How's your dad?" a familiar voice asked from the door.

Trish turned. One of her resident butterflies took a leap of pure joy. "Hi, Red. He's fi—how'd you know something was wrong?"

"Guard said your dad wasn't here last night or this morning. I knew he wouldn't leave you alone here unless something was really wrong."

Trish swallowed the lump that threatened her throat. "He got wet in that rainstorm—chilled—and now he has a fever."

"So he's in bed?"

Trish nodded.

Eric appeared to be thinking hard. "Tell you what, I'll be right back." He dog-trotted up the aisle and out the barn.

Trish carried her saddle and bridle to the stall. Gallop was on the chart for Spitfire's work for the morning. She'd just have to take this one step at a time.

She was ready to mount when Eric reappeared—with help.

"Meet Romero and Juan."

Trish smiled at the two dark-haired young men.

"They'll clean out the stall while you ride. Then help you wash him down if you'd like. They're good with horses."

"Thank you." Trish nodded at each of them.

"Oh, they don't speak English," Red added.

"*Gracias,*" Trish felt her tongue trip over the simple word. You'd think she'd never taken beginning Spanish, let alone three years of it. But then, words like *pitchfork* and *manure* hadn't been part of the curriculum either. She headed for the tools stored in the tack box.

"I'll see you out on the track," Red said as he gave her a leg up. "Don't worry about these guys. They know what to do."

"Thanks." Trish stared down into eyes blue enough to drown in. She adjusted her helmet and nudged Spitfire forward. Her throat felt dry. She wasn't coming down with something—was she?

It was almost possible to forget her worries with the breeze fresh in her face and Spitfire tugging at the bit. She kept him to a walk for half a circuit, then let him slow-gallop. He didn't fight her for more this morning, as if he knew she had enough to think about. Eric, mounted on a feisty gray, walked a circuit with her.

Later, she realized how much she enjoyed his teasing. Laughing felt good, but a clean stall and extra hands to help her wash the colt down and walk him out felt even better.

"You going for breakfast?" Eric showed up just as Trish had said her last *muchas gracias.*

"No. I need to get back to my dad. Thanks for finding me help." Trish opened her car door. "See ya."

Red leaned on the open door. "Where y'all staying?"

"The Louisville Inn. Why?"

"I'll call you later to see how things are going." He touched a finger to his helmet and trotted off.

Trish fixed a tray of food at the hotel buffet and carried it up to the suite. Her father was still asleep. She'd heard him coughing and wandering about several times during the night.

"Dad?" She moved things aside and set the tray on the nightstand. "I brought you breakfast."

"How's Spitfire?" Hal turned on his back and looked at her with real awareness for the first time since the chill. He cleared his throat.

Trish propped a couple of pillows behind his head and handed him a glass of orange juice. "He's fine, I'm fine, and you're looking better." She lifted the plastic dome off the plate and set the tray across his knees. "I'll go make some coffee."

She caught herself humming as she filled the pot. Amazing how her father's feeling better put a song in her heart.

"How are you handling everything?"

"Fine. Red brought me two stable hands and they cleaned out the stall while I worked Spitfire. Then I held him while they washed him down. I tried to talk some with them, but my Spanish is so slow they must think I'm an idiot."

Hal smiled around a bite of scrambled eggs. "I'm so proud of you, I can never begin to tell you how much. Thanks for the breakfast. Food tastes good this morning—finally."

Trish brought him a cup of coffee. "I'm going back to school Spitfire after the day's program starts. Since that's what you had on the schedule, I see no need to change it."

"Have you talked with your mother?"

"Not since Monday." Trish curled up in a chair and sipped her orange juice. "I'll call her tonight. You sound better, so we won't be lying."

"I'll take it easy today, but tomorrow I should be able to help. Tee, I've been thinking. Maybe we should hire Patrick O'Hern, that ex-trainer I introduced you to the other day. That would take some of the pressure off you."

"Why not wait and see? My two helpers are doing fine." Trish nibbled a piece of toast. "Not to change the subject, but Equinox is stabled right next to us. He's kind of high-strung."

"If we hired Patrick, he could become a permanent employee. We've been understaffed too long."

Trish looked at her father closely. He was serious about this. "We've gotten along okay up to now."

"I know." Hal handed her the tray. "I can't eat any more. I'll rest awhile, then get a shower. Can't believe how weak I am again."

"You were sick, running a fever, what'd you expect?"

"Yes, Dr. Evanston." A smile lifted a corner of his mouth. "How's your homework coming?"

"That's where I'm going now." She took the tray and placed it outside their door. Then, with books spread around her on the sofa, she attacked the list of assignments. That way she was able to blot out the idea of someone strange joining Runnin' On Farm.

When the phone rang, she about leaped out of her skin. What would she say to her mother? She picked it up before it could ring again. At the sound of Red's voice, she heaved a sigh of relief.

"Dad's sleeping again but feeling some better. Got him to eat a little."

"Is there anything I can do for you?"

Trish felt a warm glow in her heart. It was nice to know that someone cared. "No, but thanks. I'll be back later for schooling. Good luck on your mounts today."

She hung up the phone and stared at the framed print of the great horse Secretariat on the wall. The horse seemed to be looking right at her. It was a friendly look.

"You want some lunch before I go back?" she asked several hours later. Besides her homework, she'd written cards to Rhonda, Brad, her mom, and David.

Hal had taken a shower and was almost sleeping again. "No, thanks."

"How about if I call room service and they bring you a tray in about an hour?"

"Okay. But maybe you should put off the schooling."

"We'll be fine. Oh, and Spitfire needs new shoes, or the ones he has reset. One's loose."

"How about Friday?"

"Sure." Trish dialed room service and ordered soup and more juice for her father.

Back at the track, the second race was being run. She and Spitfire just hung out for a while. She sat crosslegged in the corner of his stall, stroking his nose and scratching his ears. He nibbled on her fingers and blew in her bangs. She heard a whinny from the stalls behind them.

"Sounds like someone else has arrived." Spitfire raised his head and answered with a nicker of his own. "Sure, sure, tell him how good you are." She tickled the whiskers on his upper lip.

Schooling went as smooth as a well-rehearsed play. Spitfire followed his lines perfectly as they trailed behind the horses heading to the paddock for the fourth race. She stood him in the stall for a while, then walked around the paddock, pointing out the Chrysler Triple Crown emblem on a white wall and all the bright flowers. Spitfire seemed to understand every word.

"Look at that black," someone in the crowd commented.

"Which race is he in?"

Trish wanted to tell them but kept walking Spitfire.

Red waved to her before the trainer boosted him into the saddle. "How's it going?"

"Fine. Good luck." Spitfire played with the chain on his lead strap when the mounted horses left the paddock to meet the ponies lined up just outside the tunnel. Another parade to post had begun. The crowd flowed back to find their seats.

"Hi, Mom." Trish caught the phone on the first ring again that night. Hal had eaten dinner and dozed off. Trish and her mother talked about what was happening at home and the track before Trish asked Hal to pick up the extension. "See ya, Mom. Next week, right? Here's Dad." She hung up before she could hear her mother pause—or decline.

"Your grandparents are coming here for the Derby," Hal told her when she went in to kiss him good-night. "They'll be here next Friday."

"Good. What about Mom?"

Hal just shrugged his shoulders.

A nightmare attacked Trish again that night. This time it was a replay of the family reliving the accident at Portland Meadows. In the dream her mother cried—forever. Trish licked her dry lips and forced her eyes open. Another race was coming up—a big one. Was she ready for it? How would she control the butterflies that already flitted when she thought ahead?

She hated to close her eyes again.

Remember the name of Jesus? Her little voice was being helpful this time. What a nice change.

Trish closed her eyes and let the name of Jesus in big letters scroll across her mind. There He sat, smiling at all the children. She could never resist smiling back. And going right to sleep.

She'd just walked Spitfire back from another schooling session the next afternoon when a voice yelled to her. "Hey, Trish! Ya got company!"

Chapter 13

"Mom, you came!" Trish flew down the aisle and threw herself into her mother's arms. "And David." She strangled him with a hug next. "You guys are really here!"

"Why didn't you tell me earlier your father was sick?" Marge whispered into her daughter's ear as she hugged Trish again.

"He wouldn't let me."

Marge sighed. "I figured as much. How bad is he?"

"Better." Trish turned to her brother. "Some track, isn't it, Davey boy. Wait'll you see the rest. I can show you around after I feed the kid here."

Spitfire nickered when he saw David. "Hey, old man. You remember me, huh?" Spitfire bopped David's Seattle Mariner's baseball hat onto the dirt aisle. David picked it up and dusted off the brim. "Sure does. He act this way with anyone else, or does he save it all for me?"

Trish laughed at the sneaky expression on Spitfire's face. "He loves you, that's all." She showed David where they kept everything and measured out the evening feed.

"Hi, Trish, need some help?" Red stuck his head in the door.

"No, thanks. Hey, meet my family. They just got here. Mom, David, this is Eric Holloran, better known as Red. He's a jockey here."

"Pleased to meet y'all." Red shook hands.

"How'd you do?" Trish asked.

"One win, a place, and a fourth. My checkbook is singing for joy. You still need the boys in the morning?"

"No, David here needs to work his muscles. And I'm glad you did well."

"Gotta run. Nice to meet y'all." He hesitated. "Can I buy you a Coke or something?"

"Thanks, but we're heading for the hotel as soon as we finish chores. Dad doesn't know they're here yet."

"Okay. See ya."

David looked from the retreating jockey to Trish. "Is there something going on here I should know about?"

Trish felt a blush creep up her neck. "David!"

Marge leaned against the half wall, smiling at her daughter. "He seems like a very nice young man."

David snorted. He dumped the feed in Spitfire's box. "Let's go see Dad."

"You guys wait out here," Trish said twenty minutes later as she dug in her pocket for the hotel key. "Dad needs a good surprise." She opened the door to the dark suite. "Dad?" She flicked on the light switch by the door.

"In here." Hal's voice sounded as if he just woke up.

"There's someone here who needs to talk with you."

"Okay, just a minute."

Trish clapped a hand over her mouth to stifle the giggles that bubbled up like a shaken soda can. She glanced at David to see the same look on his face. Marge had her tongue stuck in her cheek.

Hal wore his robe over a pair of jeans and was brushing his hair back with his hands as he came around the corner. The look on his face made the secrecy well worthwhile. He hugged Marge first, and with her tucked against his side, he wrapped his other arm around his son's neck and squeezed hard.

Trish could also tell from her dad's look that he was thinking, "Thank you, God," just like she was. Her mother had come, fear or not. They were together, the way they should be. Trish felt a weight float away from her shoulders that she hadn't realized was so heavy.

They ordered room service and sat around catching up for the next couple of hours.

"Good news," Marge said at one point. "Grandpa and Grandma are coming for sure; said they wouldn't miss it. They'll arrive on Friday."

"Will they stay long enough to go sightseeing with us?" Trish asked.

Marge shrugged. "Got me. You know what a rush they're always in to get back to their volunteering. I think they're busier now than when they were working."

Trish fell asleep that night with a smile on her face. Her family was all together.

"This area doesn't look at all like I expected," David said as he and Trish drove to the track the next morning.

"I know. The bluegrass country is really around Lexington. But wait till you see the Ohio River. It's huge. We haven't been anywhere yet since Dad got sick. Maybe this weekend." She parked by their barn. "We need to get you a badge later."

If it weren't for the difference in scenery, Trish would have felt as if she were home. She and David worked together like the team they'd become since their father's illness began. Having her brother there made her even more aware how much she'd missed him.

"Slow gallop now," David reminded her as he gave her a leg up. Spitfire stood quietly. "Is he feeling all right?" David nodded at the horse.

"Sure, why?"

"Well, he—he's quieter. Not such a clown."

Trish leaned forward and smoothed Spitfire's mane to one side. "I don't know. He seems to realize this is serious business. But you missed out on a real tantrum with the thunderstorm. Like at the airport. He *doesn't* like loud noises."

It had rained during the night and the morning air smelled fresh-washed and rose-petal soft on Trish's skin. She walked the colt once around the track, staying close by the outside rail. The rising sunlight sparkled on the twin spires above the grandstand.

At the second round, they broke into a slow gallop. Spitfire settled into the rocking gait, ears pricked, always aware of the horses working around him but not concerned. Trish relaxed along with him. There was no place on earth she'd rather be.

Red saluted her with his whip as he galloped by.

Trish pointed out the sights on the backside as she and David jogged over to the track kitchen for breakfast. On the way back they stopped at the office for his badge.

At ten the farrier arrived with his tools to shoe the colt. Spitfire stood like a perfect gentleman, only rubbing his forehead on Trish's chest as she held him.

Saturday morning after the chores were done, Hal called Trish and David into the office. "I think it's time we brought in someone else to help us," he said. "Now, I don't want you to think it's because you haven't been doing a good job. You know better than that." He smoothed back a lock of hair that fell over Trish's cheek. "I just think we need to make life easier for all of us, and thanks to Spitfire's win at Santa Anita, we can afford it."

"You have someone in mind?" David asked.

Hal nodded. "His name is Patrick O'Hern. Trish met him earlier this week. He had a tremendous reputation until . . ."

"Until—" David interrupted a long pause.

"Well, he—ummm—"

Warning bells went off in Trish's mind. Her father was on his helping-others mode again. What had Patrick done?

"He became an alcoholic after his wife died and his whole life fell apart." Hal said the words in a rush, as if he couldn't wait to get them out. "But with God's help, he's turned his life around. I feel privileged to work with him. The man knows more about horses and racing than—"

"It's okay, Dad." David nodded and shrugged at the same time. "We trust you. If you think Patrick is who we need, that's great. Right, Trish?"

Trish nodded. "Sure. I liked him." But a squirmy little doubt dug in at the back of her mind.

"It's settled then. I'll page him and see if he can meet us up at the track kitchen."

The meeting with Patrick went according to Hal's plan. The man would start work on Monday.

The pace stepped up after the weekend. It seemed there were more reporters each day. Trish began to wonder where they all came from. All the Derby entries were now on site. As Trish watched the other horses work, she tried to compare them to Spitfire.

"You're just prejudiced," David said after one of her comments about the bad temper of the chestnut called Going South. His trainer had posted a sign warning visitors to keep back.

"Where'd you ever get that idea?" Trish tried to look innocent, but the mischief dancing in her eyes gave her away.

They all fell easily into the new routine. Since Patrick stayed on the grounds, he fed Spitfire in the morning so Trish and David could sleep in a bit later. Then David mucked out the stall while Trish took Spitfire out on the track. The colt and Patrick hit it off from the first moment Patrick slipped the black a carrot chunk.

"Breeze him five furlongs," Hal said as Patrick boosted Trish up on Tuesday morning. "Trot once around to warm him up, then let him loose in front of the wooden stands." He pointed to the wooden bleachers constructed for owners and trainers by the gate to the track. "Patrick and I'll clock you from there."

Spitfire seemed to sense this morning was different. He played with the bit and danced sideways on the far turn. Trish snapped her goggles into place. As they came around the near turn, she angled him to the rail and let him extend to a gallop.

"Okay, fella, let's get ready," she crooned into his twitching ears. At the furlong marker she gave him his head and shouted, "Go, Spitfire!" She crouched high over his withers as he exploded under her. With each stride he gained speed, like a sprinter off the mark. She remained in the high position, hands firm and encouraging. She almost missed the fifth marker, and the sixth passed before she could bring him down. They cantered on around the track.

The grin on her father's face told her all she needed to know. But her internal stopwatch already knew the colt had run well. The only question—could he last the mile and a quarter? Santa Anita had been a mile and an eighth. An eighth of a mile, one furlong, didn't seem far, unless you were running on pure heart by then. Races could be won or lost in the last stride.

"Here, lass, I'll walk 'im." Patrick reached for the lead shank.

"No, that's okay, I need something to keep busy. You guys are doing all the hard stuff." Trish relaxed after walking Spitfire out. His knee stayed cool to the touch, as if there had never been an injury. One more big relief.

Each day her internal aerial troupe took to practicing new routines. Anytime she thought of the coming race she could feel the butterflies leaping, fluttering, and diving.

"You okay?" Red asked her Wednesday morning at the kitchen.

"Why?"

" 'Cause you've been stirrin' those eggs 'stead of eating them." He pointed to her plate.

"Guess I'm just not hungry."

"She always like this?" Red asked David. The two had become good friends in a short time.

Now Trish had two big brothers bossing her around. Except that when her hand touched Red's, it didn't feel the same as when she brushed David's. *Think about that later!* she ordered, after her shoulder tingled from Red's casual touch.

Thursday morning arrived either too soon or not soon enough—Trish wasn't sure which. This was *the* day for choosing post positions. She woke up to a mist hovering just above the ground. At the track, horses seemed to float in and out, like phantoms in a ghostly dance.

Marge and Hal attended the breakfast for owners, but Trish, David, and Patrick stayed with Spitfire, finishing morning chores. They went through the routine without talking, grabbed a quick bite to eat, and headed for the museum. Red had advised them to get there early, since the place would be packed.

The statue of Secretariat with its blanket of roses had been moved, and a podium with microphones was set up in its place in the oval room of the museum. Stage lights made the area brighter than day. TV crews were setting up their cameras, with cables snaking across the carpet.

As the time drew nearer, the room filled with spectators, owners, trainers, officials; and reporters with tape recorders, camcorders, and clipboards. Everyone was handed a sheet of paper with the twelve horses running listed.

"Here." Hal handed each of them a gold baseball cap with "Spitfire" lettered in crimson. "I meant to give you these before you left this morning. How'd everything go?"

"Fine." Trish bent the brim and settled her cap in place. "How was the breakfast?" She grinned at her mother. Even Marge, dressed in her navy silk suit, wore the crimson and gold hat.

Just then the lights went out. A multi-projector slide show set to music and narration sprang to life on a continuous screen that circled the room just under the second-floor railing. Trish felt a lump in her throat as she watched the life of a Thoroughbred from foaling to the Derby. She kept turning to watch the scenes unfold as heroes of past Derbies galloped across the screen. A field of red tulips around the entire screen brought an "oooh" from many spectators. Haunting strains of "My Old Kentucky Home" faded away as the screen flashed names of this year's contenders. Spitfire, Going South, Nancy's Request, Nomatterwhat, First Admiral. Trish had to turn to keep reading. Dun Rovin', Equinox, Waring Prince, Who Sez, Spanish Dancer, That's All, and Sea Urchin. One of those names would be added to the list of greats.

The lights came back on. Now all Trish could see was the broad back of the man standing in front of her. The ceremony began. A horse's name was called, a number drawn from a container. The race secretary then placed that number beside the horse's name on a board for all to see.

Trish watched the people around her mark their papers. She didn't even have a pencil. A group cheered when Who Sez drew position one. Number twelve for Spanish Dancer didn't thrill his owners. Spitfire's name was halfway down the list. What would his number be?

Trish's butterflies went berserk.

Chapter 14

Spitfire, position six." The waiting was over.

Trish listened with only half an ear as the remaining numbers were called. Number six meant they'd be right in the middle of the field.

As soon as the last number was posted, a reporter shoved a microphone in front of her father. Hal smiled at the question.

"You're right, the weather could indeed be in our favor. When you come from the Pacific Northwest, your horse better not mind the rain. Our colt runs well on a wet track. And position six can be either an asset or a handicap, depending on how fast he breaks."

He turned to answer another question. "No, there's been no problem with his knee for the last couple of weeks. Running at Santa Anita caused only a mild inflammation, nothing to be concerned about."

Nothing to be concerned about! Trish caught herself before she made any noises. *She'd* been concerned, that's for sure. If the press only knew all that had gone on.

She'd just thought about leaving when a young woman asked her a question. "That fatal accident out in Portland, you were involved in it, weren't you?"

Trish thought fast. "Yes. But I wasn't hurt much, a mild concussion."

"Do you feel that affected your riding? How about if you get caught in the middle during the Derby?"

Trish took a deep breath. Should she tell them she lost two races after that and considered backing out of another? No, this wasn't the place for total honesty.

"How can it *not* affect you when a friend is killed? But you go on. You ride each race as it comes. And you do your best. Guess that's about all you can do. Spitfire and me—we'll do our best."

"Good answer," David whispered in her ear as the reporters left to talk to others.

Hal was answering a man with ABC lettered on his microphone. Marge had a smile pasted on her face. Trish could tell the glue was wearing thin and the smile might slip off. She signaled David and the two of them took their mother's arms. "Let's go look at the trophies."

They could identify the owners and trainers by the groups gathered around them. The crowd was thinning out now, and the television crews were dismantling the cameras and rolling up their cables.

"How was the breakfast?" Trish shifted her attention from the humongous silver bowl in the trophy case to her mother.

"Huge. Hundreds of people."

"How about the trainers' dinner?" David asked.

"The hotel was beautiful and the food great but . . ."

Trish and David waited for her to go on.

"But—well, we met some very nice people." She paused, thinking. "I guess things are just different here."

Trish looked around the room. "I guess."

"Like back in there. It's a fashion show. We just don't do things that way at home."

Trish grinned. "That's why I like it better down at the barns. Horses are easier than people. Did you see that woman all in white?"

"If those rocks she wore were real—" David shook his head.

"And the broad-brimmed hat. Why y'all don't know how na-ahce it is to see ya he-ah." Trish copied the accent and the gestures perfectly.

"Trish." Marge strangled on the laugh and bit her lip to keep from choking.

"We better get outta here before you get us in trouble." David appeared to be suffering from the same choking problem as his mother. He took both their arms and walked them past the visitor's information desk and out the front doors. When they reached the sunshine, they looked at each other and let the laughter spill. Hal found them a bit later, still giggling.

"Okay, what's going on?"

Trish and her mother looked at each other and started in again. Finally Trish took a deep breath and forced herself to look at her father, her face serious. "Y'all just don't dress us ra-aght, Daddy de-ah."

"The woman in white?"

"Oh, you noticed." Marge slipped her arm through Hal's.

"How could I not?" Hal shook his head. "Let's go check on Spitfire."

More reporters and writers crowded around them when they arrived back at the stable. Trish was beginning to understand what famous people meant when they talked about living in a fish bowl. She was scratching Spitfire's cheek with his head draped over her shoulder in his favorite position when someone asked if they could take her picture. Spitfire flinched as the flash blinded his eyes.

It was a relief when they headed back to the hotel.

"That slide show was the neatest thing I've seen." Trish popped the top on her can of Diet Coke and drank deeply.

"It really was." Marge leaned back in a chair. She slipped off her shoes and flexed her toes. "I'd love to see it again."

"The schedule is posted for showings." Hal stretched his arms over his head. "There any coffee left?"

David poured a cup for himself and one for his dad. "What a mass of people. This whole week is just one big party."

"No, it's lots of parties. Speaking of which, we have another one to attend tonight. The Churchill Downs Derby party." Hal looked at Marge.

"Do we *have* to?"

"We don't *have* to do anything. I'm sure they won't miss us, since I've heard there are usually about five hundred people at this one. Besides, according to our daughter here, I don't dress you right. For dinner at the famous Galt House, that is."

Trish scrunched her eyebrows at him. "You don't say it right either."

"By the way, Red was asking for you."

Trish felt the heat blossom on her neck. "Oh?"

"Said he'd see you at evening feed if not before." Hal had a knowing twinkle in his eye.

Trish felt the blush spread to her cheekbones.

"Seems like a right nice young man."

"Da-ad!" She held her Coke can to her cheek. This was crazy. She didn't *like* him—did she? Did he like her? Her father certainly seemed to think so. She threw a decorator pillow at David to wipe the smirk off his face.

"Just think, less than forty-eight hours." David shook his head. "And it's Derby time."

"Thanks a bunch." Now her butterflies leaped into life. A swallow of soda sent them into a frenzy. "You guys are really a big help."

"You kids want to go to the parade?" Hal set his coffee cup on the table.

Trish thought a minute. All those people. "How can we? Spitfire needs to eat about that time. The parade is late afternoon. I'd rather go somewhere for dinner that has great food, just us."

And that's what they did. By the time they were stuffed with hush puppies and babyback ribs, Trish was ready for bed. Mornings came so early.

"You and that black colt, lass, you're some pair," Patrick said the next morning as Trish leaped to the ground. "You both seem to know what the other's thinking. That'll be hard to beat out there."

"That means a lot, coming from you," Trish said. It was the first real compliment Patrick had given her. "I sure hope you're right."

They'd just finished breakfast when Hal and Marge ushered the two newcomers into the track kitchen. Trish leaped from her seat and threw her arms first around her grandfather, then her grandmother. Her grandmother's familiar lavender perfume lingered in the air.

"Can you believe we're all really meeting in Kentucky? I'm so glad you came." She stepped back to give them the once-over. "You look great."

While her grandfather seemed a bit more stooped in the shoulders, Trish didn't see any sign that he had been sick. Actually the two of them looked more alike than ever.

"Hello, David." The slender woman with snow-white hair leaned over to kiss his cheek.

By the time Hal had introduced Patrick, Trish had brought a tray with coffee for everyone.

"Are any of them decaf?" her grandmother asked. "I really must be careful, you know."

"I remembered. Those two on the outside are for you two." Trish handed one to her grandfather. She caught her father's wink as she handed him a cup. Careful was the operative word. When she thought about it, Trish knew where her mother got the worries—from *her* mother.

When Patrick excused himself, Trish followed suit.

"We'll be down later," her father said.

That afternoon was the running of the Oaks. Trish leaned on the iron rail around their box and watched both the spectators and the race. Tomorrow she would be up in the jockey room—waiting.

A chestnut filly with two white socks won by a length. The jockey riding her, Jerry Jones, would be up on Nomatterwhat the next afternoon. He was known to bring in winners.

"Firefly would have taken it," Trish said to no one in particular. "Sure wish we could have brought her."

"She'll have her chance." Hal tapped her on the shoulder with his program. "And so will you."

Trish wondered later what he meant by that. As she flipped to her other side—for the third time—in bed that night, she couldn't quit thinking about the coming race. What if someone fell? What if Spitfire got hurt? What if they lost? What if they won? The what-ifs were driving her right out of her mind.

She tried to pray. The questions paraded across her mind instead. She recited her Bible verses. Ahhhh, she felt a little calmer. *Relax,* she ordered her muscles. They ignored her.

Maybe they should have gone to one of the parties they'd been invited to. Then she wouldn't have so much time to think. She turned over—again.

Finally Trish sat up in bed and turned on the light. The soft glow burnished the curve of the carved eagle wings. Trish smoothed a finger over the intricate carving. Her song "Raise you up on eagle's wings, bear you on the breath of God . . ." drifted through her restlessness.

What would it be like to catch the air currents and spiral higher and higher? To feel the wind in your wings? She sighed. She knew what it felt like to be held "in the palm of His hand."

"Thank you, Father," she breathed. "Thank you."

The peace of sleep was shattered by screams and groans. By sirens and shock. By dirt and blood. The nightmare rocked through her with a vengeance.

Trish jerked upright, gasping for air. She'd felt as if someone were sitting on her chest. She propped her shoulders against the head of the bed and waited for her heart to stop pounding. It was just a nightmare. And nightmares were always worse than reality.

You're scared! her little nagger whispered. *You have the big race tomorrow—no—today, and you're scared to bits. Look at you shake. You shouldn't be afraid.*

Trish clapped her hands over her ears, but it didn't help. She *shouldn't* be scared. But then, who wouldn't be. The Kentucky Derby was a *big* deal. Half the world would be watching.

That thought didn't help at all. Instead, she got up and went to the bathroom. She got a drink of water and climbed back into bed. This time she painted and repainted a picture of Jesus on her mental screen until she slipped off to sleep.

Her butterflies leaped into life with the buzz of the alarm. It would have been nice if they'd overslept.

As usual, Patrick had already fed the hungry black colt. He hummed a happy tune as he polished their racing saddle.

After greeting him, Trish whistled softly. Spitfire, his head already over the web gate, nickered his happiness at seeing her. He nuzzled her cheek and whiskered her hand, begging for his carrot treat. Trish didn't disappoint him.

The sky was overcast as Trish trotted him out onto the track half an hour later. The forecast was for possible thundershowers.

"And you don't like thunder, do you?" Trish carried on a conversation with his ears. They twitched backward and pricked forward again, keeping track of everything around them. Trish rose in her stirrups as they trotted around the track. When he settled to a slow jog, she sat down again and enjoyed the ride. A pounding trot hadn't helped her stomach any.

Her father was answering questions again when they returned to the stall. Patrick and David washed the colt down, getting their own steam bath in the process. Trish washed Spitfire's face with a soft sponge. He nibbled at the sponge, then shook his head, spraying her with water.

"Knock it off." She raised an arm to keep the drops out of her eyes. Spitfire curled his upper lip, as if he were laughing at her. They scraped him dry, blanketed him, and then Trish took the lead shank to walk him out. David had already cleaned the stall and spread new straw.

Trish missed her messed-up conversations with her two Spanish-speaking helpers. They'd called Spitfire *muy cabrillo,* beautiful horse.

"How you feelin'?" Red fell into step beside her.

"Scared. You just startled me."

"You were kinda off in dreamland."

"No, I wasn't." But Trish knew her mind had been somewhere else. That was dangerous. She needed to concentrate on Spitfire in case something spooked him.

"You going for breakfast?"

Trish shot him a pained look.

"Oh. Butterflies?"

"A belly full."

"You better eat something. I'll see you later up in the jockey room. You play pool?"

Trish shook her head. How would she get through all those hours up in the jockey room?

"How about Ping-Pong then? We'll find something to make the time pass. See ya." He trotted off.

"Do you think he ever walks?" Spitfire shook his head.

Trish managed to get down a piece of toast. She bypassed the milk and drank apple juice instead.

"You'll be fine." Her father had his mind-reading skills in gear.

"Wish I could stay down at the barn with you guys. At least I'd have something to do there."

"I know this is different and difficult. But the day'll be gone before you know it."

Trish nodded, but this time she doubted her father was right.

Spitfire shone from all the brushing. His hooves gleamed, mane and tail waved, flowing free just as Trish liked. Neither she nor her father cared for the decorative braiding some stables used. The tack was soaped and polished.

It was quiet around the stalls. Once in a while a visitor dropped by, but horses and people were both getting a rest. Trish leaned back in the lawn chair. If only she could stay here.

"You want me to walk you over?" David asked.

Trish glanced at her watch. It was time. Why did she feel like she was being walked to the execution block?

Patrick clasped her cold hands in his warm ones. "Don't be worryin', lass. Just give it your best."

Trish nodded. She was afraid if she opened her mouth, the butterflies would strangle her.

In spite of the lowering sky, the infield was fast filling with spectators. All the grandstand and bleacher area had been reserved weeks before, but crowds had poured into the infield since the gates opened at eight.

"Did you see the car?" David nudged her arm. They were almost at the tunnel.

"The red one?"

"Yeah. Just think, it'll be yours when you win. A red Chrysler Le Baron convertible."

"I can't think about that now." Trish chewed her lip. Her swallower was too dry to work.

David handed her her sports bag at the bottom of the stairs to the second-story jockey rooms. "See you in the saddling stalls."

Trish stepped on the escalator. She turned once and waved to David, who waited at the bottom.

Frances Brown was the only one in the women's jockey room. She sat at her desk, reading a coffee-table-size book. "Hi, Trish. I brought this in for everyone to look at." She turned to the front cover. The title, *Kentucky Derby,* was lettered in white above a racing Thoroughbred. "The pictures are fantastic. I've never seen a better book."

An hour later Trish was still reading it. The pictures were great but so was the text. She learned things about the history of the track and racing she'd never heard before.

Since the first race of the day was at eleven-thirty, several other women came in. Trish was the only female riding in the Derby. She put the book down when she heard someone call her name.

"Trish, Red's in the other room asking for you." Frances smiled at her. "Glad you like my book."

"Where did you get it? I want one."

"At the museum gift store. You go eat something if you can. You'll feel better."

Trish wasn't so sure. At the roar of the crowd on the monitor, her butterflies thought the applause was for them. They added new routines to their show. Trish wrapped both arms around her middle. *Please, God, help me.*

Chapter

15

It was raining.

Trish stood at the window looking out over the rooftops of the grandstand. The rain looked like sheets of gauze blowing in the wind. She'd watched race number two on the monitor. It had finished just before the rain veil hit.

She heard the click of pool balls from the table behind her.

"What's a five-letter word for dog?" asked a jockey who was working a crossword puzzle at one of the tables.

"Hound."

"Thanks."

Trish didn't turn around until Red handed her a Diet Coke. Then she leaned her hips against the windowsill and looked up at the monitor. Another previous race was running.

"I watch those all the time." Red gestured toward the screen. "Helps to understand each jockey's style."

"Where do you watch, here?"

"Over in the museum. It's a big screen too, so you can see more. Plus the track has a video library."

"Wish I could be down at the barn. At least there's something to do there."

"Pretty quiet yet. Spitfire's probably sleeping. With the all-night partying on the streets around the area, the horses need some extra sleep too."

"I suppose." She rotated her neck. "Usually I have at least a couple of mounts, more like three or four. That keeps me hustling. Or I help David on the backside."

"Trish." He paused. "How long you gonna be around after the race?"

She shrugged. "Depends on how we do. Dad just says wait till after the Derby, then he'll decide."

"But you're entered in all three races of the Triple Crown?"

She nodded. "Why?"

It was his turn to shrug. "I'd like to spend some time with you. Maybe a drive or a movie. Something."

"Oh." Trish took a long swallow of her Coke. She looked up to find those blue-blue eyes studying her. "I'll ask my dad."

"Good. See you later. Gotta get ready for my next ride." His grin made her feel good.

"Good luck."

Trish returned to the women's room to find Frances swapping tales with one of the jockeys. They broke off to watch the fourth race. Red brought his mount up on the outside, hanging back with another horse until the stretch.

"Now!" Trish joined in the hollering, cheering him on.

Red went to the whip and bore down on the leader. He won by a length. When the camera showed the winner, you could hardly recognize horse or rider for the mud. But Red's grin was contagious even over the television.

The rain had quit but the track was now officially listed as muddy. From the looks of the last riders, muddy was an understatement.

Maybe the rain lulled them to sleep. Trish suddenly realized her stomach was butterfly-free. She sprayed furniture polish on her five pairs of goggles and wiped them off, stacking them together, ready to snap over her helmet. Then she buffed her boots. *When did the butterflies disappear?*

She didn't know, but didn't really care either. The peace she'd prayed for had crept right in. She felt good. It wouldn't be long now.

She was all stretched and ready when the call came.

"Give it all you've got," Frances told her. "It's about time we had a woman in that red horseshoe."

"Thanks." A couple of butterflies tried to break out, but Trish swallowed them down. On the scale, her total weight with saddle and lead registered 126 pounds, like every other Derby jockey. She followed the others down the stairs and through the lines of waving and shouting spectators to the paddock. It wasn't raining.

Trish breathed in deeply of the fresh-washed air and rotated her shoulders. Her parents and grandparents were dressed in their best. David and Patrick waited with Spitfire. The colt nickered when he saw Trish.

"You ready?" Hal asked.

At Trish's nod, David punched her lightly on the shoulder. "You can do it."

Trish kissed Spitfire on his nose. He wuffled in her ear as she hugged him. "This is it, fella. You ready to show them what we can do?"

"Riders up." The official call was clear.

Trish felt a lump grow in her throat when she looked into her father's eyes. "I love you," she whispered in his ear as she threw her arms around his neck and hugged him. She hugged her mother next. "Thanks for being here."

Marge nodded. Her sniff told of tears hovering.

Then Trish hugged her grandparents. "I can't tell you how glad I am you came."

"We wouldn't have missed it," her grandfather said.

Trish took a moment, looking deep into David's eyes. "I'm glad you're my brother. We couldn't have made it without you."

David gave her a quick hug, the kind that brothers give when they're more used to swats and jabs. "Just win for us."

Patrick touched her hand. "We'll all be praying, lass."

Hal gave her a leg up and squeezed her knee. "You know what to do. God bless."

Patrick led them out to join the line in position number six. There was no turning back now.

Trish's pony rider picked her up at the tunnel. The gray horse wore roses in his braided tail and mane. As Spitfire cleared the tunnel, Trish heard the bands playing and everyone singing "My Old Kentucky Home." She reached forward to pat her horse's black neck. Head high, ears forward, Spitfire waltzed to the music. The way he floated over the ground couldn't be described any other way. They turned and trotted back before the grandstand again. Trish saw lightning fork from the dark sky to the west. Thunder rumbled in the distance.

Equinox trotted in front of them, giving his handler a bad time. Sweat already darkened his shoulders.

As they cantered toward the backside, Trish could feel Spitfire relax even more. The only thing bothering her was the dense black cloud that blanketed the sky above the barns. If only it would hold off until after the race.

The wind picked up even as the parade of horses began entering the starting gate. Number one, Who Sez, refused to go in. Four green-jacketed gatemen got behind and shoved the horse into the gate. The next four walked right in. Equinox reared when the lead was transferred from pony rider to handler. The jockey clung like the professional he was, but Trish knew he must feel shaky about it.

Spitfire danced to the side but obeyed when Trish ordered him forward. He stood quietly in the gate. Dun Rovin' on their right acted spooky, tossing his head and rocking back and forth.

"Watch him," his handler said from his place up on the side of the gate by the horse's head.

Trish kept her eyes straight ahead, focused on the spot between Spitfire's ears. He was balanced, ready.

As Spanish Dancer, number twelve, stepped into the gate, the entire area turned blue-white. Thunder crashed right on top of them. The gates sprang open.

Spitfire threw up his head. Off balance, he slipped at the bound from the gate. Equinox bumped hard against him.

Trish fought to hold his head up. Spitfire gained his footing, but by the time they were running true, the field had left them behind.

"Okay, fella, bad start, so now we gotta make up for it." Trish's steady

125

voice cheered him on. They were two lengths off the pace as they passed the stands for the first time.

It looked like a wall of haunches ahead of them as the last four horses ran shoulder to shoulder. Trish waited patiently until one drifted to the outer rail and she had a hole to drive through. She took it without a flinch.

They came out of the clubhouse turn running neck and neck with number eight in the middle of the field. Trish eased Spitfire to the right until they ran on the outside.

Two lengths in front of them, the horse on the inside was bumped and crashed into the rail.

The jockey flying over the horse's head barely registered, it happened so fast. "Come on, fella," Trish crooned around the clench in her gut. Only three horses pounded on ahead of them. Trish could tell the going was slow, but Spitfire didn't mind.

She had pulled down three goggles already. The horse in front seemed to stop, he slowed so much. Spitfire was running easily in third. At the mile marker, Trish made her move.

"Okay, Spitfire, this is it." She crouched tight over his neck, feeling herself part of her colt—as if they were one body, one mind. And that mind was on the two horses leading.

Spitfire stretched out. He picked up the pace, running as if the track were dry and fast.

"Come on, Spitfire!" Trish hollered in his twitching ears.

The second-place horse fell back in a couple of strides. Only Nomatterwhat was left.

One furlong, an eighth of a mile, to go. Trish willed her black colt to give it all he had. She could see the white posts ahead.

"Now, boy, now!" They drew even.

Jones went to the whip. Neck and neck, they thundered toward the finish line.

Spitfire stretched his nose past the sorrel. Then his neck. His shoulders. He won by three-quarters of a length.

"Yowee!" Trish yelled at the top of her lungs. She straightened her legs, standing in the stirrups to slow Spitfire down. "You did it, you gorgeous hunk of horseflesh, you did it!"

Tears streamed down her face, creating furrows in the mud.

"Thank you, Father, thank you. The Derby. We won the Derby!" She turned and cantered back to the finish line. Past the screaming and cheering crowd, past the cameras lining the inside rail, to that grassy horseshoe outlined in red tulips.

Trish stopped in the center of the track and turned Spitfire to face the crowds, to receive his applause, his just due. "You did it, fella. See how good it feels?" She raised a mud-crusted arm and waved. As her arm came down, she leaned forward and hugged her horse's neck. The applause thundered louder.

David and Patrick reached them first. David slapped her on the knee and pumped Trish's hand. "I didn't think you two would pull it off after a start like that."

"My old heart nearly stopped." Patrick patted his chest. "As I said, you two are really something."

"I told you he doesn't like thunder." Trish looked across the crowd for her father. He had Marge by the arm, helping her negotiate the rutted and muddy track. Behind them, two men in business suits assisted her grandparents. Trish could see Marge had been crying, in fact, still was. The radiant smile she lifted for her daughter said the tears were those of joy.

"All I can say is thank you, God," Hal said as he clenched Trish's hand.

"You're safe," Marge said around her tears.

"And we won." Trish swallowed hard.

"Come on." Hal grasped the reins and led them through the mob and into the horseshoe.

Spitfire stood, head high as the officials draped a blanket of red roses across his withers. Cameras clicked while a sheaf of roses was handed to Trish. More cameras flashed in the dimming light. Trish leaped lightly to the ground. She reached up and pulled Spitfire's head down for a quick scratch and a hug.

At that moment, Spitfire noticed David's hat. He flipped the brim with his nose and sent it flying.

David looked at Trish and shook his head. "Can't you teach this clown any manners?" People around them laughed and applauded again.

"Come on, old son." Patrick slipped a halter over Spitfire's head. "Let's get you to the testing barn." As he led the colt away, Trish and her parents were escorted up the white ramp of the horseshoe to stand behind the row of four silver trophies. The large fancy one was given each year to the winner, then returned to the museum with the winner's name engraved on it.

"This is unusual," the master of ceremonies announced. "This time all these trophies go to the same family. Owner and trainer, Hal Evanston. Jockey, his daughter, sixteen-year-old Tricia Evanston. This bunch keeps things in the family."

Trish, Hal, and Marge waved again. Trish couldn't look at her mother, for she knew she'd cry in earnest then.

Hal stepped up to the microphone. "I can't begin to tell you how I feel. I thank all of you, and our heavenly Father for making this day happen." He waved again. "And yes, we'll be going on to the Preakness, God willing."

Trish felt a leap of excitement. Could anything top this?

"And now, the first female jockey in history to win the Kentucky Derby, Tricia Evanston."

Trish cleared her throat. She looked across the sea of people filling the stands. Reporters with cameras and camcorders crowded the infield in front of her.

"Every jockey dreams of being up here one day. I don't think the feeling would be any different, whether you're a man or a woman. This is my dream come true, helping my father make *his* dream come true. Thank you."

"Stay right here," the master of ceremonies said, and he introduced the representative of the Chrysler Corporation.

"It is my great pleasure to present you, Tricia Evanston, with the keys to that Le Baron convertible over there." He placed them in her hand. "Is this your first car?"

Trish nodded. "Thank you," she stammered. She'd forgotten about the car. What would her mother say about this?

After answering more questions, shaking all the hands that reached for them, smiling for the cameras, and answering *more* questions, the security officers opened a pathway through the crowds and escorted the Evanston family across the track and into the tunnel.

"Way to go, Trish," a familiar voice called from the stands above her head. Trish looked up to wave at Red.

The escort took them upstairs to the director's office, where more congratulations were extended. Trish wished David were able to be with them. Instead, he had joined Patrick and Spitfire back at the testing barn.

"Trish, I'm Bill Williams from *Sports Illustrated.*"

Trish shook his hand. "I'm glad to meet you."

"Before you change, could we go out to the backside and get some more pictures of you and Spitfire? I'd like a headshot of the two of you for the cover of our next issue."

Trish looked around for her father. He was talking with someone across the room. "I—I guess." *The cover of* Sports Illustrated. *What's Rhonda gonna say about this?* She almost giggled at the thought. *And what's Mom gonna say?*

What could she say?

"You better wash your face first," Marge whispered in Trish's ear. Trish excused herself and did just that.

They all trekked across to the backside to barn 41. Patrick had Spitfire all washed and dried, but quickly slipped the white bridle back in place. Spitfire draped his head over Trish's shoulder, as he loved to do, and pricked his ears when someone snapped their fingers behind the photographer's head.

"Thank you," Williams said. "And I can call you at the Inn for an interview time?"

Trish nodded. "That would be fine."

"We have another reception." Hal laid his hand on Trish's shoulder. "You better go change."

Marge reached to hug her daughter before she left. "I was so scared and so proud at the same time, I didn't know what to do but pray. I thank God for taking care of you, and for prayer. I couldn't have gotten through this otherwise."

"Mom, I'm so proud of you." Trish hugged her mother back. "No matter how afraid you were, you came through. You came and watched me race. Dad and I really needed you."

Hal wrapped his arms around both of them. "That's right. We're in this together. And now it's on to Pimlico."

Spitfire shoved his head between them and blew in Trish's ear. He was ready too, for another carrot and more scratching.

ACKNOWLEDGMENTS

My thanks to Emergency Medical Technician Ted Bingham, who told me procedures for emergency vehicles. My favorite medical expert is Karen Chafin, whose nursing experience is invaluable when I need a quick medical question answered. She's also my sister—I'm blessed.

Several hours listening to jockey Patty (P. J.) Cooksey, trainer Glinny Dunlop Bartram, and jockey room mother Frances Brown swap horse stories in the women's jockey room at Churchill Downs was worth the entire trip to Kentucky, even if I hadn't been able to see the Derby. Thanks to all of you for enriching my stories by increasing my knowledge.

Linda Wood introduced us to Churchill Downs, the site and the people. Thanks for sharing your time and knowledge.

So many people answer so many questions for me. Thank you all.

CALL FOR COURAGE

BOOK FIVE

To Ruby MacDonald and Pat Rushford,
my first dedicated critique group
and lasting friends.

We owe each other our successes.

Chapter 01

This was turning out to be a year of firsts. First race, first win, first trip to California, and now the first female to win the Kentucky Derby. Sixteen-year-old Tricia Evanston hugged the tall, black colt she and her father had raised and trained. Spitfire lived up to his name.

Back at Churchill Downs on Sunday morning, Trish still rode the high from yesterday's win. Their dream had come true. She and Spitfire had won the Kentucky Derby!

"Spitfire, you crazy horse, stop it now." Trish tried to insert at least a hint of command in her tone but failed miserably. *Serious* just didn't seem to fit into her vocabulary this morning. The laughter kept bubbling, joined by giggles.

Spitfire might be the newly crowned winner of the Kentucky Derby, but he loved hats—as in flipping them off favored people's heads. This morning, the flying hat of fedora vintage belonged to assistant trainer Patrick O'Hern.

"You should see the look on your face," Trish said, smiling at the more than slightly rounded ex-jockey. A halo of white hair fringed his shiny bald head.

"I'll put me a look on 'is face!" Patrick leaned over to grab his hat, but a playful breeze joined in the prank, bowling the grungy hat a step or three across the gravel.

Trish leaned against the wall of barn 41, her legs feeling like cooked spaghetti from all the laughing.

David kept a wary eye on the black colt and a hand on his favorite Seattle Mariner's baseball cap as he reached for Patrick's dust-covered hat.

"You know, if you two were wearing Runnin' On Farm hats, he'd leave you alone," Trish said. "He knows those hats are in his honor."

David gave her one of his smart-big-brother to dumb-little-sister looks. "Why don't you just get up on him and work off some of his orneriness?"

Trish tossed the reins she held over the animal's black head and turned for a leg up. Patrick gave her the boost. Trish let her legs dangle below the stirrups as she gathered her reins. "Y'all see if you can stay out of trouble now, ya he-ah?" Her laughter floated back on the breeze as she nudged her horse into a trot.

Trish and Spitfire stopped beside the track entry. She watched other horses coming and going as she slid her feet into the iron stirrups. With hands crossed on the colt's withers, she kept her reins collected but at rest.

Spitfire, head raised, sniffed the morning scents of horse, damp sand, sweat, and the lingering aroma of the crowds from the day before. He blew, nostrils flaring with the force.

If Trish closed her eyes she could still see and hear the cheering spectators. Even though it had been pouring rain, she and Spitfire had taken their bow. What a feeling—to win the Kentucky Derby on the colt bred on their own farm!

"Can't ya just see it all," a familiar voice interrupted her daydreaming. Red Holloran, with hair that gave him the nickname and a smile to melt any female heart, sat on the back of a dark bay. He gazed around the track with Trish. "Never thought you'd do it after that start."

"We Evanstons don't give up easily." Trish nudged Spitfire forward. They turned counterclockwise on the track and walked their horses side by side along the outer rail.

"I noticed. You see the morning paper?"

"Nope."

"You'll love your picture." Red grinned at her.

"I'll bet. Monster from the mud lagoon. They shoulda made me take a shower before I got on the scale. Coming from behind on a sloppy track like that one—" Trish shook her head. "If a person didn't know we wore crimson and gold silks, they never would have been able to tell yesterday, at least not from my front. And Spitfire was just as bad." She leaned forward to stroke the horse's arched neck. "Weren't ya, fella?" Spitfire pulled at the bit, a gentle tug that politely begged for more than a walk.

Trish obliged and posted to a lazy jog.

"How do ya like that new car?" Red kept pace.

"My mother is going to have a fit." Trish shook her head. "Can you see me—at sixteen—tooling around Vancouver, Washington—where it rains three hundred days out of the year—in a bright red Chrysler LeBaron convertible?" Trish settled back in the saddle. "She'll have a cow."

"Your mother seems like a real nice lady to me."

"She is. But she's not *your* mother. And *you're* not her only daughter. The daughter she'd much rather see *not* racing Thoroughbreds."

"Well, she can't make you give the car back."

"No, but she *can* keep me from driving it."

"Would she?"

"I don't know." Trish frowned. "We haven't always gotten along the best. She and I—well, we have different ideas of what I should do with my life."

"What do you want to do?"

"Ride, race." Trish glanced up to the empty stands where a couple of men in green and white uniforms cleaned up trash. "To keep on doing what I'm doing—full-time."

"And your mother?"

"She wants me to go to school, get good grades, and go on to college— also with good grades, so I can have a good, safe life."

"Nothing wrong with that."

Trish raised her eyebrows at Red. "Would you?"

"No. But it *is* important to finish school."

Trish sighed. "I know." She turned Spitfire off toward the barn. "See ya later."

"When do you leave for Baltimore?" Red raised his voice.

"Thursday, I think," Trish yelled back. She felt her butterflies take an experimental leap when she thought of the race ahead. Baltimore, Maryland. Home of Pimlico Race Course, where the Preakness Stakes was the next jewel in the Triple Crown of Thoroughbred horse racing. The Derby was the first, the Preakness in two weeks, and the Belmont two weeks later.

"David?" Trish asked in the car on the way back to the hotel. They'd left Patrick grooming Spitfire, his hat hung safely on a nail in the tackroom.

"What?"

"Has Mom said anything about the car?" Trish concentrated on her driving, trying to sound casual. She could feel David studying her. "Well?"

"You mean your convertible?"

"You know that's what I mean; don't be difficult."

"I wouldn't plan on driving it to school every day, and it's a good thing you have money to pay the insurance. Other than that, I think she's kind of waiting to see what'll happen."

"What do you mean, what'll happen?"

"What she said was, 'I absolutely refuse to worry about Trish driving around in a red convertible until I have to.' "

Trish saw the humor in that. Her mother was trying very hard not to worry anymore. But as she had said, worrying was as much a part of her nature as the color of her eyes.

Trish was also beginning to understand about worry. It was an easy habit to fall into. But as her little voice kept reminding her, worry and faith didn't go well together.

"We were beginning to think you got lost," her father said when the two young people entered the family hotel suite. Hal glanced at his watch. "We're meeting Grandpa and Grandma at the restaurant in half an hour. The Finleys are coming too, so you'd better hustle."

"You see the papers?" Trish didn't wait for an answer when she spotted the opened newspapers on the coffee table. "Oh yuck!" She stared from the picture back to her father. "I look awful. You can hardly even tell it's me."

David looked over her shoulder. "Looks like you took a mud bath. Hey, we oughta blow these up poster size."

Trish jabbed him in the gut with her elbow. "Sure, highlight of my life and I'm covered with mud. And Spitfire's not any better." She studied the pictures again and wrinkled her nose in distaste. "These *would* be in color too."

"Well, the trophy's shiny and the roses are red; what more could you ask for?" Hal handed her another paper. "The articles are good, but you'll have to read them later. The grands are leaving for home today, so we need to spend what time we can with them."

Trish nearly bumped into the wall as she read one article on the way to the bathroom. The headline "First Female to Win the Roses" gave her goose bumps. She plugged in the curling iron, washed, then brushed her teeth. As she brushed she studied the face in the mirror. Hazel eyes, like her mother's, remained the same. Determined chin, only more so. Though her bangs were smashed flat from her helmet, the hot iron would take care of that. Her hair still curled just above her shoulders if she left it loose. *You'd think there'd be a difference after the big win yesterday,* she thought.

Trish pulled a summer-green cotton sweater over her head and stepped into a pair of white jeans. Three rolls with the iron, a brush job, hair clipped back, and she was ready. No time for makeup. She'd already heard her father making noises like they were late.

They ate at a fish house that overlooked the broad Ohio River. Just upriver they could see a paddle wheeler docked.

"I wish we could have eaten there." Trish pointed to the newly painted white vessel. "Wouldn't it be fun to cruise down the river like they did in the old days?"

"You'd have hated all the skirts and petticoats," Marge reminded her. "And the parasols. Just think how many dresses and skirts you *don't* wear now."

Trish nodded at her mother. "You're right." She stared at the glistening boat again. "But still . . ."

They had all served themselves at the elaborate buffet and returned to the room they'd reserved. It was private and had a sweeping view of the river. Everyone sat at one long table, with Hal at the head.

"You sure pulled off a good one yesterday," Adam Finley, a horse owner and trainer from central California, told Trish as he pulled out his chair and sat across from her. She'd gotten to know Adam and his wife on the trip to Santa Anita in April. "I thought Martha would squeeze my arm to death when that black colt of yours reared in the starting gate."

"He doesn't like thunder." Trish shuddered at the memory. It hadn't been one of her better moments either.

"I don't know how you can get out there like that, with all that danger around you. Why, one jockey was ridden right into the rail." Trish's grandmother, Gloria Johnson, shook her head. A frown creased her forehead as she looked from Marge to Hal as if they'd lost their wits. "To think you'd let your daughter . . ."

Her husband, David, interrupted with a smile. "Now, dear, you promised."

In the last few days Trish had really begun to understand where her mother got the worry habit. It was obviously an inherited trait.

Trish looked up in time to catch a wink from her father. He'd been reading her mind again. Trish checked to see how her mother was reacting.

Marge was shaking her head. She rolled her eyes heavenward when she caught Trish's questioning look.

Trish pressed her lips together to keep a grin from breaking out. Her mom had caught on.

"So, Trish," Adam Finley said, leaning across the table. "How about coming down and riding for me this summer? You remember we talked about it in April?"

How could she forget? What a dream it would be to race again in California. But at the same time she wished she could get the man to lower his voice. She stole a peek at her mother. She'd heard all right. Her frown said it all.

"I—uh, of course I remember. I'm just not sure what we're doing yet."

"Trish, you promised to make up that chemistry class this summer." Marge's tone didn't offer any outs.

Adam looked from Trish to her mother. "I see."

"Now you've stuck your foot in your mouth," Adam's wife, Martha, who appeared everyone's image of the perfect grandmother, scolded her husband. "You get so excited, you think everyone should think like you do."

"Well . . ." Adam paused. "Trish *is* an amazing rider for one so young. I like the way she handles horses."

"Thank you," Trish responded. Her mother didn't look one bit happy.

"We'll see what we can work out," Hal said as he pushed his chair back. "And now, I have some announcements to make."

As soon as all eyes were on him he began. "First, congratulations, Trish. You have no idea how proud I am of you and Spitfire. Yesterday, you made one of my dreams come true. Thank you."

Trish could feel the heat blazing into her cheeks when everyone began applauding. She chewed her lip, then rose and took a quick bow. "Thanks, everybody." She could feel tears swimming at the back of her eyes at the look of love and pride on her father's face. Trish tried to blink them back and almost made it. "I thought all my tears ran out yesterday."

"Somehow *I* never seem to run out." Marge blew her nose and sniffed again.

Chuckles, like dry leaves before a wind, blew around the table.

"And secondly, BlueMist Farms has offered to buy shares in Spitfire with the agreement that he will retire to stud there. Two other people want in too, so I'll have a lawyer draw up the papers and Spitfire will be legally syndicated, if that is okay with everyone."

"If I'm not one of those people you mentioned, I'd like in on the syndication too," Adam said. "You just tell me your price per share and how many you'll offer."

"We'll work something out." Hal nodded. "I'd be pleased to have you in with us, Adam."

Trish heard the exchange with one part of her brain, but the other part was in shock. So soon? She hadn't thought of the colt leaving home till sometime in the far distant future. And then, not really. But many farms retired a stud colt after winning the Derby. And Spitfire carried good lines. His father, Seattle Slew, won the Triple Crown in 1977.

But Spitfire was hers. How could she let him go? And no one else could ride him. He wouldn't let anyone. Trish chewed on her thumbnail. She hadn't thought about Spitfire leaving Runnin' On Farm.

"You know we're not set up for a stud farm," David whispered in her ear.

"I know." Trish took a deep breath. "I just hadn't thought about it."

"You okay, Tee?" Hal had picked up her distress.

Trish nodded. She squared her shoulders but didn't dare look directly at her father. She knew she'd break into tears right there.

"Think about Miss Tee," David added.

A smile tickled the corner of Trish's mouth. The little filly that had been born on her birthday always brought a happy reaction in her. At eight months, Miss Tee was just beginning her training.

"As I was saying earlier, I just don't understand why Trish—"

"Now, Mother . . ." Grandpa Johnson patted his wife's hand. He checked his watch. "I really think we'd better get on the road. I hate to leave you all, but I don't drive after dark anymore and Florida is a ways off. So thank you for a good time and this fine meal." He pulled out his wife's chair after he stood. "Come on, Mother. Let's get all the hugging and crying done so we can be going."

Trish pushed back her own chair. "Sorry I didn't get to spend more time with you," she said as she gave her grandfather a big hug. "Thanks for coming."

"You too, Grandma," she added. "Maybe you'll fly up for Pimlico. That's not too far away from Florida." Trish hugged the gray-haired woman who was short like herself.

"I don't know, dear. Watching you up on that black horse of yours nearly worried me to death. Now, you be careful." She stepped back and shook her head.

"I will, I promise," Trish said.

The Finleys left for the airport soon after the Evanstons waved off the departing grandparents. Hal had his arms around both Marge and Trish as they all stood in the parking lot waving good-bye.

"Well, let's get back to the hotel. We have a lot to do before we leave tomorrow," Hal said.

"I thought we were leaving for Pimlico on Thursday." Trish looked up at her father.

"We are. But I have to fly home to Vancouver for a chemotherapy treatment. Your mother is going with me and we plan to be back on Wednesday."

"But I thought . . ." Trish started to say. Her little nagging voice didn't give her a chance to finish. *No, you weren't thinking at all. Not about your father and the cancer. You just think about horse racing.*

Chapter
02

I wish Dad were still here." Trish flopped back on her bed on Monday morning.

"Well, he's not and you're wasting time." David whirled around and headed for the door.

"What's the matter with you?"

"Nothing!"

"Right." Trish grabbed her windbreaker and trotted after him. David nearly ran to the elevator, or at least it seemed that way to Trish. *I didn't oversleep. No one's called. What set him off?* Trish's mind played with the questions while she studied the stern profile of her usually easygoing brother as they waited for the hotel elevator.

"Let's take the stairs." David wheeled to the right and pushed open the exit door. As they clattered down six flights of stairs, Trish's mind took up the game again. Even the set of David's shoulders declared his . . . anger? Resentment? Disgust? Trish wasn't sure. Just keeping up was effort enough.

"Okay, what is it?" She crossed her arms over her chest after snapping her seat belt in the rental car.

David's sigh sounded as if it had been trapped inside long enough to build up steam. "Does it ever occur to you that sometimes I get tired of being in charge?"

Trish was taken aback. "No. I mean, I guess I thought we kinda shared that, the responsibility and all. It's not like Dad does this on purpose. Leaving, I mean." She felt as if her words and thoughts rattled together and came out broken. "Besides, we have Patrick now."

"I know." David gripped the top of the steering wheel and leaned his forehead on his hands. "I guess part of it is this awful feeling I have in the pit of my stomach."

"Awful feeling? About what? Did Dad say something to you before they left this morning? I just gave them a hug and fell back to sleep."

"I don't know. No, nothing was said. Maybe it's just Dad's leaving us here."

"At least you don't have to talk with that guy from *Sports Illustrated* again. All by yourself."

"I'll be there if you need me," David reminded his sister.

"I meant without Dad. He always says exactly the right thing. I sound like someone with half a brain."

"Well, the article *is* mostly about you and Spitfire. Besides, you know what kind of questions they'll ask. Think of your answers in advance."

Trish nodded. Silence fell while they both looked out the window of the car. A flicker of red caught Trish's eye as a scarlet cardinal lighted on one of the blossom-frosted branches of the dogwood tree in front of them.

"Look," Trish whispered. "Halfway up the tree on the right." She breathed a sigh of delight as a dull-colored female joined her mate on the branch. The little male glistened like a ruby jewel set among the creamy blossoms.

"Well, we better get going." David reached for the ignition key and then paused. "We'd better be praying, Tee."

"For what? Right now things are going pretty smooth."

"I don't know, but I have a feeling." David turned his head to back the car out of the parking space. "A bad feeling."

Trish mentally sorted through her favorite Bible verses. They were printed on three-by-five cards and tacked above her desk at home. Her father had started the collection during his first hospital stay the previous fall. Finally she settled on "In everything give thanks." It was hard to pray when she didn't know what to pray for.

What if you really don't like what's coming? her nagging little voice inquired. *Then you're going to feel pretty stupid giving thanks for it.* Some days her inner voice seemed to be a help, but more often it nagged at her—like today.

Glad for the reprieve, Trish leaped from the car as soon as David parked beside barn 41, near their stall. A silver and blue horse van was stationed in the road waiting to load. The sounds of an early-morning track were music to Trish's ears. Horses nickering, a sharp whinny, people laughing, the rhythmic grunts of a galloping horse counterpoint with pounding hooves on the dirt track, a bird warbling his sunrise song in one of the gigantic oak trees.

Spitfire nickered as soon as he heard Trish greet Patrick. He tossed his head, spraying her with drops from his recent drink, then wuffled her hair and nosed her hands for the carrot she always carried. Trish gave him his treat and scratched behind his ears and down his cheek. The colt leaned his head against her chest and closed his eyes in bliss.

"If I didn't know better, I'd say you'll be a-spoilin' him rotten." Patrick shook his head, but his smile told Trish that he understood the special relationship she and Spitfire shared. "Come on, old son." Patrick slipped into the stall and saddled the colt with practiced ease. "You be in bad need of a good run."

Trish fitted the headstall over the soft black ears and buckled the chin strap. Spitfire answered a whinny from a horse a few stalls down.

"Ouch, right in my ear." Trish rubbed her ringing ear. "Did you have to be so loud?"

"He's just letting 'em all know he's king." Patrick smoothed the already gleaming black shoulder as he unhooked the green web gate across the stall entrance. "Now, you trot once around and then gallop nice and easy another. Let him get the kinks out." Patrick boosted Trish into the saddle. "We'll give him a short work tomorrow."

Trish nodded. She slid her feet into the iron stirrups and clucked her horse forward. Spitfire walked with that loose-limbed gait that told Trish he was completely relaxed. His stride lengthened as they approached the entrance to the track, and Trish went to a post as he trotted out to the left.

The soothing rhythm made it too easy for her mind to keep chewing on David's comment. If *he* had a bad feeling—David wasn't one to talk much about his feelings. And for him to—Trish jerked her attention back to the present. She had to concentrate on riding. Accidents happened too easily when a rider let the mind wander.

"Wish I could just keep riding," Trish muttered when she slid to the ground, much too soon for her liking.

While she'd tried to think of answers for her interviewer, Trish knew that journalists often threw a curve.

And that's exactly what he did.

"Where will you be riding after the Belmont?" Bill Williams looked up from his writing pad.

"I—I'm not sure." Trish couldn't think up anything but the truth. "You see, I promised to make up a chemistry class this summer. The school let me drop it when I was having too much trouble with that and racing and all the other stuff going on."

"By other stuff, you mean your father's illness?"

Trish nodded. *Why, oh why, had she mentioned the chemistry?* "Dad and I originally talked about Longacres in Seattle, but I've been invited to ride in California too, so—"

"Is chemistry really so important?"

"No, but my promise is." Trish felt a flush start up her neck. *How could she switch the subject?*

"Other young riders get their GED or hire a tutor. Or just drop out of school. What do you think you'll do?"

Trish took a deep breath. "My mom would never let me get my GED or drop out. She thinks college is really important."

"What do *you* think?"

"Well . . ." Trish paused to give her brain time to get in gear before she said something she'd be sorry for. "School is important. But so is racing. Somehow we'll just have to work it all out."

When Williams finally said good-bye, Trish felt like she'd been scrubbed and hung up to dry like the bandages that swung from the wire along the aisle. She left the tack room and slipped under the web gate in Spitfire's stall.

"Come on, you guys, let's eat." She gave Spitfire a quick hug. "I'd rather wash ten horses than go through an interview again."

"You sounded pretty cool to me." David picked up the bucket full of grooming gear. Trish watched as David put all the brushes and cloths away in the tack box. His whistle told her he'd gotten rid of the bad feeling he'd had. She knew where it had gone. Right to the pit of her stomach.

"Hey, what's the matter with our Derby winner?" Red held the door for them as they entered the track kitchen. "You look like you lost your best friend."

I did, Trish almost answered. Her father had flown back home for treatment that morning.

"She just had a go-round with that writer from *Sports Illustrated,*" David answered for her. "She got caught on 'where are you racing after Belmont'?"

"Well?" Red grinned at her. "Where are you?"

"I wish I knew." Trish picked up a tray and set it down hard on the counter. Here she was a Derby winner, and right now she felt about as low as the last-place rider.

Temper, temper. And if there was any way to strangle her resident critic, that would be fine too.

Trish ignored the three men talking around her as she mixed black cherry yogurt with crunchy dry cereal. While the combination didn't look the greatest, it tasted good and was good for her. *Why did I bring up the chemistry? Now Mom will feel—who knows what she'll feel? Right now I feel like hiding and bawling for a week or two.* She licked the yogurt off her spoon. She could feel the tears burning the back of her eyelids.

This is stupid. You have nothing to cry about, her little nagger leaped back into the act.

"I'll see you guys back at the barn." Trish picked up her tray and left, ignoring their protests. But no matter how fast she walked, she couldn't get away from the thoughts swirling in her head.

Good Christians don't get down like this. You should be ashamed of yourself. You have so much to be grateful for.

It's okay, buddy, you're just tired. We've been through a lot the last few days. And besides, your dad just left. That's always hard.

Trish decided she liked the second voice better. And it was true. She knew all about adrenaline highs, the kind that carry you through the excitement and then dump you down the next day.

"God, help us," she pleaded as she slipped into Spitfire's stall and sank down in the straw in the corner. "Please take care of my dad—and us." Spitfire snuffled her hair and licked away a tear that had escaped and trickled down her cheek. Trish laid her head on her arms and let the tears roll. Spitfire stood over her, as if keeping guard.

By the time the others returned, slightly red eyes and a wayward sniff or two were the only signs of the storm that had passed.

The sound of laughter drew Trish to the tack room. She leaned against the doorway as Patrick, deep in his story, bent forward to deliver the punch line. Red and David, both with saddle-soaped cloths in their hands, listened and cleaned tack at the same time.

When her chuckle chimed in with the others, Patrick waved Trish to a chair without a break in his monologue. She settled back for a pleasant time. His stories could go on all day and into the night if encouraged.

Two hours later and feeling more like herself, Trish took advantage of a break and stood up. Her sides ached from laughing. The tack room looked like Mr. Clean had just sent his whirlwind through.

"I need to go study for a while. Those finals are coming right up," Trish announced.

"Need some help?" Red looked up with a hopeful grin.

"Thanks, but no thanks. Besides, what do you know about government in Washington State?"

"I could ask you questions."

"Sure," David added. "About racing times and track conditions."

Red snapped a rag at David's knee. "Thanks. You're a big help."

David tossed Trish the car keys. "Pick me up after evening feed."

"I'll bring him back." Red turned his teasing gaze up to Trish. "That way you can study without interruption. Then maybe we can all go to a movie later."

Patrick walked Trish to the car. "Sure you'll be all right now?"

"Thanks for the stories." Trish leaned on the open car door. "You always make me feel better."

"Now, you'd be a-tellin' me if I can help?"

Trish nodded. "Thanks again."

Tuesday morning dawned heavily overcast, with predictions of rain. Even the breeze felt wet in her face as Trish galloped Spitfire around the track. While she kept him controlled, he still had a sweat-popping run. As she walked him around to cool him down, Trish thought back to the night before.

The three of them had gone to a movie, and sitting next to Red made her feel warm and restless. Until he took her hand in his—then she just felt warm. A feeling that was just right. David had punched her lightly on the arm on the way out of the theater. Just thinking about it sent a blush to her neck. So far she hadn't seen Red again this morning. How would she act? What should she say?

Chapter 03

She didn't have to say or do anything. Trish didn't see Red all Tuesday morning. Or that afternoon.

"And what might be botherin' my girl today?" Patrick asked after lunch at the track kitchen.

"She's in love." David dodged Trish's well-aimed fist. "First love." He ducked again.

Laughter twinkled from Patrick's sky-blue eyes. "And I wouldn't have to be a-askin' who the young man might be."

"I'm not in *love*." Trish ignored the blush she felt creeping up her neck. "I'm in . . . like."

Patrick and David looked over their shoulders at each other, then fought to keep from exploding.

"If you two can't act any more mature than that, I'll just go on back to the hotel and get to work. *Somebody* has to be an adult around here." Trish rose to her feet, her chin tilted in a determined don't-mess-with-me angle.

"Tricia Evanston?"

Trish stopped before she bumped into the young man she recognized as one of the jockey agents.

"Yes." She set her tray back down on the table.

"My name is Jonathan Smith." He extended his hand. "Do you have a minute?"

Trish nodded as she shook his hand. "Sure. You want to talk here?"

"This will be fine." He nodded as Trish introduced David and Patrick. "Good to see you again, Patrick. Glad to have you back." He settled into the chair on the other side of Trish. "Is it true that you haven't signed with an agent?"

Trish nodded. "I haven't needed to. In Portland I had all the mounts I could handle."

"Well, a trainer came and asked me to get you to ride for him tomorrow afternoon." Smith checked a paper he took from his pocket. "That would be in the third race. Are you interested?"

"Of course." Trish leaned forward. She clenched her fists to keep her hands from clapping.

"You understand that you'll need to sign a contract with me?"

Trish nodded. She had known that one day it would come to this. But she thought she'd have to find an agent herself—not that one would find her. And in Kentucky.

Jonathan pulled a folded paper from his shirt pocket. "It's very simple, really. You can look it over if you like." He handed Trish the typed form.

"I'd like my father to read this, if that's okay." Trish scanned the simple document. Her eyes stopped at the paragraph that detailed the fees. While twenty-five percent was normal, she hated giving the agent that much of her winnings.

"Dad's not here," David reminded her softly.

Trish caught her bottom lip between her teeth. "You need this signed before tomorrow?"

The man nodded.

"One thing you should know. I don't take a jockey fee when I ride Spitfire, or any of our own horses, for that matter. That means you wouldn't get any money either."

Jonathan tipped back on the legs of the chair. He crossed his arms over his chest, appearing to be deep in thought. "Usually an agent gets his cut on any ride." He thumped his chair back solidly on the floor. "Let's be honest, Tricia. You are in a strong position to win the Preakness or at least come in the money. That makes you a valuable property, to me or any other agent. And face it, I'm in the business to make money too. But I can only charge you for the mounts I get for you." A smile worked its way up to his eyes. "One thing I'll make sure of, you'll be racing more and more for farms other than your father's."

Trish handed the contract to David. "What do you think?" she asked as he and Patrick finished reading it.

"It's standard," Patrick replied. "And besides, if he doesn't do a good job for you, you can fire him and hire someone else."

Trish grinned at the twinkle she saw dancing in the old man's eyes. She reached across the table and pulled a pen from David's pocket. After signing her name, she handed the paper back to the agent.

"Thank you." Jonathan refolded the paper and put it back in his pocket. "I'll see if I can get more mounts for you before you leave— Thursday, right?"

Trish nodded. "Early, most likely."

"And you want to ride at Pimlico." It was more a statement than a question.

Trish nodded again.

"Good. I'll be talking with you." He shook hands with her and the others, and strode out of the room.

Trish settled back against her chair and stretched her arms above her head. "Well, that's done." Doubts chased each other through her mind like kids playing tag.

"You needn't worry about whether you did the right thing, you know," Patrick said, reading her mind. "As long as you're under age and all."

"He's right," David added. "Dad could cancel the contract if he thought you weren't being treated right."

Trish frowned. "But I gave my word."

"I know," Patrick said. "Just be rememberin' that Jonathan works for *you*. You don't work for him." He pushed his chair back and rose to his feet. "And now, I'll be getting back to our prince, and you can get back to your books. The day'll be gone before we know it."

Returning to the hotel, Trish hit the books with a flourish. She read two chapters for history, then started on *War and Peace* for English. It didn't take long to realize she should have started the book much earlier. She was still trying to figure out who all the characters were when the phone rang.

"Jonathan Smith here," the man responded to her greeting. "I have another mount for you tomorrow, if you'd like it. Seventh race, a claiming for fillies and mares."

"Great—uh, let me check something." Trish shuffled some papers by the phone. "Dad's put in a claim for Sarah's Pride in that race. Will that be a problem?"

"Shouldn't. That's not the horse I have for you. You'll take it then?"

"Yes—and thanks." Trish could feel a smile stretching her cheeks, causing bubbles of happiness to rise and float above her head. As they popped, they showered giggles all over her. *Wait till I tell David—and Red.* When she thought of Red the bubbles bounced higher. *And Dad. If only he were here. I'll have to call him tonight.* Two mounts for Wednesday. In Kentucky—at Churchill Downs. Not bad for a sixteen-year-old kid from Vancouver, Washington—definitely *not* the horse capital of the world.

Trish had a hard time getting back into *War and Peace.*

Good thing I read fast, she thought as she drove to the track to pick up David, *or that book could take a year.* She waved at the guard on the gate and drove back to barn 41. Spitfire nickered as soon as she whistled; a horse on the other side of the barn answered him. David, Red, and Patrick lounged in the tack room.

"How'd you do today?" she asked Red.

He shook his head. "Good thing they pay something for those of us who don't come in the money. Otherwise my bank account would be in reverse."

"Like that nag you had in the last race?" David asked as he stretched his hands above his head.

"You gotta understand, boy," Patrick got in his digs, "that horse couldn't even go backward—it just quit."

Trish grinned at the teasing. It was nice not to be the brunt of it for a change. "What races are you in tomorrow?"

Red squinted his eyes, trying to remember. "Think I have three so far. First, fifth, and seventh." He nodded. "Yeah, that's right."

"Shame you're not up in the third. Then I could beat you in two races."

Red thumped his chair back on all four legs. "You got another mount? Way to go! That calls for a celebration! Come on, I'm buying you a super-size Diet Coke. You two wanna join us?" He threw an arm around Trish's shoulders and waited for an answer.

Patrick and David looked at each other and shrugged, slowly pulling themselves up from their chairs.

"You're sure we won't be in the way?" Patrick's face looked unchar-acteristically innocent—almost cherubic.

Trish felt like stomping on his foot, but the weight of Red's arm seemed to lock her jaw and her feet. He tugged her around, and she kept pace with the three of them as they walked to the car.

They ordered dinner, and the time passed in a haze of laughter. Pat-rick topped every story anyone started. The waitress must have thought they were high on something. They were—on happiness.

That night Trish called Rhonda. She broke out in giggles as she told her about Red.

"You really like him, don't you?"

"I guess so. Remember your teasing me about Doug Ramstead last fall?" Trish twirled her hair around a finger. "And I never even got to go out with him."

"Yeah. He's still a hunk too."

"Well, Red's *here.* Wish you could meet him. He and David pick on me about as much as Brad and David did, but it's different. Really different."

"I miss you," Rhonda wailed.

"Yeah, me too. David's flying home for Brad's graduation. Wish I could. Just think, one more of our musketeers is done with Prairie High. Only you and I'll be left."

"Yeah. And you're never here."

When Trish hung up half an hour later, she winced at the thought of the phone bill. Talking from halfway across the country wasn't the same as a mile away. She lay back on her bed and thought of all the news Rhonda had told her about school. If only Rhonda could come to Kentucky.

It seemed as if school and Vancouver were in another life. *Distance does that,* she remembered her father saying.

Thinking about him made Trish jerk upright and dial Runnin' On Farm. There was no answer. She checked her watch. Nine-thirty eastern time meant six-thirty at home.

"David." She stood and walked into the living room, where he was watching television. "There's no answer at home. Where do you think Mom and Dad are?" A frown wrinkled her forehead.

David blinked awake and rubbed his eyes. A yawn caught him before he could answer. He checked his watch. Seeing the time brought him instantly awake.

"You suppose they're at the hospital?" He ran a hand through the dark curls that fell on his forehead.

Trish walked across the room to the window and stared out, her teeth tugging her bottom lip. "David, remember that bad feeling you had? Well, I've got it now."

Trish awoke to the phone ringing on Wednesday morning. Her heart seemed to leap right out of her chest. She fumbled for both the phone and the lamp switch. *What's wrong with Spitfire?* chased *Could it be Dad?* through her brain.

"Hello?" Even her voice sounded scared.

"Good morning, Tee."

Trish collapsed back against the pillows. "Hi, Mom. What's wrong?"

"We just wanted to get in touch with you two before you left for the track. Sorry to call so early."

"That's okay." Trish leaned over to shut off the alarm. "It was time to get up anyway. How's Dad?"

"Not doing real well right now. He had a bad reaction to the chemo and the doctor wants to do more tests."

"More tests?"

"It's routine at this point, and they may have to change his medication. Anyway, we won't be flying back today as we'd planned. Dad says he'll call you this evening and let you know whether to go on without us or not."

Trish felt as if she'd been punched in the gut. "But—but . . . Is Dad there? Can I talk with him?"

"He's at the hospital now, and finally sleeping. He was up and down all night. I just came home to check on things here and pick up some clean clothes." Marge's voice had an edge of worry to it again. She took a deep breath. "How are things going there?"

For an instant Trish couldn't even remember why she'd tried to call the night before. "We called last night. I knew something was wrong when no one answered." She paused for her thoughts to catch up with her. "Tell Dad I signed with an agent. I have two mounts this afternoon."

"Are you sure that's the best thing to do? You know you'll be heading back to school as soon as Belmont is over." Her mother's worry was more obvious now.

"Mo-om."

"I'm sorry, Trish. I can't even think straight right now. Just be careful. Tell David we'll talk to him tonight. Good-bye now."

Trish stared at the phone in her hand. *If only I could have talked with Dad.* She could feel the tears prick at the back of her eyes.

Don't be such a baby, her little nagger scolded. *He was at the hospital, not the farm. You know, if you'd pray more . . .* Trish slammed the receiver down. She felt like slamming something else.

She stomped into the other room. "David." She shook his shoulder. "David, how could you sleep through the phone and everything?"

David pulled a pillow over his head, then flipped over with a suddenly wide-awake glare. "What do you mean, the phone?"

"Mom called. They're not coming today and maybe not even tomorrow."

"Dad's worse?" He was really awake now.

"I don't know how bad. He's in the hospital. More tests." Trish balled a section of her nightshirt in her fist. "What do we do now?" she pleaded.

"We take care of Spitfire. Then you study, and ride this afternoon." David reached for his jeans draped across the bottom of his bed. "And we pray like crazy. Now get going. We leave in ten minutes."

Trish wanted to argue—or smack him for his methodical tone. Bet-

26

ter yet, she felt like locking herself in the bathroom and turning on the shower so no one could hear her scream.

Instead, she dragged herself back to her room and started dressing. *God, what are you doing with my dad? Why can't things get better instead of worse? Why don't you just leave us alone?*

David and Trish hardly talked on the way to the track. Patrick had Spitfire fed and groomed by the time they arrived.

"Sorry we're late," David said. "Things aren't good at home."

That's the understatement of the year, Trish thought as she leaned against Spitfire's shoulder and rubbed his neck. The colt snuffled her hair and whiskered her cheek as if to cheer her up.

"They know, lass," Patrick said softly behind her. "Animals always know when those they love are hurtin'."

Trish felt the tears again. She buried her face in Spitfire's mane. "Dad's got to get better again. We need him here. I need him. I—" She sniffed back the tears. "Patrick, do you pray?"

"Of course, lass. How else could I be livin' and workin' again? Only God could cure a drunk like me." He swiped a finger across his eyes. "And your father now—he gave me this job. And I'm thinkin' it's to be takin' care of more than a horse. I'd like to give back some of what your father gave me."

Trish turned and let the old trainer put his arms around her. He patted her back, all the while crooning to her as he did with Spitfire. The music worked the same magic on humans as it did on horses.

Trish mopped her eyes again. "Well, let's get this kid out on the track." She nodded at Spitfire, who pricked his ears at David's tuneless whistle in the aisle. "Thanks, Patrick."

"Your dad'll be here soon." Patrick patted Trish's shoulder. "I feel it in my bones."

"You okay?" David asked when he gave her a leg up. Concern darkened his eyes.

Trish nodded. "We'll make it." She gathered her reins and clucked Spitfire forward.

You know, if you were really a good Christian, you wouldn't worry about your dad like this, her nagger gloated. *And what happened to the old I-will-not-cry Trish?*

God loves you no matter what, her other little voice responded. *Remember, He knows what He's doing now just like He has in the past. Remember when you fell apart in the parking lot at Portland Meadows? God'll take care of you now too.*

Trish shut both voices off by shoving her boots into the iron stirrups and nudging Spitfire into a trot. But it sure was nice to know *someone* was on her side.

Red saluted her with his whip as he slow-galloped a bay around the track. "See you later?" His question floated back on the slight breeze.

Now that Spitfire was warmed up, Trish turned the colt clockwise and gave him enough rein for a steady gallop. Spitfire pulled at the restraint, pleading for a chance to run. Trish only laughed at him when he tossed his head at her refusal.

"You big goof. You think you can run anytime you want." She rode high in the stirrups, her weight helping to keep the horse under control. "I should be working those two I'm riding today."

Spitfire flicked his ears back and forth, listening to her voice while keeping track of everything around him.

"You know, if you'd just let someone else ride you like this in the morning, I could go home for Brad's graduation," Trish spoke to the horse. "I might as well be tied in the stall with you."

The colt snorted, shaking his head as if he disagreed with her.

Trish felt as if someone had smacked her between the shoulder blades. What had she just said?

Her nagger didn't miss a beat. *Sure. Here you are doing what every jockey dreams of, and you're griping. There's just no pleasing you, is there? Where's that attitude of gratitude you're supposed to have anyway?*

"Sorry, fella," Trish muttered to her horse. "It's not your fault we let you get used to only me for a rider." She shrugged off the negative feelings and concentrated on the remaining ride. When she pulled Spitfire back down to a trot, he hadn't run enough to work up a decent sweat.

"You sure are in good condition," Trish told him as they trotted out the track entrance. "I should be running a track myself." Spitfire nodded his agreement. "What do you know about it?" Trish laughed as she jumped to the ground, giving him a playful scratch under his forelock.

"I've gotta go meet my horses and trainers for this afternoon," Trish said after giving Spitfire a last pat. "So don't wait breakfast for me. I'll have to leave for the hotel right after."

Trish checked the barn numbers that her agent Jonathan had written down for her. Numbers 20 and 22—both of them housed the horses of smaller farms.

"Mr. Danielson around?" she asked a young Hispanic man grooming a horse.

"*Sí, él está ahí.*" He pointed to the office as he spoke.

Trish listened hard as her brain translated the words. She smiled back at him. "*Gracias.*" She'd probably do better in Spanish if she'd just make a point of talking to the people around the track. *If they'd only speak slower.*

When Trish approached the office she could hear two men arguing inside.

"But you don't know anything about her," one said.

"She won the Derby, didn't she?" answered the other. "That's enough for me."

"She only won because she was riding her father's colt. No one else would let her near their horses."

Trish felt her ears burning. The flush crept all the way up her face. She walked back outside the barn and leaned against the wall. *Guess I'll just have to prove that I can ride,* she thought. She pushed the hurt she felt down where she couldn't feel it, at least for the moment.

In a few seconds a man wearing a brown sweater strode out of the barn, and with the voice of the one who questioned her ability, he spoke to one of the grooms. Taking a deep breath and pasting a smile on her face, Trish walked back into the barn.

"Mr. Danielson?" She cleared her throat. "I'm Tricia Evanston."

Danielson glanced from Trish to the back of the man striding across the hot-walking area.

Trish lifted her chin to boost her confidence. No matter what anyone thought, she wasn't going to back down on her commitment.

The man nodded slightly as if reading her mind. Then he smiled and extended his hand. "Glad to meet you, Tricia. How about taking this fellow out for a warm-up? Juan, saddle Jiminy for her, please."

The dark bay horse sported a white star between his eyes. Instead of looking friendly and curious like most horses did, he laid his ears back and reached out as if to take a nip.

Trish stopped and studied the animal. "Is he nasty mean or just a tease?"

Danielson grabbed the halter and rubbed the horse's cheek. "Jiminy here is nothing but a big bluff. He thinks he's tough, but—"

"He's really a big softy," Trish finished for him. She extended her palm with a piece of carrot in it. "We have one like him at home, but you have to watch out, because he'll *really* nip you." Trish reached up to scratch the horse's ears and under the short mane.

"He's been in the money twice but never won," Danielson filled her in on the horse's history. "Then he pulled a muscle, and is just coming back." By this time the horse was saddled and Danielson gave Trish a leg up. "Take him half a circuit at a walk and then jog the rest."

Trish kept up her usual stream of singsong chatter as they circled the track, and Jiminy settled into a ground-eating stride when she turned him to the left. He watched all the action around them as though a spectator instead of a participant. When Trish nudged him to a trot, he settled easily into the gait.

"We're gonna have to light a fire under you, old man," Trish muttered as she rode back to the barn. "I'll see you this afternoon." She slipped Jiminy another carrot chunk as soon as the groom removed the bridle.

"That's a good way to make him your slave for life." Danielson tipped his hat back, then ran a hand down the gelding's shoulder and right foreleg. "Okay, take him away." A woman took the lead and led the horse off to the hot walker.

"I need to meet another trainer," Trish said as she and Danielson walked back to the office. "So if there's nothing else, I'll see you in the saddling paddock, third race."

"Fine. And by the way, Tricia, don't let some things you might hear get to you." The twinkle in the man's deep blue eyes told Trish he knew she'd overheard the earlier conversation.

Trish grinned back. "Thanks."

She located the next trainer leaning on the fence watching the action on the track. By the time they'd met and talked, it was eight o'clock. His mare had been warmed up earlier. Trish checked her watch. She didn't have a lot of time before she had to be back in the jockey room.

Praying on her way back to the hotel, Trish stopped to catch a fast-food breakfast, knowing the buffet at the hotel would be closed by now. "God, please help me to keep my mind on my work," she prayed aloud, in case God could hear better that way.

In her room she reviewed the characters in *War and Peace* and read further. "These Russian names are gonna do me in," she muttered. "How will I ever write a book report? I can't pronounce the names, let alone spell them."

When it was time to leave for the track, she stuffed the novel and her history book into her sports bag. She could resume study in the jockey room. On the drive out she tried to concentrate on getting geared up for the race. When thoughts of her father intruded, she gritted her teeth and did what he'd always told her to do: *Stick in a Bible verse so the fear can't take over.* Finally, she resorted to a song. "He will raise you up on eagle's wings, bear you . . ." Boy, did she ever need those eagle's wings once again.

"Tricia, there's a redheaded young man out here asking for you." Frances Brown, keeper of the women's jockey room, leaned against the door frame. Trish was camped on one of the beds, making it a study hall. "He seems to have a special interest in you."

Trish couldn't help but respond to the grin that crinkled Frances's face clear up to her eyes. At the thought of Red, a fuzzy feeling warmed Trish's middle. She marked her place in her history book and leaped off the bed. So much for good intentions to study.

"Hi, Trish—got time for a quick soda?" Red greeted her in one breath.

"Sure." Trish smiled back at him. When they bumped shoulders walking into the rec room, she thought back to the time Red had held her hand at the movie. Would he hold it again? The thought sent a familiar flush up her neck. If only she didn't blush so easily.

As soon as they took their sodas to a table and sat down, a couple of other jockeys joined them. It wasn't long before Red was the center of the group. He seemed to draw attention wherever he went. Trish hid her smile behind her paper cup. It felt good to know he had come especially for her.

When Trish followed the other jockeys down the stairs and out to the saddling paddock for the third race, she felt the old familiar butterflies take a couple of practice leaps before beginning their regular show. By the time she fell into step with the trainer Danielson, they were in rare form. Trish swallowed hard. *Settle down.*

"Now, you can use that whip to keep old Jiminy's mind on his business," Danielson said as he gave Trish a leg up. "I like my horses to come from behind, but take advantage of that number two position. Don't let him drift out."

Trish nodded, stuffing her reluctance to use a whip back where it belonged. All horses weren't trained like those at Runnin' On Farm.

Jiminy behaved like a veteran as he galloped out to the starting gate and walked in flat-footed. Trish tightened the reins, forcing him to center his weight on his haunches and prepare for the start.

As the gate clanged open, Jiminy leaped forward in perfect time. Ears pricked, he suddenly seemed to realize what he was supposed to be doing—racing.

"Yeah, that's the way!" Trish shouted at him as they surged past the number one horse and took the rail. "Come on, come on, don't be lazy now." She kept a firm hold on his mouth so he couldn't drift and bump into another horse. With only six furlongs to run, they couldn't miss a beat.

Jiminy held his number one position through the turn and into the final stretch. When two other horses pulled up even with them, Trish went to the whip. Jiminy flattened his black ears and obeyed quickly. His stride lengthened, while heavy grunts matched the pounding of his feet.

One horse kept the pace and began to pull ahead.

Trish encouraged Jiminy again with her voice and the leather whip. Each stride brought the white columns closer. One more command screamed at the twitching ears and they flashed across the wire. They'd won by a nose.

That'll show 'em, Trish thought as she accepted congratulations from the trainer and the owner. She recognized the owner as the man in the brown sweater that morning, the one who'd said she couldn't ride anything but Spitfire.

She smiled for the cameras. This photo would go in a frame on her wall.

When she pulled a fourth place out of a field of ten in the seventh race, Trish didn't feel too badly. The mare she rode tried to quit in the stretch but Trish had kept her running. That in itself was something to be proud of. She had shown her skill as a jockey again.

Besides, Sarah's Pride, the filly her father had put claiming money on, had won. Runnin' On Farm now owned a new horse. Trish followed David and Patrick as they led their new acquisition back to the barn.

"Ya done good, lass," Patrick said. "Guess that'll show 'em what you're made of."

Trish grinned. "Feels good."

When they got back to the hotel that evening, the message light was flashing on their phone.

"Sorry, kids," Hal's voice sounded both sad and weak when they returned his call. "I just won't make it in time. You'll have to go on to Pimlico without me."

Chapter
05

But, Dad, what's wrong? Why can't you come now?"

"Trish—"

"Are you sicker and not telling us?" Trish could hardly keep the tears from choking her voice.

"Tee, listen to me. I don't want to talk about this over the phone. All the arrangements for your trip are in place, and Mom and I'll just be a bit later, that's all. Besides, this way I won't have to make that long drive. We'll fly directly to Baltimore."

"I guess."

"Now, is David there? Put him on the other phone."

"I'm here, Dad. Have been all along."

Hal finished giving them directions to the Crosskeys Inn and on how to manage the trip. "You'll meet Mel Howell at Pimlico. I've already talked with him. Oh, and Trish?"

"Yeah."

"I think you should ride in the van just in case the horses need you. I love you kids more than you'll ever know."

After they said good-bye, Trish returned the receiver to its cradle and sprawled spread-eagle across her bed. Nothing was turning out as it was supposed to. Her father had been getting better before they started traveling. Maybe they shouldn't have come to Kentucky. Would staying home have helped? Maybe her mother had been right all along.

Later that night Trish couldn't get comfortable in bed. She turned one way and then the other. She punched the pillows up and kicked the bedspread off. Kicking felt good. *If only there were some way to kick the cancer.* Finally she turned the light back on, propped herself up on two pillows, and reached for the carved eagle her father had placed on her nightstand before he left. She smoothed a finger over the perfectly carved feathers. "If only we could soar like you," she whispered.

Placing the figure back under the light, Trish picked up her Bible. The verse in Isaiah 40 hadn't changed, but the first words caught her attention. *"Those who wait upon the Lord . . ."* She read them again. Waiting had never been one of her favorite pastimes.

Her father was learning to wait. He'd said so.

She'd rather have the eagle's wings *now*. She read the rest of the verse. *"They shall run and not be weary, they shall walk and not faint."* Boy, did she need these promises now. She shut the book and closed her eyes. The words to pray wouldn't come, only a picture of an eagle catching the thermals and soaring above the cliffs.

Finally, Trish snapped off the light and burrowed under the covers. "Thank you, God—I think. Please take care of my dad." The next thing she knew the alarm was ringing.

Dawn had pinked the sky by the time Trish and David drove through the gates at Churchill Downs. They'd taken the time to pack up and check out of the hotel.

At the stall both horses were still eating. Trish told Patrick what her father had said, then opened the tack boxes to begin packing for the trip. Everything was in order—ropes wound neatly, buckets stacked. Even the feed sacks were tied off.

"Patrick, you're super." Trish turned and smiled her appreciation. "Thank you."

"David and I did that yesterday, figuring we'd be leaving early. All that's left is the stuff from this morning." Patrick tipped his fedora back and scratched his forehead. "I'm all packed too, so after you loosen 'em up, we'll be ready to load."

Trish felt herself saying good-bye to Churchill Downs as she trotted Spitfire around the track. It wasn't like at home where she knew she'd be back in the fall. After all, how many times did a West Coast farm get to bring a horse to the Derby?

"Maybe I'll ride here sometime on my own. What do you think?" Spitfire twitched his ears and shook his head. "Thanks for the vote of confidence." She patted his neck and tightened him down to a walk. "Maybe we'll get to bring you here for the Breeder's Cup in October. What would you think of that?" Spitfire snorted. "Was that a yes or a no?" The black colt tugged on the bit and pranced sideways as they left the track. "See if I ask your opinion again." Trish jumped to the ground and handed the reins over to Patrick. She gave Spitfire a quick scratch while David switched the saddle to Sarah's Pride.

"How's our girl this morning?" Trish spoke softly to the bright-sorrel filly. With one hand clamped on the reins under the filly's chin, Trish used the other to work magic around the horse's ears and down her cheek. Sarah's Pride pricked her ears and nosed Trish's shoulder. She dropped her head lower to make it easier for Trish to reach under the bridle behind her ears. Trish smoothed the forelock and rubbed down the horse's neck.

"You'll be puttin' her to sleep that way," Patrick said as he watched Trish get better acquainted.

"Well, we better not do that." Trish raised her knee, and with David's assistance swung smoothly into the saddle. "Come on, girl, let's see how you behave."

Sarah's Pride wanted to run. She snorted and pranced, throwing in a bounce or two to keep Trish alert. Halfway around the first turn, the filly shied at a blowing paper. A few strides farther she stopped to stare at something only she could see.

By the time they returned to the barn, Trish felt as if she'd been working Gatesby, the horse who gave her so much trouble at home.

"No wonder she doesn't usually win," Trish said as she slid to the ground. "She can't keep her mind on what she's doing. If she races like she works—" Trish shook her head. "And look at her, she's lathered from just that bit we did. My girl, even I know you've got some conditioning ahead of you." Trish slipped the filly a carrot piece.

"Never mind, lass. We'll turn her into a racehorse yet." Patrick stripped off the tack while David brought out the wash gear. Once the filly was washed down and scraped dry, Trish took the lead.

"I'll walk her. Then let's eat. That truck'll be here anytime."

Red fell into step beside Trish after a couple of rounds on the sanded walking circle. "Hi. Guess you're leaving pretty soon, huh?"

"Yeah. Dad's meeting us in Baltimore."

"Um-m-m." Red seemed uncomfortable. "I'll be back in a minute."

Trish watched him trot back to their stalls. "What's the matter with him?" The filly kept on walking.

"Here, let me finish." David reached for the lead shank as soon as he joined her.

"What's up?" She looked from her brother to Red.

"I need to talk with you a minute." Red nodded toward the grassy area behind the barns. "How about over there?"

"Fine, I guess." She looked at David, who just shrugged. "But I don't have much time."

"You rode really well yesterday." Red kicked a stone in front of them.

"Thanks." Trish's shoulder felt warm where it rubbed against his. If only he'd take her hand again. If only she were brave enough to take his.

Red kicked the stone again. It skittered across the gravel. Sounds from the barns faded into the distance.

"I—I'm really going to miss you." Red turned to Trish, and they stopped under a spreading oak tree. "I have something for you—to remember me by. But I'll see you again."

Trish swallowed against the tight knot in her throat. She drew circles in the dewy grass with the toe of her boot.

"Here." Red took her hand in his and placed a small box in it.

The knot turned into a lump in Trish's throat that threatened to choke her.

"Open it." Red leaned closer.

Trish smoothed the blue velvet of the flat box and finally opened it.

She gasped at the sight of a finely etched gold cross on a delicate chain. "Oh, Red, it's beautiful!" Her smile trembled, threatening tears.

"You like it then?"

"Oh yes." Trish lifted the cross and draped the chain across her palm.

"Here, let me put it on for you." Red took it from her, looped the chain around her neck, and fastened the clasp. "Now you have something to remember me by." He turned her to face him again and placed his lips on hers. It was a first kiss—tentative and sweet.

"Thank you—for the cross," Trish whispered as she stepped back. "But I didn't need anything to remind me of you."

Red smiled. "I'll see you at Belmont for sure, Pimlico if I can possibly make it." He brushed a lock of hair from her cheek. "I want to be there when you take the Triple Crown."

Trish nodded, but couldn't speak. Her voice was lost somewhere in the sadness of leaving.

Red threaded his fingers through hers, and they ambled back to the barn.

Trish wiped the tears from her cheeks as they drove out the gates of Churchill Downs. She waved to Red once more, and settled back for the trip. Everything had conspired to speed them on their way, and the horses had loaded as if they were looking forward to a new place. There hadn't been a line in the track kitchen, and the truck had arrived early.

Trish had been pleasantly surprised when the truck drove up. Fred Robertson, the driver who had taken them in from the airport, had requested the trip.

The drive was long but uneventful. Trish checked on the horses when they stopped for lunch. Spitfire nickered when he heard her voice and snuffled her hair as she checked the tie ropes and water buckets.

After lunch Trish slept for a couple of hours. It kept her from thinking about having left Red and about the fact that her father was not with them. It was a good thing Fred had lots of stories to tell about racing and about the country they were passing through. His company helped Trish through her sadness.

They pulled up to the gate at Pimlico at seven o'clock. Racing was over for the day and the evening chores finished. The area was quiet. Trish stifled a feeling of disappointment as she compared the old track at Pimlico to Churchill Downs.

Fred read her feelings and said, "Not to worry. This place may not be as fancy as the Downs, but wait till you see how they treat you here. You and that black colt of yours are stars now, and Mel will take good care of you."

"Mel?"

"Here he comes now. Mel Howell is chief of security for the Maryland Racing Association. He has a headful of tales you won't believe."

Trish watched the man with military bearing approach them. His smile erased any stiffness as he stuck his hand in the truck window to shake hands with Robertson.

"Good to see you, you old horse hauler. Been some time since you made it all the way to Baltimore."

"Ah know. But ah brought you someone mahghty special. Tricia Evanston, meet Mel Howell. That's her brother and trainer in the car behind us."

"Welcome, Tricia. I've been looking forward to meeting the young lady who's set everyone on their ears. I hear you won yesterday too."

Trish felt as if she'd just met an old friend. "Thank you. It's hard to believe I'm really here."

"Well, let's get you settled. Spitfire's stall is all ready. Fred, you know the way to the stakes barn. I'll ride in the car so I can meet the others."

Robertson eased the van through the gate and past several barns that glowed a faded rose in the evening light. The stakes barn was last, at the northernmost corner of the backside. It sported a fresh coat of tan paint with white trim. Potted shrubs and freshly raked sand aisles set the stakes barn apart from the gentle decay of the other barns.

As soon as the truck stopped, Trish leaped down from the cab and swung open the doors to the van. Spitfire nickered and tossed his head. Sarah's Pride turned her head as far as the tie-downs allowed and joined the greeting.

"You two ready to go for a walk?" Trish asked as she palmed a piece of carrot for each. "Bet you're hungry too." As soon as she heard the ramp clang into position, she slipped the knot on Spitfire's lead and led him toward the door. She started down the ramp, but Spitfire paused in the opening. His challenging whinny floated on the evening air. Horses answered from barns on two sides of them. He trumpeted again, pawing the straw in the truck with one front hoof.

"Show-off." Trish tugged on the lead. Spitfire shook himself, then followed her down the padded ramp, his hooves thudding a rhythm that hinted at excitement.

"Yours is stall number ten. We left it in sand like your father requested, and there's plenty of straw in place. We've put your filly in the barn there." Mel pointed to the barn that nearly formed a T with the stakes barn, except for the drive between them. He turned to Patrick. "Sure is good to see you back in the business. We saved you a spot upstairs in the same barn, if that's okay."

"Good to be back." Patrick tipped his hat off his forehead. "Looks like most of your boarders are already here." He gestured to the horses that watched out their stall doors.

"Only two more after you. The guards are all in place. You can sleep easy tonight."

Trish kept an ear on their conversation and an eye on the trailer where Sarah's Pride had joined David at the doorway. Like Spitfire, she announced her arrival and waited for the responses. Then she danced down the incline like a little girl let out to play.

Trish and David walked the two horses around the stakes barn several times while Patrick oversaw the tack box moving and prepared the evening feed.

Fred waited until they had the horses bedded down and had hauled Patrick's suitcases up to his room. He shook hands all around and stopped at Trish.

"Ah'll be praying for you," he said softly, "and yuh daddy. It's been mah privilege to be your driver."

Trish started to shake his hand but instead threw her arms around his neck and hugged him. "Thank you. You made both our drives a lot of fun—and I even learned something. Lots of things, in fact." She stepped back in time to see a tear brighten his eyes. "Wish you could stay for the next trip."

"Me too." He pulled his hat on his head. "Y'all take care now." With a final wave he climbed back into his truck and drove off.

Trish watched until the taillights cleared the gate. She seemed to be saying an awful lot of good-byes lately.

As the truck drove out, a long white limo pulled in and drove right up to the barn. A uniformed man stepped out.

"I'd like you to meet your personal driver for the time you're at Pimlico," Mel said. "Trish and David Evanston, this is Hank Benson. Hank is a police officer here and volunteers to drive on his off hours."

Trish felt her jaw drop open and hang suspended. *A limo—and driver—for us?* She turned to David. He was trying to remain cool. He kept his jaw in place, but he couldn't talk either.

"Well, that's a first." Patrick shook his head. "Ya been flummoxed, I'd say. Downright flummoxed."

Trish forced her eyes off the limo and asked, "Flummoxed? Patrick, you made that word up."

"Me?" Patrick had his most-innocent look firmly in place—if the laughter shaking his shoulders didn't dislodge it. "You know, lass, pole-axed." At her look of total confusion, he turned to Mel for help.

"Surprised. Shocked." Mel pushed his white Pimlico hat back on his head and shrugged.

"Right." Trish shook her head. Adults didn't always make sense.

"I'm pleased to meet all of you." Hank Benson smiled around the circle. "Now, if you'd like, I'll put your suitcases in the trunk."

"You can leave your car here," Mel told David. "Just take your gear and lock it up. No one will bother it."

While David went to get their suitcases, Mel said, "I'll be around after morning works to take you and David on a tour of Pimlico. If you have any questions, we can answer them for you then. There's a good restaurant at the Crosskeys, and of course a kitchen here at the track for the morning."

Trish couldn't keep from giggling as she settled against the soft leather seat in the limo. Her fingers itched to push all the buttons on the panel to see what they were for. The TV was obvious. There was also a stereo, and a mini-refrigerator stocked with soft drinks and ice.

"Trish, knock it off," David hissed. "You're as bad as a little kid." His fingers ignored his own words and pressed a button that rolled down the window between them and the driver.

"Anything I can help you with?" Benson's voice sounded metallic over the intercom. "Help yourselves to drinks and snacks. Glasses are behind that sliding panel if you'd like ice."

Trish melted back against the seat after fixing her Diet Coke. "Now *this* is the life."

Hank Benson clicked the intercom back on. "We've been following your career, Trish. My daughter, Genny, thinks the sun rises and sets on you."

"How old is she?" Trish tried to rest her glass casually on the leather arm beside her.

"Twelve, and horse-crazy is far too weak a description of her. Says she's going to be a jockey just like you. Maybe sometime while you're here she can meet you."

"Sure. Would she like to meet Spitfire too?"

"Do kids like ice cream?" Hank chuckled. "She has pictures of the two of you on her bedroom walls." He swung the long vehicle into an underground parking garage and stopped in front of the glass doors marked Entrance. "Now let's get you settled. What time would you like me to pick you up in the morning?"

"Would five be okay?" David suggested.

"You know, you can sleep in a bit if you want. Morning works last until nine-thirty." Hank slid out of the driver's side and came around to open the passenger door. "Might as well take it easy while you can. Besides, the reporters will mob you once you're at the track."

Trish felt her butterflies take a dive. She still didn't feel comfortable talking to the press. *What if I sound like an idiot?* "Six would be great."

The bellboy showed them to connecting rooms. "You can still order from room service," he said, "but the dining room is about to close."

David thanked him, even remembering to give him a tip. He handed Trish a menu and studied one himself. As soon as they'd called in their order, Trish dialed Runnin' On Farm to let her parents know they'd arrived safely.

There was no answer.

Chapter
06

 T ry the hospital," David said.

"I thought sure they'd be home by now." Trish ran her hand through her bangs.

"I know, but try." David dug in his billfold for the number. "Here."

Trish breathed a sigh of relief when Marge answered the phone to Hal's hospital room. "Hi, Mom. What's happening?"

"You guys made it okay?"

"Sure. How's Dad?" Trish held the phone away from her ear so David could hear too.

"He's better tonight. Here, you can talk with him."

Trish held the receiver so hard her fingers cramped. "Hi, Dad. We miss you." She tried to swallow the gravel in her throat so her voice would sound normal.

"Hi, Tee. I miss you guys too. Is David there?" Hal's voice sounded faint, as if he were far away from the phone.

"Right here." David cleared his throat.

"Now I don't want you to worry, but we won't be coming until

Saturday. We should have test results back tomorrow and then we can leave. Mom's booked the tickets for Saturday morning."

"You sure you're not holding out on us?" Trish couldn't keep her tone light. While her father sounded calm, something inside her felt like screaming.

"We'll talk about all that's happened when we get there. Both horses shipped okay?"

"Yeah, and settled in fine." David tilted the receiver so he could talk easier. "Patrick is great. We couldn't do it without him."

"Wait till you meet Mel Howell," Trish added. She couldn't just listen, she had so much to tell her dad. "Oh, and wait till you see our limo! David and I almost got lost in it." She felt her butterflies leap for joy when her father chuckled softly.

Trish hadn't begun to touch on all she wanted to say before her father said he'd see them Saturday and hung up. She sank down on the edge of the bed.

"Did he sound weaker, or am I just making things up?"

David started clipping his nails. The clicking sound was distracting and annoyed Trish.

"David!"

He took a deep breath and looked up to meet Trish's stare. "Yes. And no, you're not making things up. I'll—" A knock on the door interrupted him. "There's our dinner."

Trish felt her stomach rumble as a waiter rolled in a white cloth-covered table. Silver domes covered the plates and a trio of yellow daisies bobbed in a bud vase. Even their Diet Cokes were served in crystal goblets.

When the waiter raised the domes, Trish snickered at the cheeseburgers and fries. They should have ordered steak or chicken. The table was much too fancy for burgers.

David tipped the waiter and sank into a chair. "I can't decide if I'm just beat, or really starved." He offered Trish the ketchup first, then doused his fries with it. "I should have ordered a chocolate shake. We earned a treat today."

Later, in bed, Trish flicked off the lamp. Light from an outside spotlight outlined her window where she hadn't pulled the drape all the way shut. At home the yard light always cast friendly shadows into her room. Vancouver seemed so far away. About as far away as God right now.

In the morning reporters were waiting for Trish. When Hank eased the limo to a stop, she noticed a woman with a tape recorder, and a man leaning against the stakes barn wall with a camera slung around his neck. They seemed to be together.

Trish wished she could slip down and disappear through the cracks in the seat. Maybe she could make a quick exit out the opposite side of the car and go directly to Spitfire's stall.

Reading her thoughts, David jabbed her with his elbow. "Come on, chicken liver. You'll do fine."

Easy for you to say, Trish thought. *You're not the one to look like an idiot if you say the wrong thing.* She took a deep breath and followed David out the open door. Hank Benson winked at her, giving her the high sign with his thumb on the door.

Trish pasted a smile on her face. She could hear her father's voice in her ear: *"Smiling makes you feel better about yourself, even if you don't feel like it. And it always makes other people think better of you."* So keep on smiling, she ordered her face. *And knock it off,* she commanded her inner aerial troop. *You can do your acrobatics later.*

"Good morning, what can I do for you?" she heard herself say.

That's the way, girl, her inner voice cheered her on. For a change, the nagging twin must have been sleeping.

"Just a few questions," the female journalist said. She clicked on the recorder. "You don't mind, do you?" She nodded at her equipment. When Trish shook her head, the woman continued. "How does it feel to be the first female to win the Kentucky Derby?"

"Probably the same as the guys feel. Happy, excited, like a dream come true. Most of them have worked longer for it than I have. So I guess that makes me appreciate the honor even more."

"They say the only reason you won is because you were on your father's horse."

Trish could feel the hair bristling on the back of her neck. "I know that's what some people are saying, but I helped raise that horse and I trained him, with my dad's instructions. We're a team, all of our family." She unclenched her fists. "And I've won a lot of races when I wasn't riding Spitfire, even in Kentucky."

"I hear your father is very sick. What will you do if he can't make the trip?"

Trish gritted her teeth. A quick *Father, help!* winged skyward as she scrambled for an answer. "Then Spitfire and I will race like my dad taught us. You can't do more than your best. And we don't do less."

Trish glanced up to see David's arm raised in victory. The approval made her bolder. "You see, we believe God is with us and guides us, around a racetrack or . . ." She took another deep breath and lifted her chin a fraction. "In a hospital."

The reporter seemed at a loss for words. "Why—uh—thank you, Tricia. I'm sure you have plenty of work to do this morning. And good luck here at Pimlico." She put her microphone away and gestured to the cameraman to follow her.

Luck, schmuck. Trish kept the words inside while her smile stayed in place. "It was nice meeting you." Feeling as if she had the last word, Trish stuffed her hands in her pockets and went in search of Patrick.

"I tried." Trish plunked down on a bale of hay in the tack room.

"I'm sure you did fine. Ya needn't be worryin' yerself." Patrick's brogue always thickened when he felt deeply about something. "Besides, most o' the time, them reporters don't get half what you say. Get yerself up there on that colt. You'll feel better."

"You're right." Trish nodded, slapped her hands on her knees, and nodded again. "At least Spitfire doesn't ask questions."

The dirt road to the track seemed long as Trish and Spitfire passed by the rows of barns. While the buildings seemed shabby, the morning orchestra was the same as on tracks everywhere—metal jangling, horses snorting and nickering, stable folk laughing, a shout or whistle thrown in for counterpoint. It was comfortable music, the kind that Trish planned always to be a part of.

When they turned left on the track, Spitfire continued making inspection with his eyes and ears. His long, loose-limbed walk ate up the mile-long track. Trish pointed to the infield at a small yellow and white building with a red roof, topped by a curious weather vane of a jockey mounted on a horse.

"Bet that's the winner's circle." Trish stopped her horse so they could get a better look at the circle of low, perfectly trimmed shrubbery. Two rows of white picket fence led from the track to the circle. "We're gonna be in there a week from Saturday, ya hear?" Spitfire snorted and went back to walking.

The glassed-in grandstand reminded Trish of Portland Meadows, but it was in better shape. Morning sun reflected off the huge panes. Die-hard spectators trained their binoculars on the working horses.

Trish nudged Spitfire into a trot for the second circuit. His easy attitude seemed to say, "A track is a track. Nothing to get excited about."

Sarah's Pride didn't agree with him. When Trish took her out, she tracked every shadow and shied at a few of her own imagination. And she didn't want to walk. Her stiff-legged trot forced Trish to post and finally rise in the stirrups. The filly even shied away when another horse came up beside her.

Patrick had walked to the track with them so he could watch the work. He shook his head when Trish brought the sweating filly to a stop in front of him.

"I'm not sure who got more of a workout, her or me," Trish grumbled, but her smile and the way she stroked the filly's neck showed she didn't mean it. "You gotta settle down," she crooned to the filly's still-twitching ears. "You can't win any races if you use up all your energy before the gate opens."

Patrick stroked his chin with one hand. "I'm thinkin' we'll do blinders on her. And lots of galloping."

Trish nodded. "Hear that, girl? Patrick will turn you into a winner yet." She turned out the gate and followed the fence line back to the barn. Patrick remained behind to watch some of the other horses work.

Mel Howell met them after breakfast. "You ready for the grand tour?" His beeper squawked and he raised a hand while he spoke into the small black box. Then he smiled again. "Sorry for the interruption. Now, where were we?"

An hour and a half later Trish felt as if she'd been toured by a walking, talking, Thoroughbred-racing encyclopedia. Mel showed them the grave of Barney, the track dog, in a corner near the stakes barn. Then he led them up and down, around and through the grandstand complex, all the while sharing anecdotes from Pimlico history. When he walked them out to the infield area that Trish had admired earlier, Mel confirmed her guess. This was the winner's circle for the Preakness. The yellow and white building was the remaining cupola from the old grandstand that had burned years before.

"The blanket of flowers for the winner is woven of chrysanthemums, actually," Mel continued his flow of information. "We have to dye the centers to match the traditional black-eyed Susans, because that flower doesn't bloom till later in the summer."

Trish shook her head. "At least no one has to worry about thorns like on the roses at Churchill." She remembered getting stuck by one the trimmers had overlooked. "Do you have bands and guards like they do there?"

"Of course. And extra guards around the stakes barn as soon as the entries begin to arrive. Safety's my job, besides making sure all you celebrities feel comfortable here, and welcome."

Trish and David smiled at each other and then at him. "Celebrities?" Trish still didn't think of herself as one. At Mel's nod, she shrugged and grinned again. "Whatever. But thank you for all you've done for us. We've never had a limo and driver before."

"You suppose this is what rock stars feel like?" David asked after they returned to the barn and told Patrick about their tour.

"I don't know." Trish stretched her arms over her head. "But I kinda like it." She wrapped her arms around Spitfire's neck as he leaned his head over her shoulder in his favorite position. "How about you, fella?" Spitfire bobbed his head, his usual plea for more scratching. "All right. All right."

Trish had just bemoaned the fact of having to return to the hotel to break open *War and Peace* again, when a man introduced himself as an agent. "I talked with Jonathan Smith," he said, "and he told me to get you some mounts if I could. One of my boys cracked a collarbone yesterday and can't ride for the rest of the week. Would you be interested in two races this afternoon?"

Trish felt a jolt of excitement. "Sure. I'm not licensed in Maryland yet, though. Is there time?"

"If you hustle. Come on, I'll walk you through the process. Or run you through, in this case."

"But I don't have enough money with me. Do I have time to go back to the hotel?"

"Not really."

"Here." Patrick dug out his wallet. "You can pay me back later." He handed her several twenties.

"Thanks, Patrick. Bet you didn't know you'd have to be my guardian angel when you signed on for this job." Trish blew him a kiss as she walked backward beside the trotting agent. Together they jogged back toward the grandstand where the offices were located.

At least this way I'll get to race this track before the Preakness, Trish thought as she slipped into the unfamiliar blue and black silks. She hadn't had a chance to meet either the trainer or the horse but it wouldn't be long now. She watched the first race of the day on the monitor.

At the call for the jockeys, Trish trotted up the stairs to the men's jockey room where the scale was located. A valet there handed her the saddle and weights to bring her up to the required 121 pounds. Off to one side she could hear a couple of guys talking—about her. Even her ears blushed as she felt the warmth spread all the way up from her toes.

"Good luck," the steward told her. At least he had a friendly smile on his face.

Trish sighed. *Oh well, this is probably what it will always be like at first. I'll have to prove myself at every track in the country, no matter how many races I win.* She trooped back down the stairs with the other jockeys for race two.

She felt at home in the saddling paddock, because like Portland Meadows it was located under the grandstand. She was in stall five.

Trish introduced herself to both the trainer and the owner. "I'm pleased to have you ride for me," the older woman of the two said, her accent definitely sounding south of the Mason-Dixon Line. "We've been following your career with interest."

"Thank you," Trish replied. Strange wasn't the word for this situation. Usually, even if a woman partly owned a horse, a man was either in charge or was the trainer.

The younger woman grinned at her. "My name's Jennifer Hasseltine, and contrary to my appearance I've been training for the last eight years. Mrs. Bovier is one of my favorite owners. And Johnny Be Late"—she stroked the gelding's gray neck—"is one terrific fella. The boards out there show him the favorite, but we don't need the numbers to tell us how great he is."

The horse nuzzled Trish's hand for more after munching her proffered carrot. Trish looked the horse in the eye and saw both desire and a calm spirit. The gray held his head proudly, as if he knew what they were saying and agreed completely.

"He reminds me of old Dan'l at home. That gray horse taught me a lot about racing and horses in general." She scratched his cheek and up behind the ears. Johnny Be Late blew in her face.

"Riders up!"

After a knee up, Trish settled herself in the saddle and smoothed a stubborn lock of gray mane to the right side. She patted Johnny's neck in the process.

"He's a sprinter," Jennifer said, "and with six furlongs you better take him to the front and let him go. Watch out for number four; he should be your main contender."

Trish nodded. It *really* seemed strange to be taking orders from a woman, but she liked it.

The parade to the post gave her the same thrill here as at home. When the bugle blew she and Johnny were ready to perform. Her horse was all collected power as they cantered back past the grandstands and out to the starting gate. He walked into his assigned gate and waited like a true professional.

Trish slipped into her normal singsong that calmed both her and her mount. She felt him gather under her, and when the gate clanged open he was ready. He surged forward neck and neck with number four, and the two of them set the pace. Down the backstretch and into the turn, this was definitely a two-horse race.

Coming out of the turn on the outside, Trish relaxed her hold on the reins. The gray pulled ahead one stride, then another. Number four picked up the pace and drew even again.

"Okay, fella, let's get this over with," Trish sang to the flicking ears. This time Johnny pulled away, and kept pulling away. Each stride drove them farther ahead until they won by two lengths.

Trish gave the gelding his moment in front of the crowd. "See, fella, that's you they're cheering. You ran a fine race."

Jennifer grinned up at Trish as she led the horse into the winner's circle. "He's good, isn't he?" She scratched under Johnny's forelock. "You rode him well."

"He was easy," Trish said as she smiled for the photographer. She leaped to the ground and stripped off the saddle.

"You can ride for me anytime," Mrs. Bovier told Trish. "I like your style. You didn't need the whip and you didn't use it."

"Thank you, my pleasure." Trish felt a warm glow in her middle. It was nice to be complimented on something she believed in so strongly. She never went to the whip unless she was forced to.

The next race wasn't so easy. She found herself boxed in right from the beginning. Rather than drive between two horses that yielded only a slight opening, Trish pulled back and to the outside. She was still off the pace going into the final turn, but her horse lengthened his stride and drove down the stretch like a runaway locomotive. They passed two horses with one leading and with a furlong to go.

"Come on, you can do it!" Her words seemed to fly off on the wind. With all her encouragement, they pulled up to the stirrup, then the neck, and with one stride—Trish wasn't sure who won. Had his whiskers been over the wire first? Only the camera would tell.

"And that's number three, Hot Shot, owned by Springhill Farms and ridden by Tricia Evanston." The speaker sounded tinny but the message rang true. She'd won two at Pimlico. And this one surprised everyone.

"That was some ride," Patrick said when she joined him and David at the rail for the running of the seventh race.

"Cut it kinda close." David shook his head. "I think you've made your mark here at Pimlico."

The Saturday morning papers agreed.

"Kinda nice, wouldn't you say?" Trish asked Spitfire during their long gallop a bit later. Spitfire snorted. "All the publicity; you're famous now. How does it feel?" Spitfire shook his head. "Wish Red were here," Trish spoke her thoughts. "He's more fun to talk to than you." Spitfire snorted again. At the thought of their first kiss, Trish felt tingly in her middle. It *would* be nice to see Red again.

There wasn't much time for conversation on the gallop with Sarah's Pride.

"Tomorrow we'll run her with blinders." Patrick pushed back his hat and scratched his forehead. "She pulled out on you when that sorrel came up beside you. She always do that?"

"Seems to." Trish helped David finish scraping the sleek red hide. "Let's get done here. I'm starved."

That afternoon's program didn't go as well. Trish again had two mounts, but she only pulled off a place. In the other race not only was she boxed in, but the horse got bumped and finished second to last.

"Mom and Dad in yet?" Trish asked after a quick change in the jockey room. "I made reservations at a restaurant down at the inner harbor. The woman at the hotel desk said it was a really great place to eat."

"They're here," David answered. "But Dad's already gone to bed. Trish, he doesn't look good at all."

Chapter 07

Not good" didn't begin to cover how bad Trish's father looked.

"Go ahead, wake him," her mother said. "He wants you to."

Trish crammed her fist against her teeth to keep from crying out. *How can he look so much worse? He hasn't even been gone a week.* She tiptoed forward to stand next to the bed. "Dad?" She touched the bruised hand lying on top of the covers. When Hal didn't respond, she turned a questioning look to her mother.

Marge nodded.

"Dad." Louder this time. Trish gently shook his shoulder.

Her father's eyelids fluttered. His eyes seemed sunken back in his head, and the skin of his face looked gray against the sharp cheekbones. He had lost weight again. It was obvious by the creases from his nose to the corners of his mouth. Slowly, as though moving against a heavy weight, Hal's eyes opened.

"Trish." He turned his hand to take hers. "Sorry I'm so tired." His voice faded in and out like an out-of-tune radio. "David, we—we'll talk in the morning, okay?" His eyes closed again before anyone could even answer.

Trish watched him breathe. Each breath seemed a struggle, yet the effort hardly raised the blanket. *Where has my strong, dark-haired, laughing dad with the broad shoulders gone?* Trish thought. *The one who tossed me into my racing saddle as if I were a featherweight. The one who used to race me up from the barns at home? The man who knew God and trusted Him—my father.*

She stroked the back of his hand where an IV had infiltrated and left terrible bruises. His hands had always calmed both Trish and the horses. Now they looked too thin for any kind of strength. He coughed, but even in sleep he'd learned to be careful not to cough too hard.

Trish wiped her cheeks and eyes with her other hand.

Marge handed her some tissues.

Trish had almost forgotten her mother and brother were there. All her love and strength focused on her father. She drew in a deep breath that snagged on the lump in her throat.

Then Trish heard the others leave the room. "God, you promised to hear our prayers, and we prayed for my dad to get better. You promised. You promised." Her whisper faded away as the tears chased each other down her cheeks.

Trish quietly left the room, then leaned against the door frame of the connecting living room. She crossed her arms and braced her fists under her armpits to keep from shaking.

"What's going on?" she pleaded with her mother.

"The doctors are trying a new method of treatment and your father reacted to it. He couldn't keep anything down for two days, but insisted we come ahead anyway. Then we couldn't get a direct flight, so the trip wore him out more than it should have."

"He looks terrible."

"I know. But a lot of that is because of exhaustion. He never sleeps well in the hospital."

"Why are they trying a new treatment?" David asked.

"I promised your father I'd let him tell you about this last week."

"Promises don't mean much," Trish blurted, then turned to her bedroom and closed the door behind her.

After changing into pajamas, she climbed into bed. Who cared about dinner? She didn't want to talk to anyone. With pillows propped behind her, Trish leaned against the headboard. *If Dad is getting better like we all thought, why the new treatment? If he isn't getting better, what's going on? Is he worse?* She thought back to the weekend before. He hadn't seemed worse. No coughing to speak of. He'd handled all the Derby stuff.

Trish tried to distract herself by examining her fingernails. None of this made any sense. Was God letting them down? She chewed on a torn cuticle until it bled. "Ouch." She pressed her thumb on the skin to stop the bleeding.

What Scripture verses would help now? None came to mind.

Trish picked up *War and Peace.* Maybe reading would calm her mind. Half an hour later she dumped the book on the floor. She couldn't hear anyone in the next room. Her watch read 8:30. She snapped off the light and snuggled down under the covers. The Jacuzzi from Kentucky would be real welcome about now.

After rolling over and smashing her pillow for the umpteenth time, Trish turned the light on again. She glared at the ceiling where she was sure her prayers were floating. Where had God gone? Picking up the eagle, she smoothed the carved wings. Suddenly she threw back the covers and, carrying the eagle, tiptoed into her parents' room. She carefully set it on the nightstand where her father would see it when he woke up.

The door to their parents' room was still closed when she and David left for the track in the morning. Drizzly skies matched Trish's mood. A stiff wind blew the cold right through her as she galloped Spitfire and then Sarah's Pride. Even the horses seemed glad to get back out of the weather. It felt more like Portland than Baltimore. She couldn't have been prepared for weather on the East Coast. She'd never been there before. *And we probably shouldn't be here now,* she thought.

Trish finished her chores without speaking to anyone. Patrick gave up after one look at her face. David never tried. He didn't seem any better off than she was.

But by the time Hank Benson drove the limo through the gate, the sun and the clouds were playing a fast game of peek-a-boo. On the ride back to the hotel, Trish thought about Sundays at home. Chores, a good breakfast, and church. Then time to play with Miss Tee in the afternoon when the racing season was finished in Portland. She and Rhonda would probably go riding. The four musketeers would hang out somewhere. *Whatever we did, we would have fun. Even if it was studying together.*

Her last thought reminded Trish of finals. She'd better get in and hit the books again. She was only about three-fourths through the list, and all her assignments had to go back with David so he could bring her more. She shook her head.

"You okay?" David asked when they reached the door to their hotel suite.

"Yeah, sure." Frown lines deepened on her forehead. How could she be okay when her father looked so awful?

When they entered the suite it was like going through a time warp. Hal had showered and shaved and was sitting up in a chair reading the newspaper.

"Good morning. Breakfast should be here any minute." His smile hid the lines Trish had seen the night before.

"D-Dad," Trish stammered in shock.

Hal teasingly touched his cheek, chin, and nose. "I think it's me. Last time I checked the mirror anyway." He laid the paper aside. "Haven't you a hug for me, Trish? I came a long way to get one."

Trish flew across the room and threw herself into his arms, with David right behind her. "But last night you—you looked—" She laid her head on his chest and soaked his robe lapel with her tears.

"I know, Tee. I know." He patted her back with one hand and reached for David's with the other. "I had hoped to get some rest so we could talk last night, but that trip wiped me out. Your mother and I really needed the sleep last night."

"The time change didn't help either." Marge stood beside them, her hand on David's shoulder.

There was a knock at the door. "That's breakfast. We went ahead and ordered for you. I knew you'd be starved." Marge went to open the door.

A waiter wheeled a white-clad table in, placed it in front of Hal's chair, and raised two leaves, turning it into a larger round table. He skillfully arranged the place settings, poured ice water in the glasses, and pointed out the items. There was a basket of rolls and muffins, two carafes of coffee, fresh-squeezed orange juice, milk, and plates of pancakes, bacon, eggs, and hash browns.

"Looks great," David said enthusiastically as he moved chairs into place. He walked the waiter to the door and tipped him.

Trish lifted the silver lid from her plate. "It even smells good."

"Let's say grace together." Hal reached for Trish's and Marge's hands on either side of him. Then David joined the circle.

"Father, we thank you for this food. Thanks too for a safe trip and for taking good care of our family. Thank you for a new morning, a new day in which to praise you. Amen." He opened his eyes and looked intently at each of them. "You have no idea how precious you are to me."

Trish bit her bottom lip to keep the tears from flowing. She lifted the silver dome again to inhale the aroma of fresh bacon and hot cakes. That bought her time to get the tears swallowed. She didn't want to cry again this morning. It was a time to be happy. They were all together.

She stole a peek at David. He was drinking his orange juice, not looking at anyone. Marge's hand covered Hal's, and her eyes were wet with tears.

"We sure missed you two," Trish managed. "But we made it. Things have been running pretty smoothly." She spread butter on her pancakes and poured syrup as though it were a typical Sunday morning. "I think Spitfire missed you too."

Marge shook her head and quipped, "Too bad he couldn't have joined us for breakfast."

"Now that would not have been a bad idea," Hal said, waving his fork. "Then I wouldn't have to drive clear over there to watch him. And Trish would have more study time."

Trish shook her head and groaned. "Don't mention studying. Have any of you ever read *War and Peace*?"

"Yeah, it's a real snoozer." David poured coffee for himself, then his parents.

"It's a classic," Marge said, sipping her coffee. "A wonderful story."

Trish and David exchanged glances. Their eyes said *Parents!*

"Mother," David said seriously, "you'd have to be looney-tunes to love *War and Peace*."

"Thank you for that comment on my taste in literature. Coming from someone who thinks the funnies and the sports page are all that matters in a newspaper, I'm complimented."

Trish let her family's laughter and good-natured banter flow around her like a warm tide. She ignored the dark lines and gray tinge of her father's face. And when his trembling hands raised the coffee cup to his lips, she looked the other way. Nothing would spoil this moment for her.

The coffee drinkers were on their second cups, and Trish swirled the last bit of orange juice around the bottom of her glass. Wishing they'd ordered more, she relished the last drops.

"So, Dad, what's going on with you?" David asked casually.

David, how could you? Trish felt like screaming at him.

Hal pulled on an ear and ran a finger around the rim of his cup. Finally he raised his gaze.

If Trish had never seen haunted eyes, she was seeing them now. She clenched her teeth against the pain she knew was coming.

"Well, the tumors in my lungs haven't grown any."

Trish let out the breath she'd been holding.

"But they found—" Hal swallowed, then continued. "The cancer has metastasized; that is, it's traveled to somewhere else—to the liver and pancreas, in my case. That's why the doctors decided to try a new protocol."

Trish felt as if she were trying to swim to a surface that was out of reach. She was drowning.

"But—but I thought God was healing you! You said He always answers our prayers!"

"He does, Trish, He does." Her father leaned toward her. "Or I wouldn't be here now. Remember, they didn't hold out much hope last fall when they found the first tumors. And those shrunk."

"But now it's worse?" Trish stared into her father's dark brown eyes. "Is that what you mean?"

"I mean that we continue to pray. We know that God knows what He's doing—"

"Maybe you do, but not me. I don't know any such thing right now." Trish pushed herself to her feet, catching the chair before it toppled to the floor. When would she be able to breathe again? "Excuse me." Her voice stuck in her throat. She felt as if she were slogging through mud on her way to her bedroom. She closed the door carefully behind her, as if being quiet would change what her father had just said.

She collapsed on the bed, clutching a pillow under her chin. "God, you'd better not let my father die. You promised to make him better. I read those words, I even memorized them. You said, 'By His stripes you are healed.' " She beat her fist into the pillow.

"My Dad trusts you. You can't let him down." She rolled over and wrapped her arms around the pillow. "You can't. You can't." She let the tears flow.

The pain in her chest clawed deeper. Was this what a broken heart felt like? She wiped her eyes and sat up. It seemed like hours had passed when she pulled off her boots and shoved her feet into her running shoes.

"I'll come with you," David said when she opened the door to leave.

"No!"

"Sorry, no choice. You can't run around here by yourself."

"You're not my boss!" Trish threw the words over her shoulder as she thundered down the stairs.

David never responded. He just kept a few paces behind her.

Trish's feet pounded the gravel, then the concrete sidewalk. She crossed a grassy field, ran up a hill, gasping for breath but refusing to stop. Downhill she picked up speed. At the bottom she slipped in a patch of mud but caught herself and ran on.

David dogged her steps. Trish could hear him struggle for breath too. The challenge? To run David into the ground. Her sides screamed with pain—her lungs, her legs. Finally she dropped to her hands and knees under a tree—and threw up. She gagged and retched and heaved again till there was nothing left but a feeling of complete exhaustion.

When she could move, Trish crawled to the trunk of the tree and leaned against it.

David lay on the grass nearby, his face on his arms.

"You didn't have to come." Trish finally spoke.

"I know."

Trish sat with her back against the tree, her knees drawn up to her chest. She closed her eyes, listening—*for what?* Her nagger could finally make himself heard above the poundings in her body.

You blew it again. Every time you hit a problem you blow it. Trish shoved herself to her feet. "Let's see about getting back. Any idea which way to go?"

David pointed to the left.

It *was* a long walk back.

For the next two days, Trish felt as if she were on a roller coaster. One minute she'd be up—mostly when she was at the track. Then all the fears would catch up and she'd crash down again. She gave up praying. Why pray when God wasn't listening anyway? Her Bible verses? Hardly! She gritted her teeth and kept on.

Working the horses, schooling Spitfire and Sarah's Pride, and studying. She smiled when she was supposed to, answered when people spoke to her, was polite when journalists asked her questions.

She even joked with the trainer for Nomatterwhat. He had a good sense of humor even if his horse didn't.

Trish could keep the mask in place. She knew she could. She *didn't* open her Bible. She *didn't* allow the songs in, and she stayed away from the carved eagle—and her father. The latter wasn't so difficult. He slept most of the time.

One night she found a familiar three-by-five card on her nightstand. Her father's usually bold printing was a bit shaky but the verse was plain. *"I will never leave nor forsake"* (Hebrews 13:5).

Ha! What a joke! Trish wanted to rip the card up. Instead, she stuck it in her history book. She could deal with this setback. After all, she was tough. Wasn't she?

Chapter
08

Let him out for half a mile, no more," Hal told Trish on Wednesday morning. "The stopwatches will be on you."

Trish nodded. She smoothed Spitfire's mane to the right and stroked his neck. "Okay, fella, let's do it." She trotted him around the track and broke into a slow gallop just before the half-mile pole. As they passed the marker, she let him loose.

Spitfire showed top form as he fairly sizzled around the track. He was still picking up speed as they flashed past the finish line. Trish stood high in her stirrups to bring him back down. "Easy now. Come on, you know the rules. Save it for Saturday."

Spitfire shook his head. He wanted, needed to run—all out.

"Don't tell me, let me guess." Trish grinned at the three men who waited for her at the exit gate. Patrick and David both clasped stopwatches in their hands. "Wasn't he fantastic?"

Patrick nodded. "That he was, lass." He grabbed his hat just in time. Spitfire was getting sneakier in his hat tosses. "You black clown, you." Patrick rubbed the top of his bald head and settled the fedora back in place—firmly.

Trish couldn't help giggling. Spitfire wore his "Who me?" look, his head slightly off to the side in case someone planned on smacking him. David loved it when *he* wasn't the object of Spitfire's pranks. Hal leaned against the fence, a grin erasing the look of weariness that now seemed permanently grooved on his face.

"So, what do you think?" David asked after stealing a peek at his watch.

Trish concentrated. "Ummm—forty-nine and three."

"Wrong. Forty-nine and one," David gloated. "You're off by two tenths of a second."

"Your watch keeps getting more and more accurate, Tee." Hal stroked Spitfire's nose. "An accurate internal stopwatch is the one thing that sets *great* jockeys apart from the rest. Did you push him?"

"Not really. But I can always tell the time easier on Spitfire. I s'pose it's 'cause I know him so well." She leaned forward to give Spitfire a hug. He tossed his head and flipped David's Runnin' On Farm hat off in the process. Trish giggled again. "See you guys at the barn before we get into any more trouble here."

Trish caught herself humming on the walk back to the barn. No matter how hard she tried, the melody broke through: "I will raise you up. . . ." She rotated her shoulders to release some of the tension. If only she could be riding and racing all the time, without a moment to think about what was happening in the rest of her life.

While the Evanstons were skipping most of the festivities of Preakness week, Thursday morning proved the exception. Trish and David finished up the chores quickly so they could join their parents and Patrick at the Sports Palace for the post position breakfast.

"Mr. Finley!" Trish was surprised to see him.

"It's Adam, remember? It's good to see you, Trish. You didn't think we would miss this, did you?" Adam and his wife, Martha, circled the white-clothed table to give Trish a hug.

"Hang in there," Martha whispered in Trish's ear.

Trish felt the familiar burning behind her eyes. She blinked it back.

"Mr. and Mrs. Shipson." Trish shook hands with the owners of BlueMist Farms.

"Congratulations on your riding," the silver-haired Donald Shipson told her. "Spitfire looks magnificent."

"Thank you."

"My dear, you are a credit to women everywhere," Bernice Shipson added in her soft Kentucky drawl. "We have a filly entered in tomorrow's third we'd like you to ride."

"Be glad to," Trish answered, smiling. This woman was easy to like. If Spitfire had to go to another farm, at least these people seemed like family.

Trish caught Patrick's nod of approval as she slid into the chair next to her father. He reached over and patted her hand, sending a warm glow all the way to her heart.

Crystal chandeliers, plush carpet, beautiful table settings, all set off the richness of the Sports Palace. Here the wealthy came to play, but Trish didn't feel out of place. Her family had earned their position here by right of excellence. Her gaze wandered to the gallery of oil portraits of jockeys who had won the Preakness. The display extended around the corners of the room. Would *her* picture join the elite one day?

Trish could feel her butterflies trying out their wings as the drawing got under way. They were seventh on the list of nine.

Nomatterwhat headed the list. The Steward drew number three. The numbers ninth, fifth, seventh, and eighth followed. Trish clenched her fists in her lap. Did they have to take so long between draws? A cheer went up. Equinox drew the post. The next number would be theirs.

Hal draped his hand across the back of her chair and gripped Trish's shoulder. She flashed him a quick smile and turned back to watch the draw.

"Position number two. Spitfire, owned by Hal Evanston." *Between Equinox and Nomatterwhat,* Trish thought. *One's a pain in the neck and the other our chief contender from the Derby.*

Trish dragged in a deep breath. At least they didn't have as far to run this time. They could take the pole and just run the others into the ground.

"That'll be good," Hal said. He nodded and patted Trish's shoulder.

As soon as the final two numbers were called, the crowd was on its feet, including the media. Several reporters gathered around the

Evanstons, questions tumbling out. Trish listened with one ear while David slipped away. She couldn't get away if she wanted to; her father stood, putting his hand on her shoulder.

"What about your health, Mr. Evanston?" one of the reporters asked. "Could that keep you from running in the Belmont?"

Hal smiled. "We have to win here first. I learned a long time ago to take one race at a time. In fact, to take one day at a time. You can't live tomorrow until it comes. As to my health, I am in God's hands. There is no safer place to be. I trust Him absolutely to do what is best for me and my family."

"And the colt—Tricia, you ride Spitfire every day. His leg any problem?"

Trish lifted her chin and banished the tears that threatened at her father's words. She squared her shoulders. "Spitfire's in great shape. You know his time from yesterday, and there's been no swelling for weeks now. We're as ready as we can be."

"You'll be retiring him to stud at BlueMist Farms then, right after the Belmont?"

"That's the plan, but we haven't put a timetable on it yet," Hal answered.

Trish felt her father leaning more of his weight on the hand that rested on her shoulder. She glanced at her mother. Marge nodded, acknowledging that she knew what was happening.

Trish took a deep breath. "That's enough for today, folks. You know that we'll be around if you have more questions later. Thank you very much." She slipped her arm around her father's waist.

As the reporters left to search for other stories, Trish pulled out a chair with one hand and eased her father into it with the other.

"You did just fine, lass," Patrick spoke in her ear so only she heard him. "Good timing."

Trish stood with her hand on her father's shoulder while he talked with the Finleys and Shipsons. Marge had taken the chair beside him. Trish could feel her father's weariness under her hand. She wanted to throw both arms around him, to give him her strength, to fight off the disease that was causing him pain.

You've got guts, Dad, she wanted to tell him. *When you believe in something you both walk it and talk it. Standing up there like that announcing your faith to the world—and this isn't the first time.* She thought back to the ceremonies after the Derby. He'd given God the glory then too.

On the way back to the barns Trish heard an argument going on in her head again. One side demanded she stay mad at God. The other insisted she needed all the strength only her heavenly Father could give her. And the courage her father had.

Courage. Guts. Peace. Her father had it all.

Trish had a lot of anger. And resentment.

She slipped into Spitfire's stall and slid down to sit in the straw in the corner. Spitfire nuzzled her hair, then cocked his back leg and dozed off again.

Trish crossed her arms over her bent knees and rested her forehead on her arms. She tried to pray, but the ceiling here seemed as tight as the hotel's. Why wasn't God hearing her?

You're still angry, her little voice slipped in now that things were quiet. *Tell Him about that.*

"So, God, I'm angry. I'm so mad I don't even want to talk with you. I just want to scream and pound things. I want to run away from all these problems and have them all better when I come back." Tears slipped down her cheeks and clogged her throat. "You can heal my Dad. I know you can. So why is he worse? I don't understand."

Spitfire wuffled in Trish's ear. When she raised her face, he licked the tears off her cheek. "Spitfire, I just don't understand." She rubbed the soft spot between his nostrils. "I don't know what to do. How can I have the courage my father has?"

She pulled a piece of hay out of the sling and chewed on it. "Do you think God's gonna help me?" She pulled the horse's head down lower so she could rub under his forelock. Spitfire closed his eyes in bliss. "Sometimes I don't much like God, you know."

She chewed some more. "Do you think Dad . . . no—" She shook her head. "I haven't been very nice to him lately—to anyone." She tilted her head back and stared at the ceiling. Spitfire blew softly on her face and licked away another tear.

"One day at a time. That's all I gotta take." Trish drew circles on her knees with a fingernail. "Huh, one minute at a time is more like it."

She sat silently for a while. Spitfire dozed off again. "Jesus, please help me. I need you so badly." Her nose ran and then her eyes. She wiped them on her sleeve. But this time, bit by bit, the peace she needed so desperately slipped into the stall and snuggled around her shoulders—and into the corners of her mind.

Patrick found Trish sometime later—curled up in the straw, sound asleep.

The peace stayed with her all day and through the night. When her nagger tried to get on her case in the morning, she just shook her head and shut him down.

"Better today?" Patrick asked as he boosted Trish into the saddle for morning works.

She smiled down at him. "Better."

That afternoon she met the Shipsons and their trainer in the saddling paddock. Their filly sniffed Trish's outstretched hand and up her arm to her head and shoulders. When she finished her inspection, Trish gave her a chunk of carrot and rubbed the satiny bay cheek.

"You're a pretty nice girl, aren't you?" Trish murmured in the filly's ear. "You think we can take this race? I do."

"She's in top condition," the trainer said. "Watch her, because she likes to set the pace and can run herself out. She placed at the Oaks; should have won it."

"Riders up!"

Mr. Shipson grasped Trish's knee and tossed her into the saddle. "She likes distance. I think the two of you will be a good match."

The blood-bay filly danced behind the lead pony. Head high, ears catching every sound, she listened to Trish's crooning and acknowledged the applause from the stands.

"You're a natural ham, aren't you?" Trish chuckled as the filly gave an extra bounce. On the canter back to the starting gates, the filly kept the pace with her lead pony, hoarding her strength for the race ahead.

"Good girl." Trish stroked the black mane and sleek red neck as they stood quietly in the gate waiting for the others to calm down. Trish gathered her reins and settled into the saddle.

The filly broke clean and fast. She had the post in three strides because the number one horse missed a beat at the gate. They had the lead going into the turn and there never was a serious contender. They won by three lengths.

"I don't know what happened to the rest of them," Trish said as she met the Shipsons in front of the winner's circle. "We just went for a fast ride all by ourselves."

"I said I thought the two of you would click," Shipson said as he led the filly into the winner's circle next to the grandstand.

After pictures, Trish looked across the heads of the crowd to the yellow and white building in the infield with the horse-and-jockey weather vane. *That's for tomorrow,* she thought as she leaped to the ground. *Spitfire and me. We'll take the Preakness—for my dad.*

Chapter
09

How can a morning like this feel so normal? Trish thought as she trotted Spitfire around the track. The rising sun had already burned off most of the fog. A wisp or two clung to the weather vane above the infield cupola at the winner's circle.

"Today's a big one," she announced as they passed the grandstand. "Middle jewel in the Triple Crown. You ready?" Spitfire snorted and jigged sideways. He tossed his head and pulled at the bit. "No, no running now. You save it all for the last sixteenth of a mile. That's when it counts."

Trish looked up at the grandstand with spotters already clinging to the fence. The yellow and black band underneath the glassed-in stands glowed in the morning sun. Each box logged two years, and the name of the Preakness winner for that year. Trish closed her eyes for a moment to picture *Spitfire* in big letters. Black on yellow.

"We can do it, fella. We can." They turned off the track and walked the easy rise to the stakes barn.

"How's the lad?" Patrick asked when Trish dismounted.

"Ready."

"And the lass?" His grin crinkled his eyes.

"No butterflies." Trish laid a hand on her middle. "Hey, you guys sleepin' in there or what?" She stuck her tongue in her cheek and cocked her head. "Guess they are. How nice."

"Good. You just keep calm. The filly here is ready for a long gallop. Work some of the sass out of her."

By the time they returned, Trish could feel the work. Sarah's Pride had tried to pull Trish's arms right out of their sockets—all the way. When Trish forced the filly down to a trot, the pace had pounded like a pile driver. The kid just wouldn't settle down and go easy.

"She can be a real handful," Trish said, rubbing her arms. "If we can get her to quit wasting her energy on nothing, we should have a winner." She stood in front of the steaming chestnut and looked the horse right in the eyes. "Shoulda called you Ain't Behavin' or some such. Whoever trained you—" She shook her head. "Well, they didn't do us any favors."

Sarah's Pride rubbed her forehead on Trish's chest. Tired, she needed some loving, not a scolding. Trish obliged as David and Patrick washed the horse down and scraped her dry.

As Trish thought ahead to the big event, her butterflies awoke and took an experimental flutter, as though warming up for the big one.

Hal joined them for breakfast. "How you doing this morning?" he asked Trish as they set their trays down at the formica table.

"Pretty good, actually," Trish answered. "Maybe I'm getting used to this or something." She spread strawberry jam on her toast. "What about you?"

"Other than three reporters already this morning, everything's fine." They shared a smile, then Trish heard a voice behind her:

"Excuse me. Tricia Evanston? May I ask you a question or two?"

Trish groaned but smiled as she turned around to face the reporter. "Sure. Be glad to."

To the first question Trish answered, "How do I feel this morning? Excited. Spitfire and me—we're ready. If all goes as it should, we'll have a real good race today."

"Boy, if you aren't getting the words down smooth." David poked her shoulder as he sat down beside her after the reporter had left.

"As they say, Davey boy, practice makes perfect." Trish sipped her apple juice.

"Naw, there's a new way to say that. Perfect practice makes perfect. And my sister is not perfect."

"Well," Hal added, "you have to admit she's been getting lots of practice."

"Yeah, but at what?"

Trish basked in the comfortable teasing pattern. If she didn't look at the lines on her father's face, she could pretend everything was all right.

But it isn't, her little nagger got his digs in. *So don't try to pretend. You're a big girl now; accept life as it is.* The butterflies seemed to agree as they took flying leaps, clear up into her throat.

Trish sighed. But instead of letting her shoulders droop, she straightened up.

"You okay?" Hal whispered.

Trish nodded. She swallowed the flutter in her throat. "Just my friends here." She patted her middle. "Guess they didn't want to miss the action after all."

She checked into the jockey room, armed with her schoolbooks. A wistful thought took her back to Churchill Downs and the women's jockey room there. Here there weren't even windows. She felt as if she were in a box. The only contacts with the outside were the monitor and an intercom so she could hear the calls.

Trish settled into a chair and pulled out her assignment list. Only three things left to check off. Her history paper only needed a final draft, so she started on that. Copying didn't take a whole lot of concentration.

As the day's program flashed on the screen, Trish could hear the roar of the spectators. They'd already announced a record crowd for this running of the Preakness.

At race six, Trish put away her books and began to get ready. She polished her boots and sprayed her goggles, layering them on her helmet. Stretching took another fifteen minutes as she went through her routine, feeling the pull in each muscle with the hamstring stretches and curls. Lying back on the floor, breathing deeply, she closed her eyes. "Jesus," she prayed, "we both know this is a biggie. Help us do our best. But most important, make my dad stronger. Fight off the cancer for him. And like him, help me to give you the glory. Amen."

An arm over her eyes, Trish lay there. The same peace she'd found in Spitfire's stall was like a pillow under her now. God had heard her. She knew that for certain. And He cared.

At the call, she checked her appearance in the mirror. Spotless white pants, black boots, crimson and gold silks, and around her neck—an etched cross on a fine gold chain. She fingered the cross. It would have been nice to have Red here. One more friend to miss. Like Rhonda and Brad. She laughed at her reflection in the mirror. And then again, maybe not *exactly* like Rhonda and Brad. She saluted the mirror image and left the room, carefully closing the door behind her.

Once weighed in, she joined the other jockeys waiting for the call to go down to the horses. "Good luck," one of the men said.

"You too." At the call, Trish followed them down the stairs and out across the dirt track to the turf course. Only during the running of the Preakness were the horses saddled in the infield. Yellow poles designated the spot for each entry. Spitfire waited by post two.

He nickered when he saw Trish.

"Missed me, did you?" She smoothed his forelock and rubbed his ears.

"We're praying for you," Hal whispered in Trish's ear as he hugged her.

David swallowed before he could speak. "Go for the glory."

Patrick waited beside the colt's shoulder. Trish started to shake his hand, but instead threw her arms around his neck and hugged him hard. "You'll do it, lass." She raised her leg to meet his waiting hands, and with a smooth, swift motion, settled into the saddle. When she looked down, she could see his eyes were suspiciously bright.

Trish sniffed and wiped her eyes. The smile she gave the most important men in her life rivaled the warmth of the sun. "I love you." She picked up her reins. "Okay, fella. Let's do it."

David led Spitfire, and Hal walked alongside with his hand on Trish's knee. As they stepped onto the dirt track, the pony rider met them. Hal gave his daughter one last pat as the bugler raised the shiny brass horn. The notes floated on the air. Parade to post. The Preakness had begun.

Spitfire took the word *parade* to heart. Perfectly collected, neck arched, he jogged in step with his leader. The sun glinted blue on his shiny black hide. Muscles rippled, the mane and tail feathered in the breeze. Spitfire was everything a Thoroughbred should be. He snorted at the turn and cantered back past the stands to thunderous applause.

"You know it, fella. They're yelling for you." Trish rode high in her stirrups, in perfect symmetry with her horse. When they approached the starting gate Spitfire waited his turn.

Equinox refused to enter the gate. It took four gatemen to finally shove him into place.

Spitfire walked right in and stood perfectly at ease.

Nomatterwhat also needed encouragement. He'd acted cantankerous ever since the parade began, trying to outrun his pony and refusing to maintain his place in line. The remaining six filed into their assigned places.

Equinox reared in the stall.

Trish caught sight of the jockey bailing off rather than being squeezed between horse and gate. Spitfire stood still, listening to Trish's voice as she continued her soothing song.

One of the handlers led Equinox around and back into the gate. The jockey swung back aboard.

Trish breathed a sigh of relief and settled herself for the break. Spitfire tensed, his weight on his haunches, his focus on the track ahead.

The gates clanged open. "They're off!"

Spitfire broke in perfect stride. Equinox hung back. Nomatterwhat came into perfect sync with Spitfire. As they passed the grandstand for the first time, the two ran neck and neck, Spitfire on the inside.

Going into the first turn, Jones took Nomatterwhat into the lead by half a length. Trish kept a tight rein, letting the other horse set a faster pace. Through the backstretch they thundered stride on stride; Spitfire's nose seemed glued to Jones' stirrup. The remaining field spread out behind them.

Going into the turn, Trish loosed the reins a fraction. Spitfire's stride lengthened. He gained with each thrust of his haunches.

Jones went to the whip. Coming out of the turn, Spitfire paced him, stride for stride. But down the final stretch it was Spitfire going away.

Trish heard the thunder of Spitfire's hooves, his breath like a freight train. The crowd screamed, waves of sound bashing against their eardrums.

And it was Spitfire by one length. By two. The winner of the Preakness—Spitfire by three lengths. As they flashed across the finish line, Trish raised her whip in salute.

Tears streamed down her face. "Thank you, God. We did it. For my dad!" She listened for the announcer.

"And the winner of the Preakness is Spitfire—owned by Hal Evanston and ridden by his daughter, Tricia Evanston."

Trish and Spitfire cantered on around the track accepting the roar of the crowd as their due. At the sixteenth pole, an official opened the railing and waved her in. Trish trotted her horse back around the turf course, stopped Spitfire in front of the stands, and turned to face the crowd.

Head high, nostrils still flared red and breathing hard, Spitfire surveyed his kingdom. Trish stroked his neck, letting him accept the applause.

"It's ours, fella. Middle jewel of the Triple Crown. Your name is history now." She turned him toward the winner's circle where her family waited.

"Congratulations, Tricia." Mel Howell appeared beside her. He grasped the reins under Spitfire's chin and led them toward the cupola. White picket fences kept back the crowds and the press in the infield. Manicured shrubs outlined the flower-bordered circle. The huge silver Woodlawn Cup shone in its place of honor.

Trish smiled and waved till it felt as if her face would crack. She let the tears flow unchecked when she saw her parents, arm in arm in front of the red banner-decked porch of the cupola. Patrick and David met her at the circle.

David raised two fingers in what looked like a peace sign. Trish nodded. Two down.

"I knew you could do it, lass. You and the clown here." Patrick thumped her knee and Spitfire's shoulder. He took the reins so Mel could help with the blanket of flowers. Yellow chrysanthemums with the brown painted centers, the blanket was draped over the horse's withers.

Trish felt the weight across her knees, like a heavy quilt. With one hand she smoothed the blossoms, waving with the other. Flashbulbs popped, video cameras recorded the moment.

Her father gripped Trish's hand. No words were necessary. The love and pride in his eyes said it all.

Trish leaped to the ground, right into her mother's arms. Marge hugged her hard, then wiped tears from both their cheeks.

Trish hugged Spitfire one more time before an official from the detention barn led him away to be tested. Mel motioned Trish to the scale, where once she was weighed, the race was declared official. She followed her family up to the railed podium.

Announcer John McKay, known everywhere as the voice of Thoroughbred horse racing, first greeted them, then led them to the microphones. "And now, I give you the owner of this year's Preakness winner, Hal Evanston," his voice boomed over the applause of the crowd.

Hal stood a moment, surveying the sea of spectators. "I can't begin to thank you all enough for the way you've made us feel welcome here. Winning the Preakness with a colt from our own farm and my daughter riding it—well, it's beyond what most men dream of. I thank our heavenly Father for the privilege of being here, for keeping everyone safe in this race, and for my family, without whom none of this would be possible." He raised one hand to wave and clasped Marge to his side with the other.

"And now, the young woman you've all been waiting for—" McKay announced, pausing, "—winning jockey, Tricia Evanston! As you can see, they're keeping the trophies in the family."

Trish looked up at her father, then out at the crowd. She clenched the mike tightly in her hand to keep it from shaking. "Only one person a year gets to stand here for this honor. No one could be more proud than I am right now. Or more thankful. I have a lot to be thankful for. My father is standing here in spite of a killer disease. As he has said so many times, we are in God's hands." Trish choked on the last words. "There's no safer or better place to be. Thank you."

The crowd thundered again as she and her father hugged each other. They raised a replica of the Woodlawn Trophy for another photo, but the one that would make most newspapers was the one of father and daughter in each other's arms.

"And now—" McKay introduced the Chrysler representative, who in turn presented a set of keys to Trish.

"These are for that red Chrysler LeBaron convertible waiting right over there. How does it feel to own two cars?"

Trish took the mike again. "It feels great and I love it. But this one's for my brother, David." She grabbed his hand and stuffed the keys into it. "He earned it—the hard way."

"Trish, you can't—" David blurted.

"Oh, yes I can." Trish handed the mike back, and the crowd applauded again.

"I think she's got you, son," Hal said with a laugh. "You'll look good in it. Red seems to suit you both."

"Right. *Both* our kids in red convertibles," Marge moaned. "In Washington—where it rains all the time."

"Mo-ther." Trish and David echoed the lament of children everywhere.

Chapter
10

And now the most important question—" McKay paused for effect. "Will you be going on to Belmont?"

"God willing," Hal replied. "We'll give Spitfire a bit of a rest and leave on Wednesday."

"And there you have it, folks. Hal Evanston, owner of Spitfire, the winner of the first two legs of the Chrysler Triple Crown Challenge. Will this black colt be the first winner of the five-million-dollar bonus? We'll know in two weeks."

Hal, Trish, David, and Marge waved again then, escorted by Mel Howell and several security people, trekked across the track and up to the Sports Palace for more celebration.

Trish watched her father closely. Was it exhaustion that made him look weaker or was it her imagination? Maybe they should just leave so he could get some rest. She stood behind him with her hand on his shoulder when he finally sat down.

Marge stood at his side. "Don't worry, Tee," Marge whispered under cover of someone else's question.

"Don't worry?" Trish whispered back, a smile tugging at the corners of her mouth. *Worrying is what got you into so much trouble. Must be a family trait.* Her thoughts flashed back to her grandmother at the Derby. Now, there was a worrier if ever there was one. When Trish looked back at her mother, she saw a younger form of her grandmother.

"At least I'm more like Dad's side of the family," Trish said in an undertone.

Marge raised her eyebrows.

"They don't worry so much."

Marge shook her head and chuckled. "No, I don't think you inherited the worry gene. I'm glad."

Then why do you worry? her little nagger leaped into the act. *You know better. It never does any good. Your worrying can't make your dad any better. In fact, it probably makes him worse.*

"Thanks a bunch," Trish muttered.

"What's that?" Hal turned his head to look up at her. He patted her hand at the same time.

"Nothing . . . I . . ."

"Well, Trish." Adam Finley took her hand. "We sure are proud of you. Martha and I . . . well, we feel you're part of our family now."

"And we couldn't be more pleased if you were our own daughter," Martha said as she gave Trish a hug.

"Thank you. Maybe being part owners in Spitfire makes us all one family in a way."

"Family's better than business partners any day." Martha's blue eyes twinkled above a merry smile.

"You think you'll have any trouble deciding what to do with that five mil?" Adam teased Trish.

"We've gotta win it first, but it sure would buy a couple of good yearlings."

"Well, you certainly don't need to think about buying a car," Adam joked.

Trish laughed and glanced at her mother to catch her reaction. They hadn't really talked about the convertibles yet. Her mother and father had always said no car until after high school graduation. And now she had two—that is, she and David. What if she won a third?

Hal patted her hand again. "What do you say we take a break here and head on back to the stakes barn. David and Patrick could maybe use some help."

Things had quieted at the barns. Patrick greeted them, then finished talking with a reporter.

"How's it going?" Hal asked after sinking into a lawn chair. He tipped his head back and rotated his neck. When he opened his eyes again, Trish could tell it was an effort.

"The problem's back." Patrick sat down beside Hal. "Spitfire's foreleg is hot and swollen. We've got it iced, and tomorrow I'll start the ultrasound. He's had a nice feed. He earned it."

"How bad is it?"

"We'll know more in the morning."

"And the reporters?"

"They couldn't miss the ice pack."

Trish left them talking and slipped into the stall where David was refilling the ice pack that stretched from shoulder to hoof. "Want me to do that?"

"No, we're about done. How's Dad?"

"He looks so tired he scares me. But Mom says not to worry."

"Right." David rolled his eyes and shook his head.

The morning papers ran banner headlines: "Spitfire, Son of Seattle Slew!" The first line read, "Can he follow in his daddy's hoofprints?" Another article mentioned the recurring leg problem.

Trish read them all. The last winner of the Triple Crown was Affirmed in 1978, the year after Seattle Slew took it. There'd been only eleven winners in all the years of racing. Could Spitfire really do it? Could he win at a mile and a half, the length of the Belmont track? Trish's butterflies took a flying leap.

On the limo ride back to the track Sunday morning, a thought kept nagging at the back of Trish's mind. Maybe they should forget the Belmont and just ship home. In the long run it might be better for both her father and Spitfire. Both of them would get the rest they needed.

She resolved to bring it up when both Patrick and her father were together.

"How is he?" Trish asked as soon as she saw Patrick.

"Not good, lass." The usual twinkle was missing from his eyes. "But I'm not sure it's real bad either. From what your father says, the lad pulls out of this pretty fast. It's just that every incident may damage that muscle more." He stroked Spitfire's shoulder while he spoke. "I don't know what to recommend."

"Will shipping him make it worse?" Trish stroked Spitfire's nose that was already draped over her shoulder.

"Not to my thinkin'. As your dad says—"

"I know," Trish interrupted, "we'll take it one day at a time."

Patrick shrugged and nodded.

Dad looks so terrible. Trish's thoughts kept pace with the filly's slow gallop. As if she sensed a problem, Sarah's Pride settled into the pace and maintained it without her usual fits and shies. As she rode, Trish's thoughts continued. She should be on top of the world, and instead she felt as if she were under it—holding it up.

"We sure enjoyed watching you win yesterday," Hank Benson told her on the ride back to the hotel. "My Genny was screaming, jumping up and down. I thought she'd burst her buttons when you entered the winner's circle. Says she wants to be just like you someday."

"You should have brought her out to the barn afterward."

"We knew you'd be busy. All those reporters and important people. I know what it's like for the winner." He smiled over his shoulder.

"Would you like to bring Genny along when you come to take us back to the track later this afternoon? She could meet Spitfire, maybe have her picture taken with him."

"You sure about that?"

"Sure. I'd love to meet her too. I remember when I was twelve. I thought Bill Shoemaker was—well, movie stars have never been a big deal to me, but that man was."

"Yeah, he was the greatest. Shame about that accident. Just after he retired too."

"I know." The limo stopped in front of the hotel entrance. "Tell Genny I'm looking forward to meeting her."

Hal was asleep again.

"He ate a good breakfast, though," Marge said. "He wanted to wait for you kids but he was too hungry."

"That's a good sign." Trish flopped in a chair. "How is he otherwise?"

"Yesterday wore him out."

"Yesterday wore us all out," David added. "I think I could sleep all afternoon."

After they'd finished breakfast, that's just what they did. Trish was amazed when she opened one eye to check the clock. *Four!* She stretched and yawned. So much for studying. The limo was due back in half an hour.

"Your dad says you take riding lessons," Trish said to Genny after they'd been introduced. "Tell me about them."

Genny sat in the seat with her back to the driver. She had long dark hair, held back by a red headband, and she wore jeans and a red turtleneck. She leaned forward as she spoke, her hands on her knees. After telling about her classes, she asked, "How do I get to be a jockey like you?"

"You keep riding, and when you're older start asking if you can exercise horses for one of the farms. You may have to clean stalls to get in, but keep asking. One time they'll need someone, and if you're good, you're on your way. There's one thing though—do you like to get up early in the morning?"

Genny flinched a bit and wrinkled her nose. "Not really."

"Well, morning works start at four-thirty or five, you know."

When they arrived at the track, Patrick was measuring the horses' evening feed. Trish handed Genny a couple of pieces of carrot from the bag in the cooler.

Spitfire nickered as soon as he heard Trish's voice. He reached his nose out as far as he could to greet her, a soundless nicker fluttering his nostrils.

"You old silly." Trish rubbed his nose and smoothed his forelock. With one hand gripping his halter, Trish motioned Genny closer. "Spitfire, meet Genny." Spitfire reached out and sniffed Genny's arm and up her shoulder. He inspected her hair, then down to her palm, where he lipped his carrot and munched.

"I think he likes you," Trish said.

"He likes anyone who brings him carrots." David leaned on the handle of his pitchfork. With a quick motion, Spitfire sent David's crimson and gold baseball hat floating to the ground. "Spitfire, you—you!"

"You should have brought him a carrot," Genny said innocently, a gleam dancing in her eye.

"Thanks." David grinned at her as he bent over to pick up his hat. "Just be glad you're not wearing a hat."

"How about if your dad takes a picture of you and Spitfire?" Trish asked.

"And you?" Genny wondered.

Trish nodded. "If you like." Trish turned her back so Spitfire could drape his head over her shoulder. Genny stood on the other side of the horse. Hank took several shots, reminding them each time to smile.

Genny's grin dimmed the lights. "Thank you, Trish. And Spitfire." She fed him her last bit of carrot. "You're the neatest."

On the way back to the hotel, Genny asked Trish to sign her program from the day before. By the time they parted, Trish felt almost as if she had a little sister. "You write to me now," Trish said, "and keep up your lessons. Maybe we'll be riding in the same race someday. You never know."

Trish let out a sigh as she and David entered the hotel. Spitfire hadn't gotten any worse. Maybe they should go on after all.

"You did good." David tapped her on the shoulder.

His praise flew straight to her heart. "Thanks. I needed that."

Hal listened carefully that night when Trish suggested they might all be better off if they flew back to Portland rather than continue on to Belmont.

"What do you think, David?" Hal asked.

David paused, his forehead wrinkled in thought. "I'm not the one that's sick. We won't know about Spitfire's leg, but it could be fine in the next couple of days. It's you we're worried about."

That word again, Trish thought. *From now on the W word should be outlawed in our family.*

"Marge, what about you?"

"You're awfully close to your dream to quit now."

Trish stared at her mother. She could feel her mouth drop open—and stay that way.

"Patrick?" The trainer had joined them for dinner.

"I can't be walkin' in your shoes. Who but God can know the future?"

Hal leaned back in his chair, his fingers steepled under his chin. The light from the lamp slashed deep shadows in his face. Trish shuddered. He'd lost more weight, she was sure of it.

"One day at a time," he finally said. "We're in God's hands—one day at a time. We'll make the final decision on Tuesday night."

It rained all day Monday. Trish spent the time studying. David and Patrick kept doctoring Spitfire's leg. Hal slept. Marge stayed busy knitting a sweater.

Before she went to sleep that night, Trish finished reading *War and Peace.* Now she just had to write the report and the assignment list was finished. Her prayers remained the same. "Please make my dad better. And Spitfire too."

On Tuesday the rain continued. Hal polled them all that evening. After listening to everyone's comments, he announced, "We leave for Belmont at nine a.m."

Trish wasn't sure if she was happy or sad.

Both horses loaded without any trouble in the morning. Spitfire wasn't limping but the leg was still warm to the touch.

Trish felt that old familiar lump in her throat as she said good-bye to Mel Howell and their limo driver, Hank Benson. "You made me really feel good here," she said. "You sure you don't want to come along to

Belmont?" After shaking hands, she climbed up in the cab of the horse van. The driver wasn't friendly like Hank or Fred Robertson.

Trish turned in the seat to get a last glimpse of Pimlico as they pulled out of the long drive. A new rental car followed right behind them with David driving.

Trish settled back in the seat. Her father had said they'd be there in about five hours. She rolled her jacket up and propped it against the window. Any time was a good time to catch a few extra Z's.

Trish wasn't sure how long they'd been driving, but she'd awakened as they crossed the river and entered the New Jersey Turnpike. Paying to drive on a freeway was a whole new concept to her. So far they'd stopped several times to pay the toll.

Up ahead construction warning signs flashed. A lighted sign overhead posted the speed limit and how far the slow-down would last. She settled back against her jacket.

Then the screech of brakes jerked her fully awake. Lights from the car ahead fishtailed in front of them. The van driver hit his brakes and in the same motion swerved to the left to avoid an accident.

Another car crashed into the rear of the truck. The screeching and rending of metal pierced the air. Trish felt her body slam against the seat belt, and her head hit the side window.

Was it David who crashed into us?

Then she heard Spitfire scream, and everything went silent.

Chapter
11

The blow to Trish's head left her dizzy. All she could think of was Spitfire. Was he hurt? Or just frightened?

Trish unsnapped her seat belt as soon as the truck came to a halt, and with a groan she pushed the door open and dropped to the ground. Her shoulder had apparently hit the side window too.

"Easy, fella," she called. *How do I get the van door open?* Everything was tipped at a crazy angle. She could hear the horses shifting and sliding around. Then she thought of the driver and dashed around the front of the truck and pulled the driver's door open. He was slumped against the steering wheel, but at least he was breathing, and moving slightly. "You okay?" she whispered, not seeing any blood.

"I think so," he managed. "Check on the horses."

Spitfire! I've got to get to him. Trish ran to the back of the van. It was then that she saw the smoking car with the front end pushed in. At least it wasn't their rental car.

By this time Trish could hear car doors slamming. Someone was moaning—or crying. She could also hear the horses snorting, their hooves thudding as they scrambled to find footing on the slanted floor. Trish clambered up the side of the van, bracing her feet in the slot that held the ramp. She reached the door handles but gravity sucked the doors shut. No matter how she strained, she couldn't open them.

Then Spitfire screamed again.

Trish wiped moisture from her right eye. When she glanced down she saw blood on her hand. She tried to keep her voice firm but fear made it wobble. She sucked in a deep breath. *Where are David and Patrick? Are they hurt too? God, please help us!* "Easy, fella, take it easy now," she spoke through the doors, but her voice broke on a sob. "Come on, Spitfire, just stand still until I can help you."

What were only minutes passing seemed like hours to Trish. She tugged again on the door handles. For once in her life, she wished she were taller.

"It's okay, Tee." David pulled himself up beside her. "We'll get it open." He grasped the handles firmly. "Now when I lift, you grab the edge. Together, we can do it." David worked from the ramp slot and Trish dropped to the ground. When he cracked the door, she threw her weight into the effort and pushed it upright. David shifted position and the door fell open.

Trish scrambled into the van. At the sight of her, Spitfire whinnied and Sarah's Pride slipped, thudding her knee against the wall of her stall.

"Easy now, you two," Trish crooned. Her voice choked when she saw blood flowing down Spitfire's cheek from a gash above his eye. Wild-eyed, he snorted and lunged against the tie ropes. The acrid smell of smoke drifted in from the smoldering car, and Trish sneezed as she fumbled for the ties.

"Here, let me help you." David jerked one lead free. "Let's turn them both so they face up the slant. Then they should be able to stand without slipping around."

Together they backed Spitfire out of the padded stall and faced him toward the door.

"Where's Patrick?" Trish asked as she stroked Spitfire's neck and face. The colt shuddered under her soothing hands.

"With Dad and Mom. The driver of the car that rear-ended you is hurt pretty badly. Hold on to Spitfire and I'll go tell Mom and Dad you're okay. Then I'll come back for the filly."

In what seemed like seconds, David was back in the van. "Okay, girl, let's get you moved out too." He eased Sarah's Pride back and let her gain her footing.

By the time both horses were calmed down, Trish could hear sirens approaching.

"How's your driver?" David nodded toward the front of the van.

"Pretty groggy, but I didn't see any blood. He said he thought he was okay." Trish wiped her face again. This time she flinched.

"You better leave that alone," David said. "Looks like it's quit bleeding."

"How's Dad?"

"I'm not sure. We told him to stay in the car, but you know Dad. Once I pulled the driver from the crashed car, Mom took over, and I came to help you."

"Where's all the smoke coming from?"

"The car behind us. I thought it was going to blow up. We used a fire extinguisher he had in the trunk."

Trish shuddered. "David, how bad was this accident, anyway?"

"I'm not sure," David answered. "Three or four cars were involved, at least."

Spitfire leaned his head against Trish's chest, smearing blood on her shirt. Trish rubbed his ears. *Where else is he hurt? How about his leg?* The questions raced through Trish's mind like a rabbit evading a hungry wolf.

A state patrolman appeared at the door. "You kids okay in there? How about the horses?"

"You'd better check on the van driver. Anything here can wait," Trish answered.

"This could have been really bad, Tee." David rubbed the filly's ears and neck.

"Our guardian angels were working overtime again?"

"For sure."

More sirens could be heard in the distance. Spitfire shifted uneasily, but Trish was able to calm him again.

"It's like we're in no-man's-land. Why doesn't someone come and tell us what's happening?" Trish blinked against the pain that thudded by her right eye. She was beginning to feel panicky. "How is Dad?"

Just then Patrick stuck his head in the door and swung himself up into the van. "The ambulance finally got here." He looked at Trish. "You'd better let the medics have a look at you too." He patted both horses. "Looks like Spitfire got clipped good," he murmured, inspecting the gash. "Anything else?" He turned to Trish again.

"I don't know. We haven't checked under the sheets."

Patrick looked at Spitfire's legs first, then the filly's. "Okay so far." He rolled back the crimson sheet. The colt flinched when Patrick touched his right shoulder. He carefully probed the area. "Pretty bad bruise. Maybe a pulled muscle. Has he been favoring this leg?"

"Not really, at least I don't think so." Trish tried to think about when they moved the horses. "No, he was moving pretty freely."

Patrick checked over the rest of the colt's body, then started on the filly. "Her knees are a bit skinned. That's all I can find now. It's a miracle, that's what I say."

"How's my dad?" Trish finally asked.

"Last I saw, he was directing traffic. He's the one who found someone with a car phone and called for help. Between your mother and David— well, the man behind you will be thankin' them for his life."

"What was the matter with him? Why'd he follow so close? You'd think he'd know better. Signs had been flashing for—"

"Now, lass," Patrick soothed, "let's just be thankful it wasn't any worse."

"I knew we should have gone home. Spitfire probably won't even be able to run, and Dad sure didn't need all this."

"Knock it off, Tee," David ordered. "Let's just get through this, and then we'll have time to sort it all out."

"Time? We *never* have enough time for anything."

David ignored her.

Trish leaned against a stall post. Suddenly she was too tired to think or move.

An emergency medical technician from an ambulance spoke to them at the van doors. "I hear we have a head wound in here." When he saw Trish, he smiled. "I guess you're it. How about letting those two guys handle the horses, and you come out here where we can check you over?"

Trish handed the lead to Patrick. She stroked Spitfire's nose. "Now, you behave, you hear?" she spoke firmly to him. She almost jumped down, until her pounding head made her think better of it. She sat carefully on the loading edge of the van and let the EMT help her to the ground.

"Anything hurt besides your head?" the young man asked as he flashed a light in each of her eyes to check for dilation of the pupils.

"My shoulder's sore, but that's all. And I've had a concussion before, so I know what one feels like. This isn't it." Trish felt limp and drained— like a balloon with the helium gone out.

"You can sit down." He unfolded a collapsible stool. "This is going to sting some, but we need to clean the wound. It isn't deep; head wounds tend to bleed a lot." He opened gauze packs and antiseptic as he spoke.

A woman in uniform came up and slapped a blood pressure cuff on Trish's arm. "Mmmm—you're gonna have a shiner there. Just missed your eye. What'd you hit, anyway?"

"The latch on the wind-wing window, I think."

"I take it you were wearing your seat belt."

Trish nodded.

"Blood pressure's fine. How'd you get so much blood on your shirt? You couldn't have lost that much."

Trish winced when she shook her head. "No, my horse got a gash above his eye too. If he wasn't so black, he'd have a shiner tomorrow like mine."

"Aren't you Tricia Evanston?" A man with a camcorder on his shoulder flashed a press pass. "And your horse, Spitfire—is he injured?"

"We're both okay. You can check with Patrick inside the box." Trish winced again at the sting of the antiseptic.

"Close your eye," the EMT ordered.

Trish followed his instructions. It felt good to be taken care of.

"There, I've butterflied the wound together. You may want to have stitches, but it isn't an area that takes a lot of stress. Some doctors don't like to put in facial stitches unless it's absolutely necessary." He finished taping a gauze pad in place, then took an ice pack out of his bag and smacked it to start the chemical reaction. "Here, you better ice it."

Trish put the ice pack to her face. She could feel it turning cold as the chemicals worked together. "You have one of these for Spitfire too?"

The young man laughed and smacked another pack. "Sure. Any horse that's this close to the Triple Crown deserves an ice pack if he needs it." He handed it up to Patrick.

Trish looked up to see her parents coming toward the van. "Hi! Are you guys all right?" Smiling hurt the side of her face. "Ouch!"

The EMT handed Trish a glass of water and two white tablets. "Here, these will help the pain."

Trish swallowed the tablets and stood to receive her mother's embrace. "Some trip, huh?"

"Are you all right, Trish?" Marge asked.

"I'll be fine, Mom. It's just a scratch."

Hal came to Trish's other side. "Thank God it wasn't any worse. Looks like you could have a shiner, though, Tee."

"That's what they say."

"Take it easy for the next day or two," the EMT told Trish as he folded his kit away and started to leave. "And I hope you win the Belmont."

"Thank you!"

"And thank you for taking care of her," Marge added. "All of you have been wonderful."

"You take some credit too, ma'am. You and your son did just the right thing. If that car had blown—" He left, shaking his head.

As the last ambulance drove away, tow trucks arrived, and Trish climbed back up into the van to hold Spitfire while the horse van was pulled back onto the highway. It wasn't long before another driver arrived to replace the one who'd been taken to the hospital.

Trish, David, and Patrick settled the horses again.

"We'll stop for lunch at the next rest stop," Hal said before climbing back into the car. "I think we all need a break. Trish, do you want to ride in the car and let Patrick take your place?"

"No, Dad. I don't want to leave Spitfire. We'll be fine." Trish climbed back into the truck cab. She looked down at the front of her shirt. "Looks like we've been through a war or something."

The new driver, named Sam, agreed with her. He was an older man with a ready smile.

They didn't take a long lunch break, but it was still rush hour as they neared New York City. Trish tried to catch a glimpse of the Statue of Liberty as they crossed the Verrazano Bridge, but it was too hazy. Sam pointed out sights as they drove up the Shore Parkway. Trish saw the signs to Coney Island, then the tops of the amusement rides off to the right. They passed JFK airport, where more construction slowed the already bumper-to-bumper crawl.

After they exited the Cross Island Parkway, it seemed to Trish as if they passed Belmont Park signs for miles of almost country-like road before they turned in at gate 6. Sam stopped at the guard gate and flashed his pass.

The uniformed guard consulted his clipboard. "Go on down Gallant Fox Road and turn left on Secretariat Avenue. Runnin' On Farm will be sharing barn 12 with BlueMist Farms. We expected you long before now."

"There was an accident on the New Jersey turnpike," Sam told the man. "It took me some time to get there to replace our other driver."

"Everything okay?" The guard peered into the truck.

Trish felt like sliding to the floor. She knew how bad she must look.

News traveled faster than the speed of the van, because a crowd gathered around the west end of barn 12. Trish waited until David opened her door.

"I don't want any more pictures," she whispered as she slipped to the ground. "Stay with me, okay?"

David nodded, but Trish could tell by the look on his face that he thought she was just being a typical girl. Flashbulbs popped when she and Spitfire appeared at the head of the ramp. The colt was limping noticeably.

Chapter 12

"How bad do you think it is?" Trish asked as Patrick probed the colt's shoulder and examined the muscles down his right leg. "Wouldn't you know it, the same leg got it again."

"Better'n two lame legs, though." Patrick ducked under Spitfire's neck and checked the other side. "Let's get 'em settled in and the ice packs in place. I'll start the ultrasound in the morning."

Trish measured grain and carried the buckets to each of the stalls. Her right shoulder ached with the strain, and her head pounded. She felt like hiding somewhere and letting the tears roll. *Like that would do any good,* she thought.

David had taken their parents to the Floral Park Hotel, where Hal had made reservations. That left Trish to walk the filly to loosen her up. Once around the sandy aisle of the long green barn was enough.

When she got back, one of the grooms from BlueMist Farms was helping Patrick with Spitfire's ice packs. Two others had moved the Runnin' On Farm equipment into an empty stall.

Trish breathed a sigh of relief. Her father had been right. They really did need more help. Sarah's Pride stuck her nose in the feed bucket and switched her tail. She already seemed to feel at home.

Trish leaned against the wall in Spitfire's stall while he ate. She was too tired to volunteer for the moving process. Spitfire lifted his nose and blew the smell of sweet feed in Trish's face, along with several flakes of grain. "Thanks. You're a big help, pal." She wiped her face with one hand and flinched when she touched the bandage over her eye.

"That place is just too far from the track," David grumbled when he walked back into the barn. "It felt like we drove on forever."

"There aren't many decent hotels around here anymore," Patrick said. "This area has really gone downhill the last few years. Most of the hotels are out by the airport."

"Were you able to get a place on the grounds?" David asked Patrick.

He nodded, checking the ice pack again without looking up. "That I did. Now, why don't you two take dinner back to the hotel and get some extra shut-eye. The lad here won't be workin' in the morning, so you can take your time about showing up. We have to be off the track by nine-thirty."

Trish checked Spitfire's eye again. Now that it had been cleaned up, she could tell it was just a surface wound.

"I'll put some antiseptic on that when he's finished eating," Patrick said. "Be on your way now."

Holding her head up was too much effort, so Trish let it fall against the headrest on the back of the car seat. They stopped for tacos at a fast-food place. While the food smelled good, Trish hardly felt like eating anything.

At the hotel, they found Hal sound asleep. Trish ate half a taco and shoved the rest away. "Mom, can you fix me an ice pack? I'm going to bed." She only woke enough to mumble "thanks" when Marge came into the room and removed the pack an hour later.

In the morning Trish gasped at the freak that stared back at her in the mirror. Her right temple and upper cheek had swelled and turned a reddish purple. The puffiness nearly closed her eye.

Her shoulder felt better after a hot shower pounded the stiffness out.

She rotated it. "Ouch!" *Guess I won't do that again. Maybe I'll let David ride the filly this morning.* She looked longingly back at her bed.

David thumped on the door. "Come on, there's work to do. And I'm hungry."

At the thought of food, Trish's stomach rumbled. "I'm coming." She grabbed a windbreaker and checked the mirror one more time. "Yuck!" She stuck her tongue out at the reflection and dashed out the door.

"How is he?" she asked Patrick as soon as she walked into the barn.

Patrick raised an eyebrow. "I'm a-thinkin' he's looking a sight better'n you, if you don't mind me sayin' so."

"Thank you, that's just what I needed this morning." Spitfire nickered his welcome. "How ya doing, fella?" Trish stroked his cheek. With the brown canvas pack on his leg and the swelling above his eye, Spitfire didn't look like a stakes-race contender. Especially not the mile-and-a-half Belmont. They only had ten days to go.

"Well, see you later," Trish said, tickling the whiskery spot on her horse's upper lip. "I gotta take care of the girl here."

Sarah's Pride seemed content to walk today. They followed other horses down the narrow, tree-lined street to the entrance to the track. Some farms had hanging flower baskets decorating the overhangs of the white-trimmed barns. The grass along the curbs was neat and lush.

It was all Trish could do to keep her mouth shut. The place was incredible. And she'd thought Churchill Downs was big. "What do you think that noise is?" she asked David as he plodded beside them.

"You got me. Sounds like high-powered sprinklers of some kind, but I don't see any."

"Could it be crickets?"

David shook his head. "They don't make *that* much noise."

Trish stopped the filly beside a traffic guard at the crossroads. "What's all that noise we hear?" she asked.

The guard looked surprised, then a grin split his face. "Ah, them's cicadas."

At the look of bafflement on Trish's face, he explained. "They's a large insect in the elm trees. You hear 'em in the spring and summer when the weather turns hot."

"How do you spell what you called them?"

He wrinkled his brow. "C—sounds like an S; then I, then C—sounds like a K; then A-D-A. Accent in the middle, on the C-A. Where you from?"

"Washington."

"D.C.?"

"No, State."

"Ah-h-h, then you must be Tricia Evanston. Hear you had an accident yesterday. That colt of yours gonna make it?"

"Time'll tell," David answered for Trish.

"Well, good luck to you." The guard tipped his hat. "And welcome to Belmont."

"Thanks!"

Trish left David and guided Sarah's Pride through the gates. The mile-and-a-half track seemed twice as big as any Trish had known. Portland Meadows, backside and all, would have fit nicely on the infield. The grass and shrubs were neatly trimmed, and a couple of ponds glinted in the sunlight out beyond the tote boards.

And the grandstand. "Wow! Can you believe all this?" Trish said to no one. The filly shook her head. The wide concrete pad in front of the cantilevered stands reminded Trish of Santa Anita. She could see three levels of seats with only the top one glassed in. Flower boxes with trailing plants graced the front of the second level all the way down to the open seats.

The lighted tote board read WELCOME TO BELMONT PARK.

Trish clucked the filly into a trot at the far turn. A breeze carried a woodsy smell from the trees that lined the track. As the filly trotted up the far side, Trish caught a glimpse of houses through the trees. Otherwise, it felt as if they were out in the country. Two other tracks lay off to the left as they rounded the final turn, then more barns came into view.

"Can you believe it?" Trish asked David when he met her at the exit gate. "This place is huge."

"You haven't seen half of it," David said, walking beside them. "It's like a town all its own. Only instead of houses, the streets are lined with barns."

Back at the hotel, Hal didn't feel up to doing the necessary paper work yet, so Trish hit her schoolbooks. Marge had brought her more homework assignments, including a Shakespearean play and two more history papers to write. Because Trish wouldn't be in class, her teacher thought written papers would make up for the lectures.

"How're you doing?" Marge tapped on Trish's door later in the afternoon.

Trish groaned. "Come on in, Mom. I can't begin to keep all these characters straight." She slapped her hand on the cover of *King Lear.* "Why couldn't we at least have had one of the comedies for a change?"

"I remember reading one of the historical plays," Marge said. "We had a slumber party and everyone read the different parts. Even Henry IV can be pretty hilarious at three in the morning." Marge sank down in the chair across from Trish at a small table.

"Then what did you do?"

"Well, it was the night before the final, so we all trooped off to class and wrote like mad. Then I came home and crashed."

"Did you pass?"

Marge raised one eyebrow. "I got an A. That's the best way to study Shakespeare." She ran her fingers through her hair. "If I can find a *King Lear* at the bookstore, I'll help you if you'd like."

"If we can find a bookstore."

"That too. You want a Diet Coke or something?"

Trish chewed on the end of her pencil. "Sure. How's Dad?"

"Sleeping." Marge rose to her feet. "I'll be right back. You want anything else?"

"Another ice pack?" Trish pushed gingerly at the bandage over her puffy eye. "Maybe I should wear a mask or something."

Marge shook her head and left quietly. She returned a short time later with soda and ice pack in hand. "Why don't you lie down with this for a while, Trish." She applied a damp washcloth first, and then the ice pack. "Thank God it missed your eye."

"I know." Trish closed her eyes and let the cold seep in. It felt so good.

The next day, after morning works, Hal appeared at the barn. "Let's go get the paper work done, David. We can drive over there. We'll pay the fees and then scratch later if we have to. Patrick, how does he look?"

"I've been using the ultrasound and ice. Think we'll walk him a little this afternoon to limber him up some; see how badly he limps."

"I know you're doing everything you can. What do you think about that maiden race for fillies and mares on Wednesday for Sarah's Pride? Do you think she's ready for that caliber of field?"

Patrick thought a moment. "Either that or another claimer. She needs a race pretty soon. Uh-huh, that'd be a good one for her."

"Well, let's get over there," Hal said. "You ready to come now too?" he spoke to Patrick.

As Trish started to climb into the car, Shipson's trainer, Wayne Connery, stopped her. "We have a filly running this afternoon. Would you like the mount? Are you licensed yet?"

"On my way right now, and I'd love to ride her. What race?"

"Fourth. That okay?"

"Great. See you then." Trish plunked herself back against the seat. "All right!"

Hal turned to look over his shoulder. "Are you going to be able to wear goggles over that cheek?"

Trish fingered the bandage. "I think so. It won't be the worst thing I've raced with. Glad I've been around the track a couple of times."

Patrick consulted his racing form. "That race is six furlongs. You'll start halfway up the backstretch. One long, easy turn."

"Cinch."

And it was. Trish took the filly into the lead from the first and won going away. She accepted congratulations from the Shipsons and leaped to the ground. The winner's circle at Belmont sparkled like a movie set. Potted plants bloomed everywhere, and there were brick risers that made it easy to get a crowd in the picture. There was even an awning over the scale.

"I could get to like this," Trish told David that evening.

Saturday morning Hal suggested they all ride the train into New York City and take a bus tour of Manhattan.

"You sure you feel up to it?" Trish questioned.

"We'll take it easy. Who knows when we'll get back to this side of the country."

Trish looked at her mother, who had the same question in her eyes. Marge nodded.

By the end of the day Trish thought her jaw must be double-hinged, it dropped open so many times. Grand Central Station arched high above them till the ceiling seemed to disappear in the dimness. People rushed every which way to trains, and there were shops along the corridors.

The Grayline bus tour lasted five short hours and took them down Fifth Avenue from Harlem to Battery Park, where they could see the Statue of Liberty in the harbor. They passed Central Park, museums, luxury hotels, and numberless skyscrapers of every description.

"I've never seen so many tall buildings," Trish said in awe.

"That's because nowhere else *has* this many high-rises." The tour guide grinned at her. "Only Manhattan Island was formed from a bedrock base strong enough for all the buildings." From upper to midtown to lower Manhattan the sights continued. Fifth Avenue, Broadway, Rockefeller Center, the famous names rolled off the guide's tongue.

"That's where the glittering ball falls on New Year's Eve." The guide pointed to a building on Times Square. "You've seen it on TV, I'm sure."

Trish nodded as she craned her neck to see Madison Square Garden. "That's the entrance?" She couldn't believe her eyes. All the things she'd heard of happening there, and the front of it looked like a second-rate theater marquee.

At the end of the tour, Trish sighed. "There's just too much to see here. We need to come back again."

"We could go to the theater," Marge said wistfully.

"Or shopping!" Trish enthused. "Wouldn't Rhonda love to go shopping here?"

David shook his head. "Not me. Where are we going for dinner? I'm starved."

"You're always hungry." Marge poked him in the arm. "Let's get some bagels and cream cheese for breakfast."

"Breakfast? You mean we're skipping dinner?"

"Of course not," Hal reassured him. "How about pizza? They say New York pizza is like no other."

Trish flagged a cab down, and after a short ride they found a pizza place.

"That *was* good," David remarked after everyone had stuffed themselves.

Trish smiled at the grin on her brother's face. Only food could bring that look. But all the way back on the train she thought about the pills she'd seen her father take throughout the day. Since when did he take so many pills, and what were they all for?

Chapter
13

On the train returning to Belmont, Hal dozed. He had also napped when the tour bus stopped at St. John's Cathedral, and again when they toured Chinatown. Trish was glad he had made it through the day. Now he looked as if he had stretched his limit.

The next morning, when Trish and David returned to the hotel after morning works, Hal was up and dressed.

"Dad?" Trish gathered courage to broach the subject that was bothering her.

Hal looked up from the newspaper he was reading. "What is it, Tee? You sound awfully serious."

"What are all those pills you've been taking?"

Hal laid the paper in his lap. "Mostly pain pills."

Trish felt her heart clench in her chest. "Is it that bad?"

"If I don't take the pills it is. The doctors told me to be sure to stay on top of it. The body has to fight harder to heal itself when the pain is too severe."

Trish sank down on the floor beside her father's chair. "Is that why you sleep so much? The pills make you sleepy?"

"Somewhat. But fighting cancer, or any illness for that matter, takes a lot of energy."

"Why didn't you tell me?" She leaned her head on his knees.

"Oh, Tee. You've had so much on your mind lately. The racing, Spitfire's injury, then the accident. I didn't want you to worry about me."

Marge sat down on the arm of the chair. "That's my job. You both know how good I am at worrying. Besides, taking care of your father gives me something to do."

Trish smiled. "Isn't there anything I can do?"

Hal smoothed Trish's hair, and his love for her warmed her spirit. "Keep praying, Tee. Enjoy the moments we can spend together. We're all doing what we can. The rest is in God's hands."

Trish nodded, but secretly she thought, *Seems to me God isn't doing too well right now.*

Her nagger cut in, *You haven't been praying for your dad very much.*

Trish had a hard time ignoring that accusation. It was true. She hadn't been praying consistently, and she hadn't been reviewing her verses either. Would she *ever* learn?

"What else haven't you told me?" Trish asked her dad.

Hal was silent until Trish looked up at him. Had he fallen asleep?

"Nothing that I can think of. You know I've always tried to be honest with you kids."

Trish nodded. She knew he had.

"All I know, Tee, is that Jesus promised to never leave us alone. No matter what happens." He lifted her chin with one finger. "Do you believe that?"

Trish nodded. She couldn't speak.

"Then we just take one day at a time."

"Speaking of time—" Marge looked at her watch. "We need to get David to the airport. You coming along, Trish?"

"No, I better hit the books again. There won't be much time this next week."

David set his suitcase on a chair. "See you Tuesday, Tee."

"Yeah. Tell Rhonda hi for me. And Brad. You've got his present?"

David nodded. "In the suitcase. Anything else?"

"No. Just have fun for me."

After her family had left, Trish stared for a long time at her history book without seeing the print. Vancouver seemed so far away. It was hard to believe that she'd really go back to school after the Belmont, like nothing had ever happened. She propped her chin on her knee. Her life had changed in the last few months. Would it ever be the same again? Did she want to go back to her old life?

That night Trish made sure she spent time praying—not just the quickies she'd been saying. She thanked God for taking care of all of them, for guarding them during the accident, for helping them win the two races. When she begged Him to make her dad better again, the tears slipped down her cheeks. "I *need* my dad," she whispered.

Just before she fell asleep, a new thought came to her mind. Even though she was unhappy with God, it wasn't like last year. She couldn't shut Him out. God seemed more real right now.

God was in her first thoughts in the morning too. Trish shook her head. Could she call God sneaky? It seemed to fit. The thought stayed with her all the way to the track.

"Breeze her three furlongs," Patrick said as he tossed Trish into the saddle on Monday morning. "Don't let her drift out on you and be sure you pull her down right away."

"She doesn't seem to mind the blinders." Trish stroked the filly's fiery red neck and smoothed her mane.

"Let's see what happens if another horse runs with you," Patrick said. "If all goes okay, we'll work her out of the starting gate after that."

Sarah's Pride seemed to know something was up. She jigged sideways until Patrick demanded she behave. Once on the track, she played crab, trotting sideways again. Trish straightened her out once, then again. The third time she pulled the filly to a stop.

"Now you're gonna stand here until you can behave." Trish refused to let up until the filly stood still for an entire minute. Sarah's Pride got the hint. Trish wasn't putting up with any more shenanigans.

When Trish turned the filly at the far turn, she nudged her into a jog. With the release of the reins at the mile-and-a-quarter post, the filly leaped forward. She ran straight and true, ignoring the other horses on the track.

"Thatta girl," Trish chanted as she pulled the horse back to a canter after they'd flashed past Patrick and his stopwatch. Trish didn't need the grin on Patrick's face to tell her they'd done well.

The filly snorted and fidgeted in the starting gate. When the gate swung open she reared instead of starting clean. But by the fourth break she settled down. Her twitching ears seemed to focus on Trish's commands and the break was clean and fast.

"Good girl. That's the way," Trish praised her mount.

"I'm thinkin' one more day at this'll do it." Patrick held the reins and removed the hood. "There now. See you back at the barn."

When she was finished with Sarah's Pride, Trish led Spitfire clear around the barn and then out to a rail-fenced grassy area by their barn to graze. He walked the distance, head up, eyes bright, without a limp.

"Enjoy." Trish loosened the lead so Spitfire could put his head down and graze. The sun sparkled on his blue-black hide. The cicadas chorused in the trees while Spitfire munched grass. Somewhere, someone had been mowing grass; the sweet perfume of it floated on the slight breeze. Trish breathed it in. She enjoyed the sights, sounds, and smells of Belmont in early summer. Five days to go.

Studying for the rest of the day did not come near the top of Trish's wish list—but she did it anyway. Finals were scheduled for the week after they got home. She didn't need her mother to remind her of that.

Tuesday morning Patrick saddled Spitfire. "Just walk him down past the stands and back. The mile and a half is too far right now."

Spitfire walked carefully, a bit stiff-legged. But he didn't limp. As soon as they returned to the barn, Patrick applied the ice pack again.

That afternoon Trish and Patrick schooled Sarah's Pride. They followed the line of horses down through the underpass and up to the saddling paddock.

Shade and sunlight dappled the white-roofed, open-air stalls. Huge elm and oak trees created a park around the circular walking lane where spectators stood on brick risers to watch the pre-post parade. White metal fences with cutouts of running horses edged the tiers.

A cast-iron statue of Secretariat in full speed graced the center, surrounded by red geraniums. A white wrought-iron chair gave visitors to the legend of racing a place to rest. Beyond rose the three-story arched windows of the clubhouse.

Trish was having a falling-jaw attack again. The place was incredible. She could tell Belmont Park cost money—lots of money. Racing in New York was *big* business.

She chuckled to herself. It all compared to Portland Meadows like the sun to the moon. Sarah's Pride nudged her in the back as if to say, "Quit gawking and start walking."

That evening David returned from his trip to Vancouver. Trish studied again while her parents went to the airport. When David walked into the suite, he was carrying a thin package under his arm.

"How was the graduation? Did Brad get his second scholarship? Did you see Rhonda? How's Miss Tee?" Trish bubbled over with questions. "For me?" she asked as David handed her the package.

"Open it. Then I'll answer all your questions."

Trish carefully untied the curled crimson and gold ribbon, then removed the brown wrapping paper. Two pieces of posterboard were taped together to make a huge card. It depicted an old, broken-down black nag stumbling across the page. A square bandage covered one haunch; the lower lip hung nearly to the sprung knees. A woman jockey sat on the swayback, her legs clapped to the bony ribs.

Trish giggled. "Did Rhonda draw this?" The caption read "On to Belmont." Inside the card, the horse had shaped up considerably. It held a rose in its teeth and the jockey waved a trophy. The inside words read, "Trish did it her way. Congratulations!" The signatures of Prairie students covered every inch of the inside and back of the card. Trish turned it over and back again, sniffling as she read. The teachers had signed it too. In the right lower corner, Rhonda had drawn a red heart and signed her name across it.

Trish handed the card to her mother while she went to get a tissue.

"Can you believe it?" she said, sinking into a chair, her legs dangling over the arm. "Wow." She blew her nose again.

Hal and Marge chuckled as they looked at the card, then handed it back to Trish. "You'll need a couple of hours just to read all the messages," Marge said. "They must have worked on it for days."

"I wish Brad and Rhonda were here. Remember when they showed up for our first race? They were whooping and hollering; I was afraid the security guards were going to throw them out. Then I was afraid they wouldn't." She shook her head. "Guess I don't embarrass so easily anymore." She looked at the inside of the card again. Brad had signed his name on the end of the horse's nose.

"So how was everything?" Trish asked again.

David told her everything he could remember, and then Trish prompted him with more questions. "Seems like we've been away from home forever," he finally said. "Miss Tee and Double Diamond have both grown some. Poor old Caesar thinks we've all deserted him. He wouldn't let me out of his sight." David stretched both arms above his head. "I'm beat. Talk about a fast trip." He turned to Trish. "How's Spitfire doing?"

"I walked him today."

"Do you think you'll race him?" David looked to his father.

"Who knows." Hal leaned back in his chair. "He favors the leg, even though he walked without limping. Patrick is doing all he can, packs and ultrasound. We'll keep going like we're in the running, and decide on Friday."

Trish huddled in her chair. Friday. Three days away. Was there any chance they could do it?

On Wednesday morning Trish walked Spitfire again. She trotted the filly to loosen her up. Sarah's Pride would have her chance in the afternoon.

In the jockey room, Trish studied while waiting for the race. *I must be getting better disciplined,* Trish thought. *I can study anywhere.* She glared at the new list of assignments David had brought her. She'd *better* be able to study anywhere with all she had to do. She tapped her pencil thoughtfully. Her mother had only mentioned studying. Maybe she'd given up nagging.

Or maybe you're doing much better on your own, and she thinks so too, Trish's little voice reminded her.

Or she's so worried about your dad, she doesn't have time to think about your studies. Her nagger had to get in his two cents' worth.

Trish glanced up at the monitor. They were running the third race. She finished dressing, ready to walk out the door when the call came to weigh in.

Hal, Patrick, and David waited for her in the paddock. Sarah's Pride pranced her way right into the hearts of the spectators.

"That's Tricia Evanston!" someone exclaimed.

"Hey, Trish, how about an autograph?" A man held out his program and a pen.

Trish signed her name with a flourish. Two other programs appeared in front of her.

"Sure hope Spitfire will be ready to run." One woman shook her head. "Shame to come so far and have to scratch."

"Yes, ma'am," Trish agreed. "We need all the prayers we can get."

A tiny little lady with snow-white hair reached out and patted Trish's arm. "I've been praying for him, and your father too. God hears us."

Trish covered the woman's hand with her own. "Thank you very much."

At the call for riders up, Trish joined the men walking the flame-red filly around the paddock. She shook her head, amazed at the intricate ways God used to get through to her.

Patrick gave her a leg up. "Now, lass, keep in mind that ye carry that whip for a reason. Use it if you have to. This girl needs a win bad. And it wouldn't be a-hurtin' you either."

Trish fingered the whip. She hated to use it. But she nodded down at Patrick. "You know best."

Hal nodded. "He does."

Sarah's Pride put on a real show on the parade to post. She danced and snorted. As they cantered back past the grandstand, she kept trying to race her pony rider. But when the gate swung open and the race began, she was content to run with the field. Two horses broke away and lengthened their lead.

Trish held the filly steady around the turn, keeping her from drifting to the outside. Down the stretch she hollered in the filly's ear and shifted her weight—anything to get the horse running harder. Finally she went to the whip.

Sarah's Pride leaped forward at the crack and drove between the two front-runners. Trish smacked her again. Neck and neck, the three pounded for the wire. One more thwack and the filly surged forward, one long line from nose to streaming tail.

"Photo finish!" the announcer and tote board declared at once.

Trish cantered on partway around the track, then turned and trotted back to the winner's circle. The three contenders walked around in circles while the rest of the field were stripped of their tack and led off to the barns.

"And that's number five, Sarah's Pride. Owned by Hal Evanston and ridden by Tricia Evanston. Ladies and gentlemen, that was the closest race I've ever called. Place goes to number three, with number one a show. The three were only separated by whiskers."

As the announcer spoke, Trish turned the filly to face the grandstand for the applause. "That's for you, girl. See how good it feels?" The filly stood, head up, accepting her due. "That's what this is all about, you know—winning." The filly nodded.

Patrick took the reins and led them into the winner's circle. The aisle led past red and white baskets of flowers, and the circle was decorated with potted trees and plants, also with blooms of red and white.

"You think she got the idea?" Hal asked as they posed for pictures.

"We'll know for sure next race, but I think so." Trish leaped to the ground and stripped off her saddle so she could weigh in.

"You and Patrick did a fine job with her," Hal said to Trish after David had led the filly off to the detention barn for testing.

"Thanks, but it took a special eye to choose her. You know how to pick 'em, Dad." She tucked her helmet under her arm and rubbed carefully at the edge of her injured eye. The bruise had faded to an ugly green and yellow. "You know what's neat? That purse paid for her."

Hal pulled both Trish and her mother close. "How about some lunch up in the clubhouse?"

Trish looked down at her dirty silks. "Like this?"

Hal stepped back to take a look. "Okay, you get five minutes to change. We'll go get a table. And tonight we'll go see the Empire State Building—after dark."

Trish trotted off happily. Why couldn't things just stay like this?

Chapter
14

Spectacular was too small a word to describe the view. Trish leaned on the metal railing around the top floor of the Empire State Building, looking toward upper Manhattan. Central Park lay like an oblong black hole between the lighted streets and tall buildings. Skyscrapers glittered against the night sky. A man next to them knew the city, and Trish listened as he pointed out the various buildings to his companion.

Walking around the observation deck, the Evanstons looked toward the downtown financial district. The twin World Trade towers dominated the skyline.

"There are so many buildings, and they're all so different," Trish commented, leaning her chin on her hands against the railing. "What do you suppose it's like up here in a windstorm?"

"The building sways," Hal answered.

"Wow!"

"It feels like it's swaying now," Marge said. "Some of these tiles move when you step on them, and I'm sure the building is moving."

"Awww, Mom," David teased her. "You just need something to worry about."

"Well, worriers have *very* vivid imaginations," Marge acknowledged. She clung to Hal's arm. "So I'm entitled. Don't you think we've seen enough now? We've been around three times."

"In a minute." Hal laid his hand over hers. "Listen. You can hear the roar of the city clear up here. Just think of all the people crammed on this small island."

"Think I'll stick to the country," David observed. "I thought Portland was a pretty big city, until now."

Trish looked up. White moths danced in the spotlights. Higher up, the spire flashed red lights. A helicopter clattered past, then swung out over the Hudson River. Trish dragged her feet back to the first elevator. The building was so tall it took two elevators to return them to street level.

On the way out they read the signs and studied displays that told the story of the Empire State Building. For many years it had been the tallest building in the world. Now the Sears Tower in Chicago was the largest. A plaque listed the names of construction workers who had won awards for their skills.

"What a nice thing to do," Marge said. "It's easy to forget the contribution that everyday people make in this world."

"Our name is on a trophy or two," Trish said. "And Spitfire will be famous forever."

"That's true," Marge agreed. "And your name has gone down in the annals of Thoroughbred racing too. How does it feel to be world-famous at sixteen?"

Trish tipped her head to the side and rolled her lips together. "I don't *feel* any different than I did before the Derby. I'm still the same old me." She raised her arms and twirled in a circle. "Do I look any different?"

"Nope. Just as dopey as ever." David ducked before Trish could punch his shoulder. "I know one thing that's different."

"What's that?" Hal asked as he guided them all toward the exit.

"We have a lot more money than we did. Those purses we've won take the pressure off, at least for a while."

"True," Hal acknowledged.

David flagged down a cab. After they'd all climbed inside, Hal continued. "We'll do things like pay off the mortgage on the farm, make some investments, set money aside for college for each of you . . ."

Trish flinched at the mention of college. She wanted to race, not study.

"Just think, you can go to whatever college you wish." Marge settled back against the seat. "And not have to worry about money."

"What would you like?" Hal took Marge's hand. "As a sort of reward for all the stress we've put you through?"

Marge thought a moment. "A new car, I guess. The poor old station wagon has seen a lot of miles."

"How about a red convertible?" Trish muttered under her breath. David snorted, and Hal swallowed a chuckle.

A smile tugged at the corners of Marge's mouth. "Sure. Three red convertibles sitting in our front yard . . ." She laughed lightly. "The neighbors will think we've gone into the car business." She shook her head. "No, make mine something with a solid top. I don't want to have to worry about water dripping in during the winter. One of those minivans would be nice."

Trish tried to hear the conversation without missing all the sights. They'd just crossed the Brooklyn Bridge.

"And what would you like, Tee?" Hal asked.

"More horses," she answered without a thought. "We could go to the January yearling sale at Santa Anita. And breed all the mares to better stallions."

Hal raised his hand. "Okay, okay. We get the picture."

"What about you, Davey boy?" Trish asked.

"I already have what I wanted—thanks to you." He tapped Trish's knee. "A decent car. College was my next dream. What can I say?"

Trish felt a warm glow of pride and deep happiness surround her family. "What about you, Dad?"

"Having money has never been a big issue with me. . . ." He put his arm around Marge. "With us. But knowing that all of you are provided for takes a big load off my mind. I think I'd like to buy something for the church—maybe a bus or a van. David, why don't you look into that when we get home."

Trish rested her head on her father's shoulder. *What we need most can't be bought. God, please make my dad better.*

Hal leaned on David and Marge for support on the way up to their suite. While he made a joke of it, Trish could tell by the way his steps faltered that he was exhausted. And the post position draw was in the morning.

Patrick had Trish walk Spitfire around the entire track at morning works.

"I don't think he'll make it," she heard one railbird say. "He ain't run all week."

Trish leaned forward to rub Spitfire's neck. "A lot he knows about it," she whispered in the horse's ear. She relaxed in the saddle and let her feet dangle below the stirrups. "You just keep getting better. We'll show 'em."

Reporters asked the same question they always asked. "Will he run?" One of the more ambitious ones walked beside Trish on their way back to the barn. "What do you think your father will do?"

"We're just taking a day at a time. We have up to the morning of the race to scratch if we have to." Trish had made the comment so many times she felt like a stuck needle on a record.

When she walked into the dining room for the post position draw, Trish had a surprise. Adam and Martha Finley stood talking with her mother and father.

"Hear you brought that filly in by a whisker," Adam said after he greeted her. "I didn't think you could do it."

"Patrick suggested the blinkers. I think she'll do all right now. She found out what winning is all about, and she liked the applause." Trish turned to greet Martha and found herself enveloped in a warm hug.

"I knew you could do it," she whispered in Trish's ear. "You've got that magic touch."

"Thanks." Trish hugged her back. "You always make me feel so good."

The crowd quieted as the officials filed to the front of the room. Each person had been given a list of the seven horses entered in the race. By now Trish could pick out the owners, trainers, and jockey for each horse. The groups huddled together, waiting for the program to begin.

Nomatterwhat drew the post position. A cheer went up from his group. Equinox drew number six. Others were called; number two, number four.

Spitfire's name was next to last. "Number seven. Spitfire in gate seven."

"Right next to Equinox again," Trish mumbled. "At least we won't have to wait in the gate while the rest of them calm down."

With the drawing of the last number, the ceremony was over. Before the officials had left the podium, a reporter had his mike in front of Hal's face.

"Will Spitfire be well enough to run?"

His question lacked originality, in Trish's estimation. She mouthed the words along with her father. "We are taking . . ."

"Has the colt been limping? Will you breeze him tomorrow?"

Hal shook his head to both questions. "I'm sorry I can't be of more help. We just don't know for sure."

"Tough break, to come so far and have an accident on the turnpike."

The Shipsons joined the group, and the reporter left. "I hear congratulations are in order for you, young lady." Mr. Shipson extended his hand. "Both for winning with the filly and bringing ours in too. Have you thought about racing in Kentucky next year?"

Trish looked to see if her mother had heard the comment.

"Don't get your hopes up," Finley put in. "We asked her first. And California is closer to Washington than Kentucky is."

Trish caught Patrick's eye and he winked at her. She glanced at her father. He was slumped in the chair, and looked as though his shoulders were too heavy to hold up.

When her mother, Martha Finley, and Bernice Shipson suggested a shopping trip, Trish turned it down. Although the idea of shopping in New York City was tempting, Trish had something she had to do and this would give her the opportunity.

"I need to study, and Patrick may have me walk Spitfire this evening," she said. "But thanks anyway. Have fun, Mom. Why don't you buy yourself something nice—like a new dress for the winner's circle." She smiled. "You haven't had a new dress for a long time."

Marge studied her daughter suspiciously. "Take care of your dad, then. And study hard. We probably won't be back until late." She kissed Hal. "Get some rest now, okay?"

Hal nodded. "You have a good time, Marge. And take your daughter's suggestion."

Trish drove her father back to the hotel and helped him to his room.

"Thanks, Tee." Hal sank down on the bed. "I know I'll feel better after I sleep awhile." He reached for his pills and took a couple with a glass of water from the nightstand.

He lay down, and Trish untied his shoes and slipped them off. "Are you hurting bad?"

"Just staying on top of it." He stretched out, and Trish pulled the sheet up. "Right now I could use those eagle's wings."

Trish smiled, but said nothing. Within seconds Hal was asleep.

He looks like an old man. The thought struck Trish with the force of a mule kick. *Where has my real father gone?*

Later that afternoon, when Hal was awake, Trish went out and bought fried chicken and took it back to the hotel.

When she and her father were seated at the table, she cleared her throat and began. "Remember last night in the taxi when you asked what I wanted to do with some of the money?"

Hal nodded. "Yes?"

"Well, what I really want—" She paused and looked her father straight in the eye. "Is there any place—like a hospital—that you could go for some other kind of treatment? Maybe some experimental stuff—something that would work better for you? We can afford it now. Even another country, if necessary." She finished quickly before the tears choked her up. "Have you thought about that?"

"No, not really. Since they found the new tumors all I could think of was getting back to you—to the tracks. How about if when we get home we talk to the doctors? They've had time now to study my situation, and may have some new recommendations. Actually, they weren't too happy with me when I walked out on them."

"Walked out on them?"

"That's right. We had to get back here."

Trish nodded. "But you'll really look into it then?"

"Yes, Trish, I promise."

Trish fell asleep that night with one thought on her mind. Tomorrow they would decide. Would Spitfire race on Saturday or not?

Friday morning dawned with a drizzle. Trish alternately walked and trotted Spitfire around the track. She could feel a difference in him. He seemed to both walk and trot on his tiptoes. He was ready to run.

When Trish brought Sarah's Pride back to the barn after an easy gallop of the entire track, she could feel water dripping off the end of her nose. She sniffed as she leaped to the ground.

Before she knew what was happening, strong arms circled her waist and whirled her around in a strong hug.

"Red!" She looked into his face. "You came!" She hugged him again. "What took you so long?"

"Is that all you can say"—Red nearly squished her hand—"after I drove most of the night to get here?"

Trish looked at David and Patrick standing nearby. She could feel the heat begin to rise from her toes up. By the time her neck and cheeks were hot, she felt as if she could light up the barn. Somehow the day didn't seem gray anymore.

Patrick winked at her, and David rolled his eyes.

Red broke the tension by asking, "You about ready for some breakfast?"

"Uh—yeah—maybe—" Trish took a deep breath and looked at David. "I'd better help with the chores first, though."

"Aw, go on. We're almost done. Catch up with you over at the kitchen."

Trish couldn't ignore the fact that Red was still holding her hand. The tingle up her arm made her throat dry. But that didn't keep her from talking. And laughing—for no reason at all. By the time they walked into the cafeteria they'd caught up on each other's news, and Trish felt back to normal—sort of.

After breakfast Hal met them all back at the barn. "Well, what do you think, Patrick? Is it a go—or no?"

Trish felt as if her heart were in her throat. At least it was pounding about five times faster than normal. She watched Patrick's face, trying to out-guess him.

"Well, we haven't galloped him. I don't know what that might do to his leg." He paused, as if studying something on the wall.

Trish wanted to scream at him to hurry.

"But there's been no heat or swelling for the last couple of days. The lad walks like he's on top o' the world."

Hal studied his hands. "If we run him, we could lame him for life, right?" He raised his head and looked at Patrick.

Patrick started to shake his head, then frowned. "Not sure I'd go quite that far. Could take him some time to heal though."

Trish chewed on the cuticle of her thumb. She felt sick to her stomach. Would they *ever* make the decision? She glanced at David. He was clipping his fingernails—a sure sign he was worried.

Looks to me like running in the Belmont is more important to you than Spitfire's leg, Trish's little nagger spoke out of nowhere.

Trish gritted her teeth. *I just want to know what we're going to do. That's all.*

Right?

She heard a nicker down the long, sandy aisle. Spitfire stuck his head over the gate and answered.

"If you want my true, gut opinion," Patrick broke the silence, "I say go for it. I think he can do it."

Hal let out a sigh that sounded as if he hadn't breathed for the last five minutes. "Then that's what we'll do."

Thank you, God! Thank you, thank you, thank you! Trish jumped up and down and ran the few steps to stand in front of Spitfire. She placed her hands on both sides of his face and looked him straight in the eye. "We're gonna run tomorrow, old man. And it's gonna take all we got."

Spitfire blew in Trish's face, then dropped his head against her chest. Running was tomorrow. Right now he wanted a good scratching. Trish obliged him.

That night Hal took their extended family, which included Red, Patrick, and the Finleys, out for a steak dinner. "We have lots to celebrate," he told them as they sat around the table. "Whether we win or lose tomorrow, we've given it all we've got. What more can anyone do?"

"To Trish and Spitfire." Adam raised his glass of iced tea. As the others joined in the toast, Trish raised her glass too. Her butterflies took a flying leap at the same time. A toast of their own, perhaps?

Tomorrow afternoon the final race for the Triple Crown would take place. Trish stared at her plate when the waitress placed it in front of her. The steak had sounded so good—*before* the inner aerial display. She picked at her food, moving it around her plate while enjoying the conversation around the table.

That is, until her father choked. He coughed and gagged and covered his mouth with a napkin. When he was unable to stop coughing, Marge thumped his back. David was on his feet, ready to apply the Heimlich maneuver if necessary.

"Dad, are you all right?" Panic made Trish's voice sound shrill.

Hal shook his head and coughed again. This time he blinked and breathed deeply. "Yes, I got it out." He coughed again, more softly this time, but couldn't seem to stop altogether.

When he finally wiped his mouth with his napkin, Trish saw a smear of blood across his lips and cheek. "Dad!"

Hal looked at her, then down at his napkin. "Oh, God, no." He wiped his mouth again and took a sip of water.

"I think we better get you to a hospital and check this out." Marge laid her hand on his shoulder. "The rest of you finish your dinner. We'll probably be back at the hotel before you are."

Trish shoved her chair back so hard it crashed to the floor. "I'll drive."

"No, I will." David took Trish by the arm. "Come on."

"Do you want me to call an ambulance?" the maitre d' asked.

"No, just tell me where the nearest hospital is." David listened carefully to the instructions.

"Right, go three blocks, turn left, go one mile and left again at the sign to Mercy Hospital."

David almost shoved Trish ahead of him. "I'll bring the car around. You help Mom with Dad."

Hal seemed better in the car. He breathed carefully, as though afraid a deep breath would start the coughing again.

"They'll just check me over and send me back to the hotel," he grumbled. "All this over a piece of meat caught in my throat."

It seemed as if they'd been waiting for hours when a nurse came into the emergency room fifteen minutes later. She led the way to a white-curtained cubicle, and they all trooped in.

The nurse patted the table and looked at Hal. "Sit right up here and the doctor will be with you in a moment." Then she picked up a clipboard and started asking questions.

Now I know what Mom felt like after my accidents, Trish thought. The questions seemed to go on forever.

A tall man with iron-gray hair parted the curtains. "I'm Dr. Silverstein. The restaurant called and said you'd choked on a piece of meat." As he spoke, he took out his stethoscope and applied it to Hal's chest. "And you had blood on your napkin after that."

Trish clenched her fists until she could feel the nails digging into her palms. *Hurry up!*

"Why don't you young people step into the waiting room? I'll let you know as soon as I find anything."

Trish shook her head stubbornly, but David took her by the arm.

"It's okay, Trish," Hal said. "I'm not going anywhere."

Trish flipped through a magazine, not seeing the words or pictures. All she *could* see was the blood on the napkin.

David slouched in the chair beside her. Then he sat up and leaned forward, dropping his head and clasping his hands. After getting up and walking around the room, he sat down again to repeat the pattern.

Trish's nerves couldn't have been more frazzled if someone had stood at a blackboard and dragged their nails across it.

Hearing footsteps in the hall, Trish looked up immediately. Marge came to sit in the chair beside her. "They've decided to keep your father overnight for observation and some X-rays. Let's go get him settled."

"Overnight? What's wrong?" Trish blinked to keep the tears back.

"The doctor thinks there's fluid in your father's lungs." Marge fiddled with her purse. "The X-rays will tell us more."

When they arrived at the door to Hal's room, he was already in bed. Trish flew into his outstretched arms. "It's okay," he murmured, stroking her hair. "You and David go on back to the hotel and get some sleep."

"No, I want to stay here." Trish raised her tear-stained face. "I can sleep in that chair."

"No, that's my chair," Marge said, standing beside the bed. She put her hand on Trish's shoulder. "We're not that far away from the hotel. If you need us, just call."

"Besides, you have to be at your best tomorrow," Hal reminded her. "We'll let them check me out, and I'll see you before you head for the jockey room."

Trish could hear the rattle in her father's chest. She'd heard it before. Back in September, when all this started.

"Don't worry. I'll be better in the morning." Hal kissed Trish's forehead. "And remember that I love you."

Trish bit her lip and nodded. "Me too. Good night." She whirled and dashed out of the room.

David hurried after her without saying a word.

Worry nagged at Trish all the way back to the hotel. *Worry!* That's what got her mother into so much trouble. Why was it so easy to say don't worry, and so hard not to?

She went to her father's room at the hotel and picked up the carved eagle. As she crawled into bed, she pictured the verses on her wall at home. She needed some promises. *"Do not be not afraid . . ."* That was a good one for tonight. *"I will never leave you . . ."*

"Please, heavenly Father, take care of *my* father tonight. I love him so much, and I know you do, too. The race is tomorrow. He needs to be there. I need him to be there. Thank you for being with us." With Trish's "amen" she was asleep.

🐎

In the morning she awoke with a start. Her heart leaped. *This is the day!* She checked the clock. It was just seven. After digging the phone book out of the drawer, she looked up hospitals and ran her finger down the M's. Mercy Hospital. She dialed the number.

"Room 736, please."

The phone rang. And rang. There was no answer.

Chapter
15

David had awakened instantly. "Call the nurse's station," he told her.

Trish's teeth chattered. She felt as if she were standing in a deep freeze.

"M-my father—Hal Evanston," she stuttered. "There was no answer to the phone in his room."

"They've taken him down to X-ray," the nurse's voice soothed. "Your mother went with him. Should I have her call you when she can?"

"No." Trish shook her head methodically. "No, we'll call later. Just tell them that we called—please."

"Of course."

Trish put down the receiver, and a band of ice circled her heart.

When she and David arrived at the track, reporters swarmed the area.

"I can't talk to them," Trish told David pleadingly. "Not right now. You and Patrick handle it."

Working the horses brought a measure of peace to Trish's mind. Her father had promised to be at the track before she left for the jockey room. He always kept his promises.

But he didn't come. Nine o'clock passed. Nine-thirty.

David called the hospital again, and when he returned to tell Trish their father was down for more tests, she said, "I'm going to the hospital."

"You can't. There's no time." David grabbed her by the shoulders. "You heard what Dad said. He'll be here. You just concentrate on the job you have to do. We've come too far to mess up now."

"But, David—"

"He's right, lass," Patrick rejoined. "You know what your dad would want you to do." He set down a can of saddle soap. "I know it's a long time to wait up there, but we'll get any message to you that's necessary."

"Come on, Trish." Red took her hand. "I'll walk you over."

"Me too." David picked up her schoolbooks. "Wouldn't want you to be bored."

Trish stopped in front of Spitfire. "Sure would rather stay with you, fella." She rubbed his ears and smoothed his forelock. "You get ready now, you hear? This is the big one." Spitfire sniffed her pockets, lipped the carrot off her palm, and licked her cheek for good measure. Trish threw her arms around his neck and buried her face in his mane. Her shoulders shook but no sound came.

David and Red waited patiently.

Trish wiped her eyes and swallowed hard. "Okay, let's go." Together they turned and headed down the street to the clubhouse.

"I'll let you know as soon as I hear anything, I promise," David assured her outside the jockey room.

Trish nodded. She took her books, squeezed Red's hand, and stumbled into the jockey room—to wait.

Her mind was a jumble of prayers, promises, and worry. When she tried to relax with deep breathing, her insides joined the jumble.

At noon Trish called the hospital herself. Her mother answered the phone on the second ring.

"Yes, Trish, we're on our way. The doctors are having a fit but your father refuses to listen. Here, you want to talk to him?"

Trish strangled the receiver with her hand. Her throat clenched so tight she didn't think she'd be able to talk. But her father's welcome voice broke the dam for her.

"It's okay, Tee," she finally heard him say. "Come on now, you'll be all right. We're coming, but I may not make it to the saddling paddock. Look for me in the winner's circle."

"Dad, I'm so scared."

"I know. But it's okay. Just go out there and ride. Go for the glory."

Trish sniffed and fumbled in her pocket for a tissue. "Thanks. I love you."

"I know that. And I love you too. See you soon."

What did her father mean by soon? The fifth race came and went. Trish began her pre-race routine. She sprayed her goggles, polished her boots, brushed her hair. She even added extra deodorant—she'd need it today for sure. Then she was down on the floor doing stretches.

When the call came she was dressed and ready. "This is it, God. For *your* glory." She walked out the door and over to the men's jockey room to weigh in.

"Mom and Dad are on their way," David called, as Trish walked with the other jockeys down the incline to the saddling paddock.

"I know. I talked to them." Trish stepped in front of Spitfire and leaned her forehead against his. "Well, fella, can you run a mile and a half today? We gotta do it—for Dad."

The noise of the crowd receded. It was as though there were a crystal bell around Trish's head. She could see what was going on, but the noise and the pressure were at bay. She was in a literal sea of peace.

"You'll do it, lass." Patrick gave her a leg up at the call.

With David and Patrick on either side, they followed the rest of the field up the incline and under the clubhouse.

The last bugle notes of the parade to post hovered on the slight breeze as Trish picked up her pony rider on the edge of the track. The track was listed as fast, the sun warm but not hot.

As they stepped onto the track, Trish heard her father's voice in her mind: *"Remember, you're a winner. And winners never quit."* She leaned forward and stroked Spitfire's neck.

"They're cheering for you," she crooned, acknowledging the applause of the crowd. Then they were chanting, "Spitfire—Spitfire—Spitfire."

For one brief moment Trish wanted to turn and run. But she looked between Spitfire's ears at the track ahead. *I can do all things through Christ who strengthens me.* The verse put steel in her spine. She squared her shoulders and let the thunder of the crowd set her blood to pumping. *I can do all things. . . .* They cantered back past the crowd toward the starting gates.

Equinox was typically obnoxious. He didn't get any better with another race. Trish shook her head. They'd never let a horse get away with that kind of behavior on their farm. Spitfire waited patiently for his turn. He entered the gate and settled for the break.

The shot. The gate clanged open.

"They're off!"

Spitfire broke clean and settled into an easy stride. He ran, head up, ears pricked, as if they were out for a joyride. He and Trish seemed of one mind as they let two others set the pace. Patrick had reminded Trish to lay back and let the others wear themselves out. The real race would begin after the mile marker.

Trish loosened the reins. Spitfire snorted and flew past the third-place runner. He took the rail, two lengths behind the two dueling for the lead. Going into the turn it was Who Sez and Nomatterwhat, neck and neck. They pounded out of the turn and Who Sez faltered.

Spitfire passed him as if the gray were standing still. Now it was Nomatterwhat and Spitfire, just like in the last two races. Only now Nomatterwhat led by two lengths.

At the mile-and-a-quarter pole Trish crouched tight against Spitfire's neck, making herself as small as possible to cut the wind. "Okay, fella, this is it," she urged him forward. Her arms and legs lifted the horse onward. Stride for stride they gained on the lead.

Trish could hear the stands going wild. Her heart thundered with Spitfire's heaving grunts. Neck and neck for two strides and Spitfire began to pull away. Ahead by a nose, by a neck. Nomatterwhat disappeared from their view. They flashed across the finish line, ahead by a length. Trish raised her arm. Victory. Spitfire had won the Triple Crown!

Tears made rivulets down Trish's dusty face. "You did it! We did it!" She raised her face to the heavens. "Thank you, God. We did it!" She turned and cantered back to stand her horse in front of the clubhouse crowd.

Applause rolled over them in waves. Spitfire stood, sides heaving but head up accepting the accolades like the king he was. Trish turned him toward the winner's circle. She felt him falter, then walk carefully as though he were in pain.

A crowd surged in and around the winner's circle. Huge cameras eyed them from every angle. Trish searched the crowd, looking for only one face. When she couldn't find her father, she started to dismount.

"No, lass." Patrick grabbed the reins.

"You can't fail him now," David hissed at her. "Let's just get through the ceremony."

Trish blinked back the tears and smiled at the Finleys and the Shipsons. She smiled when the cameramen asked her to, and raised her arms so they could drape the blanket of white carnations across her lap and Spitfire's withers. She smiled again. Her cheeks felt as if they were cracked.

As the cameras flashed again and the announcer began his spiel, Trish heard another voice. This one from the man she loved above all others—her father. *"I have fought the good fight, Tee. I have won my race. Remember that I love you."*

"Dad's gone, isn't he?" she asked David, searching for the truth in his eyes.

David nodded and reached up to grasp her hand. "They got a message to us after the race had started."

Trish leaned against Spitfire's neck, fighting the knife thrust of the awful reality. *My father . . .* She pushed herself upright. Teeth clenched against the tears streaming down her face, Trish turned to face the cameras. With his life and his love her father had taught her courage. She raised her arm, the victory salute.

ACKNOWLEDGMENTS

My special thanks to Mel Howell, head of security for the Maryland Racing Commission, for sharing his fund of racing knowledge and his time with us at Pimlico. Thanks too to all those friendly people who answered my questions at Belmont and Aquaduct. All of you helped make our New York trip a special event.